THE MAGIC OF OZ

THE MAGIC OF OZ

BOOKS ELEVEN THROUGH FIFTEEN OF THE OZ SERIES

L. FRANK BAUM

FALL RIVER PRESS

New York

FALL RIVER PRESS

New York

An Imprint of Sterling Publishing
1166 Avenue of the Americas
New York, NY 10036

The Lost Princess of Oz was originally published in 1917.
The Tin Woodman of Oz was originally published in 1918.
The Magic of Oz was originally published in 1919.
Glinda of Oz was originally published in 1920.
Little Wizard Stories of Oz was originally published in 1913.

ISBN 978-1-4351-6173-3

Manufactured in the United States of America

2 4 6 8 10 9 7 5 3 1

www.sterlingpublishing.com

Contents

Introduction

BETWEEN 1900 AND 1920 L. FRANK BAUM PUBLISHED FOURTEEN NOVELS
and one collection of short stories, all set in his marvelous Land of Oz. During that
interval Baum tried several times to put Oz behind him and devote his attention
to other literary projects. But he had succeeded wildly in his effort to create, as he
wrote in his introduction to *The Wonderful Wizard of Oz*, "a modernized fairy tale"
in which—in contrast to classic fairy tales—"the wonderment and joy are retained
and the heart-aches and nightmares are left out." None of Baum's non-Oz titles were
as popular as the books in the Oz canon and, if we are to believe the introductory
note "To My Readers" that he wrote for each of them, the adoring audience of young
readers that they cultivated showered him with letters that kept him coming back to
entertain them.

The four novels collected in this volume—*The Lost Princess of Oz* (1917), *The
Tin Woodman of Oz* (1918), *The Magic of Oz* (1919), and *Glinda of Oz* (1920)—are
the last four that Baum wrote for the series. Both *The Magic of Oz* and *Glinda of
Oz* were published after his death on May 5, 1919, ten days short of his sixty-third
birthday. (*The Royal Book of Oz*, published in 1921 under Baum's byline, was actually
the work of Ruth Plumly Johnson, the first of several writers sanctioned by Baum's
publisher to extend the Oz canon.) Baum had completed each far enough in advance
of its successor to tease readers in the book's introductory note with a hint of surprises to come in the next novel. He knew how to keep his readers entertained, and
the plots of these books follow the pattern he had established in their predecessors,
introducing his core cast of characters to new adventures and perils in their travels
to different lands and kingdoms in his imaginary world. These characters include
Dorothy Gale of Kansas, now a princess of Oz; the Scarecrow, the Cowardly Lion,
and the Tin Woodman who accompanied Dorothy on her first adventure; the great
Wizard of Oz, a fraudulent humbug turned benefactor and patron of Dorothy and
her friends; Glinda, the Good Witch of the South; and Princess Ozma, the ruler of
Oz. Over the course of these novels, the characters are swept up in intrigues of the
kind that drove the plots of earlier Oz novels: attempts by malefactors to seize control of the kingdom of Oz in *The Lost Princess of Oz* and *The Magic of Oz* and war
between opposing kingdoms in *Glinda of Oz*. *The Tin Woodman of Oz* hearkens back
to the very first Oz adventure, providing the backstory of how Jack Chopper, the
Tin Woodman, had the parts of his body replaced by tin pieces, and—in a potentially

macabre scene defused with the sort of humor typical of the Oz books—allowing him to actually converse with his still living human head. Secondary characters including the young boy Button-Bright, the young girls Trot and Betsy Bobbin, the Shaggy Man, Jack Pumpkinhead, the Saw-Horse, Tik-Tok the mechanical man, and the egg-fearing Nome King all contribute to these novels' incidents.

The short story collection *Little Wizard Stories of Oz* was first published in 1913. Although it features many of the same characters who appear in the Oz novels, Baum wrote them to appeal to an even younger readership than for those books. It's not hard to figure out why he did. By the time the book was published, the Oz novels had shaped the imaginations of a generation of readers who were themselves preparing to bring children into the world. Baum clearly felt that it was important to have a new set of Oz adventures tailor-made for the new generation of readers.

In his note "To My Readers" for *The Tin Woodman of Oz*, Baum answered a college professor's question regarding the age of readers for whom his books were intended by quoting from three enthusiastic fan letters: one from a five-year-old boy, one from a thirteen-year-old girl, and one from a seventy-year old married couple. Baum concluded that "my books are intended for all those whose hearts are young, no matter what their ages may be." May the stories collected in *The Magic of Oz* be enjoyed by readers who appreciate them for the spirit in which Baum wrote them.

THE LOST PRINCESS OF OZ

Contents

CHAPTER I

A TERRIBLE LOSS

THERE COULD BE NO DOUBT OF THE FACT: PRINCESS OZMA, THE LOVELY girl Ruler of the Fairyland of Oz, was lost. She had completely disappeared. Not one of her subjects—not even her closest friends—knew what had become of her.

It was Dorothy who first discovered it. Dorothy was a little Kansas girl who had come to the Land of Oz to live and had been given a delightful suite of rooms in Ozma's royal palace, just because Ozma loved Dorothy and wanted her to live as near her as possible, so the two girls might be much together.

Dorothy was not the only girl from the outside world who had been welcomed to Oz and lived in the royal palace. There was another named Betsy Bobbin, whose adventures had led her to seek refuge with Ozma, and still another named Trot, who had been invited, together with her faithful companion Cap'n Bill, to make her home in this wonderful fairyland. The three girls all had rooms in the palace and were great chums; but Dorothy was the dearest friend of their gracious Ruler and only she at any hour dared to seek Ozma in her royal apartments. For Dorothy had lived in Oz much longer than the other girls and had been made a Princess of the realm.

Betsy was a year older than Dorothy and Trot was a year younger, yet the three were near enough of an age to become great play-mates and to have nice times together. It was while the three were talking together one morning in Dorothy's room that Betsy proposed they make a journey into the Munchkin Country, which was one of the four great countries of the Land of Oz ruled by Ozma.

"I've never been there yet," said Betsy Bobbin, "but the Scarecrow once told me it is the prettiest country in all Oz."

"I'd like to go, too," added Trot.

"All right," said Dorothy. "I'll go and ask Ozma. Perhaps she will let us take the Saw-Horse and the Red Wagon, which would be much nicer for us than having to walk all the way. This Land of Oz is a pretty big place, when you get to all the edges of it."

So she jumped up and went along the halls of the splendid palace until she came to the royal suite, which filled all the front of the second floor. In a little waiting room sat Ozma's maid, Jellia Jamb, who was busily sewing.

"Is Ozma up yet?" inquired Dorothy.

"I don't know, my dear," replied Jellia. "I haven't heard a word from her this morning. She hasn't even called for her bath or her breakfast, and it is far past her usual time for them."

"That's strange!" exclaimed the little girl.

"Yes," agreed the maid, "but of course no harm could have happened to her. No one can die or be killed in the Land of Oz and Ozma is herself a powerful fairy, and she has no enemies, so far as we know. Therefore I am not at all worried about her, though I must admit her silence is unusual."

"Perhaps," said Dorothy, thoughtfully, "she has overslept. Or she may be reading, or working out some new sort of magic to do good to her people."

"Any of these things may be true," replied Jellia Jamb, "so I haven't dared disturb our royal mistress. You, however, are a privileged character, Princess, and I am sure that Ozma wouldn't mind at all if you went in to see her."

"Of course not," said Dorothy, and opening the door of the outer chamber she went in. All was still here. She walked into another room, which was Ozma's boudoir, and then, pushing back a heavy drapery richly broidered with threads of pure gold, the girl entered the sleeping-room of the fairy Ruler of Oz. The bed of ivory and gold was vacant; the room was vacant; not a trace of Ozma was to be found.

Very much surprised, yet still with no fear that anything had happened to her friend, Dorothy returned through the boudoir to the other rooms of the suite. She went into the music room, the library, the laboratory, the bath, the wardrobe and even into the great throne room, which adjoined the royal suite, but in none of these places could she find Ozma.

So she returned to the anteroom where she had left the maid, Jellia Jamb, and said:

"She isn't in her rooms now, so she must have gone out."

"I don't understand how she could do that without my seeing her," replied Jellia, "unless she made herself invisible."

"She isn't there, anyhow," declared Dorothy.

"Then let us go find her," suggested the maid, who appeared to be a little uneasy. So they went into the corridors and there Dorothy almost stumbled over a queer girl who was dancing lightly along the passage.

"Stop a minute, Scraps!" she called. "Have you seen Ozma this morning?"

"Not I!" replied the queer girl, dancing nearer. "I lost both my eyes in a tussle with the Woozy, last night, for the creature scraped 'em both off my face with his square paws. So I put the eyes in my pocket and this morning Button-Bright led me to Aunt Em, who sewed 'em on again. So I've seen nothing at all to-day, except during the last five minutes. So of course I haven't seen Ozma."

"Very well, Scraps," said Dorothy, looking curiously at the eyes, which were merely two round black buttons sewed upon the girl's face.

There were other things about Scraps that would have seemed curious to one seeing her for the first time. She was commonly called "The Patchwork Girl"

because her body and limbs were made from a gay-colored patchwork quilt which had been cut into shape and stuffed with cotton. Her head was a round ball stuffed in the same manner and fastened to her shoulders. For hair, she had a mass of brown yarn and to make a nose for her a part of the cloth had been pulled out into the shape of a knob and tied with a string to hold it in place. Her mouth had been carefully made by cutting a slit in the proper place and lining it with red silk, adding two rows of pearls for teeth and a bit of red flannel for a tongue.

In spite of this queer make-up, the Patchwork Girl was magically alive and had proved herself not the least jolly and agreeable of the many quaint characters who inhabit the astonishing Fairyland of Oz. Indeed, Scraps was a general favorite, although she was rather flighty and erratic and did and said many things that surprised her friends. She was seldom still, but loved to dance, to turn handsprings and somersaults, to climb trees and to indulge in many other active sports.

"I'm going to search for Ozma," remarked Dorothy, "for she isn't in her rooms and I want to ask her a question."

"I'll go with you," said Scraps, "for my eyes are brighter than yours and they can see farther."

"I'm not sure of that," returned Dorothy. "But come along, if you like."

Together they searched all through the great palace and even to the farthest limits of the palace grounds, which were quite extensive, but nowhere could they find a trace of Ozma. When Dorothy returned to where Betsy and Trot awaited her, the little girl's face was rather solemn and troubled, for never before had Ozma gone away without telling her friends where she was going, or without an escort that befitted her royal state.

She was gone, however, and none had seen her go. Dorothy had met and questioned the Scarecrow, Tik-Tok, the Shaggy Man, Button-Bright, Cap'n Bill, and even the wise and powerful Wizard of Oz, but not one of them had seen Ozma since she parted with her friends the evening before and had gone to her own rooms.

"She didn't say anything las' night about going anywhere," observed little Trot.

"No, and that's the strange part of it," replied Dorothy. "Usually Ozma lets us know of everything she does."

"Why not look in the Magic Picture?" suggested Betsy Bobbin. "That will tell us where she is, in just one second."

"Of course!" cried Dorothy. "Why didn't I think of that before?" And at once the three girls hurried away to Ozma's boudoir, where the Magic Picture always hung.

This wonderful Magic Picture was one of the royal Ozma's greatest treasures. There was a large gold frame, in the center of which was a bluish-gray canvas on which various scenes constantly appeared and disappeared. If one who stood before it wished to see what any person—anywhere in the world—was doing, it was only necessary to make the wish and the scene in the Magic Picture would shift to the scene where that person was and show exactly what he or she was then engaged in doing. So the girls knew it would be easy for them to wish to see Ozma, and from the picture they could quickly learn where she was.

Dorothy advanced to the place where the picture was usually protected by thick satin curtains, and pulled the draperies aside. Then she stared in amazement, while her two friends uttered exclamations of disappointment.

The Magic Picture was gone. Only a blank space on the wall behind the curtains showed where it had formerly hung.

CHAPTER II

THE TROUBLES OF GLINDA THE GOOD

THAT SAME MORNING THERE WAS GREAT EXCITEMENT IN THE CASTLE OF THE powerful Sorceress of Oz, Glinda the Good. This castle, situated in th Quadling Country, far south of the Emerald City where Ozma ruled, was a splendid structure of exquisite marbles and silver grilles. Here the Sorceress lived, surrounded by a bevy of the most beautiful maidens of Oz, gathered from all the four countries of that fairyland as well as from the magnificent Emerald City itself, which stood in the place where the four countries cornered.

It was considered a great honor to be allowed to serve the good Sorceress, whose arts of magic were used only to benefit the Oz people. Glinda was Ozma's most valued servant, for her knowledge of sorcery was wonderful and she could accomplish almost anything that her mistress, the lovely girl Ruler of Oz, wished her to.

Of all the magical things which surrounded Glinda in her castle there was none more marvelous than her Great Book of Records. On the pages of this Record Book were constantly being inscribed—day by day and hour by hour—all the important events that happened anywhere in the known world, and they were inscribed in the book at exactly the moment the events happened. Every adventure in the Land of Oz and in the big outside world, and even in places that you and I have never heard of, were recorded accurately in the Great Book, which never made a mistake and stated only the exact truth. For that reason nothing could be concealed from Glinda the Good, who had only to look at the pages of the Great Book of Records to know everything that had taken place. That was one reason she was such a great Sorceress, for the records made her wiser than any other living person.

This wonderful book was placed upon a big gold table that stood in the middle of Glinda's drawing-room. The legs of the table, which were incrusted with precious gems, were firmly fastened to the tiled floor and the book itself was chained to the table and locked with six stout golden padlocks, the keys to which Glinda carried on a chain that was secured around her own neck.

The pages of the Great Book were larger in size than those of an American newspaper and although they were exceedingly thin there were so many of them that they made an enormous, bulky volume. With its gold cover and gold clasps the book was so heavy that three men could scarcely have lifted it. Yet this morning, when Glinda entered her drawing-room after breakfast, the good Sorceress was amazed to discover that her Great Book of Records had mysteriously disappeared.

Advancing to the table, she found the chains had been cut with some sharp instrument, and this must have been done while all in the castle slept. Glinda was shocked and grieved. Who could have done this wicked, bold thing? And who could wish to deprive her of her Great Book of Records?

The Sorceress was thoughtful for a time, considering the consequences of her loss. Then she went to her Room of Magic to prepare a charm that would tell her who had stolen the Record Book. But when she unlocked her cupboard and threw open the doors, all of her magical instruments and rare chemical compounds had been removed from the shelves.

The Sorceress was now both angry and alarmed. She sat down in a chair and tried to think how this extraordinary robbery could have taken place. It was evident that the thief was some person of very great power, or the theft could never have been accomplished without her knowledge. But who, in all the Land of Oz, was powerful and skillful enough to do this awful thing? And who, having the power, could also have an object in defying the wisest and most talented Sorceress the world has ever known?

Glinda thought over the perplexing matter for a full hour, at the end of which time she was still puzzled how to explain it. But although her instruments and chemicals were gone, her knowledge of magic had not been stolen, by any means, since no thief, however skillful, can rob one of knowledge, and that is why knowledge is the best and safest treasure to acquire. Glinda believed that when she had time to gather more magical herbs and elixirs and to manufacture more magical instruments she would be able to discover who the robber was, and what had become of her precious Book of Records.

"Whoever has done this," she said to her maidens, "is a very foolish person, for in time he is sure to be found out and will then be severely punished."

She now made a list of the things she needed and dispatched messengers to every part of Oz with instructions to obtain them and bring them to her as soon as possible.

And one of her messengers met the little Wizard of Oz, who was seated on the back of the famous live Saw-Horse and was clinging to its neck with both his arms; for the Saw-Horse was speeding to Glinda's castle with the velocity of the wind, bearing the news that Royal Ozma, Ruler of all the great Land of Oz, had suddenly disappeared and no one in the Emerald City knew what had become of her.

"Also," said the Wizard as he stood before the astonished Sorceress, "Ozma's Magic Picture is gone, so we cannot consult it to discover where she is. So I came to you for assistance as soon as we realized our loss. Let us look in the Great Book of Records."

"Alas," returned the Sorceress sorrowfully, "we cannot do that, for the Great Book of Records has also disappeared!"

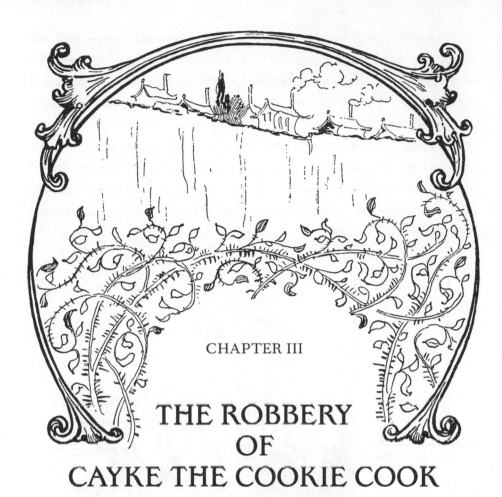

CHAPTER III

THE ROBBERY
OF
CAYKE THE COOKIE COOK

ONE MORE IMPORTANT THEFT WAS REPORTED IN THE LAND OF OZ THAT eventful morning, but it took place so far from either the Emerald City or the castle of Glinda the Good that none of those persons we have mentioned learned of the robbery until long afterward.

In the far southwestern corner of the Winkie Country is a broad tableland that can be reached only by climbing a steep hill, whichever side one approaches it. On the hillside surrounding this tableland are no paths at all, but there are quantities of bramble-bushes with sharp prickers on them, which prevent any of the Oz people who live down below from climbing up to see what is on top. But on top live the Yips, and although the space they occupy is not great in extent the wee country is all their own. The Yips had never—up to the time this story begins—left their broad tableland to go down into the Land of Oz, nor had the Oz people ever climbed up to the Country of the Yips.

Living all alone as they did, the Yips had queer ways and notions of their own and did not resemble any other people of the Land of Oz. Their houses were scattered all over the flat surface; not like a city, grouped together, but set wherever their owners' fancy dictated, with fields here, trees there, and odd little paths connecting the houses one with another.

It was here, on the morning when Ozma so strangely disappeared from the Emerald City, that Cayke the Cookie Cook discovered that her diamond-studded gold dishpan had been stolen, and she raised such a hue-and-cry over her loss and wailed and shrieked so loudly that many of the Yips gathered around her house to inquire what was the matter.

It was a serious thing, in any part of the Land of Oz, to accuse one of stealing, so when the Yips heard Cayke the Cookie Cook declare that her jeweled dishpan had been stolen they were both humiliated and disturbed and forced Cayke to go with them to the Frogman to see what could be done about it.

I do not suppose you have ever before heard of the Frogman, for like all other dwellers on that tableland he had never been away from it, nor had anyone come up there to see him. The Frogman was, in truth, descended from the common frogs of Oz, and when he was first born he lived in a pool in the Winkie Country and was much like any other frog. Being of an adventurous nature, however, he soon hopped out of his pool and began to travel, when a big bird came along and seized him in its beak and started to fly away with him to its nest. When high in the air, the frog wriggled so frantically that he got loose and fell down—down—down into a small hidden pool on the tableland of the Yips. Now that pool, it seems, was unknown to the Yips because it was surrounded by thick bushes and was not near to any dwelling, and it proved to be an enchanted pool, for the frog grew very fast and very big, feeding on the magic skosh which is found nowhere else on earth except in that one pool. And the skosh not only made the frog very big, so that when he stood on his hind legs he was as tall as any Yip in the country, but it made him unusually intelligent, so that he soon knew more than the Yips did and was able to reason and to argue very well indeed.

No one could expect a frog with these talents to remain in a hidden pool, so he finally got out of it and mingled with the people of the tableland, who were amazed at his appearance and greatly impressed by his learning. They had never seen a frog before and the frog had never seen a Yip before, but as there were plenty of Yips and only one frog, the frog became the most important. He did not hop any more, but stood upright on his hind legs and dressed himself in fine clothes and sat in chairs and did all the things that people do; so he soon came to be called the Frogman, and that is the only name he has ever had.

After some years had passed the people came to regard the Frogman as their adviser in all matters that puzzled them. They brought all their difficulties to him and when he did not know anything he pretended to know it, which seemed to answer just as well. Indeed, the Yips thought the Frogman was much wiser than he really was, and he allowed them to think so, being very proud of his position of authority.

There was another pool on the tableland, which was not enchanted but contained good clear water and was located close to the dwellings. Here the people built the Frogman a house of his own, close to the edge of the pool, so that he could take a bath or a swim whenever he wished. He usually swam in the pool in the early morning, before anyone else was up, and during the day he dressed himself in his beautiful clothes and sat in his house and received the visits of all the Yips who came to him to ask his advice.

The Frogman's usual costume consisted of knee-breeches made of yellow satin plush, with trimmings of gold braid and jeweled knee-buckles; a white satin vest with silver buttons in which were set solitaire rubies; a swallow-tailed coat of bright yellow; green stockings and red leather shoes turned up at the toes and having diamond buckles. He wore, when he walked out, a purple silk hat and carried a gold-headed cane. Over his eyes he wore great spectacles with gold rims, not because his eyes were bad but because the spectacles made him look wise, and so distinguished and gorgeous was his appearance that all the Yips were very proud of him.

There was no King or Queen in the Yip Country, so the simple inhabitants naturally came to look upon the Frogman as their leader as well as their Counsellor in all times of emergency. In his heart the big frog knew he was no wiser than the Yips, but for a frog to know as much as a person was quite remarkable, and the Frogman was shrewd enough to make the people believe he was far more wise than he really was. They never suspected he was a humbug, but listened to his words with great respect and did just what he advised them to do.

Now, when Cayke the Cookie Cook raised such an outcry over the theft of her diamond-studded dishpan, the first thought of the people was to take her to the Frogman and inform him of the loss, thinking that of course he could tell her where to find it.

He listened to the story with his big eyes wide open behind his spectacles, and said in his deep, croaking voice, "If the dishpan is stolen, somebody must have taken it."

"But who?" asked Cayke, anxiously. "Who is the thief?"

"The one who took the dishpan, of course," replied the Frogman, and hearing this all the Yips nodded their heads gravely and said to one another:

"It is absolutely true!"

"But I want my dishpan!" cried Cayke.

"No one can blame you for that wish," remarked the Frogman.

"Then tell me where I may find it," she urged.

The look the Frogman gave her was a very wise look and he rose from his chair and strutted up and down the room with his hands under his coat-tails, in a very pompous and imposing manner. This was the first time so difficult a matter had been brought to him and he wanted time to think. It would never do to let them suspect his ignorance and so he thought very, very hard how best to answer the woman without betraying himself.

"I beg to inform you," said he, "that nothing in the Yip Country has ever been stolen before."

"We know that, already," answered Cayke the Cookie Cook, impatiently.

"Therefore," continued the Frogman, "this theft becomes a very important matter."

"Well, where is my dishpan?" demanded the woman.

"It is lost; but it must be found. Unfortunately, we have no policemen or detectives to unravel the mystery, so we must employ other means to regain the lost article. Cayke must first write a Proclamation and tack it to the door of her house, and the Proclamation must read that whoever stole the jeweled dishpan must return it at once."

"But suppose no one returns it," suggested Cayke.

"Then," said the Frogman, "that very fact will be proof that no one has stolen it."

Cayke was not satisfied, but the other Yips seemed to approve the plan highly. They all advised her to do as the Frogman had told her to, so she posted the sign on her door and waited patiently for someone to return the dishpan—which no one ever did.

Again she went, accompanied by a group of her neighbors, to the Frogman, who by this time had given the matter considerable thought. Said he to Cayke:

"I am now convinced that no Yip has taken your dishpan, and, since it is gone from the Yip Country, I suspect that some stranger came from the world down below us, in the darkness of night when all of us were asleep, and took away your treasure. There can be no other explanation of its disappearance. So, if you wish to recover that golden, diamond-studded dishpan, you must go into the lower world after it."

This was indeed a startling proposition. Cayke and her friends went to the edge of the flat tableland and looked down the steep hillside to the plains below. It was so far to the bottom of the hill that nothing there could be seen very distinctly and it seemed to the Yips very venturesome, if not dangerous, to go so far from home into an unknown land.

However, Cayke wanted her dishpan very badly, so she turned to her friends and asked:

"Who will go with me?"

No one answered the question, but after a period of silence one of the Yips said:

"We know what is here, on the top of this flat hill, and it seems to us a very pleasant place; but what is down below we do not know. The chances are it is not so pleasant, so we had best stay where we are."

"It may be a far better country than this is," suggested the Cookie Cook.

"Maybe, maybe," responded another Yip, "but why take chances? Contentment with one's lot is true wisdom. Perhaps, in some other country, there are better cookies than you cook; but as we have always eaten your cookies, and liked them— except when they are burned on the bottom—we do not long for any better ones."

Cayke might have agreed to this argument had she not been so anxious to find her precious dishpan, but now she exclaimed impatiently:

"You are cowards—all of you! If none of you are willing to explore with me the great world beyond this small hill, I will surely go alone."

"That is a wise resolve," declared the Yips, much relieved. "It is your dishpan that is lost, not ours; and, if you are willing to risk your life and liberty to regain it, no one can deny you the privilege."

While they were thus conversing the Frogman joined them and looked down at the plain with his big eyes and seemed unusually thoughtful. In fact, the Frogman was thinking that he'd like to see more of the world. Here in the Yip Country he had become the most important creature of them all and his importance was getting to be a little tame. It would be nice to have other people defer to him and ask his advice and there seemed no reason, so far as he could see, why his fame should not spread throughout all Oz.

He knew nothing of the rest of the world, but it was reasonable to believe that there were more people beyond the mountain where he now lived than there were Yips, and if he went among them he could surprise them with his display of wisdom and make them bow down to him as the Yips did. In other words, the Frogman was ambitious to become still greater than he was, which was impossible if he always remained upon this mountain. He wanted others to see his gorgeous clothes and listen to his solemn sayings, and here was an excuse for him to get away from the Yip Country. So he said to Cayke the Cookie Cook:

"*I* will go with you, my good woman," which greatly pleased Cayke because she felt the Frogman could be of much assistance to her in her search.

But now, since the mighty Frogman had decided to undertake the journey, several of the Yips who were young and daring at once made up their minds to go along; so the next morning after breakfast the Frogman and Cayke the Cookie Cook and nine of the Yips started to slide down the side of the mountain. The bramble bushes and cactus plants were very prickly and uncomfortable to the touch, so the Frogman commanded the Yips to go first and break a path, so that when he followed them he would not tear his splendid clothes. Cayke, too, was wearing her best dress, and was likewise afraid of the thorns and prickers, so she kept behind the Frogman.

They made rather slow progress and night overtook them before they were halfway down the mountainside, so they found a cave in which they sought shelter until morning. Cayke had brought along a basket full of her famous cookies, so they all had plenty to eat.

On the second day the Yips began to wish they had not embarked on this adventure. They grumbled a good deal at having to cut away the thorns to make the path for the Frogman and the Cookie Cook, for their own clothing suffered many tears, while Cayke and the Frogman traveled safely and in comfort.

"If it is true that anyone came to our country to steal your diamond dishpan," said one of the Yips to Cayke, "it must have been a bird, for no person in the form of a man, woman or child could have climbed through these bushes and back again."

"And, allowing he could have done so," said another Yip, "the diamond-studded gold dishpan would not have repaid him for his troubles and his tribulations."

"For my part," remarked a third Yip, "I would rather go back home and dig and polish some more diamonds, and mine some more gold, and make you another dishpan, than be scratched from head to heel by these dreadful bushes. Even now, if my mother saw me, she would not know I am her son."

Cayke paid no heed to these mutterings, nor did the Frogman. Although their journey was slow it was being made easy for them by the Yips, so they had nothing to complain of and no desire to turn back.

Quite near to the bottom of the great hill they came upon a deep gulf, the sides of which were as smooth as glass. The gulf extended a long distance—as far as they could see, in either direction—and although it was not very wide it was far too wide for the Yips to leap across it. And, should they fall into it, it was likely they might never get out again.

"Here our journey ends," said the Yips. "We must go back again."

Cayke the Cookie Cook began to weep.

"I shall never find my pretty dishpan again—and my heart will be broken!" she sobbed.

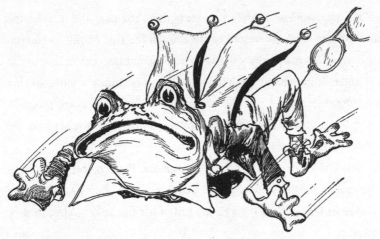

The Frogman went to the edge of the gulf and with his eye carefully measured the distance to the other side.

"Being a frog," said he, "I can leap, as all frogs do; and, being so big and strong, I am sure I can leap across this gulf with ease. But the rest of you, not being frogs, must return the way you came."

"We will do that with pleasure," cried the Yips and at once they turned and began to climb up the steep mountain, feeling they had had quite enough of this unsatisfactory adventure. Cayke the Cookie Cook did not go with them, however. She sat on a rock and wept and wailed and was very miserable.

"Well," said the Frogman to her, "I will now bid you good-bye. If I find your diamond-decorated gold dishpan I will promise to see that it is safely returned to you."

"But I prefer to find it myself!" she said. "See here, Frogman, why can't you carry me across the gulf when you leap it? You are big and strong, while I am small and thin."

The Frogman gravely thought over this sugges-tion. It was a fact that Cayke the Cookie Cook was not a heavy person. Perhaps he could leap the gulf with her on his back.

"If you are willing to risk a fall," said he, "I will make the attempt."

At once she sprang up and grabbed him around his neck with both her arms. That is, she grabbed him where his neck ought to be, for the Frogman had no neck at all. Then he squatted down, as frogs do when they leap, and with his powerful rear legs he made a tremendous jump.

Over the gulf he sailed, with the Cookie Cook on his back, and he had leaped so hard—to make sure of not falling in—that he sailed over a lot of bramble-bushes that grew on the other side and landed in a clear space which was so far beyond the gulf that when they looked back they could not see it at all.

Cayke now got off the Frogman's back and he stood erect again and carefully brushed the dust from his velvet coat and rearranged his white satin necktie.

"I had no idea I could leap so far," he said wonderingly. "Leaping is one more accomplishment I can now add to the long list of deeds I am able to perform."

"You are certainly fine at leap-frog," said the Cookie Cook, admiringly; "but, as you say, you are wonderful in many ways. If we meet with any people down here I am sure they will consider you the greatest and grandest of all living creatures."

"Yes," he replied, "I shall probably astonish strangers, because they have never before had the pleasure of seeing me. Also they will marvel at my great learning. Every time I open my mouth, Cayke, I am liable to say something important."

"That is true," she agreed, "and it is fortunate your mouth is so very wide and opens so far, for otherwise all the wisdom might not be able to get out of it."

"Perhaps nature made it wide for that very reason," said the Frogman. "But come; let us now go on, for it is getting late and we must find some sort of shelter before night overtakes us."

CHAPTER IV

AMONG THE WINKIES

THE SETTLED PARTS OF THE WINKIE COUNTRY ARE FULL OF HAPPY AND CON-
tented people who are ruled by a tin Emperor named Nick Chopper, who in turn is
a subject of the beautiful girl Ruler, Ozma of Oz. But not all of the Winkie Country
is fully settled. At the east, which part lies nearest the Emerald City, there are beautiful farmhouses and roads, but as you travel west you first come to a branch of the
Winkie River, beyond which there is a rough country where few people live, and
some of these are quite unknown to the rest of the world. After passing through this
rude section of territory, which no one ever visits, you would come to still another
branch of the Winkie River, after crossing which you would find another well-settled
part of the Winkie Country, extending westward quite to the Deadly Desert that
surrounds all the Land of Oz and separates that favored fairyland from the more
common outside world. The Winkies who live in this west section have many tin
mines, from which metal they make a great deal of rich jewelry and other articles, all
of which are highly esteemed in the Land of Oz because tin is so bright and pretty,
and there is not so much of it as there is of gold and silver.

Not all the Winkies are miners, however, for some till the fields and grow grains for food, and it was at one of these far west Winkie farms that the Frogman and Cayke the Cookie Cook first arrived after they had descended from the mountain of the Yips.

"Goodness me!" cried Nellary, the Winkie wife, when she saw the strange couple approaching her house. "I have seen many queer creatures in the Land of Oz, but none more queer than this giant frog, who dresses like a man and walks on his hind legs. Come here, Wiljon," she called to her husband, who was eating his breakfast, "and take a look at this astonishing freak."

Wiljon the Winkie came to the door and looked out. He was still standing in the doorway when the Frogman approached and said with a haughty croak:

"Tell me, my good man, have you seen a diamond-studded gold dishpan?"

"No; nor have I seen a copper-plated lobster," replied Wiljon, in an equally haughty tone.

The Frogman stared at him and said:

"Do not be insolent, fellow!"

"No," added Cayke the Cookie Cook, hastily, "you must be very polite to the great Frogman, for he is the wisest creature in all the world."

"Who says that?" inquired Wiljon.

"He says so himself," replied Cayke, and the Frogman nodded and strutted up and down, twirling his gold-headed cane very gracefully.

"Does the Scarecrow admit that this overgrown frog is the wisest creature in the world?" asked Wiljon.

"I do not know who the Scarecrow is," answered Cayke the Cookie Cook.

"Well, he lives at the Emerald City, and he is supposed to have the finest brains in all Oz. The Wizard gave them to him, you know."

"Mine grew in my head," said the Frogman pompously, "so I think they must be better than any wizard brains. I am so wise that sometimes my wisdom makes my head ache. I know so much that often I have to forget part of it, since no one creature, however great, is able to contain so much knowledge."

"It must be dreadful to be stuffed full of wisdom," remarked Wiljon reflectively, and eyeing the Frogman with a doubtful look. "It is my good fortune to know very little."

"I hope, however, you know where my jeweled dishpan is," said the Cookie Cook anxiously.

"I do not know even that," returned the Winkie. "We have trouble enough in keeping track of our own dishpans, without meddling with the dishpans of strangers."

Finding him so ignorant, the Frogman proposed that they walk on and seek Cayke's dishpan elsewhere. Wiljon the Winkie did not seem greatly impressed by the great Frogman, which seemed to that personage as strange as it was disappointing; but others in this unknown land might prove more respectful.

"I'd like to meet that Wizard of Oz," remarked Cayke, as they walked along a path. "If he could give a Scarecrow brains he might be able to find my dishpan."

"Poof!" grunted the Frogman scornfully. "I am greater than any wizard. Depend on me. If your dishpan is anywhere in the world I am sure to find it."

"If you do not, my heart will be broken," declared the Cookie Cook in a sorrowful voice.

For a while the Frogman walked on in silence. Then he asked:

"Why do you attach so much importance to a dishpan?"

"It is the greatest treasure I possess," replied the woman. "It belonged to my mother and to all my grandmothers, since the beginning of time. It is, I believe, the very oldest thing in all the Yip Country—or was while it was there—and," she added, dropping her voice to an awed whisper, "it has magic powers!"

"In what way?" inquired the Frogman, seeming to be surprised at this statement.

"Whoever has owned that dishpan has been a good cook, for one thing. No one else is able to make such good cookies as I have cooked, as you and all the Yips know. Yet, the very morning after my dishpan was stolen, I tried to make a batch of cookies and they burned up in the oven! I made another batch that proved too tough to eat, and I was so ashamed of them that I buried them in the ground. Even the third batch of cookies, which I brought with me in my basket, were pretty poor stuff and no better than any woman could make who does not own my diamond-studded gold dishpan. In fact, my good Frogman, Cayke the Cookie Cook will never be able to cook good cookies again until her magic dishpan is restored to her."

"In that case," said the Frogman with a sigh, "I suppose we must manage to find it."

CHAPTER V

OZMA'S FRIENDS
ARE PERPLEXED

"REALLY," SAID DOROTHY, LOOKING SOLEMN, "THIS IS VERY S'PRISING. We can't even find a shadow of Ozma anywhere in the Em'rald City; and, wherever she's gone, she's taken her Magic Picture with her."

She was standing in the courtyard of the palace with Betsy and Trot, while Scraps, the Patchwork Girl, danced around the group, her hair flying in the wind.

"P'raps," said Scraps, still dancing, "someone has stolen Ozma."

"Oh, they'd never dare do that!" exclaimed tiny Trot.

"And stolen the Magic Picture, too, so the thing can't tell where she is," added the Patchwork Girl.

"That's nonsense," said Dorothy. "Why, ev'ryone loves Ozma. There isn't a person in the Land of Oz who would steal a single thing she owns."

"Huh!" replied the Patchwork Girl. "You don't know ev'ry person in the Land of Oz."

"Why don't I?"

"It's a big country," said Scraps. "There are cracks and corners in it that even Ozma doesn't know of."

"The Patchwork Girl's just daffy," declared Betsy.

"No, she's right about that," replied Dorothy thoughtfully. "There are lots of queer people in this fairyland who never come near Ozma or the Em'rald City. I've seen some of 'em myself, girls; but I haven't seen all, of course, and there might be some wicked persons left in Oz, yet, though I think the wicked witches have all been destroyed."

Just then the Wooden Saw-Horse dashed into the courtyard with the Wizard of Oz on his back.

"Have you found Ozma?" cried the Wizard when the Saw-Horse stopped beside them.

"Not yet," said Dorothy. "Doesn't Glinda know where she is?"

"No. Glinda's Book of Records and all her magic instruments are gone. Someone must have stolen them."

"Goodness me!" exclaimed Dorothy, in alarm. "This is the biggest steal I ever heard of. Who do you think did it, Wizard?"

"I've no idea," he answered. "But I have come to get my own bag of magic tools and carry them to Glinda. She is so much more powerful than I that she may be able to discover the truth by means of my magic, quicker and better than I could myself."

"Hurry, then," said Dorothy, "for we've all gotten terr'bly worried."

The Wizard rushed away to his rooms but presently came back with a long, sad face.

"It's gone!" he said.

"What's gone?" asked Scraps.

"My black bag of magic tools. Someone must have stolen it!"

They looked at one another in amazement.

"This thing is getting desperate," continued the Wizard. "All the magic that belongs to Ozma, or to Glinda, or to me, has been stolen."

"Do you suppose Ozma could have taken them, herself, for some purpose?" asked Betsy.

"No, indeed," declared the Wizard. "I suspect some enemy has stolen Ozma and, for fear we would follow and recapture her, has taken all our magic away from us."

"How dreadful!" cried Dorothy. "The idea of anyone wanting to injure our dear Ozma! Can't we do anything to find her, Wizard?"

"I'll ask Glinda. I must go straight back to her and tell her that my magic tools have also disappeared. The good Sorceress will be greatly shocked, I know."

With this, he jumped upon the back of the Saw-Horse again, and the quaint steed, which never tired, dashed away at full speed.

The three girls were very much disturbed in mind. Even the Patchwork Girl was more quiet than usual and seemed to realize that a great calamity had overtaken them all. Ozma was a fairy of considerable power, and all the creatures in Oz, as well as the three mortal girls from the outside world, looked upon her as their protector and friend. The idea of their beautiful girl Ruler's being overpowered by an enemy and dragged from her splendid palace a captive was too astonishing for them to comprehend, at first. Yet what other explanation of the mystery could there be?

"Ozma wouldn't go away willingly, without letting us know about it," asserted Dorothy, "and she wouldn't steal Glinda's Great Book of Records, or the Wizard's magic, 'cause she could get them any time, just by asking for 'em. I'm sure some wicked person has done all this."

"Someone in the Land of Oz?" asked Trot.

"Of course. No one could get across the Deadly Desert, you know, and no one but an Oz person could know about the Magic Picture and the Book of Records and the Wizard's magic, or where they were kept, and so be able to steal the whole outfit before we could stop 'em. It must be someone who lives in the Land of Oz."

"But who—who—who?" asked Scraps. "That's the question. Who?"

"If we knew," replied Dorothy, severely, "we wouldn't be standing here doing nothing."

Just then two boys entered the courtyard and approached the group of girls. One boy was dressed in the fantastic Munchkin costume—a blue jacket and knickerbockers, blue leather shoes and a blue hat with a high peak and tiny silver bells dangling from its rim—and this was Ojo the Lucky, who had once come from the Munchkin Country of Oz and now lived in the Emerald City. The other boy was an American, from Philadelphia, and had lately found his way to Oz in the company of Trot and Cap'n Bill. His name was Button-Bright; that is, everyone called him by that name, and knew no other.

Button-Bright was not quite as big as the Munchkin boy, but he wore the same kind of clothes, only they were of different colors. As the two came up to the girls, arm in arm, Button-Bright remarked:

"Hello, Dorothy. They say Ozma is lost."

"*Who* says so?" she asked.

"Ev'rybody's talking about it, in the City," he replied.

"I wonder how the people found it out?" Dorothy asked.

"I know," said Ojo. "Jellia Jamb told them. She has been asking everywhere if anyone has seen Ozma."

"That's too bad," observed Dorothy, frowning.

"Why?" asked Button-Bright.

"There wasn't any use making all our people unhappy, till we were dead certain that Ozma can't be found."

"Pshaw," said Button-Bright, "it's nothing to get lost. I've been lost lots of times."

"That's true," admitted Trot, who knew that the boy had a habit of getting lost and then finding himself again; "but it's diff'rent with Ozma. She's the Ruler of all this big fairyland, and we're 'fraid that the reason she's lost is because somebody has stolen her away."

"Only wicked people steal," said Ojo. "Do you know of any wicked people in Oz, Dorothy?"

"No," she replied.

"They're here, though," cried Scraps, dancing up to them and then circling around the group. "Ozma's stolen; someone in Oz stole her; only wicked people steal; so someone in Oz is wicked!"

There was no denying the truth of this statement. The faces of all of them were now solemn and sorrowful.

"One thing is sure," said Button-Bright, after a time, "if Ozma has been stolen, someone ought to find her and punish the thief."

"There may be a lot of thieves," suggested Trot gravely, "and in this fairy country they don't seem to have any soldiers or policemen."

"There is one soldier," claimed Dorothy. "He has green whiskers and a gun and is a Major-General; but no one is afraid of either his gun or his whiskers, 'cause he's so tender-hearted that he wouldn't hurt a fly."

"Well, a soldier is a soldier," said Betsy, "and perhaps he'd hurt a wicked thief if he wouldn't hurt a fly. Where is he?"

"He went fishing about two months ago and hasn't come back yet," explained Button-Bright.

"Then I can't see that he will be of much use to us in this trouble," sighed little Trot. "But p'raps Ozma, who is a fairy, can get away from the thieves without any help from anybody."

"She *might* be able to," answered Dorothy, reflectively, "but if she had the power to do that, it isn't likely she'd have let herself be stolen. So the thieves must have been even more powerful in magic than our Ozma."

There was no denying this argument and, although they talked the matter over all the rest of that day, they were unable to decide how Ozma had been stolen against her will or who had committed the dreadful deed.

Toward evening the Wizard came back, riding slowly upon the Saw-Horse because he felt discouraged and perplexed. Glinda came, later, in her aerial chariot drawn by twenty milk-white swans, and she also seemed worried and unhappy. More of Ozma's friends joined them and that evening they all had a long talk together.

"I think," said Dorothy, "we ought to start out right away in search of our dear Ozma. It seems cruel for us to live comf'tably in her palace while she is a pris'ner in the power of some wicked enemy."

"Yes," agreed Glinda the Sorceress, "someone ought to search for her. I cannot go myself, because I must work hard in order to create some new instruments of sorcery by means of which I may rescue our fair Ruler. But if you can find her, in the meantime, and let me know who has stolen her, it will enable me to rescue her much more quickly."

"Then we'll start to-morrow morning," decided Dorothy. "Betsy and Trot and I won't waste another minute."

"I'm not sure you girls will make good detectives," remarked the Wizard; "but I'll go with you, to protect you from harm and to give you my advice. All my wizardry, alas, is stolen, so I am now really no more a wizard than any of you; but I will try to protect you from any enemies you may meet."

"What harm could happen to us in Oz?" inquired Trot.

"What harm happened to Ozma?" returned the Wizard. "If there is an Evil Power abroad in our fairyland, which is able to steal not only Ozma and her Magic Picture, but Glinda's Book of Records and all her magic, and my black bag containing all my tricks of wizardry, then that Evil Power may yet cause us considerable injury. Ozma is a fairy, and so is Glinda, so no power can kill or destroy them; but you girls are all mortals, and so are Button-Bright and I, so we must watch out for ourselves."

"Nothing can kill me," said Ojo, the Munchkin boy.

"That is true," replied the Sorceress, "and I think it may be well to divide the searchers into several parties, that they may cover all the land of Oz more quickly. So I will send Ojo and Unc Nunkie and Dr. Pipt into the Munchkin Country, which they are well acquainted with; and I will send the Scarecrow and the Tin Woodman into the Quadling Country, for they are fearless and brave and never tire; and to the Gillikin Country, where many dangers lurk, I will send the Shaggy Man and his brother, with Tik-Tok and Jack Pumpkinhead. Dorothy may make up her own party and travel into the Winkie Country. All of you must inquire everywhere for Ozma and try to discover where she is hidden."

They thought this a very wise plan and adopted it without question. In Ozma's absence Glinda the Good was the most important person in Oz and all were glad to serve under her direction.

CHAPTER VI

THE
SEARCH PARTY

NEXT MORNING, AS SOON AS THE SUN WAS UP, GLINDA FLEW BACK TO HER castle, stopping on the way to instruct the Scarecrow and the Tin Woodman, who were at that time staying at the college of Professor H. M. Woggle-Bug, T. E., and taking a course of his Patent Educational Pills. On hearing of Ozma's loss they started at once for the Quadling Country to search for her.

As soon as Glinda had left the Emerald City, Tik-Tok and the Shaggy Man and Jack Pumpkinhead, who had been present at the conference, began their journey into the Gillikin Country, and an hour later Ojo and Unc Nunkie joined Dr. Pipt and together they traveled toward the Munchkin Country. When all these searchers were gone, Dorothy and the Wizard completed their own preparations.

The Wizard hitched the Saw-Horse to the Red Wagon, which would seat four very comfortably. He wanted Dorothy, Betsy, Trot and the Patchwork Girl to ride in the wagon, but Scraps came up to them mounted upon the Woozy, and the Woozy said he would like to join the party. Now this Woozy was a most peculiar

animal, having a square head, square body, square legs and square tail. His skin was very tough and hard, resembling leather, and while his movements were somewhat clumsy the beast could travel with remarkable swiftness. His square eyes were mild and gentle in expression and he was not especially foolish. The Woozy and the Patchwork Girl were great friends and so the Wizard agreed to let the Woozy go with them.

Another great beast now appeared and asked to go along. This was none other than the famous Cowardly Lion, one of the most interesting creatures in all Oz. No lion that roamed the jungles or plains could compare in size or intelligence with this Cowardly Lion, who—like all animals living in Oz—could talk, and who talked with more shrewdness and wisdom than many of the people did. He said he was cowardly because he always trembled when he faced danger, but he had faced danger many times and never refused to fight when it was necessary. This Lion was a great favorite with Ozma and always guarded her throne on state occasions. He was also an old companion and friend of the Princess Dorothy, so the girl was delighted to have him join the party.

"I'm so nervous over our dear Ozma," said the Cowardly Lion in his deep, rumbling voice, "that it would make me unhappy to remain behind while you are trying to find her. But do not get into any danger, I beg of you, for danger frightens me terribly."

"We'll not get into danger if we can poss'bly help it," promised Dorothy; "but we shall do anything to find Ozma, danger or no danger."

The addition of the Woozy and the Cowardly Lion to the party gave Betsy Bobbin an idea and she ran to the marble stables at the rear of the palace and brought out her mule, Hank by name. Perhaps no mule you ever saw was so lean and bony and altogether plain looking as this Hank, but Betsy loved him dearly because he was faithful and steady and not nearly so stupid as most mules are considered to be. Betsy had a saddle for Hank and declared she would ride on his back, an arrangement approved by the Wizard because it left only four of the party to ride on the seats of the Red Wagon—Dorothy and Button-Bright and Trot and himself.

An old sailor-man, who had one wooden leg, came to see them off and suggested that they put a supply of food and blankets in the Red Wagon, inasmuch as they were uncertain how long they would be gone. This sailor-man was called Cap'n Bill. He was a former friend and comrade of Trot and had encountered many adventures in company with the little girl. I think he was sorry he could not go with her on this trip, but Glinda the Sorceress had asked Cap'n Bill to remain in the Emerald City and take charge of the royal palace while everyone else was away, and the one-legged sailor had agreed to do so.

They loaded the back end of the Red Wagon with everything they thought they might need, and then they formed a procession and marched from the palace through the Emerald City to the great gates of the wall that surrounded this beautiful capital of the Land of Oz. Crowds of citizens lined the streets to see them pass and to cheer them and wish them success, for all were grieved over Ozma's loss and anxious that she be found again.

First came the Cowardly Lion; then the Patchwork Girl riding upon the Woozy; then Betsy Bobbin on her mule Hank; and finally the Saw-Horse drawing the Red Wagon, in which were seated the Wizard and Dorothy and Button-Bright and Trot. No one was obliged to drive the Saw-Horse, so there were no reins to his harness; one had only to tell him which way to go, fast or slow, and he understood perfectly.

It was about this time that a shaggy little black dog who had been lying asleep in Dorothy's room in the palace woke up and discovered he was lonesome. Everything seemed very still throughout the great building, and Toto—that was the little dog's name—missed the customary chatter of the three girls. He never paid much atten-tion to what was going on around him and, although he could speak, he seldom said anything; so the little dog did not know about Ozma's loss or that everyone had gone in search of her. But he liked to be with people, and especially with his own mistress, Dorothy, and having yawned and stretched himself and found the door of the room ajar he trotted out into the corridor and went down the stately marble stairs to the hall of the palace, where he met Jellia Jamb.

"Where's Dorothy?" asked Toto.

"She's gone to the Winkie Country," answered the maid.

"When?"

"A little while ago," replied Jellia.

Toto turned and trotted out into the palace garden and down the long driveway until he came to the streets of the Emerald City. Here he paused to listen and, hearing sounds of cheering, he ran swiftly along until he came in sight of the Red Wagon and the Woozy and the Lion and the Mule and all the others. Being a wise little dog, he decided not to show himself to Dorothy just then, lest he be sent back home; but he never lost sight of the party of travelers, all of whom were so eager to get ahead that they never thought to look behind them.

When they came to the gates in the city wall the Guardian of the Gates came out to throw wide the golden portals and let them pass through.

"Did any strange person come in or out of the city on the night before last, when Ozma was stolen?" asked Dorothy.

"No, indeed, Princess," answered the Guardian of the Gates.

"Of course not," said the Wizard. "Anyone clever enough to steal all the things we have lost would not mind the barrier of a wall like this, in the least. I think the thief must have flown through the air, for otherwise he could not have stolen from Ozma's royal palace and Glinda's far-away castle in the same night. Moreover, as there are no airships in Oz and no way for airships from the outside world to get into this country, I believe the thief must have flown from place to place by means of magic arts which neither Glinda nor I understand."

On they went, and before the gates closed behind them Toto managed to dodge through them. The country surrounding the Emerald City was thickly settled and for a while our friends rode over nicely paved roads which wound through a fertile country dotted with beautiful houses, all built in the quaint Oz fashion. In the course of a few hours, however, they had left the tilled fields and entered the Country of the Winkies, which occupies a quarter of all the territory in the Land of Oz but is not so well known as many other parts of Ozma's fairyland. Long before night the travelers had crossed the Winkie River near to the Scarecrow's Tower (which was now vacant) and had entered the Rolling Prairie where few people live. They asked everyone they met for news of Ozma, but none in this district had seen her or even knew that she had been stolen. And by nightfall they had passed all the farmhouses and were obliged to stop and ask for shelter at the hut of a lonely shepherd. When they halted, Toto was not far behind. The little dog halted, too, and stealing softly around the party he hid himself behind the hut.

The shepherd was a kindly old man and treated the travelers with much courtesy. He slept out of doors that night, giving up his hut to the three girls, who made their beds on the floor with the blankets they had brought in the Red Wagon. The Wizard and Button-Bright also slept out of doors, and so did the Cowardly Lion and Hank the Mule. But Scraps and the Saw-Horse did not sleep at all and the Woozy could stay awake for a month at a time, if he wished to, so these three sat in a little group by themselves and talked together all through the night.

In the darkness, the Cowardly Lion felt a shaggy little form nestling beside his own, and he said sleepily:

"Where did you come from, Toto?"

"From home," said the dog. "If you roll over, roll the other way, so you won't smash me."

"Does Dorothy know you are here?" asked the Lion.

"I believe not," admitted Toto, and he added, a little anxiously: "Do you think, friend Lion, we are now far enough from the Emerald City for me to risk showing myself? Or will Dorothy send me back because I wasn't invited?"

"Only Dorothy can answer that question," said the Lion. "For my part, Toto, I consider this affair none of my business, so you must act as you think best."

Then the huge beast went to sleep again and Toto snuggled closer to his warm, hairy body and also slept. He was a wise little dog, in his way, and didn't intend to worry when there was something much better to do.

In the morning the Wizard built a fire, over which the girls cooked a very good breakfast.

Suddenly Dorothy discovered Toto sitting quietly before the fire and the little girl exclaimed:

"Goodness me, Toto! Where did you come from?"

"From the place you cruelly left me," replied the dog in a reproachful tone.

"I forgot all about you," admitted Dorothy, "and if I hadn't I'd prob'ly left you with Jellia Jamb, seeing this isn't a pleasure trip but stric'ly business. But, now that you're here, Toto, I s'pose you'll have to stay with us, unless you'd rather go back again. We may get ourselves into trouble, before we're done, Toto."

"Never mind that," said Toto, wagging his tail. "I'm hungry, Dorothy."

"Breakfas'll soon be ready and then you shall have your share," promised his little mistress, who was really glad to have her dog with her. She and Toto had traveled together before, and she knew he was a good and faithful comrade.

When the food was cooked and served the girls invited the old shepherd to join them in their morning meal. He willingly consented and while they ate he said to them:

"You are now about to pass through a very dangerous country, unless you turn to the north or to the south to escape its perils."

"In that case," said the Cowardly Lion, "let us turn, by all means, for I dread to face dangers of any sort."

"What's the matter with the country ahead of us?" inquired Dorothy.

"Beyond this Rolling Prairie," explained the shepherd, "are the Merry-Go-Round Mountains, set close together and surrounded by deep gulfs, so that no one is

able to get past them. Beyond the Merry-Go-Round Mountains it is said the Thistle-Eaters and the Herkus live."

"What are they like?" demanded Dorothy.

"No one knows, for no one has ever passed the Merry-Go-Round Mountains," was the reply; "but it is said that the Thistle-Eaters hitch dragons to their chariots and that the erkus are waited upon by giants whom they have conquered and made their slaves."

"Who says all that?" asked Betsy.

"It is common report," declared the shepherd. "Everyone believes it."

"I don't see how they know," remarked little Trot, "if no one has been there."

"Perhaps the birds who fly over that country brought the news," suggested Betsy.

"If you escaped those dangers," continued the shepherd, "you might encounter others, still more serious, before you came to the next branch of the Winkie River. It is true that beyond that river there lies a fine country, inhabited by good people, and if you reached there you would have no further trouble. It is between here and the west branch of the Winkie River that all dangers lie, for that is the unknown territory that is inhabited by terrible, lawless people."

"It may be, and it may not be," said the Wizard. "We shall know when we get there."

"Well," persisted the shepherd, "in a fairy country such as ours every undiscovered place is likely to harbor wicked creatures. If they were not wicked, they would discover themselves, and by coming among us submit to Ozma's rule and be good and considerate, as are all the Oz people whom we know."

"That argument," stated the little Wizard, "convinces me that it is our duty to go straight to those unknown places, however dangerous they may be; for it is surely some cruel and wicked person who has stolen our Ozma, and we know it would be folly to search among good people for the culprit. Ozma may not be hidden in the secret places of the Winkie Country, it is true, but it is our duty to travel to every spot, however dangerous, where our beloved Ruler is likely to be imprisoned."

"You're right about that," said Button-Bright approvingly. "Dangers don't hurt us; only things that happen ever hurt anyone, and a danger is a thing that might happen, and might not happen, and sometimes don't amount to shucks. I vote we go ahead and take our chances."

They were all of the same opinion, so they packed up and said good-bye to the friendly shepherd and proceeded on their way.

CHAPTER VII

THE MERRY-GO-ROUND MOUNTAINS

THE ROLLING PRAIRIE WAS NOT DIFFICULT TO TRAVEL OVER, ALTHOUGH IT WAS all up-hill and down-hill, so for a while they made good progress. Not even a shepherd was to be met with now, and the farther they advanced the more dreary the landscape became. At noon they stopped for a "picnic luncheon," as Betsy called it, and then they again resumed their journey. All the animals were swift and tireless and even the Cowardly Lion and the Mule found they could keep up with the pace of the Woozy and the Saw-Horse.

It was the middle of the afternoon when first they came in sight of a cluster of low mountains. These were cone-shaped, rising from broad bases to sharp peaks at the tops. From a distance the mountains appeared indistinct and seemed rather small—more like hills than mountains—but as the travelers drew nearer they noted a most unusual circumstance: the hills were all whirling around, some in one direction and some the opposite way.

"I guess these are the Merry-Go-Round Mountains, all right," said Dorothy.

"They must be," said the Wizard.

"They go 'round, sure enough," agreed Trot, "but they don't seem very merry."

There were several rows of these mountains, extending both to the right and to the left, for miles and miles. How many rows there might be, none could tell, but between the first row of peaks could be seen other peaks, all steadily whirling around one way or another. Continuing to ride nearer, our friends watched these hills attentively, until at last, coming close up, they discovered there was a deep but narrow gulf around the edge of each mountain, and that the mountains were set so close together that the outer gulf was continuous and barred farther advance.

At the edge of the gulf they all dismounted and peered over into its depths. There was no telling where the bottom was, if indeed there was any bottom at all. From where they stood it seemed as if the mountains had been set in one great hole in the ground, just close enough together so they would not touch, and that each mountain was supported by a rocky column beneath its base which extended far down in the black pit below. From the land side it seemed impossible to get across the gulf or, succeeding in that, to gain a foothold on any of the whirling mountains.

"This ditch is too wide to jump across," remarked Button-Bright.

"P'raps the Lion could do it," suggested Dorothy.

"What, jump from here to that whirling hill?" cried the Lion indignantly. "I should say not! Even if I landed there, and could hold on, what good would it do? There's another spinning mountain beyond it, and perhaps still another beyond that. I don't believe any living creature could jump from one mountain to another, when both are whirling like tops and in different directions."

"I propose we turn back," said the Wooden Saw-Horse, with a yawn of his chopped-out mouth, as he stared with his knot eyes at the Merry-Go-Round Mountains.

"I agree with you," said the Woozy, wagging his square head.

"We should have taken the shepherd's advice," added Hank the Mule.

The others of the party, however they might be puzzled by the serious problem that confronted them, would not allow themselves to despair.

"If we once get over these mountains," said Button-Bright, "we could probably get along all right."

"True enough," agreed Dorothy. "So we must find some way, of course, to get past these whirligig hills. But how?"

"I wish the Ork was with us," sighed Trot.

"But the Ork isn't here," said the Wizard, "and we must depend upon ourselves to conquer this difficulty. Unfortunately, all my magic has been stolen; otherwise I am sure I could easily get over the mountains."

"Unfortunately," observed the Woozy, "none of us has wings. And we're in a magic country without any magic."

"What is that around your waist, Dorothy?" asked the Wizard.

"That? Oh, that's just the Magic Belt I once captured from the Nome King," she replied.

"A Magic Belt! Why, that's fine. I'm sure a Magic Belt would take you over these hills."

"It might, if I knew how to work it," said the little girl. "Ozma knows a lot of its magic, but I've never found out about it. All I know is that while I am wearing it nothing can hurt me."

"Try wishing yourself across, and see if it will obey you," suggested the Wizard.

"But what good would that do?" asked Dorothy. "If I got across, it wouldn't help the rest of you, and I couldn't go alone among all those giants and dragons, while you stayed here."

"True enough," agreed the Wizard, sadly; and then, after looking around the group, he inquired, "What is that on your finger, Trot?"

"A ring. The Mermaids gave it to me," she explained, "and if ever I'm in trouble when I'm on the water, I can call the Mermaids and they'll come and help me. But the Mermaids can't help me on the land, you know, 'cause they swim, and—and—they haven't any legs."

"True enough," repeated the Wizard, more sadly.

There was a big, broad-spreading tree near the edge of the gulf and as the sun was hot above them they all gathered under the shade of the tree to study the problem of what to do next.

"If we had a long rope," said Betsy, "we could fasten it to this tree and let the other end of it down into the gulf and all slide down it."

"Well, what then?" asked the Wizard.

"Then, if we could manage to throw the rope up the other side," explained the girl, "we could all climb it and be on the other side of the gulf."

"There are too many 'ifs' in that suggestion," remarked the little Wizard. "And you must remember that the other side is nothing but spinning mountains, so we couldn't possibly fasten a rope to them—even if we had one."

"That rope idea isn't half bad, though," said the Patchwork Girl, who had been dancing dangerously near to the edge of the gulf.

"What do you mean?" asked Dorothy.

The Patchwork Girl suddenly stood still and cast her button eyes around the group.

"Ha, I have it!" she exclaimed. "Unharness the Saw-Horse, somebody; my fingers are too clumsy."

"Shall we?" asked Button-Bright doubtfully, turning to the others.

"Well, Scraps has a lot of brains, even if she is stuffed with cotton," asserted the Wizard. "If her brains can help us out of this trouble, we ought to use them."

So he began unharnessing the Saw-Horse, and Button-Bright and Dorothy helped him. When they had removed the harness the Patchwork Girl told them to take it all apart and buckle the straps together, end to end. And, after they had done this, they found they had one very long strap that was stronger than any rope.

"It would reach across the gulf, easily," said the Lion, who with the other animals had sat on his haunches and watched this proceeding. "But I don't see how it could be fastened to one of those dizzy mountains."

Scraps had no such notion as that in her baggy head. She told them to fasten one end of the strap to a stout limb of the tree, pointing to one which extended quite to the edge of the gulf. Button-Bright did that, climbing the tree and then crawling out upon the limb until he was nearly over the gulf. There he managed to fasten the strap, which reached to the ground below, and then he slid down it and was caught by the Wizard, who feared he might fall into the chasm.

Scraps was delighted. She seized the lower end of the strap and telling them all to get out of her way she went back as far as the strap would reach and then made a sudden run toward the gulf. Over the edge she swung, clinging to the strap until it had gone as far as its length permitted, when she let go and sailed gracefully through the air until she alighted upon the mountain just in front of them.

Almost instantly, as the great cone continued to whirl, she was sent flying against the next mountain in the rear, and that one had only turned halfway around when Scraps was sent flying to the next mountain behind it. Then her patchwork form disappeared from view entirely and the amazed watchers under the tree wondered what had become of her.

"She's gone, and she can't get back," said the Woozy.

"My, how she bounded from one mountain to another!" exclaimed the Lion.

"That was because they whirl so fast," the Wizard explained. "Scraps had nothing to hold on to and so of course she was tossed from one hill to another. I'm afraid we shall never see the poor Patchwork Girl again."

"*I* shall see her," declared the Woozy. "Scraps is an old friend of mine and, if there are really Thistle-Eaters and Giants on the other side of those tops, she will need someone to protect her. So, here I go!"

He seized the dangling strap firmly in his square mouth and in the same way that Scraps had done swung himself over the gulf. He let go the strap at the right moment and fell upon the first whirling mountain. Then he bounded to the next one back of it—not on his feet but "all mixed up," as Trot said—and then he shot across to another mountain, disappearing from view just as the Patchwork Girl had done.

"It seems to work, all right," remarked Button-Bright. "I guess I'll try it."

"Wait a minute," urged the Wizard. "Before any more of us make this desperate leap into the beyond, we must decide whether all will go, or if some of us will remain behind."

"Do you s'pose it hurt them much, to bump against those mountains?" asked Trot.

"I don't s'pose anything could hurt Scraps or the Woozy," said Dorothy, "and nothing can hurt me, because I wear the Magic Belt. So, as I'm anxious to find Ozma, I mean to swing myself across, too."

"I'll take my chances," decided Button-Bright.

"I'm sure it will hurt dreadfully, and I'm afraid to do it," said the Lion, who was already trembling; "but I shall do it if Dorothy does."

"Well, that will leave Betsy and the Mule and Trot," said the Wizard; "for of course, I shall go, that I may look after Dorothy. Do you two girls think you can find your way back home again?" he asked, addressing Trot and Betsy.

"I'm not afraid; not much, that is," said Trot. "It looks risky, I know, but I'm sure I can stand it if the others can."

"If it wasn't for leaving Hank," began Betsy in a hesitating voice; but the Mule interrupted her by saying:

"Go ahead, if you want to, and I'll come after you. A mule is as brave as a lion, any day."

"Braver," said the Lion, "for I'm a coward, friend Hank, and you are not. But of course the Saw-Horse—"

"Oh, nothing ever hurts me," asserted the Saw-Horse calmly. "There's never been any question about my going. I can't take the Red Wagon, though."

"No, we must leave the wagon," said the Wizard; "and also we must leave our food and blankets, I fear. But if we can defy these Merry-Go-Round Mountains to stop us we won't mind the sacrifice of some of our comforts."

"No one knows where we're going to land!" remarked the Lion, in a voice that sounded as if he were going to cry.

"We may not land at all," replied Hank; "but the best way to find out what will happen to us is to swing across as Scraps and the Woozy have done."

"I think I shall go last," said the Wizard; "so who wants to go first?"

"I'll go," decided Dorothy.

"No, it's my turn first," said Button-Bright. "Watch me!"

Even as he spoke the boy seized the strap and after making a run swung himself across the gulf. Away he went, bumping from hill to hill until he disappeared. They listened intently, but the boy uttered no cry until he had been gone some moments, when they heard a faint "Hullo-a!" as if called from a great distance.

The sound gave them courage, however, and Dorothy picked up Toto and held him fast under one arm while with the other hand she seized the strap and bravely followed after Button-Bright.

When she struck the first whirling mountain she fell upon it quite softly, but before she had time to think she flew through the air and lit with a jar on the side of the next mountain. Again she flew, and alighted; and again, and still again, until after five successive bumps she fell sprawling upon a green meadow and was so dazed and bewildered by her bumpy journey across the Merry-Go-Round Mountains that she lay quite still for a time, to collect her thoughts. Toto had escaped from her arms just as she fell, and he now sat beside her panting with excitement.

Then Dorothy realized that someone was helping her to her feet, and here was Button-Bright on one side of her and Scraps on the other, both seeming to be unhurt. The next object her eyes fell upon was the Woozy, squatting upon his square back end and looking at her reflectively, while Toto barked joyously to find his mistress unhurt after her whirlwind trip.

"Good!" said the Woozy; "here's another and a dog, both safe and sound. But my word, Dorothy, you flew some! If you could have seen yourself, you'd have been absolutely astonished."

"They say 'Time flies,'" laughed Button-Bright; "but Time never made a quicker journey than that."

Just then, as Dorothy turned around to look at the whirling mountains, she was in time to see tiny Trot come flying from the nearest hill to fall upon the soft grass not a yard away from where she stood. Trot was so dizzy she couldn't stand, at first, but she wasn't at all hurt and presently Betsy came flying to them and would have bumped into the others had they not retreated in time to avoid her.

Then, in quick succession, came the Lion, Hank and the Saw-Horse, bounding from mountain to mountain to fall safely upon the greensward. Only the Wizard was now left behind and they waited so long for him that Dorothy began to be worried. But suddenly he came flying from the nearest mountain and tumbled heels over head beside them. Then they saw that he had wound two of their blankets around his body, to keep the bumps from hurting him, and had fastened the blankets with some of the spare straps from the harness of the Saw-Horse.

CHAPTER VIII

THE MYSTERIOUS CITY

THERE THEY SAT UPON THE GRASS, THEIR HEADS STILL SWIMMING FROM their dizzy flights, and looked at one another in silent bewilderment. But presently, when assured that no one was injured, they grew more calm and collected, and the Lion said with a sigh of relief:

"Who would have thought those Merry-Go-Round Mountains were made of rubber?"

"Are they really rubber?" asked Trot.

"They must be," replied the Lion, "for otherwise we would not have bounded so swiftly from one to another without getting hurt."

"That is all guesswork," declared the Wizard, unwinding the blankets from his body, "for none of us stayed long enough on the mountains to discover what they are made of. But where are we?"

"That's guesswork," said Scraps. "The shepherd said the Thistle-Eaters live this side of the mountains and are waited on by giants."

"Oh no," said Dorothy; "it's the Herkus who have giant slaves, and the Thistle-Eaters hitch dragons to their chariots."

"How could they do that?" asked the Woozy. "Dragons have long tails, which would get in the way of the chariot wheels."

"And, if the Herkus have conquered the giants," said Trot, "they must be at least twice the size of giants. P'raps the Herkus are the biggest people in all the world!"

"Perhaps they are," assented the Wizard, in a thoughtful tone of voice. "And perhaps the shepherd didn't know what he was talking about. Let us travel on toward the west and discover for ourselves what the people of this country are like."

It seemed a pleasant enough country, and it was quite still and peaceful when they turned their eyes away from the silently whirling mountains. There were trees here and there and green bushes, while throughout the thick grass were scattered brilliantly colored flowers. About a mile away was a low hill that hid from them all the country beyond it, so they realized they could not tell much about the country until they had crossed the hill.

The Red Wagon having been left behind, it was now necessary to make other arrangements for traveling. The Lion told Dorothy she could ride upon his back, as she had often done before, and the Woozy said he could easily carry both Trot and the Patchwork Girl. Betsy still had her mule, Hank, and Button-Bright and the Wizard could sit together upon the long, thin back of the Saw-Horse, but they took care to soften their seat with a pad of blankets before they started. Thus mounted, the adventurers started for the hill, which was reached after a brief journey.

As they mounted the crest and gazed beyond the hill they discovered not far away a walled city, from the towers and spires of which gay banners were flying. It was not a very big city, indeed, but its walls were very high and thick and it appeared that the people who lived there must have feared attack by a powerful enemy, else they would not have surrounded their dwellings with so strong a barrier.

There was no path leading from the mountains to the city, and this proved that the people seldom or never visited the whirling hills; but our friends found the grass soft and agreeable to travel over and with the city before them they could not well lose their way. When they drew nearer to the walls, the breeze carried to their ears the sound of music—dim at first but growing louder as they advanced.

"That doesn't seem like a very terr'ble place," remarked Dorothy.

"Well, it *looks* all right," replied Trot, from her seat on the Woozy, "but looks can't always be trusted."

"*My* looks can," said Scraps. "I *look* patchwork, and I *am* patchwork, and no one but a blind owl could ever doubt that I'm the Patchwork Girl." Saying which she turned a somersault off the Woozy and, alighting on her feet, began wildly dancing about.

"Are owls ever blind?" asked Trot.

"Always, in the daytime," said Button-Bright. "But Scraps can see with her button eyes both day and night. Isn't it queer?"

"It's queer that buttons can see at all," answered Trot; "but—good gracious! what's become of the city?"

"I was going to ask that myself," said Dorothy. "It's gone!"

The animals came to a sudden halt, for the city had really disappeared—walls and all—and before them lay the clear, unbroken sweep of the country.

"Dear me!" exclaimed the Wizard. "This is rather disagreeable. It is annoying to travel almost to a place and then find it is not there."

"Where can it be, then?" asked Dorothy. "It cert'nly was there a minute ago."

"I can hear the music yet," declared Button-Bright, and when they all listened the strains of music could plainly be heard.

"Oh! There's the city—over at the left," called Scraps, and turning their eyes they saw the walls and towers and fluttering banners far to the left of them.

"We must have lost our way," suggested Dorothy.

"Nonsense," said the Lion. "I, and all the other animals, have been tramping straight toward the city ever since we first saw it."

"Then how does it happen—"

"Never mind," interrupted the Wizard, "we are no farther from it than we were before. It is in a different direction, that's all; so let us hurry and get there before it again escapes us."

So on they went directly toward the city, which seemed only a couple of miles distant; but when they had traveled less than a mile it suddenly disappeared again. Once more they paused, somewhat discouraged, but in a moment the button eyes of Scraps again discovered the city, only this time it was just behind them, in the direction from which they had come.

"Goodness gracious!" cried Dorothy. "There's surely something wrong with that city. Do you s'pose it's on wheels, Wizard?"

"It may not be a city at all," he replied, looking toward it with a speculative glance.

"What *could* it be, then?"

"Just an illusion."

"What's that?" asked Trot.

"Something you think you see and don't see."

"I can't believe that," said Button-Bright. "If we only saw it, we might be mistaken, but if we can see it and hear it, too, it must be there."

"Where?" asked the Patchwork Girl.

"Somewhere near us," he insisted.

"We will have to go back, I suppose," said the Woozy, with a sigh.

So back they turned and headed for the walled city until it disappeared again, only to reappear at the right of them. They were constantly getting nearer to it, however, so they kept their faces turned toward it as it flitted here and there to all points of the compass. Presently the Lion, who was leading the procession, halted abruptly and cried out: "Ouch!"

"What's the matter?" asked Dorothy.

"Ouch—ouch!" repeated the Lion, and leaped backward so suddenly that Dorothy nearly tumbled from his back. At the same time Hank the Mule yelled "Ouch!" almost as loudly as the Lion had done, and he also pranced backward a few paces.

"It's the thistles," said Betsy. "They prick their legs."

Hearing this, all looked down, and sure enough the ground was thick with thistles, which covered the plain from the point where they stood way up to the walls of the mysterious city. No pathways through them could be seen at all; here the soft grass ended and the growth of thistles began.

"They're the prickliest thistles I ever felt," grumbled the Lion. "My legs smart yet from their stings, though I jumped out of them as quickly as I could."

"Here is a new difficulty," remarked the Wizard in a grieved tone. "The city has stopped hopping around, it is true; but how are we to get to it over this mass of prickers?"

"They can't hurt *me*," said the thick-skinned Woozy, advancing fearlessly and trampling among the thistles.

"Nor me," said the Wooden Saw-Horse.

"But the Lion and the Mule cannot stand the prickers," asserted Dorothy, "and we can't leave them behind."

"Must we all go back?" asked Trot.

"Course not!" replied Button-Bright scornfully. "Always, when there's trouble, there's a way out of it, if you can find it."

"I wish the Scarecrow was here," said Scraps, standing on her head on the Woozy's square back. "His splendid brains would soon show us how to conquer this field of thistles."

"What's the matter with your brains?" asked the boy.

"Nothing," she said, making a flip-flop into the thistles and dancing among them without feeling their sharp points. "I could tell you in half a minute how to get over the thistles, if I wanted to."

"Tell us, Scraps!" begged Dorothy.

"I don't want to wear my brains out with overwork," replied the Patchwork Girl.

"Don't you love Ozma? And don't you want to find her?" asked Betsy reproachfully.

"Yes indeed," said Scraps, walking on her hands as an acrobat does at the circus.

"Well, we can't find Ozma unless we get past these thistles," declared Dorothy.

Scraps danced around them two or three times, without reply. Then she said:

"Don't look at me, you stupid folks. Look at those blankets."

The Wizard's face brightened at once.

"Of course!" he exclaimed. "Why didn't we think of those blankets before?"

"Because you haven't magic brains," laughed Scraps. "Such brains as you have are of the common sort that grow in your heads, like weeds in a garden. I'm sorry for you people who have to be born in order to be alive."

But the Wizard was not listening to her. He quickly removed the blankets from the back of the Saw-Horse and spread one of them upon the thistles, just next the grass. The thick cloth rendered the prickers harmless, so the Wizard walked over this first blanket and spread the second one farther on, in the direction of the phantom city.

"These blankets," said he, "are for the Lion and the Mule to walk upon. The Saw-Horse and the Woozy can walk on the thistles."

So the Lion and the Mule walked over the first blanket and stood upon the second one until the Wizard had picked up the one they had passed over and spread it in front of them, when they advanced to that one and waited while the one behind them was again spread in front.

"This is slow work," said the Wizard, "but it will get us to the city after a while."

"The city is a good half mile away, yet," announced Button-Bright.

"And this is awful hard work for the Wizard," added Trot.

"Why couldn't the Lion ride on the Woozy's back?" asked Dorothy. "It's a big, flat back, and the Woozy's mighty strong. Perhaps the Lion wouldn't fall off."

"You may try it, if you like," said the Woozy to the Lion. "I can take you to the city in a jiffy and then come back for Hank."

"I'm—I'm afraid," said the Cowardly Lion. He was twice as big as the Woozy.

"Try it," pleaded Dorothy.

"And take a tumble among the thistles?" asked the Lion reproachfully. But when the Woozy came close to him the big beast suddenly bounded upon its back and man-

aged to balance himself there, although forced to hold his four legs so close together that he was in danger of toppling over. The great weight of the monster Lion did not seem to affect the Woozy, who called to his rider, "Hold on tight!" and ran swiftly over the thistles toward the city.

The others stood on the blanket and watched the strange sight anxiously. Of course, the Lion couldn't "hold on tight" because there was nothing to hold to, and he swayed from side to side as if likely to fall off any moment. Still, he managed to stick to the Woozy's back until they were close to the walls of the city, when he leaped to the ground. Next moment the Woozy came dashing back at full speed.

"There's a little strip of ground next the wall where there are no thistles," he told them, when he had reached the adventurers once more. "Now then, friend Hank, see if you can ride as well as the Lion did."

"Take the others first," proposed the Mule. So the Saw-Horse and the Woozy made a couple of trips over the thistles to the city walls and carried all the people in safety, Dorothy holding little Toto in her arms. The travelers then sat in a group on a little hillock, just outside the wall, and looked at the great blocks of gray stone and waited for the Woozy to bring Hank to them. The Mule was very awkward and his legs trembled so badly that more than once they thought he would tumble off, but finally he reached them in safety and the entire party was now reunited. More than that, they had reached the city that had eluded them for so long and in so strange a manner.

"The gates must be around the other side," said the Wizard. "Let us follow the curve of the wall until we reach an opening in it."

"Which way?" asked Dorothy.

"We must guess that," he replied. "Suppose we go to the left? One direction is as good as another."

They formed in marching order and went around the city wall to the left. It wasn't a big city, as I have said, but to go way around it, outside the high wall, was quite a walk, as they became aware. But around it our adventurers went, without finding any sign of a gateway or other opening. When they had returned to the little mound from which they had started, they dismounted from the animals and again seated themselves on the grassy mound.

"It's mighty queer, isn't it?" asked Button-Bright.

"There must be *some* way for the people to get out and in," declared Dorothy. "Do you s'pose they have flying machines, Wizard?"

"No," he replied, "for in that case they would be flying all over the Land of Oz, and we know they have not done that. Flying machines are unknown here. I think it more likely that the people use ladders to get over the walls."

"It would be an awful climb, over that high stone wall," said Betsy.

"Stone, is it?" cried Scraps, who was again dancing wildly around, for she never tired and could never keep still for long.

"Course it's stone," answered Betsy scornfully. "Can't you see?"

"Yes," said Scraps, going closer. "I can *see* the wall, but I can't *feel* it." And then, with her arms outstretched, she did a very queer thing. She walked right into the wall and disappeared.

"For goodness sake!" cried Dorothy amazed, as indeed they all were.

CHAPTER IX

THE HIGH COCO-LORUM OF THI

AND NOW THE PATCHWORK GIRL CAME DANCING OUT OF THE WALL AGAIN.

"Come on!" she called. "It isn't there. There isn't any wall at all."

"What? No wall?" exclaimed the Wizard.

"Nothing like it," said Scraps. "It's a make-believe. You see it, but it isn't. Come on into the city; we've been wasting time."

With this she danced into the wall again and once more disappeared. Button-Bright, who was rather venturesome, dashed away after her and also became invisible to them. The others followed more cautiously, stretching out their hands to feel the wall and finding, to their astonishment, that they could feel nothing because nothing opposed them. They walked on a few steps and found themselves in the streets of a very beautiful city. Behind them they again saw the wall, grim and forbidding as ever; but now they knew it was merely an illusion, prepared to keep strangers from entering the city.

But the wall was soon forgotten, for in front of them were a number of quaint people who stared at them in amazement, as if wondering where they had come from. Our friends forgot their good manners, for a time, and returned the stares with interest, for so remarkable a people had never before been discovered in all the remarkable Land of Oz.

Their heads were shaped like diamonds and their bodies like hearts. All the hair they had was a little bunch at the tip top of their diamond-shaped heads and their eyes were very large and round and their noses and mouths very small. Their clothing was tight-fitting and of brilliant colors, being handsomely embroidered in quaint designs with gold or silver threads; but on their feet they wore sandals, with no stockings whatever. The expression of their faces was pleasant enough, although they now showed surprise at the appearance of strangers so unlike themselves, and our friends thought they seemed quite harmless.

"I beg your pardon," said the Wizard, speaking for his party, "for intruding upon you uninvited, but we are traveling on important business and find it necessary to visit your city. Will you kindly tell us by what name your city is called?"

They looked at one another uncertainly, each expecting some other to answer. Finally, a short one whose heart-shaped body was very broad replied:

"We have no occasion to call our city anything. It is where we live, that is all."

"But by what name do others call your city?" asked the Wizard.

"We know of no others, except yourselves," said the man. And then he inquired: "Were you born with those queer forms you have, or has some cruel magician transformed you to them from your natural shapes?"

"These are our natural shapes," declared the Wizard, "and we consider them very good shapes, too."

The group of inhabitants was constantly being enlarged by others who joined it. All were evidently startled and uneasy at the arrival of strangers.

"Have you a King?" asked Dorothy, who knew it was better to speak with someone in authority. But the man shook his diamond-like head.

"What is a King?" he asked.

"Isn't there anyone who rules over you?" inquired the Wizard.

"No," was the reply, "each of us rules himself; or, at least, tries to do so. It is not an easy thing to do, as you probably know."

The Wizard reflected.

"If you have disputes among you," said he, after a little thought, "who settles them?"

"The High Coco-Lorum," they answered in a chorus.

"And who is he?"

"The judge who enforces the laws," said the man who had first spoken.

"Then he is the principal person here?" continued the Wizard.

"Well, I would not say that," returned the man in a puzzled way. "The High Coco-Lorum is a public servant. However, he represents the laws, which we must all obey."

"I think," said the Wizard, "we ought to see your High Coco-Lorum and talk with him. Our mission here requires us to consult one high in authority, and the High Coco-Lorum ought to be high, whatever else he is."

The inhabitants seemed to consider this proposition reasonable, for they nodded their diamond-shaped heads in approval. So the broad one who had been their spokesman said: "Follow me," and, turning, led the way along one of the streets.

The entire party followed him, the natives falling in behind. The dwellings they passed were quite nicely planned and seemed comfortable and convenient. After leading them a few blocks their conductor stopped before a house which was neither better nor worse than the others. The doorway was shaped to admit the strangely formed bodies of these people, being narrow at the top, broad in the middle and tapering at the bottom. The windows were made in much the same way, giving the house a most peculiar appearance. When their guide opened the gate a music-box concealed in the gate-post began to play, and the sound attracted the attention of the High Coco-Lorum, who appeared at an open window and inquired:

"What has happened now?"

But in the same moment his eyes fell upon the strangers and he hastened to open the door and admit them—all but the animals, which were left outside with the throng of natives that had now gathered. For a small city there seemed to be a large number of inhabitants, but they did not try to enter the house and contented themselves with staring curiously at the strange animals. Toto followed Dorothy.

Our friends entered a large room at the front of the house, where the High Coco-Lorum asked them to be seated.

"I hope your mission here is a peaceful one," he said, looking a little worried, "for the Thists are not very good fighters and object to being conquered."

"Are your people called Thists?" asked Dorothy.

"Yes. I thought you knew that. And we call our city Thi."

"Oh!"

"We are Thists because we eat thistles, you know," continued the High Coco-Lorum.

"Do you really eat those prickly things?" inquired Button-Bright wonderingly.

"Why not?" replied the other. "The sharp points of the thistles cannot hurt us, because all our insides are gold-lined."

"Gold-lined!"

"To be sure. Our throats and stomachs are lined with solid gold, and we find the thistles nourishing and good to eat. As a matter of fact, there is nothing else in our country that is fit for food. All around the City of Thi grow countless thistles, and all we need do is to go and gather them. If we wanted anything else to eat we would have to plant it, and grow it, and harvest it, and that would be a lot of trouble and make us work, which is an occupation we detest."

"But tell me, please," said the Wizard, "how does it happen that your city jumps around so, from one part of the country to another?"

"The city doesn't jump; it doesn't move at all," declared the High Coco-Lorum. "However, I will admit that the land that surrounds it has a trick of turning this way or that; and so, if one is standing upon the plain and facing north, he is likely to find himself suddenly facing west—or east—or south. But once you reach the thistle fields you are on solid ground."

"Ah, I begin to understand," said the Wizard, nodding his head. "But I have another question to ask: How does it happen that the Thists have no King to rule over them?"

"Hush!" whispered the High Coco-Lorum, looking uneasily around to make sure they were not overheard. "In reality, I am the King, but the people don't know it. They think they rule themselves, but the fact is I have everything my own way. No one else knows anything about our laws, and so I make the laws to suit myself. If any oppose me, or question my acts, I tell them it's the law, and that settles it. If I called myself King, however, and wore a crown and lived in royal state, the people would not like me, and might do me harm. As the High Coco-Lorum of Thi, I'm considered a very agreeable person."

"It seems a very clever arrangement," said the Wizard. "And now, as you are the principal person in Thi, I beg you to tell us if the Royal Ozma is a captive in your city."

"No," answered the diamond-headed man, "we have no captives. No strangers but yourselves are here, and we have never before heard of the Royal Ozma."

"She rules over all of Oz," said Dorothy, "and so she rules your city and you, because you are in the Winkie Country, which is a part of the Land of Oz."

"It may be," returned the High Coco-Lorum, "for we do not study geography and have never inquired whether we live in the Land of Oz or not. And any Ruler who rules us from a distance, and unknown to us, is welcome to the job. But what has happened to your Royal Ozma?"

"Someone has stolen her," said the Wizard. "Do you happen to have any talented magician among your people—one who is especially clever, you know?"

"No, none especially clever. We do some magic, of course, but it is all of the ordinary kind. I do not think any of us has yet aspired to stealing Rulers, either by magic or otherwise."

"Then we've come a long way for nothing!" exclaimed Trot regretfully.

"But we are going farther than this," asserted the Patchwork Girl, bending her stuffed body backward until her yarn hair touched the floor and then walking around on her hands with her feet in the air.

The High Coco-Lorum watched Scraps admiringly.

"You may go farther on, of course," said he, "but I advise you not to. The Herkus live back of us, beyond the thistles and the twisting lands, and they are not very nice people to meet, I assure you."

"Are they giants?" asked Betsy.

"They are worse than that," was the reply. "They have giants for their slaves and they are so much stronger than giants that the poor slaves dare not rebel, for fear of being torn to pieces."

"How do you know?" asked Scraps.

"Everyone says so," answered the High Coco-Lorum.

"Have you seen the Herkus yourself?" inquired Dorothy.

"No, but what everyone says must be true; otherwise, what would be the use of their saying it?"

"We were told, before we got here, that you people hitch dragons to your chariots," said the little girl.

"So we do," declared the High Coco-Lorum. "And that reminds me that I ought to entertain you, as strangers and my guests, by taking you for a ride around our splendid City of Thi."

He touched a button and a band began to play; at least, they heard the music of a band, but couldn't tell where it came from.

"That tune is the order to my charioteer to bring around my dragon-chariot," said the High Coco-Lorum. "Every time I give an order it is in music, which is a much more pleasant way to address servants than in cold, stern words."

"Does this dragon of yours bite?" asked Button-Bright.

"Mercy, no! Do you think I'd risk the safety of my innocent people by using a biting dragon to draw my chariot? I'm proud to say that my dragon is harmless—unless his steering-gear breaks—and he was manufactured at the famous dragon-factory in this City of Thi. Here he comes and you may examine him for yourselves."

They heard a low rumble and a shrill squeaking sound and, going out to the front of the house, they saw coming around the corner a car drawn by a gorgeous jeweled dragon, which moved its head to right and left and flashed its eyes like the headlights of an automobile and uttered a growling noise as it slowly moved toward them.

When it stopped before the High Coco-Lorum's house Toto barked sharply at the sprawling beast, but even tiny Trot could see that the dragon was not alive. Its scales were of gold and each one was set with sparkling jewels, while it walked in such a stiff, regular manner that it could be nothing else than a machine. The chariot that trailed behind it was likewise of gold and jewels, and when they entered it they found there were no seats. Everyone was supposed to stand up while riding.

The charioteer was a little diamond-headed fellow who straddled the neck of the dragon and moved the levers that made it go.

"This," said the High Coco-Lorum, pompously, "is a wonderful invention. We are all very proud of our auto-dragons, many of which are in use by our wealthy inhabitants. Start the thing going, charioteer!"

The charioteer did not move.

"You forgot to order him in music," suggested Dorothy.

"Ah, so I did." He touched a button and a music-box in the dragon's head began to play a tune. At once the little charioteer pulled over a lever and the dragon began to move—very slowly and groaning dismally as it drew the clumsy chariot after it. Toto trotted between the wheels. The Saw-Horse, the Mule, the Lion and the Woozy followed after and had no trouble in keeping up with the machine; indeed, they had to go slow to keep from running into it. When the wheels turned another music-box concealed somewhere under the chariot played a lively march tune which was in striking contrast with the dragging movement of the strange vehicle and Button-Bright decided that the music he had heard when they first sighted this city was nothing else than a chariot plodding its weary way through the streets.

All the travelers from the Emerald City thought this ride the most uninteresting and dreary they had ever experienced, but the High Coco-Lorum seemed to think it was grand. He pointed out the different buildings and parks and fountains, in much the same way that the conductor does on an American "sight-seeing wagon" does, and being guests they were obliged to submit to the ordeal. But they became a little worried when their host told them he had ordered a banquet prepared for them in the City Hall.

"What are we going to eat?" asked Button-Bright suspiciously.

"Thistles," was the reply; "fine, fresh thistles, gathered this very day."

Scraps laughed, for she never ate anything, but Dorothy said in a protesting voice:

"*Our* insides are not lined with gold, you know."

"How sad!" exclaimed the High Coco-Lorum; and then he added, as an afterthought, "but we can have the thistles boiled, if you prefer."

"I'm 'fraid they wouldn't taste good, even then," said little Trot. "Haven't you anything else to eat?"

The High Coco-Lorum shook his diamond-shaped head.

"Nothing that I know of," said he. "But why should we have anything else, when we have so many thistles? However, if you can't eat what we eat, don't eat anything. We shall not be offended and the banquet will be just as merry and delightful."

Knowing his companions were all hungry, the Wizard said:

"I trust you will excuse us from the banquet, sir, which will be merry enough without us, although it is given in our honor. For, as Ozma is not in your city, we must leave here at once and seek her elsewhere."

"Sure we must!" Dorothy, and she whispered to Betsy and Trot: "I'd rather starve somewhere else than in this city, and—who knows?—we may run across somebody who eats reg'lar food and will give us some."

So, when the ride was finished, in spite of the protests of the High Coco-Lorum they insisted on continuing their journey.

"It will soon be dark," he objected.

"We don't mind the darkness," replied the Wizard.

"Some wandering Herku may get you."

"Do you think the Herkus would hurt us?" asked Dorothy.

"I cannot say, not having had the honor of their acquaintance. But they are said to be so strong that, if they had any other place to stand upon, they could lift the world."

"All of them together?" asked Button-Bright wonderingly.

"Any one of them could do it," said the High Coco-Lorum.

"Have you heard of any magicians being among them?" asked the Wizard, knowing that only a magician could have stolen Ozma in the way she had been stolen.

"I am told it is quite a magical country," declared the High Coco-Lorum, "and magic is usually performed by magicians. But I have never heard that they have any invention or sorcery to equal our wonderful auto-dragons."

They thanked him for his courtesy and, mounting their own animals, rode to the farther side of the city and right through the Wall of Illusion out into the open country.

"I'm glad we got away so easily," said Betsy. "I didn't like those queer-shaped people."

"Nor did I," agreed Dorothy. "It seems dreadful to be lined with sheets of pure gold and have nothing to eat but thistles."

"They seemed happy and contented, though," remarked the Wizard, "and those who are contented have nothing to regret and nothing more to wish for."

CHAPTER X

TOTO LOSES SOMETHING

FOR A WHILE THE TRAVELERS WERE CONSTANTLY LOSING THEIR DIRECTION, for beyond the thistle fields they again found themselves upon the turning-lands, which swung them around in such a freakish manner that first they were headed one way and then another. But by keeping the City of Thi constantly behind them the adventurers finally passed the treacherous turning-lands and came upon a stony country where no grass grew at all. There were plenty of bushes, however, and although it was now almost dark, the girls discovered some delicious yellow berries growing upon the bushes, one taste of which set them all to picking as many as they could find. The berries relieved their pangs of hunger, for a time, and as it now became too dark to see anything they camped where they were.

The three girls lay down upon one of the blankets—all in a row—and the Wizard covered them with the other blanket and tucked them in. Button-Bright crawled under the shelter of some bushes and was asleep in half a minute. The Wizard sat down with his back to a big stone and looked at the stars in the sky and thought gravely upon the dangerous adventure they had undertaken, wondering if they would ever be able to find their beloved Ozma again. The animals lay in a group by themselves, a little distance from the others.

"I've lost my growl!" said Toto, who had been very silent and sober all that day. "What do you suppose has become of it?"

"If you had asked me to keep track of your growl, I might be able to tell you," remarked the Lion sleepily. "But, frankly, Toto, I supposed you were taking care of it yourself."

"It's an awful thing to lose one's growl," said Toto, wagging his tail disconsolately. "What if you lost your roar, Lion? Wouldn't you feel terrible?"

"My roar," replied the Lion, "is the fiercest thing about me. I depend on it to frighten my enemies so badly that they won't dare to fight me."

"Once," said the Mule, "I lost my bray, so that I couldn't call to Betsy to let her know I was hungry. That was before I could talk, you know, for I had not yet come into the Land of Oz, and I found it was certainly very uncomfortable not to be able to make a noise."

"You make enough noise now," declared Toto. "But none of you have answered my question: Where is my growl?"

"You may search *me*," said the Woozy. "I don't care for such things myself."

"You snore terribly," asserted Toto.

"It may be," said the Woozy. "What one does when asleep one is not accountable for. I wish you would wake me up, some time when I'm snoring, and let me hear the sound. Then I can judge whether it is terrible or delightful."

"It isn't pleasant, I assure you," said the Lion, yawning.

"To me it seems wholly unnecessary," declared Hank the Mule.

"You ought to break yourself of the habit," said the Saw-Horse. "You never hear me snore, because I never sleep. I don't even whinny, as those puffy meat horses do. I wish that whoever stole Toto's growl had taken the Mule's bray and the Lion's roar and the Woozy's snore at the same time."

"Do you think, then, that my growl was stolen?"

"You have never lost it before, have you?" inquired the Saw-Horse.

"Only once, when I had a sore throat from barking too long at the moon."

"Is your throat sore now?" asked the Woozy.

"No," replied the dog.

"I can't understand," said Hank, "why dogs bark at the moon. They can't scare the moon, and the moon doesn't pay any attention to the bark. So why do dogs do it?"

"Were you ever a dog?" asked Toto.

"No, indeed," replied Hank. "I am thankful to say I was created a mule—the most beautiful of all beasts—and have always remained one."

The Woozy sat upon his square haunches to examine Hank with care.

"Beauty," said he, "must be a matter of taste. I don't say your judgment is bad, friend Hank, or that you are so vulgar as to be conceited. But if you admire big waggy ears, and a tail like a paint-brush, and hoofs big enough for an elephant, and a long neck and a body so skinny that one can count the ribs with one eye shut—if that's your idea of beauty, Hank—then either you or I must be much mistaken."

"You're full of edges," sneered the Mule. "If I were square, as you are, I suppose you'd think me lovely."

"Outwardly, dear Hank, I would," replied the Woozy. "But to be really lovely one must be beautiful without and within."

The Mule couldn't deny this statement, so he gave a disgusted grunt and rolled over so that his back was toward the Woozy. But the Lion, regarding the two calmly with his great yellow eyes, said to the dog:

"My dear Toto, our friends have taught us a lesson in humility. If the Woozy and the Mule are indeed beautiful creatures, as they seem to think, you and I must be decidedly ugly."

"Not to ourselves," protested Toto, who was a shrewd little dog. "You and I, Lion, are fine specimens of our own races. I am a fine dog and you are a fine lion. Only in point of comparison, one with another, can we be properly judged, so I will leave it to the poor old Saw-Horse to decide which is the most beautiful animal among us all. The Saw-Horse is wood, so he won't be prejudiced and will speak the truth."

"I surely will," responded the Saw-Horse, wagging his ears, which were chips set in his wooden head. "Are you all agreed to accept my judgment?"

"We are!" they declared, each one hopeful.

"Then," said the Saw-Horse, "I must point out to you the fact that you are all meat creatures, who tire unless they sleep, and starve unless they eat, and suffer from thirst unless they drink. Such animals must be very imperfect, and imperfect creatures cannot be beautiful. Now, *I* am made of wood."

"You surely have a wooden head," said the Mule.

"Yes, and a wooden body and wooden legs—which are as swift as the wind and as tireless. I've heard Dorothy say that 'handsome is as handsome does,' and I surely perform my duties in a handsome manner. Therefore, if you wish my honest judgment, I will confess that among us all I am the most beautiful."

The Mule snorted, and the Woozy laughed; Toto had lost his growl and could only look scornfully at the Saw-Horse, who stood in his place unmoved. But the Lion stretched himself and yawned, saying quietly:

"Were we all like the Saw-Horse we would all be Saw-Horses, which would be too many of the kind; were we all like Hank, we would be a herd of mules; if like Toto, we would be a pack of dogs; should we all become the shape of the Woozy, he would no longer be remarkable for his unusual appearance. Finally, were you all like me, I would consider you so common that I would not care to associate with you. To be individual, my friends, to be different from others, is the only way to become distinguished from the common herd. Let us be glad, therefore, that we differ from one another in form and in disposition. Variety is the spice of life and we are various enough to enjoy one another's society; so let us be content."

"There is some truth in that speech," remarked Toto reflectively. "But how about my lost growl?"

"The growl is of importance only to you," responded the Lion, "so it is your business to worry over the loss, not ours. If you love us, do not afflict your burdens on us; be unhappy all by yourself."

"If the same person stole my growl who stole Ozma," said the little dog, "I hope we shall find him very soon and punish him as he deserves. He must be the most cruel person in all the world, for to prevent a dog from growling when it is his nature to growl is just as wicked, in my opinion, as stealing all the magic in Oz."

CHAPTER XI

BUTTON-BRIGHT
LOSES HIMSELF

THE PATCHWORK GIRL, WHO NEVER SLEPT AND WHO COULD SEE VERY WELL in the dark, had wandered among the rocks and bushes all night long, with the result that she was able to tell some good news the next morning.

"Over the crest of the hill before us," she said, "is a big grove of trees of many kinds, on which all sorts of fruits grow. If you will go there you will find a nice breakfast awaiting you."

This made them eager to start, so as soon as the blankets were folded and strapped to the back of the Saw-Horse they all took their places on the animals and set out for the big grove Scraps had told them of.

As soon as they got over the brow of the hill they discovered it to be a really immense orchard, extending for miles to the right and left of them. As their way led straight through the trees they hurried forward as fast as possible.

The first trees they came to bore quinces, which they did not like. Then there were rows of citron trees and then crab apples and afterward limes and lemons. But beyond these they found a grove of big golden oranges, juicy and sweet, and the fruit hung low on the branches, so they could pluck it easily.

They helped themselves freely and all ate oranges as they continued on their way. Then, a little farther along, they came to some trees bearing fine red apples, which they also feasted on, and the Wizard stopped here long enough to tie a lot of the apples in one end of a blanket.

"We do not know what will happen to us after we leave this delightful orchard," he said, "so I think it wise to carry a supply of apples with us. We can't starve as long as we have apples, you know."

Scraps wasn't riding the Woozy just now. She loved to climb the trees and swing herself by the branches from one tree to another. Some of the choicest fruit was gathered by the Patchwork Girl from the very highest limbs and tossed down to the others.

Suddenly, Trot asked, "Where's Button-Bright?" and when the others looked for him, they found the boy had disappeared.

"Dear me!" cried Dorothy. "I guess he's lost again, and that will mean our waiting here until we can find him."

"It's a good place to wait," suggested Betsy, who had found a plum tree and was eating some of its fruit.

"How can you wait here, and find Button-Bright, at one and the same time?" inquired the Patchwork Girl, hanging by her toes on a limb just over the heads of the three mortal girls.

"Perhaps he'll come back here," answered Dorothy.

"If he tries that, he'll prob'ly lose his way," said Trot. "I've known him to do that, lots of times. It's losing his way that gets him lost."

"Very true," said the Wizard. "So all the rest of you must stay here while I go look for the boy."

"Won't *you* get lost, too?" asked Betsy.

"I hope not, my dear."

"Let *me* go," said Scraps, dropping lightly to the ground. "I can't get lost, and I'm more likely to find Button-Bright than any of you."

Without waiting for permission, she darted away through the trees and soon disappeared from their view.

"Dorothy," said Toto, squatting beside his little mistress, "I've lost my growl."

"How did that happen?" she asked.

"I don't know," replied Toto. "Yesterday morning the Woozy nearly stepped on me and I tried to growl at him and found I couldn't growl a bit."

"Can you bark?" inquired Dorothy.

"Oh, yes, indeed!"

"Then never mind the growl," said she.

"But what will I do when I get home to the Glass Cat and the Pink Kitten?" asked the little dog in an anxious tone.

"They won't mind, if you can't growl at them, I'm sure," said Dorothy. "I'm sorry for you, of course, Toto, for it's just those things we can't do that we want to do most of all; but before we get back you may find your growl again."

"Do you think the person who stole Ozma stole my growl?"

Dorothy smiled.

"Perhaps, Toto."

"Then he's a scoundrel!" cried the little dog.

"Anyone who would steal Ozma is as bad as bad can be," agreed Dorothy, "and when we remember that our dear friend, the lovely Ruler of Oz, is lost, we ought not to worry over just a growl."

Toto was not entirely satisfied with this remark, for the more he thought upon his lost growl the more important his misfortune became. When no one was looking he went away among the trees and tried his best to growl—even a little bit—but could not manage to do so. All he could do was bark, and a bark cannot take the place of a growl, so he sadly returned to the others.

Now, Button-Bright had no idea that he was lost, at first. He had merely wandered from tree to tree, seeking the finest fruit, until he discovered he was alone in the great orchard. But that didn't worry him just then and seeing some apricot trees farther on he went to them; then he discovered some cherry trees; just beyond these were some tangerines.

"We've found 'most ev'ry kind of fruit but peaches," he said to himself, "so I guess there are peaches here, too, if I can find the trees."

He searched here and there, paying no attention to his way, until he found that the trees surrounding him bore only nuts. He put some walnuts in his pockets and kept on searching and at last—right among the nut trees—he came upon one solitary peach tree. It was a graceful, beautiful tree, but although it was thickly leaved it bore no fruit except one large, splendid peach, rosy-cheeked and fuzzy and just right to eat.

Button-Bright had some trouble getting that lonesome peach, for it hung far out of reach; but he climbed the tree nimbly and crept out on the branch on which it grew and after several trials, during which he was in danger of falling, he finally managed to pick it. Then he got back to the ground and decided the fruit was well worth his trouble. It was delightfully fragrant and when he bit into it he found it the most delicious morsel he had ever tasted.

"I really ought to divide it with Trot and Dorothy and Betsy," he said; "but p'rhaps there are plenty more in some other part of the orchard."

In his heart he doubted this statement, for this was a solitary peach tree, while all the other fruits grew upon many trees set close to one another; but that one luscious bite made him unable to resist eating the rest of it and soon the peach was all gone except the pit.

Button-Bright was about to throw this peach-pit away when he noticed that it was of pure gold. Of course this surprised him, but so many things in the Land of Oz were surprising that he did not give much thought to the golden peach-pit. He put it in his pocket, however, to show to the girls, and five minutes afterward had forgotten all about it.

For now he realized that he was far separated from his companions, and knowing that this would worry them and delay their journey, he began to shout as loud as he could. His voice did not penetrate very far among all those trees, and after shouting a dozen times and getting no answer, he sat down on the ground and said:

"Well, I'm lost again. It's too bad, but I don't see how it can be helped."

As he leaned his back against a tree he looked up and saw a Bluefinch fly down from the sky and alight upon a branch just before him. The bird looked and looked at him. First it looked with one bright eye and then turned its head and looked at him with the other eye. Then, fluttering its wings a little, it said:

"Oho! So you've eaten the enchanted peach, have you?"

"Was it enchanted?" asked Button-Bright.

"Of course," replied the Bluefinch. "Ugu the Shoemaker did that."

"But why? And how was it enchanted? And what will happen to one who eats it?" questioned the boy.

"Ask Ugu the Shoemaker; he knows," said the bird, pruning its feathers with its bill.

"And who is Ugu the Shoemaker?"

"The one who enchanted the peach and placed it here—in the exact center of the Great Orchard—so no one would ever find it. We birds didn't dare to eat it; we are too wise for that. But you are Button-Bright, from the Emerald City, and you— you—YOU ate the enchanted peach! You must explain to Ugu the Shoemaker why you did that."

And then, before the boy could ask any more questions, the bird flew away and left him alone.

Button-Bright was not much worried to find that the peach he had eaten was enchanted. It certainly had tasted very good and his stomach didn't ache a bit. So again he began to reflect upon the best way to rejoin his friends.

"Whichever direction I follow is likely to be the wrong one," he said to himself, "so I'd better stay just where I am and let *them* find *me*—if they can."

A White Rabbit came hopping through the orchard and paused a little way off to look at him.

"Don't be afraid," said Button-Bright; "I won't hurt you."

"Oh, I'm not afraid for myself," returned the White Rabbit. "It's you I'm worried about."

"Yes; I'm lost," said the boy.

"I fear you are, indeed," answered the Rabbit. "Why on earth did you eat the enchanted peach?"

The boy looked at the excited little animal thoughtfully.

"There were two reasons," he explained. "One reason was that I like peaches, and the other reason was that I didn't know it was enchanted."

"That won't save you from Ugu the Shoemaker," declared the White Rabbit and it scurried away before the boy could ask any more questions.

"Rabbits and birds," he thought, "are timid creatures and seem afraid of this shoemaker—whoever he may be. If there was another peach half as good as that other, I'd eat it in spite of a dozen enchantments or a hundred shoemakers!"

Just then Scraps came dancing along and saw him sitting at the foot of the tree.

"Oh, here you are!" she said. "Up to your old tricks, eh? Don't you know it's impolite to get lost and keep everybody waiting for you? Come along, and I'll lead you back to Dorothy and the others."

Button-Bright rose slowly to accompany her.

"That wasn't much of a loss," he said cheerfully. "I haven't been gone half a day, so there's no harm done."

Dorothy, however, when the boy rejoined the party, gave him a good scolding.

"When we're doing such an important thing as searching for Ozma," said she, "it's naughty for you to wander away and keep us from getting on. S'pose she's a pris'ner—in a dungeon cell!—do you want to keep our dear Ozma there any longer than we can help?"

"If she's in a dungeon cell, how are you going to get her out?" inquired the boy.

"Never you mind; we'll leave that to the Wizard; he's sure to find a way."

The Wizard said nothing, for he realized that without his magic tools he could do no more than any other person. But there was no use reminding his companions of that fact; it might discourage them.

"The important thing just now," he remarked, "is to find Ozma; and, as our party is again happily reunited, I propose we move on."

As they came to the edge of the Great Orchard the sun was setting and they knew it would soon be dark. So it was decided to camp under the trees, as another broad plain was before them. The Wizard spread the blankets on a bed of soft leaves and presently all of them except Scraps and the Saw-Horse were fast asleep. Toto snuggled close to his friend the Lion, and the Woozy snored so loudly that the Patchwork Girl covered his square head with her apron to deaden the sound.

CHAPTER XII

THE CZAROVER OF HERKU

Trot wakened just as the sun rose and, slipping out of the blankets, went to the edge of the Great Orchard and looked across the plain. Something glittered in the far distance.

"That looks like another city," she said half aloud.

"And another city it is," declared Scraps, who had crept to Trot's side unheard, for her stuffed feet made no sound. "The Saw-Horse and I made a journey in the dark, while you were all asleep, and we found over there a bigger city than Thi. There's a wall around it, too, but it has gates and plenty of pathways."

"Did you go in?" asked Trot.

"No, for the gates were locked and the wall was a real wall. So we came back here again. It isn't far to the city. We can reach it in two hours after you've had your breakfasts."

Trot went back and, finding the other girls now awake, told them what Scraps had said. So they hurriedly ate some fruit—there were plenty of plums and fijoas in this part of the orchard—and then they mounted the animals and set out upon the journey to the strange city. Hank the Mule had breakfasted on grass and the Lion had stolen away and found a breakfast to his liking; he never told what it was, but Dorothy hoped the little rabbits and the field mice had kept out of his way. She warned Toto not to chase birds and gave the dog some apple, with which he was quite content. The Woozy was as fond of fruit as of any other food, except honey, and the Saw-Horse never ate at all.

Except for their worry over Ozma they were all in good spirits as they proceeded swiftly over the plain. Toto still worried over his lost growl, but like a wise little dog kept his worry to himself. Before long the city grew nearer and they could examine it with interest.

In outward appearance the place was more imposing than Thi, and it was a square city, with a square, four-sided wall around it and on each side was a square gate of burnished copper. Everything about the city looked solid and substantial; there were no banners flying and the towers that rose above the city wall seemed bare of any ornament whatever.

A path led from the fruit orchard directly to one of the city gates, showing that the inhabitants preferred fruit to thistles. Our friends followed this path to the gate, which they found fast shut. But the Wizard advanced and pounded upon it with his fist, saying in a loud voice: "Open!"

At once there rose above the great wall a row of immense heads, all of which looked down at them as if to see who was intruding. The size of these heads was astonishing and our friends at once realized that they belonged to giants, who were standing within the city. All had thick, bushy hair and whiskers, on some the hair being white and on others black or red or yellow, while the hair of a few was just turning gray, showing that the giants were of all ages. However fierce the heads might seem the eyes were mild in expression, as if the creatures had been long subdued, and their faces expressed patience rather than ferocity.

"What's wanted?" asked one old giant, in a low, grumbling voice.

"We are strangers and we wish to enter the city," replied the Wizard.

"Do you come in war or peace?" asked another.

"In peace, of course," retorted the Wizard, and he added impatiently: "Do we look like an army of conquest?"

"No," said the first giant who had spoken, "you look like innocent tramps; but one never can tell by appearances. Wait here until we report to our masters. No one can enter here without the permission of Vig, the Czarover."

"Who's that?" inquired
Dorothy. But the heads had
all bobbed down and disappeared behind the walls, so
there was no answer.

They waited a long time
before the gate rolled back with
a rumbling sound and a loud voice
cried: "Enter!" But they lost no time in taking
advantage of the invitation.

On either side of the broad street that
led into the city from the gate stood a row
of huge giants—twenty of them on a
side and all standing so close together
that their elbows touched. They wore
uniforms of blue and yellow and were armed
with clubs as big around as tree-trunks. Each giant had around his neck a broad band
of gold, riveted on, to show he was a slave.

As our friends entered, riding upon the Lion, the Woozy, the Saw-Horse and
the Mule, the giants half turned and walked in two files on either side of them, as if
escorting them on their way. It looked to Dorothy as if all her party had been made

prisoners, for even mounted on their animals their heads scarcely reached to the knees of the marching giants. The girls and Button-Bright were anxious to know what sort of a city they had entered, and what the people were like who had made these powerful creatures their slaves. Through the legs of the giants, as they walked, Dorothy could see rows of houses on each side the street and throngs of people standing on the sidewalks; but the people were of ordinary size and the only remarkable thing about them was the fact that they were dreadfully lean and thin. Between their skin and their bones there seemed to be little or no flesh, and they were mostly stoop-shouldered and weary looking, even to the little children.

More and more Dorothy wondered how and why the great giants had ever submitted to become slaves of such skinny, languid masters, but there was no chance to question anyone until they arrived at a big palace located in the heart of the city. Here the giants formed lines to the entrance and stood still while our friends rode into the courtyard of the palace. Then the gates closed behind them and before them was a skinny little man who bowed low and said in a sad voice:

"If you will be so obliging as to dismount, it will give me pleasure to lead you into the presence of the World's Most Mighty Ruler, Vig the Czarover."

"I don't believe it!" said Dorothy indignantly.

"What don't you believe?" asked the man.

"I don't believe your Czarover can hold a candle to our Ozma."

"He wouldn't hold a candle under any circumstances, or to any living person," replied the man very seriously, "for he has slaves to do such things and the Mighty Vig is too dignified to do anything that others can do for him. He even obliges a slave to sneeze for him, if ever he catches cold. However, if you dare to face our powerful Ruler, follow me."

"We dare anything," said the Wizard, "so go ahead."

Through several marble corridors having lofty ceilings they passed, finding each corridor and doorway guarded by servants; but these servants of the palace were of the people and not giants, and they were so thin that they almost resembled skeletons. Finally they entered a great circular room with a high domed ceiling, where the Czarover sat on a throne cut from a solid block of white marble and decorated with purple silk hangings and gold tassels.

The Ruler of these people was combing his eyebrows when our friends entered the throne-room and stood before him, but he put the comb in his pocket and examined the strangers with evident curiosity. Then he said:

"Dear me, what a surprise! You have really shocked me. For no outsider has ever before come to our City of Herku, and I cannot imagine why *you* have ventured to do so."

"We are looking for Ozma, the Supreme Ruler of the Land of Oz," replied the Wizard.

"Do you see her anywhere around here?" asked the Czarover.

"Not yet, Your Majesty; but perhaps you may tell us where she is."

"No; I have my hands full keeping track of my own people. I find them hard to manage because they are so tremendously strong."

"They don't look very strong," said Dorothy. "It seems as if a good wind would blow 'em way out of the city, if it wasn't for the wall."

"Just so—just so," admitted the Czarover. "They really look that way, don't they? But you must never trust to appearances, which have a way of fooling one. Perhaps you noticed that I prevented you from meeting any of my people. I protected you with my giants while you were on the way from the gates to my palace, so that not a Herku got near you."

"Are your people so dangerous, then?" asked the Wizard.

"To strangers, yes; but only because they are so friendly. For, if they shake hands with you, they are likely to break your arms or crush your fingers to a jelly."

"Why?" asked Button-Bright.

"Because we are the strongest people in all the world."

"Pshaw!" exclaimed the boy. "That's bragging. You prob'ly don't know how strong other people are. Why, once I knew a man in Philadelphi' who could bend iron bars with just his hands!"

"But—mercy me!—it's no trick to bend iron bars," said His Majesty. "Tell me, could this man crush a block of stone with his bare hands?"

"No one could do that," declared the boy.

"If I had a block of stone I'd show you," said the Czarover, looking around the room. "Ah, here is my throne. The back is too high, anyhow, so I'll just break off a piece of that."

He rose to his feet and tottered in an uncertain way around the throne. Then he took hold of the back and broke off a piece of marble over a foot thick.

"This," said he, coming back to his seat, "is very solid marble and much harder than ordinary stone. Yet I can crumble it easily with my fingers—a proof that I am very strong."

Even as he spoke he began breaking off chunks of marble and crumbling them as one would a bit of earth. The Wizard was so astonished that he took a piece in his own hands and tested it, finding it very hard indeed.

Just then one of the giant servants entered and exclaimed:

"Oh, Your Majesty, the cook has burned the soup! What shall we do?"

"How dare you interrupt me?" asked the Czarover, and grasping the immense giant by one of his legs he raised him in the air and threw him headfirst out of an open window.

"Now, tell me," he said, turning to Button-Bright, "could your man in Philadelphia crumble marble in his fingers?"

"I guess not," said Button-Bright, much impressed by the skinny monarch's strength.

"What makes you so strong?" inquired Dorothy.

"It's the zosozo," he explained, "which is an invention of my own. I and all my people eat zosozo, and it gives us tremendous strength. Would you like to eat some?"

"No, thank you," replied the girl. "I—I don't want to get so thin."

"Well, of course one can't have strength and flesh at the same time," said the Czarover. "Zosozo is pure energy, and it's the only compound of its sort in existence. I never allow our giants to have it, you know, or they would soon become our masters, since they are bigger that we; so I keep all the stuff locked up in my private laboratory. Once a year I feed a teaspoonful of it to each of my people—men, women and children—so every one of them is nearly as strong as I am. Wouldn't you like a dose, sir?" he asked, turning to the Wizard.

"Well," said the Wizard, "if you would give me a little zosozo in a bottle, I'd like to take it with me on my travels. It might come in handy, on occasion."

"To be sure. I'll give you enough for six doses," promised the Czarover. "But don't take more than a teaspoonful at a time. Once Ugu the Shoemaker took two teaspoonsful, and it made him so strong that when he leaned against the city wall he pushed it over, and we had to build it up again."

"Who is Ugu the Shoemaker?" asked Button-Bright curiously, for he now remembered that the bird and the rabbit had claimed Ugu the Shoemaker had enchanted the peach he had eaten.

"Why, Ugu is a great magician, who used to live here. But he's gone away, now," replied the Czarover.

"Where has he gone?" asked the Wizard quickly.

"I am told he lives in a wickerwork castle in the mountains to the west of here. You see, Ugu became such a powerful magician that he didn't care to live in our city any longer, for fear we would discover some of his secrets. So he went to the mountains and built him a splendid wicker castle, which is so strong that even I and my people could not batter it down, and there he lives all by himself."

"This is good news," declared the Wizard, "for I think this is just the magician we are searching for. But why is he called Ugu the Shoemaker?"

"Once he was a very common citizen here and made shoes for a living," replied the monarch of Herku. "But he was descended from the greatest wizard and sorcerer who ever lived—in this or in any other country—and one day Ugu the Shoemaker discovered all the magical books and recipes of his famous great-grandfather, which had been hidden away in the attic of his house. So he began to study the papers and books and to practice magic, and in time he became so skillful that, as I said, he scorned our city and built a solitary castle for himself."

"Do you think," asked Dorothy anxiously, "that Ugu the Shoemaker would be wicked enough to steal our Ozma of Oz?"

"And the Magic Picture?" asked Trot.

"And the Great Book of Records of Glinda the Good?" asked Betsy.

"And my own magic tools?" asked the Wizard.

"Well," replied the Czarover, "I won't say that Ugu is wicked, exactly, but he is very ambitious to become the most powerful magician in the world, and so I suppose he would not be too proud to steal any magic things that belonged to anybody else—if he could manage to do so."

"But how about Ozma? Why would he wish to steal *her?*" questioned Dorothy.

"Don't ask me, my dear. Ugu doesn't tell me why he does things, I assure you."

"Then we must go and ask him ourselves," declared the little girl.

"I wouldn't do that, if I were you," advised the Czarover, looking first at the three girls and then at the boy and the little Wizard and finally at the stuffed Patchwork Girl. "If Ugu has really stolen your Ozma, he will probably keep her a prisoner, in spite of all your threats or entreaties. And, with all his magical knowledge, he would be a dangerous person to attack. Therefore, if you are wise, you will go home again and find a new Ruler for the Emerald City and the Land of Oz. But perhaps it isn't Ugu the Shoemaker who has stolen your Ozma."

"The only way to settle that question," replied the Wizard, "is to go to Ugu's castle and see if Ozma is there. If she is, we will report the matter to the great

Sorceress, Glinda the Good, and I'm pretty sure she will find a way to rescue our darling Ruler from the Shoemaker."

"Well, do as you please," said the Czarover, "but if you are all transformed into hummingbirds or caterpillars, don't blame me for not warning you."

They stayed the rest of that day in the City of Herku and were fed at the royal table of the Czarover and given sleeping rooms in his palace. The strong monarch treated them very nicely and gave the Wizard a little golden vial of zosozo, to use if ever he or any of his party wished to acquire great strength.

Even at the last, the Czarover tried to persuade them not to go near Ugu the Shoemaker, but they were resolved on the venture and the next morning bade the friendly monarch a cordial good-bye and, mounting upon their animals, left the Herkus and the City of Herku and headed for the mountains that lay to the west.

CHAPTER XIII

THE TRUTH POND

I<small>T SEEMS A LONG TIME SINCE WE HAVE HEARD ANYTHING OF THE</small> F<small>ROGMAN</small> and Cayke the Cookie Cook, who had left the Yip Country in search of the diamond-studded gold dishpan which had been mysteriously stolen the same night that Ozma had disappeared from the Emerald City. But you must remember that while the Frogman and the Cookie Cook were preparing to descend from their mountain-top, and even while on their way to the farmhouse of Wiljon the Winkie, Dorothy and the Wizard and their friends were encountering the adventures we have just related.

So it was that on the very morning when the travelers from the Emerald City bade farewell to the Czarover of the City of Herku, Cayke and the Frogman awoke in a grove in which they had passed the night sleeping on beds of leaves. There were plenty of farmhouses in the neighborhood, but no one seemed to welcome the puffy, haughty Frogman or the little dried-up Cookie Cook, and so they slept comfortably enough underneath the trees of the grove.

The Frogman wakened first, on this morning, and after going to the tree where Cayke slept and finding her still wrapped in slumber, he decided to take a little walk and seek some breakfast. Coming to the edge of the grove he observed, half a mile away, a pretty yellow house that was surrounded by a yellow picket fence, so he walked toward this house and on entering the yard found a Winkie woman picking up sticks with which to build a fire to cook her morning meal.

"For goodness sakes!" she exclaimed on seeing the Frogman, "what are you doing out of your frog-pond?"

"I am traveling in search of a jeweled gold dishpan, my good woman," he replied, with an air of great dignity.

"You won't find it here, then," said she. "Our dishpans are tin, and they're good enough for anybody. So go back to your pond and leave me alone."

She spoke rather crossly and with a lack of respect that greatly annoyed the Frogman.

"Allow me to tell you, madam," said he, "that although I am a frog I am the Greatest and Wisest Frog in all the world. I may add that I possess much more wisdom than any Winkie—man or woman—in this land. Wherever I go, people fall on their knees before me and render homage to the Great Frogman! No one else knows so much as I; no one else is so grand—so magnificent!"

"If you know so much," she retorted, "why don't you know where your dishpan is instead of chasing around the country after it?"

"Presently," he answered, "I am going where it is; but just now I am traveling and have had no breakfast. Therefore I honor you by asking you for something to eat."

"Oho! The Great Frogman is hungry as any tramp, is he? Then pick up these sticks and help me to build the fire," said the woman contemptuously.

"Me! The Great Frogman pick up sticks?" he exclaimed in horror. "In the Yip Country, where I am more honored and powerful than any King could be, people weep with joy when I ask them to feed me."

"Then that's the place to go for your breakfast," declared the woman.

"I fear you do not realize my importance," urged the Frogman. "Exceeding wisdom renders me superior to menial duties."

"It's a great wonder to me," remarked the woman, carrying her sticks to the house, "that your wisdom doesn't inform you that you'll get no breakfast here," and she went in and slammed the door behind her.

The Frogman felt he had been insulted, so he gave a loud croak of indignation and turned away. After going a short distance he came upon a faint path which led across a meadow in the direction of a grove of pretty trees, and thinking this circle of evergreens must surround a house—where perhaps he would be kindly received— he decided to follow the path. And by and by he came to the trees, which were set close together, and pushing aside some branches he found no house inside the circle, but instead a very beautiful pond of clear water.

Now the Frogman, although he was so big and well educated, and now aped the ways and customs of human beings, was still a frog. As he gazed at this solitary, deserted pond, his love for water returned to him with irresistible force.

"If I cannot get a breakfast I may at least have a fine swim," said he, and pushing his way between the trees he reached the bank. There he took off his fine clothing, laying his shiny purple hat and his gold-headed cane beside it. A moment later he sprang with one leap into the water and dived to the very bottom of the pond.

The water was deliciously cool and grateful to his thick, rough skin, and the Frogman swam around the pond several times before he stopped to rest. Then he floated upon the surface and examined the pond with some curiosity. The bottom and sides were all lined with glossy tiles of a light pink color; just one place in the bottom, where the water bubbled up from a hidden spring, had been left free. On the banks the green grass grew to the edge of the pink tiling.

And now, as the Frogman examined the place, he found that on one side of the pool, just above the water line, had been set a golden plate on which some words were deeply engraved. He swam toward this plate and on reaching it read the following inscription:

This is
THE TRUTH POND
Whoever bathes in this
water must always
afterward tell
THE TRUTH

This statement startled the Frogman. It even worried him, so that he leaped upon the bank and hurriedly began to dress himself.

"A great misfortune has befallen me," he told himself, "for hereafter I cannot tell people I am wise, since it is not the truth. The truth is that my boasted wisdom

is all a sham, assumed by me to deceive people and make them defer to me. In truth, no living creature can know much more than his fellows, for one may know one thing, and another know another thing, so that wisdom is evenly scattered throughout the world. But—ah, me!—what a terrible fate will now be mine. Even Cayke the Cookie Cook will soon discover that my knowledge is no greater than her own; for having bathed in the enchanted water of the Truth Pond, I can no longer deceive her or tell a lie."

More humbled than he had been for many years, the Frogman went back to the grove where he had left Cayke and found the woman now awake and washing her face in a tiny brook.

"Where has Your Honor been?" she asked.

"To a farmhouse to ask for something to eat," said he, "but the woman refused me."

"How dreadful!" she exclaimed. "But never mind; there are other houses, where the people will be glad to feed the Wisest Creature in all the World."

"Do you mean yourself?" he asked.

"No, I mean you."

The Frogman felt strongly impelled to tell the truth, but struggled hard against it. His reason told him there was no use in letting Cayke know he was not wise, for then she would lose much respect for him, but each time he opened his mouth to speak he realized he was about to tell the truth and shut it again as quickly as possible. He tried to talk about something else, but the words necessary to undeceive the woman would force themselves to his lips in spite of all his struggles. Finally, knowing that he must either remain dumb or let the truth prevail, he gave a low groan of despair and said:

"Cayke, I am *not* the Wisest Creature in all the World; I am not wise at all."

"Oh, you must be!" she protested. "You told me so yourself, only last evening."

"Then last evening I failed to tell you the truth," he admitted, looking very shamefaced, for a frog. "I am sorry I told you this lie, my good Cayke; but, if you must know the truth, the whole truth and nothing but the truth, I am not really as wise as you are."

The Cookie Cook was greatly shocked to hear this, for it shattered one of her most pleasing illusions. She looked at the gorgeously dressed Frogman in amazement.

"What has caused you to change your mind so suddenly?" she inquired.

"I have bathed in the Truth Pond," he said, "and whoever bathes in that water is ever afterward obliged to tell the truth."

"You were foolish to do that," declared the woman. "It is often very embarrassing to tell the truth. I'm glad *I* didn't bathe in that dreadful water!"

The Frogman looked at his companion thoughtfully.

"Cayke," said he, "I want you to go to the Truth Pond and take a bath in its water. For if we are to travel together and encounter unknown adventures, it would not be fair that I alone must always tell you the truth, while you could tell me whatever you pleased. If we both dip in the enchanted water there will be no chance in the future of our deceiving one another."

"No," she asserted, shaking her head positively, "I won't do it, Your Honor. For, if I told you the truth, I'm sure you wouldn't like me. No Truth Pond for me. I'll be just as I am, an honest woman who can say what she wants to without hurting anyone's feelings."

With this decision the Frogman was forced to be content, although he was sorry the Cookie Cook would not listen to his advice.

CHAPTER XIV

THE UNHAPPY FERRYMAN

LEAVING THE GROVE WHERE THEY HAD SLEPT, THE FROGMAN AND THE Cookie Cook turned to the east to seek another house and after a short walk came to one where the people received them very politely. The children stared rather hard at the big, pompous Frogman, but the woman of the house, when Cayke asked for something to eat, at once brought them food and said they were welcome to it.

"Few people in need of help pass this way," she remarked, "for the Winkies are all prosperous and love to stay in their own homes. But perhaps you are not a Winkie," she added.

"No," said Cayke, "I am a Yip, and my home is on a high mountain at the southeast of your country."

"And the Frogman—is he also a Yip?"

"I do not know what he is, other than a very remarkable and highly educated creature," replied the Cookie Cook. "But he has lived many years among the Yips, who have found him so wise and intelligent that they always go to him for advice."

"May I ask why you have left your home, and where you are going?" said the Winkie woman.

Then Cayke told her of the diamond-studded gold dishpan and how it had been mysteriously stolen from her house, after which she had discovered that she could no longer cook good cookies. So she had resolved to search until she found her dishpan again, because a Cookie Cook who cannot cook good cookies is not of much use. The Frogman, who had wanted to see more of the world, had accompanied her to assist in the search. When the woman had listened to this story, she asked:

"Then you have no idea, as yet, who has stolen your dishpan?"

"I only know it must have been some mischievous fairy, or a magician, or some such powerful person, because none other could have climbed the steep mountain to the Yip Country. And who else could have carried away my beautiful, magic dishpan without being seen?"

The woman thought about this during the time that Cayke and the Frogman ate their breakfast. When they had finished she said:

"Where are you going next?"

"We have not decided," answered the Cookie Cook.

"Our plan," explained the Frogman, in his important way, "is to travel from place to place until we learn where the thief is located, and then to force him to return the dishpan to its proper owner."

"The plan is all right," agreed the woman, "but it may take you a long time before you succeed, your method being sort of haphazard and indefinite. However, I advise you to travel toward the east."

"Why?" asked the Frogman.

"Because if you went west you would soon come to the desert, and also because in this part of the Winkie Country no one steals, so your time here would be wasted. But toward the east, beyond the river, live many strange people whose honesty I would not vouch for. Moreover, if you journey far enough east and cross the river for a second time, you will come to the Emerald City, where there is much magic and sorcery. The Emerald City is ruled by a dear little girl called Ozma, who also rules the Emperor of the Winkies and all the Land of Oz. So, as Ozma is a fairy, she may be able to tell you just who has taken your precious dishpan. Provided, of course, you do not find it before you reach her."

"This seems to be to be excellent advice," said the Frogman, and Cayke agreed with him.

"The most sensible thing for you to do," continued the woman, "would be to return to your home and use another dishpan, learning to cook cookies as other people cook cookies, without the aid of magic. But if you cannot be happy without the magic dishpan you have lost, you are likely to learn more about it in the Emerald City than at any other place in Oz."

They thanked the good woman and on leaving her house faced the east and continued in that direction all the way. Toward evening they came to the west branch of the Winkie River and there, on the river bank, found a ferryman who lived all alone in a little yellow house.

This ferryman was a Winkie with a very small head and a very large body. He was sitting in his doorway as the travelers approached him and did not even turn his head to look at them.

"Good evening," said the Frogman.

The ferryman made no reply.

"We would like some supper and the privilege of sleeping in your house until morning," continued the Frogman. "At daybreak we would like some breakfast and then we would like to have you row us across the river."

The ferryman neither moved nor spoke. He sat in his doorway and looked straight ahead.

"I think he must be deaf and dumb," Cayke whispered to her companion. Then she stood directly in front of the ferryman and putting her mouth close to his ear she yelled as loudly as she could:

"Good evening!"

The ferryman scowled.

"Why do you yell at me, woman?" he asked.

"Can you hear what I say?" asked in her ordinary tone of voice.

"Of course," replied the man.

"Then why didn't you answer the Frogman?"

"Because," said the ferryman, "I don't understand the frog language."

"He speaks the same words that I do and in the same way," declared Cayke.

"Perhaps," replied the ferryman; "but to me his voice sounded like a frog's croak. I know that in the Land of Oz animals can speak our language, and so can the birds and bugs and fishes; but in *my* ears, they sound merely like growls and chirps and croaks."

"Why is that?" asked the Cookie Cook in surprise.

"Once, many years ago, I cut the tail off a fox which had taunted me; and I stole some birds' eggs from a nest to make an omelet with, and also I pulled a fish from the river and left it lying on the bank to gasp for lack of water until it died. I don't know why I did those wicked things, but I did them. So the Emperor of the Winkies—who is the Tin Woodman and has a very tender tin heart—punished me by denying me

any communication with beasts, birds or fishes. I cannot understand them when they speak to me, although I know that other people can do so, nor can the creatures understand a word I say to them. Every time I meet one of them I am reminded of my former cruelty, and it makes me very unhappy."

"Really," said Cayke, "I'm sorry for you, although the Tin Woodman is not to blame for punishing you."

"What is he mumbling about?" asked the Frogman.

"He is talking to me, but you don't understand him," she replied. And then she told him of the ferryman's punishment and afterward explained to the ferryman that they wanted to stay all night with him and be fed.

He gave them some fruit and bread, which was the only sort of food he had, and he allowed Cayke to sleep in a room of his cottage. But the Frogman he refused to admit to his house, saying that the frog's presence made him miserable and unhappy. At no time would he look directly at the Frogman, or even toward him, fearing he would shed tears if he did so; so the big frog slept on the river bank, where he could hear little frogs croaking in the river all the night through. But that did not keep him awake; it merely soothed him to slumber, for he realized how much superior he was to them.

Just as the sun was rising on a new day the ferryman rowed the two travelers across the river—keeping his back to the Frogman all the way—and then Cayke thanked him and bade him good-bye and the ferryman rowed home again.

On this side of the river there were no paths at all, so it was evident they had reached a part of the country little frequented by travelers. There was a marsh at the south of them, sandhills at the north and a growth of scrubby underbrush leading toward a forest at the east. So the east was really the least difficult way to go and that direction was the one they had determined to follow.

Now the Frogman, although he wore green patent-leather shoes with ruby buttons, had very large and flat feet, and when he tramped through the scrub his weight crushed down the underbrush and made a path for Cayke to follow him. Therefore they soon reached the forest, where the tall trees were set far apart but were so leafy that they shaded all the spaces between them with their branches.

"There are no bushes here," said Cayke, much pleased, "so we can now travel faster and with more comfort."

CHAPTER XV

THE BIG
LAVENDER BEAR

IT WAS A PLEASANT PLACE TO WANDER AND THE TWO TRAVELERS WERE proceeding at a brisk pace when suddenly a voice shouted:

"Halt!"

They looked around in surprise, seeing at first no one at all. Then from behind a tree there stepped a brown fuzzy bear whose head came about as high as Cayke's waist—and Cayke was a small woman. The bear was chubby as well as fuzzy; his body was even puffy, while his legs and arms seemed jointed at the knees and elbows and fastened to his body by pins or rivets. His ears were round in shape and stuck out in a comical way, while his round black eyes were bright and sparkling as beads. Over his shoulder the little brown bear bore a gun with a tin barrel. The barrel had a cork in the end of it and a string was attached to the cork and to the handle of the gun.

Both the Frogman and Cayke gazed hard at this curious bear, standing silent for some time. But finally the Frogman recovered from his surprise and remarked:

"It seems to me that you are stuffed with sawdust and ought not to be alive."

"That's all you know about it," answered the little Brown Bear in a squeaky voice. "I am stuffed with a very good quality of curled hair and my skin is the "best plush that was ever made. As for my being alive, that is my own affair and cannot concern you at all—except that it gives me the privilege to say you are my prisoners."

"Prisoners! Why do you speak such nonsense?" the Frogman angrily. "Do you think we are afraid of a toy bear with a toy gun?"

"You ought to be," was the confident reply, "for I am merely the sentry guarding the way to Bear Center, which is a city containing hundreds of my race, who are ruled by a very powerful sorcerer known as the Lavender Bear. He ought to be a purple color, you know, seeing he is a King, but he's only light lavender, which is, of course, second-cousin to royal purple. So unless you come with me peaceably, as my prisoners, I shall fire my gun and bring a hundred bears—of all sizes and colors—to capture you."

"Why do you wish to capture us?" inquired the Frogman, who had listened to his speech with much astonishment.

"I don't wish to, as a matter of fact," replied the little Brown Bear, "but it is my duty to, because you are now trespassing on the domain of His Majesty the King of Bear Center. Also I will admit that things are rather quiet in our city, just now, and the excitement of your capture, followed by your trial and execution, should afford us much entertainment."

"We defy you!" said the Frogman.

"Oh, no; don't do that," pleaded Cayke, speaking to her companion. "He says his King is a sorcerer, so perhaps it is he or one of his bears who ventured to steal my jeweled dishpan. Let us go to the City of the Bears and discover if my dishpan is there."

"I must now register one more charge against you," remarked the little Brown Bear, with evident satisfaction. "You have just accused us of stealing, and that is such a dreadful thing to say that I am quite sure our noble King will command you to be executed."

"But how could you execute us?" inquired the Cookie Cook.

"I've no idea. But our King is a wonderful inventor and there is no doubt he can find a proper way to destroy you. So, tell me, are you going to struggle, or will you go peaceably to meet your doom?"

It was all so ridiculous that Cayke laughed aloud and even the Frogman's wide mouth curled in a smile. Neither was a bit afraid to go to the Bear City and it seemed to both that there was a possibility they might discover the missing dishpan. So the Frogman said:

"Lead the way, little Bear, and we will follow without a struggle."

"That's very sensible of you; very sensible, indeed," declared the Brown Bear. "So—for-ward *march*!" and with the command he turned around and began to waddle along a path that led between the trees.

Cayke and the Frogman, as they followed their conductor, could scarce forbear laughing at his stiff, awkward manner of walking and, although he moved his stuffy legs fast, his steps were so short that they had to go slowly in order not to run into him. But after a time they reached a large, circular space in the center of the forest, which was clear of any stumps or underbrush. The ground was covered by a soft, gray moss, pleasant to tread upon. All the trees surrounding this space seemed to be hollow and had round holes in their trunks, set a little way above the ground, but otherwise there was nothing unusual about the place and nothing, in the opinion of the prisoners, to indicate a settlement. But the little Brown Bear said in a proud and impressive voice (although it still squeaked):

"This is the wonderful city known to fame as Bear Center!"

"But there are no houses; there are no bears living here at all!" exclaimed Cayke.

"Oh, indeed!" retorted their captor and raising his gun he pulled the trigger. The cork flew out of the tin barrel with a loud "pop!" and at once from every hole in every tree within view of the clearing appeared the head of a bear. They were of many colors and of many sizes, but all were made in the same manner as the bear who had met and captured them.

At first a chorus of growls arose and then a sharp voice cried:

"What has happened, Corporal Waddle?"

"Captives, Your Majesty!" answered the Brown Bear. "Intruders upon our domain and slanderers of our good name."

"Ah, that's important," answered the voice.

Then from out the hollow trees tumbled a whole regiment of stuffed bears, some carrying tin swords, some popguns and others long spears with gay ribbons tied to the handles. There were hundreds of them, altogether, and they quietly formed a circle around the Frogman and the Cookie Cook but kept at a distance and left a large space for the prisoners to stand in.

Presently this circle parted and into the center of it stalked a huge toy bear of a lovely lavender color. He walked upon his hind legs, as did all the others, and on his head he wore a tin crown set with diamonds and amethysts, while in one paw he carried a short wand of some glittering metal that resembled silver but wasn't.

"His Majesty the King!" shouted Corporal Waddle, and all the bears bowed low. Some bowed so low that they lost their balance and toppled over, but they soon scrambled up again and the Lavender King squatted on his haunches before the prisoners and gazed at them steadily with his bright pink eyes.

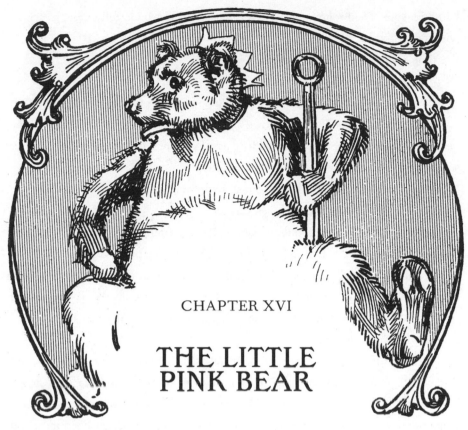

CHAPTER XVI

THE LITTLE PINK BEAR

"ONE PERSON AND ONE FREAK," SAID THE BIG LAVENDER BEAR, WHEN HE had carefully examined the strangers.

"I am sorry to hear you call poor Cayke the Cookie Cook a Freak," remonstrated the Frogman.

"She is the Person," asserted the King. "Unless I am mistaken, it is you who are the Freak."

The Frogman was silent, for he could not truthfully deny it.

"Why have you dared intrude in my forest?" demanded the Bear King.

"We didn't know it *was* your forest," said Cayke, "and we are on our way to the far east, where the Emerald City is."

"Ah, it's a long way from here to the Emerald City," remarked the King. "It is so far away, indeed, that no bear among us has ever been there. But what errand requires you to travel such a distance?"

"Someone has stolen my diamond-studded gold dishpan," explained Cayke; "and, as I cannot be happy without it, I have decided to search the world over until

I find it again. The Frogman, who is very learned and wonderfully wise, has come with me to give me his assistance. Isn't it kind of him?"

The King looked at the Frogman.

"What makes you so wonderfully wise?" he asked.

"I'm not," was the candid reply. "The Cookie Cook, and some others in the Yip Country, think because I am a big frog and talk and act like a man, that I must be very wise. I have learned more than a frog usually knows, it is true, but I am not yet so wise as I hope to become at some future time."

The King nodded, and when he did so something squeaked in his chest.

"Did Your Majesty speak?" asked Cayke.

"Not just then," answered the Lavender Bear, seeming to be somewhat embarrassed. "I am so built, you must know, that when anything pushes against my chest, as my chin accidentally did just then, I make that silly noise. In this city it isn't considered good manners to notice. But I like your Frogman. He is honest and truthful, which is more than can be said of many others. As for your late lamented dishpan, I'll show it to you."

With this he waved three times the metal wand which he held in his paw and instantly there appeared upon the ground, midway between the King and Cayke, a big round pan made of beaten gold. Around the top edge was a row of small diamonds; around the center of the pan was another row of larger diamonds; and at the bottom was a row of exceedingly large and brilliant diamonds. In fact, they all sparkled magnificently and the pan was so big and broad that it took a lot of diamonds to go around it three times.

Cayke stared so hard that her eyes seemed about to pop out of her head.

"O-o-o-oh!" she exclaimed, drawing a deep breath of delight.

"Is this your dishpan?" inquired the King.

"It is—it is!" cried the Cookie Cook, and rushing forward she fell on her knees and threw her arms around the precious pan. But her arms came together without meeting any resistance at all. Cayke tried to seize the edge, but found nothing to grasp. The pan was surely there, she thought, for she could see it plainly; but it was not solid; she could not feel it at all. With a moan of astonishment and despair she raised her head to look at the Bear King, who was watching her actions curiously. Then she turned to the pan again, only to find it had completely disappeared.

"Poor creature!" murmured the King pityingly. "You must have thought, for the moment, that you had actually recovered your dishpan. But what you saw was

merely the image of it, conjured up by means of my magic. It is a pretty dishpan, indeed, though rather big and awkward to handle. I hope you will some day find it."

Cayke was grievously disappointed. She began to cry, wiping her eyes on her apron. The King turned to the throng of toy bears surrounding him and asked:

"Has any of you ever seen this golden dishpan before?"

"No," they answered in a chorus.

The King seemed to reflect. Presently he inquired, "Where is the Little Pink Bear?"

"At home, Your Majesty," was the reply.

"Fetch him here," commanded the King.

Several of the bears waddled over to one of the trees and pulled from its hollow a tiny pink bear, smaller than any of the others. A big white bear carried the pink one in his arms and set it down beside the King, arranging the joints of its legs so that it would stand upright.

This Pink Bear seemed lifeless until the King turned a crank which protruded from its side, when the little creature turned its head stiffly from side to side and said in a small shrill voice:

"Hurrah for the King of Bear Center!"

"Very good," said the big Lavender Bear; "he seems to be working very well today. Tell me, my Pink Pinkerton, what has become of this lady's jeweled dishpan?"

"U—u—u," said the Pink Bear, and then stopped short.

The King turned the crank again.

"U-g-u the Shoemaker has it," said the Pink Bear.

"Who is Ugu the Shoemaker?" demanded the King, again turning the crank.

"A magician who lives on a mountain in a wickerwork castle," was the reply.

"Where is this mountain?" was the next question.

"Nineteen miles and three furlongs from Bear Center to the northeast."

"And is the dishpan still at the castle of Ugu the Shoemaker?" asked the King.

"It is."

The King turned to Cayke.

"You may rely on this information," said he. "The Pink Bear can tell us anything we wish to know, and his words are always words of truth."

"Is he alive?" asked the Frogman, much interested in the Pink Bear.

"Something animates him—when you turn his crank," replied the King. "I do not know if it is life, or what it is, or how it happens that the Little Pink Bear can answer correctly every question put to him. We discovered his talent a long time ago and whenever we wish to know anything—which is not very often—we ask the Pink Bear. There is no doubt whatever, madam, that Ugu the Magician has your dishpan, and if you dare to go to him you may be able to recover it. But of that I am not certain."

"Can't the Pink Bear tell?" asked Cayke anxiously.

"No, for that is in the future. He can tell anything that has happened, but nothing that is going to happen. Don't ask me why, for I don't know."

"Well," said the Cookie Cook after a little thought, "I mean to go to this magician, anyhow, and tell him I want my dishpan. I wish I knew what Ugu the Shoemaker is like."

"Then I'll show him to you," promised the King. "But do not be frightened; it won't be Ugu, remember, but only his image."

With this he waved his metal wand and in the circle suddenly appeared a thin little man, very old and skinny, who was seated on a wicker stool before a wicker table. On the table lay a Great Book with gold clasps. The Book was open and the man was reading in it. He wore great spectacles, which were fastened before his eyes by means of a ribbon that passed around his head and was tied in a bow at the neck. His hair was very thin and white; his skin, which clung fast to his bones, was brown and seared with furrows; he had a big, fat nose and little eyes set close together.

On no account was Ugu the Shoemaker a pleasant person to gaze at. As his image appeared before them, all were silent and intent until Corporal Waddle, the Brown Bear, became nervous and pulled the trigger of his gun. Instantly, the cork flew out of the tin barrel with a loud "pop!" that made them all jump. And, at this sound, the image of the magician vanished.

"So! *that's* the thief, is it?" said Cayke, in an angry voice. "I should think he'd be ashamed of himself for stealing a poor woman's diamond dishpan! But I mean to face him in his wicker castle and force him to return my property."

"To me," said the Bear King, reflectively, "he looked like a dangerous person. I hope he won't be so unkind as to argue the matter with you."

The Frogman was much disturbed by the vision of Ugu the Shoemaker, and Cayke's determination to go to the magician filled her companion with misgivings. But he would not break his pledged word to assist the Cookie Cook and after breathing a deep sigh of resignation he asked the King:

"Will Your Majesty lend us this Pink Bear who answers questions, that we may take him with us on our journey? He would be very useful to us and we will promise to bring him safely back to you."

The King did not reply at once; he seemed to be thinking.

"*Please* let us take the Pink Bear," begged Cayke. "I'm sure he would be a great help to us."

"The Pink Bear," said the King, "is the best bit of magic I possess, and there is not another like him in the world. I do not care to let him out of my sight; nor do I wish to disappoint you; so I believe I will make the journey in your company and carry my Pink Bear with me. He can walk, when you wind the other side of him, but so slowly and awkwardly that he would delay you. But if I go along I can carry him in my arms, so I will join your party. Whenever you are ready to start, let me know."

"But—Your Majesty!" exclaimed Corporal Waddle in protest, "I hope you do not intend to let these prisoners escape without punishment."

"Of what crime do you accuse them?" inquired the King.

"Why, they trespassed on your domain, for one thing," said the Brown Bear.

"We didn't know it was private property, Your Majesty," said the Cookie Cook.

"And they asked if any of us had stolen the dishpan!" continued Corporal Waddle indignantly. "That is the same thing as calling us thieves and robbers, and bandits and brigands, is it not?"

"Every person has the right to ask questions," said the Frogman.

"But the Corporal is quite correct," declared the Lavender Bear. "I condemn you both to death, the execution to take place ten years from this hour."

"But we belong in the Land of Oz, where no one ever dies," Cayke reminded him.

"Very true," said the King. "I condemn you to death merely as a matter of form. It sounds quite terrible, and in ten years we shall have forgotten all about it. Are you ready to start for the wicker castle of Ugu the Shoemaker?"

"Quite ready, Your Majesty."

"But who will rule in your place, while you are gone?" asked a big Yellow Bear.

"I myself will rule while I am gone," was the reply. "A King isn't required to stay at home forever, and if he takes a notion to travel, whose business is it but his own? All I ask is that you bears behave yourselves while I am away. If any of you is naughty, I'll send him to some girl or boy in America to play with."

This dreadful threat made all the toy bears look solemn. They assured the King, in a chorus of growls, that they would be good. Then the big Lavender Bear picked up the little Pink Bear and after tucking it carefully under one arm he said "Good-bye till I come back!" and waddled along the path that led through the forest. The Frogman and Cayke the Cookie Cook also said good-bye to the bears and then followed after the King, much to the regret of the little Brown Bear, who pulled the trigger of his gun and popped the cork as a parting salute.

CHAPTER XVII

THE MEETING

WHILE THE FROGMAN AND HIS PARTY WERE ADVANCING FROM THE WEST,
Dorothy and her party were advancing from the east, and so it happened that on
the following night they all camped at a little hill that was only a few miles from the
wicker castle of Ugu the Shoemaker. But the two parties did not see one another that
night, for one camped on one side of the hill while the other camped on the opposite
side. But the next morning the Frogman thought he would climb the hill and see
what was on top of it, and at the same time Scraps, the Patchwork Girl, also decided
to climb the hill to find if the wicker castle was visible from its top. So she stuck her
head over an edge just as the Frogman's head appeared over another edge and both,
being surprised, kept still while they took a good look at one another.

Scraps recovered from her astonishment first and bounding upward she turned
a somersault and landed sitting down and facing the big Frogman, who slowly
advanced and sat opposite her.

"Well met, Stranger!" cried the Patchwork Girl with a whoop of laughter. "You
are quite the funniest individual I have seen in all my travels."

"Do you suppose I can be any funnier than you?" asked the Frogman, gazing at her in wonder.

"I'm not funny to myself, you know," returned Scraps. "I wish I were. And perhaps you are so used to your own absurd shape that you do not laugh whenever you see your reflection in a pool, or in a mirror."

"No," said the Frogman gravely, "I do not. I used to be proud of my great size and vain of my culture and education, but since I bathed in the Truth Pond I sometimes think it is not right that I should be different from all other frogs."

"Right or wrong," said the Patchwork Girl, "to be different is to be distinguished. Now, in my case, I'm just like all other Patchwork Girls because I'm the only one there is. But, tell me, where did you come from?"

"The Yip Country," said he.

"Is that in the Land of Oz?"

"Of course," replied the Frogman.

"And do you know that your Ruler, Ozma of Oz, has been stolen?"

"I was not aware that I had a Ruler, so of course I couldn't know that she was stolen."

"Well, you have. All the people of Oz," explained Scraps, "are ruled by Ozma, whether they know it or not. And she has been stolen. Aren't you angry? Aren't you indignant? Your Ruler, whom you didn't know you had, has positively been stolen!"

"That is queer," remarked the Frogman thoughtfully. "Stealing is a thing practically unknown in Oz, yet this Ozma has been taken and a friend of mine has also had her dishpan stolen. With her I have traveled all the way from the Yip Country in order to recover it."

"I don't see any connection between a Royal Ruler of Oz and a dishpan!" declared Scraps.

"They've both been stolen, haven't they?"

"True. But why can't your friend wash her dishes in another dishpan?" asked Scraps.

"Why can't you use another Royal Ruler? I suppose you prefer the one who is lost, and my friend wants her own dishpan, which is made of gold and studded with diamonds and has magic powers."

"Magic, eh?" exclaimed Scraps. "*There* is a link that connects the two steals, anyhow, for it seems that all the magic in the Land of Oz was stolen at the same time, whether it was in the Emerald City or in Glinda's castle or in the Yip Country. Seems mighty strange and mysterious, doesn't it?"

"It used to seem that way to me," admitted the Frogman, "but we have now discovered who took our dishpan. It was Ugu the Shoemaker."

"Ugu? Good gracious! That's the same magician we think has stolen Ozma. We are now on our way to the castle of this Shoemaker."

"So are we," said the Frogman.

"Then follow me, quick! and let me introduce you to Dorothy and the other girls and to the Wizard of Oz and all the rest of us."

She sprang up and seized his coat-sleeve, dragging him off the hilltop and down the other side from that whence he had come. And at the foot of the hill the Frogman was astonished to find the three girls and the Wizard and Button-Bright, who were surrounded by a wooden Saw-Horse, a lean Mule, a square Woozy and a Cowardly Lion. A little black dog ran up and smelled at the Frogman, but couldn't growl at him.

"I've discovered another party that has been robbed," shouted Scraps as she joined them. "This is their leader and they're all going to Ugu's castle to fight the wicked Shoemaker!"

They regarded the Frogman with much curiosity and interest and, finding all eyes fixed upon him, the newcomer arranged his necktie and smoothed his beautiful vest and swung his gold-headed cane like a regular dandy. The big spectacles over his eyes quite altered his froglike countenance and gave him a learned and impressive look. Used as she was to seeing strange creatures in the Land of Oz, Dorothy was amazed at discovering the Frogman. So were all her companions. Toto wanted to growl at him, but couldn't, and he didn't dare bark. The Saw-Horse snorted rather contemptuously, but the Lion whispered to the wooden steed: "Bear with this strange creature, my friend, and remember he is no more extraordinary than you are. Indeed, it is more natural for a frog to be big than for a Saw-Horse to be alive."

On being questioned, the Frogman told them the whole story of the loss of Cayke's highly prized dishpan and their adventures in search of it. When he came to tell of the Lavender Bear King and of the Little Pink Bear who could tell anything you wanted to know, his hearers became eager to see such interesting animals.

"It will be best," said the Wizard, "to unite our two parties and share our fortunes together, for we are all bound on the same errand and as one band we may more easily defy this shoemaker magician than if separate. Let us be allies."

"I will ask my friends about that," replied the Frogman, and climbed over the hill to find Cayke and the toy bears. The Patchwork Girl accompanied him and when they came upon the Cookie Cook and the Lavender Bear and the Pink Bear it was hard to tell which of the lot was the most surprised.

"Mercy me!" cried Cayke, addressing the Patchwork Girl. "However did you come alive?"

Scraps stared at the bears.

"Mercy me!" she echoed; "you are stuffed, as I am, with cotton, and yet you appear to be living. That makes me feel ashamed, for I have prided myself on being the only live cotton-stuffed person in Oz."

"Perhaps you are," returned the Lavender Bear, "for I am stuffed with extra-quality curled hair, and so is the Little Pink Bear."

"You have relieved my mind of a great anxiety," declared the Patchwork Girl, now speaking more cheerfully. "The Scarecrow is stuffed with straw, and you with hair, so I am still the Original and Only Cotton-Stuffed!"

"I hope I am too polite to criticize cotton, as compared with curled hair," said the King, "especially as you seem satisfied with it."

Then the Frogman told of his interview with the party from the Emerald City and added that the Wizard of Oz had invited the bears and Cayke and himself to travel in company with them to the castle of Ugu the Shoemaker. Cayke was much pleased, but the Bear King looked solemn. He set the Little Pink Bear on his lap and turned the crank in its side and asked:

"Is it safe for us to associate with those people from the Emerald City?"

And the Pink Bear at once replied:

> "Safe for you and safe for me;
> Perhaps no others safe will be."

"That 'perhaps' need not worry us," said the King; "so let us join the others and offer them our protection."

Even the Lavender Bear was astonished, however, when on climbing over the hill he found on the other side the group of queer animals and the people from the Emerald City. The bears and Cayke were received very cordially, although Button-Bright was cross when they wouldn't let him play with the Little Pink Bear. The three girls greatly admired the toy bears, and especially the pink one, which they longed to hold.

"You see," explained the Lavender King, in denying them this privilege, "he's a very valuable bear, because his magic is a correct guide on all occasions, and especially if one is in difficulties. It was the Pink Bear who told us that Ugu the Shoemaker had stolen the Cookie Cook's dishpan."

"And the King's magic is just as wonderful," added Cayke, "because it showed us the Magician himself."

"What did he look like?" inquired Dorothy.

"He was dreadful!"

"He was sitting at a table and examining an immense Book which had three golden clasps," remarked the King.

"Why, that must have been Glinda's Great Book of Records!" exclaimed Dorothy. "If it is, it proves that Ugu the Shoemaker stole Ozma, and with her all the magic in the Emerald City."

"And my dishpan," said Cayke. And the Wizard added:

"It also proves that he is following our adventures in the Book of Records, and therefore knows that we are seeking him and that we are determined to find him and reach Ozma at all hazards."

"If we can," added the Woozy, but everybody frowned at him.

The Wizard's statement was so true that the faces around him were very serious until the Patchwork Girl broke into a peal of laughter.

"Wouldn't it be a rich joke if he made prisoners of us, too?" she said.

"No one but a crazy Patchwork Girl would consider that a joke," grumbled Button-Bright. And then the Lavender Bear King asked:

"Would you like to see this magical shoemaker?"

"Wouldn't he know it?" Dorothy inquired.

"No, I think not."

Then the King waved his metal wand and before them appeared a room in the wicker castle of Ugu. On the wall of the room hung Ozma's Magic Picture, and seated before it was the Magician. They could see the Picture as well as he could, because it faced them, and in the Picture was the hillside where they were now sitting, all their forms being reproduced in miniature. And, curiously enough, within the scene of the Picture was the scene they were now beholding, so they knew that the Magician was at this moment watching them in the Picture, and also that he saw himself and the room he was in become visible to the people on the hillside. Therefore he knew very well that they were watching him while he was watching them.

In proof of this, Ugu sprang from his seat and turned a scowling face in their direction; but now he could not see the travelers who were seeking him, although they could still see him. His actions were so distinct, indeed, that it seemed he was actually before them.

"It is only a ghost," said the Bear King. "It isn't real at all, except that it shows us Ugu just as he looks and tells us truly just what he is doing."

"I don't see anything of my lost growl, though," said Toto, as if to himself.

Then the vision faded away and they could see nothing but the grass and trees and bushes around them.

CHAPTER XVIII

THE CONFERENCE

"Now, then," said the Wizard, "let us talk this matter over and decide what to do when we get to Ugu's wicker castle. There can be no doubt that the Shoemaker is a powerful Magician, and his powers have been increased a hundred-fold since he secured the Great Book of Records, the Magic Picture, all of Glinda's recipes for sorcery, and my own black bag—which was full of tools of wizardry. The man who could rob us of those things, and the man with all their powers at his command, is one who may prove somewhat difficult to conquer; therefore we should plan our actions well before we venture too near to his castle."

"I didn't see Ozma in the Magic Picture," said Trot. "What do you suppose Ugu has done with her?"

"Couldn't the Little Pink Bear tell us what he did with Ozma?" asked Button-Bright.

"To be sure," replied the Lavender King; "I'll ask him."

So he turned the crank in the Little Pink Bear's side and inquired: "Did Ugu the Shoemaker steal Ozma of Oz?"

"Yes," answered the Little Pink Bear.

"Then what did he do with her?" asked the King.

"Shut her up in a dark place," answered the Little Pink Bear.

"Oh, that must be a dungeon cell!" cried Dorothy, horrified. "How dreadful!"

"Well, we must get her out of it," said the Wizard. "That is what we came for and of course we must rescue Ozma. But—how?"

Each one looked at some other one for an answer, and all shook their heads in a grave and dismal manner. All but Scraps, who danced around them gleefully.

"You're afraid," said the Patchwork Girl, "because so many things can hurt your meat bodies. Why don't you give it up and go home? How can you fight a great magician when you have nothing to fight with?"

Dorothy looked at her reflectively.

"Scraps," said she, "you know that Ugu couldn't hurt you, a bit, whatever he did; nor could he hurt *me*, 'cause I wear the Nome King's Magic Belt. S'pose just we two go on together, and leave the others here to wait for us?"

"No, no!" said the Wizard positively. "That won't do at all. Ozma is more powerful than either of you, yet she could not defeat the wicked Ugu, who has shut her up in a dungeon. We must go to the Shoemaker in one mighty band, for only in union is there strength."

"That is excellent advice," said the Lavender Bear, approvingly.

"But what can we do, when we get to Ugu?" inquired the Cookie Cook anxiously.

"Do not expect a prompt answer to that important question," replied the Wizard, "for we must first plan our line of conduct. Ugu knows, of course, that we are after him, for he has seen our approach in the Magic Picture, and he has read of all we have done up to the present moment in the Great Book of Records. Therefore we cannot expect to take him by surprise."

"Don't you suppose Ugu would listen to reason?" asked Betsy. "If we explained to him how wicked he has been, don't you think he'd let poor Ozma go?"

"And give me back my dishpan?" added the Cookie Cook eagerly.

"Yes, yes; won't he say he's sorry and get on his knees and beg our pardon?" cried Scraps, turning a flip-flop to show her scorn of the suggestion. "When Ugu the Shoemaker does that, please knock at the front door and let me know."

The Wizard sighed and rubbed his bald head with a puzzled air.

"I'm quite sure Ugu will not be polite to us," said he, "so we must conquer this cruel magician by force, much as we dislike to be rude to anyone. But none of you has yet suggested a way to do that. Couldn't the Little Pink Bear tell us how?" he asked, turning to the Bear King.

"No, for that is something that is *going* to happen," replied the Lavender Bear. "He can only tell us what already *has* happened."

Again they were grave and thoughtful. But after a time, Betsy said in a hesitating voice:

"Hank is a great fighter; perhaps he could conquer the magician."

The Mule turned his head to look reproachfully at his old friend, the young girl.

"Who can fight against magic?" he asked.

"The Cowardly Lion could," said Dorothy.

The Lion, who was lying with his front legs spread out, his chin on his paws, raised his shaggy head.

"I can fight when I'm not afraid," said he calmly; "but the mere mention of a fight sets me to trembling."

"Ugu's magic couldn't hurt the Saw-Horse," suggested tiny Trot.

"And the Saw-Horse couldn't hurt the Magician," declared that wooden animal.

"For my part," said Toto, "I am helpless, having lost my growl."

"Then," said Cayke the Cookie Cook, "we must depend upon the Frogman. His marvelous wisdom will surely inform him how to conquer the wicked Magician and restore to me my dishpan."

All eyes were now turned questioningly upon the Frogman. Finding himself the center of observation, he swung his gold-headed cane, adjusted his big spectacles and after swelling out his chest, sighed and said in a modest tone of voice:

"Respect for truth obliges me to confess that Cayke is mistaken in regard to my superior wisdom. I am not very wise. Neither have I had any practical experience in conquering magicians. But let us consider this case. What is Ugu, and what is a magician? Ugu is a renegade shoemaker and a magician is an ordinary man who, having learned how to do magical tricks, considers himself above his fellows. In this case, the Shoemaker has been naughty enough to steal a lot of magical tools and things that did not belong to him, and it is more wicked to steal than to be a magician. Yet, with all the arts at his command, Ugu is still a man, and surely there are ways in which a man may be conquered. How, do you say, how? Allow me to state that I don't know. In my judgment we cannot decide how best to act until we get to Ugu's castle. So let us go to it and take a look at it. After that we may discover an idea that will guide us to victory."

"That may not be a wise speech, but it sounds good," said Dorothy approvingly. "Ugu the Shoemaker is not only a common man, but he's a wicked man and a cruel man and deserves to be conquered. We mustn't have any mercy on him till Ozma is set free. So let's go to his castle, as the Frogman says, and see what the place looks like."

No one offered any objection to this plan and so it was adopted. They broke camp and were about to start on the journey to Ugu's castle when they discovered that Button-Bright was lost again. The girls and the Wizard shouted his name, and the Lion roared and the Donkey brayed and the Frogman croaked and the Big Lavender Bear growled (to the envy of Toto, who couldn't growl but barked his loudest) yet none of them could make Button-Bright hear. So after vainly searching for the boy a full hour, they formed a procession and proceeded in the direction of the wicker castle of Ugu the Shoemaker.

"Button-Bright's always getting lost," said Dorothy. "And, if he wasn't always getting found again, I'd prob'ly worry. He may have gone ahead of us, and he may have gone back; but, wherever he is, we'll find him sometime and somewhere, I'm almost sure."

CHAPTER XIX

UGU
THE SHOEMAKER

A CURIOUS THING ABOUT UGU THE SHOEMAKER WAS THAT HE DIDN'T suspect, in the least, that he was wicked. He wanted to be powerful and great and he hoped to make himself master of all the Land of Oz, that he might compel everyone in that fairy country to obey him, His ambition blinded him to the rights of others and he imagined anyone else would act just as he did if anyone else happened to be as clever as himself.

When he inhabited his little shoemaking shop in the City of Herku he had been discontented, for a shoemaker is not looked upon with high respect and Ugu knew that his ancestors had been famous magicians for many centuries past and therefore his family was above the ordinary. Even his father practiced magic, when Ugu was a boy, but his father had wandered away from Herku and had never come back again. So, when Ugu grew up, he was forced to make shoes for a living, knowing nothing of the magic of his forefathers. But one day, in searching through the attic of his house, he discovered all the books of magical recipes and many magical instruments which had formerly been in use in his family. From that day he stopped making shoes and began to study magic. Finally he aspired to become the greatest magician in Oz, and for days and weeks and months he thought on a plan to render all the other sorcerers and wizards, as well as those with fairy powers, helpless to oppose him.

From the books of his ancestors, he learned the following facts:

(1) That Ozma of Oz was the fairy Ruler of the Emerald City and the Land of Oz, and that she could not be destroyed by any magic ever devised. Also, by means of her Magic Picture she would be able to discover anyone who approached her royal palace with the idea of conquering it.

(2) That Glinda the Good was the most powerful Sorceress in Oz, among her other magical possessions being the Great Book of Records, which told her all that happened anywhere in the world. This Book of Records was very dangerous to Ugu's plans and Glinda was in the service of Ozma and would use her arts of sorcery to protect the girl Ruler.

(3) That the Wizard of Oz, who lived in Ozma's palace, had been taught much powerful magic by Glinda and had a bag of magic tools with which he might be able to conquer the Shoemaker.

(4) That there existed in Oz—in the Yip Country—a jeweled dishpan made of gold, which dishpan would grow large enough for a man to sit inside it. Then, when he grasped both the golden handles, the dishpan would transport him in an instant to any place he wished to go within the borders of the Land of Oz.

No one now living, except Ugu, knew of the powers of the Magic Dishpan; so, after long study, the shoemaker decided that if he could manage to secure the dishpan he could, by its means, rob Ozma and Glinda and the Wizard of Oz of all their magic, thus becoming himself the most powerful person in all the land.

His first act was to go away from the City of Herku and build for himself the Wicker Castle in the hills. Here he carried his books and instruments of magic and here for a full year he diligently practiced all the magical arts learned from his ancestors. At the end of that time, he could do a good many wonderful things.

Then, when all his preparations were made, he set out for the Yip Country and climbing the steep mountain at night he entered the house of Cayke the Cookie Cook and stole her diamond-studded gold dishpan while all the Yips were asleep, Taking his prize outside, he set the pan upon the ground and uttered the required magic word. Instantly the dishpan grew as large as a big washtub and Ugu seated himself in it and grasped the two handles. Then he wished himself in the great drawing-room of Glinda the Good.

He was there in a flash. First he took the Great Book of Records and put it in the dishpan. Then he went to Glinda's laboratory and took all her rare chemical compounds and her instruments of sorcery, placing these also in the dishpan, which he caused to grow large enough to hold them. Next he seated himself amongst the treasures he had stolen and wished himself in the room in Ozma's palace which the

Wizard occupied and where he kept his bag of magic tools. This bag Ugu added to his plunder and then wished himself in the apartments of Ozma.

Here he first took the Magic Picture from the wall and then seized all the other magical things which Ozma possessed. Having placed these in the dishpan he was about to climb in himself when he looked up and saw Ozma standing beside him. Her fairy instinct had warned her that danger was threatening her, so the beautiful girl Ruler rose from her couch and leaving her bedchamber at once confronted the thief.

Ugu had to think quickly, for he realized that if he permitted Ozma to rouse the inmates of her palace all his plans and his present successes were likely to come to naught. So he threw a scarf over the girl's head, so she could not scream, and pushed her into the dishpan and tied her fast, so she could not move. Then he climbed in beside her and wished himself in his own wicker castle. The Magic Dishpan was there in an instant, with all its contents, and Ugu rubbed his hands together in triumphant joy as he realized that he now possessed all the important magic in the Land of Oz and could force all the inhabitants of that fairyland to do as he willed.

So quickly had his journey been accomplished that before daylight the robber magician had locked Ozma in a room, making her a prisoner, and had unpacked and arranged all his stolen goods. The next day he placed the Book of Records on his table and hung the Magic Picture on his wall and put away in his cupboards and drawers all the elixirs and magic compounds he had stolen. The magical instruments he polished and arranged, and this was fascinating work and made him very happy. The only thing that bothered him was Ozma. By turns the imprisoned Ruler wept and scolded the Shoemaker, haughtily threatening him with dire punishment for the wicked deeds he had done. Ugu became somewhat afraid of his fairy prisoner, in spite of the fact that he believed he had robbed her of all her powers; so he performed an enchantment that quickly disposed of her and placed her out of his sight and hearing. After that, being occupied with other things, he soon forgot her.

But now, when he looked into the Magic Picture and read the Great Book of Records, the Shoemaker learned that his wickedness was not to go unchallenged. Two important expeditions had set out to find him and force him to give up his stolen property. One was the party headed by the Wizard and Dorothy, while the other consisted of Cayke and the Frogman. Others were also searching, but not in the right places. These two groups, however, were headed straight for the wicker castle and so Ugu began to plan how best to meet them and to defeat their efforts to conquer him.

CHAPTER XX

MORE SURPRISES

ALL THAT FIRST DAY AFTER THE UNION OF THE TWO PARTIES OUR FRIENDS marched steadily toward the wicker castle of Ugu the Shoemaker. When night came they camped in a little grove and passed a pleasant evening together, although some of them were worried because Button-Bright was still lost.

"Perhaps," said Toto, as the animals lay grouped together for the night, "this Shoemaker who stole my growl, and who stole Ozma, has also stolen Button-Bright."

"How do you know that the Shoemaker stole your growl?" demanded the Woozy.

"He has stolen about everything else of value in Oz, hasn't he?" replied the dog.

"He has stolen everything he wants, perhaps," agreed the Lion; "but what could anyone want with your growl?"

"Well," said the dog, wagging his tail slowly, "my recollection is that it was a wonderful growl, soft and low and—and—"

"And ragged at the edges," said the Saw-Horse.

"So," continued Toto, "if that magician hadn't any growl of his own, he might have wanted mine and stolen it."

"And, if he has, he will soon wish he hadn't," remarked the Mule. "Also, if he has stolen Button-Bright he will be sorry."

"Don't you like Button-Bright, then?" asked the Lion in surprise.

"It isn't a question of liking him," replied the Mule. "It's a question of watching him and looking after him. Any boy who causes his friends so much worry isn't worth having around. I never get lost."

"If you did," said Toto, "no one would worry a bit. I think Button-Bright is a very lucky boy, because he always gets found."

"See here," said the Lion, "this chatter is keeping us all awake and to-morrow is likely to be a busy day. Go to sleep and forget your quarrels."

"Friend Lion," retorted the dog, "if I hadn't lost my growl you would hear it now. I have as much right to talk as you have to sleep."

The Lion sighed.

"If only you had lost your voice, when you lost your growl," said he, "you would be a more agreeable companion."

But they quieted down, after that, and soon the entire camp was wrapped in slumber.

Next morning they made an early start but had hardly proceeded on their way an hour when, on climbing a slight elevation, they beheld in the distance a low mountain, on top of which stood Ugu's wicker castle. It was a good-sized building and rather pretty because the sides, roofs and domes were all of wicker closely woven, as it is in fine baskets.

"I wonder if it is strong?" said Dorothy musingly, as she eyed the queer castle.

"I suppose it is, since a magician built it," answered the Wizard. "With magic to protect it, even a paper castle might be as strong as if made of stone. This Ugu must be a man of ideas, because he does things in a different way from other people."

"Yes; no one else would steal our dear Ozma," sighed tiny Trot.

"I wonder if Ozma is there?" said Betsy, indicating the castle with a nod of her head.

"Where else could she be?" asked Scraps.

"S'pose we ask the Pink Bear," suggested Dorothy.

That seemed a good idea, so they halted the procession and the Bear King held the little Pink Bear on his lap and turned the crank in its side and asked:

"Where is Ozma of Oz?"

And the little Pink Bear answered:

"She is in a hole in the ground, a half mile away, at your left."

"Good gracious!" cried Dorothy. "Then she is not in Ugu's castle at all."

"It is lucky we asked that question," said the Wizard; "for, if we can find Ozma and rescue her, there will be no need for us to fight that wicked and dangerous magician."

"Indeed!" said Cayke. "Then what about my dishpan?"

The Wizard looked puzzled at her tone of remonstrance, so she added:

"Didn't you people from the Emerald City promise that we would all stick together, and that you would help me to get my dishpan if I would help you to get your Ozma? And didn't I bring to you the little Pink Bear, which has told you where Ozma is hidden?"

"She's right," said Dorothy to the Wizard. "We must do as we agreed."

"Well, first of all, let us go and rescue Ozma," proposed the Wizard. "Then our beloved Ruler may be able to advise us how to conquer Ugu the Shoemaker."

So they turned to the left and marched for half a mile until they came to a small but deep hole in the ground. At once all rushed to the brim to peer into the hole, but instead of finding there Princess Ozma of Oz, all that they saw was Button-Bright, who was lying asleep on the bottom.

Their cries soon wakened the boy, who sat up and rubbed his eyes. When he recognized his friends he smiled sweetly, saying: "Found again!"

"Where is Ozma?" inquired Dorothy anxiously.

"I don't know," answered Button-Bright from the depths of the hole. "I got lost, yesterday, as you may remember, and in the night, while I was wandering around in the moonlight, trying to find my way back to you, I suddenly fell into this hole."

"And wasn't Ozma in it then?"

"There was no one in it but me, and I was sorry it wasn't entirely empty. The sides are so steep I can't climb out, so there was nothing to be done but sleep until someone found me. Thank you for coming. If you'll please let down a rope I'll empty this hole in a hurry."

"How strange!" said Dorothy, greatly disappointed. "It's evident the Pink Bear didn't tell us the truth."

"He never makes a mistake," declared the Lavender Bear King, in a tone that showed his feelings were hurt. And then he turned the crank of the little Pink Bear again and asked:

"Is this the hole that Ozma of Oz is in?"

"Yes," answered the Pink Bear.

"That settles it," said the King positively. "Your Ozma is in this hole in the ground."

"Don't be silly," returned Dorothy impatiently. "Even your beady eyes can see there is no one in the hole but Button-Bright."

"Perhaps Button-Bright is Ozma," suggested the King.

"And perhaps he isn't! Ozma is a girl, and Button-Bright is a boy."

"Your Pink Bear must be out of order," said the Wizard; "for, this time at least, his machinery has caused him to make an untrue statement."

The Bear King was so angry at this remark that he turned away, holding the Pink Bear in his paws, and refused to discuss the matter in any further way.

"At any rate," said the Frogman, "the Pink Bear has led us to your boy friend and so enabled you to rescue him."

Scraps was leaning so far over the hole, trying to find Ozma in it, that suddenly she lost her balance and pitched in headforemost. She fell upon Button-Bright and tumbled him over, but he was not hurt by her soft stuffed body and only laughed at the mishap. The Wizard buckled some straps together and let one end of them down into the hole, and soon both Scraps and the boy had climbed up and were standing safely beside the others.

They looked once more for Ozma, but the hole was now absolutely vacant. It was a round hole, so from the top they could plainly see every part of it. Before they left the place Dorothy went to the Bear King and said:

"I'm sorry we couldn't believe what the little Pink Bear said, 'cause we don't want to make you feel bad by doubting him. There must be a mistake, somewhere, and we prob'ly don't understand just what the little Pink Bear means. Will you let me ask him one more question?"

The Lavender Bear King was a good-natured bear, considering how he was made and stuffed and jointed, so he accepted Dorothy's apology and turned the crank and allowed the little girl to question his wee Pink Bear.

"Is Ozma *really* in this hole?" asked Dorothy.

"No," said the little Pink Bear.

This surprised everybody. Even the Bear King was now puzzled by the contradictory statements of his oracle.

"Where *is* she?" asked the King.

"Here, among you," answered the little Pink Bear.

"Well," said Dorothy, "this beats me, entirely! I guess the little Pink Bear has gone crazy."

"Perhaps," called Scraps, who was rapidly turning "cart-wheels" all around the perplexed group, "Ozma is invisible."

"Of course!" cried Betsy. "That would account for it."

"Well, I've noticed that people can speak, even when they've been made invisible," said the Wizard. And then he looked all around him and said in a solemn voice: "Ozma, are you here?"

There was no reply. Dorothy asked the question, too, and so did Button-Bright and Trot and Betsy, but none received any reply at all.

"It's strange—it's terrible strange!" muttered Cayke the Cookie Cook. "I was sure that the little Pink Bear always tells the truth."

"I still believe in his honesty," said the Frogman, and this tribute so pleased the Bear King that he gave these last speakers grateful looks, but still gazed sourly on the others.

"Come to think of it," remarked the Wizard, "Ozma couldn't be invisible, for she is a fairy and fairies cannot be made invisible against their will. Of course she could be imprisoned by the magician, or even enchanted, or transformed, in spite of her fairy powers; but Ugu could not render her invisible by any magic at his command."

"I wonder if she's been transformed into Button-Bright?" said Dorothy nervously. Then she looked steadily at the boy and asked: "Are you Ozma? Tell me truly!"

Button-Bright laughed.

"You're getting rattled, Dorothy," he replied. "Nothing ever enchants *me*. If I were Ozma, do you think I'd have tumbled into that hole?"

"Anyhow," said the Wizard, "Ozma would never try to deceive her friends, or prevent them from recognizing her, in whatever form she happened to be. The puzzle is still a puzzle, so let us go on to the wicker castle and question the magician himself. Since it was he who stole our Ozma, Ugu is the one who must tell us where to find her."

CHAPTER XXI

MAGIC AGAINST MAGIC

THE WIZARD'S ADVICE WAS GOOD, SO AGAIN THEY STARTED IN THE direction of the low mountain on the crest of which the wicker castle had been built. They had been gradually advancing up hill, so now the elevation seemed to them more like a round knoll than a mountain-top. However, the sides of the knoll were sloping and covered with green grass, so there was a stiff climb before them yet.

Undaunted, they plodded on and had almost reached the knoll when they suddenly observed that it was surrounded by a circle of flame. At first the flames barely rose above the ground, but presently they grew higher and higher until a circle of flaming tongues of fire taller than any of their heads quite surrounded the hill on which the wicker castle stood. When they approached the flames the heat was so intense that it drove them back again.

"This will never do for me!" exclaimed the Patchwork Girl. "I catch fire very easily."

"It won't do for me, either," grumbled the Saw-Horse, prancing to the rear.

"I also strongly object to fire," said the Bear King, following the Saw-Horse to a safe distance and hugging the little Pink Bear with his paws.

"I suppose the foolish Shoemaker imagines these blazes will stop us," remarked the Wizard, with a smile of scorn for Ugu. "But I am able to inform you that this is merely a simple magic trick which the robber stole from Glinda the Good, and by good fortune I know how to destroy these flames, as well as how to produce them. Will some one of you kindly give me a match?"

You may be sure the girls carried no matches, nor did the Frogman or Cayke or any of the animals. But Button-Bright, after searching carefully through his pockets, which contained all sorts of useful and useless things, finally produced a match and handed it to the Wizard, who tied it to the end of a branch which he tore from a small tree growing near them. Then the little Wizard carefully lighted the match and running forward thrust it into the nearest flame. Instantly the circle of fire began to die away and soon vanished completely, leaving the way clear for them to proceed.

"That was funny!" laughed Button-Bright.

"Yes," agreed the Wizard, "it seems odd that a little match could destroy such a great circle of fire, but when Glinda invented this trick she believed no one would ever think of a match being a remedy for fire. I suppose even Ugu doesn't know how we managed to quench the flames of his barrier, for only Glinda and I know the secret. Glinda's Book of Magic, which Ugu stole, told how to make the flames, but not how to put them out."

They now formed in marching order and proceeded to advance up the slope of the hill; but had not gone far when before them rose a wall of steel, the surface of which was thickly covered with sharp, gleaming points resembling daggers. The wall completely surrounded the wicker castle and its sharp points prevented anyone from climbing it. Even the Patchwork Girl might be ripped to pieces if she dared attempt it.

"Ah!" exclaimed the Wizard cheerfully, "Ugu is now using one of my own tricks against me. But this is more serious than the Barrier of Fire, because the only way to destroy the wall is to get on the other side of it."

"How can that be done?" asked Dorothy.

The Wizard looked thoughtfully around his little party and his face grew troubled.

"It's a pretty high wall," he sadly remarked. "I'm pretty sure the Cowardly Lion could not leap over it."

"I'm sure of that, too!" said the Lion with a shudder of fear. "If I foolishly tried such a leap I would be caught on those dreadful spikes."

"I think I could do it, sir," said the Frogman, with a bow to the Wizard. "It is an up-hill jump, as well as being a high jump, but I'm considered something of a jumper by my friends in the Yip Country and I believe a good strong leap will carry me to the other side."

"I'm sure it would," agreed the Cookie Cook.

"Leaping, you know, is a froglike accomplishment," continued the Frogman, modestly, "but please tell me what I am to do when I reach the other side of the wall."

"You're a brave creature," said the Wizard, admiringly. "Has anyone a pin?"

Betsy had one, which she gave him.

"All you need do," said the Wizard to the Frogman, giving him the pin, "is to stick this into the other side of the wall."

"But the wall is of steel!" exclaimed the big frog.

"I know; at least, it *seems* to be steel; but do as I tell you. Stick the pin into the wall and it will disappear."

The Frogman took off his handsome coat and carefully folded it and laid it on the grass. Then he removed his hat and laid it, together with his gold-headed cane, beside the coat. He then went back a way and made three powerful leaps, in rapid succession. The first two leaps took him to the wall and the third leap carried him well over it, to the amazement of all. For a short time he disappeared from their view, but when he had obeyed the Wizard's injunction and had thrust the pin into the wall, the huge barrier vanished and showed them the form of the Frogman, who now went to where his coat lay and put it on again.

"We thank you very much," said the delighted Wizard. "That was the most wonderful leap I ever saw and it has saved us from defeat by our enemy. Let us now hurry on to the castle before Ugu the Shoemaker thinks up some other means to stop us."

"We must have surprised him, so far," declared Dorothy.

"Yes, indeed. The fellow knows a lot of magic—all of our tricks and some of his own," replied the Wizard. "So, if he is half as clever as he ought to be, we shall have trouble with him yet."

He had scarcely spoken these words when out from the gates of the wicker castle marched a regiment of soldiers, clad in gay uniforms and all bearing long, pointed spears and sharp battle-axes. These soldiers were girls, and the uniforms were short

skirts of yellow and black satin, golden shoes, bands of gold across their foreheads and necklaces of glittering jewels. Their jackets were scarlet, braided with silver cords. There were hundreds of these girl-soldiers, and they were more terrible than beautiful, being strong and fierce in appearance. They formed a circle all around the castle and faced outward, their spears pointed toward the invaders and their battle-axes held over their shoulders, ready to strike.

Of course our friends halted at once, for they had not expected this dreadful array of soldiery. The Wizard seemed puzzled and his companions exchanged discouraged looks.

"I'd no idea Ugu had such an army as that," said Dorothy. "The castle doesn't look big enough to hold them all."

"It isn't," declared the Wizard.

"But they all marched out of it."

"They seemed to; but I don't believe it is a real army at all. If Ugu the Shoemaker had so many people living with him, I'm sure the Czarover of Herku would have mentioned the fact to us."

"They're only girls!" laughed Scraps.

"Girls are the fiercest soldiers of all," declared the Frogman. "They are more brave than men and they have better nerves. That is probably why the magician uses them for soldiers and has sent them to oppose us."

No one argued this statement, for all were staring hard at the line of soldiers, which now, having taken a defiant position, remained motionless.

"Here is a trick of magic new to me," admitted the Wizard, after a time. "I do not believe the army is real, but the spears may be sharp enough to prick us, nevertheless, so we must be cautious. Let us take time to consider how to meet this difficulty."

While they were thinking it over, Scraps danced closer to the line of girl soldiers. Her button eyes sometimes saw more than did the natural eyes of her comrades and so, after staring hard at the magician's army, she boldly advanced and danced right through the threatening line! On the other side, she waved her stuffed arms and called out:

"Come on, folks. The spears can't hurt you."

"Ah!" said the Wizard, gayly, "an optical illusion, as I thought. Let us all follow the Patchwork Girl."

The three little girls were somewhat nervous in attempting to brave the spears and battle-axes, but after the others had safely passed the line they ventured to follow. And when all had passed through the ranks of the girl army, the army itself magically disappeared from view.

All this time our friends had been getting farther up the hill and nearer to the wicker castle. Now, continuing their advance, they expected something else to oppose their way, but to their astonishment nothing happened and presently they arrived at the wicker gates, which stood wide open, and boldly entered the domain of Ugu the Shoemaker.

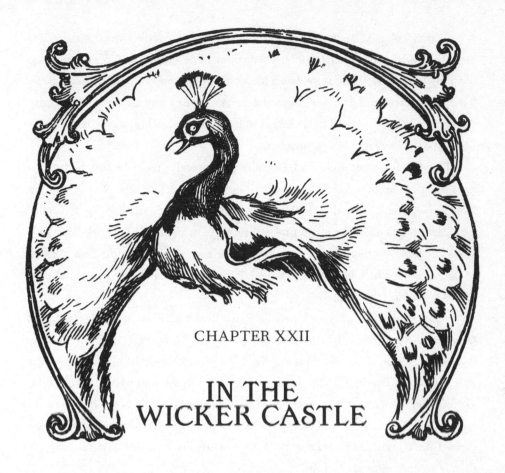

CHAPTER XXII

IN THE
WICKER CASTLE

No sooner were the Wizard of Oz and his followers well within the castle entrance when the big gates swung to with a clang and heavy bars dropped across them. They looked at one another uneasily, but no one cared to speak of the incident. If they were indeed prisoners in the wicker castle it was evident they must find a way to escape, but their first duty was to attend to the errand on which they had come and seek the Royal Ozma, whom they believed to be a prisoner of the magician, and rescue her.

They found they had entered a square courtyard, from which an entrance led into the main building of the castle. No person had appeared to greet them, so far, although a gaudy peacock, perched upon the wall, cackled with laughter and said in its sharp, shrill voice: "Poor fools! Poor fools!"

"I hope the peacock is mistaken," remarked the Frogman, but no one else paid any attention to the bird. They were a little awed by the stillness and loneliness of the place.

As they entered the doors of the castle, which stood invitingly open, these also closed behind them and huge bolts shot into place. The animals had all accompanied the party into the castle, because they felt it would be dangerous for them to separate. They were forced to follow a zigzag passage, turning this way and that, until finally they entered a great central hall, circular in form and with a high dome from which was suspended an enormous chandelier.

The Wizard went first, and Dorothy, Betsy and Trot followed him, Toto keeping at the heels of his little mistress. Then came the Lion, the Woozy and the Saw-Horse; then Cayke the Cookie Cook and Button-Bright; then the Lavender Bear carrying the Pink Bear, and finally the Frogman and the Patchwork Girl, with Hank the Mule tagging behind. So it was the Wizard who caught the first glimpse of the big domed hall, but the others quickly followed and gathered in a wondering group just within the entrance.

Upon a raised platform at one side was a heavy table on which lay Glinda's Great Book of Records; but the platform was firmly fastened to the floor and the table was fastened to the platform and the Book was chained fast to the table—just as it had been when it was kept in Glinda's palace. On the wall over the table hung Ozma's Magic Picture. On a row of shelves at the opposite side of the hall stood all the chemicals and essences of magic and all the magical instruments that had been stolen from Glinda and Ozma and the Wizard, with glass doors covering the shelves so that no one could get at them.

And in a far corner sat Ugu the Shoemaker, his feet lazily extended, his skinny hands clasped behind his head. He was leaning back at his ease and calmly smoking a long pipe. Around the magician was a sort of cage, seemingly made of golden bars set wide apart, and at his feet—also within the cage—reposed the long-sought diamond-studded dishpan of Cayke the Cookie Cook.

Princess Ozma of Oz was nowhere to be seen.

"Well, well," said Ugu, when the invaders had stood in silence for a moment, staring about them, "this visit is an unexpected pleasure, I assure you. I knew you were coming, and I know why you are here. You are not welcome, for I cannot use any of you to my advantage, but as you have insisted on coming I hope you will make the afternoon call as brief as possible. It won't take long to transact your business with me. You will ask me for Ozma, and my reply will be that you may find her—if you can."

"Sir," answered the Wizard, in a tone of rebuke, "you are a very wicked and cruel person. I suppose you imagine, because you have stolen this poor woman's dishpan and all the best magic in Oz, that you are more powerful than we are and will be able to triumph over us."

"Yes," said Ugu the Shoemaker, slowly filling his pipe with fresh tobacco from a silver bowl that stood beside him, "that is exactly what I imagine. It will do you no good to demand from me the girl who was formerly the Ruler of Oz, because I will not tell you where I have hidden her—and you can't guess in a thousand years. Neither will I restore to you any of the magic I have captured. I am not so foolish. But bear this in mind: I mean to be the Ruler of Oz myself, hereafter, so I advise you to be careful how you address your future Monarch."

"Ozma is still Ruler of Oz, wherever you may have hidden her," declared the Wizard. "And bear this in mind, miserable Shoemaker: We intend to find her and to rescue her, in time, but our first duty and pleasure will be to conquer you and then punish you for your misdeeds."

"Very well; go ahead and conquer," said Ugu. "I'd really like to see how you can do it."

Now, although the little Wizard had spoken so boldly, he had at the moment no idea how they might conquer the magician. He had that morning given the Frogman, at his request, a dose of zosozo from his bottle, and the Frogman had promised to fight a good fight if it was necessary; but the Wizard knew that strength alone could not avail against magical arts. The toy Bear King seemed to have some pretty good magic, however, and the Wizard depended to an extent on that. But something ought to be done right away, and the Wizard didn't know what it was.

While he considered this perplexing question and the others stood looking at him as their leader, a queer thing happened. The floor of the great circular hall, on which they were standing, suddenly began to tip. Instead of being flat and level it became a slant, and the slant grew steeper and steeper until none of the party could manage to stand upon it. Presently they all slid down to the wall, which was now under them, and then it became evident that the whole vast room was slowly turning upside-down! Only Ugu the Shoemaker, kept in place by the bars of his golden cage, remained in his former position, and the wicked magician seemed to enjoy the surprise of his victims immensely.

First, they all slid down to the wall back of them, but as the room continued to turn over they next slid down the wall and found themselves at the bottom of the great dome, bumping against the big chandelier which, like everything else, was now upside-down.

The turning movement now stopped and the room became stationary. Looking far up, they saw Ugu suspended in his cage at the very top, which had once been the floor.

"Ah," said he, grinning down at them, "the way to conquer is to act, and he who acts promptly is sure to win. This makes a very good prison, from which I am sure you cannot escape. Please amuse yourselves in any way you like, but I must beg you to excuse me, as I have business in another part of my castle."

Saying this, he opened a trap door in the floor of his cage (which was now over his head) and climbed through it and disappeared from their view. The diamond dishpan still remained in the cage, but the bars kept it from falling down on their heads.

"Well, I declare!" said the Patchwork Girl, seizing one of the bars of the chandelier and swinging from it, "we must peg one for the Shoemaker, for he has trapped us very cleverly."

"Get off my foot, please," said the Lion to the Saw-Horse.

"And oblige me, Mr. Mule," remarked the Woozy, "by taking your tail out of my left eye."

"It's rather crowded down here," explained Dorothy, "because the dome is rounding and we have all slid into the middle of it. But let us keep as quiet as possible until we can think what's best to be done."

"Dear, dear!" wailed Cayke; "I wish I had my darling dishpan," and she held her arms longingly toward it.

"I wish I had the magic on those shelves up there," sighed the Wizard.

"Don't you s'pose we could get to it?" asked Trot anxiously.

"We'd have to fly," laughed the Patchwork Girl.

But the Wizard took the suggestion seriously, and so did the Frogman. They talked it over and soon planned an attempt to reach the shelves where the magical instruments were. First the Frogman lay against the rounding dome and braced his foot on the stem of the chandelier; then the Wizard climbed over him and lay on the dome with his feet on the Frogman's shoulders; the Cookie Cook came next; then Button-Bright climbed to the woman's shoulders; then Dorothy climbed up, and Betsy and Trot, and finally the Patchwork Girl, and all their lengths made a long line that reached far up the dome but not far enough for Scraps to touch the shelves.

"Wait a minute; perhaps I can reach the magic," called the Bear King, and began scrambling up the bodies of the others. But when he came to the Cookie Cook his soft paws tickled her side so that she squirmed and upset the whole line. Down they

came, tumbling in a heap against the animals, and although no one was much hurt it was a bad mix-up, and the Frogman, who was at the bottom, almost lost his temper before he could get on his feet again.

Cayke positively refused to try what she called "the pyramid act" again, and as the Wizard was now convinced they could not reach the magic tools in that manner, the attempt was abandoned.

"But *something* must be done," said the Wizard, and then he turned to the Lavender Bear and asked: "Cannot Your Majesty's magic help us to escape from here?"

"My magic powers are limited," was the reply. "When I was stuffed, the fairies stood by and slyly dropped some magic into my stuffing. Therefore I can do any of the magic that's inside me, but nothing else. You, however, are a wizard, and a wizard should be able to do anything."

"Your Majesty forgets that my tools of magic have been stolen," said the Wizard sadly, "and a wizard without tools is as helpless as a carpenter without a hammer or saw."

"Don't give up," pleaded Button-Bright, "'cause if we can't get out of this queer prison, we'll all starve to death."

"Not I!" laughed the Patchwork Girl, now standing on top of the chandelier, at the place that was meant to be the bottom of it.

"Don't talk of such dreadful things," said Trot, shuddering. "We came here to capture the Shoemaker, didn't we?"

"Yes, and to save Ozma," said Betsy.

"And here we are, captured ourselves, and my darling dishpan up there in plain sight!" wailed the Cookie Cook, wiping her eyes on the tail of the Frogman's coat.

"Hush!" called the Lion with a low, deep growl. "Give the Wizard time to think."

"He has plenty of time," said Scraps. "What he needs is the Scarecrow's brains."

After all, it was little Dorothy who came to their rescue, and her ability to save them was almost as much a surprise to the girl as it was to her friends. Dorothy had been secretly testing the powers of her Magic Belt, which she had once captured from the Nome King, and experimenting with it in various ways, ever since she had started on this eventful journey. At different times she had stolen away from the others of her party and in solitude had tried to find out what the Magic Belt could do and what it could not do. There were a lot of things it could not do, she discovered, but she learned some things about the Belt which even her girl friends did not suspect she knew.

For one thing, she had remembered that when the Nome King owned it the Magic Belt used to perform transformations, and by thinking hard she had finally recalled the way in which such transformations had been accomplished. Better than this, however, was the discovery that the Magic Belt would grant its wearer one wish a day. All she need do was close her right eye and wiggle her left toe and then draw a long breath and make her wish. Yesterday she had wished in secret for a box of caramels, and instantly found the box beside her. To-day she had saved her daily wish, in case she might need it in an emergency, and the time had now come when she must use the wish to enable her to escape with her friends from the prison in which Ugu had caught them.

So, without telling anyone what she intended to do—for she had only used the wish once and could not be certain how powerful the Magic Belt might be—Dorothy closed her right eye and wiggled her left big toe and drew a long breath and wished with all her might. The next moment the room began to revolve again, as slowly as before, and by degrees they all slid to the side wall and down the wall to the floor—all but Scraps, who was so astonished that she still clung to the chandelier. When the big hall was in its proper position again and the others stood firmly upon the floor of it, they looked far up the dome and saw the Patchwork Girl swinging from the chandelier.

"Good gracious!" cried Dorothy. "How ever will you get down?"

"Won't the room keep turning?" asked Scraps.

"I hope not. I believe it has stopped for good," said Princess Dorothy.

"Then stand from under, so you won't get hurt!" shouted the Patchwork Girl, and as soon as they had obeyed this request she let go the chandelier and came tumbling down heels over head and twisting and turning in a very exciting manner. Plump! she fell on the tiled floor and they ran to her and rolled her and patted her into shape again.

CHAPTER XXIII

THE DEFIANCE OF UGU THE SHOEMAKER

The delay caused by Scraps had prevented anyone from running to the shelves to secure the magic instruments so badly needed. Even Cayke neglected to get her diamond-studded dishpan because she was watching the Patchwork Girl. And now the magician had opened his trap door and appeared in his golden cage again, frowning angrily because his prisoners had been able to turn their upside-down prison right-side-up.

"Which of you has dared defy my magic?" he shouted in a terrible voice.

"It was I," answered Dorothy calmly.

"Then I shall destroy you, for you are only an Earth girl and no fairy," he said, and began to mumble some magic words.

Dorothy now realized that Ugu must be treated as an enemy, so she advanced toward the corner in which he sat, saying as she went:

"I am not afraid of you, Mr. Shoemaker, and I think you'll be sorry, pretty soon, that you're such a bad man. You can't destroy me and I won't destroy you, but I'm going to punish you for your wickedness."

Ugu laughed, a laugh that was not nice to hear, and then he waved his hand. Dorothy was halfway across the room when suddenly a wall of glass rose before her and stopped her progress. Through the glass she could see the magician sneering at her because she was a weak little girl, and this provoked her. Although the glass wall obliged her to halt she instantly pressed both hands to her Magic Belt and cried in a loud voice:

"Ugu the Shoemaker, by the magic virtues of the Magic Belt, I command you to become a dove!"

The magician instantly realized he was being enchanted, for he could feel his form changing. He struggled desperately against the enchantment, mumbling magic words and making magic passes with his hands. And in one way he succeeded in defeating Dorothy's purpose, for while his form soon changed to that of a gray dove, the dove was of an enormous size—bigger even than Ugu had been as a man—and this feat he had been able to accomplish before his powers of magic wholly deserted him.

And the dove was not gentle, as doves usually are, for Ugu was terribly enraged at the little girl's success. His books had told him nothing of the Nome King's Magic Belt, the Country of the Nomes being outside the Land of Oz. He knew, however, that he was likely to be conquered unless he made a fierce fight, so he spread his wings and rose in the air and flew directly toward Dorothy. The Wall of Glass had disappeared the instant Ugu became transformed.

Dorothy had meant to command the Belt to transform the magician into a Dove of Peace, but in her excitement she forgot to say more than "dove," and now Ugu was not a Dove of Peace by any means, but rather a spiteful Dove of War. His size made his sharp beak and claws very dangerous, but Dorothy was not afraid when he came darting toward her with his talons outstretched and his sword-like beak open. She knew the Magic Belt would protect its wearer from harm.

But the Frogman did not know that fact and became alarmed at the little girl's seeming danger. So he gave a sudden leap and leaped full upon the back of the great dove.

Then began a desperate struggle. The dove was as strong as Ugu had been, and in size it was considerably bigger than the Frogman. But the Frogman had eaten the zosozo and it had made him fully as strong as Ugu the Dove. At the first leap he bore the dove to the floor, but the giant bird got free and began to bite and claw the Frogman, beating him down with its great wings whenever he attempted to rise. The thick, tough skin of the big frog was not easily damaged, but Dorothy feared for her cham-

pion and by again
using the transforma-
tion power of the Magic Belt she
made the dove grow small, until it
was no larger than a canary bird.

Ugu had not lost his knowledge of magic
when he lost his shape as a man, and he now realized it was hopeless to oppose the power
of the Magic Belt and knew that his only hope of escape lay in instant action. So he
quickly flew into the golden jeweled dishpan he had stolen from Cayke the Cookie Cook
and, as birds can talk as well as beasts or men in the Fairyland of Oz, he muttered the
magic word that was required and wished himself in the Country of the Quadlings—
which was as far away from the wicker castle as he believed he could get.

Our friends did not know, of course, what Ugu was about to do. They saw the dishpan tremble an instant and then disappear, the dove disappearing with it, and although they waited expectantly for some minutes for the magician's return, Ugu did not come back again.

"Seems to me," said the Wizard in a cheerful voice, "that we have conquered the wicked magician more quickly than we expected to."

"Don't say 'we'—Dorothy did it!" cried the Patchwork Girl, turning three somersaults in succession and then walking around on her hands. "Hurrah for Dorothy!"

"I thought you said you did not know how to use the magic of the Nome King's Belt," said the Wizard to Dorothy.

"I didn't know, at that time," she replied, "but afterward I remembered how the Nome King once used the Magic Belt to enchant people and transform 'em into ornaments and all sorts of things; so I tried some enchantments in secret and after awhile I transformed the Saw-Horse into a potato-masher and back again, and the Cowardly Lion into a pussycat and back again, and then I knew the thing would work all right."

"When did you perform those enchantments?" asked the Wizard, much surprised.

"One night when all the rest of you were asleep but Scraps, and she had gone chasing moonbeams."

"Well," remarked the Wizard, "your discovery has certainly saved us a lot of trouble, and we must all thank the Frogman, too, for making such a good fight. The dove's shape had Ugu's evil disposition inside it, and that made the monster bird dangerous."

The Frogman was looking sad because the bird's talons had torn his pretty clothes, but he bowed with much dignity at this well-deserved praise. Cayke, however, had squatted on the floor and was sobbing bitterly.

"My precious dishpan is gone!" she wailed. "Gone, just as I had found it again!"

"Never mind," said Trot, trying to comfort her, "it's sure to be *some*where, so we'll cert'nly run across it some day."

"Yes, indeed," added Betsy; "now that we have Ozma's Magic Picture, we can tell just where the Dove went with your dishpan."

They all approached the Magic Picture, and Dorothy wished it to show the enchanted form of Ugu the Shoemaker, wherever it might be. At once there appeared in the frame of the Picture a scene in the far Quadling Country, where the Dove was perched disconsolately on the limb of a tree and the jeweled dishpan lay on the ground just underneath the limb.

"But where is the place—how far or how near?" asked Cayke anxiously.

"The Book of Records will tell us that," answered the Wizard. So they looked in the Great Book and read the following:

Ugu the Magician, being transformed into a dove by Princess Dorothy of Oz, has used the magic of the golden dishpan to carry him instantly to the northeast corner of the Quadling Country.

"That's all right," said Dorothy. "Don't worry, Cayke, for the Scarecrow and the Tin Woodman are in that part of the country, looking for Ozma, and they'll surely find your dishpan."

"Good gracious!" exclaimed Button-Bright. "We've forgot all about Ozma. Let's find out where the magician hid her."

Back to the Magic Picture they trooped, but when they wished to see Ozma, wherever she might be hidden, only a round black spot appeared in the center of the canvas.

"I don't see how *that* can be Ozma!" said Dorothy, much puzzled.

"It seems to be the best the Magic Picture can do, however," said the Wizard, no less surprised. "If it's an enchantment, it looks as if the magician had transformed Ozma into a chunk of pitch."

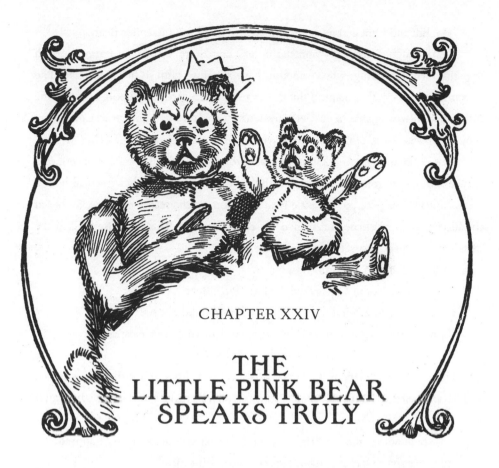

CHAPTER XXIV

THE
LITTLE PINK BEAR
SPEAKS TRULY

FOR SEVERAL MINUTES THEY ALL STOOD STARING AT THE BLACK SPOT ON the canvas of the Magic Picture, wondering what it could mean.

"P'r'aps we'd better ask the little Pink Bear about Ozma," suggested Trot.

"Pshaw!" said Button-Bright, "he don't know anything."

"He never makes a mistake," declared the King.

"He did once, surely," said Betsy. "But perhaps he wouldn't make a mistake again."

"He won't have the chance," grumbled the Bear King.

"We might hear what he has to say," said Dorothy. "It won't do any harm to ask the Pink Bear where Ozma is."

"I will not have him questioned," declared the King, in a surly voice. "I do not intend to allow my little Pink Bear to be again insulted by your foolish doubts. He never makes a mistake."

"Didn't he say Ozma was in that hole in the ground?" asked Betsy.

"He did; and I am certain she was there," replied the Lavender Bear.

Scraps laughed jeeringly and the others saw there was no use arguing with the stubborn Bear King, who seemed to have absolute faith in his Pink Bear. The Wizard, who knew that magical things can usually be depended upon, and that the little Pink Bear was able to answer questions by some remarkable power of magic, thought it wise to apologize to the Lavender Bear for the unbelief of his friends, at the same time urging the King to consent to question the Pink Bear once more. Cayke and the Frogman also pleaded with the big Bear, who finally agreed, although rather ungraciously, to put the little Bear's wisdom to the test once more. So he sat the little one on his knee and turned the crank and the Wizard himself asked the questions in a very respectful tone of voice.

"Where is Ozma?" was his first query.

"Here, in this room," answered the little Pink Bear.

They all looked around the room, but of course did not see her.

"In what part of the room is she?" was the Wizard's next question.

"In Button-Bright's pocket," said the little Pink Bear.

This reply amazed them all, you may be sure, and although the three girls smiled and Scraps yelled: "Hoo-ray!" in derision, the Wizard turned to consider the matter with grave thoughtfulness.

"In which one of Button-Bright's pockets is Ozma?" he presently inquired.

"In the lefthand jacket-pocket," said the little Pink Bear.

"The pink one has gone crazy!" exclaimed Button-Bright, staring hard at the little bear on the big bear's knee.

"I am not so sure of that," declared the Wizard. "If Ozma proves to be really in your pocket, then the little Pink Bear spoke truly when he said Ozma was in that hole in the ground. For at that time you were also in the hole, and after we had pulled you out of it the little Pink Bear said Ozma was not in the hole."

"He never makes a mistake," asserted the Bear King, stoutly.

"Empty that pocket, Button-Bright, and let's see what's in it," requested Dorothy.

So Button-Bright laid the contents of his left jacket-pocket on the table. These proved to be a peg-top, a bunch of string, a small rubber ball and a golden peach-pit.

"What's this?" asked the Wizard, picking up the peach-pit and examining it closely.

"Oh," said the boy, "I saved that to show to the girls, and then forgot all about it. It came out of a lonesome peach that I found in the orchard back yonder, and which I ate while I was lost. It looks like gold, and I never saw a peach-pit like it before."

"Nor I," said the Wizard, "and that makes it seem suspicious."

All heads were bent over the golden peach-pit. The Wizard turned it over several times and then took out his pocket-knife and pried the pit open.

As the two halves fell apart a pink, cloud-like haze came pouring from the golden peach-pit, almost filling the big room, and from the haze a form took shape and settled beside them. Then, as the haze faded away, a sweet voice said: "Thank you, my friends!" and there before them stood their lovely girl Ruler, Ozma of Oz.

With a cry of delight Dorothy rushed forward and embraced her. Scraps turned gleeful flip-flops all around the room. Button-Bright gave a low whistle of astonishment. The Frogman took off his tall hat and bowed low before the beautiful girl who had been freed from her enchantment in so startling a manner. For a time no sound was heard beyond the low murmur of delight that came from the amazed group, but presently the growl of the big Lavender Bear grew louder and he said in a tone of triumph:

"He never makes a mistake!"

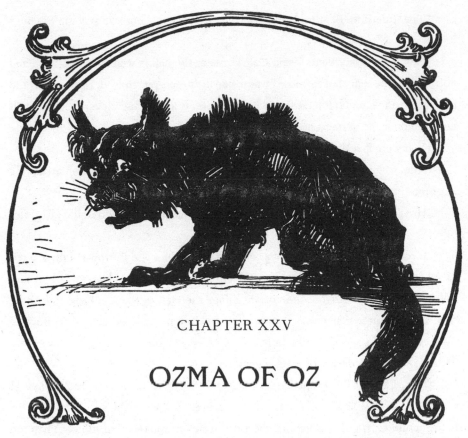

CHAPTER XXV

OZMA OF OZ

"IT'S FUNNY," SAID TOTO, STANDING BEFORE HIS FRIEND THE LION AND wagging his tail, "but I've found my growl at last! I am positive, now, that it was the cruel magician who stole it."

"Let's hear your growl," requested the Lion.

"Gr-r-r-r-r!" said Toto.

"That is fine," declared the big beast. "It isn't as loud or as deep as the growl of the big Lavender Bear, but it is a very respectable growl for a small dog. Where did you find it, Toto?"

"I was smelling in the corner, yonder," said Toto, "when suddenly a mouse ran out—and I growled!"

The others were all busy congratulating Ozma, who was very happy at being released from the confinement of the golden peach-pit, where the magician had placed her with the notion that she never could be found or liberated.

"And only to think," cried Dorothy, "that Button-Bright has been carrying you in his pocket all this time, and we never knew it!"

"The little Pink Bear told you," said the Bear King, "but you wouldn't believe him."

"Never mind, my dears," said Ozma graciously; "all is well that ends well, and you couldn't be expected to know I was inside the peach-pit. Indeed, I feared I would remain a captive much longer than I did, for Ugu is a bold and clever magician and he had hidden me very securely."

"You were in a fine peach," said Button-Bright; "the best I ever ate."

"The magician was foolish to make the peach so tempting," remarked the Wizard; "but Ozma would lend beauty to any transformation."

"How did you manage to conquer Ugu the Shoemaker?" inquired the girl Ruler of Oz.

Dorothy started to tell the story and Trot helped her, and Button-Bright wanted to relate it in his own way, and the Wizard tried to make it clear to Ozma, and Betsy had to remind them of important things they left out, and all together there was such a chatter that it was a wonder that Ozma understood any of it. But she listened patiently, with a smile on her lovely face at their eagerness, and presently had gleaned all the details of their adventures.

Ozma thanked the Frogman very earnestly for his assistance and she advised Cayke the Cookie Cook to dry her weeping eyes, for she promised to take her to the Emerald City and see that her cherished dishpan was restored to her. Then the beautiful Ruler took a chain of emeralds from around her own neck and placed it around the neck of the little Pink Bear.

"Your wise answers to the questions of my friends," said she, "helped them to rescue me. Therefore I am deeply grateful to you and to your noble King."

The bead eyes of the little Pink Bear stared unresponsive to this praise until the Big Lavender Bear turned the crank in its side, when it said in its squeaky voice:

"I thank Your Majesty."

"For my part," returned the Bear King, "I realize that you were well worth saving, Miss Ozma, and so I am much pleased that we could be of service to you. By means of my magic wand I have been creating exact images of your Emerald City and your Royal Palace, and I must confess that they are more attractive than any places I have ever seen—not excepting Bear Center."

"I would like to entertain you in my palace," returned Ozma, sweetly, "and you are welcome to return with me and to make me a long visit, if your bear subjects can spare you from your own kingdom."

"As for that," answered the King, "my kingdom causes me little worry, and I often find it somewhat tame and uninteresting. Therefore I am in no hurry to return to it and will be glad to accept your kind invitation. Corporal Waddle may be trusted to care for my bears in my absence."

"And you'll bring the little Pink Bear?" asked Dorothy eagerly.

"Of course, my dear; I would not willingly part with him."

They remained in the wicker castle for three days, carefully packing all the magical things that had been stolen by Ugu and also taking whatever in the way of magic the shoemaker had inherited from his ancestors.

"For," said Ozma, "I have forbidden any of my subjects except Glinda the Good and the Wizard of Oz to practice magical arts, because they cannot be trusted to do good and not harm. Therefore Ugu must never again be permitted to work magic of any sort."

"Well," remarked Dorothy cheerfully, "a dove can't do much in the way of magic, anyhow, and I'm going to keep Ugu in the form of a dove until he reforms and becomes a good and honest shoemaker."

When everything was packed and loaded on the backs of the animals, they set out for the river, taking a more direct route than that by which Cayke and the Frogman had come. In this way they avoided the Cities of Thi and Herku and Bear Center and after a pleasant journey reached the Winkie River and found a jolly ferryman who had a fine big boat and was willing to carry the entire party by water to a place quite near to the Emerald City.

The river had many windings and many branches, and the journey did not end in a day, but finally the boat floated into a pretty lake which was but a short distance from Ozma's home. Here the jolly ferryman was rewarded for his labors and then the entire party set out in a grand procession to march to the Emerald City.

News that the Royal Ozma had been found spread quickly throughout the neighborhood and both sides of the road soon became lined with loyal subjects of the beautiful and beloved Ruler. Therefore Ozma's ears heard little but cheers and her eyes beheld little else than waving handkerchiefs and banners during all the triumphal march from the lake to the city's gates.

And there she met a still greater concourse, for all the inhabitants of the Emerald City turned out to welcome her return and several bands played gay music and all the houses were decorated with flags and bunting and never before were the people so joyous and happy as at this moment when they welcomed home their girl

Ruler. For she had been lost and was now found again, and surely that was cause for rejoicing.

Glinda was at the royal palace to meet the returning party and the good Sorceress was indeed glad to have her Great Book of Records returned to her, as well as all the precious collection of magic instruments and elixirs and chemicals that had been stolen from her castle. Cap'n Bill and the Wizard at once hung the Magic Picture upon the wall of Ozma's boudoir and the Wizard was so light-hearted that he did several tricks with the tools in his black bag to amuse his companions and prove that once again he was a powerful wizard.

For a whole week there was feasting and merriment and all sorts of joyous festivities at the palace, in honor of Ozma's safe return. The Lavender Bear and the little Pink Bear received much attention and were honored by all, much to the Bear King's satisfaction. The Frogman speedily became a favorite at the Emerald City and the Shaggy Man and Tik-Tok and Jack Pumpkinhead, who had now returned from their search, were very polite to the big frog and made him feel quite at home. Even the Cookie Cook, because she was quite a stranger and Ozma's guest, was shown as much deference as if she had been a queen.

"All the same, Your Majesty," said Cayke to Ozma, day after day, with tiresome repetition, "I hope you will soon find my jeweled dishpan, for never can I be quite happy without it."

CHAPTER XXVI

DOROTHY FORGIVES

THE GRAY DOVE WHICH HAD ONCE BEEN UGU THE SHOEMAKER SAT ON ITS tree in the far Quadling Country and moped, chirping dismally and brooding over its misfortunes. After a time the Scarecrow and the Tin Woodman came along and sat beneath the tree, paying no heed to the mutterings of the gray dove.

The Tin Woodman took a small oilcan from his tin pocket and carefully oiled his tin joints with it. While he was thus engaged the Scarecrow remarked:

"I feel much better, dear comrade, since we found that heap of nice clean straw and you stuffed me anew with it."

"And I feel much better now that my joints are oiled," returned the Tin Woodman, with a sigh of pleasure. "You and I, friend Scarecrow, are much more easily cared for than those clumsy meat people, who spend half their time dressing in fine clothes and who must live in splendid dwellings in order to be contented and happy. You and I do not eat, and so we are spared the dreadful bother of getting three meals a day. Nor do we waste half our lives in sleep, a condition that causes the meat people to lose all consciousness and become as thoughtless and helpless as logs of wood."

"You speak truly," responded the Scarecrow, tucking some wisps of straw into his breast with his padded fingers. "I often feel sorry for the meat people, many of whom are my friends. Even the beasts are happier than they, for they require less to make them content. And the birds are the luckiest creatures of all, for they can fly swiftly where they will and find a home at any place they care to perch; their food consists of seeds and grains they gather from the fields and their drink is a sip of water from some running brook. If I could not be a Scarecrow—or a Tin Woodman—my next choice would be to live as a bird does."

The gray dove had listened carefully to this speech and seemed to find comfort in it, for it hushed its moaning. And just then the Tin Woodman discovered Cayke's dishpan, which was on the ground quite near to him.

"Here is a rather pretty utensil," he said, taking it in his tin hands to examine it, "but I would not care to own it. Whoever fashioned it of gold and covered it with diamonds did not add to its usefulness, nor do I consider it as beautiful as the bright dishpans of tin one usually sees. No yellow color is ever so handsome as the silver sheen of tin," and he turned to look at his tin legs and body with approval.

"I cannot quite agree with you there," replied the Scarecrow. "My straw stuffing has a light yellow color, and it is not only pretty to look at but it crunkles most delightfully when I move."

"Let us admit that all colors are good in their proper places," said the Tin Woodman, who was too kind-hearted to quarrel; "but you must agree with me that a dishpan that is yellow is unnatural. What shall we do with this one, which we have just found?"

"Let us carry it back to the Emerald City," suggested the Scarecrow. "Some of our friends might like to have it for a foot-bath, and in using it that way its golden color and sparkling ornaments would not injure its usefulness."

So they went away and took the jeweled dishpan with them. And after wandering through the country for a day or so longer, they learned the news that Ozma had been found. Therefore they straightway returned to the Emerald City and presented the dishpan to Princess Ozma as a token of their joy that she had been restored to them.

Ozma promptly gave the diamond-studded gold dishpan to Cayke the Cookie Cook, who was so delighted at regaining her lost treasure that she danced up and down in glee and then threw her skinny arms around Ozma's neck and kissed her gratefully. Cayke's mission was now successfully accomplished, but she was having such a good time at the Emerald City that she seemed in no hurry to go back to the Country of the Yips.

It was several weeks after the dishpan had been restored to the Cookie Cook when one day, as Dorothy was seated in the royal gardens with Trot and Betsy beside her, a gray dove came flying down and alighted at the girl's feet.

"I am Ugu the Shoemaker," said the dove in a soft, mourning voice, "and I have come to ask you to forgive me for the great wrong I did in stealing Ozma and the magic that belonged to her and to others."

"Are you sorry, then?" asked Dorothy, looking hard at the bird.

"I am *very* sorry," declared Ugu. "I've been thinking over my misdeeds for a long time, for doves have little else to do but think, and I'm surprised that I was such a wicked man and had so little regard for the rights of others. I am now convinced that even had I succeeded in making myself Ruler of all Oz I should not have been happy, for many days of quiet thought have shown me that only those things one acquires honestly are able to render one content."

"I guess that's so," said Trot.

"Anyhow," said Betsy, "the bad man seems truly sorry, and if he has now become a good and honest man we ought to forgive him."

"I fear I cannot become a good man again," said Ugu, "for the transformation I am under will always keep me in the form of a dove. But, with the kind forgiveness of my former enemies, I hope to become a very good dove, and highly respected."

"Wait here till I run for my Magic Belt," said Dorothy, "and I'll transform you back to your reg'lar shape in a jiffy."

"No—don't do that!" pleaded the dove, fluttering its wings in an excited way. "I only want your forgiveness; I don't want to be a man again. As Ugu the Shoemaker I was skinny and old and unlovely; as a dove I am quite pretty to look at. As a man I was ambitious and cruel, while as a dove I can be content with my lot and happy in my simple life. I have learned to love the free and independent life of a bird and I'd rather not change back."

"Just as you like, Ugu," said Dorothy, resuming her seat. "Perhaps you are right, for you're certainly a better dove than you were a man, and if you should ever backslide, an' feel wicked again, you couldn't do much harm as a gray dove."

"Then you forgive me for all the trouble I caused you?" he asked earnestly.

"Of course; anyone who's sorry just *has* to be forgiven."

"Thank you," said the gray dove, and flew away again.

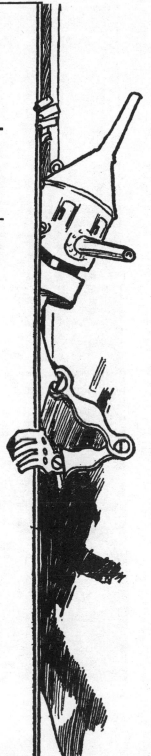

THE **TIN**
WOODMAN
OF

Contents

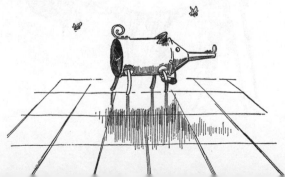

CHAPTER I

WOOT THE WANDERER

THE TIN WOODMAN SAT ON HIS GLITTERING TIN throne in the handsome tin hall of his splendid tin castle in the Winkie Country of the Land of Oz. Beside him, in a chair of woven straw, sat his best friend, the Scarecrow of Oz. At times they spoke to one another of curious things they had seen and strange adventures they had known since first they two had met and become comrades. But at times they were silent, for these things had been talked over many times between them, and they found themselves contented in merely being together, speaking now and then a brief sentence to prove they were wide awake and attentive. But then, these two quaint persons never slept. Why should they sleep, when they never tired?

And now, as the brilliant sun sank low over the Winkie Country of Oz, tinting the glistening tin towers and tin minarets of the tin castle with glorious sunset hues, there approached along a winding pathway Woot the Wanderer, who met at the castle entrance a Winkie servant.

The servants of the Tin Woodman all wore tin helmets and tin breastplates and uniforms covered with tiny tin discs sewed closely together on silver cloth, so that their bodies sparkled as beautifully as did the tin castle—and almost as beautifully as did the Tin Woodman himself.

Woot the Wanderer looked at the man servant—all bright and glittering—and at the magnificent castle—all bright and glittering—and as he looked his eyes grew big with wonder. For Woot was not very big and not very old and, wanderer though he was, this proved the most gorgeous sight that had ever met his boyish gaze.

"Who lives here?" he asked.

"The Emperor of the Winkies, who is the famous Tin Woodman of Oz," replied the servant, who had been trained to treat all strangers with courtesy.

"A Tin Woodman? How queer!" exclaimed the little wanderer.

"Well, perhaps our Emperor *is* queer," admitted the servant; "but he is a kind master and as honest and true as good tin can make him; so we, who gladly serve him, are apt to forget that he is not like other people."

"May I see him?" asked Woot the Wanderer, after a moment's thought.

"If it please you to wait a moment, I will go and ask him," said the servant, and then he went into the hall where the Tin Woodman sat with his friend the Scarecrow. Both were glad to learn that a stranger had arrived at the castle, for this would give them something new to talk about, so the servant was asked to admit the boy at once.

By the time Woot the Wanderer had passed through the grand corridors—all lined with ornamental tin—and under stately tin archways and through the many tin rooms all set with beautiful tin furniture, his eyes had grown bigger than ever and his whole little body thrilled with amazement. But, astonished though he was, he was able to make a polite bow before the throne and to say in a respectful voice: "I salute Your Illustrious Majesty and offer you my humble services."

"Very good!" answered the Tin Woodman in his accustomed cheerful manner. "Tell me who you are, and whence you come."

"I am known as Woot the Wanderer," answered the boy, "and I have come, through many travels and by roundabout ways, from my former home in a far corner of the Gillikin Country of Oz."

"To wander from one's home," remarked the Scarecrow, "is to encounter dangers and hardships, especially if one is made of meat and bone. Had you no friends in that corner of the Gillikin Country? Was it not homelike and comfortable?"

To hear a man stuffed with straw speak, and speak so well, quite startled Woot, and perhaps he stared a bit rudely at the Scarecrow. But after a moment he replied:

"I had home and friends, your Honorable Strawness, but they were so quiet and happy and comfortable that I found them dismally stupid. Nothing in that corner of Oz interested me, but I believed that in other parts of the country I would find strange people and see new sights, and so I set out upon my wandering journey. I have been a wanderer for nearly a full year, and now my wanderings have brought me to this splendid castle."

"I suppose," said the Tin Woodman, "that in this year you have seen so much that you have become very wise."

"No," replied Woot, thoughtfully, "I am not at all wise, I beg to assure Your Majesty. The more I wander the less I find that I know, for in the Land of Oz much wisdom and many things may be learned."

"To learn is simple. Don't you ask questions?" inquired the Scarecrow.

"Yes; I ask as many questions as I dare; but some people refuse to answer questions."

"That is not kind of them," declared the Tin Woodman. "If one does not ask for information he seldom receives it; so I, for my part, make it a rule to answer any civil question that is asked me."

"So do I," added the Scarecrow, nodding.

"I am glad to hear this," said the Wanderer, "for it makes me bold to ask for something to eat."

"Bless the boy!" cried the Emperor of the Winkies; "how careless of me not to remember that wanderers are usually hungry. I will have food brought you at once."

Saying this he blew upon a tin whistle that was suspended from his tin neck, and at the summons a servant appeared and bowed low. The Tin Woodman ordered food for the stranger, and in a few minutes the servant brought in a tin tray heaped with a choice array of good things to eat, all neatly displayed on tin dishes that were polished till they shone like mirrors. The tray was set upon a tin table drawn before the throne, and the servant placed a tin chair before the table for the boy to seat himself.

"Eat, friend Wanderer," said the Emperor cordially, "and I trust the feast will be to your liking. I, myself, do not eat, being made in such manner that I require no food to keep me alive. Neither does my friend the Scarecrow. But all my Winkie people eat, being formed of flesh, as you are, and so my tin cupboard is never bare, and strangers are always welcome to whatever it contains."

The boy ate in silence for a time, being really hungry, but after his appetite was somewhat satisfied, he said:

"How happened Your Majesty to be made of tin, and still be alive?"

"That," replied the tin man, "is a long story."

"The longer the better," said the boy. "Won't you please tell me the story?"

"If you desire it," promised the Tin Woodman, leaning back in his tin throne and crossing his tin legs. "I haven't related my history in a long while, because everyone here knows it nearly as well as I do. But you, being a stranger, are no doubt curious to learn how I became so beautiful and prosperous, so I will recite for your benefit my strange adventures."

"Thank you," said Woot the Wanderer, still eating.

"I was not always made of tin," began the Emperor, "for in the beginning I was a man of flesh and bone and blood and lived in the Munchkin Country of Oz. There I was, by trade, a woodchopper, and contributed my share to the comfort of the Oz people by chopping up the trees of the forest to make firewood, with which the women would cook their meals while the children warmed themselves about the fires. For my home I had a little hut by the edge of the forest, and my life was one of much content until I fell in love with a beautiful Munchkin girl who lived not far away."

"What was the Munchkin girl's name?" asked Woot.

"Nimmie Amee. This girl, so fair that the sunsets blushed when their rays fell upon her, lived with a powerful witch who wore silver shoes and who had made the poor child her slave. Nimmie Amee was obliged to work from morning till night for the old Witch of the East, scrubbing and sweeping her hut and cooking her meals and washing her dishes. She had to cut firewood, too, until I found her one day in the forest and fell in love with her. After that, I always brought plenty of firewood to Nimmie Amee and we became very friendly. Finally I asked her to marry me, and she agreed to do so, but the Witch happened to overhear our conversation and it made her very angry, for she did not wish her slave to be taken away from her. The Witch commanded me never to come near Nimmie Amee again, but I told her I was

my own master and would do as I pleased, not realizing that this was a careless way to speak to a Witch.

"The next day, as I was cutting wood in the forest, the cruel Witch enchanted my axe, so that it slipped and cut off my right leg."

"How dreadful!" cried Woot the Wanderer.

"Yes, it was a seeming misfortune," agreed the Tin Man, "for a one-legged woodchopper is of little use in his trade. But I would not allow the Witch to conquer me so easily. I knew a very skillful mechanic at the other side of the forest, who was my friend, so I hopped on one leg to him and asked him to help me. He soon made me a new leg out of tin and fastened it cleverly to my meat body. It had joints at the knee and at the ankle and was almost as comfortable as the leg I had lost."

"Your friend must have been a wonderful workman!" exclaimed Woot.

"He was, indeed," admitted the Emperor. "He was a tinsmith by trade and could make anything out of tin. When I returned to Nimmie Amee, the girl was delighted and threw her arms around my neck and kissed me, declaring she was proud of me. The Witch saw the kiss and was more angry than before. When I went to work in the forest, next day, my axe, being still enchanted, slipped and cut off my other leg. Again I hopped—on my tin leg—to my friend the tinsmith, who kindly made me another tin leg and fastened it to my body. So I returned joyfully to Nimmie Amee, who was much pleased with my glittering legs and promised that when we were wed she would always keep them oiled and polished. But the Witch was more furious than ever, and as soon as I raised my axe to chop, it twisted around and cut off one of my arms. The tinsmith made me a tin arm and I was not much worried, because Nimmie Amee declared she still loved me."

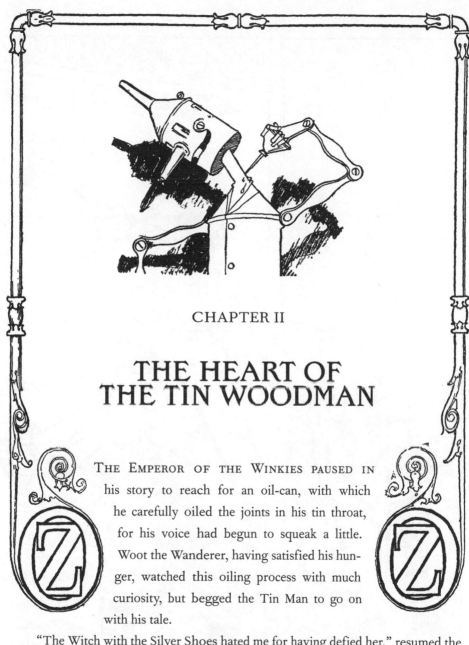

CHAPTER II

THE HEART OF
THE TIN WOODMAN

THE EMPEROR OF THE WINKIES PAUSED IN his story to reach for an oil-can, with which he carefully oiled the joints in his tin throat, for his voice had begun to squeak a little. Woot the Wanderer, having satisfied his hunger, watched this oiling process with much curiosity, but begged the Tin Man to go on with his tale.

"The Witch with the Silver Shoes hated me for having defied her," resumed the Emperor, his voice now sounding clear as a bell, "and she insisted that Nimmie Amee should never marry me. Therefore she made the enchanted axe cut off my other arm, and the tinsmith also replaced that member with tin, including these finely-jointed hands that you see me using. But, alas! after that, the axe, still enchanted by the cruel Witch, cut my body in two, so that I fell to the ground. Then the Witch, who was

watching from a near-by bush, rushed up and seized the axe and chopped my body into several small pieces, after which, thinking that at last she had destroyed me, she ran away laughing in wicked glee.

"But Nimmie Amee found me. She picked up my arms and legs and head, and made a bundle of them and carried them to the tinsmith, who set to work and made me a fine body of pure tin. When he had joined the arms and legs to the body, and set my head in the tin collar, I was a much better man than ever, for my body could not ache or pain me, and I was so beautiful and bright that I had no need of clothing. Clothing is always a nuisance, because it soils and tears and has to be replaced; but my tin body only needs to be oiled and polished.

"Nimmie Amee still declared she would marry me, as she still loved me in spite of the Witch's evil deeds. The girl declared I would make the brightest husband in all the world, which was quite true. However, the Wicked Witch was not yet defeated. When I returned to my work the axe slipped and cut off my head, which was the only meat part of me then remaining. Moreover, the old woman grabbed up my severed head and carried it away with her and hid it. But Nimmie Amee came into the forest and found me wandering around helplessly, because I could not see where to go, and she led me to my friend the tinsmith. The faithful fellow at once set to work to make me a tin head, and he had just completed it when Nimmie Amee came running up with my old head, which she had stolen from the Witch. But, on reflection, I considered the tin head far superior to the meat one—I am wearing it yet, so you can see its beauty and grace of outline—and the girl agreed with me that a man all made of tin was far more perfect than one formed of different materials. The tinsmith was as proud of his workmanship as I was, and for three whole days, all admired me and praised my beauty.

"Being now completely formed of tin, I had no more fear of the Wicked Witch, for she was powerless to injure me. Nimmie Amee said we must be married at once, for then she could come to my cottage and live with me and keep me bright and sparkling.

"'I am sure, my dear Nick,' said the brave and beautiful girl—my name was then Nick Chopper, you should be told—'that you will make the best husband any girl could have. I shall not be obliged to cook for you, for now you do not eat; I shall not have to make your bed, for tin does not tire or require sleep; when we go to a dance, you will not get weary before the music stops and say you want to go home. All day long, while you are chopping wood in the forest, I shall be able to amuse myself in my own way—a privilege few wives enjoy. There is no temper in your new head, so you will not get angry with me. Finally, I shall take pride in being the wife of the only live Tin Woodman in all the world!' Which shows that Nimmie Amee was as wise as she was brave and beautiful."

"I think she was a very nice girl," said Woot the Wanderer. "But, tell me, please, why were you not killed when you were chopped to pieces?"

"In the Land of Oz," replied the Emperor, "no one can ever be killed. A man with a wooden leg or a tin leg is still the same man; and, as I lost parts of my meat body by degrees, I always remained the same person as in the beginning, even though in the end I was all tin and no meat."

"I see," said the boy, thoughtfully. "And did you marry Nimmie Amee?"

"No," answered the Tin Woodman, "I did not. She said she still loved me, but I found that I no longer loved her. My tin body contained no heart, and without a heart no one can love. So the Wicked Witch conquered in the end, and when I left the Munchkin Country of Oz, the poor girl was still the slave of the Witch and had to do her bidding day and night."

"Where did you go?" asked Woot.

"Well, I first started out to find a heart, so I could love Nimmie Amee again; but hearts are more scarce than one would think. One day, in a big forest that was strange to me, my joints suddenly became rusted, because I had forgotten to oil them. There I stood, unable to move hand or foot. And there I continued to stand—while days came and went—until Dorothy and the Scarecrow came along and rescued me. They oiled my joints and set me free, and I've taken good care never to rust again."

"Who was this Dorothy?" questioned the Wanderer.

"A little girl who happened to be in a house when it was carried by a cyclone all the way from Kansas to the Land of Oz. When the house fell, in the Munchkin Country, it fortunately landed on the Wicked Witch and smashed her flat. It was a big house, and I think the Witch is under it yet."

"No," said the Scarecrow, correcting him, "Dorothy says the Witch turned to dust, and the wind scattered the dust in every direction."

"Well," continued the Tin Woodman, "after meeting the Scarecrow and Dorothy, I went with them to the Emerald City, where the Wizard of Oz gave me a heart. But the Wizard's stock of hearts was low, and he gave me a Kind Heart instead of a Loving Heart, so that I could not love Nimmie Amee any more than I did when I was heartless."

"Couldn't the Wizard give you a heart that was both Kind and Loving?" asked the boy.

"No; that was what I asked for, but he said he was so short on hearts, just then, that there was but one in stock, and I could take that or none at all. So I accepted it, and I must say that for its kind it is a very good heart indeed."

"It seems to me," said Woot, musingly, "that the Wizard fooled you. It can't be a very Kind Heart, you know."

"Why not?" demanded the Emperor.

"Because it was unkind of you to desert the girl who loved you, and who had been faithful and true to you when you were in trouble. Had the heart the Wizard gave you been a Kind Heart, you would have gone back home and made the beautiful Munchkin girl your wife, and then brought her here to be an Empress and live in your splendid tin castle."

The Tin Woodman was so surprised at this frank speech that for a time he did nothing but stare hard at the boy Wanderer. But the Scarecrow wagged his stuffed head and said in a positive tone:

"This boy is right. I've often wondered, myself, why you didn't go back and find that poor Munchkin girl."

Then the Tin Woodman stared hard at his friend the Scarecrow. But finally he said in a serious tone of voice:

"I must admit that never before have I thought of such a thing as finding Nimmie Amee and making her Empress of the Winkies. But it is surely not too late, even now, to do this, for the girl must still be living in the Munchkin Country. And, since this strange Wanderer has reminded me of Nimmie Amee, I believe it is my duty to set out and find her. Surely it is not the girl's fault that I no longer love her, and so, if I can make her happy, it is proper that I should do so, and in this way reward her for her faithfulness."

"Quite right, my friend!" agreed the Scarecrow.

"Will you accompany me on this errand?" asked the Tin Emperor.

"Of course," said the Scarecrow.

"And will you take me along?" pleaded Woot the Wanderer in an eager voice.

"To be sure," said the Tin Woodman, "if you care to join our party. It was you who first told me it was my duty to find and marry Nimmie Amee, and I'd like you to know that Nick Chopper, the Tin Emperor of the Winkies, is a man who never shirks his duty, once it is pointed out to him."

"It ought to be a pleasure, as well as a duty, if the girl is so beautiful," said Woot, well pleased with the idea of the adventure.

"Beautiful things may be admired, if not loved," asserted the Tin Man. "Flowers are beautiful, for instance, but we are not inclined to marry them. Duty, on the contrary, is a bugle call to action, whether you are inclined to act, or not. In this case, I obey the bugle call of duty."

"When shall we start?" inquired the Scarecrow, who was always glad to embark upon a new adventure. "I don't hear any bugle, but when do we go?"

"As soon as we can get ready," answered the Emperor. "I'll call my servants at once and order them to make preparations for our journey."

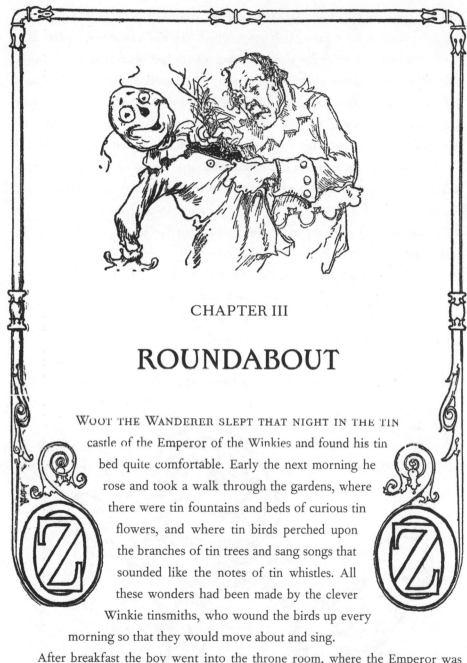

CHAPTER III

ROUNDABOUT

WOOT THE WANDERER SLEPT THAT NIGHT IN THE TIN castle of the Emperor of the Winkies and found his tin bed quite comfortable. Early the next morning he rose and took a walk through the gardens, where there were tin fountains and beds of curious tin flowers, and where tin birds perched upon the branches of tin trees and sang songs that sounded like the notes of tin whistles. All these wonders had been made by the clever Winkie tinsmiths, who wound the birds up every morning so that they would move about and sing.

After breakfast the boy went into the throne room, where the Emperor was having his tin joints carefully oiled by a servant, while other servants were stuffing sweet, fresh straw into the body of the Scarecrow.

Woot watched this operation with much interest, for the Scarecrow's body was only a suit of clothes filled with straw. The coat was buttoned tight to keep the packed straw from falling out and a rope was tied around the waist to hold it in shape and prevent the straw from sagging down. The Scarecrow's head was a gunnysack filled with bran, on which the eyes, nose and mouth had been painted. His hands were white cotton gloves stuffed with fine straw. Woot noticed that even when carefully stuffed and patted into shape, the straw man was awkward in his movements and decidedly wobbly on his feet, so the boy wondered if the Scarecrow would be able to travel with them all the way to the forests of the Munchkin Country of Oz.

The preparations made for this important journey were very simple. A knapsack was filled with food and given Woot the Wanderer to carry upon his back, for the food was for his use alone. The Tin Woodman shouldered an axe which was sharp and brightly polished, and the Scarecrow put the Emperor's oil-can in his pocket, that he might oil his friend's joints should they need it.

"Who will govern the Winkie Country during your absence?" asked the boy.

"Why, the country will run itself," answered the Emperor. "As a matter of fact, my people do not need an Emperor, for Ozma of Oz watches over the welfare of all her subjects, including the Winkies. Like a good many kings and emperors, I have a grand title, but very little real power, which allows me time to amuse myself in my own way. The people of Oz have but one law to obey, which is: 'Behave Yourself,'

so it is easy for them to abide by this Law, and you'll notice they behave very well. But it is time for us to be off, and I am eager to start because I suppose that that poor Munchkin girl is anxiously awaiting my coming."

"She's waited a long time already, seems to me," remarked the Scarecrow, as they left the grounds of the castle and followed a path that led eastward.

"True," replied the Tin Woodman; "but I've noticed that the last end of a wait, however long it has been, is the hardest to endure; so I must try to make Nimmie Amee happy as soon as possible."

"Ah; that proves you have a Kind Heart," remarked the Scarecrow, approvingly.

"It's too bad he hasn't a Loving Heart," said Woot. "This Tin Man is going to marry a nice girl through kindness, and not because he loves her, and somehow that doesn't seem quite right."

"Even so, I am not sure it isn't best for the girl," said the Scarecrow, who seemed very intelligent for a straw man, "for a loving husband is not always kind, while a kind husband is sure to make any girl content."

"Nimmie Amee will become an Empress!" announced the Tin Woodman, proudly. "I shall have a tin gown made for her, with tin ruffles and tucks on it, and she shall have tin slippers, and tin earrings and bracelets, and wear a tin crown on her head. I am sure that will delight Nimmie Amee, for all girls are fond of finery."

"Are we going to the Munchkin Country by way of the Emerald City?" inquired the Scarecrow, who looked upon the Tin Woodman as the leader of the party.

"I think not," was the reply. "We are engaged upon a rather delicate adventure, for we are seeking a girl who fears her former lover has forgotten her. It will be rather hard for me, you must admit, when I confess to Nimmie Amee that I have come to marry her because it is my duty to do so, and therefore the fewer witnesses there are to our meeting the better for both of us. After I have found Nimmie Amee and she has managed to control her joy at our reunion, I shall take her to the Emerald City and introduce her to Ozma and Dorothy, and to Betsy Bobbin and Tiny Trot, and all our other friends; but, if I remember rightly, poor Nimmie Amee has a sharp tongue when angry, and she may be a trifle angry with me, at first, because I have been so long in coming to her."

"I can understand that," said Woot gravely. "But how can we get to that part of the Munchkin Country where you once lived without passing through the Emerald City?"

"Why, that is easy," the Tin Man assured him.

"I have a map of Oz in my pocket," persisted the boy, "and it shows that the Winkie Country, where we now are, is at the west of Oz, and the Munchkin Country at the east, while directly between them lies the Emerald City."

"True enough; but we shall go toward the north, first of all, into the Gillikin Country, and so pass around the Emerald City," explained the Tin Woodman.

"That may prove a dangerous journey," replied the boy. "I used to live in one of the top corners of the Gillikin Country, near to Oogaboo, and I have been told that in this northland country are many people whom it is not pleasant to meet. I was very careful to avoid them during my journey south."

"A Wanderer should have no fear," observed the Scarecrow, who was wobbling along in a funny, haphazard manner, but keeping pace with his friends.

"Fear does not make one a coward," returned Woot, growing a little red in the face, "but I believe it is more easy to avoid danger than to overcome it. The safest way is the best way, even for one who is brave and determined."

"Do not worry, for we shall not go far to the north," said the Emperor. "My one idea is to avoid the Emerald City without going out of our way more than is necessary. Once around the Emerald City we will turn south into the Munchkin Country, where the Scarecrow and I are well acquainted and have many friends."

"I have traveled some in the Gillikin Country," remarked the Scarecrow, "and while I must say I have met some strange people there at times, I have never yet been harmed by them."

"Well, it's all the same to me," said Woot, with assumed carelessness. "Dangers, when they cannot be avoided, are often quite interesting, and I am willing to go wherever you two venture to go."

So they left the path they had been following and began to travel toward the northeast, and all that day they were in the pleasant Winkie Country, and all the people they met saluted the Emperor with great respect and wished him good luck on his journey. At night they stopped at a house where they were well entertained and where Woot was given a comfortable bed to sleep in.

"Were the Scarecrow and I alone," said the Tin Woodman, "we would travel by night as well as by day; but with a meat person in our party, we must halt at night to permit him to rest."

"Meat tires, after a day's travel," added the Scarecrow, "while straw and tin never tire at all. Which proves," said he, "that we are somewhat superior to people made in the common way."

Woot could not deny that he was tired, and he slept soundly until morning, when he was given a good breakfast, smoking hot.

"You two miss a great deal by not eating," he said to his companions.

"It is true," responded the Scarecrow. "We miss suffering from hunger, when food cannot be had, and we miss a stomach-ache, now and then."

As he said this, the Scarecrow glanced at the Tin Woodman, who nodded his assent.

All that second day they traveled steadily, entertaining one another the while with stories of adventures they had formerly met and listening to the Scarecrow recite poetry. He had learned a great many poems from Professor Woggle-Bug and loved to repeat them whenever anybody would listen to him. Of course Woot and the Tin Woodman now listened, because they could not do otherwise—unless they rudely ran away from their stuffed comrade.

One of the Scarecrow's recitations was like this:

> "What sound is so sweet
>   As the straw from the wheat
>   When it crunkles so tender and low?
>   It is yellow and bright,
>   So it gives me delight
>   To crunkle wherever I go.
>
> "Sweet, fresh, golden Straw!
>   There is surely no flaw
>   In a stuffing so clean and compact.
>   It creaks when I walk,
>   And it thrills when I talk,
>   And its fragrance is fine, for a fact.
>
> "To cut me don't hurt,
>   For I've no blood to squirt,
>   And I therefore can suffer no pain;
>   The straw that I use
>   Doesn't lump up or bruise,
>   Though it's pounded again and again!

"I know it is said
That my beautiful head
Has brains of mixed wheat-straw and bran,
But my thoughts are so good
I'd not change, if I could,
For the brains of a common meat man.

"Content with my lot,
I'm glad that I'm not
Like others I meet day by day;
If my insides get musty,
Or mussed-up, or dusty,
I get newly stuffed right away."

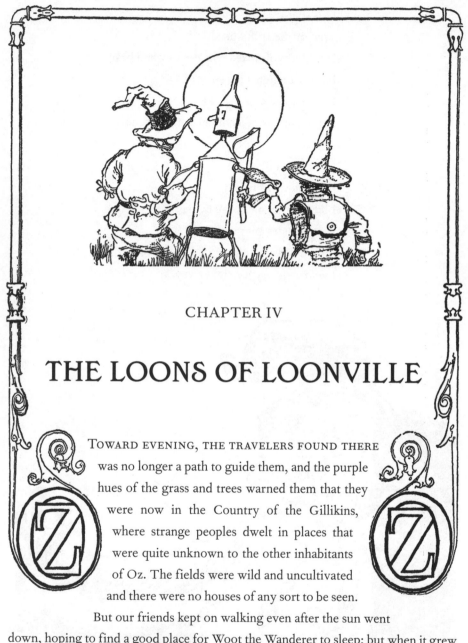

CHAPTER IV

THE LOONS OF LOONVILLE

Toward evening, the travelers found there was no longer a path to guide them, and the purple hues of the grass and trees warned them that they were now in the Country of the Gillikins, where strange peoples dwelt in places that were quite unknown to the other inhabitants of Oz. The fields were wild and uncultivated and there were no houses of any sort to be seen.

But our friends kept on walking even after the sun went down, hoping to find a good place for Woot the Wanderer to sleep; but when it grew quite dark and the boy was weary with his long walk, they halted right in the middle of a field and allowed Woot to get his supper from the food he carried in his knapsack. Then the Scarecrow laid himself down, so that Woot could use his stuffed body as a pillow, and the Tin Woodman stood up beside them all night, so the dampness of the ground might not rust his joints or dull his brilliant polish. Whenever the dew settled on his body he carefully wiped it off with a cloth, and so in the morning the Emperor shone as brightly as ever in the rays of the rising sun.

They wakened the boy at daybreak, the Scarecrow saying to him:

"We have discovered something queer, and therefore we must counsel together what to do about it."

"What have you discovered?" asked Woot, rubbing the sleep from his eyes with his knuckles and giving three wide yawns to prove he was fully awake.

"A Sign," said the Tin Woodman. "A Sign, and another path."

"What does the Sign say?" inquired the boy.

"It says that 'All Strangers are Warned not to Follow this Path to Loonville,'" answered the Scarecrow, who could read very well when his eyes had been freshly painted.

"In that case," said the boy, opening his knapsack to get some breakfast, "let us travel in some other direction."

But this did not seem to please either of his companions.

"I'd like to see what Loonville looks like," remarked the Tin Woodman.

"When one travels, it is foolish to miss any interesting sight," added the Scarecrow.

"But a warning means danger," protested Woot the Wanderer, "and I believe it sensible to keep out of danger whenever we can."

They made no reply to this speech for a while. Then said the Scarecrow:

"I have escaped so many dangers, during my lifetime, that I am not much afraid of anything that can happen."

"Nor am I!" exclaimed the Tin Woodman, swinging his glittering axe around his tin head, in a series of circles. "Few things can injure tin, and my axe is a powerful weapon to use against a foe. But our boy friend," he continued, looking solemnly at Woot, "might perhaps be injured if the people of Loonville are really dangerous; so I propose he waits here while you and I, Friend Scarecrow, visit the forbidden City of Loonville."

"Don't worry about me," advised Woot, calmly. "Wherever you wish to go, I will go, and share your dangers. During my wanderings I have found it more wise to keep out of danger than to venture in, but at that time I was alone, and now I have two powerful friends to protect me."

So, when he had finished his breakfast, they all set out along the path that led to Loonville.

"It is a place I have never heard of before," remarked the Scarecrow, as they approached a dense forest. "The inhabitants may be people, of some sort, or they may be animals, but whatever they prove to be, we will have an interesting story to relate to Dorothy and Ozma on our return."

The path led into the forest, but the big trees grew so closely together and the vines and underbrush were so thick and matted that they had to clear a path at each step in order to proceed. In one or two places the Tin Man, who went first to clear the way, cut the branches with a blow of his axe. Woot followed next, and last of the three came the Scarecrow, who could not have kept the path at all had not his comrades broken the way for his straw-stuffed body.

Presently the Tin Woodman pushed his way through some heavy underbrush, and almost tumbled headlong into a vast cleared space in the forest. The clearing was circular, big and roomy, yet the top branches of the tall trees reached over and formed a complete dome or roof for it. Strangely enough, it was not dark in this immense natural chamber in the woodland, for the place glowed with a soft, white light that seemed to come from some unseen source.

In the chamber were grouped dozens of queer creatures, and these so astonished the Tin Man that Woot had to push his metal body aside, that he might see, too. And the Scarecrow pushed Woot aside, so that the three travelers stood in a row, staring with all their eyes.

The creatures they beheld were round and ball-like; round in body, round in legs and arms, round in hands and feet and round of head. The only exception to the roundness was a slight hollow on the top of each head, making it saucer-shaped instead of dome-shaped. They wore no clothes on their puffy bodies, nor had they any hair. Their skins were all of a light gray color, and their eyes were mere purple spots. Their noses were as puffy as the rest of them.

"Are they rubber, do you think?" asked the Scarecrow, who noticed that the creatures bounded, as they moved, and seemed almost as light as air.

"It is difficult to tell what they are," answered Woot, "they seem to be covered with warts."

The Loons—for so these folks were called—had been doing many things, some playing together, some working at tasks and some gathered in groups to talk; but at the sound of strange voices, which echoed rather loudly through the clearing, all turned in the direction of the intruders. Then, in a body, they all rushed forward, running and bounding with tremendous speed.

The Tin Woodman was so surprised by this sudden dash that he had no time to raise his axe before the Loons were on them. The creatures swung their puffy hands, which looked like boxing-gloves, and pounded the three travelers as hard as they could, on all sides. The blows were quite soft and did not hurt our friends at all, but the onslaught quite bewildered them, so that in a brief period all three were knocked over and fell flat upon the ground. Once down, many of the Loons held them, to prevent their getting up again, while others wound long tendrils of vines about them, binding their arms and legs to their bodies and so rendering them helpless.

"Aha!" cried the biggest Loon of all; "we've got 'em safe; so let's carry 'em to King Bal and have 'em tried, and condemned and perforated!"

They had to drag their captives to the center of the domed chamber, for their weight, as compared with that of the Loons, prevented their being carried. Even the Scarecrow was much heavier than the puffy Loons. But finally the party halted before a raised platform, on which stood a sort of throne, consisting of a big, wide chair with a string tied to one arm of it. This string led upward to the roof of the dome.

Arranged before the platform, the prisoners were allowed to sit up, facing the empty throne.

"Good!" said the big Loon who had commanded the party. "Now to get King Bal to judge these terrible creatures we have so bravely captured."

As he spoke he took hold of the string and began to pull as hard as he could. One or two of the others helped him and pretty soon, as they drew in the cord, the leaves above them parted and a Loon appeared at the other end of the string. It didn't take long to draw him down to the throne, where he seated himself and was tied in, so he wouldn't float upward again.

"Hello," said the King, blinking his purple eyes at his followers; "what's up now!"

"Strangers, Your Majesty—strangers and captives," replied the big Loon, pompously.

"Dear me! I see 'em. I see 'em very plainly," exclaimed the King, his purple eyes bulging out as he looked at the three prisoners. "What curious animals! Are they dangerous, do you think, my good Panta?"

"I'm 'fraid so, Your Majesty. Of course, they may not be dangerous, but we mustn't take chances. Enough accidents happen to us poor Loons as it is, and my advice is to condemn and perforate 'em as quickly as possible."

"Keep your advice to yourself," said the monarch, in a peeved tone. "Who's King here, anyhow? You or Me?"

"We made you our King because you have less common sense than the rest of us," answered Panta Loon, indignantly. "I could have been King myself, had I wanted to, but I didn't care for the hard work and responsibility."

As he said this, the big Loon strutted back and forth in the space between the throne of King Bal and the prisoners, and the other Loons seemed much impressed by his defiance. But suddenly there came a sharp report and Panta Loon instantly disappeared, to the great astonishment of the Scarecrow, the Tin Woodman and Woot the Wanderer, who saw on the spot where the big fellow had stood a little heap of flabby, wrinkled skin that looked like a collapsed rubber balloon.

"There!" exclaimed the King; "I expected that would happen. The conceited rascal wanted to puff himself up until he was bigger than the rest of you, and this is the result of his folly. Get the pump working, some of you, and blow him up again."

"We will have to mend the puncture first, Your Majesty," suggested one of the Loons, and the prisoners noticed that none of them seemed surprised or shocked at the sad accident to Panta.

"All right," grumbled the King. "Fetch Til to mend him."

One or two ran away and presently returned, followed by a lady Loon wearing huge, puffed-up rubber skirts. Also she had a purple feather fastened to a wart on the top of her head, and around her waist was a sash of fibre-like vines, dried and tough, that looked like strings.

"Get to work, Til," commanded King Bal. "Panta has just exploded."

The lady Loon picked up the bunch of skin and examined it carefully until she discovered a hole in one foot. Then she pulled a strand of string from her sash, and drawing the edges of the hole together, she tied them fast with the string, thus

making one of those curious warts which the strangers had noticed on so many Loons. Having done this, Til Loon tossed the bit of skin to the other Loons and was about to go away when she noticed the prisoners and stopped to inspect them.

"Dear me!" said Til; "what dreadful creatures. Where did they come from?"

"We captured them," replied one of the Loons.

"And what are we going to do with them?" inquired the girl Loon.

"Perhaps we'll condemn 'em and puncture 'em," answered the King.

"Well," said she, still eyeing the captives, "I'm not sure they'll puncture. Let's try it, and see."

One of the Loons ran to the forest's edge and quickly returned with a long, sharp thorn. He glanced at the King, who nodded his head in assent, and then he rushed forward and stuck the thorn into the leg of the Scarecrow. The Scarecrow merely smiled and said nothing, for the thorn didn't hurt him at all.

Then the Loon tried to prick the Tin Woodman's leg, but the tin only blunted the point of the thorn.

"Just as I thought," said Til, blinking her purple eyes and shaking her puffy head; but just then the Loon stuck the thorn into the leg of Woot the Wanderer, and while it had been blunted somewhat, it was still sharp enough to hurt.

"Ouch!" yelled Woot, and kicked out his leg with so much energy that the frail bonds that tied him burst apart. His foot caught the Loon—who was leaning over him—full on his puffy stomach, and sent him shooting up into the air. When he was high over their heads he exploded with a loud "pop" and his skin fell to the ground.

"I really believe," said the King, rolling his spot-like eyes in a frightened way, "that Panta was right in claiming these prisoners are dangerous. Is the pump ready?"

Some of the Loons had wheeled a big machine in front of the throne and now took Panta's skin and began to pump air into it. Slowly it swelled out until the King cried "Stop!"

"No, no!" yelled Panta, "I'm not big enough yet."

"You're as big as you're going to be," declared the King. "Before you exploded you were bigger than the rest of us, and that caused you to be proud and over-bearing. Now you're a little smaller than the rest, and you will last longer and be more humble."

"Pump me up—pump me up!" wailed Panta "If you don't you'll break my heart."

"If we do we'll break your skin," replied the King.

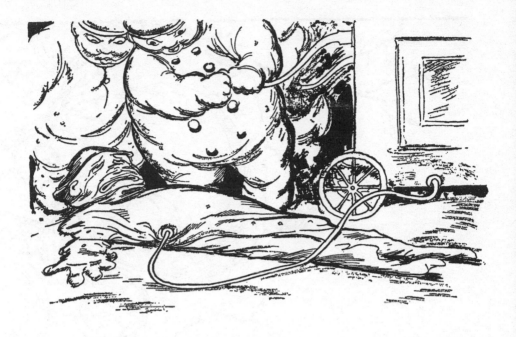

So the Loons stopped pumping air into Panta, and pushed him away from the pump. He was certainly more humble than before his accident, for he crept into the background and said nothing more.

"Now pump up the other one," ordered the King. Til had already mended him, and the Loons set to work to pump him full of air.

During these last few moments none had paid much attention to the prisoners, so Woot, finding his legs free, crept over to the Tin Woodman and rubbed the bonds that were still around his arms and body against the sharp edge of the axe, which quickly cut them.

The boy was now free, and the thorn which the Loon had stuck into his leg was lying unnoticed on the ground, where the creature had dropped it when he exploded. Woot leaned forward and picked up the thorn, and while the Loons were busy watching the pump, the boy sprang to his feet and suddenly rushed upon the group.

"Pop"—"pop"—"pop!" went three of the Loons, when the Wanderer pricked them with his thorn, and at the sounds the others looked around and saw their danger. With yells of fear they bounded away in all directions, scattering about the clearing, with Woot the Wanderer in full chase. While they could run much faster than the boy, they often stumbled and fell, or got in one another's way, so he managed to catch several and prick them with his thorn.

It astonished him to see how easily the Loons exploded. When the air was let out of them they were quite helpless. Til Loon was one of those who ran against his thorn and many others suffered the same fate. The creatures could not escape from the enclosure, but in their fright many bounded upward and caught branches of the trees, and then climbed out of reach of the dreaded thorn.

Woot was getting pretty tired chasing them, so he stopped and came over, panting, to where his friends were sitting, still bound.

"Very well done, my Wanderer," said the Tin Woodman. "It is evident that we need fear these puffed-up creatures no longer, so be kind enough to unfasten our bonds and we will proceed upon our journey."

Woot untied the bonds of the Scarecrow and helped him to his feet. Then he freed the Tin Woodman, who got up without help. Looking around them, they saw that the only Loon now remaining within reach was Bal Loon, the King, who had remained seated in his throne, watching the punishment of his people with a bewildered look in his purple eyes.

"Shall I puncture the King?" the boy asked his companions.

King Bal must have overheard the question, for he fumbled with the cord that fastened him to the throne and managed to release it. Then he floated upward until he reached the leafy dome, and parting the branches he disappeared from sight. But the string that was tied to his body was still connected with the arm of the throne, and they knew they could pull His Majesty down again, if they wanted to.

"Let him alone," suggested the Scarecrow. "He seems a good enough king for his peculiar people, and after we are gone, the Loons will have something of a job to pump up all those whom Woot has punctured."

"Every one of them ought to be exploded," declared Woot, who was angry because his leg still hurt him.

"No," said the Tin Woodman, "that would not be just fair. They were quite right to capture us, because we had no business to intrude here, having been warned to keep away from Loonville. This is their country, not ours, and since the poor things can't get out of the clearing, they can harm no one save those who venture here out of curiosity, as we did."

"Well said, my friend," agreed the Scarecrow. "We really had no right to disturb their peace and comfort; so let us go away."

They easily found the place where they had forced their way into the enclosure, so the Tin Woodman pushed aside the underbrush and started first along the path.

The Scarecrow followed next and last came Woot, who looked back and saw that the Loons were still clinging to their perches on the trees and watching their former captives with frightened eyes.

"I guess they're glad to see the last of us," remarked the boy, and laughing at the happy ending of the adventure, he followed his comrades along the path.

CHAPTER V

MRS. YOOP, THE GIANTESS

When they had reached the end of the path, where they had first seen the warning sign, they set off across the country in an easterly direction. Before long they reached Rolling Lands, which were a succession of hills and valleys where constant climbs and descents were required, and their journey now became tedious, because on climbing each hill, they found before them nothing in the valley below it—except grass, or weeds or stones.

Up and down they went for hours, with nothing to relieve the monotony of the landscape, until finally, when they had topped a higher hill than usual, they discovered a cup-shaped valley before them in the center of which stood an enormous castle, built of purple stone. The castle was high and broad and long, but had no turrets and towers. So far as they could see, there was but one small window and one big door on each side of the great building.

"This is strange!" mused the Scarecrow. "I'd no idea such a big castle existed in this Gillikin Country. I wonder who lives here?"

"It seems to me, from this distance," remarked the Tin Woodman, "that it's the biggest castle I ever saw. It is really too big for any use, and no one could open or shut those big doors without a step-ladder."

"Perhaps, if we go nearer, we shall find out whether anybody lives there or not," suggested Woot. "Looks to me as if nobody lived there."

On they went, and when they reached the center of the valley, where the great stone castle stood, it was beginning to grow dark. So they hesitated as to what to do.

"If friendly people happen to live here," said Woot. "I shall be glad of a bed; but should enemies occupy the place, I prefer to sleep upon the ground."

"And if no one at all lives here," added the Scarecrow, "we can enter, and take possession, and make ourselves at home."

While speaking he went nearer to one of the great doors, which was three times as high and broad as any he had ever seen in a house before, and then he discovered, engraved in big letters upon a stone over the doorway, the words:

YOOP CASTLE

"Oho!" he exclaimed; "I know the place now. This was probably the home of Mr. Yoop, a terrible giant whom I have seen confined in a cage, a long way from here. Therefore this castle is likely to be empty and we may use it in any way we please."

"Yes, yes," said the Tin Emperor, nodding; "I also remember Mr. Yoop. But how are we to get into his deserted castle? The latch of the door is so far above our heads that none of us can reach it."

They considered this problem for a while, and then Woot said to the Tin Man:

"If I stand upon your shoulders, I think I can unlatch the door."

"Climb up, then," was the reply, and when the boy was perched upon the tin shoulders of Nick Chopper, he was just able to reach the latch and raise it.

At once the door swung open, its great hinges making a groaning sound as if in protest, so Woot leaped down and followed his companions into a big, bare hallway. Scarcely were the three inside, however, when they heard the door slam shut behind them, and this astonished them because no one had touched it. It had closed of its own accord, as if by magic. Moreover, the latch was on the outside, and the thought occurred to each one of them that they were now prisoners in this unknown castle.

"However," mumbled the Scarecrow, "we are not to blame for what cannot be helped; so let us push bravely ahead and see what may be seen."

It was quite dark in the hallway, now that the outside door was shut, so as they stumbled along a stone passage they kept close together, not knowing what danger was likely to befall them.

Suddenly a soft glow enveloped them. It grew brighter, until they could see their surroundings distinctly. They had reached the end of the passage and before them was another huge door. This noiselessly swung open before them, without the help of anyone, and through the doorway they observed a big chamber, the walls of which were lined with plates of pure gold, highly polished.

This room was also lighted, although they could discover no lamps, and in the center of it was a great table at which sat an immense woman. She was clad in silver robes embroidered with gay floral designs, and wore over this splendid raiment a short apron of elaborate lace-work. Such an apron was no protection, and was not in keeping with the handsome gown, but the huge woman wore it, nevertheless. The table at which she sat was spread with a white cloth and had golden dishes upon it, so the travelers saw that they had surprised the Giantess while she was eating her supper.

She had her back toward them and did not even turn around, but taking a biscuit from a dish she began to butter it and said in a voice that was big and deep but not especially unpleasant:

"Why don't you come in and allow the door to shut? You're causing a draught, and I shall catch cold and sneeze. When I sneeze, I get cross, and when I get cross I'm liable to do something wicked. Come in, you foolish strangers; come in!"

Being thus urged, they entered the room and approached the table, until they stood where they faced the great Giantess. She continued eating, but smiled in a curious way as she looked at them. Woot noticed that the door had closed silently after they had entered, and that didn't please him at all.

"Well," said the Giantess, "what excuse have you to offer?"

"We didn't know anyone lived here, Madam," explained the Scarecrow; "so, being travelers and strangers in these parts, and wishing to find a place for our boy friend to sleep, we ventured to enter your castle."

"You knew it was private property, I suppose?" said she, buttering another biscuit.

"We saw the words, 'Yoop Castle,' over the door, but we knew that Mr. Yoop is a prisoner in a cage in a far-off part of the land of Oz, so we decided there was no one now at home and that we might use the castle for the night."

"I see," remarked the Giantess, nodding her head and smiling again in that curious way—a way that made Woot shudder. "You didn't know that Mr. Yoop was married, or that after he was cruelly captured his wife still lived in his castle and ran it to suit herself."

"Who captured Mr. Yoop?" asked Woot, looking gravely at the big woman.

"Wicked enemies. People who selfishly objected to Yoop's taking their cows and sheep for his food. I must admit, however, that Yoop had a bad temper, and had the habit of knocking over a few houses, now and then, when he was angry. So one day the little folks came in a great crowd and captured Mr. Yoop, and carried him away to a cage somewhere in the mountains. I don't know where it is, and I don't care, for my husband treated me badly at times, forgetting the respect a giant owes to a giantess. Often he kicked me on my shins, when I wouldn't wait on him. So I'm glad he is gone."

"It's a wonder the people didn't capture you, too," remarked Woot.

"Well, I was too clever for them," said she, giving a sudden laugh that caused such a breeze that the wobbly Scarecrow was almost blown off his feet and had to grab his friend Nick Chopper to steady himself. "I saw the people coming," continued Mrs. Yoop, "and knowing they meant mischief I transformed myself into a mouse and hid in a cupboard. After they had gone away, carrying my shin-kicking husband with them, I transformed myself back to my former shape again, and here I've lived in peace and comfort ever since."

"Are you a Witch, then?" inquired Woot.

"Well, not exactly a Witch," she replied, "but I'm an Artist in Transformations. In other words, I'm more of a Yookoohoo than a Witch, and of course you know that the Yookoohoos are the cleverest magic-workers in the world."

The travelers were silent for a time, uneasily considering this statement and the effect it might have on their future. No doubt the Giantess had wilfully made them her prisoners; yet she spoke so cheerfully, in her big voice, that until now they had not been alarmed in the least.

By and by the Scarecrow, whose mixed brains had been working steadily, asked the woman:

"Are we to consider you our friend, Mrs. Yoop, or do you intend to be our enemy?"

"I never have friends," she said in a matter-of-fact tone, "because friends get too familiar and always forget to mind their own business. But I am not your enemy; not yet, anyhow. Indeed, I'm glad you've come, for my life here is rather lonely. I've

had no one to talk to since I transformed Polychrome, the Daughter of the Rainbow, into a canary-bird."

"How did you manage to do that?" asked the Tin Woodman, in amazement. "Polychrome is a powerful fairy!"

"She was," said the Giantess; "but now she's a canary-bird. One day after a rain, Polychrome danced off the Rainbow and fell asleep on a little mound in this valley, not far from my castle. The sun came out and drove the Rainbow away, and before Poly wakened, I stole out and transformed her into a canary-bird in a gold cage studded with diamonds. The cage was so she couldn't fly away. I expected she'd sing and talk and we'd have good times together; but she has proved no company for me at all. Ever since the moment of her transformation, she has refused to speak a single word."

"Where is she now?" inquired Woot, who had heard tales of lovely Polychrome and was much interested in her.

"The cage is hanging up in my bedroom," said the Giantess, eating another biscuit.

The travelers were now more uneasy and suspicious of the Giantess than before. If Polychrome, the Rainbow's Daughter, who was a real fairy, had been transformed and enslaved by this huge woman, who claimed to be a Yookoohoo, what was liable to happen to them? Said the Scarecrow, twisting his stuffed head around in Mrs. Yoop's direction:

"Do you know, Ma'am, who we are?"

"Of course," said she; "a straw man, a tin man and a boy."

"We are very important people," declared the Tin Woodman.

"All the better," she replied. "I shall enjoy your society the more on that account. For I mean to keep you here as long as I live, to amuse me when I get lonely. And," she added slowly, "in this Valley no one ever dies."

They didn't like this speech at all, so the Scarecrow frowned in a way that made Mrs. Yoop smile, while the Tin Woodman looked so fierce that Mrs. Yoop laughed. The Scarecrow suspected she was going to laugh, so he slipped behind his friends to escape the wind from her breath. From this safe position he said warningly:

"We have powerful friends who will soon come to rescue us."

"Let them come," she returned, with an accent of scorn. "When they get here they will find neither a boy, nor a tin man, nor a scarecrow, for tomorrow morning I intend to transform you all into other shapes, so that you cannot be recognized."

This threat filled them with dismay. The good-natured Giantess was more terrible than they had imagined. She could smile and wear pretty clothes and at the same time be even more cruel than her wicked husband had been.

Both the Scarecrow and the Tin Woodman tried to think of some way to escape from the castle before morning, but she seemed to read their thoughts and shook her head.

"Don't worry your poor brains," said she. "You can't escape me, however hard you try. But why should you wish to escape? I shall give you new forms that are much better than the ones you now have. Be contented with your fate, for discontent leads to unhappiness, and unhappiness, in any form, is the greatest evil that can befall you."

"What forms do you intend to give us?" asked Woot earnestly.

"I haven't decided, as yet. I'll dream over it tonight, so in the morning I shall have made up my mind how to transform you. Perhaps you'd prefer to choose your own transformations?"

"No," said Woot, "I prefer to remain as I am."

"That's funny," she retorted. "You are little, and you're weak; as you are, you're not much account, anyhow. The best thing about you is that you're alive, for I shall be able to make of you some sort of live creature which will be a great improvement on your present form."

She took another biscuit from a plate and dipped it in a pot of honey and calmly began eating it.

The Scarecrow watched her thoughtfully.

"There are no fields of grain in your Valley," said he; "where, then, did you get the flour to make your biscuits?"

"Mercy me! do you think I'd bother to make biscuits out of flour?" she replied. "That is altogether too tedious a process for a Yookoohoo. I set some traps this afternoon and caught a lot of field-mice, but as I do not like to eat mice, I transformed them into hot biscuits for my supper. The honey in this pot was once a wasp's nest, but since being transformed it has become sweet and delicious. All I need do, when I wish to eat, is to take something I don't care to keep, and transform it into any sort of food I like, and eat it. Are you hungry?"

"I don't eat, thank you," said the Scarecrow.

"Nor do I," said the Tin Woodman.

"I have still a little natural food in my knapsack," said Woot the Wanderer, "and I'd rather eat that than any wasp's nest."

"Every one to his taste," said the Giantess carelessly, and having now finished her supper she rose to her feet, clapped her hands together, and the supper table at once disappeared.

CHAPTER VI

THE MAGIC OF
A YOOKOOHOO

WOOT HAD SEEN VERY LITTLE OF MAGIC DURING
his wanderings, while the Scarecrow and the Tin
Woodman had seen a great deal of many sorts in
their lives, yet all three were greatly impressed
by Mrs. Yoop's powers. She did not affect
any mysterious airs or indulge in chants or
mystic rites, as most witches do, nor was the
Giantess old and ugly or disagreeable in face
or manner. Nevertheless, she frightened her prisoners
more than any witch could have done.

"Please be seated," she said to them, as she sat herself down in a great arm-chair
and spread her beautiful embroidered skirts for them to admire. But all the chairs in
the room were so high that our friends could not climb to the seats of them. Mrs.
Yoop observed this and waved her hand, when instantly a golden ladder appeared
leaning against a chair opposite her own.

"Climb up," said she, and they obeyed, the Tin Man and the boy assisting the more clumsy Scarecrow. When they were all seated in a row on the cushion of the chair, the Giantess continued: "Now tell me how you happened to travel in this direction, and where you came from and what your errand is."

So the Tin Woodman told her all about Nimmie Amee, and how he had decided to find her and marry her, although he had no Loving Heart. The story seemed to amuse the big woman, who then began to ask the Scarecrow questions and for the first time in her life heard of Ozma of Oz, and of Dorothy and Jack Pumpkinhead and Dr. Pipt and Tik-Tok and many other Oz people who are well known in the Emerald City. Also Woot had to tell his story, which was very simple and did not take long. The Giantess laughed heartily when the boy related their adventure at Loonville, but said she knew nothing of the Loons because she never left her Valley.

"There are wicked people who would like to capture me, as they did my giant husband, Mr. Yoop," said she; "so I stay at home and mind my own business."

"If Ozma knew that you dared to work magic without her consent, she would punish you severely," declared the Scarecrow, "for this castle is in the Land of Oz, and no persons in the Land of Oz are permitted to work magic except Glinda the Good and the little Wizard who lives with Ozma in the Emerald City."

"*That* for your Ozma!" exclaimed the Giantess, snapping her fingers in derision. "What do I care for a girl whom I have never seen and who has never seen me?"

"But Ozma is a fairy," said the Tin Woodman, "and therefore she is very powerful. Also, we are under Ozma's protection, and to injure us in any way would make her extremely angry."

"What I do here, in my own private castle in this secluded Valley—where no one comes but fools like you—can never be known to your fairy Ozma," returned the Giantess. "Do not seek to frighten me from my purpose, and do not allow yourselves to be frightened, for it is best to meet bravely what cannot be avoided. I am now going to bed, and in the morning I will give you all new forms, such as will be more interesting to me than the ones you now wear. Good night, and pleasant dreams."

Saying this, Mrs. Yoop rose from her chair and walked through a doorway into another room. So heavy was the tread of the Giantess that even the walls of the big stone castle trembled as she stepped. She closed the door of her bedroom behind her, and then suddenly the light went out and the three prisoners found themselves in total darkness.

The Tin Woodman and the Scarecrow didn't mind the dark at all, but Woot the Wanderer felt worried to be left in this strange place in this strange manner, without being able to see any danger that might threaten.

"The big woman might have given me a bed, anyhow," he said to his companions, and scarcely had he spoken when he felt something press against his legs, which were then dangling from the seat of the chair. Leaning down, he put out his hand and found that a bedstead had appeared, with mattress, sheets and covers, all complete. He lost no time in slipping down upon the bed and was soon fast asleep.

During the night the Scarecrow and the Emperor talked in low tones together, and they got out of the chair and moved all about the room, feeling for some hidden spring that might open a door or window and permit them to escape.

Morning found them still unsuccessful in the quest and as soon as it was daylight Woot's bed suddenly disappeared, and he dropped to the floor with a thump that quickly wakened him. And after a time the Giantess came from her bedroom, wearing another dress that was quite as elaborate as the one in which she had been attired the evening before, and also wearing the pretty lace apron. Having seated herself in a chair, she said:

"I'm hungry; so I'll have breakfast at once."

She clapped her hands together and instantly the table appeared before her, spread with snowy linen and laden with golden dishes. But there was no food upon the table, nor anything else except a pitcher of water, a bundle of weeds and a handful of pebbles. But the Giantess poured some water into her coffee-pot, patted it once or twice with her hand, and then poured out a cupful of steaming hot coffee.

"Would you like some?" she asked Woot.

He was suspicious of magic coffee, but it smelled so good that he could not resist it; so he answered: "If you please, Madam."

The Giantess poured out another cup and set it on the floor for Woot. It was as big as a tub, and the golden spoon in the saucer beside the cup was so heavy the boy could scarcely lift it. But Woot managed to get a sip of the coffee and found it delicious.

Mrs. Yoop next transformed the weeds into a dish of oatmeal, which she ate with good appetite.

"Now, then," said she, picking up the pebbles. "I'm wondering whether I shall have fish-balls or lamb-chops to complete my meal. Which would you prefer, Woot the Wanderer?"

"If you please, I'll eat the food in my knapsack," answered the boy. "Your magic food might taste good, but I'm afraid of it."

The woman laughed at his fears and transformed the pebbles into fish-balls.

"I suppose you think that after you had eaten this food it would turn to stones again and make you sick," she remarked; "but that would be impossible. *Nothing I transform ever gets back to its former shape again*, so these fish-balls can never more be pebbles. That is why I have to be careful of my transformations," she added, busily eating while she talked, "for while I can change forms at will I can never change them back again—which proves that even the powers of a clever Yookoohoo are limited. When I have transformed you three people, you must always wear the shapes that I have given you."

"Then please don't transform us," begged Woot, "for we are quite satisfied to remain as we are."

"I am not expecting to satisfy you, but intend to please myself," she declared, "and my pleasure is to give you new shapes. For, if by chance your friends came in search of you, not one of them would be able to recognize you."

Her tone was so positive that they knew it would be useless to protest. The woman was not unpleasant to look at; her face was not cruel; her voice was big but gracious in tone; but her words showed that she possessed a merciless heart and no pleadings would alter her wicked purpose.

Mrs. Yoop took ample time to finish her breakfast and the prisoners had no desire to hurry her, but finally the meal was concluded and she folded her napkin and made the table disappear by clapping her hands together. Then she turned to her captives and said:

"The next thing on the programme is to change your forms."

"Have you decided what forms to give us?" asked the Scarecrow, uneasily.

"Yes; I dreamed it all out while I was asleep. This Tin Man seems a very solemn person"—indeed, the Tin Woodman was looking solemn, just then, for he was greatly disturbed—"so I shall change him into an Owl."

All she did was to point one finger at him as she spoke, but immediately the form of the Tin Woodman began to change and in a few seconds Nick Chopper, the Emperor of the Winkies, had been transformed into an Owl, with eyes as big as saucers and a hooked beak and strong claws. But he was still tin. He was a Tin Owl, with tin legs and beak and eyes and feathers. When he flew to the back of a chair and perched upon it, his tin feathers rattled against one another with a tinny clatter.

The Giantess seemed much amused by the Tin Owl's appearance, for her laugh was big and jolly.

"You're not liable to get lost," said she, "for your wings and feathers will make a racket wherever you go. And, on my word, a Tin Owl is so rare and pretty that it is an improvement on the ordinary bird. I did not intend to make you tin, but I forgot to wish you to be meat. However, tin you were, and tin you are, and as it's too late to change you, that settles it."

Until now the Scarecrow had rather doubted the possibility of Mrs. Yoop's being able to transform him, or his friend the Tin Woodman, for they were not made as ordinary people are. He had worried more over what might happen to Woot than to himself, but now he began to worry about himself.

"Madam," he said hastily, "I consider this action very impolite. It may even be called rude, considering we are your guests."

"You are not guests, for I did not invite you here," she replied.

"Perhaps not; but we craved hospitality. We threw ourselves upon your mercy, so to speak, and we now find you have no mercy. Therefore, if you will excuse the expression, I must say it is downright wicked to take our proper forms away from us and give us others that we do not care for."

"Are you trying to make me angry?" she asked, frowning.

"By no means," said the Scarecrow; "I'm just trying to make you act more ladylike."

"Oh, indeed! In my opinion, Mr. Scarecrow, you are now acting like a bear—so a Bear you shall be!"

Again the dreadful finger pointed, this time in the Scarecrow's direction, and at once his form began to change. In a few seconds he had become a small Brown Bear, but he was stuffed with straw as he had been before, and when the little Brown Bear shuffled across the floor he was just as wobbly as the Scarecrow had been and moved just as awkwardly.

Woot was amazed, but he was also thoroughly frightened.

"Did it hurt?" he asked the little Brown Bear.

"No, of course not," growled the Scarecrow in the Bear's form; "but I don't like walking on four legs; it's undignified."

"Consider my humiliation!" chirped the Tin Owl, trying to settle its tin feathers smoothly with its tin beak. "And I can't see very well, either. The light seems to hurt my eyes."

"That's because you are an Owl," said Woot. "I think you will see better in the dark."

"Well," remarked the Giantess, "I'm very well pleased with these new forms, for my part, and I'm sure you will like them better when you get used to them. So now," she added, turning to the boy, "it is *your* turn."

"Don't you think you'd better leave me as I am?" asked Woot in a trembling voice.

"No," she replied, "I'm going to make a monkey of you. I love monkeys—they're so cute!—and I think a Green Monkey will be lots of fun and amuse me when I am sad."

Woot shivered, for again the terrible magic finger pointed, and pointed directly his way. He felt himself changing; not so very much, however, and it didn't hurt him a bit. He looked down at his limbs and body and found that his clothes were gone and his skin covered with a fine, silk-like green fur. His hands and feet were now those of a monkey. He realized he really was a monkey, and his first feeling was one of anger. He began to chatter as monkeys do. He bounded to the seat of a giant chair, and then to its back and with a wild leap sprang upon the laughing Giantess. His idea was to seize her hair and pull it out by the roots, and so have revenge for her wicked transformations. But she raised her hand and said:

"Gently, my dear Monkey—gently! You're not angry; you're happy as can be!"

Woot stopped short. No; he wasn't a bit angry now; he felt as good-humored and gay as ever he did when a boy. Instead of pulling Mrs. Yoop's hair, he perched on her shoulder and smoothed her soft cheek with his hairy paw. In return, she smiled at the funny green animal and patted his head.

"Very good," said the Giantess. "Let us all become friends and be happy together. How is my Tin Owl feeling?"

"Quite comfortable," said the Owl. "I don't like it, to be sure, but I'm not going to allow my new form to make me unhappy. But, tell me, please: what is a Tin Owl good for?"

"You are only good to make me laugh," replied the Giantess.

"Will a stuffed Bear also make you laugh?" inquired the Scarecrow, sitting back on his haunches to look up at her.

"Of course," declared the Giantess; "and I have added a little magic to your transformations to make you all contented with wearing your new forms. I'm sorry I didn't think to do that when I transformed Polychrome into a Canary-Bird. But perhaps, when she sees how cheerful you are, she will cease to be silent and sullen and take to singing. I will go get the bird and let you see her."

With this, Mrs. Yoop went into the next room and soon returned bearing a golden cage in which sat upon a swinging perch a lovely yellow Canary.

"Polychrome," said the Giantess, "permit me to introduce to you a Green Monkey, which used to be a boy called Woot the Wanderer, and a Tin Owl, which

used to be a Tin Woodman named Nick Chopper, and a straw-stuffed little Brown Bear which used to be a live Scarecrow."

"We already know one another," declared the Scarecrow. "The bird is Polychrome, the Rainbow's Daughter, and she and I used to be good friends."

"Are you really my old friend, the Scarecrow?" asked the bird, in a sweet, low voice.

"There!" cried Mrs. Yoop; "that's the first time she has spoken since she was transformed."

"I am really your old friend," answered the Scarecrow; "but you must pardon me for appearing just now in this brutal form."

"I am a bird, as you are, dear Poly," said the Tin Woodman; "but, alas! a Tin Owl is not as beautiful as a Canary-Bird."

"How dreadful it all is!" sighed the Canary. "Couldn't you manage to escape from this terrible Yookoohoo?"

"No," answered the Scarecrow, "we tried to escape, but failed. She first made us her prisoners and then transformed us. But how did she manage to get *you*, Polychrome?"

"I was asleep, and she took unfair advantage of me," answered the bird sadly. "Had I been awake, I could easily have protected myself."

"Tell me," said the Green Monkey earnestly, as he came close to the cage, "what must we do, Daughter of the Rainbow, to escape from these transformations? Can't you help us, being a Fairy?"

"At present I am powerless to help even myself," replied the Canary.

"That's the exact truth!" exclaimed the Giantess, who seemed pleased to hear the bird talk, even though it complained; "you are all helpless and in my power, so you may as well make up your minds to accept your fate and be content. Remember that you are transformed for good, since no magic on earth can break your enchantments. I am now going out for my morning walk, for each day after breakfast I walk sixteen times around my castle for exercise. Amuse yourselves while I am gone, and when I return I hope to find you all reconciled and happy."

So the Giantess walked to the door by which our friends had entered the great hall and spoke one word: "Open!" Then the door swung open and after Mrs. Yoop had passed out it closed again with a snap as its powerful bolts shot into place. The Green Monkey had rushed toward the opening, hoping to escape, but he was too late and only got a bump on his nose as the door slammed shut.

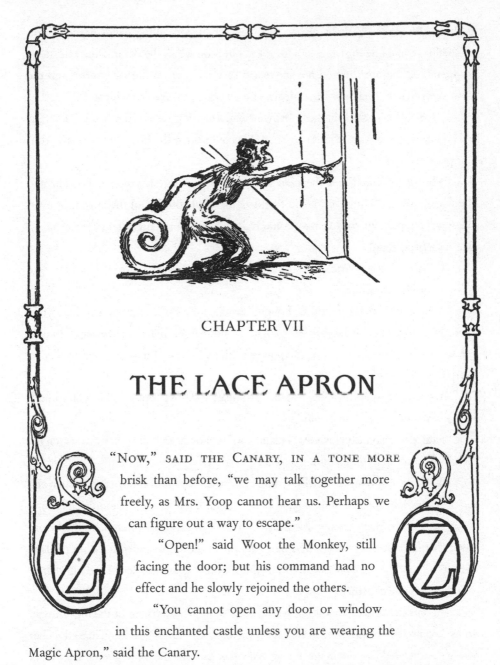

CHAPTER VII

THE LACE APRON

"Now," said the Canary, in a tone more brisk than before, "we may talk together more freely, as Mrs. Yoop cannot hear us. Perhaps we can figure out a way to escape."

"Open!" said Woot the Monkey, still facing the door; but his command had no effect and he slowly rejoined the others.

"You cannot open any door or window in this enchanted castle unless you are wearing the Magic Apron," said the Canary.

"What Magic Apron do you mean?" asked the Tin Owl, in a curious voice.

"The lace one, which the Giantess always wears. I have been her prisoner, in this cage, for several weeks, and she hangs my cage in her bedroom every night, so that she can keep her eye on me," explained Polychrome the Canary. "Therefore I have discovered that it is the Magic Apron that opens the doors and windows, and nothing else can move them. When she goes to bed, Mrs. Yoop hangs her apron on the bedpost, and one morning she forgot to put it on when she commanded the door to open, and the door would not move. So then she put on the lace apron and the door obeyed her. That was how I learned the magic power of the apron."

"I see—I see!" said the little Brown Bear, wagging his stuffed head. "Then, if we could get the apron from Mrs. Yoop, we could open the doors and escape from our prison."

"That is true, and it is the plan I was about to suggest," replied Polychrome the Canary-Bird. "However, I don't believe the Owl could steal the apron, or even the Bear, but perhaps the Monkey could hide in her room at night and get the apron while she is asleep."

"I'll try it!" cried Woot the Monkey. "I'll try it this very night, if I can manage to steal into her bedroom."

"You mustn't think about it, though," warned the bird, "for she can read your thoughts whenever she cares to do so. And do not forget, before you escape, to take me with you. Once I am out of the power of the Giantess, I may discover a way to save us all."

"We won't forget our fairy friend," promised the boy; "but perhaps you can tell me how to get into the bedroom."

"No," declared Polychrome, "I cannot advise you as to that. You must watch for a chance, and slip in when Mrs. Yoop isn't looking."

They talked it over for a while longer and then Mrs. Yoop returned. When she entered, the door opened suddenly, at her command, and closed as soon as her huge form had passed through the doorway. During that day she entered her bedroom several times, on one errand or another, but always she commanded the door to close behind her and her prisoners found not the slightest chance to leave the big hall in which they were confined.

The Green Monkey thought it would be wise to make a friend of the big woman, so as to gain her confidence, so he sat on the back of her chair and chattered to her while she mended her stockings and sewed silver buttons on some golden shoes that were as big as row-boats. This pleased the Giantess and she would pause at times to pat the Monkey's head. The little Brown Bear curled up in a corner and lay still all day. The Owl and the Canary found they could converse together in the bird language, which neither the Giantess nor the Bear nor the Monkey could understand; so at times they twittered away to each other and passed the long, dreary day quite cheerfully.

After dinner Mrs. Yoop took a big fiddle from a big cupboard and played such loud and dreadful music that her prisoners were all thankful when at last she stopped and said she was going to bed.

After cautioning the Monkey and Bear and Owl to behave themselves during the night, she picked up the cage containing the Canary and, going to the door of her bedroom, commanded it to open. Just then, however, she remembered she had left her fiddle lying upon a table, so she went back for it and put it away in the cupboard, and while her back was turned the Green Monkey slipped through the open door into her bedroom and hid underneath the bed. The Giantess, being sleepy, did not notice this, and entering her room she made the door close behind her and then hung the bird-cage on a peg by the window. Then she began to undress, first taking off the lace apron and laying it over the bedpost, where it was within easy reach of her hand.

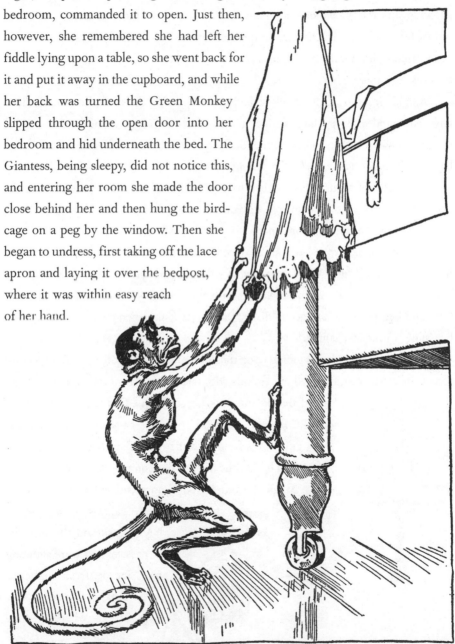

As soon as Mrs. Yoop was in bed the lights all went out, and Woot the Monkey crouched under the bed and waited patiently until he heard the Giantess snoring. Then he crept out and in the dark felt around until he got hold of the apron, which he at once tied around his own waist.

Next, Woot tried to find the Canary, and there was just enough moonlight showing through the window to enable him to see where the cage hung; but it was out of his reach. At first he was tempted to leave Polychrome and escape with his other friends, but remembering his promise to the Rainbow's Daughter Woot tried to think how to save her.

A chair stood near the window, and this—showing dimly in the moonlight—gave him an idea. By pushing against it with all his might, he found he could move the giant chair a few inches at a time. So he pushed and pushed until the chair was beneath the bird-cage, and then he sprang noiselessly upon the seat—for his monkey form enabled him to jump higher than he could do as a boy—and from there to the back of the chair, and so managed to reach the cage and take it off the peg. Then down he sprang to the floor and made his way to the door.

"Open!" he commanded, and at once the door obeyed and swung open, But his voice wakened Mrs. Yoop, who gave a wild cry and sprang out of bed with one bound. The Green Monkey dashed through the doorway, carrying the cage with him, and before the Giantess could reach the door it slammed shut and imprisoned her in her own bed-chamber!

The noise she made, pounding upon the door, and her yells of anger and dreadful threats of vengeance, filled all our friends with terror, and Woot the Monkey was so

excited that in the dark he could not find the outer door of the hall. But the Tin Owl could see very nicely in the dark, so he guided his friends to the right place and when all were grouped before the door Woot commanded it to open. The Magic Apron proved as powerful as when it had been worn by the Giantess, so a moment later they had rushed through the passage and were standing in the fresh night air outside the castle, free to go wherever they willed.

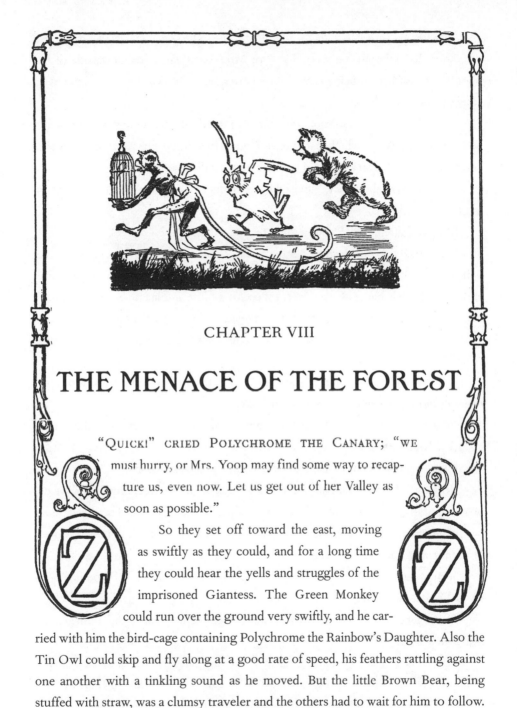

CHAPTER VIII

THE MENACE OF THE FOREST

"Quick!" cried Polychrome the Canary; "we must hurry, or Mrs. Yoop may find some way to recapture us, even now. Let us get out of her Valley as soon as possible."

So they set off toward the east, moving as swiftly as they could, and for a long time they could hear the yells and struggles of the imprisoned Giantess. The Green Monkey could run over the ground very swiftly, and he carried with him the bird-cage containing Polychrome the Rainbow's Daughter. Also the Tin Owl could skip and fly along at a good rate of speed, his feathers rattling against one another with a tinkling sound as he moved. But the little Brown Bear, being stuffed with straw, was a clumsy traveler and the others had to wait for him to follow.

However, they were not very long in reaching the ridge that led out of Mrs. Yoop's Valley, and when they had passed this ridge and descended into the next valley they stopped to rest, for the Green Monkey was tired.

"I believe we are safe, now," said Polychrome, when her cage was set down and the others had all gathered around it, "for Mrs. Yoop dares not go outside of her own Valley, for fear of being captured by her enemies. So we may take our time to consider what to do next."

"I'm afraid poor Mrs. Yoop will starve to death, if no one lets her out of her bedroom," said Woot, who had a heart as kind as that of the Tin Woodman. "We've taken her Magic Apron away, and now the doors will never open."

"Don't worry about that," advised Polychrome. "Mrs. Yoop has plenty of magic left to console her."

"Are you sure of that?" asked the Green Monkey.

"Yes, for I've been watching her for weeks," said the Canary. "She has six magic hairpins, which she wears in her hair, and a magic ring which she wears on her thumb and which is invisible to all eyes except those of a fairy, and magic bracelets on both her ankles. So I am positive that she will manage to find a way out of her prison."

"She might transform the door into an archway," suggested the little Brown Bear.

"That would be easy for her," said the Tin Owl; "but I'm glad she was too angry to think of that before we got out of her Valley."

"Well, we have escaped the big woman, to be sure," remarked the Green Monkey, "but we still wear the awful forms the cruel Yookoohoo gave us. How are we going to get rid of these shapes, and become ourselves again?"

None could answer that question. They sat around the cage, brooding over the problem, until the Monkey fell asleep. Seeing this, the Canary tucked her head under her wing and also slept, and the Tin Owl and the Brown Bear did not disturb them until morning came and it was broad daylight.

"I'm hungry," said Woot, when he wakened, for his knapsack of food had been left behind at the castle.

"Then let us travel on until we can find something for you to eat," returned the Scarecrow Bear.

"There is no use in your lugging my cage any farther," declared the Canary. "Let me out, and throw the cage away. Then I can fly with you and find my own breakfast of seeds. Also I can search for water, and tell you where to find it."

So the Green Monkey unfastened the door of the golden cage and the Canary hopped out. At first she flew high in the air and made great circles overhead, but after a time she returned and perched beside them.

"At the east, in the direction we were following," announced the Canary, "there is a fine forest, with a brook running through it. In the forest there may be fruits or nuts growing, or berry bushes at its edge, so let us go that way."

They agreed to this and promptly set off, this time moving more deliberately. The Tin Owl, which had guided their way during the night, now found the sunshine very trying to his big eyes, so he shut them tight and perched upon the back of the little Brown Bear, which carried the Owl's weight with ease. The Canary sometimes perched upon the Green Monkey's shoulder and sometimes fluttered on ahead of the party, and in this manner they traveled in good spirits across that valley and into the next one to the east of it.

This they found to be an immense hollow, shaped like a saucer, and on its farther edge appeared the forest which Polychrome had seen from the sky.

"Come to think of it," said the Tin Owl, waking up and blinking comically at his friends, "there's no object, now, in our traveling to the Munchkin Country. My idea in going there was to marry Nimmie Amee, but however much the Munchkin girl may have loved a Tin Woodman, I cannot reasonably expect her to marry a Tin Owl."

"There is some truth in that, my friend," remarked the Brown Bear. "And to think that I, who was considered the handsomest Scarecrow in the world, am now condemned to be a scrubby, no-account beast, whose only redeeming feature is that he is stuffed with straw!"

"Consider *my* case, please," said Woot. "The cruel Giantess has made a monkey of a boy, and that is the most dreadful deed of all!"

"Your color is rather pretty," said the Brown Bear, eyeing Woot critically. "I have never seen a pea-Green Monkey before, and it strikes me you are quite gorgeous."

"It isn't so bad to be a bird," asserted the Canary, fluttering from one to another with a free and graceful motion, "but I long to enjoy my own shape again."

"As Polychrome, you were the loveliest maiden I have ever seen—except, of course, Ozma," said the Tin Owl; "so the Giantess did well to transform you into the loveliest of all birds, if you were to be transformed at all. But tell me, since you are a fairy, and have a fairy wisdom: do you think we shall be able to break these enchantments?"

"Queer things happen in the Land of Oz," replied the Canary, again perching on the Green Monkey's shoulder and turning one bright eye thoughtfully toward her questioner. "Mrs. Yoop has declared that none of her transformations can ever be changed,

even by herself, but I believe that if we could get to Glinda, the Good Sorceress, she might find a way to restore us to our natural shapes. Glinda, as you know, is the most powerful Sorceress in the world, and there are few things she cannot do if she tries."

"In that case," said the Little Brown Bear, "let us return southward and try to get to Glinda's castle. It lies in the Quadling Country, you know, so it is a good way from here."

"First, however, let us visit the forest and search for something to eat," pleaded Woot. So they continued on to the edge of the forest, which consisted of many tall and beautiful trees. They discovered no fruit trees, at first, so the Green Monkey pushed on into the forest depths and the others followed close behind him.

They were traveling quietly along, under the shade of the trees, when suddenly an enormous jaguar leaped upon them from a limb and with one blow of his paw sent the little Brown Bear tumbling over and over until he was stopped by a tree-trunk. Instantly they all took alarm. The Tin Owl shrieked: "Hoot—hoot!" and flew straight up to the branch of a tall tree, although he could scarcely see where he was going. The Canary swiftly darted to a place beside the Owl, and the Green Monkey sprang up, caught a limb, and soon scrambled to a high perch of safety.

The Jaguar crouched low and with hungry eyes regarded the little Brown Bear, which slowly got upon its feet and asked reproachfully:

"For goodness sake, Beast, what were you trying to do?"

"Trying to get my breakfast," answered the Jaguar with a snarl, "and I believe I've succeeded. You ought to make a delicious meal—unless you happen to be old and tough."

"I'm worse than that, considered as a breakfast," said the Bear, "for I'm only a skin stuffed with straw, and therefore not fit to eat."

"Indeed!" cried the Jaguar, in a disappointed voice; "then you must be a magic Bear, or enchanted, and I must seek my breakfast from among your companions."

With this he raised his lean head to look up at the Tin Owl and the Canary and the Monkey, and he lashed his tail upon the ground and growled as fiercely as any jaguar could.

"My friends are enchanted, also," said the little Brown Bear.

"All of them?" asked the Jaguar.

"Yes. The Owl is tin, so you couldn't possibly eat him. The Canary is a fairy—Polychrome, the Daughter of the Rainbow—and you never could catch her because she can easily fly out of your reach."

"There still remains the Green Monkey," remarked the Jaguar hungrily. "He is neither made of tin nor stuffed with straw, nor can he fly. I'm pretty good at climbing trees, myself, so I think I'll capture the Monkey and eat him for my breakfast."

Woot the Monkey, hearing this speech from his perch on the tree, became much frightened, for he knew the nature of jaguars and realized they could climb trees and leap from limb to limb with the agility of cats. So he at once began to scamper through the forest as fast as he could go, catching at a branch with his long monkey arms and swinging his green body through space to grasp another branch in a neighboring tree, and so on, while the Jaguar followed him from below, his eyes fixed steadfastly on his prey. But presently Woot got his feet tangled in the Lace Apron, which he was still wearing, and that tripped him in his flight and made him fall to the ground, where the Jaguar placed one huge paw upon him and said grimly:

"I've got you, now!"

The fact that the Apron had tripped him made Woot remember its magic powers, and in his terror he cried out: "Open!" without stopping to consider how this command might save him. But, at the word, the earth opened at the exact spot where he lay under the Jaguar's paw, and his body sank downward, the earth closing over it again. The last thing Woot the Monkey saw, as he glanced upward, was the Jaguar peering into the hole in astonishment.

"He's gone!" cried the beast, with a long-drawn sigh of disappointment; "he's gone, and now I shall have no breakfast."

The clatter of the Tin Owl's wings sounded above him, and the little Brown Bear came trotting up and asked:

"Where is the Monkey? Have you eaten him so quickly?"

"No, indeed," answered the Jaguar. "He disappeared into the earth before I could take one bite of him!"

And now the Canary perched upon a stump, a little way from the forest beast, and said:

"I am glad our friend has escaped you; but, as it is natural for a hungry beast to wish his breakfast, I will try to give you one."

"Thank you," replied the Jaguar. "You're rather small for a full meal, but it's kind of you to sacrifice yourself to my appetite."

"Oh, I don't intend to be eaten, I assure you," said the Canary, "but as I am a fairy I know something of magic, and though I am now transformed into a bird's shape, I am sure I can conjure up a breakfast that will satisfy you."

"If you can work magic, why don't you break the enchantment you are under and return to your proper form?" inquired the beast doubtingly.

"I haven't the power to do that," answered the Canary, "for Mrs. Yoop, the Giantess who transformed me, used a peculiar form of Yookoohoo magic that is unknown to me. However, she could not deprive me of my own fairy knowledge, so I will try to get you a breakfast."

"Do you think a magic breakfast would taste good, or relieve the pangs of hunger I now suffer?" asked the Jaguar.

"I am sure it would. What would you like to eat?"

"Give me a couple of fat rabbits," said the beast.

"Rabbits! No, indeed. I'd not allow you to eat the dear little things," declared Polychrome the Canary.

"Well, three or four squirrels, then," pleaded the Jaguar.

"Do you think me so cruel?" demanded the Canary, indignantly. "The squirrels are my especial friends."

"How about a plump owl?" asked the beast. "Not a tin one, you know, but a real meat owl."

"Neither beast nor bird shall you have," said Polychrome in a positive voice.

"Give me a fish, then; there's a river a little way off," proposed the Jaguar.

"No living thing shall be sacrificed to feed you," returned the Canary.

"Then what in the world do you expect me to eat?" said the Jaguar in a scornful tone.

"How would mush-and-milk do?" asked the Canary.

The Jaguar snarled in derision and lashed his tail against the ground angrily.

"Give him some scrambled eggs on toast, Poly," suggested the Bear Scarecrow. "He ought to like that."

"I will," responded the Canary, and fluttering her wings she made a flight of three circles around the stump. Then she flew up to a tree and the Bear and the Owl and the Jaguar saw that upon the stump had appeared a great green leaf upon which was a large portion of scrambled eggs on toast, smoking hot.

"There!" said the Bear; "eat your breakfast, friend Jaguar, and be content."

The Jaguar crept closer to the stump and sniffed the fragrance of the scrambled eggs. They smelled so good that he tasted them, and they tasted so good that he ate the strange meal in a hurry, proving he had been really hungry.

"I prefer rabbits," he muttered, licking his chops, "but I must admit the magic breakfast has filled my stomach full, and brought me comfort. So I'm much obliged for the kindness, little Fairy, and I'll now leave you in peace."

Saying this, he plunged into the thick underbrush and soon disappeared, although they could hear his great body crashing through the bushes until he was far distant.

"That was a good way to get rid of the savage beast, Poly," said the Tin Woodman to the Canary; "but I'm surprised that you didn't give our friend Woot a magic breakfast, when you knew he was hungry."

"The reason for that," answered Polychrome, "was that my mind was so intent on other things that I quite forgot my power to produce food by magic. But where *is* the monkey boy?"

"Gone!" said the Scarecrow Bear, solemnly. "The earth has swallowed him up."

CHAPTER IX

THE QUARRELSOME DRAGONS

THE GREEN MONKEY SANK GENTLY INTO THE earth for a little way and then tumbled swiftly through space, landing on a rocky floor with a thump that astonished him. Then he sat up, found that no bones were broken, and gazed around him.

He seemed to be in a big underground cave, which was dimly lighted by dozens of big round discs that looked like moons. They were not moons, however, as Woot discovered when he had examined the place more carefully. They were eyes. The eyes were in the heads of enormous beasts whose bodies trailed far behind them. Each beast was bigger than an elephant, and three times as long, and there were a dozen or more of the creatures scattered here and there about the cavern. On their bodies were big scales, as round as pie-plates, which were beautifully tinted in shades of green, purple and orange. On the ends of their long tails were clusters of jewels. Around the great, moon-like eyes were circles of diamonds which sparkled in the subdued light that glowed from the eyes.

Woot saw that the creatures had wide mouths and rows of terrible teeth and, from tales he had heard of such beings, he knew he had fallen into a cavern inhabited by the great Dragons that had been driven from the surface of the earth and were only allowed to come out once in a hundred years to search for food. Of course he had never seen Dragons before, yet there was no mistaking them, for they were unlike any other living creatures.

Woot sat upon the floor where he had fallen, staring around, and the owners of the big eyes returned his look, silently and motionless. Finally one of the Dragons which was farthest away from him asked, in a deep, grave voice:

"What was that?"

And the greatest Dragon of all, who was just in front of the Green Monkey, answered in a still deeper voice:

"It is some foolish animal from Outside."

"Is it good to eat?" inquired a smaller Dragon beside the great one. "I'm hungry."

"Hungry!" exclaimed all the Dragons, in a reproachful chorus; and then the great one said chidingly: "Tut-tut, my son! You've no reason to be hungry at *this* time."

"Why not?" asked the little Dragon. "I haven't eaten anything in eleven years."

"Eleven years is nothing," remarked another Dragon, sleepily opening and closing his eyes; "*I* haven't feasted for eighty-seven years, and I dare not get hungry for a dozen or so years to come. Children who eat between meals should be broken of the habit."

"All I had, eleven years ago, was a rhinoceros, and that's not a full meal at all," grumbled the young one. "And, before that, I had waited sixty-two years to be fed; so it's no wonder I'm hungry."

"How old are you now?" asked Woot, forgetting his own dangerous position in his interest in the conversation.

"Why, I'm—I'm— How old am I, Father?" asked the little Dragon.

"Goodness gracious! what a child to ask questions. Do you want to keep me thinking all the time? Don't you know that thinking is very bad for Dragons?" returned the big one, impatiently.

"How old am I, Father?" persisted the small Dragon.

"About six hundred and thirty, I believe. Ask your mother."

"No; don't!" said an old Dragon in the background; "haven't I enough worries, what with being wakened in the middle of a nap, without being obliged to keep track of my children's ages?"

"You've been fast asleep for over sixty years, Mother," said the child Dragon. "How long a nap do you wish?"

"I should have slept forty years longer. And this strange little green beast should be punished for falling into our cavern and disturbing us."

"I didn't know you were here, and I didn't know I was going to fall in," explained Woot.

"Nevertheless, here you are," said the great Dragon, "and you have carelessly wakened our entire tribe; so it stands to reason you must be punished."

"In what way?" inquired the Green Monkey, trembling a little.

"Give me time and I'll think of a way. You're in no hurry, are you?" asked the great Dragon.

"No, indeed," cried Woot. "Take your time. I'd much rather you'd all go to sleep again, and punish me when you wake up in a hundred years or so."

"Let me eat him!" pleaded the littlest Dragon.

"He is too small," said the father. "To eat this one Green Monkey would only serve to make you hungry for more, and there *are* no more."

"Quit this chatter and let me get to sleep," protested another Dragon, yawning in a fearful manner, for when he opened his mouth a sheet of flame leaped forth from it and made Woot jump back to get out of its way.

In his jump he bumped against the nose of a Dragon behind him, which opened its mouth to growl and shot another sheet of flame at him. The flame was bright, but not very hot, yet Woot screamed with terror and sprang forward with a great bound. This time he landed on the paw of the great Chief Dragon, who angrily raised his other front paw and struck the Green Monkey a fierce blow. Woot went sailing through the air and fell sprawling upon the rocky floor far beyond the place where the Dragon Tribe was grouped.

All the great beasts were now thoroughly wakened and aroused, and they blamed the monkey for disturbing their quiet. The littlest Dragon darted after Woot and the others turned their unwieldy bodies in his direction and followed, flashing from their eyes and mouths flames which lighted up the entire cavern.

Woot almost gave him-
self up for lost, at that moment,
but he scrambled to his feet and
dashed away to the farthest end of
the cave, the Dragons following more
leisurely because they were too clumsy to
move fast. Perhaps they thought there was no
need of haste, as the Monkey could not escape from the cave. But, away up at the
end of the place, the cavern floor was heaped with tumbled rocks, so Woot, with
an agility born of fear, climbed from rock to rock until he found himself crouched
against the cavern roof. There he waited, for he could go no farther, while on over

the tumbled rocks slowly crept the Dragons—the littlest one coming first because he was hungry as well as angry.

The beasts had almost reached him when Woot, remembering his lace apron—now sadly torn and soiled—recovered his wits and shouted: "Open!" At the cry a hole appeared in the roof of the cavern, just over his head, and through it the sunlight streamed full upon the Green Monkey.

The Dragons paused, astonished at the magic and blinking at the sunlight, and this gave Woot time to climb through the opening. As soon as he reached the surface of the earth the hole closed again, and the boy monkey realized, with a thrill of joy, that he had seen the last of the dangerous Dragon family.

He sat upon the ground, still panting hard from his exertions, when the bushes before him parted and his former enemy, the Jaguar, appeared.

"Don't run," said the woodland beast, as Woot sprang up; "you are perfectly safe, so far as I am concerned, for since you so mysteriously disappeared I have had my breakfast. I am now on my way home, to sleep the rest of the day."

"Oh, indeed!" returned the Green Monkey, in a tone both sorry and startled. "Which of my friends did you manage to eat?"

"None of them," returned the Jaguar, with a sly grin. "I had a dish of magic scrambled eggs—on toast—and it wasn't a bad feast, at all. There isn't room in me for even you, and I don't regret it because I judge, from your green color, that you are not ripe, and would make an indifferent meal. We jaguars have to be careful of our digestions. Farewell, Friend Monkey. Follow the path I made through the bushes and you will find your friends."

With this the Jaguar marched on his way and Woot took his advice and followed the trail he had made until he came to the place where the little Brown Bear, and

the Tin Owl, and the Canary were conferring together and wondering what had become of their comrade, the Green Monkey.

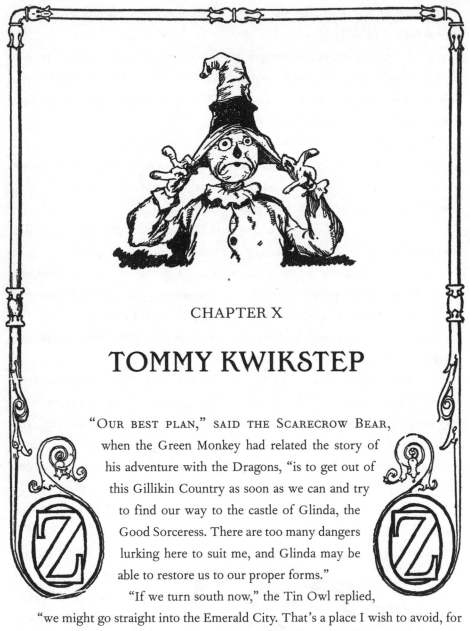

CHAPTER X

TOMMY KWIKSTEP

"Our best plan," said the Scarecrow Bear, when the Green Monkey had related the story of his adventure with the Dragons, "is to get out of this Gillikin Country as soon as we can and try to find our way to the castle of Glinda, the Good Sorceress. There are too many dangers lurking here to suit me, and Glinda may be able to restore us to our proper forms."

"If we turn south now," the Tin Owl replied, "we might go straight into the Emerald City. That's a place I wish to avoid, for I'd hate to have my friends see me in this sad plight," and he blinked his eyes and fluttered his tin wings mournfully.

"But I am certain we have passed beyond Emerald City," the Canary assured him, sailing lightly around their heads. "So, should we turn south from here, we would pass into the Munchkin Country, and continuing south we would reach the Quadling Country where Glinda's castle is located."

"Well, since you're sure of that, let's start right away," proposed the Bear. "It's a long journey, at the best, and I'm getting tired of walking on four legs."

"I thought you never tired, being stuffed with straw," said Woot.

"I mean that it annoys me, to be obliged to go on all fours, when two legs are my proper walking equipment," replied the Scarecrow. "I consider it beneath my dignity. In other words, my remarkable brains can tire, through humiliation, although my body cannot tire."

"That is one of the penalties of having brains," remarked the Tin Owl with a sigh. "I have had no brains since I was a man of meat, and so I never worry. Nevertheless, I prefer my former manly form to this owl's shape and would be glad to break Mrs. Yoop's enchantment as soon as possible. I am so noisy, just now, that I disturb myself," and he fluttered his wings with a clatter that echoed throughout the forest.

So, being all of one mind, they turned southward, traveling steadily on until the woods were left behind and the landscape turned from purple tints to blue tints, which assured them they had entered the Country of the Munchkins.

"Now I feel myself more safe," said the Scarecrow Bear. "I know this country pretty well, having been made here by a Munchkin farmer and having wandered over these lovely blue lands many times. Seems to me, indeed, that I even remember that group of three tall trees ahead of us; and, if I do, we are not far from the home of my friend Jinjur."

"Who is Jinjur?" asked Woot, the Green Monkey.

"Haven't you heard of Jinjur?" exclaimed the Scarecrow, in surprise.

"No," said Woot. "Is Jinjur a man, a woman, a beast or a bird?"

"Jinjur is a girl," explained the Scarecrow Bear. "She's a fine girl, too, although a bit restless and liable to get excited. Once, a long time ago, she raised an army of girls and called herself 'General Jinjur.' With her army she captured the Emerald City, and drove me out of it, because I insisted that an army in Oz was highly improper. But Ozma punished the rash girl, and afterward Jinjur and I became fast friends. Now Jinjur lives peacefully on a farm, near here, and raises fields of cream-puffs, chocolate-caramels and macaroons. They say she's a pretty good farmer, and in addition to that she's an artist, and paints pictures so perfect that one can scarcely tell them from nature. She often repaints my face for me, when it gets worn or mussy, and the lovely expression I wore when the Giantess transformed me was painted by Jinjur only a month or so ago."

"It was certainly a pleasant expression," agreed Woot.

"Jinjur can paint anything," continued the Scarecrow Bear, with enthusiasm, as they walked along together. "Once, when I came to her house, my straw was old and crumpled, so that my body sagged dreadfully. I needed new straw to replace the old, but Jinjur had no straw on all her ranch and I was really unable to travel farther until I had been restuffed. When I explained this to Jinjur, the girl at once painted a straw-stack which was so natural that I went to it and secured enough straw to fill all my body. It was a good quality of straw, too, and lasted me a long time."

This seemed very wonderful to Woot, who knew that such a thing could never happen in any place but a fairy country like Oz.

The Munchkin Country was much nicer than the Gillikin Country, and all the fields were separated by blue fences, with grassy lanes and paths of blue ground, and the land seemed well cultivated. They were on a little hill looking down upon this favored country, but had not quite reached the settled parts, when on turning a bend in the path they were halted by a form that barred their way.

A more curious creature they had seldom seen, even in the Land of Oz, where curious creatures abound. It had the head of a young man—evidently a Munchkin—with a pleasant face and hair neatly combed. But the body was very long, for it had twenty legs—ten legs on each side—and this caused the body to stretch out and lie in a horizontal position, so that all the legs could touch the ground and stand firm. From the shoulders extended two small arms; at least, they seemed small beside so many legs.

This odd creature was dressed in the regulation clothing of the Munchkin people, a dark blue coat neatly fitting the long body and each pair of legs having a pair of sky-blue trousers, with blue-tinted stockings and blue leather shoes turned up at the pointed toes.

"I wonder who you are?" said Polychrome the Canary, fluttering above the strange creature, who had probably been asleep on the path.

"I sometimes wonder, myself, who I am," replied the many-legged young man; "but, in reality, I am Tommy Kwikstep, and I live in a hollow tree that fell to the ground with age. I have polished the inside of it, and made a door at each end, and that's a very comfortable residence for me because it just fits my shape."

"How did you happen to have such a shape?" asked the Scarecrow Bear, sitting on his haunches and regarding Tommy Kwikstep with a serious look. "Is the shape natural?"

"No; it was wished on me," replied Tommy, with a sigh. "I used to be very active and loved to run errands for anyone who needed my services. That was how

I got my name of Tommy Kwikstep. I could run an errand more quickly than any other boy, and so I was very proud of myself. One day, however, I met an old lady who was a fairy, or a witch, or something of the sort, and she said if I would run an errand for her—to carry some magic medicine to another old woman—she would grant me just one Wish, whatever the Wish happened to be. Of course I consented and, taking the medicine, I hurried away. It was a long distance, mostly up hill, and my legs began to grow weary. Without thinking what I was doing I said aloud: 'Dear me; I wish I had twenty legs!' and in an instant I became the unusual creature you see beside you. Twenty legs! Twenty on one man! You may count them, if you doubt my word."

"You've got 'em, all right," said Woot the Monkey, who had already counted them.

"After I had delivered the magic medicine to the old woman, I returned and tried to find the witch, or fairy, or whatever she was, who had given me the unlucky wish, so she could take it away again. I've been searching for her ever since, but never can I find her," continued poor Tommy Kwikstep, sadly.

"I suppose," said the Tin Owl, blinking at him, "you can travel very fast, with those twenty legs."

"At first I was able to," was the reply; "but I traveled so much, searching for the fairy, or witch, or whatever she was, that I soon got corns on my toes. Now, a corn on one toe is not so bad, but when you have a hundred toes—as I have—and get corns on most of them, it is far from pleasant. Instead of running, I now painfully crawl, and although I try not to be discouraged I do hope I shall find that witch or fairy, or whatever she was, before long."

"I hope so, too," said the Scarecrow. "But, after all, you have the pleasure of knowing you are unusual, and therefore remarkable among the people of Oz. To be just like other persons is small credit to one, while to be unlike others is a mark of distinction."

"That *sounds* very pretty," returned Tommy Kwikstep, "but if you had to put on ten pair of trousers every morning, and tie up twenty shoes, you would prefer not to be so distinguished."

"Was the witch, or fairy, or whatever she was, an old person, with wrinkled skin and half her teeth gone?" inquired the Tin Owl.

"No," said Tommy Kwikstep.

"Then she wasn't Old Mombi," remarked the transformed Emperor.

"I'm not interested in who it wasn't, so much as I am in who it was," said the twenty-legged young man. "And, whatever or whomsoever she was, she has managed to keep out of my way."

"If you found her, do you suppose she'd change you back into a two-legged boy?" asked Woot.

"Perhaps so, if I could run another errand for her and so earn another wish."

"Would you really like to be as you were before?" asked Polychrome the Canary, perching upon the Green Monkey's shoulder to observe Tommy Kwikstep more attentively.

"I would, indeed," was the earnest reply.

"Then I will see what I can do for you," promised the Rainbow's Daughter, and flying to the ground she took a small twig in her bill and with it made several mystic figures on each side of Tommy Kwikstep.

"Are you a witch, or fairy, or something of the sort?" he asked as he watched her wonderingly.

The Canary made no answer, for she was busy, but the Scarecrow Bear replied: "Yes; she's something of the sort, and a bird of a magician."

The twenty-legged boy's transformation happened so queerly that they were all surprised at its method. First, Tommy Kwikstep's last two legs disappeared; then the next two, and the next, and as each pair of legs vanished his body shortened. All this while Polychrome was running around him and chirping mystical words, and when all the young man's legs had disappeared but two he noticed that the Canary was still busy and cried out in alarm:

"Stop—stop! Leave me *two* of my legs, or I shall be worse off than before."

"I know," said the Canary. "I'm only removing with my magic the corns from your last ten toes."

"Thank you for being so thoughtful," he said gratefully, and now they noticed that Tommy Kwikstep was quite a nice looking young fellow.

"What will you do now?" asked Woot the Monkey.

"First," he answered, "I must deliver a note which I've carried in my pocket ever since the witch, or fairy, or whatever she was, granted my foolish wish. And I am resolved never to speak again without taking time to think carefully on what I am going to say, for I realize that speech without thought is dangerous. And after I've delivered the note, I shall run errands again for anyone who needs my services."

So he thanked Polychrome again and started away in a different direction from their own, and that was the last they saw of Tommy Kwikstep.

CHAPTER XI

JINJUR'S RANCH

As they followed a path down the blue-grass hillside, the first house that met the view of the travelers was joyously recognized by the Scarecrow Bear as the one inhabited by his friend Jinjur, so they increased their speed and hurried toward it.

On reaching the place, however, they found the house deserted. The front door stood open, but no one was inside. In the garden surrounding the house were neat rows of bushes bearing cream-puffs and macaroons, some of which were still green, but others ripe and ready to eat. Farther back were fields of caramels, and all the land seemed well cultivated and carefully tended. They looked through the fields for the girl farmer, but she was nowhere to be seen.

"Well," finally remarked the little Brown Bear, "let us go into the house and make ourselves at home. That will be sure to please my friend Jinjur, who happens to be away from home just now. When she returns, she will be greatly surprised."

"Would she care if I ate some of those ripe cream-puffs?" asked the Green Monkey.

"No, indeed; Jinjur is very generous. Help yourself to all you want," said the Scarecrow Bear.

So Woot gathered a lot of the cream-puffs that were golden yellow and filled with a sweet, creamy substance, and ate until his hunger was satisfied. Then he entered the house with his friends and sat in a rocking-chair—just as he was accustomed to do when a boy. The Canary perched herself upon the mantel and daintily plumed her feathers; the Tin Owl sat on the back of another chair; the Scarecrow squatted on his hairy haunches in the middle of the room.

"I believe I remember the girl Jinjur," remarked the Canary, in her sweet voice. "She cannot help us very much, except to direct us on our way to Glinda's castle, for she does not understand magic. But she's a good girl, honest and sensible, and I'll be glad to see her."

"All our troubles," said the Owl with a deep sigh, "arose from my foolish resolve to seek Nimmie Amee and make her Empress of the Winkies, and while I wish to reproach no one, I must say that it was Woot the Wanderer who put the notion into my head."

"Well, for my part, I am glad he did," responded the Canary. "Your journey resulted in saving me from the Giantess, and had you not traveled to the Yoop Valley, I would still be Mrs. Yoop's prisoner. It is much nicer to be free, even though I still bear the enchanted form of a Canary-Bird."

"Do you think we shall ever be able to get our proper forms back again?" asked the Green Monkey earnestly.

Polychrome did not make reply at once to this important question, but after a period of thoughtfulness she said:

"I have been taught to believe that there is an antidote for every magic charm, yet Mrs. Yoop insists that no power can alter her transformations. I realize that my own fairy magic cannot do it, although I have thought that we Sky Fairies have more power than is accorded to Earth Fairies. The Yookoohoo magic is admitted to be very strange in its workings and different from the magic usually practiced, but perhaps Glinda or Ozma may understand it better than I. In them lies our only hope. Unless they can help us, we must remain forever as we are."

"A Canary-Bird on a Rainbow wouldn't be so bad," asserted the Tin Owl, winking and blinking with his round tin eyes, "so if you can manage to find your Rainbow again you need have little to worry about."

"That's nonsense, Friend Chopper," exclaimed Woot. "I know just how Polychrome feels. A beautiful girl is much superior to a little yellow bird, and a boy—such as I was—far better than a green monkey. Neither of us can be happy again unless we recover our rightful forms."

"I feel the same way," announced the stuffed Bear. "What do you suppose my friend the Patchwork Girl would think of me, if she saw me wearing this beastly shape?"

"She'd laugh till she cried," admitted the Tin Owl. "For my part, I'll have to give up the notion of marrying Nimmie Amee, but I'll try not to let that make me unhappy. If it's my duty, I'd like to do my duty, but if magic prevents my getting married I'll flutter along all by myself and be just as contented."

Their serious misfortunes made them all silent for a time, and as their thoughts were busy in dwelling upon the evils with which fate had burdened them, none noticed that Jinjur had suddenly appeared in the doorway and was looking at them in astonishment. The next moment her astonishment changed to anger, for there, in her best rocking-chair, sat a Green Monkey. A great shiny Owl perched upon another chair and a Brown Bear squatted upon her parlor rug. Jinjur did not notice the Canary, but she caught up a broomstick and dashed into the room, shouting as she came:

"Get out of here, you wild creatures! How dare you enter my house?"

With a blow of her broom she knocked the Brown Bear over, and the Tin Owl tried to fly out of her reach and made a great clatter with his tin wings. The Green Monkey was so startled by the sudden attack that he sprang into the fire-place—where there was fortunately no fire—and tried to escape by climbing up the chimney. But he found the opening too small, and so was forced to drop down again. Then he crouched trembling in the fireplace, his pretty green hair all blackened with soot and covered with ashes. From this position Woot watched to see what would happen next.

"Stop, Jinjur—stop!" cried the Brown Bear, when the broom again threatened him. "Don't you know me? I'm your old friend the Scarecrow?"

"You're trying to deceive me, you naughty beast! I can see plainly that you are a bear, and a mighty poor specimen of a bear, too," retorted the girl.

"That's because I'm not properly stuffed," he assured her. "When Mrs. Yoop transformed me, she didn't realize I should have more stuffing."

"Who is Mrs. Yoop?" inquired Jinjur, pausing with the broom still upraised.

"A Giantess in the Gillikin Country."

"Oh; I begin to understand. And Mrs. Yoop transformed you? You are really the famous Scarecrow of Oz?"

"I *was*, Jinjur. Just now I'm as you see me—a miserable little Brown Bear with a poor quality of stuffing. That Tin Owl is none other than our dear Tin Woodman— Nick Chopper, the Emperor of the Winkies—while this Green Monkey is a nice little boy we recently became acquainted with, Woot the Wanderer."

"And I," said the Canary, flying close to Jinjur, "am Polychrome, the Daughter of the Rainbow, in the form of a bird."

"Goodness me!" cried Jinjur, amazed; "that Giantess must be a powerful Sorceress, and as wicked as she is powerful."

"She's a Yookoohoo," said Polychrome. "Fortunately, we managed to escape from her castle, and we are now on our way to Glinda the Good to see if she possesses the power to restore us to our former shapes."

"Then I must beg your pardons; all of you must forgive me," said Jinjur, putting away the broom. "I took you to be a lot of wild, unmannerly animals, as was quite natural. You are very welcome to my home and I'm sorry I haven't the power to help you out of your troubles. Please use my house and all that I have, as if it were your own."

At this declaration of peace, the Bear got upon his feet and the Owl resumed his perch upon the chair and the Monkey crept out of the fireplace. Jinjur looked at Woot critically, and scowled.

"For a Green Monkey," said she, "you're the blackest creature I ever saw. And you'll get my nice clean room all dirty with soot and ashes. Whatever possessed you to jump up the chimney?"

"I—I was scared," explained Woot, somewhat ashamed.

"Well, you need renovating, and that's what will happen to you, right away. Come with me!" she commanded.

"What are you going to do?" asked Woot.

"Give you a good scrubbing," said Jinjur.

Now, neither boys nor monkeys relish being scrubbed, so Woot shrank away from the energetic girl, trembling fearfully. But Jinjur grabbed him by his paw and dragged him out to the back yard, where, in spite of his whines and struggles, she plunged him into a tub of cold water and began to scrub him with a stiff brush and a cake of yellow soap.

This was the hardest trial that Woot had endured since he became a monkey, but no protest had any influence with Jinjur, who lathered and scrubbed him in a business-like manner and afterward dried him with a coarse towel.

The Bear and the Owl gravely watched this operation and nodded approval when Woot's silky green fur shone clear and bright in the afternoon sun. The Canary seemed much amused and laughed a silvery ripple of laughter as she said:

"Very well done, my good Jinjur; I admire your energy and judgment. But I had no idea a monkey could look so comical as this monkey did while he was being bathed."

"I'm *not* a monkey!" declared Woot, resentfully; "I'm just a boy in a monkey's shape, that's all."

"If you can explain to me the difference," said Jinjur, "I'll agree not to wash you again—that is, unless you foolishly get into the fireplace. All persons are usually judged by the shapes in which they appear to the eyes of others. Look at *me*, Woot; what am *I*?"

Woot looked at her.

"You're as pretty a girl as I've ever seen," he replied.

Jinjur frowned. That is, she tried hard to frown.

"Come out into the garden with me," she said, "and I'll give you some of the most delicious caramels you ever ate. They're a new variety, that no one can grow but me, and they have a heliotrope flavor."

CHAPTER XII

OZMA AND DOROTHY

IN HER MAGNIFICENT PALACE IN THE EMERALD City, the beautiful girl Ruler of all the wonderful Land of Oz sat in her dainty boudoir with her friend Princess Dorothy beside her. Ozma was studying a roll of manuscript which she had taken from the Royal Library, while Dorothy worked at her embroidery and at times stooped to pat a shaggy little black dog that lay at her feet. The little dog's name was Toto, and he was Dorothy's faithful companion.

To judge Ozma of Oz by the standards of our world, you would think her very young—perhaps fourteen or fifteen years of age—yet for years she had ruled the Land of Oz and had never seemed a bit older. Dorothy appeared much younger than Ozma. She had been a little girl when first she came to the Land of Oz, and she was a little girl still, and would never seem to be a day older while she lived in this wonderful fairyland.

Oz was not always a fairyland, I am told. Once it was much like other lands, except it was shut in by a dreadful desert of sandy wastes that lay all around it, thus preventing its people from all contact with the rest of the world. Seeing this isolation, the fairy band of Queen Lurline, passing over Oz while on a journey, enchanted the country and so made it a Fairyland. And Queen Lurline left one of her fairies to rule this enchanted Land of Oz, and then passed on and forgot all about it.

From that moment no one in Oz ever died. Those who were old remained old; those who were young and strong did not change as years passed them by; the children remained children always, and played and romped to their hearts' content, while all the babies lived in their cradles and were tenderly cared for and never grew up. So people in Oz stopped counting how old they were in years, for years made no difference in their appearance and could not alter their station. They did not get sick, so there were no doctors among them. Accidents might happen to some, on rare occasions, it is true, and while no one could die naturally, as other people do, it was possible that one might be totally destroyed. Such incidents, however, were very unusual, and so seldom was there anything to worry over that the Oz people were as happy and contented as can be.

Another strange thing about this fairy Land of Oz was that whoever managed to enter it from the outside world came under the magic spell of the place and did not change in appearance as long as they lived there. So Dorothy, who now lived with Ozma, seemed just the same sweet little girl she had been when first she came to this delightful fairyland.

Perhaps all parts of Oz might not be called truly delightful, but it was surely delightful in the neighborhood of the Emerald City, where Ozma reigned. Her loving influence was felt for many miles around, but there were places in the mountains of the Gillikin Country, and the forests of the Quadling Country, and perhaps in far-away parts of the Munchkin and Winkie Countries, where the inhabitants were somewhat rude and uncivilized and had not yet come under the spell of Ozma's wise and kindly rule. Also, when Oz first became a fairyland, it harbored several witches and magicians and sorcerers and necromancers, who were scattered in various parts, but most of these had been deprived of their magic powers, and Ozma had issued a royal edict forbidding anyone in her dominions to work magic except Glinda the Good and the Wizard of Oz. Ozma herself, being a real fairy, knew a lot of magic, but she only used it to benefit her subjects.

This little explanation will help you to understand better the story you are reading, but most of it is already known to those who are familiar with the Oz people whose adventures they have followed in other Oz books.

Ozma and Dorothy were fast friends and were much together. Everyone in Oz loved Dorothy almost as well as they did their lovely Ruler, for the little Kansas girl's good fortune had not spoiled her or rendered her at all vain. She was just the same brave and true and adventurous child as before she lived in a royal palace and became the chum of the fairy Ozma.

In the room in which the two sat—which was one of Ozma's private suite of apartments—hung the famous Magic Picture. This was the source of constant interest to little Dorothy. One had but to stand before it and wish to see what any person was doing, and at once a scene would flash upon the magic canvas which showed exactly where that person was, and like our own moving pictures would reproduce the actions of that person as long as you cared to watch them. So today, when Dorothy tired of her embroidery, she drew the curtains from before the Magic Picture and wished to see what her friend Button-Bright was doing. Button-Bright, she saw, was playing ball with Ojo, the Munchkin boy, so Dorothy next wished to

see what her Aunt Em was doing. The picture showed Aunt Em quietly engaged in darning socks for Uncle Henry, so Dorothy wished to see what her old friend the Tin Woodman was doing.

The Tin Woodman was then just leaving his tin castle in the company of the Scarecrow and Woot the Wanderer. Dorothy had never seen this boy before, so she wondered who he was. Also she was curious to know where the three were going, for she noticed Woot's knapsack and guessed they had started on a long journey. She asked Ozma about it, but Ozma did not know.

That afternoon Dorothy again saw the travelers in the Magic Picture, but they were merely tramping through the country and Dorothy was not much interested in them. A couple of days later, however, the girl, being again with Ozma, wished to see her friends, the Scarecrow and the Tin Woodman in the Magic Picture, and on this occasion found them in the great castle of Mrs. Yoop, the Giantess, who was at the time about to transform them. Both Dorothy and Ozma now became greatly interested and watched the transformations with indignation and horror.

"What a wicked Giantess!" exclaimed Dorothy.

"Yes," answered Ozma, "she must be punished for this cruelty to our friends, and to the poor boy who is with them."

After this they followed the adventure of the little Brown Bear and the Tin Owl and the Green Monkey with breathless interest, and were delighted when they escaped from Mrs. Yoop. They did not know, then, who the Canary was, but realized it must be the transformation of some person of consequence, whom the Giantess had also enchanted.

When, finally, the day came when the adventurers headed south into the Munchkin Country, Dorothy asked anxiously:

"Can't something be done for them, Ozma? Can't you change 'em back into their own shapes? They've suffered enough from these dreadful transformations, seems to me."

"I've been studying ways to help them, ever since they were transformed," replied Ozma. "Mrs. Yoop is now the only Yookoohoo in my dominions, and the Yookoohoo magic is very peculiar and hard for others to understand, yet I am resolved to make the attempt to break these enchantments. I may not succeed, but I shall do the best I can. From the directions our friends are taking, I believe they are going to pass by Jinjur's Ranch, so if we start now we may meet them there. Would you like to go with me, Dorothy?"

"Of course," answered the little girl; "I wouldn't miss it for anything."

"Then order the Red Wagon," said Ozma of Oz, "and we will start at once."

Dorothy ran to do as she was bid, while Ozma went to her Magic Room to make ready the things she believed she would need. In half an hour the Red Wagon stood before the grand entrance of the palace, and before it was hitched the Wooden Saw-Horse, which was Ozma's favorite steed.

This Saw-Horse, while made of wood, was very much alive and could travel swiftly and without tiring. To keep the ends of his wooden legs from wearing down short, Ozma had shod the Saw-Horse with plates of pure gold. His harness was studded with brilliant emeralds and other jewels and so, while he himself was not at all handsome, his outfit made a splendid appearance.

Since the Saw-Horse could understand her spoken words, Ozma used no reins to guide him. She merely told him where to go. When she came from the palace with Dorothy, they both climbed into the Red Wagon and then the little dog, Toto, ran up and asked:

"Are you going to leave me behind, Dorothy?" Dorothy looked at Ozma, who smiled in return and said:

"Toto may go with us, if you wish him to."

So Dorothy lifted the little dog into the wagon, for, while he could run fast, he could not keep up with the speed of the wonderful Saw-Horse.

Away they went, over hills and through meadows, covering the ground with astonishing speed. It is not surprising, therefore, that the Red Wagon arrived before Jinjur's house just as that energetic young lady had finished scrubbing the Green Monkey and was about to lead him to the caramel patch.

CHAPTER XIII

THE RESTORATION

THE TIN OWL GAVE A HOOT OF DELIGHT WHEN he saw the Red Wagon draw up before Jinjur's house, and the Brown Bear grunted and growled with glee and trotted toward Ozma as fast as he could wobble. As for the Canary, it flew swiftly to Dorothy's shoulder and perched there, saying in her ear:

"Thank goodness you have come to our rescue!"

"But who are you?" asked Dorothy

"Don't you know?" returned the Canary.

"No; for the first time we noticed you in the Magic Picture, you were just a bird, as you are now. But we've guessed that the giant woman had transformed you, as she did the others."

"Yes; I'm Polychrome, the Rainbow's Daughter," announced the Canary.

"Goodness me!" cried Dorothy. "How dreadful."

"Well, I make a rather pretty bird, I think," returned Polychrome, "but of course I'm anxious to resume my own shape and get back upon my rainbow."

"Ozma will help you, I'm sure," said Dorothy. "How does it feel, Scarecrow, to be a Bear?" she asked, addressing her old friend.

"I don't like it," declared the Scarecrow Bear. "This brutal form is quite beneath the dignity of a wholesome straw man."

"And think of me," said the Owl, perching upon the dashboard of the Red Wagon with much noisy clattering of his tin feathers. "Don't I look horrid, Dorothy, with eyes several sizes too big for my body, and so weak that I ought to wear spectacles?"

"Well," said Dorothy critically, as she looked him over, "you're nothing to brag of, I must confess. But Ozma will soon fix you up again."

The Green Monkey had hung back, bashful at meeting two lovely girls while in the form of a beast; but Jinjur now took his hand and led him forward while she introduced him to Ozma, and Woot managed to make a low bow, not really ungraceful, before Her Girlish Majesty, the Ruler of Oz.

"You have all been forced to endure a sad experience," said Ozma, "and so I am anxious to do all in my power to break Mrs. Yoop's enchantments. But first tell me how you happened to stray into that lonely Valley where Yoop Castle stands."

Between them they related the object of their journey, the Scarecrow Bear telling of the Tin Woodman's resolve to find Nimmie Amee and marry her, as a just reward for her loyalty to him. Woot told of their adventures with the Loons of Loonville, and the Tin Owl described the manner in which they had been captured and transformed by the Giantess. Then Polychrome related her story, and when all had been told, and Dorothy had several times reproved Toto for growling at the Tin Owl, Ozma remained thoughtful for a while, pondering upon what she had heard. Finally she looked up, and with one of her delightful smiles, said to the anxious group:

"I am not sure my magic will be able to restore every one of you, because your transformations are of such a strange and unusual character. Indeed, Mrs. Yoop was quite justified in believing no power could alter her enchantments. However, I am sure I can restore the Scarecrow to his original shape. He was stuffed with straw from the beginning, and even the Yookoohoo magic could not alter that. The Giantess was merely able to make a bear's shape of a man's shape, but the bear is stuffed with straw, just as the man was. So I feel confident I can make a man of the bear again."

"Hurrah!" cried the Brown Bear, and tried clumsily to dance a jig of delight.

"As for the Tin Woodman, his case is much the same," resumed Ozma, still smiling. "The power of the Giantess could not make him anything but a tin creature, whatever shape she transformed him into, so it will not be impossible to restore him to his manly form. Anyhow, I shall test my magic at once, and see if it will do what I have promised."

She drew from her bosom a small silver wand and, making passes with the wand over the head of the Bear, she succeeded in the brief space of a moment in breaking his enchantment. The original Scarecrow of Oz again stood before them, well stuffed with straw and with his features nicely painted upon the bag which formed his head.

The Scarecrow was greatly delighted, as you may suppose, and he strutted proudly around while the powerful fairy, Ozma of Oz, broke the enchantment that had transformed the Tin Woodman and made a Tin Owl into a Tin Man again.

"Now, then," chirped the Canary, eagerly; "I'm next, Ozma!"

"But your case is different," replied Ozma, no longer smiling but wearing a grave expression on her sweet face. "I shall have to experiment on you, Polychrome, and I may fail in all my attempts."

She then tried two or three different methods of magic, hoping one of them would succeed in breaking Polychrome's enchantment, but still the Rainbow's Daughter remained a Canary-Bird. Finally, however, she experimented in another way. She transformed the Canary into a Dove, and then transformed the Dove into a Speckled Hen, and then changed the Speckled Hen into a rabbit, and then the rabbit into a Fawn. And at the last, after mixing several powders and sprinkling them upon the Fawn, the Yookoohoo enchantment was suddenly broken and before them stood one of the daintiest and loveliest creatures in any fairyland in the world. Polychrome was as sweet and merry in disposition as she was beautiful, and when she danced and capered around in delight, her beautiful hair floated around her like a golden mist and her many-hued raiment, as soft as cobwebs, reminded one of drifting clouds in a summer sky.

Woot was so awed by the entrancing sight of this exquisite Sky Fairy that he quite forgot his own sad plight until he noticed Ozma gazing upon him with an intent expression that denoted sympathy and sorrow. Dorothy whispered in her friend's ear, but the Ruler of Oz shook her head sadly.

Jinjur, noticing this and understanding Ozma's looks, took the paw of the Green Monkey in her own hand and patted it softly.

"Never mind," she said to him. "You are a very beautiful color, and a monkey can climb better than a boy and do a lot of other things no boy can ever do."

"What's the matter?" asked Woot, a sinking feeling at his heart. "Is Ozma's magic all used up?"

Ozma herself answered him.

"Your form of enchantment, my poor boy," she said pityingly, "is different from that of the others. Indeed, it is a form that is impossible to alter by any magic known to fairies or Yookoohoos. The wicked Giantess was well aware, when she gave you the form of a green monkey, that the Green Monkey must exist in the Land of Oz for all future time."

Woot drew a long sigh.

"Well, that's pretty hard luck," he said bravely, "but if it can't be helped I must endure it; that's all. I don't like being a monkey, but what's the use of kicking against my fate?"

They were all very sorry for him, and Dorothy anxiously asked Ozma:

"Couldn't Glinda save him?"

"No," was the reply. "Glinda's power in transformations is no greater than my own. Before I left my palace I went to my Magic Room and studied Woot's case very carefully. I found that no power can do away with the Green Monkey. He might transfer, or exchange his form with some other person, it is true; but the Green Monkey we cannot get rid of by any magic arts known to science."

"But—see here," said the Scarecrow, who had listened intently to this explanation, "why not put the monkey's form on some one else?"

"Who would agree to make the change?" asked Ozma. "If by force we caused anyone else to become a green monkey, we would be as cruel and wicked as Mrs. Yoop. And what good would an exchange do?" she continued. "Suppose, for instance, we worked the enchantment, and made Toto into a green monkey. At the same moment Woot would become a little dog."

"Leave me out of your magic, please," said Toto, with a reproachful growl. "I wouldn't become a green monkey for anything."

"And I wouldn't become a dog," said Woot. "A green monkey is much better than a dog, it seems to me."

"That is only a matter of opinion," answered Toto.

"Now, here's another idea," said the Scarecrow. "My brains are working finely today, you must admit. Why not transform Toto into Woot the Wanderer, and then have them exchange forms? The dog would become a green monkey and the Monkey would have his own natural shape again."

"To be sure!" cried Jinjur. "That's a fine idea."

"Leave me out of it," said Toto. "I won't do it."

"Wouldn't you be willing to become a Green Monkey—see what a pretty color it is—so that this poor boy could be restored to his own shape?" asked Jinjur, pleadingly.

"No," said Toto.

"I don't like that plan the least bit," declared Dorothy, "for then I wouldn't have any little dog."

"But you'd have a Green Monkey in his place," persisted Jinjur, who liked Woot and wanted to help him.

"I don't want a Green Monkey," said Dorothy positively.

"Don't speak of this again, I beg of you," said Woot. "This is my own misfortune and I would rather suffer it alone than deprive Princess Dorothy of her dog, or deprive the dog of his proper shape. And perhaps even Her Majesty, Ozma of Oz, might not be able to transform anyone else into the shape of Woot the Wanderer."

"Yes; I believe I might do that," Ozma returned; "but Woot is quite right; we are not justified in inflicting upon anyone—man or dog—the form of a Green Monkey. Also it is certain that in order to relieve the boy of the form he now wears, we must give it to someone else, who would be forced to wear it always."

"I wonder," said Dorothy, thoughtfully, "if we couldn't find someone in the Land of Oz who would be willing to become a green monkey? Seems to me a monkey is active and spry, and he can climb trees and do a lot of clever things, and green isn't a bad color for a monkey—it makes him unusual."

"I wouldn't ask anyone to take this dreadful form," said Woot; "it wouldn't be right, you know. I've been a monkey for some time, now, and I don't like it. It makes me ashamed to be a beast of this sort when by right of birth I'm a boy; so I'm sure it would be wicked to ask anyone else to take my place."

They were all silent, for they knew he spoke the truth. Dorothy was almost ready to cry with pity and Ozma's sweet face was sad and disturbed. The Scarecrow rubbed and patted his stuffed head to try to make it think better, while the Tin Woodman went into the house and began to oil his tin joints so that the sorrow of his friends might not cause him to weep. Weeping is liable to rust tin, and the Emperor prided himself upon his highly polished body—now doubly dear to him because for a time he had been deprived of it.

Polychrome had danced down the garden paths and back again a dozen times, for she was seldom still a moment, yet she had heard Ozma's speech and understood very well Woot's unfortunate position. But the Rainbow's Daughter, even while dancing, could think and reason very clearly, and suddenly she solved the problem in the nicest possible way. Coming close to Ozma, she said:

"Your Majesty, all this trouble was caused by the wickedness of Mrs. Yoop, the Giantess. Yet even now that cruel woman is living in her secluded castle, enjoying the thought that she has put this terrible enchantment on Woot the Wanderer. Even now she is laughing at our despair because we can find no way to get rid of the Green Monkey. Very well, we do not wish to get rid of it. Let the woman who created the form wear it herself, as a just punishment for her wickedness. I am sure your fairy power can give to Mrs. Yoop the form of Woot the Wanderer—even at this distance from her—and then it will be possible to exchange the two forms. Mrs. Yoop will become the Green Monkey, and Woot will recover his own form again."

Ozma's face brightened as she listened to this clever proposal.

"Thank you, Polychrome," said she. "The task you propose is not so easy as you suppose, but I will make the attempt, and perhaps I may succeed."

CHAPTER XIV

THE GREEN MONKEY

THEY NOW ENTERED THE HOUSE, AND AS AN interested group, watched Jinjur, at Ozma's command, build a fire and put a kettle of water over to boil. The Ruler of Oz stood before the fire silent and grave, while the others, realizing that an important ceremony of magic was about to be performed, stood quietly in the background so as not to interrupt Ozma's proceedings. Only Polychrome kept going in and coming out, humming softly to herself as she danced, for the Rainbow's Daughter could not keep still for long, and the four walls of a room always made her nervous and ill at ease. She moved so noiselessly, however, that her movements were like the shifting of sunbeams and did not annoy anyone.

When the water in the kettle bubbled, Ozma drew from her bosom two tiny packets containing powders. These powders she threw into the kettle and after briskly stirring the contents with a branch from a macaroon bush, Ozma poured the mystic broth upon a broad platter which Jinjur had placed upon the table. As the broth cooled it became as silver, reflecting all objects from its smooth surface like a mirror.

While her companions gathered around the table, eagerly attentive—and Dorothy even held little Toto in her arms that he might see—Ozma waved her wand over the mirror-like surface. At once it reflected the interior of Yoop Castle, and in the big hall sat Mrs. Yoop, in her best embroidered silken robes, engaged in weaving a new lace apron to replace the one she had lost.

The Giantess seemed rather uneasy, as if she had a faint idea that someone was spying upon her, for she kept looking behind her and this way and that, as though expecting danger from an unknown source. Perhaps some Yookoohoo instinct warned her. Woot saw that she had escaped from her room by some of the magical means at her disposal, after her prisoners had escaped her. She was now occupying the big hall of her castle as she used to do. Also Woot thought, from the cruel expression on the face of the Giantess, that she was planning revenge on them, as soon as her new magic apron was finished.

But Ozma was now making passes over the platter with her silver wand, and presently the form of the Giantess began to shrink in size and to change its shape. And now, in her place sat the form of Woot the Wanderer, and as if suddenly realizing her transformation Mrs. Yoop threw down her work and rushed to a looking-glass that stood against the wall of her room. When she saw the boy's form reflected as her own, she grew violently angry and dashed her head against the mirror, smashing it to atoms.

Just then Ozma was busy with her magic wand, making strange figures, and she had also placed her left hand firmly upon the shoulder of the Green Monkey. So now, as all eyes were turned upon the platter, the form of Mrs. Yoop gradually changed again. She was slowly transformed into the Green Monkey, and at the same time Woot slowly regained his natural form.

It was quite a surprise to them all when they raised their eyes from the platter and saw Woot the Wanderer standing beside Ozma. And, when they glanced at the platter again, it reflected nothing more than the walls of the room in Jinjur's house in which they stood. The magic ceremonial was ended, and Ozma of Oz had triumphed over the wicked Giantess.

"What will become of her, I wonder?" said Dorothy, as she drew a long breath.

"She will always remain a Green Monkey," replied Ozma, "and in that form she will be unable to perform any magical arts whatsoever. She need not be unhappy, however, and as she lives all alone in her castle she probably won't mind the transformation very much after she gets used to it."

"Anyhow, it serves her right," declared Dorothy, and all agreed with her.

"But," said the kind hearted Tin Woodman, "I'm afraid the Green Monkey will starve, for Mrs. Yoop used to get her food by magic, and now that the magic is taken away from her, what can she eat?"

"Why, she'll eat what other monkeys do," returned the Scarecrow. "Even in the form of a Green Monkey, she's a very clever person, and I'm sure her wits will show her how to get plenty to eat."

"Don't worry about her," advised Dorothy. "She didn't worry about you, and her condition is no worse than the condition she imposed on poor Woot. She can't starve *to death* in the Land of Oz, that's certain, and if she gets hungry at times it's no more than the wicked thing deserves. Let's forget Mrs. Yoop; for, in spite of her being a Yookoohoo, our fairy friends have broken all of her transformations."

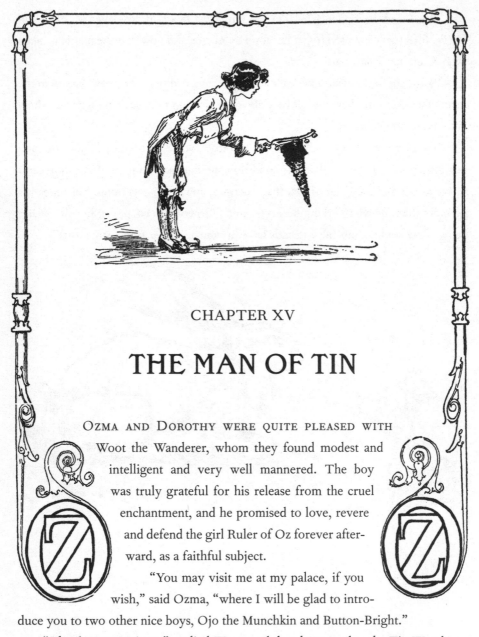

CHAPTER XV

THE MAN OF TIN

OZMA AND DOROTHY WERE QUITE PLEASED WITH Woot the Wanderer, whom they found modest and intelligent and very well mannered. The boy was truly grateful for his release from the cruel enchantment, and he promised to love, revere and defend the girl Ruler of Oz forever afterward, as a faithful subject.

"You may visit me at my palace, if you wish," said Ozma, "where I will be glad to introduce you to two other nice boys, Ojo the Munchkin and Button-Bright."

"Thank Your Majesty," replied Woot, and then he turned to the Tin Woodman and inquired: "What are your further plans, Mr. Emperor? Will you still seek Nimmie Amee and marry her, or will you abandon the quest and return to the Emerald City and your own castle?"

The Tin Woodman, now as highly polished and well-oiled as ever, reflected a while on this question and then answered:

"Well, I see no reason why I should not find Nimmie Amee. We are now in the Munchkin Country, where we are perfectly safe, and if it was right for me, before our enchantment, to marry Nimmie Amee and make her Empress of the Winkies, it must be right now, when the enchantment has been broken and I am once more myself. Am I correct, friend Scarecrow?"

"You are, indeed," answered the Scarecrow. "No one can oppose such logic."

"But I'm afraid you don't love Nimmie Amee," suggested Dorothy.

"That is just because I can't love anyone," replied the Tin Woodman. "But, if I cannot love my wife, I can at least be kind to her, and all husbands are not able to do that."

"Do you s'pose Nimmie Amee still loves you, after all these years?" asked Dorothy.

"I'm quite sure of it, and that is why I am going to her to make her happy. Woot the Wanderer thinks I ought to reward her for being faithful to me after my meat body was chopped to pieces and I became tin. What do *you* think, Ozma?"

Ozma smiled as she said:

"I do not know your Nimmie Amee, and so I cannot tell what she most needs to make her happy. But there is no harm in your going to her and asking her if she still wishes to marry you. If she does, we will give you a grand wedding at the Emerald City and, afterward, as Empress of the Winkies, Nimmie Amee would become one of the most important ladies in all Oz."

So it was decided that the Tin Woodman would continue his journey, and that the Scarecrow and Woot the Wanderer should accompany him, as before. Polychrome also decided to join their party, somewhat to the surprise of all.

"I hate to be cooped up in a palace," she said to Ozma, "and of course the first time I meet my Rainbow I shall return to my own dear home in the skies, where my fairy sisters are even now awaiting me and my father is cross because I get lost so often. But I can find my Rainbow just as quickly while traveling in the Munchkin Country as I could if living in the Emerald City—or any other place in Oz—so I shall go with the Tin Woodman and help him woo Nimmie Amee."

Dorothy wanted to go, too, but as the Tin Woodman did not invite her to join his party, she felt she might be intruding if she asked to be taken. She hinted, but she found he didn't take the hint. It is quite a delicate matter for one to ask a girl to marry him, however much she loves him, and perhaps the Tin Woodman did not desire to have too many looking on when he found his old sweetheart, Nimmie

Amee. So Dorothy contented herself with the thought that she would help Ozma prepare a splendid wedding feast, to be followed by a round of parties and festivities when the Emperor of the Winkies reached the Emerald City with his bride.

Ozma offered to take them all in the Red Wagon to a place as near to the great Munchkin forest as a wagon could get. The Red Wagon was big enough to seat them all, and so, bidding good-bye to Jinjur, who gave Woot a basket of ripe cream-puffs and caramels to take with him, Ozma commanded the Wooden Saw-Horse to start, and the strange creature moved swiftly over the lanes and presently came to the Road of Yellow Bricks. This road led straight to a dense forest, where the path was too narrow for the Red Wagon to proceed farther, so here the party separated.

Ozma and Dorothy and Toto returned to the Emerald City, after wishing their friends a safe and successful journey, while the Tin Woodman, the Scarecrow, Woot the Wanderer and Polychrome, the Rainbow's Daughter, prepared to push their way through the thick forest. However, these forest paths were well known to the Tin Man and the Scarecrow, who felt quite at home among the trees.

"I was born in this grand forest," said Nick Chopper, the Tin Emperor, speaking proudly, "and it was here that the Witch enchanted my axe and I lost different parts of my meat body until I became all tin. Here, also—for it is a big forest—Nimmie Amee lived with the Wicked Witch, and at the other edge of the trees stands the cottage of my friend Ku-Klip, the famous tinsmith who made my present beautiful form."

"He must be a clever workman," declared Woot, admiringly.

"He is simply wonderful," declared the Tin Woodman.

"I shall be glad to make his acquaintance," said Woot.

"If you wish to meet with real cleverness," remarked the Scarecrow, "you should visit the Munchkin farmer who first made me. I won't say that my friend the Emperor isn't all right for a tin man, but any judge of beauty can understand that a Scarecrow is far more artistic and refined."

"You are too soft and flimsy," said the Tin Woodman.

"You are too hard and stiff," said the Scarecrow, and this was as near to quarreling as the two friends ever came. Polychrome laughed at them both, as well she might, and Woot hastened to change the subject.

At night they all camped underneath the trees. The boy ate cream-puffs for supper and offered Polychrome some, but she preferred other food and at daybreak sipped the dew that was clustered thick on the forest flowers. Then they tramped onward again, and presently the Scarecrow paused and said:

"It was on this very spot that Dorothy and I first met the Tin Woodman, who was rusted so badly that none of his joints would move. But after we had oiled him up, he was as good as new and accompanied us to the Emerald City."

"Ah, that was a sad experience," asserted the Tin Woodman soberly. "I was caught in a rainstorm while chopping down a tree for exercise, and before I realized it, I was firmly rusted in every joint. There I stood, axe in hand, but unable to move, for days and weeks and months! Indeed, I have never known exactly how long the time was; but finally along came Dorothy and I was saved. See! This is the very tree I was chopping at the time I rusted."

"You cannot be far from your old home, in that case," said Woot.

"No; my little cabin stands not a great way off, but there is no occasion for us to visit it. Our errand is with Nimmie Amee, and her house is somewhat farther away, to the left of us."

"Didn't you say she lives with a Wicked Witch, who makes her a slave?" asked the boy.

"She did, but she doesn't," was the reply. "I am told the Witch was destroyed when Dorothy's house fell on her, so now Nimmie Amee must live all alone. I haven't seen her, of course, since the Witch was crushed, for at that time I was standing rusted in the forest and had been there a long time, but the poor girl must have felt very happy to be free from her cruel mistress."

"Well," said the Scarecrow, "let's travel on and find Nimmie Amee. Lead on, Your Majesty, since you know the way, and we will follow."

So the Tin Woodman took a path that led through the thickest part of the forest, and they followed it for some time. The light was dim here, because vines and bushes and leafy foliage were all about them, and often the Tin Man had to push aside the branches that obstructed their way, or cut them off with his axe. After they had proceeded some distance, the Emperor suddenly stopped short and exclaimed: "Good gracious!"

The Scarecrow, who was next, first bumped into his friend and then peered around his tin body, and said in a tone of wonder:

"Well, I declare!"

Woot the Wanderer pushed forward to see what was the matter, and cried out in astonishment:

"For goodness sake!"

Then the three stood motionless, staring hard, until Polychrome's merry laughter rang out behind them and aroused them from their stupor.

In the path before them stood a tin man who was the exact duplicate of the Tin Woodman. He was of the same size, he was jointed in the same manner, and he was made of shining tin from top to toe. But he stood immovable, with his tin jaws half parted and his tin eyes turned upward. In one of his hands was held a long, gleaming sword. Yes, there was the difference, the only thing that distinguished him from the Emperor of the Winkies. This tin man bore a sword, while the Tin Woodman bore an axe.

"It's a dream; it *must* be a dream!" gasped Woot.

"That's it, of course," said the Scarecrow; "there couldn't be *two* Tin Woodmen."

"No," agreed Polychrome, dancing nearer to the stranger, "this one is a Tin Soldier. Don't you see his sword?"

The Tin Woodman cautiously put out one tin hand and felt of his double's arm. Then he said in a voice that trembled with emotion:

"Who are you, friend?"

There was no reply.

"Can't you see he's rusted, just as you were once?" asked Polychrome, laughing again. "Here, Nick Chopper, lend me your oil-can a minute!"

The Tin Woodman silently handed her his oil-can, without which he never traveled, and Polychrome first oiled the stranger's tin jaws and then worked them gently to and fro until the Tin Soldier said:

"That's enough. Thank you. I can now talk. But please oil my other joints."

Woot seized the oil-can and did this, but all the others helped wiggle the soldier's joints as soon as they were oiled, until they moved freely.

The Tin Soldier seemed highly pleased at his release. He strutted up and down the path, saying in a high, thin voice:

> "The Soldier is a splendid man
>   When marching on parade,
>   And when he meets the enemy
>   He never is afraid.
>   He rights the wrongs of nations,
>   His country's flag defends,
>   The foe he'll fight with great delight,
>   But seldom fights his friends."

CHAPTER XVI

CAPTAIN FYTER

"ARE YOU REALLY A SOLDIER?" ASKED WOOT, when they had all watched this strange tin person parade up and down the path and proudly flourish his sword.

"I was a soldier," was the reply, "but I've been a prisoner to Mr. Rust so long that I don't know exactly *what* I am."

"But—dear me!" cried the Tin Woodman, sadly perplexed; "how came you to be made of tin?"

"That," answered the Soldier, "is a sad, sad story. I was in love with a beautiful Munchkin girl, who lived with a Wicked Witch. The Witch did not wish me to marry the girl, so she enchanted my sword, which began hacking me to pieces. When I lost my legs I went to the tinsmith, Ku-Klip, and he made me some tin legs. When I lost my arms, Ku-Klip made me tin arms, and when I lost my head he made me this fine one out of tin. It was the same way with my body, and finally I was all tin. But I was not unhappy, for Ku-Klip made a good job of me, having had experience in making another tin man before me."

"Yes," observed the Tin Woodman, "it was Ku-Klip who made me. But, tell me, what was the name of the Munchkin girl you were in love with?"

"She is called Nimmie Amee," said the Tin Soldier.

Hearing this, they were all so astonished that they were silent for a time, regarding the stranger with wondering looks. Finally the Tin Woodman ventured to ask:

"And did Nimmie Amee return your love?"

"Not at first," admitted the Soldier. "When first I marched into the forest and met her, she was weeping over the loss of her former sweetheart, a woodman whose name was Nick Chopper."

"That is me," said the Tin Woodman.

"She told me he was nicer than a soldier, because he was all made of tin and shone beautifully in the sun. She said a tin man appealed to her artistic instincts more than an ordinary meat man, as I was then. But I did not despair, because her tin sweetheart had disappeared, and could not be found. And finally Nimmie Amee permitted me to call upon her and we became friends. It was then that the Wicked Witch discovered me and became furiously angry when I said I wanted to marry the girl. She enchanted my sword, as I said, and then my troubles began. When I got my tin legs, Nimmie Amee began to take an interest in me; when I got my tin arms, she began to like me better than ever, and when I was all made of tin, she said I looked like her dear Nick Chopper and she would be willing to marry me.

"The day of our wedding was set, and it turned out to be a rainy day. Nevertheless I started out to get Nimmie Amee, because the Witch had been absent for some time, and we meant to elope before she got back. As I traveled the forest paths the rain wetted my joints, but I paid no attention to this because my thoughts were all on my wedding with beautiful Nimmie Amee and I could think of nothing else until suddenly my legs stopped moving. Then my arms rusted at the joints and I became frightened and cried for help, for now I was unable to oil myself. No one heard my calls and before long my jaws rusted, and I was unable to utter another sound. So I stood helpless in this spot, hoping some wanderer would come my way and save me. But this forest path is seldom used, and I have been standing here so long that I have lost all track of time. In my mind I composed poetry and sang songs, but not a sound have I been able to utter. But this desperate condition has now been relieved by your coming my way and I must thank you for my rescue."

"This is wonderful!" said the Scarecrow, heaving a stuffy, long sigh. "I think Ku-Klip was wrong to make two tin men, just alike, and the strangest thing of all is that both you tin men fell in love with the same girl."

"As for that," returned the Soldier, seriously, "I must admit I lost my ability to love when I lost my meat heart. Ku-Klip gave me a tin heart, to be sure, but it doesn't love anything, as far as I can discover, and merely rattles against my tin ribs, which makes me wish I had no heart at all."

"Yet, in spite of this condition, you were going to marry Nimmie Amee?"

"Well, you see I had promised to marry her, and I am an honest man and always try to keep my promises. I didn't like to disappoint the poor girl, who had been disappointed by one tin man already."

"That was not my fault," declared the Emperor of the Winkies, and then he related how he, also, had rusted in the forest and after a long time had been rescued by Dorothy and the Scarecrow and had traveled with them to the Emerald City in search of a heart that could love.

"If you have found such a heart, sir," said the Soldier, "I will gladly allow you to marry Nimmie Amee in my place."

"If she loves you best, sir," answered the Woodman, "I shall not interfere with your wedding her. For, to be quite frank with you, I cannot yet love Nimmie Amee as I did before I became tin."

"Still, one of you ought to marry the poor girl," remarked Woot; "and, if she likes tin men, there is not much choice between you. Why don't you draw lots for her?"

"That wouldn't be right," said the Scarecrow.

"The girl should be permitted to choose her own husband," asserted Polychrome. "You should both go to her and allow her to take her choice. Then she will surely be happy."

"That, to me, seems a very fair arrangement," said the Tin Soldier.

"I agree to it," said the Tin Woodman, shaking the hand of his twin to show the matter was settled. "May I ask your name, sir?" he continued.

"Before I was so cut up," replied the other, "I was known as Captain Fyter, but afterward I was merely called 'The Tin Soldier.'"

"Well, Captain, if you are agreeable, let us now go to Nimmie Amee's house and let her choose between us."

"Very well; and if we meet the Witch, we will both fight her—you with your axe and I with my sword."

"The Witch is destroyed," announced the Scarecrow, and as they walked away he told the Tin Soldier of much that had happened in the Land of Oz since he had stood rusted in the forest.

"I must have stood there longer than I had imagined," he said thoughtfully.

CHAPTER XVII

THE WORKSHOP OF KU-KLIP

IT WAS NOT MORE THAN A TWO HOURS' JOURNEY to the house where Nimmie Amee had lived, but when our travelers arrived there they found the place deserted. The door was partly off its hinges, the roof had fallen in at the rear and the interior of the cottage was thick with dust. Not only was the place vacant, but it was evident that no one had lived there for a long time.

"I suppose," said the Scarecrow, as they all stood looking wonderingly at the ruined house, "that after the Wicked Witch was destroyed, Nimmie Amee became lonely and went somewhere else to live."

"One could scarcely expect a young girl to live all alone in a forest," added Woot. "She would want company, of course, and so I believe she has gone where other people live."

"And perhaps she is still crying her poor little heart out because no tin man comes to marry her," suggested Polychrome.

"Well, in that case, it is the clear duty of you two tin persons to seek Nimmie Amee until you find her," declared the Scarecrow.

"I do not know where to look for the girl," said the Tin Soldier, "for I am almost a stranger to this part of the country."

"I was born here," said the Tin Woodman, "but the forest has few inhabitants except the wild beasts. I cannot think of anyone living near here with whom Nimmie Amee might care to live."

"Why not go to Ku-Klip and ask him what has become of the girl?" proposed Polychrome.

That struck them all as being a good suggestion, so once more they started to tramp through the forest, taking the direct path to Ku-Klip's house, for both the tin twins knew the way, having followed it many times.

Ku-Klip lived at the far edge of the great forest, his house facing the broad plains of the Munchkin Country that lay to the eastward. But, when they came to this residence by the forest's edge, the tinsmith was not at home.

It was a pretty place, all painted dark blue with trimmings of lighter blue. There was a neat blue fence around the yard and several blue benches had been placed underneath the shady blue trees which marked the line between forest and plain. There was a blue lawn before the house, which was a good sized building. Ku-Klip lived in the front part of the house and had his work-shop in the back part, where he had also built a lean-to addition, in order to give him more room.

Although they found the tinsmith absent on their arrival, there was smoke coming out of his chimney, which proved that he would soon return.

"And perhaps Nimmie Amee will be with him," said the Scarecrow in a cheerful voice.

While they waited, the Tin Woodman went to the door of the workshop and, finding it unlocked, entered and looked curiously around the room where he had been made.

"It seems almost like home to me," he told his friends, who had followed him in. "The first time I came here I had lost a leg, so I had to carry it in my hand while I hopped on the other leg all the way from the place in the forest where the enchanted axe cut me. I remember that old Ku-Klip carefully put my meat leg into a barrel—I think that is the same barrel, still standing in the corner yonder—and then at once

he began to make a tin leg for me. He worked fast and with skill, and I was much interested in the job."

"My experience was much the same," said the Tin Soldier. "I used to bring all the parts of me, which the enchanted sword had cut away, here to the tinsmith, and Ku-Klip would put them into the barrel."

"I wonder," said Woot, "if those cast-off parts of you two unfortunates are still in that barrel in the corner?"

"I suppose so," replied the Tin Woodman. "In the Land of Oz no part of a living creature can ever be destroyed."

"If that is true, how was that Wicked Witch destroyed?" inquired Woot.

"Why, she was very old and was all dried up and withered before Oz became a fairyland," explained the Scarecrow. "Only her magic arts had kept her alive so long, and when Dorothy's house fell upon her she just turned to dust, and was blown away and scattered by the wind. I do not think, however, that the parts cut away from these two young men could ever be entirely destroyed and, if they are still in those barrels, they are likely to be just the same as when the enchanted axe or sword severed them."

"It doesn't matter, however," said the Tin Woodman; "our tin bodies are more brilliant and durable, and quite satisfy us."

"Yes, the tin bodies are best," agreed the Tin Soldier. "Nothing can hurt them."

"Unless they get dented or rusted," said Woot, but both the tin men frowned on him.

Scraps of tin, of all shapes and sizes, lay scattered around the workshop. Also there were hammers and anvils and soldering irons and a charcoal furnace and many other tools such as a tinsmith works with. Against two of the side walls had been built stout work-benches and in the center of the room was a long table. At the end of the shop, which adjoined the dwelling, were several cupboards.

After examining the interior of the workshop until his curiosity was satisfied, Woot said:

"I think I will go outside until Ku-Klip comes. It does not seem quite proper for us to take possession of his house while he is absent."

"That is true," agreed the Scarecrow, and they were all about to leave the room when the Tin Woodman said: "Wait a minute," and they halted in obedience to the command.

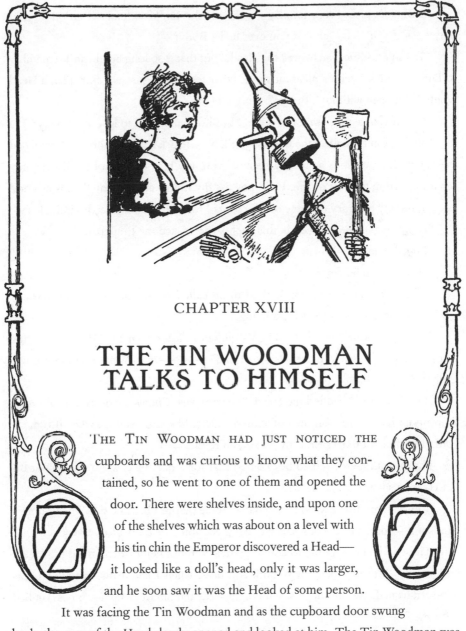

CHAPTER XVIII

THE TIN WOODMAN TALKS TO HIMSELF

THE TIN WOODMAN HAD JUST NOTICED THE cupboards and was curious to know what they contained, so he went to one of them and opened the door. There were shelves inside, and upon one of the shelves which was about on a level with his tin chin the Emperor discovered a Head— it looked like a doll's head, only it was larger, and he soon saw it was the Head of some person.

It was facing the Tin Woodman and as the cupboard door swung back, the eyes of the Head slowly opened and looked at him. The Tin Woodman was not at all surprised, for in the Land of Oz one runs into magic at every turn.

"Dear me!" said the Tin Woodman, staring hard. "It seems as if I had met you, somewhere, before. Good morning, sir!"

"You have the advantage of me," replied the Head. "I never saw you before in my life."

"Still, your face is very familiar," persisted the Tin Woodman. "Pardon me, but may I ask if you—eh—eh—if you ever had a Body?"

"Yes, at one time," answered the Head, "but that is so long ago I can't remember it. Did you think," with a pleasant smile, "that I was born just as I am? That a Head would be created without a Body?"

"No, of course not," said the other. "But how came you to lose your body?"

"Well, I can't recollect the details; you'll have to ask Ku-Klip about it," returned the Head. "For, curious as it may seem to you, my memory is not good since my separation from the rest of me. I still possess my brains and my intellect is as good as ever, but my memory of some of the events I formerly experienced is quite hazy."

"How long have you been in this cupboard?" asked the Emperor.

"I don't know."

"Haven't you a name?"

"Oh, yes," said the Head; "I used to be called Nick Chopper, when I was a woodman and cut down trees for a living."

"Good gracious!" cried the Tin Woodman in astonishment. "If you are Nick Chopper's Head, then you are *Me*—or I'm *You*—or—or— What relation are we, anyhow?"

"Don't ask me," replied the Head. "For my part, I'm not anxious to claim relationship with any common, manufactured article, like you. You may be all right in your class, but your class isn't my class. You're tin."

The poor Emperor felt so bewildered that for a time he could only stare at his old Head in silence. Then he said:

"I must admit that I wasn't at all bad looking before I became tin. You're almost handsome—for meat. If your hair was combed, you'd be quite attractive."

"How do you expect me to comb my hair without help?" demanded the Head, indignantly. "I used to keep it smooth and neat, when I had arms, but after I was removed from the rest of me, my hair got mussed, and old Ku-Klip never has combed it for me."

"I'll speak to him about it," said the Tin Woodman. "Do you remember loving a pretty Munchkin girl named Nimmie Amee?"

"No," answered the Head. "That is a foolish question. The heart in my body— when I had a body—might have loved someone, for all I know, but a head isn't made to love; it's made to think."

"Oh; do you think, then?"

"I used to think."

"You must have been shut up in this cupboard for years and years. What have you thought about, in all that time?"

"Nothing. That's another foolish question. A little reflection will convince you that I have had nothing to think about, except the boards on the inside of the cupboard door, and it didn't take me long to think of everything about those boards that could be thought of. Then, of course, I quit thinking."

"And are you happy?"

"Happy? What's that?"

"Don't you know what happiness is?" inquired the Tin Woodman.

"I haven't the faintest idea whether it's round or square, or black or white, or what it is. And, if you will pardon my lack of interest in it, I will say that I don't care."

The Tin Woodman was much puzzled by these answers. His traveling companions had grouped themselves at his back, and had fixed their eyes on the Head and listened to the conversation with much interest, but until now, they had not interrupted because they thought the Tin Woodman had the best right to talk to his own head and renew acquaintance with it.

But now the Tin Soldier remarked:

"I wonder if my old head happens to be in any of these cupboards," and he proceeded to open all the cupboard doors. But no other head was to be found on any of the shelves.

"Oh, well; never mind," said Woot the Wanderer; "I can't imagine what anyone wants of a cast-off head, anyhow."

"I can understand the Soldier's interest," asserted Polychrome, dancing around the grimy workshop until her draperies formed a cloud around her dainty form. "For sentimental reasons a man might like to see his old head once more, just as one likes to revisit an old home."

"And then to kiss it good-bye," added the Scarecrow.

"I hope that tin thing won't try to kiss me good-bye!" exclaimed the Tin Woodman's former head. "And I don't see what right you folks have to disturb my peace and comfort, either."

"You belong to me," the Tin Woodman declared.

"I do not!"

"You and I are one."

"We've been parted," asserted the Head. "It would be unnatural for me to have any interest in a man made of tin. Please close the door and leave me alone."

"I did not think that my old Head could be so disagreeable," said the Emperor. "I—I'm quite ashamed of myself; meaning you."

"You ought to be glad that I've enough sense to know what my rights are," retorted the Head. "In this cupboard I am leading a simple life, peaceful and dignified, and when a mob of people in whom I am not interested disturb me, they are the disagreeable ones; not I."

With a sigh the Tin Woodman closed and latched the cupboard door and turned away.

"Well," said the Tin Soldier, "if my old head would have treated me as coldly and in so unfriendly a manner as your old head has treated you, friend Chopper, I'm glad I could not find it."

"Yes; I'm rather surprised at my head, myself," replied the Tin Woodman, thoughtfully. "I thought I had a more pleasant disposition when I was made of meat."

But just then old Ku-Klip the Tinsmith arrived, and he seemed surprised to find so many visitors. Ku-Klip was a stout man and a short man. He had his sleeves rolled above his elbows, showing muscular arms, and he wore a leathern apron that covered all the front of him, and was so long that Woot was surprised he didn't step on it and trip whenever he walked. And Ku-Klip had a gray beard that was almost as long as his apron, and his head was bald on top and his ears stuck out from his head like two fans. Over his eyes, which were bright and twinkling, he wore big spectacles. It was easy to see that the tinsmith was a kind hearted man, as well as a merry and agreeable one.

"Oh-ho!" he cried in a joyous bass voice; "here are both my tin men come to visit me, and they and their friends are welcome indeed. I'm very proud of you two characters, I assure you, for you are so perfect that you are proof that I'm a good workman. Sit down. Sit down, all of you—if you can find anything to sit on—and tell me why you are here."

So they found seats and told him all of their adventures that they thought he would like to know. Ku-Klip was glad to learn that Nick Chopper, the Tin Woodman, was now Emperor of the Winkies and a friend of Ozma of Oz, and the tinsmith was also interested in the Scarecrow and Polychrome.

He turned the straw man around, examining him curiously, and patted him on all sides, and then said:

"You are certainly wonderful, but I think you would be more durable and steady on your legs if you were made of tin. Would you like me to—"

"No, indeed!" interrupted the Scarecrow hastily; "I like myself better as I am."

But to Polychrome the tinsmith said:

"Nothing could improve *you*, my dear, for you are the most beautiful maiden I have ever seen. It is pure happiness just to look at you."

"That is praise, indeed, from so skillful a workman," returned the Rainbow's Daughter, laughing and dancing in and out the room.

"Then it must be this boy you wish me to help," said Ku-Klip, looking at Woot.

"No," said Woot, "we are not here to seek your skill, but have merely come to you for information."

Then, between them, they related their search for Nimmie Amee, whom the Tin Woodman explained he had resolved to marry, yet who had promised to become the bride of the Tin Soldier before he unfortunately became rusted. And when the story was told, they asked Ku-Klip if he knew what had become of Nimmie Amee.

"Not exactly," replied the old man, "but I know that she wept bitterly when the Tin Soldier did not come to marry her, as he had promised to do. The old Witch was so provoked at the girl's tears that she beat Nimmie Amee with her crooked stick and then hobbled away to gather some magic herbs, with which she intended to transform the girl into an old hag, so that no one would again love her or care to marry her. It was while she was away on this errand that Dorothy's house fell on the Wicked Witch, and she turned to dust and blew away. When I heard this good news, I sent Nimmie Amee to find the silver shoes which the Witch had worn, but Dorothy had taken them with her to the Emerald City."

"Yes, we know all about those silver shoes," said the Scarecrow.

"Well," continued Ku-Klip, "after that, Nimmie Amee decided to go away from the forest and live with some people she was acquainted with who had a house on Mount Munch. I have never seen the girl since."

"Do you know the name of the people on Mount Munch, with whom she went to live?" asked the Tin Woodman.

"No, Nimmie Amee did not mention her friend's name, and I did not ask her. She took with her all that she could carry of the goods that were in the Witch's house, and she told me I could have the rest. But when I went there I found nothing worth taking except some magic powders that I did not know how to use, and a bottle of Magic Glue."

"What is Magic Glue?" asked Woot.

"It is a magic preparation with which to mend people when they cut themselves. One time, long ago, I cut off one of my fingers by accident, and I carried it to the Witch, who took down her bottle and glued it on again for me. See!" showing them his finger, "it is as good as ever it was. No one else that I ever heard of had this Magic Glue, and of course when Nick Chopper cut himself to pieces with his enchanted axe and Captain Fyter cut himself to pieces with his enchanted sword, the Witch would not mend them, or allow me to glue them together, because she had herself wickedly enchanted the axe and sword. Nothing remained but for me to make them new parts out of tin; but, as you see, tin answered the purpose very well, and I am sure their tin bodies are a great improvement on their meat bodies."

"Very true," said the Tin Soldier.

"I quite agree with you," said the Tin Woodman. "I happened to find my old head in your cupboard, a while ago, and certainly it is not as desirable a head as the tin one I now wear."

"By the way," said the Tin Soldier, "what ever became of *my* old head, Ku-Klip?"

"And of the different parts of our bodies?" added the Tin Woodman.

"Let me think a minute," replied Ku-Klip. "If I remember right, you two boys used to bring me most of your parts, when they were cut off, and I saved them in that barrel in the corner. You must not have brought me all the parts, for when I made Chopfyt I had hard work finding enough pieces to complete the job. I finally had to finish him with one arm."

"Who is Chopfyt?" inquired Woot.

"Oh, haven't I told you about Chopfyt?" exclaimed Ku-Klip. "Of course not! And he's quite a curiosity, too. You'll be interested in hearing about Chopfyt. This is how he happened:

"One day, after the Witch had been destroyed and Nimmie Amee had gone to live with her friends on Mount Munch, I was looking around the shop for something and came upon the bottle of Magic Glue which I had brought from the old Witch's house. It occurred to me to piece together the odds and ends of you two people, which of course were just as good as ever, and see if I couldn't make a man out of them. If I succeeded, I would have an assistant to help me with my work, and I thought it would be a clever idea to put to some practical use the scraps of Nick Chopper and Captain Fyter. There were two perfectly good heads in my cupboard, and a lot of feet and legs and parts of bodies in the barrel, so I set to work to see what I could do.

"First, I pieced together a body, gluing it with the Witch's Magic Glue, which worked perfectly. That was the hardest part of my job, however, because the bodies didn't match up well and some parts were missing. But by using a piece of Captain Fyter here and a piece of Nick Chopper there, I finally got together a very decent body, with heart and all the trimmings complete."

"Whose heart did you use in making the body?" asked the Tin Woodman anxiously.

"I can't tell, for the parts had no tags on them and one heart looks much like another. After the body was completed, I glued two fine legs and feet onto it. One leg was Nick Chopper's and one was Captain Fyter's and, finding one leg longer than the other, I trimmed it down to make them match. I was much disappointed to find that I had but one arm. There was an extra leg in the barrel, but I could find only one arm. Having glued this onto the body, I was ready for the head, and I had some difficulty in making up my mind which head to use. Finally I shut my eyes and reached out my hand toward the cupboard shelf, and the first head I touched I glued upon my new man."

"It was mine!" declared the Tin Soldier, gloomily.

"No, it was mine," asserted Ku-Klip, "for I had given you another in exchange for it—the beautiful tin head you now wear. When the glue had dried, my man was quite an interesting fellow. I named him Chopfyt, using a part of Nick Chopper's name and a part of Captain Fyter's name, because he was a mixture of both your cast-off parts. Chopfyt was interesting, as I said, but he did not prove a very agreeable companion. He complained bitterly because I had given him but one arm—as if it were my fault!—and he grumbled because the suit of blue Munchkin clothes, which I got for him from a neighbor, did not fit him perfectly."

"Ah, that was because he was wearing my old head," remarked the Tin Soldier. "I remember that head used to be very particular about its clothes."

"As an assistant," the old tinsmith continued, "Chopfyt was not a success. He was awkward with tools and was always hungry. He demanded something to eat six or eight times a day, so I wondered if I had fitted his insides properly. Indeed, Chopfyt ate so much that little food was left for myself; so, when he proposed, one day, to go out into the world and seek adventures, I was delighted to be rid of him. I even made him a tin arm to take the place of the missing one, and that pleased him very much, so that we parted good friends."

"What became of Chopfyt after that?" the Scarecrow inquired.

"I never heard. He started off toward the east, into the plains of the Munchkin Country, and that was the last I ever saw of him."

"It seems to me," said the Tin Woodman reflectively, "that you did wrong in making a man out of our cast-off parts. It is evident that Chopfyt could, with justice, claim relationship with both of us."

"Don't worry about that," advised Ku-Klip cheerfully; "it is not likely that you will ever meet the fellow. And, if you should meet him, he doesn't know who he is made of, for I never told him the secret of his manufacture. Indeed, you are the only ones who know of it, and you may keep the secret to yourselves, if you wish to."

"Never mind Chopfyt," said the Scarecrow. "Our business now is to find poor Nimmie Amee and let her choose her tin husband. To do that, it seems, from the information Ku-Klip has given us, we must travel to Mount Munch."

"If that's the programme, let us start at once," suggested Woot.

So they all went outside, where they found Polychrome dancing about among the trees and talking with the birds and laughing as merrily as if she had not lost her Rainbow and so been separated from all her fairy sisters.

They told her they were going to Mount Munch, and she replied:

"Very well; I am as likely to find my Rainbow there as here, and any other place is as likely as there. It all depends on the weather. Do you think it looks like rain?"

They shook their heads, and Polychrome laughed again and danced on after them when they resumed their journey.

CHAPTER XIX

THE INVISIBLE COUNTRY

THEY WERE PROCEEDING SO EASILY AND COMFORTABLY on their way to Mount Munch that Woot said in a serious tone of voice:

"I'm afraid something is going to happen."

"Why?" asked Polychrome, dancing around the group of travelers.

"Because," said the boy, thoughtfully, "I've noticed that when we have the least reason for getting into trouble, something is sure to go wrong. Just now the weather is delightful; the grass is beautifully blue and quite soft to our feet; the mountain we are seeking shows clearly in the distance and there is no reason anything should happen to delay us in getting there. Our troubles all seem to be over, and—well, that's why I'm afraid," he added, with a sigh.

"Dear me!" remarked the Scarecrow, "what unhappy thoughts you have, to be sure. This is proof that born brains cannot equal manufactured brains, for my brains dwell only on facts and never borrow trouble. When there is occasion for my brains to think, they think, but I would be ashamed of my brains if they kept shooting out thoughts that were merely fears and imaginings, such as do no good, but are likely to do harm."

"For my part," said the Tin Woodman, "I do not think at all, but allow my velvet heart to guide me at all times."

"The tinsmith filled my hollow head with scraps and clippings of tin," said the Soldier, "and he told me they would do nicely for brains, but when I begin to think, the tin scraps rattle around and get so mixed that I'm soon bewildered. So I try not to think. My tin heart is almost as useless to me, for it is hard and cold, so I'm sure the red velvet heart of my friend Nick Chopper is a better guide."

"Thoughtless people are not unusual," observed the Scarecrow, "but I consider them more fortunate than those who have useless or wicked thoughts and do not try to curb them. Your oil-can, friend Woodman, is filled with oil, but you only apply the oil to your joints, drop by drop, as you need it, and do not keep spilling it where it will do no good. Thoughts should be restrained in the same way as your oil, and only applied when necessary, and for a good purpose. If used carefully, thoughts are good things to have."

Polychrome laughed at him, for the Rainbow's Daughter knew more about thoughts than the Scarecrow did. But the others were solemn, feeling they had been rebuked, and tramped on in silence.

Suddenly Woot, who was in the lead, looked around and found that all his comrades had mysteriously disappeared. But where could they have gone to? The broad plain was all about him and there were neither trees nor bushes that could hide even a rabbit, nor any hole for one to fall into. Yet there he stood, alone.

Surprise had caused him to halt, and with a thoughtful and puzzled expression on his face he looked down at his feet. It startled him anew to discover that he had no feet. He reached out his hands, but he could not see them. He could feel his hands and arms and body; he stamped his feet on the grass and knew they were there, but in some strange way they had become invisible.

While Woot stood, wondering, a crash of metal sounded in his ears and he heard two heavy bodies tumble to the earth just beside him.

"Good gracious!" exclaimed the voice of the Tin Woodman.

"Mercy me!" cried the voice of the Tin Soldier.

"Why didn't you look where you were going?" asked the Tin Woodman reproachfully.

"I did, but I couldn't see you," said the Tin Soldier. "Something has happened to my tin eyes. I can't see you, even now, nor can I see anyone else!"

"It's the same way with me," admitted the Tin Woodman.

Woot couldn't see either of them, although he heard them plainly, and just then something smashed against him unexpectedly and knocked him over; but it was only the straw-stuffed body of the Scarecrow that fell upon him and while he could not see the Scarecrow he managed to push him off and rose to his feet just as Polychrome whirled against him and made him tumble again.

Sitting upon the ground, the boy asked:

"Can you see us, Poly?"

"No, indeed," answered the Rainbow's Daughter; "we've all become invisible."

"How did it happen, do you suppose?" inquired the Scarecrow, lying where he had fallen.

"We have met with no enemy," answered Polychrome, "so it must be that this part of the country has the magic quality of making people invisible—even fairies falling under the charm. We can see the grass, and the flowers, and the stretch of plain before us, and we can still see Mount Munch in the distance; but we cannot see ourselves or one another."

"Well, what are we to do about it?" demanded Woot.

"I think this magic affects only a small part of the plain," replied Polychrome; "perhaps there is only a streak of the country where an enchantment makes people become invisible. So, if we get together and hold hands, we can travel toward Mount Munch until the enchanted streak is passed."

"All right," said Woot, jumping up, "give me your hand, Polychrome. Where are you?"

"Here," she answered. "Whistle, Woot, and keep whistling until I come to you."

So Woot whistled, and presently Polychrome found him and grasped his hand.

"Someone must help me up," said the Scarecrow, lying near them; so they found the straw man and sat him upon his feet, after which he held fast to Polychrome's other hand.

Nick Chopper and the Tin Soldier had managed to scramble up without assistance, but it was awkward for them and the Tin Woodman said:

"I don't seem to stand straight, somehow. But my joints all work, so I guess I can walk."

Guided by his voice, they reached his side, where Woot grasped his tin fingers so they might keep together.

The Tin Soldier was standing near by and the Scarecrow soon touched him and took hold of his arm.

"I hope you're not wobbly," said the straw man, "for if two of us walk unsteadily we will be sure to fall."

"I'm not wobbly," the Tin Soldier assured him, "but I'm certain that one of my legs is shorter than the other. I can't see it, to tell what's gone wrong, but I'll limp on with the rest of you until we are out of this enchanted territory."

They now formed a line, holding hands, and turning their faces toward Mount Munch resumed their journey. They had not gone far, however, when a terrible growl saluted their ears. The sound seemed to come from a place just in front of them, so they halted abruptly and remained silent, listening with all their ears.

"I smell straw!" cried a hoarse, harsh voice, with more growls and snarls. "I smell straw, and I'm a Hip-po-gy-raf who loves straw and eats all he can find. I want to eat this straw! Where is it? Where is it?"

The Scarecrow, hearing this, trembled but kept silent. All the others were silent, too, hoping that the invisible beast would be unable to find them. But the creature sniffed the odor of the straw and drew nearer and nearer to them until he reached the Tin Woodman, on one end of the line. It was a big beast and it smelled of the Tin Woodman and grated two rows of enormous teeth against the Emperor's tin body.

"Bah! that's not straw," said the harsh voice, and the beast advanced along the line to Woot.

"Meat! Pooh, you're no good! I can't eat meat," grumbled the beast, and passed on to Polychrome.

"Sweetmeats and perfume—cobwebs and dew! Nothing to eat in a fairy like you," said the creature.

Now, the Scarecrow was next to Polychrome in the line, and he realized if the beast devoured his straw he would be helpless for a long time, because the last farmhouse was far behind them and only grass covered the vast expanse of plain. So in his fright he let go of Polychrome's hand and put the hand of the Tin Soldier in that of the Rainbow's Daughter. Then he slipped back of the line and went to the other end, where he silently seized the Tin Woodman's hand.

Meantime, the beast had smelled the Tin Soldier and found he was the last of the line.

"That's funny!" growled the Hip-po-gy-raf; "I can smell straw, but I can't find it. Well, it's here, somewhere, and I must hunt around until I *do* find it, for I'm hungry."

His voice was now at the left of them, so they started on, hoping to avoid him, and traveled as fast as they could in the direction of Mount Munch.

"I don't like this invisible country," said Woot with a shudder. "We can't tell how many dreadful, invisible beasts are roaming around us, or what danger we'll come to next."

"Quit thinking about danger, please," said the Scarecrow, warningly.

"Why?" asked the boy.

"If you think of some dreadful thing, it's liable to happen, but if you don't think of it, and no one else thinks of it, it just *can't* happen. Do you see?"

"No," answered Woot. "I won't be able to see much of anything until we escape from this enchantment."

But they got out of the invisible strip of country as suddenly as they had entered it, and the instant they got out they stopped short, for just before them was a deep ditch, running at right angles as far as their eyes could see and stopping all further progress toward Mount Munch.

"It's not so very wide," said Woot, "but I'm sure none of us can jump across it."

Polychrome began to laugh, and the Scarecrow said: "What's the matter?"

"Look at the tin men!" she said, with another burst of merry laughter.

Woot and the Scarecrow looked, and the tin men looked at themselves.

"It was the collision," said the Tin Woodman regretfully. "I knew something was wrong with me, and now I can see that my side is dented in so that I lean over toward the left. It was the Soldier's fault; he shouldn't have been so careless."

"It is your fault that my right leg is bent, making it shorter than the other, so that I limp badly," retorted the Soldier. "You shouldn't have stood where I was walking."

"You shouldn't have walked where I was standing," replied the Tin Woodman.

It was almost a quarrel, so Polychrome said soothingly:

"Never mind, friends; as soon as we have time I am sure we can straighten the Soldier's leg and get the dent out of the Woodman's body. The Scarecrow needs patting into shape, too, for he had a bad tumble, but our first task is to get over this ditch."

"Yes, the ditch is the most important thing, just now," added Woot.

They were standing in a row, looking hard at the unexpected barrier, when a fierce growl from behind them made them all turn quickly. Out of the invisible country marched a huge beast with a thick, leathery skin and a surprisingly long neck. The head on the top of this neck was broad and flat and the eyes and mouth were very big and the nose and ears very small. When the head was drawn down toward the beast's shoulders, the neck was all wrinkles, but the head could shoot up very high indeed, if the creature wished it to.

"Dear me!" exclaimed the Scarecrow, "this must be the Hip-po-gy-raf."

"Quite right," said the beast; "and you're the straw which I'm to eat for my dinner. Oh, how I love straw! I hope you don't resent my affectionate appetite?"

With its four great legs it advanced straight toward the Scarecrow, but the Tin Woodman and the Tin Soldier both sprang in front of their friend and flourished their weapons.

"Keep off!" said the Tin Woodman, warningly, "or I'll chop you with my axe."

"Keep off!" said the Tin Soldier, "or I'll cut you with my sword."

"Would you really do that?" asked the Hip-po-gy-raf, in a disappointed voice.

"We would," they both replied, and the Tin Woodman added: "The Scarecrow is our friend, and he would be useless without his straw stuffing. So, as we are comrades, faithful and true, we will defend our friend's stuffing against all enemies."

The Hip-po-gy-raf sat down and looked at them sorrowfully.

"When one has made up his mind to have a meal of delicious straw, and then finds he can't have it, it is certainly hard luck," he said. "And what good is the straw man to you, or to himself, when the ditch keeps you from going any further?"

"Well, we can go back again," suggested Woot.

"True," said the Hip-po; "and if you do, you'll be as disappointed as I am. That's some comfort, anyhow."

The travelers looked at the beast, and then they looked across the ditch at the level plain beyond. On the other side the grass had grown tall, and the sun had dried it, so there was a fine crop of hay that only needed to be cut and stacked.

"Why don't you cross over and eat hay?" the boy asked the beast.

"I'm not fond of hay," replied the Hip-po-gy-raf; "straw is much more delicious, to my notion, and it's more scarce in this neighborhood, too. Also I must confess that I can't get across the ditch, for my body is too heavy and clumsy for me to jump the distance. I can stretch my neck across, though, and you will notice that I've nibbled the hay on the farther edge—not because I liked it, but because one must eat, and if one can't get the sort of food he desires, he must take what is offered or go hungry."

"Ah, I see you are a philosopher," remarked the Scarecrow.

"No, I'm just a Hip-po-gy-raf," was the reply.

Polychrome was not afraid of the big beast. She danced close to him and said:

"If you can stretch your neck across the ditch, why not help us over? We can sit on your big head, one at a time, and then you can lift us across."

"Yes; I *can*, it is true," answered the Hip-po; "but I refuse to do it. Unless—" he added, and stopped short.

"Unless what?" asked Polychrome.

"Unless you first allow me to eat the straw with which the Scarecrow is stuffed."

"No," said the Rainbow's Daughter, "that is too high a price to pay. Our friend's straw is nice and fresh, for he was restuffed only a little while ago."

"I know," agreed the Hip-po-gy-raf. "That's why I want it. If it was old, musty straw, I wouldn't care for it."

"*Please* lift us across," pleaded Polychrome.

"No," replied the beast; "since you refuse my generous offer, I can be as stubborn as you are."

After that they were all silent for a time, but then the Scarecrow said bravely:

"Friends, let us agree to the beast's terms. Give him my straw, and carry the rest of me with you across the ditch. Once on the other side, the Tin Soldier can cut some of the hay with his sharp sword, and you can stuff me with that material until we reach a place where there is straw. It is true I have been stuffed with straw all my life and it will be somewhat humiliating to be filled with common hay, but I am willing to sacrifice my pride in a good cause. Moreover, to abandon our errand and so deprive the great Emperor of the Winkies—or this noble Soldier—of his bride, would be equally humiliating, if not more so."

"You're a very honest and clever man!" exclaimed the Hip-po-gy-raf, admiringly. "When I have eaten your head, perhaps I also will become clever."

"You're not to eat my head, you know," returned the Scarecrow hastily. "My head isn't stuffed with straw and I cannot part with it. When one loses his head he loses his brains."

"Very well, then; you may keep your head," said the beast.

The Scarecrow's companions thanked him warmly for his loyal sacrifice to their mutual good, and then he laid down and permitted them to pull the straw from his body. As fast as they did this, the Hip-po-gy-raf ate up the straw, and when all was consumed Polychrome made a neat bundle of the clothes and boots and gloves and hat and said she would carry them, while Woot tucked the Scarecrow's head under his arm and promised to guard its safety.

"Now, then," said the Tin Woodman, "keep your promise, Beast, and lift us over the ditch."

"M-m-m-mum, but that was a fine dinner!" said the Hip-po, smacking his thick lips in satisfaction, "and I'm as good as my word. Sit on my head, one at a time, and I'll land you safely on the other side."

He approached close to the edge of the ditch and squatted down. Polychrome climbed over his big body and sat herself lightly upon the flat head, holding the bundle of the Scarecrow's raiment in her hand. Slowly the elastic neck stretched out until it reached the far side of the ditch, when the beast lowered his head and permitted the beautiful fairy to leap to the ground.

Woot made the queer journey next, and then the Tin Soldier and the Tin Woodman went over, and all were well pleased to have overcome this serious barrier to their progress.

"Now, Soldier, cut the hay," said the Scarecrow's head, which was still held by Woot the Wanderer.

"I'd like to, but I can't stoop over, with my bent leg, without falling," replied Captain Fyter.

"What can we do about that leg, anyhow?" asked Woot, appealing to Polychrome.

She danced around in a circle several times without replying, and the boy feared she had not heard him; but the Rainbow's Daughter was merely thinking upon the problem, and presently she paused beside the Tin Soldier and said:

"I've been taught a little fairy magic, but I've never before been asked to mend tin legs with it, so I'm not sure I can help you. It all depends on the good will of my unseen fairy guardians, so I'll try, and if I fail, you will be no worse off than you are now."

She danced around the circle again, and then laid both hands upon the twisted tin leg and sang in her sweet voice:

> "Fairy Powers, come to my aid!
> This bent leg of tin is made;
> Make it straight and strong and true,
> And I'll render thanks to you."

"Ah!" murmured Captain Fyter in a glad voice, as she withdrew her hands and danced away, and they saw he was standing straight as ever, because his leg was as shapely and strong as it had been before his accident.

The Tin Woodman had watched Polychrome with much interest, and he now said:

"Please take the dent out of my side, Poly, for I am more crippled than was the Soldier."

So the Rainbow's Daughter touched his side lightly and sang:

> "Here's a dent by accident;
> Such a thing was never meant.
> Fairy Powers, so wondrous great,
> Make our dear Tin Woodman straight!"

"Good!" cried the Emperor, again standing erect and strutting around to show his fine figure. "Your fairy magic may not be able to accomplish all things, sweet Polychrome, but it works splendidly on tin. Thank you very much."

"The hay—the hay!" pleaded the Scarecrow's head.

"Oh, yes; the hay," said Woot. "What are you waiting for, Captain Fyter?"

At once the Tin Soldier set to work cutting hay with his sword and in a few minutes there was quite enough with which to stuff the Scarecrow's body. Woot and

Polychrome did this and it was no easy task because the hay packed together more than straw and as they had little experience in such work their job, when completed, left the Scarecrow's arms and legs rather bunchy. Also there was a hump on his back which made Woot laugh and say it reminded him of a camel, but it was the best they could do and when the head was fastened on to the body they asked the Scarecrow how he felt.

"A little heavy, and not quite natural," he cheerfully replied; "but I'll get along somehow until we reach a straw-stack. Don't laugh at me, please, because I'm a little ashamed of myself and I don't want to regret a good action."

They started at once in the direction of Mount Munch, and as the Scarecrow proved very clumsy in his movements, Woot took one of his arms and the Tin Woodman the other and so helped their friend to walk in a straight line.

And the Rainbow's Daughter, as before, danced ahead of them and behind them and all around them, and they never minded her odd ways, because to them she was like a ray of sunshine.

CHAPTER XX

OVER NIGHT

THE LAND OF THE MUNCHKINS IS FULL OF surprises, as our travelers had already learned, and although Mount Munch was constantly growing larger as they advanced toward it, they knew it was still a long way off and were not certain, by any means, that they had escaped all danger or encountered their last adventure.

The plain was broad, and as far as the eye could see, there seemed to be a level stretch of country between them and the mountain, but toward evening they came upon a hollow, in which stood a tiny blue Munchkin dwelling with a garden around it and fields of grain filling in all the rest of the hollow.

They did not discover this place until they came close to the edge of it, and they were astonished at the sight that greeted them because they had imagined that this part of the plain had no inhabitants.

"It's a very small house," Woot declared. "I wonder who lives there?"

"The way to find out is to knock on the door and ask," replied the Tin Woodman. "Perhaps it is the home of Nimmie Amee."

"Is she a dwarf?" asked the boy.

"No, indeed; Nimmie Amee is a full sized woman."

"Then I'm sure she couldn't live in that little house," said Woot.

"Let's go down," suggested the Scarecrow. "I'm almost sure I can see a straw-stack in the back yard."

They descended the hollow, which was rather steep at the sides, and soon came to the house, which was indeed rather small. Woot knocked upon a door that was not much higher than his waist, but got no reply. He knocked again, but not a sound was heard.

"Smoke is coming out of the chimney," announced Polychrome, who was dancing lightly through the garden, where cabbages and beets and turnips and the like were growing finely.

"Then someone surely lives here," said Woot, and knocked again.

Now a window at the side of the house opened and a queer head appeared. It was white and hairy and had a long snout and little round eyes. The ears were hidden by a blue sunbonnet tied under the chin.

"Oh; it's a pig!" exclaimed Woot.

"Pardon me; I am Mrs. Squealina Swyne, wife of Professor Grunter Swyne, and this is our home," said the one in the window. "What do you want?"

"What sort of a Professor is your husband?" inquired the Tin Woodman curiously.

"He is Professor of Cabbage Culture and Corn Perfection. He is very famous in his own family, and would be the wonder of the world if he went abroad," said Mrs. Swyne in a voice that was half proud and half irritable. "I must also inform you intruders that the Professor is a dangerous individual, for he files his teeth every morning until they are sharp as needles. If you are butchers, you'd better run away and avoid trouble."

"We are not butchers," the Tin Woodman assured her.

"Then what are you doing with that axe? And why has the other tin man a sword?"

"They are the only weapons we have to defend our friends from their enemies," explained the Emperor of the Winkies, and Woot added:

"Do not be afraid of us, Mrs. Swyne, for we are harmless travelers. The tin men and the Scarecrow never eat anything and Polychrome feasts only on dewdrops. As for me, I'm rather hungry, but there is plenty of food in your garden to satisfy me."

Professor Swyne now joined his wife at the window, looking rather scared in spite of the boy's assuring speech. He wore a blue Munchkin hat, with pointed crown and broad brim, and big spectacles covered his eyes. He peeked around from behind his wife and after looking hard at the strangers, he said:

"My wisdom assures me that you are merely travelers, as you say, and not butchers. Butchers have reason to be afraid of me, but you are safe. We cannot invite you in, for you are too big for our house, but the boy who eats is welcome to all the carrots and turnips he wants. Make yourselves at home in the garden and stay all night, if you like; but in the morning you must go away, for we are quiet people and do not care for company."

"May I have some of your straw?" asked the Scarecrow.

"Help yourself," replied Professor Swyne.

"For pigs, they're quite respectable," remarked Woot, as they all went toward the straw-stack.

"I'm glad they didn't invite us in," said Captain Fyter. "I hope I'm not too particular about my associates, but I draw the line at pigs."

The Scarecrow was glad to be rid of his hay, for during the long walk it had sagged down and made him fat and squatty and more bumpy than at first.

"I'm not specially proud," he said, "but I love a manly figure, such as only straw stuffing can create. I've not felt like myself since that hungry Hip-po ate my last straw."

Polychrome and Woot set to work removing the hay and then they selected the finest straw, crisp and golden, and with it stuffed the Scarecrow anew. He certainly looked better after the operation, and he was so pleased at being reformed that he tried to dance a little jig, and almost succeeded.

"I shall sleep under the straw-stack tonight," Woot decided, after he had eaten some of the vegetables from the garden, and in fact he slept very well, with the two tin men and the Scarecrow sitting silently beside him and Polychrome away somewhere in the moonlight dancing her fairy dances.

At daybreak the Tin Woodman and the Tin Soldier took occasion to polish their bodies and oil their joints, for both were exceedingly careful of their personal appearance. They had forgotten the quarrel due to their accidental bumping of one

another in the invisible country, and being now good friends the Tin Woodman polished the Tin Soldier's back for him and then the Tin Soldier polished the Tin Woodman's back.

For breakfast the Wanderer ate crisp lettuce and radishes, and the Rainbow's Daughter, who had now returned to her friends, sipped the dewdrops that had formed on the petals of the wild-flowers.

As they passed the little house to renew their journey, Woot called out:

"Good-bye, Mr. and Mrs. Swyne!"

The window opened and the two pigs looked out.

"A pleasant journey," said the Professor.

"Have you any children?" asked the Scarecrow, who was a great friend of children.

"We have nine," answered the Professor; "but they do not live with us, for when they were tiny piglets the Wizard of Oz came here and offered to care for them and to educate them. So we let him have our nine tiny piglets, for he's a good Wizard and can be relied upon to keep his promises."

"I know the Nine Tiny Piglets," said the Tin Woodman.

"So do I," said the Scarecrow. "They still live in the Emerald City, and the Wizard takes good care of them and teaches them to do all sorts of tricks."

"Did they ever grow up?" inquired Mrs. Squealina Swyne, in an anxious voice.

"No," answered the Scarecrow; "like all other children in the Land of Oz, they will always remain children, and in the case of the tiny piglets that is a good thing, because they would not be nearly so cute and cunning if they were bigger."

"But are they happy?" asked Mrs. Swyne.

"Everyone in the Emerald City is happy," said the Tin Woodman. "They can't help it."

Then the travelers said good-bye, and climbed the side of the basin that was toward Mount Munch.

CHAPTER XXI

POLYCHROME'S MAGIC

ON THIS MORNING, WHICH OUGHT TO BE THE last of this important journey, our friends started away as bright and cheery as could be, and Woot whistled a merry tune so that Polychrome could dance to the music.

On reaching the top of the hill, the plain spread out before them in all its beauty of blue grasses and wild-flowers, and Mount Munch seemed much nearer than it had the previous evening. They trudged on at a brisk pace, and by noon the mountain was so close that they could admire its appearance. Its slopes were partly clothed with pretty evergreens, and its foot-hills were tufted with a slender waving bluegrass that had a tassel on the end of every blade. And, for the first time, they perceived, near the foot of the mountain, a charming house, not of great size but neatly painted and with many flowers surrounding it and vines climbing over the doors and windows.

It was toward this solitary house that our travelers now directed their steps, thinking to inquire of the people who lived there where Nimmie Amee might be found.

There were no paths, but the way was quite open and clear, and they were drawing near to the dwelling when Woot the Wanderer, who was then in the lead of the little party, halted with such an abrupt jerk that he stumbled over backward and lay flat on his back in the meadow. The Scarecrow stopped to look at the boy.

"Why did you do that?" he asked in surprise.

Woot sat up and gazed around him in amazement.

"I—I don't know!" he replied.

The two tin men, arm in arm, started to pass them when both halted and tumbled, with a great clatter, into a heap beside Woot. Polychrome, laughing at the absurd sight, came dancing up and she, also, came to a sudden stop, but managed to save herself from falling.

Everyone of them was much astonished, and the Scarecrow said with a puzzled look:

"I don't see anything."

"Nor I," said Woot; "but something hit me, just the same."

"Some invisible person struck me a heavy blow," declared the Tin Woodman, struggling to separate himself from the Tin Soldier, whose legs and arms were mixed with his own.

"I'm not sure it was a person," said Polychrome, looking more grave than usual. "It seems to me that I merely ran into some hard substance which barred my way. In order to make sure of this, let me try another place."

She ran back a way and then with much caution advanced in a different place, but when she reached a position on a line with the others she halted, her arms outstretched before her.

"I can feel something hard—something smooth as glass," she said, "but I'm sure it is not glass."

"Let me try," suggested Woot, getting up; but when he tried to go forward, he discovered the same barrier that Polychrome had encountered.

"No," he said, "it isn't glass. But what is it?"

"Air," replied a small voice beside him. "Solid air; that's all."

They all looked downward and found a sky-blue rabbit had stuck his head out of a burrow in the ground. The rabbit's eyes were a deeper blue than his fur, and the pretty creature seemed friendly and unafraid.

"Air!" exclaimed Woot, staring in astonishment into the rabbit's blue eyes; "whoever heard of air so solid that one cannot push it aside?"

"You can't push *this* air aside," declared the rabbit, "for it was made hard by powerful sorcery, and it forms a wall that is intended to keep people from getting to that house yonder."

"Oh; it's a wall, is it?" said the Tin Woodman.

"Yes, it is really a wall," answered the rabbit, "and it is fully six feet thick."

"How high is it?" inquired Captain Fyter, the Tin Soldier.

"Oh, ever so high; perhaps a mile," said the rabbit.

"Couldn't we go around it?" asked Woot.

"Of course, for the wall is a circle," explained the rabbit. "In the center of the circle stands the house, so you may walk around the Wall of Solid Air, but you can't get to the house."

"Who put the air wall around the house?" was the Scarecrow's question.

"Nimmie Amee did that."

"Nimmie Amee!" they all exclaimed in surprise.

"Yes," answered the rabbit. "She used to live with an old Witch, who was suddenly destroyed, and when Nimmie Amee ran away from the Witch's house, she took with her just one magic formula—pure sorcery it was—which enabled her to build this air wall around her house—the house yonder. It was quite a clever idea, I think, for it doesn't mar the beauty of the landscape, solid air being invisible, and yet it keeps all strangers away from the house."

"Does Nimmie Amee live there now?" asked the Tin Woodman anxiously.

"Yes, indeed," said the rabbit.

"And does she weep and wail from morning till night?" continued the Emperor.

"No; she seems quite happy," asserted the rabbit.

The Tin Woodman seemed quite disappointed to hear this report of his old sweetheart, but the Scarecrow reassured his friend, saying:

"Never mind, Your Majesty; however happy Nimmie Amee is now, I'm sure she will be much happier as Empress of the Winkies."

"Perhaps," said Captain Fyter, somewhat stiffly, "she will be still more happy to become the bride of a Tin Soldier."

"She shall choose between us, as we have agreed," the Tin Woodman promised; "but how shall we get to the poor girl?"

Polychrome, although dancing lightly back and forth, had listened to every word of the conversation. Now she came forward and sat herself down just in front of the Blue Rabbit, her many-hued draperies giving her the appearance of some beautiful flower. The rabbit didn't back away an inch. Instead, he gazed at the Rainbow's Daughter admiringly.

"Does your burrow go underneath this Wall of Air?" asked Polychrome.

"To be sure," answered the Blue Rabbit; "I dug it that way so I could roam in these broad fields, by going out one way, or eat the cabbages in Nimmie Amee's garden by leaving my burrow at the other end. I don't think Nimmie Amee ought to mind the little I take from her garden, or the hole I've made under her magic wall. A rabbit may go and come as he pleases, but no one who is bigger than I am could get through my burrow."

"Will you allow us to pass through it, if we are able to?" inquired Polychrome.

"Yes, indeed," answered the Blue Rabbit. "I'm no especial friend of Nimmie Amee, for once she threw stones at me, just because I was nibbling some lettuce, and only yesterday she yelled 'Shoo!' at me, which made me nervous. You're welcome to use my burrow in any way you choose."

"But this is all nonsense!" declared Woot the Wanderer. "We are every one too big to crawl through a rabbit's burrow."

"We are too big now," agreed the Scarecrow, "but you must remember that Polychrome is a fairy, and fairies have many magic powers."

Woot's face brightened as he turned to the lovely Daughter of the Rainbow.

"Could you make us all as small as that rabbit?" he asked eagerly.

"I can try," answered Polychrome, with a smile.

And presently she did it—so easily that Woot was not the only one astonished. As the now tiny people grouped themselves before the rabbit's burrow the hole appeared to them like the entrance to a tunnel, which indeed it was.

"I'll go first," said wee Polychrome, who had made herself grow as small as the others, and into the tunnel she danced without hesitation. A tiny Scarecrow went next and then the two funny little tin men.

"Walk in; it's your turn," said the Blue Rabbit to Woot the Wanderer. "I'm coming after, to see how you get along. This will be a regular surprise party to Nimmie Amee."

So Woot entered the hole and felt his way along its smooth sides in the dark until he finally saw the glimmer of daylight ahead and knew the journey was almost over. Had he remained his natural size, the distance could have been covered in a few steps, but to a thumb-high Woot it was quite a promenade. When he emerged from the burrow he found himself but a short distance from the house, in the center of the vegetable garden, where the leaves of rhubarb waving above his head seemed like trees. Outside the hole, and waiting for him, he found all his friends.

"So far, so good!" remarked the Scarecrow cheerfully.

"Yes; so *far*, but no farther," returned the Tin Woodman in a plaintive and disturbed tone of voice. "I am now close to Nimmie Amee, whom I have come ever so far to seek, but I cannot ask the girl to marry such a little man as I am now."

"I'm no bigger than a toy soldier!" said Captain Fyter, sorrowfully. "Unless Polychrome can make us big again, there is little use in our visiting Nimmie Amee at all, for I'm sure she wouldn't care for a husband she might carelessly step on and ruin."

Polychrome laughed merrily.

"If I make you big, you can't get out of here again," said she, "and if you remain little Nimmie Amee will laugh at you. So make your choice."

"I think we'd better go back," said Woot seriously.

"No," said the Tin Woodman, stoutly, "I have decided that it's my duty to make Nimmie Amee happy, in case she wishes to marry me."

"So have I," announced Captain Fyter. "A good soldier never shrinks from doing his duty."

"As for that," said the Scarecrow, "tin doesn't shrink any to speak of, under any circumstances. But Woot and I intend to stick to our comrades, whatever they decide to do, so we will ask Polychrome to make us as big as we were before."

Polychrome agreed to this request and in half a minute all of them, including herself, had been enlarged again to their natural sizes. They then thanked the Blue Rabbit for his kind assistance, and at once approached the house of Nimmie Amee.

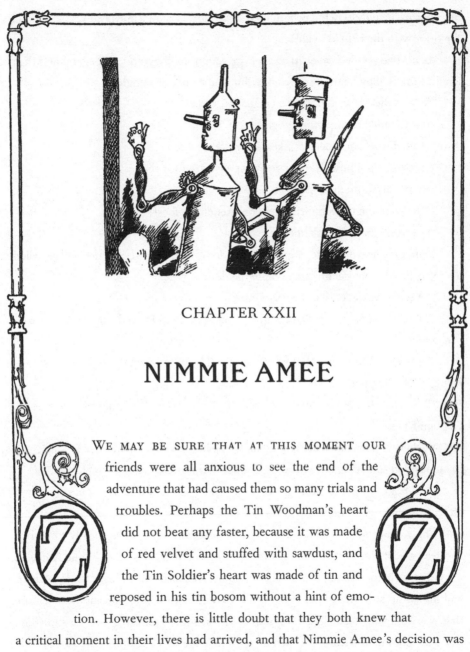

CHAPTER XXII

NIMMIE AMEE

W<small>E MAY BE SURE THAT AT THIS MOMENT OUR</small> friends were all anxious to see the end of the adventure that had caused them so many trials and troubles. Perhaps the Tin Woodman's heart did not beat any faster, because it was made of red velvet and stuffed with sawdust, and the Tin Soldier's heart was made of tin and reposed in his tin bosom without a hint of emotion. However, there is little doubt that they both knew that a critical moment in their lives had arrived, and that Nimmie Amee's decision was destined to influence the future of one or the other.

As they assumed their natural sizes and the rhubarb leaves that had before towered above their heads now barely covered their feet, they looked around the garden and found that no person was visible save themselves. No sound of activity came from the house, either, but they walked to the front door, which had a little porch built before it, and there the two tin men stood side by side while both knocked upon the door with their tin knuckles.

As no one seemed eager to answer the summons they knocked again; and then again. Finally they heard a stir from within and someone coughed.

"Who's there?" called a girl's voice.

"It's I!" cried the tin twins, together.

"How did you get there?" asked the voice.

They hesitated how to reply, so Woot answered for them:

"By means of magic."

"Oh," said the unseen girl. "Are you friends, or foes?"

"Friends!" they all exclaimed.

Then they heard footsteps approach the door, which slowly opened and revealed a very pretty Munchkin girl standing in the doorway.

"Nimmie Amee!" cried the tin twins.

"That's my name," replied the girl, looking at them in cold surprise. "But who can *you* be?"

"Don't you know me, Nimmie?" said the Tin Woodman. "I'm your old sweetheart, Nick Chopper!"

"Don't you know *me*, my dear?" said the Tin Soldier. "I'm your old sweetheart, Captain Fyter!"

Nimmie Amee smiled at them both. Then she looked beyond them at the rest of the party and smiled again. However, she seemed more amused than pleased.

"Come in," she said, leading the way inside. "Even sweethearts are forgotten after a time, but you and your friends are welcome."

The room they now entered was cosy and comfortable, being neatly furnished and well swept and dusted. But they found someone there besides Nimmie Amee. A man dressed in the attractive Munchkin costume was lazily reclining in an easy chair, and he sat up and turned his eyes on the visitors with a cold and indifferent stare that was almost insolent. He did not even rise from his seat to greet the strangers, but after glaring at them he looked away with a scowl, as if they were of too little importance to interest him.

The tin men returned this man's stare with interest, but they did not look away from him because neither of them seemed able to take his eyes off this Munchkin, who was remarkable in having one tin arm—quite like their own tin arms.

"Seems to me," said Captain Fyter, in a voice that sounded harsh and indignant, "that you, sir, are a vile impostor!"

"Gently—gently!" cautioned the Scarecrow; "don't be rude to strangers, Captain."

"Rude?" shouted the Tin Soldier, now very much provoked; "why, he's a scoundrel—a thief! *The villain is wearing my own head!*"

"Yes," added the Tin Woodman, "and he's wearing my right arm! I can recognize it by the two warts on the little finger."

"Good gracious!" exclaimed Woot. "Then this must be the man whom old Ku-Klip patched together and named Chopfyt."

The man now turned toward them, still scowling.

"Yes, that is my name," he said in a voice like a growl, "and it is absurd for you tin creatures, or for anyone else, to claim my head, or arm, or any part of me, for they are my personal property."

"You? You're a Nobody!" shouted Captain Fyter.

"You're just a mix-up," declared the Emperor.

"Now, now, gentlemen," interrupted Nimmie Amee, "I must ask you to be more respectful to poor Chopfyt. For, being my guests, it is not polite for you to insult my husband."

"Your husband!" the tin twins exclaimed in dismay.

"Yes," said she. "I married Chopfyt a long time ago, because my other two sweethearts had deserted me."

This reproof embarrassed both Nick Chopper and Captain Fyter. They looked down, shamefaced, for a moment, and then the Tin Woodman explained in an earnest voice:

"I rusted."

"So did I," said the Tin Soldier.

"I could not know that, of course," asserted Nimmie Amee. "All I knew was that neither of you came to marry me, as you had promised to do. But men are not scarce in the Land of Oz. After I came here to live, I met Mr. Chopfyt, and he was the more interesting because he reminded me strongly of both of you, as you were before you became tin. He even had a tin arm, and that reminded me of you the more."

"No wonder!" remarked the Scarecrow.

"But, listen, Nimmie Amee!" said the astonished Woot; "he really *is* both of them, for he is made of their cast-off parts."

"Oh, you're quite wrong," declared Polychrome, laughing, for she was greatly enjoying the confusion of the others. "The tin men are still themselves, as they will tell you, and so Chopfyt must be someone else."

They looked at her bewildered, for the facts in the case were too puzzling to be grasped at once.

"It is all the fault of old Ku-Klip," muttered the Tin Woodman. "He had no right to use our cast-off parts to make another man with."

"It seems he did it, however," said Nimmie Amee calmly, "and I married him because he resembled you both. I won't say he is a husband to be proud of, because he has a mixed nature and isn't always an agreeable companion. There are times when I have to chide him gently, both with my tongue and with my broomstick. But he is my husband, and I must make the best of him."

"If you don't like him," suggested the Tin Woodman, "Captain Fyter and I can chop him up with our axe and sword, and each take such parts of the fellow as belong to him. Then we are willing for you to select one of us as your husband."

"That is a good idea," approved Captain Fyter, drawing his sword.

"No," said Nimmie Amee; "I think I'll keep the husband I now have. He is now trained to draw the water and carry in the wood and hoe the cabbages and weed the flower-beds and dust the furniture and perform many tasks of a like character. A new husband would have to be scolded—and gently chided—until he learns my ways. So I think it will be better to keep my Chopfyt, and I see no reason why you should object to him. You two gentlemen threw him away when you became tin, because you had no further use for him, so you cannot justly claim him now. I advise you to go back to your own homes and forget me, as I have forgotten you."

"Good advice!" laughed Polychrome, dancing.

"Are you happy?" asked the Tin Soldier.

"Of course I am," said Nimmie Amee; "I'm the mistress of all I survey—the queen of my little domain."

"Wouldn't you like to be the Empress of the Winkies?" asked the Tin Woodman.

"Mercy, no," she answered. "That would be a lot of bother. I don't care for society, or pomp, or posing. All I ask is to be left alone and not to be annoyed by visitors."

The Scarecrow nudged Woot the Wanderer.

"That sounds to me like a hint," he said.

"Looks as if we'd had our journey for nothing," remarked Woot, who was a little ashamed and disappointed because he had proposed the journey.

"I am glad, however," said the Tin Woodman, "that I have found Nimmie Amee, and discovered that she is already married and happy. It will relieve me of any further anxiety concerning her."

"For my part," said the Tin Soldier, "I am not sorry to be free. The only thing that really annoys me is finding my head upon Chopfyt's body."

"As for that, I'm pretty sure it is *my* body, or a part of it, anyway," remarked the Emperor of the Winkies. "But never mind, friend Soldier; let us be willing to donate our cast-off members to insure the happiness of Nimmie Amee, and be thankful it is not our fate to hoe cabbages and draw water—and be chided—in the place of this creature Chopfyt."

"Yes," agreed the Soldier, "we have much to be thankful for."

Polychrome, who had wandered outside, now poked her pretty head through an open window and exclaimed in a pleased voice:

"It's getting cloudy. Perhaps it is going to rain!"

CHAPTER XXIII

THROUGH THE TUNNEL

IT DIDN'T RAIN JUST THEN, ALTHOUGH THE CLOUDS in the sky grew thicker and more threatening. Polychrome hoped for a thunder-storm, followed by her Rainbow, but the two tin men did not relish the idea of getting wet. They even preferred to remain in Nimmie Amee's house, although they felt they were not welcome there, rather than go out and face the coming storm. But the Scarecrow, who was a very thoughtful person, said to his friends:

"If we remain here until after the storm, and Polychrome goes away on her Rainbow, then we will be prisoners inside the Wall of Solid Air; so it seems best to start upon our return journey at once. If I get wet, my straw stuffing will be ruined, and if you two tin gentlemen get wet, you may perhaps rust again, and become useless. But even that is better than to stay here. Once we are free of the barrier, we have

Woot the Wanderer to help us, and he can oil your joints and restuff my body, if it becomes necessary, for the boy is made of meat, which neither rusts nor gets soggy or moldy."

"Come along, then!" cried Polychrome from the window, and the others, realizing the wisdom of the Scarecrow's speech, took leave of Nimmie Amee, who was glad to be rid of them, and said good-bye to her husband, who merely scowled and made no answer, and then they hurried from the house.

"Your old parts are not very polite, I must say," remarked the Scarecrow, when they were in the garden.

"No," said Woot, "Chopfyt is a regular grouch. He might have wished us a pleasant journey, at the very least."

"I beg you not to hold us responsible for that creature's actions," pleaded the Tin Woodman. "We are through with Chopfyt and shall have nothing further to do with him."

Polychrome danced ahead of the party and led them straight to the burrow of the Blue Rabbit, which they might have had some difficulty in finding without her. There she lost no time in making them all small again. The Blue Rabbit was busy nibbling cabbage leaves in Nimmie Amee's garden, so they did not ask his permission but at once entered the burrow.

Even now the raindrops were beginning to fall, but it was quite dry inside the tunnel and by the time they had reached the other end, outside the circular Wall of Solid Air, the storm was at its height and the rain was coming down in torrents.

"Let us wait here," proposed Polychrome, peering out of the hole and then quickly retreating. "The Rainbow won't appear until after the storm and I can make you big again in a jiffy, before I join my sisters on our bow."

"That's a good plan," said the Scarecrow approvingly. "It will save me from getting soaked and soggy."

"It will save me from rusting," said the Tin Soldier.

"It will enable me to remain highly polished," said the Tin Woodman.

"Oh, as for that, I myself prefer not to get my pretty clothes wet," laughed the Rainbow's Daughter. "But while we wait I will bid you all adieu. I must also thank you for saving me from that dreadful Giantess, Mrs. Yoop. You have been good and patient comrades and I have enjoyed our adventures together, but I am never so happy as when on my dear Rainbow."

"Will your father scold you for getting left on the earth?" asked Woot.

"I suppose so," said Polychrome gaily; "I'm always getting scolded for my mad pranks, as they are called. My sisters are so sweet and lovely and proper that they never dance off our Rainbow, and so they never have any adventures. Adventures to me are good fun, only I never like to stay too long on earth, because I really don't belong here. I shall tell my Father the Rainbow that I'll try not to be so careless again, and he will forgive me because in our sky mansions there is always joy and happiness."

They were indeed sorry to part with their dainty and beautiful companion and assured her of their devotion if they ever chanced to meet again. She shook hands with the Scarecrow a nd the Tin Men and kissed Woot the Wanderer lightly upon his forehead.

And then the rain suddenly ceased, and as the tiny people left the burrow of the Blue Rabbit, a glorious big Rainbow appeared in the sky and the end of its arch slowly descended and touched the ground just where they stood.

Woot was so busy watching a score of lovely maidens—sisters of Polychrome—who were leaning over the edge of the bow, and another score who danced gaily amid the radiance of the splendid hues, that he did not notice he was growing big again. But now Polychrome joined her sisters on the Rainbow and the huge arch lifted and slowly melted away as the sun burst from the clouds and sent its own white beams dancing over the meadows.

"Why, she's gone!" exclaimed the boy, and turned to see his companions still waving their hands in token of adieu to the vanished Polychrome.

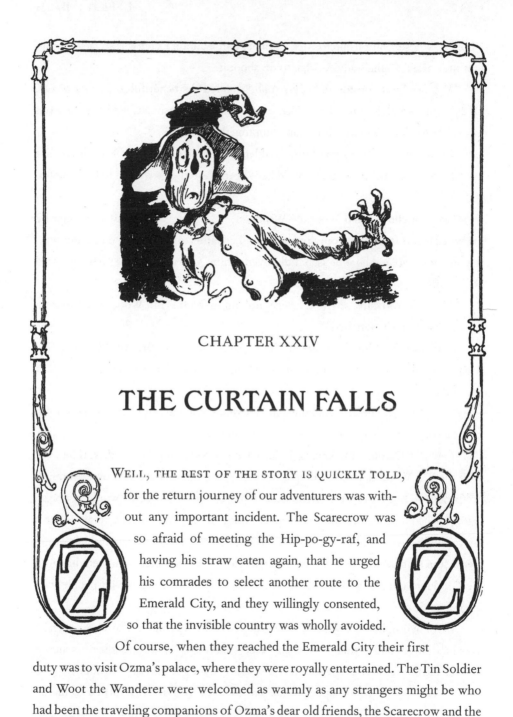

CHAPTER XXIV

THE CURTAIN FALLS

WELL, THE REST OF THE STORY IS QUICKLY TOLD, for the return journey of our adventurers was without any important incident. The Scarecrow was so afraid of meeting the Hip-po-gy-raf, and having his straw eaten again, that he urged his comrades to select another route to the Emerald City, and they willingly consented, so that the invisible country was wholly avoided.

Of course, when they reached the Emerald City their first duty was to visit Ozma's palace, where they were royally entertained. The Tin Soldier and Woot the Wanderer were welcomed as warmly as any strangers might be who had been the traveling companions of Ozma's dear old friends, the Scarecrow and the Tin Woodman.

At the banquet table that evening they related the manner in which they had discovered Nimmie Amee, and told how they had found her happily married to

Chopfyt, whose relationship to Nick Chopper and Captain Fyter was so bewildering that they asked Ozma's advice what to do about it.

"You need not consider Chopfyt at all," replied the beautiful girl Ruler of Oz. "If Nimmie Amee is content with that misfit man for a husband, we have not even just cause to blame Ku-Klip for gluing him together."

"I think it was a very good idea," added little Dorothy, "for if Ku-Klip hadn't used up your cast-off parts, they would have been wasted. It's wicked to be wasteful, isn't it?"

"Well, anyhow," said Woot the Wanderer, "Chopfyt, being kept a prisoner by his wife, is too far away from anyone to bother either of you tin men in any way. If you hadn't gone where he is and discovered him, you would never have worried about him."

"What do you care, anyhow," Betsy Bobbin asked the Tin Woodman, "so long as Nimmie Amee is satisfied?"

"And just to think," remarked Tiny Trot, "that any girl would rather live with a mixture like Chopfyt, on far-away Mount Munch, than to be the Empress of the Winkies!"

"It is her own choice," said the Tin Woodman contentedly; "and, after all, I'm not sure the Winkies would care to have an Empress."

It puzzled Ozma, for a time, to decide what to do with the Tin Soldier. If he went with the Tin Woodman to the Emperor's castle, she felt that the two tin men might not be able to live together in harmony, and moreover the Emperor would not be so distinguished if he had a double constantly beside him. So she asked Captain Fyter if he was willing to serve her as a soldier, and he promptly declared that nothing would please him more. After he had been in her service for some time, Ozma sent him into the Gillikin Country, with instructions to keep order among the wild people who inhabit some parts of that unknown country of Oz.

As for Woot, being a Wanderer by profession, he was allowed to wander wherever he desired, and Ozma promised to keep watch over his future journeys and to protect the boy as well as she was able, in case he ever got into more trouble.

All this having been happily arranged, the Tin Woodman returned to his tin castle, and his chosen comrade, the Scarecrow, accompanied him on the way. The two friends were sure to pass many pleasant hours together in talking over their recent adventures, for as they neither ate nor slept they found their greatest amusement in conversation.

THE MAGIC OF OZ

THE HUNGRY
TIGER
AND THE
COWARDLY LION

CONTENTS

MT.
MUNCH

CHAPTER I

MOUNT MUNCH

ON THE EAST EDGE OF THE LAND OF OZ, IN THE
Munchkin Country, is a big, tall hill called Mount
Munch. On one side, the bottom of this hill just touches
the Deadly Sandy Desert that separates the Fairyland
of Oz from all the rest of the world, but on the other
side, the hill touches the beautiful, fertile Country of
the Munchkins.

The Munchkin folks, however, merely stand off
and look at Mount Munch and know very little about
it; for, about a third of the way up, its sides become
too steep to climb, and if any people live upon the top
of that great towering peak that seems to reach nearly to the skies, the Munchkins
are not aware of the fact.

But people *do* live there, just the same. The top of Mount Munch is shaped like
a saucer, broad and deep, and in the saucer are fields where grains and vegetables
grow, and flocks are fed, and brooks flow and trees bear all sorts of things. There are
houses scattered here and there, each having its family of Hyups, as the people call

themselves. The Hyups seldom go down the mountain, for the same reason that the Munchkins never climb up: the sides are too steep.

In one of the houses lived a wise old Hyup named Bini Aru, who used to be a clever Sorcerer. But Ozma of Oz, who rules everyone in the Land of Oz, had made a decree that no one should practice magic in her dominions except Glinda the Good and the Wizard of Oz, and when Glinda sent this royal command to the Hyups by means of a strong-winged Eagle, old Bini Aru at once stopped performing magical arts. He destroyed many of his magic powders and tools of magic, and afterward honestly obeyed the law. He had never seen Ozma, but he knew she was his Ruler and must be obeyed.

There was only one thing that grieved him. He had discovered a new and secret method of transformations that was unknown to any other Sorcerer. Glinda the Good did not know it, nor did the little Wizard of Oz, nor Dr. Pipt nor old Mombi, nor anyone else who dealt in magic arts. It was Bini Aru's own secret. By its means, it was the simplest thing in the world to transform anyone into beast, bird or fish, or anything else, and back again, once you know how to pronounce the mystical word: "**Pyrzqxgl**."

Bini Aru had used this secret many times, but not to cause evil or suffering to others. When he had wandered far from home and was hungry, he would say: "I want to become a cow—**Pyrzqxgl!**" In an instant he would be a cow, and then he would eat grass and satisfy his hunger. All beasts and birds can talk in the Land of Oz, so when the cow was no longer hungry, it would say: "I want to be Bini Aru again: **Pyrzqxgl!!**" and the Magic Word, properly pronounced, would instantly restore him to his proper form.

Now, of course, I would not dare to write down this Magic Word so plainly if I thought my readers would pronounce it properly and so be able to transform themselves and others, but it is a fact that no one in all the world except Bini Aru, had ever (up to the time this story begins) been able to pronounce "**Pyrzqxgl**" the right way, so I think it is safe to give it to you. It might be well, however, in reading this story aloud, to be careful not to pronounce **Pyrzqxgl** the proper way, and thus avoid all danger of the secret being able to work mischief.

Bini Aru, having discovered the secret of instant transformation, which required no tools or powders or other chemicals or herbs and always worked perfectly, was reluctant to have such a wonderful discovery entirely unknown or lost to all human knowledge. He decided not to use it again, since Ozma had forbidden him to do so, but he reflected that Ozma was a girl and some time might change her mind and allow her subjects to practice magic, in which case Bini Aru could again transform himself and others at will,—unless, of course, he forgot how to pronounce **Pyrzqxgl** in the meantime.

After giving the matter careful thought, he decided to write the word, and how it should be pronounced, in some secret place, so that he could find it after many years, but where no one else could ever find it.

That was a clever idea, but what bothered the old Sorcerer was to find a secret place. He wandered all over the Saucer at the top of Mount Munch, but found no place in which to write the secret word where others might not be likely to stumble upon it. So finally he decided it must be written somewhere in his own house.

Bini Aru had a wife named Mopsi Aru who was famous for making fine huckleberry pies, and he had a son named Kiki Aru who was not famous at all. He was noted as being cross and disagreeable because he was not happy, and he was not happy because he wanted to go down the mountain and visit the big world below and his father would not let him. No one paid any attention to Kiki Aru, because he didn't amount to anything, anyway.

Once a year there was a festival on Mount Munch which all the Hyups attended. It was held in the center of the saucer-shaped country, and the day was given over to feasting and merry-making. The young folks danced and sang songs; the women spread the tables with good things to eat, and the men played on musical instruments and told fairy tales.

Kiki Aru usually went to these festivals with his parents, and then sat sullenly outside the circle and would not dance or sing or even talk to the other young people. So the festival did not make him any happier than other days, and this time he told Bini Aru and Mopsi Aru that he would not go. He would rather stay at home and be unhappy all by himself, he said, and so they gladly let him stay.

But after he was left alone Kiki decided to enter his father's private room, where he was forbidden to go, and see if he could find any of the magic tools Bini Aru used to work with when he practiced sorcery. As he went in Kiki stubbed his toe on one of the floor boards. He searched everywhere but found no trace of his father's magic. All had been destroyed.

Much disappointed, he started to go out again when he stubbed his toe on the same floor board. That set him thinking. Examining the board more closely, Kiki found it had been pried up and then nailed down again in such a manner that it was

a little higher than the other boards. But why had his father taken up the board? Had he hidden some of his magic tools underneath the floor?

Kiki got a chisel and pried up the board, but found nothing under it. He was just about to replace the board when it slipped from his hand and turned over, and he saw something written on the underside of it. The light was rather dim, so he took the board to the window and examined it, and found that the writing described exactly how to pronounce the Magic Word **Pyrzqxgl**, which would transform anyone into anything instantly, and back again when the word was repeated.

Now, at first, Kiki Aru didn't realize what a wonderful secret he had discovered; but he thought it might be of use to him and so he took a piece of paper and made on it an exact copy of the instructions for pronouncing **Pyrzqxgl**. Then he folded the paper and put it in his pocket, and replaced the board in the floor so that no one would suspect it had been removed.

After this Kiki went into the garden and sitting beneath a tree made a careful study of the paper. He had always wanted to get away from Mount Munch and visit the big world—especially the Land of Oz—and the idea now came to him that if he could transform himself into a bird, he could fly to any place he wished to go and fly back again whenever he cared to. It was necessary, however, to learn by heart the way to pronounce the Magic Word, because a bird would have no way to carry a paper with it, and Kiki would be unable to resume his proper shape if he forgot the word or its pronunciation.

So he studied it a long time, repeating it a hundred times in his mind until he was sure he would not forget it. But to make safety doubly sure he placed the paper in a tin box in a neglected part of the garden and covered the box with small stones.

By this time it was getting late in the day and Kiki wished to attempt his first transformation before his parents returned from the festival. So he stood on the front porch of his home and said:

"I want to become a big, strong bird, like a hawk—**Pyrzqxgl**!" He pronounced it the right way, so in a flash he felt that he was completely changed in form. He flapped his wings, hopped to the porch railing and said: "Caw-oo! Caw-oo!"

Then he laughed and said half aloud: "I suppose that's the funny sound this sort of a bird makes. But now let me try my wings and see if I'm strong enough to fly across the desert."

For he had decided to make his first trip to the country outside the Land of Oz. He had stolen this secret of transformation and he knew he had disobeyed the law of Oz by working magic. Perhaps Glinda or the Wizard of Oz would discover him and punish him, so it would be good policy to keep away from Oz altogether.

Slowly Kiki rose into the air, and resting on his broad wings, floated in graceful circles above the saucer-shaped mountain-top. From his height, he could see, far across the burning sands of the Deadly Desert, another country that might be pleasant to explore, so he headed that way, and with strong, steady strokes of his wings, began the long flight.

CHAPTER II

THE HAWK

EVEN A HAWK HAS TO FLY HIGH IN ORDER TO cross the Deadly Desert, from which poisonous fumes are constantly rising. Kiki Aru felt sick and faint by the time he reached good land again, for he could not quite escape the effects of the poisons. But the fresh air soon restored him and he alighted in a broad table-land which is called Hiland. Just beyond it is a valley known as Loland, and these two countries are ruled by the Gingerbread Man, John Dough, with Chick the Cherub as his Prime Minister. The hawk merely stopped here long enough to rest, and then he flew north and passed over a fine country called Merryland, which is ruled by a lovely Wax Doll. Then, following the curve of the Desert, he turned north and settled on a tree-top in the Kingdom of Noland.

Kiki was tired by this time, and the sun was now setting, so he decided to remain here till morning. From his tree-top he could see a house near by, which looked very comfortable. A man was milking a cow in the yard and a pleasant-faced woman came to the door and called him to supper.

That made Kiki wonder what sort of food hawks ate. He felt hungry, but didn't know what to eat or where to get it. Also he thought a bed would be more comfortable than a tree-top for sleeping, so he hopped to the ground and said: "I want to become Kiki Aru again—**Pyrzqxgl!**"

Instantly he had resumed his natural shape, and going to the house, he knocked upon the door and asked for some supper.

"Who are you?" asked the man of the house.

"A stranger from the Land of Oz," replied Kiki Aru.

"Then you are welcome," said the man.

Kiki was given a good supper and a good bed, and he behaved very well, although he refused to answer all the questions the good people of Noland asked him. Having escaped from his home and found a way to see the world, the young man was no longer unhappy, and so he was no longer cross and disagreeable. The people thought him a very respectable person and gave him breakfast next morning, after which he started on his way feeling quite contented.

Having walked for an hour or two through the pretty country that is ruled by King Bud, Kiki Aru decided he could travel faster and see more as a bird, so he transformed himself into a white dove and visited the great city of Nole and saw the King's palace and gardens and many other places of interest. Then he flew westward into the Kingdom of Ix, and after a day in Queen Zixi's country went on westward into the Land of Ev. Every place he visited he thought was much more pleasant than the saucer-country of the Hyups, and he decided that when he reached the finest country of all he would settle there and enjoy his future life to the utmost.

In the land of Ev he resumed his own shape again, for the cities and villages were close together and he could easily go on foot from one to another of them.

Toward evening he came to a good Inn and asked the inn-keeper if he could have food and lodging.

"You can if you have the money to pay," said the man, "otherwise you must go elsewhere."

This surprised Kiki, for in the Land of Oz they do not use money at all, everyone being allowed to take what he wishes without price. He had no money, therefore, and so he turned away to seek hospitality elsewhere. Looking through an open window

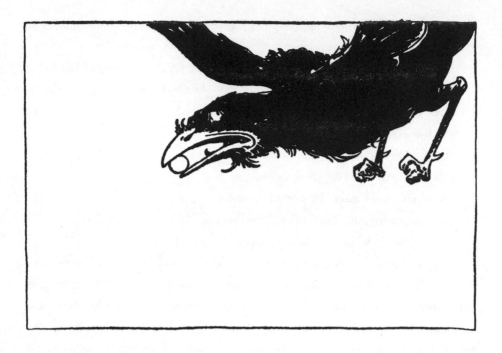

into one of the rooms of the Inn, as he passed along, he saw an old man counting on a table a big heap of gold pieces, which Kiki thought to be money. One of these would buy him supper and a bed, he reflected, so he transformed himself into a magpie and, flying through the open window, caught up one of the gold pieces in his beak and flew out again before the old man could interfere. Indeed, the old man who was robbed was quite helpless, for he dared not leave his pile of gold to chase the magpie, and before he could place the gold in a sack in his pocket the robber bird was out of sight and to seek it would be folly.

Kiki Aru flew to a group of trees and, dropping the gold piece to the ground, resumed his proper shape, and then picked up the money and put it in his pocket.

"You'll be sorry for this!" exclaimed a small voice just over his head.

Kiki looked up and saw that a sparrow, perched upon a branch, was watching him.

"Sorry for what?" he demanded.

"Oh, I saw the whole thing," asserted the sparrow. "I saw you look in the window at the gold, and then make yourself into a magpie and rob the poor man, and then I saw you fly here and make the bird into your former shape. That's magic, and magic is wicked and unlawful; and you stole money, and that's a still greater crime. You'll be sorry, some day."

"I don't care," replied Kiki Aru, scowling.

"Aren't you afraid to be wicked?" asked the sparrow.

"No, I didn't know I was being wicked," said Kiki, "but if I was, I'm glad of it. I hate good people. I've always wanted to be wicked, but I didn't know how."

"Haw, haw, haw!" laughed someone behind him, in a big voice; "that's the proper spirit, my lad! I'm glad I've met you; shake hands."

The sparrow gave a frightened squeak and flew away.

CHAPTER III

TWO BAD ONES

K‍IKI TURNED AROUND AND SAW A QUEER OLD MAN
standing near. He didn't stand straight, for he was
crooked. He had a fat body and thin legs and arms.
He had a big, round face with bushy, white whiskers
that came to a point below his waist, and white hair
that came to a point on top of his head. He wore
dull-gray clothes that were tight fitting, and his
pockets were all bunched out as if stuffed full
of something.

"I didn't know you were here," said Kiki.

"I didn't come until after you did," said the queer old man.

"Who are you?" asked Kiki.

"My name's Ruggedo. I used to be the Nome King; but I got kicked out of my
country, and now I'm a wanderer."

"What made them kick you out?" inquired the Hyup boy.

"Well, it's the fashion to kick kings nowadays. I was a pretty good King—to myself—but those dreadful Oz people wouldn't let me alone. So I had to abdicate."

"What does that mean?"

"It means to be kicked out. But let's talk about something pleasant. Who are you and where did you come from?"

"I'm called Kiki Aru. I used to live on Mount Munch in the Land of Oz, but now I'm a wanderer like yourself."

The Nome King gave him a shrewd look.

"I heard that bird say that you transformed yourself into a magpie and back again. Is that true?"

Kiki hesitated, but saw no reason to deny it. He felt that it would make him appear more important.

"Well—yes," he said.

"Then you're a wizard?"

"No; I only understand transformations," he admitted.

"Well, that's pretty good magic, anyhow," declared old Ruggedo. "I used to have some very fine magic, myself, but my enemies took it all away from me. Where are you going now?"

"I'm going into the inn, to get some supper and a bed," said Kiki.

"Have you the money to pay for it?" asked the Nome.

"I have one gold piece."

"Which you stole. Very good. And you're glad that you're wicked. Better yet. I like you, young man, and I'll go to the inn with you if you'll promise not to eat eggs for supper."

"Don't you like eggs?" asked Kiki.

"I'm afraid of 'em; they're dangerous!" said Ruggedo, with a shudder.

"All right," agreed Kiki; "I won't ask for eggs."

"Then come along," said the Nome.

When they entered the inn, the landlord scowled at Kiki and said:

"I told you I would not feed you unless you had money."

Kiki showed him the gold piece.

"And how about you?" asked the landlord, turning to Ruggedo. "Have you money?"

"I've something better," answered the old Nome, and taking a bag from one of his pockets he poured from it upon the table a mass of glittering gems—diamonds, rubies and emeralds.

The landlord was very polite to the strangers after that. He served them an excellent supper, and while they ate it, the Hyup boy asked his companion:

"Where did you get so many jewels?"

"Well, I'll tell you," answered the Nome. "When those Oz people took my kingdom away from me—just because it was my kingdom and I wanted to run it to suit myself—they said I could take as many precious stones as I could carry. So I had a lot of pockets made in my clothes and loaded them all up. Jewels are fine things to have with you when you travel; you can trade them for anything."

"Are they better than gold pieces?" asked Kiki.

"The smallest of these jewels is worth a hundred gold pieces such as you stole from the old man."

"Don't talk so loud," begged Kiki, uneasily. "Some one else might hear what you are saying."

After supper they took a walk together, and the former Nome King said:

"Do you know the Shaggy Man, and the Scarecrow, and the Tin Woodman, and Dorothy, and Ozma and all the other Oz people?"

"No," replied the boy, "I have never been away from Mount Munch until I flew over the Deadly Desert the other day in the shape of a hawk."

"Then you've never seen the Emerald City of Oz?"

"Never."

"Well," said the Nome, "I knew all the Oz people, and you can guess I do not love them. All during my wanderings I have brooded on how I can be revenged on them. Now that I've met you I can see a way to conquer the Land of Oz and be King there myself, which is better than being King of the Nomes."

"How can you do that?" inquired Kiki Aru, wonderingly.

"Never mind how. In the first place, I'll make a bargain with you. Tell me the secret of how to perform transformations and I will give you a pocketful of jewels, the biggest and finest that I possess."

"No," said Kiki, who realized that to share his power with another would be dangerous to himself.

"I'll give you two pocketsful of jewels," said the Nome.

"No," answered Kiki.

"I'll give you every jewel I possess."

"No, no, no!" said Kiki, who was beginning to be frightened.

"Then," said the Nome, with a wicked look at the boy, "I'll tell the inn-keeper that you stole that gold piece and he will have you put in prison."

Kiki laughed at the threat.

"Before he can do that," said he, "I will transform myself into a lion and tear him to pieces, or into a bear and eat him up, or into a fly and fly away where he could not find me."

"Can you really do such wonderful transformations?" asked the old Nome, looking at him curiously.

"Of course," declared Kiki. "I can transform you into a stick of wood, in a flash, or into a stone, and leave you here by the roadside."

The wicked Nome shivered a little when he heard that, but it made him long more than ever to possess the great secret. After a while he said:

"I'll tell you what I'll do. If you will help me to conquer Oz and to transform the Oz people, who are my enemies, into sticks or stones, by telling me your secret, I'll agree to make you the Ruler of all Oz, and I will be your Prime Minister and see that your orders are obeyed."

"I'll help do that," said Kiki, "but I won't tell you my secret."

The Nome was so furious at this refusal that he jumped up and down with rage and spluttered and choked for a long time before he could control his passion. But the boy was not at all frightened. He laughed at the wicked old Nome, which made him more furious than ever.

"Let's give up the idea," he proposed, when Ruggedo had quieted somewhat. "I don't know the Oz people you mention and so they are not my enemies. If they've kicked you out of your kingdom, that's your affair—not mine."

"Wouldn't you like to be king of that splendid fairyland?" asked Ruggedo.

"Yes, I would," replied Kiki Aru; "but you want to be king yourself, and we would quarrel over it."

"No," said the Nome, trying to deceive him. "I don't care to be King of Oz, come to think it over. I don't even care to live in that country. What I want first is revenge. If we can conquer Oz, I'll get enough magic then to conquer my own Kingdom of the Nomes, and I'll go back and live in my underground caverns, which

are more home-like than the top of the earth. So here's my proposition: Help me conquer Oz and get revenge, and help me get the magic away from Glinda and the Wizard, and I'll let you be King of Oz forever afterward."

"I'll think it over," answered Kiki, and that is all he would say that evening.

In the night when all in the Inn were asleep but himself, old Ruggedo the Nome, rose softly from his couch and went into the room of Kiki Aru the Hyup, and searched everywhere for the magic tool that performed his transformations. Of course, there was no such tool, and although Ruggedo searched in all the boy's pockets, he found nothing magical whatever. So he went back to his bed and began to doubt that Kiki could perform transformations.

Next morning he said:

"Which way do you travel to-day?"

"I think I shall visit the Rose Kingdom," answered the boy.

"That is a long journey," declared the Nome.

"I shall transform myself into a bird," said Kiki, "and so fly to the Rose Kingdom in an hour."

"Then transform me, also, into a bird, and I will go with you," suggested Ruggedo. "But, in that case, let us fly together to the Land of Oz, and see what it looks like."

Kiki thought this over. Pleasant as were the countries he had visited, he heard everywhere that the Land of Oz was more beautiful and delightful. The Land of Oz was his own country, too, and if there was any possibility of his becoming its King, he must know something about it.

While Kiki the Hyup thought, Ruggedo the Nome was also thinking. This boy possessed a marvelous power, and although very simple in some ways, he was determined not to part with his secret. However, if Ruggedo could get him to transport the wily old Nome to Oz, which he could reach in no other way, he might then induce the boy to follow his advice and enter into the plot for revenge, which he had already planned in his wicked heart.

"There are wizards and magicians in Oz," remarked Kiki, after a time. "They might discover us, in spite of our transformations."

"Not if we are careful," Ruggedo assured him. "Ozma has a Magic Picture, in which she can see whatever she wishes to see; but Ozma will know nothing of our going to Oz, and so she will not command her Magic Picture to show where we are or what we are doing. Glinda the Good has a Great Book called the Book of Records, in which is magically written everything that people do in the Land of Oz, just the instant they do it."

"Then," said Kiki, "there is no use our attempting to conquer the country, for Glinda would read in her book all that we do, and as her magic is greater than mine, she would soon put a stop to our plans."

"I said 'people,' didn't I?" retorted the Nome. "The book doesn't make a record of what birds do, or beasts. It only tells the doings of people. So, if we fly into the country as birds, Glinda won't know anything about it."

"Two birds couldn't conquer the Land of Oz," asserted the boy, scornfully.

"No; that's true," admitted Ruggedo, and then he rubbed his forehead and stroked his long pointed beard and thought some more.

"Ah, now I have the idea!" he declared. "I suppose you can transform us into beasts as well as birds?"

"Of course."

"And can you make a bird a beast, and a beast a bird again, without taking a human form in between?"

"Certainly," said Kiki. "I can transform myself or others into anything that can talk. There's a Magic Word that must be spoken in connection with the transformations, and as beasts and birds and dragons and fishes can talk in Oz, we may become any of these we desire to. However, if I transformed myself into a tree, I would always remain a tree, because then I could not utter the Magic Word to change the transformation."

"I see; I see," said Ruggedo, nodding his bushy, white head until the point of his hair waved back and forth like a pendulum. "That fits in with my idea, exactly. Now, listen, and I'll explain to you my plan. We'll fly to Oz as birds and settle in one of the thick forests in the Gillikin Country. There you will transform us into powerful beasts, and as Glinda doesn't keep any track of the doings of beasts we can act without being discovered."

"But how can two beasts raise an army to conquer the powerful people of Oz?" inquired Kiki.

"That's easy. But not an army of *people*, mind you. That would be quickly discovered. And while we are in Oz you and I will never resume our human forms until we've conquered the country and destroyed Glinda, and Ozma, and the Wizard, and Dorothy, and all the rest, and so have nothing more to fear from them."

"It is impossible to kill anyone in the Land of Oz," declared Kiki.

"It isn't necessary to kill the Oz people," rejoined Ruggedo.

"I'm afraid I don't understand you," objected the boy. "What will happen to the Oz people, and what sort of an army could we get together, except of people?"

"I'll tell you. The forests of Oz are full of beasts. Some of them, in the far-away places, are savage and cruel, and would gladly follow a leader as savage as themselves. They have never troubled the Oz people much, because they had no leader to urge them on, but we will tell them to help us conquer Oz and as a reward we will transform all the beasts into men and women, and let them live in the houses and enjoy all the good things; and we will transform all the people of Oz into beasts of various sorts, and send them to live in the forests and the jungles. That is a splendid idea, you must admit, and it's so easy that we won't have any trouble at all to carry it through to success."

"Will the beasts consent, do you think?" asked the boy.

"To be sure they will. We can get every beast in Oz on our side—except a few who live in Ozma's palace, and they won't count."

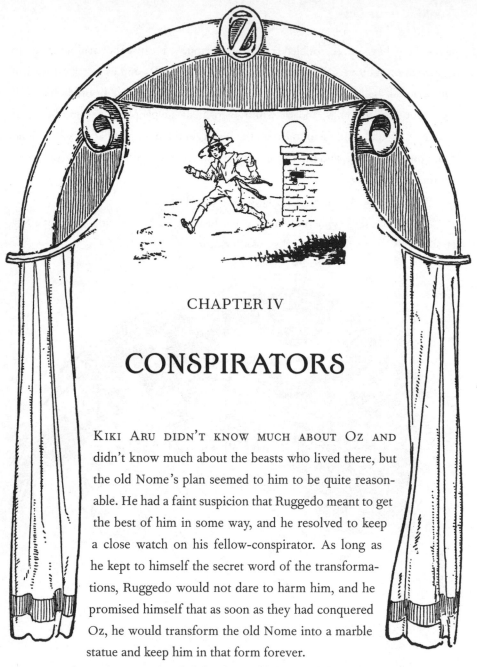

CHAPTER IV

CONSPIRATORS

KIKI ARU DIDN'T KNOW MUCH ABOUT OZ AND didn't know much about the beasts who lived there, but the old Nome's plan seemed to him to be quite reasonable. He had a faint suspicion that Ruggedo meant to get the best of him in some way, and he resolved to keep a close watch on his fellow-conspirator. As long as he kept to himself the secret word of the transformations, Ruggedo would not dare to harm him, and he promised himself that as soon as they had conquered Oz, he would transform the old Nome into a marble statue and keep him in that form forever.

Ruggedo, on his part, decided that he could, by careful watching and listening, surprise the boy's secret, and when he had learned the Magic Word he would transform Kiki Aru into a bundle of faggots and burn him up and so be rid of him.

This is always the way with wicked people. They cannot be trusted even by one another. Ruggedo thought he was fooling Kiki, and Kiki thought he was fooling Ruggedo; so both were pleased.

"It's a long way across the Desert," remarked the boy, "and the sands are hot and send up poisonous vapors. Let us wait until evening and then fly across in the night when it will be cooler."

The former Nome King agreed to this, and the two spent the rest of that day in talking over their plans. When evening came they paid the inn-keeper and walked out to a little grove of trees that stood near by.

"Remain here for a few minutes and I'll soon be back," said Kiki, and walking swiftly away, he left the Nome standing in the grove. Ruggedo wondered where he had gone, but stood quietly in his place until, all of a sudden, his form changed to that of a great eagle, and he uttered a piercing cry of astonishment and flapped his wings in a sort of panic. At once his eagle cry was answered from beyond the grove, and another eagle, even larger and more powerful than the transformed Ruggedo, came sailing through the trees and alighted beside him.

"Now we are ready for the start," said the voice of Kiki, coming from the eagle.

Ruggedo realized that this time he had been outwitted. He had thought Kiki would utter the Magic Word in his presence, and so he would learn what it was, but the boy had been too shrewd for that.

As the two eagles mounted high into the air and began their flight across the great Desert that separates the Land of Oz from all the rest of the world, the Nome said:

"When I was King of the Nomes I had a magic way of working transformations that I thought was good, but it could not compare with your secret word. I had to have certain tools and make passes and say a lot of mystic words before I could transform anybody."

"What became of your magic tools?" inquired Kiki.

"The Oz people took them all away from me—that horrid girl, Dorothy, and that terrible fairy, Ozma, the Ruler of Oz—at the time they took away my underground kingdom and kicked me upstairs into the cold, heartless world."

"Why did you let them do that?" asked the boy.

"Well," said Ruggedo, "I couldn't help it. They rolled eggs at me—*eggs*—dreadful eggs!—and if an egg even touches a Nome, he is ruined for life."

"Is any kind of an egg dangerous to a Nome?"

"Any kind and every kind. An egg is the only thing I'm afraid of."

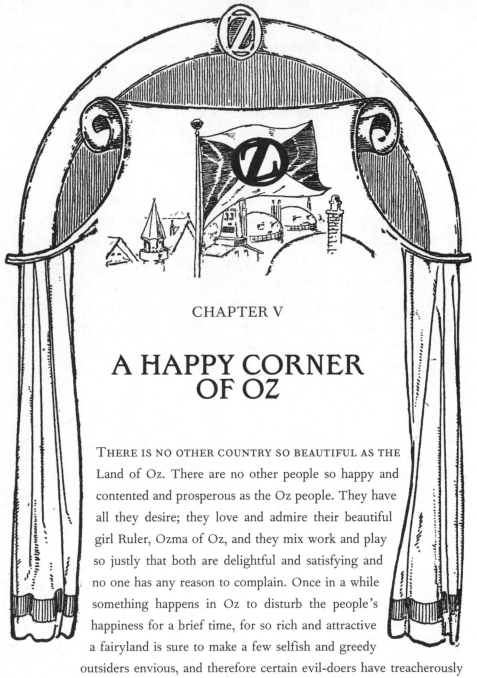

CHAPTER V

A HAPPY CORNER
OF OZ

THERE IS NO OTHER COUNTRY SO BEAUTIFUL AS THE
Land of Oz. There are no other people so happy and
contented and prosperous as the Oz people. They have
all they desire; they love and admire their beautiful
girl Ruler, Ozma of Oz, and they mix work and play
so justly that both are delightful and satisfying and
no one has any reason to complain. Once in a while
something happens in Oz to disturb the people's
happiness for a brief time, for so rich and attractive
a fairyland is sure to make a few selfish and greedy
outsiders envious, and therefore certain evil-doers have treacherously
plotted to conquer Oz and enslave its people and destroy its girl Ruler, and so gain
the wealth of Oz for themselves. But up to the time when the cruel and crafty Nome,
Ruggedo, conspired with Kiki Aru, the Hyup, all such attempts had failed. The Oz
people suspected no danger. Life in the world's nicest fairyland was one round of
joyous, happy days.

In the center of the Emerald City of Oz, the capital city of Ozma's dominions, is a vast and beautiful garden, surrounded by a wall inlaid with shining emeralds, and in the center of this garden stands Ozma's Royal Palace, the most splendid building ever constructed. From a hundred towers and domes floated the banners of Oz, which included the Ozmies, the Munchkins, the Gillikins, the Winkies and the Quadlings. The banner of the Munchkins is blue, that of the Winkies yellow; the Gillikin banner is purple, and the Quadling's banner is red. The colors of the Emerald City are of course green. Ozma's own banner has a green center, and is divided into four quarters. These quarters are colored blue, purple, yellow and red, indicating that she rules over all the countries of the Land of Oz.

This fairyland is so big, however, that all of it is not yet known to its girl Ruler, and it is said that in some far parts of the country, in forests and mountain fast-nesses, in hidden valleys and thick jungles, are people and beasts that know as little about Ozma as she knows of them. Still, these unknown subjects are not nearly so numerous as the known inhabitants of Oz, who occupy all the countries near to the Emerald City. Indeed, I'm sure it will not be long until all parts of the fairyland of Oz are explored and their peoples made acquainted with their Ruler, for in Ozma's palace are several of her friends who are so curious that they are constantly discovering new and extraordinary places and inhabitants.

One of the most frequent discoverers of these hidden places in Oz is a little Kansas girl named Dorothy, who is Ozma's dearest friend and lives in luxurious rooms in the Royal Palace. Dorothy is, indeed, a Princess of Oz, but she does not like to be called a princess, and because she is simple and sweet and does not pretend to be anything but an ordinary little girl, she is called just "Dorothy" by everybody and is the most popular person, next to Ozma, in all the Land of Oz.

One morning Dorothy crossed the hall of the palace and knocked on the door of another girl named Trot, also a guest and friend of Ozma. When told to enter, Dorothy found that Trot had company, an old sailor-man with one wooden leg and one meat leg, who was sitting by the open window puffing smoke from a corn-cob pipe. This sailor-man was named Cap'n Bill, and he had accompanied Trot to the Land of Oz and was her oldest and most faithful comrade and friend. Dorothy liked Cap'n Bill, too, and after she had greeted him, she said to Trot:

"You know, Ozma's birthday is next month, and I've been wondering what I can give her as a birthday present. She's so good to us all that we certainly ought to remember her birthday."

"That's true," agreed Trot. "I've been wondering, too, what I could give Ozma. It's pretty hard to decide, 'cause she's got already all she wants, and as she's a fairy and knows a lot about magic, she could satisfy any wish."

"I know," returned Dorothy, "but that isn't the point. It isn't that Ozma *needs* anything, but that it will please her to know we've remembered her birthday. But what shall we give her?"

Trot shook her head in despair.

"I've tried to think and I can't," she declared.

"It's the same way with me," said Dorothy.

"I know one thing that 'ud please her," remarked Cap'n Bill, turning his round face with its fringe of whiskers toward the two girls and staring at them with his big, light-blue eyes wide open.

"What is it, Cap'n Bill?"

"It's an Enchanted Flower," said he. "It's a pretty plant that stands in a golden flower-pot an' grows all sorts o' flowers, one after another. One minute a fine rose buds an' blooms, an' then a tulip, an' next a chrys—chrys—"

"—anthemum," said Dorothy, helping him.

"That's it; and next a dahlia, an' then a daffydil, an' on all through the range o' posies. Jus' as soon as one fades away, another comes, of a different sort, an' the perfume from 'em is mighty snifty, an' they keeps bloomin' night and day, year in an' year out."

"That's wonderful!" exclaimed Dorothy. "I think Ozma would like it."

"But where is the Magic Flower, and how can we get it?" asked Trot.

"Dun'no, zac'ly," slowly replied Cap'n Bill. "The Glass Cat tol' me about it only yesterday, an' said it was in some lonely place up at the nor'east o' here. The Glass Cat goes travelin' all around Oz, you know, an' the little critter sees a lot o' things no one else does."

"That's true," said Dorothy, thoughtfully. "Northeast of here must be in the Munchkin Country, and perhaps a good way off, so let's ask the Glass Cat to tell us how to get to the Magic Flower."

So the two girls, with Cap'n Bill stumping along on his wooden leg after them, went out into the garden, and after some time spent in searching, they found the Glass Cat curled up in the sunshine beside a bush, fast sleep.

The Glass Cat is one of the most curious creatures in all Oz. It was made by a famous magician named Dr. Pipt before Ozma had forbidden her subjects to work magic. Dr. Pipt had made the Glass Cat to catch mice, but the Cat refused to catch mice and was considered more curious than useful.

This astonished cat was made all of glass and was so clear and transparent that you could see through it as easily as through a window. In the top of its head,

however, was a mass of delicate pink balls which looked like jewels but were intended for brains. It had a heart made of blood-red ruby. The eyes were two large emeralds. But, aside from these colors, all the rest of the animal was of clear glass, and it had a spun-glass tail that was really beautiful.

"Here, wake up," said Cap'n Bill. "We want to talk to you."

Slowly the Glass Cat got upon its feet, yawned and then looked at the three who stood before it.

"How dare you disturb me?" it asked in a peevish voice. "You ought to be ashamed of yourselves."

"Never mind that," returned the sailor. "Do you remember tellin' me yesterday 'bout a Magic Flower in a Gold Pot?"

"Do you think I'm a fool? Look at my brains—you can see 'em work. Of course I remember!" said the cat.

"Well, where can we find it?"

"You can't. It's none of your business, anyhow. Go away and let me sleep," advised the Glass Cat.

"Now, see here," said Dorothy; "we want the Magic Flower to give to Ozma on her birthday. You'd be glad to please Ozma, wouldn't you?"

"I'm not sure," replied the creature. "Why should I want to please anybody?"

"You've got a heart, 'cause I can see it inside of you," said Trot.

"Yes; it's a pretty heart, and I'm fond of it," said the cat, twisting around to view its own body. "But it's made from a ruby, and it's hard as nails."

"Aren't you good for *anything*?" asked Trot.

"Yes, I'm pretty to look at, and that's more than can be said of you," retorted the creature.

Trot laughed at this, and Dorothy, who understood the Glass Cat pretty well, said soothingly:

"You are indeed beautiful, and if you can tell Cap'n Bill where to find the Magic Flower, all the people in Oz will praise your cleverness. The Flower will belong to Ozma, but everyone will know the Glass Cat discovered it."

This was the kind of praise the crystal creature liked.

"Well," it said, while the pink brains rolled around, "I found the Magic Flower way up in the north of the Munchkin Country where few people live or ever go. There's a river there that flows through a forest, and in the middle of the river in the middle of the forest there is a small island on which stands the gold pot in which grows the Magic Flower."

"How did you get to the island?" asked Dorothy. "Glass cats can't swim."

"No, but I'm not afraid of water," was the reply. "I just walked across the river on the bottom."

"Under the water?" exclaimed Trot.

The cat gave her a scornful look.

"How could I walk *over* the water on the *bottom* of the river? If you were transparent, anyone could see *your* brains were not working. But I'm sure you could never find the place alone. It has always been hidden from the Oz people."

"But you, with your fine pink brains, could find it again, I s'pose," remarked Dorothy.

"Yes; and if you want that Magic Flower for Ozma, I'll go with you and show you the way."

"That's lovely of you!" declared Dorothy. "Trot and Cap'n Bill will go with you, for this is to be their birthday present to Ozma. While you're gone I'll have to find something else to give her."

"All right. Come on, then, Cap'n," said the Glass Cat, starting to move away.

"Wait a minute," begged Trot. "How long will we be gone?"

"Oh, about a week."

"Then I'll put some things in a basket to take with us," said the girl, and ran into the palace to make her preparations for the journey.

CHAPTER VI

OZMA'S BIRTHDAY PRESENTS

WHEN CAP'N BILL AND TROT AND THE GLASS Cat had started for the hidden island in the far-off river to get the Magic Flower, Dorothy wondered again what she could give Ozma on her birthday. She met the Patchwork Girl and said:

"What are you going to give Ozma for a birthday present?"

"I've written a song for her," answered the strange Patchwork Girl, who went by the name of "Scraps," and who, though stuffed with cotton, had a fair assortment of mixed brains. "It's a splendid song and the chorus runs this way:

"I am crazy;

You're a daisy,

Ozma dear;

I'm demented;

You're contented,

Ozma dear;

I am patched and gay and glary;

You're a sweet and lovely fairy;

May your birthdays all be happy,

Ozma dear!"

"How do you like it, Dorothy?" inquired the Patchwork Girl.

"Is it good poetry, Scraps?" asked Dorothy, doubtfully.

"It's as good as any ordinary song," was the reply. "I have given it a dandy title, too. I shall call the song: 'When Ozma Has a Birthday, Everybody's Sure to Be Gay, for She Cannot Help the Fact That She Was Born.'"

"That's a pretty long title, Scraps," said Dorothy.

"That makes it stylish," replied the Patchwork Girl, turning a somersault and alighting on one stuffed foot. "Now-a-days the titles are sometimes longer than the songs."

Dorothy left her and walked slowly toward the palace, where she met the Tin Woodman just going up the front steps.

"What are you going to give Ozma on her birthday?" she asked.

"It's a secret, but I'll tell you," replied the Tin Woodman, who was Emperor of the Winkies. "I am having my people make Ozma a lovely girdle set with beautiful tin nuggets. Each tin nugget will be surrounded by a circle of emeralds, just to set it off to good advantage. The clasp of the girdle will be pure tin! Won't that be fine?"

"I'm sure she'll like it," said Dorothy. "Do you know what *I* can give her?"

"I haven't the slightest idea, Dorothy. It took me three months to think of my own present for Ozma."

The girl walked thoughtfully around to the back of the palace, and presently came upon the famous Scarecrow of Oz, who has having two of the palace servants stuff his legs with fresh straw.

"What are you going to give Ozma on her birthday?" asked Dorothy.

"I want to surprise her," answered the Scarecrow.

"I won't tell," promised Dorothy.

"Well, I'm having some straw slippers made for her — all straw, mind you, and braided very artistically. Ozma has always admired my straw filling, so I'm sure she'll be pleased with these lovely straw slippers."

"Ozma will be pleased with anything her loving friends give her," said the girl. "What *I'm* worried about, Scarecrow, is what to give Ozma that she hasn't got already."

"That's what worried me, until I thought of the slippers," said the Scarecrow. "You'll have to *think*, Dorothy; that's the only way to get a good idea. If I hadn't such wonderful brains, I'd never have thought of those straw foot-decorations."

Dorothy left him and went to her room, where she sat down and tried to think hard. A Pink Kitten was curled up on the window-sill and Dorothy asked her:

"What can I give Ozma for her birthday present?"

"Oh, give her some milk," replied the Pink Kitten; "that's the nicest thing I know of."

A fuzzy little black dog had squatted down at Dorothy's feet and now looked up at her with intelligent eyes.

"Tell me, Toto," said the girl; "what would Ozma like best for a birthday present?"

The little black dog wagged his tail.

"Your love," said he. "Ozma wants to be loved more than anything else."

"But I already love her, Toto!"

"Then tell her you love her twice as much as you ever did before."

"That wouldn't be true," objected Dorothy, "for I've always loved her as much as I could, and, really, Toto, I want to give Ozma some *present*, 'cause everyone else will give her a present."

"Let me see," said Toto. "How would it be to give her that useless Pink Kitten?"

"No, Toto; that wouldn't do."

"Then six kisses."

"No; that's no present."

"Well, I guess you'll have to figure it out for yourself, Dorothy," said the little dog. "To *my* notion you're more particular than Ozma will be."

Dorothy decided that if anyone could help her it would be Glinda the Good, the wonderful Sorceress of Oz who was Ozma's faithful subject and friend. But Glinda's castle was in the Quadling Country and quite a journey from the Emerald City.

So the little girl went to Ozma and asked permission to use the Wooden Saw-Horse and the royal Red Wagon to pay a visit to Glinda, and the girl Ruler kissed Princess Dorothy and graciously granted permission.

The Wooden Saw-Horse was one of the most remarkable creatures in Oz. Its body was a small log and its legs were limbs of trees stuck in the body. Its eyes were knots, its mouth was sawed in the end of the log and its ears were two chips. A small branch had been left at the rear end of the log to serve as a tail.

Ozma herself, during one of her early adventures, had brought this wooden horse to life, and so she was much attached to the queer animal and had shod the bottoms of its wooden legs with plates of gold so they would not wear out. The Saw-Horse was a swift and willing traveler, and though it could talk if need arose, it seldom said anything unless spoken to. When the Saw-Horse was harnessed to the Red Wagon there were no reins to guide him because all that was needed was to tell him where to go.

Dorothy now told him to go to Glinda's Castle and the Saw-Horse carried her there with marvelous speed.

"Glinda," said Dorothy, when she had been greeted by the Sorceress, who was tall and stately, with handsome and dignified features and dressed in a splendid and becoming gown, "what are you going to give Ozma for a birthday present?"

The Sorceress smiled and answered:

"Come into my patio[1] and I will show you."

---

1. Pronounced *pá-shi-o.*

So they entered a place that was surrounded by the wings of the great castle but had no roof, and was filled with flowers and fountains and exquisite statuary and many settees and chairs of polished marble or filigree gold. Here there were gathered fifty beautiful young girls, Glinda's handmaids, who had been selected from all parts of the Land of Oz on account of their wit and beauty and sweet dispositions. It was a great honor to be made one of Glinda's handmaidens.

When Dorothy followed the Sorceress into this delightful patio all the fifty girls were busily weaving, and their shuttles were filled with a sparkling green spun glass such as the little girl had never seen before.

"What is it, Glinda?" she asked.

"One of my recent discoveries," explained the Sorceress. "I have found a way to make threads from emeralds, by softening the stones and then spinning them into long, silken strands. With these emerald threads we are weaving cloth to make Ozma a splendid court gown for her birthday. You will notice that the threads have all the beautiful glitter and luster of the emeralds from which they are made, and so Ozma's new dress will be the most magnificent the world has ever seen, and quite fitting for our lovely Ruler of the Fairyland of Oz."

Dorothy's eyes were fairly dazed by the brilliance of the emerald cloth, some of which the girls had already woven.

"I've never seen *any*thing so beautiful!" she said, with a sigh. "But tell me, Glinda, what can *I* give our lovely Ozma on her birthday?"

The good Sorceress considered this question for a long time before she replied. Finally she said:

"Of course there will be a grand feast at the Royal Palace on Ozma's birthday, and all our friends will be present. So I suggest that you make a fine big birthday cake of Ozma, and surround it with candles."

"Oh, just a *cake*!" exclaimed Dorothy, in disappointment.

"Nothing is nicer for a birthday," said the Sorceress.

"How many candles should there be on the cake?" asked the girl.

"Just a row of them," replied Glinda, "for no one knows how old Ozma is, although she appears to us to be just a young girl—as fresh and fair as if she had lived but a few years."

"A cake doesn't seem like much of a present," Dorothy asserted.

"Make it a surprise cake," suggested the Sorceress. "Don't you remember the four and twenty blackbirds that were baked in a pie? Well, you need not use live blackbirds in your cake, but you could have some surprise of a different sort."

"Like what?" questioned Dorothy, eagerly.

"If I told you, it wouldn't be *your* present to Ozma, but *mine*," answered the Sorceress, with a smile. "Think it over, my dear, and I am sure you can originate a surprise that will add greatly to the joy and merriment of Ozma's birthday banquet."

Dorothy thanked her friend and entered the Red Wagon and told the Saw-Horse to take her back home to the palace in the Emerald City.

On the way she thought the matter over seriously of making a surprise birthday cake and finally decided what to do.

As soon as she reached home, she went to the Wizard of Oz, who had a room fitted up in one of the high towers of the palace, where he studied magic so as to be able to perform such wizardry as Ozma commanded him to do for the welfare of her subjects.

The Wizard and Dorothy were firm friends and had enjoyed many strange adventures together. He was a little man with a bald head and sharp eyes and a round, jolly face, and because he was neither haughty nor proud he had become a great favorite with the Oz people.

"Wizard," said Dorothy, "I want you to help me fix up a present for Ozma's birthday."

"I'll be glad to do anything for you and for Ozma," he answered. "What's on your mind, Dorothy?"

"I'm going to make a great cake, with frosting and candles, and all that, you know."

"Very good," said the Wizard.

"In the center of this cake I'm going to leave a hollow place, with just a roof of the frosting over it," continued the girl.

"Very good," repeated the Wizard, nodding his bald head.

"In that hollow place," said Dorothy, "I want to hide a lot of monkeys about three inches high, and after the cake is placed on the banquet table, I want the monkeys to break through the frosting and dance around on the table-cloth. Then, I want each monkey to cut out a piece of cake and hand it to a guest."

"Mercy me!" cried the little Wizard, as he chuckled with laughter. "Is that *all* you want, Dorothy?"

"Almost," said she. "Can you think of anything more the little monkeys can do, Wizard?"

"Not just now," he replied. "But where will you get such tiny monkeys?"

"That's where you're to help me," said Dorothy. "In some of those wild forests in the Gillikin Country are lots of monkeys."

"Big ones," said the Wizard.

"Well, you and I will go there, and we'll get some of the big monkeys, and you will make them small—just three inches high—by means of your magic, and we'll put the little monkeys all in a basket and bring them home with us. Then you'll train them to dance—up here in your room, where no one can see them—and on Ozma's birthday we'll put 'em into the cake and they'll know by that time just what to do."

The Wizard looked at Dorothy with admiring approval, and chuckled again.

"That's really clever, my dear," he said, "and I see no reason why we can't do it, just the way you say, if only we can get the wild monkeys to agree to it."

"Do you think they'll object?" asked the girl.

"Yes; but perhaps we can argue them into it. Anyhow it's worth trying, and I'll help you if you'll agree to let this Surprise Cake be a present to Ozma from you and me together. I've been wondering what I could give Ozma, and as I've got to train the monkeys as well as make them small, I think you ought to make me your partner."

"Of course," said Dorothy; "I'll be glad to do so."

"Then it's a bargain," declared the Wizard. "We must go to seek those monkeys at once, however, for it will take time to train them and we'll have to travel a good way to the Gillikin forests where they live."

"I'm ready to go any time," agreed Dorothy. "Shall we ask Ozma to let us take the Saw-Horse?"

The Wizard did not answer that at once. He took time to think of the suggestion.

"No," he answered at length, "the Red Wagon couldn't get through the thick forests and there's some danger to us in going into the wild places to search for monkeys. So I propose we take the Cowardly Lion and the Hungry Tiger. We can ride on their backs as well as in the Red Wagon, and if there is danger to us from other beasts, these two friendly champions will protect us from all harm."

"That's a splendid idea!" exclaimed Dorothy. "Let's go now and ask the Hungry Tiger and the Cowardly Lion if they will help us. Shall we ask Ozma if we can go?"

"I think not," said the Wizard, getting his hat and his black bag of magic tools. "This is to be a surprise for her birthday, and so she mustn't know where we're going. We'll just leave word, in case Ozma inquires for us, that we'll be back in a few days."

CHAPTER VII

THE FOREST OF GUGU

In the central western part of the Gillikin Country is a great tangle of trees called Gugu Forest. It is the biggest forest in all Oz and stretches miles and miles in every direction—north, south, east and west. Adjoining it on the east side is a range of rugged mountains covered with underbrush and small twisted trees. You can find this place by looking at the Map of the Land of Oz.

Gugu Forest is the home of most of the wild beasts that inhabit Oz. These are seldom disturbed in their leafy haunts because there is no reason why Oz people should go there, except on rare occasions, and most parts of the forest have never been seen by any eyes but the eyes of the beasts who make their home there. The biggest beasts inhabit the great forest, while the smaller ones live mostly in the mountain underbrush at the east.

Now, you must know that there are laws in the forests, as well as in every other place, and these laws are made by the beasts themselves, and are necessary to keep them from fighting and tearing one another to pieces. In Gugu Forest there is a King—an enormous yellow leopard called "Gugu"—after whom the forest is named. And this King has three other beasts to advise him in keeping the laws and maintaining order—Bru the Bear, Loo the Unicorn and Rango the Gray Ape—who are known as the King's Counsellors. All these are fierce and ferocious beasts, and hold their high offices because they are more intelligent and more feared then their fellows.

Since Oz became a fairyland, no man, woman or child ever dies in that land nor is anyone ever sick. Likewise the beasts of the forests never die, so that long years add to their cunning and wisdom, as well as to their size and strength. It is possible for beasts—or even people—to be destroyed, but the task is so difficult that it is seldom attempted. Because it is free from sickness and death is one reason why Oz is a fairyland, but it is doubtful whether those who come to Oz from the outside world, as Dorothy and Button-Bright and Trot and Cap'n Bill and the Wizard did, will live forever or cannot be injured. Even Ozma is not sure about this, and so the guests of Ozma from other lands are always carefully protected from any danger, so as to be on the safe side.

In spite of the laws of the forests there are often fights among the beasts; some of them have lost an eye or an ear or even had a leg torn off. The King and the King's Counsellors always punish those who start a fight, but so fierce is the nature of some beasts that they will at times fight in spite of laws and punishment.

Over this vast, wild Forest of Gugu flew two eagles, one morning, and near the center of the jungle the eagles alighted on a branch of a tall tree.

"Here is the place for us to begin our work," said one, who was Ruggedo, the Nome.

"Do many beasts live here?" asked Kiki Aru, the other eagle.

"The forest is full of them," said the Nome. "There are enough beasts right here to enable us to conquer the people of Oz, if we can get them to consent to join us. To do that, we must go among them and tell them our plans, so we must now decide on what shapes we had better assume while in the forest."

"I suppose we must take the shapes of beasts?" said Kiki.

"Of course. But that requires some thought. All kinds of beasts live here, and a yellow leopard is King. If we become leopards, the King will be jealous of us. If we take the forms of some of the other beasts, we shall not command proper respect."

"I wonder if the beasts will attack us?" asked Kiki.

"I'm a Nome, and immortal, so nothing can hurt me," replied Ruggedo.

"I was born in the Land of Oz, so nothing can hurt me," said Kiki.

"But, in order to carry out our plans, we must win the favor of all the animals of the forest."

"Then what shall we do?" asked Kiki.

"Let us mix the shapes of several beasts, so we will not look like any one of them," proposed the wily old Nome. "Let us have the heads of lions, the bodies of monkeys, the wings of eagles and the tails of wild asses, with knobs of gold on the end of them instead of bunches of hair."

"Won't that make a queer combination?" inquired Kiki.

"The queerer the better," declared Ruggedo.

"All right," said Kiki. "You stay here, and I'll fly away to another tree and transform us both, and then we'll climb down our trees and meet in the forest."

"No," said the Nome, "we mustn't separate. You must transform us while we are together."

"I won't do that," asserted Kiki, firmly. "You're trying to get my secret, and I won't let you."

The eyes of the other eagle flashed angrily, but Ruggedo did not dare insist. If he offended this boy, he might have to remain an eagle always and he wouldn't like that. Some day he hoped to be able to learn the secret word of the magical transformations, but just now he must let Kiki have his own way.

"All right," he said gruffly; "do as you please."

So Kiki flew to a tree that was far enough distant so that Ruggedo could not overhear him and said: "I want Ruggedo, the Nome, and myself to have the heads of lions, the bodies of monkeys, the wings of eagles and the tails of wild asses, with knobs of gold on the ends of them instead of bunches of hair—**Pyrzqxgl!**"

He pronounced the Magic Word in the proper manner and at once his form changed to the one he had described. He spread his eagle's wings and finding they were strong enough to support his monkey body and lion head he flew swiftly to the tree where he had left Ruggedo. The Nome was also transformed and was climbing down the tree because the branches all around him were so thickly entwined that there was no room between them to fly.

Kiki quickly joined his comrade and it did not take them long to reach the ground.

CHAPTER VIII

THE LI-MON-EAGS MAKE TROUBLE

THERE HAD BEEN TROUBLE IN THE FOREST OF Gugu that morning. Chipo the Wild Boar had bitten the tail off Arx the Giraffe while the latter had his head among the leaves of a tree, eating his breakfast. Arx kicked with his heels and struck Tirrip, the great Kangaroo, who had a new baby in her pouch. Tirrip knew it was the Wild Boar's fault, so she knocked him over with one powerful blow and then ran away to escape Chipo's sharp tusks. In the chase that followed a giant porcupine stuck fifty sharp quills into the Boar and a chimpanzee in a tree threw a cocoanut at the porcupine that jammed its head into its body.

All this was against the Laws of the Forest, and when the excitement was over, Gugu the Leopard King called his royal Counsellors together to decide how best to punish the offenders.

The four lords of the forest were holding solemn council in a small clearing when they saw two strange beasts approaching them—beasts the like of which they had never seen before.

Not one of the four, however, relaxed his dignity or showed by a movement that he was startled. The great Leopard crouched at full length upon a fallen tree-trunk. Bru the Bear sat on his haunches before the King; Rango the Gray Ape stood with his muscular arms folded, and Loo the Unicorn reclined, much as a horse does, between his fellow-councillors. With one consent they remained silent, eyeing with steadfast looks the intruders, who were making their way into their forest domain.

"Well met, Brothers!" said one of the strange beasts, coming to a halt beside the group, while his comrade with hesitation lagged behind.

"We are not brothers," returned the Gray Ape, sternly. "Who are you, and how came you in the forest of Gugu?"

"We are two Li-Mon-Eags," said Ruggedo, inventing the name. "Our home is in Sky Island, and we have come to earth to warn the forest beasts that the people of Oz are about to make war upon them and enslave them, so that they will become beasts of burden forever after and obey only the will of their two-legged masters."

A low roar of anger arose from the Council of Beasts.

"Who's going to do that?" asked Loo the Unicorn, in a high, squeaky voice, at the same time rising to his feet.

"The people of Oz," said Ruggedo.

"But what will we be doing?" inquired the Unicorn.

"That's what I've come to talk to you about."

"You needn't talk! We'll fight the Oz people!" screamed the Unicorn. "We'll smash 'em; we'll trample 'em; we'll gore 'em; we'll—"

"Silence!" growled Gugu the King, and Loo obeyed, although still trembling with wrath. The cold, steady gaze of the Leopard wandered over the two strange beasts. "The people of Oz," said he, "have not been our friends; they have not been our enemies. They have let us alone, and we have let them alone. There is no reason for war between us. They have no slaves. They could not use us as slaves if they should conquer us. I think you are telling us lies, you strange Li-Mon-Eag—you mixed-up beast who are neither one thing nor another."

"Oh, on my word, it's the truth!" protested the Nome in the beast's shape. "I wouldn't lie for the world; I—"

"Silence!" again growled Gugu the King; and somehow, even Ruggedo was abashed and obeyed the edict.

"What do you say, Bru?" asked the King, turning to the great Bear, who had until now said nothing.

"How does the Mixed Beast know that what he says is true?" asked the Bear.

"Why, I can fly, you know, having the wings of an Eagle," explained the Nome. "I and my comrade yonder," turning to Kiki, "flew to a grove in Oz, and there we heard the people telling how they will make many ropes to snare you beasts, and then they will surround this forest, and all other forests, and make you prisoners. So we came here to warn you, for being beasts ourselves, although we live in the sky, we are your friends."

The Leopard's lip curled and showed his enormous teeth, sharp as needles. He turned to the Gray Ape.

"What do you think, Rango?" he asked.

"Send these mixed beasts away, Your Majesty," replied the Gray Ape. "They are mischief-makers."

"Don't do that—don't do that!" cried the Unicorn, nervously. "The stranger said he would tell us what to do. Let him tell us, then. Are we fools, not to heed a warning?"

Gugu the King turned to Ruggedo.

"Speak, Stranger," he commanded.

"Well," said the Nome, "it's this way: The Land of Oz is a fine country. The people of Oz have many good things—houses with soft beds, all sorts of nice-tasting food, pretty clothes, lovely jewels, and many other things that beasts know nothing of. Here in the dark forests the poor beasts have hard work to get enough to eat and to find a bed to rest in. But the beasts are better than the people, and why should they not have all the good things the people have? So I propose that before the Oz people have the time to make all those ropes to snare you with, that all we beasts get together and march against the Oz people and capture them. Then the beasts will become the masters and the people their slaves."

"What good would that do us?" asked Bru the Bear.

"It would save you from slavery, for one thing, and you could enjoy all the fine things the Oz people have."

"Beasts wouldn't know what to do with the things people use," said the Gray Ape.

"But this is only part of my plan," insisted the Nome. "Listen to the rest of it. We two Li-Mon-Eags are powerful magicians. When you have conquered the Oz people we will transform them all into beasts, and send them to the forests to live, and we will transform all the beasts into people, so they can enjoy all the wonderful delights of the Emerald City."

For a moment no beast spoke. Then the King said: "Prove it."

"Prove what?" asked Ruggedo.

"Prove that you can transform us. If you are a magician transform the Unicorn into a man. Then we will believe you. If you fail, we will destroy you."

"All right," said the Nome. "But I'm tired, so I'll let my comrade make the transformation."

Kiki Aru had stood back from the circle, but he had heard all that was said. He now realized that he must make good Ruggedo's boast, so he retreated to the edge of the clearing and whispered the Magic Word.

Instantly the Unicorn became a fat, chubby little man, dressed in the purple Gillikin costume, and it was hard to tell which was the more astonished, the King, the Bear, the Ape or the former Unicorn.

"It's true!" shorted the man-beast. "Good gracious, look what I am! It's wonderful!"

The King of Beasts now addressed Ruggedo in a more friendly tone.

"We must believe your story, since you have given us proof of your power," said he. "But why, if you are so great a magician, cannot you conquer the Oz people without our help, and so save us the trouble?"

"Alas!" replied the crafty old Nome, "no magician is able to do everything. The transformations are easy to us because we are Li-Mon-Eags, but we cannot fight, or conquer even such weak creatures as the Oz people. But we will stay with you and advise and help you, and we will transform all the Oz people into beasts, when the time comes, and all the beasts into people."

Gugu the King turned to his Counsellors.

"How shall we answer this friendly stranger?" he asked.

Loo the former Unicorn was dancing around and cutting capers like a clown.

"On my word, Your Majesty," he said, "this being a man is more fun than being a Unicorn."

"You look like a fool," said the Gray Ape.

"Well, I *feel* fine!" declared the man-beast.

"I think I prefer to be a Bear," said Big Bru. "I was born a Bear, and I know a Bear's ways. So I am satisfied to live as a Bear lives."

"That," said the old Nome, "is because you know nothing better. When we have conquered the Oz people, and you become a man, you'll be glad of it."

The immense Leopard rested his chin on the log and seemed thoughtful.

"The beasts of the forest must decide this matter for themselves," he said. "Go you, Rango the Gray Ape, and tell your monkey tribe to order all the forest beasts to assemble in the Great Clearing at sunrise to-morrow. When all are gathered together, this mixed-up Beast who is a magician shall talk to them and tell them what he has told us. Then, if they decide to fight the Oz people, who have declared war on us, I will lead the beasts to battle."

Rango the Gray Ape turned at once and glided swiftly through the forest on his mission. The Bear gave a grunt and walked away. Gugu the King rose and stretched himself. Then he said to Ruggedo: "Meet us at sunrise to-morrow," and with stately stride vanished among the trees.

The man-unicorn, left alone with the strangers, suddenly stopped his foolish prancing.

"You'd better make me a Unicorn again," he said. "I like being a man, but the forest beasts won't know I'm their friend, Loo, and they might tear me in pieces before morning."

So Kiki changed him back to his former shape, and the Unicorn departed to join his people.

Ruggedo the Nome was much pleased with his success.

"To-morrow," he said to Kiki Aru, "we'll win over these beasts and set them to fight and conquer the Oz people. Then I will have my revenge on Ozma and Dorothy and all the rest of my enemies."

"But I am doing all the work," said Kiki.

"Never mind; you're going to be King of Oz," promised Ruggedo.

"Will the big Leopard let me be King?" asked the boy anxiously.

The Nome came close to him and whispered:

"If Gugu the Leopard opposes us, you will transform him into a tree, and then he will be helpless."

"Of course," agreed Kiki, and he said to himself: "I shall also transform this deceitful Nome into a tree, for he lies and I cannot trust him."

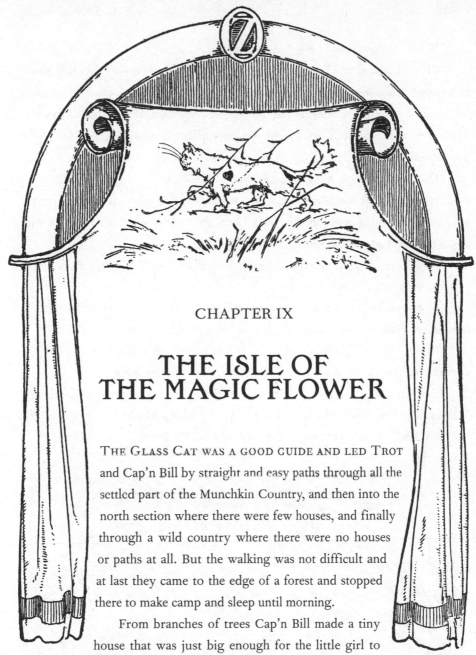

CHAPTER IX

THE ISLE OF THE MAGIC FLOWER

THE GLASS CAT WAS A GOOD GUIDE AND LED TROT and Cap'n Bill by straight and easy paths through all the settled part of the Munchkin Country, and then into the north section where there were few houses, and finally through a wild country where there were no houses or paths at all. But the walking was not difficult and at last they came to the edge of a forest and stopped there to make camp and sleep until morning.

From branches of trees Cap'n Bill made a tiny house that was just big enough for the little girl to crawl into and lie down. But first they ate some of the food Trot had carried in the basket.

"Don't you want some, too?" she asked the Glass Cat.

"No," answered the creature.

"I suppose you'll hunt around an' catch a mouse," remarked Cap'n Bill.

"Me? Catch a mouse! Why should I do that?" inquired the Glass Cat.

"Why, then you could eat it," said the sailor-man.

"I beg to inform you," returned the crystal tabby, "that I do not eat mice. Being transparent, so anyone can see through me, I'd look nice, wouldn't I, with a common mouse inside me? But the fact is that I haven't any stomach or other machinery that would permit me to eat things. The careless magician who made me didn't think I'd need to eat, I suppose."

"Don't you ever get hungry or thirsty?" asked Trot.

"Never. I don't complain, you know, at the way I'm made, for I've never yet seen any living thing as beautiful as I am. I have the handsomest brains in the world. They're pink, and you can see 'em work."

"I wonder," said Trot thoughtfully, as she ate her bread and jam, "if my brains whirl around in the same way yours do."

"No; not the same way, surely," returned the Glass Cat; "for, in that case, they'd be as good as my brains, except that they're hidden under a thick, boney skull."

"Brains," remarked Cap'n Bill, "is of all kinds and work different ways. But I've noticed that them as thinks that their brains is best is often mistook."

Trot was a little disturbed by sounds from the forest, that night, for many beasts seemed prowling among the trees, but she was confident Cap'n Bill would protect her from harm. And in fact, no beast ventured from the forest to attack them.

At daybreak they were up again, and after a simple breakfast Cap'n Bill said to the Glass Cat:

"Up anchor, Mate, and let's forge ahead. I don't suppose we're far from that Magic Flower, are we?"

"Not far," answered the transparent one, as it led the way into the forest, "but it may take you some time to get to it."

Before long they reached the bank of a river. It was not very wide, at this place, but as they followed the banks in a northerly direction it gradually broadened.

Suddenly the blue-green leaves of the trees changed to a purple hue, and Trot noticed this and said:

"I wonder what made the colors change like that?"

"It's because we have left the Munchkin Country and entered the Gillikin Country," explained the Glass Cat. "Also it's a sign our journey is nearly ended."

The river made a sudden turn, and after the travelers had passed around the bend, they saw that the stream had now become as broad as a small lake, and in the center of the Lake they beheld a little island, not more than fifty feet in extent, either way. Something glittered in the middle of this tiny island, and the Glass Cat paused on the bank and said:

"There is the gold flower-pot containing the Magic Flower, which is very curious and beautiful. If you can get to the island, your task is ended—except to carry the thing home with you."

Cap'n Bill looked at the broad expanse of water and began to whistle a low, quavering tune. Trot knew that the whistle meant that Cap'n Bill was thinking, and the old sailor didn't look at the island as much as he looked at the trees upon the bank where they stood. Presently he took from the big pocket of his coat an axe-blade, wound in an old cloth to keep the sharp edge from cutting his clothing. Then, with a large pocket knife, he cut a small limb from a tree and whittled it into a handle for his axe.

"Sit down, Trot," he advised the girl, as he worked. "I've got quite a job ahead of me now, for I've got to build us a raft."

"What do we need a raft for, Cap'n?"

"Why, to take us to the island. We can't walk under water, in the river bed, as the Glass Cat did, so we must float atop the water."

"Can you make a raft, Cap'n Bill?"

"O' course, Trot, if you give me time."

The little girl sat down on a log and gazed at the Island of the Magic Flower. Nothing else seemed to grow on the tiny isle. There was no tree, no shrub, no grass, even, as far as she could make out from that distance. But the gold pot glittered in the rays of the sun, and Trot could catch glimpses of glowing colors above it, as the Magic Flower changed from one sort to another.

"When I was here before," remarked the Glass Cat, lazily reclining at the girl's feet, "I saw two Kalidahs on this very bank, where they had come to drink."

"What are Kalidahs?" asked the girl.

"The most powerful and ferocious beasts in all Oz. This forest is their especial home, and so there are few other beasts to be found except monkeys. The monkeys are spry enough to keep out of the way of the fierce Kalidahs, which attack all other animals and often fight among themselves."

"Did they try to fight you when you saw 'em?" asked Trot, getting very much excited.

"Yes. They sprang upon me in an instant; but I lay flat on the ground, so I wouldn't get my legs broken by the great weight of the beasts, and when they tried to bite me I laughed at them and jeered them until they were frantic with rage, for they nearly broke their teeth on my hard glass. So, after a time, they discovered they could not hurt me, and went away. It was great fun."

"I hope they don't come here again to drink,—not while we're here, anyhow," returned the girl, "for I'm not made of glass, nor is Cap'n Bill, and if those bad beasts bit us, we'd get hurt."

Cap'n Bill was cutting from the trees some long stakes, making them sharp at one end and leaving a crotch at the other end. These were to bind the logs of his raft together. He had fashioned several and was just finishing another when the Glass Cat cried: "Look out! There's a Kalidah coming toward us."

Trot jumped up, greatly frightened, and looked at the terrible animal as if fascinated by its fierce eyes, for the Kalidah was looking at her, too, and its look wasn't at all friendly. But Cap'n Bill called to her: "Wade into the river, Trot, up to your knees—an' stay there!" and she obeyed him at once. The sailor-man hobbled forward, the stake in one hand and his axe in the other, and got between the girl and the beast, which sprang upon him with a growl of defiance.

Cap'n Bill moved pretty slowly, sometimes, but now he was quick as could be. As the Kalidah sprang toward him he stuck out his wooden leg and the point of it struck the beast between the eyes and sent it rolling upon the ground. Before it could

get upon its feet again the sailor pushed the sharp stake right through its body and then with the flat side of the axe he hammered the stake as far into the ground as it would go. By this means he captured the great beast and made it harmless, for try as it would, it could not get away from the stake that held it.

Cap'n Bill knew he could not kill the Kalidah, for no living thing in Oz can be killed, so he stood back and watched the beast wriggle and growl and paw the earth with its sharp claws, and then, satisfied it could not escape, he told Trot to come out of the water again and dry her wet shoes and stockings in the sun.

"Are you sure he can't get away?" she asked.

"I'd bet a cookie on it," said Cap'n Bill, so Trot came ashore and took off her shoes and stockings and laid them on the log to dry, while the sailor-man resumed his work on the raft.

The Kalidah, realizing after many struggles that it could not escape, now became quiet, but it said in a harsh, snarling voice:

"I suppose you think you're clever, to pin me to the ground in this manner. But when my friends, the other Kalidahs, come here, they'll tear you to pieces for treating me this way."

"P'raps," remarked Cap'n Bill, coolly, as he chopped at the logs, "an' p'raps not. When are your folks comin' here?"

"I don't know," admitted the Kalidah. "But when they do come, you can't escape them."

"If they hold off long enough, I'll have my raft ready," said Cap'n Bill.

"What are you going to do with a raft?" inquired the beast.

"We're goin' over to that island, to get the Magic Flower."

The huge beast looked at him in surprise a moment, and then it began to laugh. The laugh was a good deal like a roar, and it had a cruel and derisive sound, but it was a laugh nevertheless.

"Good!" said the Kalidah. "Good! Very good! I'm glad you're going to get the Magic Flower. But what will you do with it?"

"We're going to take it to Ozma, as a present on her birthday."

The Kalidah laughed again; then it became sober. "If you get to the land on your raft before my people can catch you," it said, "you will be safe from us. We can swim like ducks, so the girl couldn't have escaped me by getting into the water; but Kalidahs don't go to that island over there."

"Why not?" asked Trot.

The beast was silent.

"Tell us the reason," urged Cap'n Bill.

"Well, it's the Isle of the Magic Flower," answered the Kalidah, "and we don't care much for magic. If you hadn't had a magic leg, instead of a meat one, you couldn't have knocked me over so easily and stuck this wooden pin through me."

"I've been to the Magic Isle," said the Glass Cat, "and I've watched the Magic Flower bloom, and I'm sure it's too pretty to be left in that lonely place where only beasts prowl around it and no else sees it. So we're going to take it away to the Emerald City."

"I don't care," the beast replied in a surly tone. "We Kalidahs would be just as contented if there wasn't a flower in our forest. What good are the things anyhow?"

"Don't you like pretty things?" asked Trot.

"No."

"You ought to admire my pink brains, anyhow," declared the Glass Cat. "They're beautiful and you can see 'em work."

The beast only growled in reply, and Cap'n Bill, having now cut all his logs to a proper size, began to roll them to the water's edge and fasten them together.

CHAPTER X

STUCK FAST

THE DAY WAS NEARLY GONE WHEN, AT LAST, THE raft was ready.

"It ain't so very big," said the old sailor, "but I don't weigh much, an' you, Trot, don't weigh half as much as I do, an' the glass pussy don't count."

"But it's safe, isn't it?" inquired the girl.

"Yes; it's good enough to carry us to the island an' back again, an' that's about all we can expect of it."

Saying this, Cap'n Bill pushed the raft into the water, and when it was afloat, stepped upon it and held out his hand to Trot, who quickly followed him. The Glass Cat boarded the raft last of all.

The sailor had cut a long pole, and had also whittled a flat paddle, and with these he easily propelled the raft across the river. As they approached the island, the Wonderful Flower became more plainly visible, and they quickly decided that the Glass Cat had not praised it too highly. The colors of the flowers that bloomed in quick succession were strikingly bright and beautiful, and the shapes of the blossoms were varied and curious. Indeed, they did not resemble ordinary flowers at all.

So intently did Trot and Cap'n Bill gaze upon the Golden Flower pot that held the Magic Flower that they scarcely noticed the island itself until the raft beached upon its sands. But then the girl exclaimed: "How funny it is, Cap'n Bill, that nothing else grows here excep' the Magic Flower."

Then the sailor glanced at the island and saw that it was all bare ground, without a weed, a stone or a blade of grass. Trot, eager to examine the Flower closer, sprang from the raft and ran up the bank until she reached the Golden Flower-pot. Then she stood beside it motionless and filled with wonder. Cap'n Bill joined her, coming more leisurely, and he, too, stood in silent admiration for a time.

"Ozma will like this," remarked the Glass Cat, sitting down to watch the shifting hues of the flowers. "I'm sure she won't have as fine a birthday present from anyone else."

"Do you s'pose it's very heavy, Cap'n? And can we get it home without breaking it?" asked Trot anxiously.

"Well, I've lifted many bigger things than that," he replied; "but let's see what it weighs."

He tried to take a step forward, but could not lift his meat foot from the ground. His wooden leg seemed free enough, but the other would not budge.

"I seem stuck, Trot," he said, with a perplexed look at his foot. "It ain't mud, an' it ain't glue, but somethin's holdin' me down."

The girl attempted to lift her own feet, to go nearer to her friend, but the ground held them as fast as it held Cap'n Bill's foot. She tried to slide them, or to twist them around, but it was no use; she could not move either foot a hair's breadth.

"This is funny!" she exclaimed. "What do you s'pose has happened to us, Cap'n Bill?"

"I'm tryin' to make out," he answered. "Take off your shoes, Trot. P'raps it's the leather soles that's stuck to the ground."

She leaned down and unlaced her shoes, but found she could not pull her feet out of them. The Glass Cat, which was walking around as naturally as ever, now said:

"Your foot has got roots to it, Cap'n, and I can see the roots going into the ground, where they spread out in all directions. It's the same way with Trot. That's why you can't move. The roots hold you fast."

Cap'n Bill was rather fat and couldn't see his own feet very well, but he squatted down and examined Trot's feet and decided that the Glass Cat was right.

"This is hard luck," he declared, in a voice that showed he was uneasy at the discovery. "We're pris'ners, Trot, on this funny island, an' I'd like to know how we're ever goin' to get loose, so's we can get home again."

"Now I know why the Kalidah laughed at us," said the girl, "and why he said none of the beasts ever came to this island. The horrid creature knew we'd be caught, and wouldn't warn us."

In the meantime, the Kalidah, although pinned fast to the earth by Cap'n Bill's stake, was facing the island, and now the ugly expression which passed over its face when it defied and sneered at Cap'n Bill and Trot, had changed to one of amusement and curiosity. When it saw the adventurers had actually reached the island and were standing beside the Magic Flower, it heaved a breath of satisfaction—a long, deep breath that swelled the deep chest until the beast could feel the stake that held him move a little, as if withdrawing itself from the ground.

"Ah ha!" murmured the Kalidah, "a little more of this will set me free and allow me to escape!"

So he began breathing as hard as he could, puffing out his chest as much as possible with each indrawing breath, and by doing this he managed to raise the stake with each powerful breath, until at last the Kalidah—using the muscles of his four legs as well as his deep breaths—found itself free of the sandy soil. The stake was sticking right through him, however, so he found a rock deeply set in the bank and pressed the sharp point of the stake upon the surface of this rock until he had driven it clear through his body. Then, by getting the stake tangled among some thorny bushes, and wiggling his body, he managed to draw it out altogether.

"There!" he exclaimed, "except for those two holes in me, I'm as good as ever; but I must admit that that old wooden-legged fellow saved both himself and the girl by making me a prisoner."

Now the Kalidahs, although the most disagreeable creatures in the Land of Oz, were nevertheless magical inhabitants of a magical Fairyland, and in their natures a certain amount of good was mingled with the evil. This one was not very revengeful, and now that his late foes were in danger of perishing, his anger against them faded away.

"Our own Kalidah King," he reflected, "has certain magical powers of his own. Perhaps he knows how to fill up these two holes in my body."

So without paying any more attention to Trot and Cap'n Bill than they were paying to him, he entered the forest and trotted along a secret path that led to the hidden lair of all the Kalidahs.

While the Kalidah was making good its escape Cap'n Bill took his pipe from his pocket and filled it with tobacco and lighted it. Then, as he puffed out the smoke, he tried to think what could be done.

"The Glass Cat seems all right," he said, "an' my wooden leg didn't take roots and grow, either. So it's only flesh that gets caught."

"It's magic that does it, Cap'n!"

"I know, Trot, and that's what sticks me. We're livin' in a magic country, but neither of us knows any magic an' so we can't help ourselves."

"Couldn't the Wizard of Oz help us—or Glinda the Good?" asked the little girl.

"Ah, now we're beginnin' to reason," he answered. "I'd probably thought o' that, myself, in a minute more. By good luck the Glass Cat is free, an' so it can run back to the Emerald City an' tell the Wizard about our fix, an' ask him to come an' help us get loose."

"Will you go?" Trot asked the cat, speaking very earnestly.

"I'm no messenger, to be sent here and there," asserted the curious animal in a sulky tone of voice.

"Well," said Cap'n Bill, "you've got to go home, anyhow, 'cause you don't want to stay here, I take it. And, when you get home, it wouldn't worry you much to tell the Wizard what's happened to us."

"That's true," said the cat, sitting on its haunches and lazily washing its face with one glass paw. "I don't mind telling the Wizard—when I get home."

"Won't you go now?" pleaded Trot. "We don't want to stay here any longer than we can help, and everybody in Oz will be interested in you, and call you a hero, and say nice things about you because you helped your friends out of trouble."

That was the best way to manage the Glass Cat, which was so vain that it loved to be praised.

"I'm going home right away," said the creature, "and I'll tell the Wizard to come and help you."

Saying this, it walked down to the water and disappeared under the surface. Not being able to manage the raft alone, the Glass Cat walked on the bottom of the river as it had done when it visited the island before, and soon they saw it appear on the farther bank and trot into the forest, where it was quickly lost to sight among the trees.

Then Trot heaved a deep sigh.

"Cap'n," said she, "we're in a bad fix. There's nothing here to eat, and we can't even lie down to sleep. Unless the Glass Cat hurries, and the Wizard hurries, I don't know what's going to become of us!"

CHAPTER XI

THE BEASTS OF THE FOREST OF GUGU

THAT WAS A WONDERFUL GATHERING OF WILD animals in the Forest of Gugu next sunrise. Rango, the Gray Ape, had even called his monkey sentinels away from the forest edge, and every beast, little and big, was in the great clearing where meetings were held on occasions of great importance.

In the center of the clearing stood a great shelving rock, having a flat, inclined surface, and on this sat the stately Leopard Gugu, who was King of the Forest. On the ground beneath him squatted Bru the Bear, Loo the Unicorn, and Rango the Gray Ape, the King's three Counsellors, and in front of them stood the two strange beasts who had called themselves Li-Mon-Eags, but were really the transformations of Ruggedo the Nome, and Kiki Aru the Hyup.

Then came the beasts—rows and rows and rows of them! The smallest beasts were nearest the King's rock throne; then there were wolves and foxes, lynxes and hyenas, and the like; behind them were gathered the monkey tribes, who were hard to keep in order because they teased the other animals and were full of mischievous tricks. Back of the monkeys were the pumas, jaguars, tigers and lions, and their kind; next the bears, all sizes and colors; after them bisons, wild asses, zebras and unicorns; farther on the rhinoceri and hippopotami, and at the far edge of the forest, close to the trees that shut in the clearing, was a row of thick-skinned elephants, still as statues but with eyes bright and intelligent.

Many other kinds of beasts, too numerous to mention, were there, and some were unlike any beasts we see in the menageries and zoos in our country. Some were from the mountains west of the forest, and some from the plains at the east, and some from the river; but all present acknowledged the leadership of Gugu, who for many years had ruled them wisely and forced all to obey the laws.

When the beasts had taken their places in the clearing and the rising sun was shooting its first bright rays over the treetops, King Gugu rose on his throne. The Leopard's giant form, towering above all the others, caused a sudden hush to fall on the assemblage.

"Brothers," he said in his deep voice, "a stranger has come among us, a beast of curious form who is a great magician and is able to change the shapes of men or beasts at his will. This stranger has come to us, with another of his kind, from out of the sky, to warn us of a danger which threatens us all, and to offer us a way to escape from that danger. He says he is our friend, and he has proved to me and to my Counsellors his magic powers. Will you listen to what he has to say to you—to the message he has brought from the sky?"

"Let him speak!" came in a great roar from the great company of assembled beasts.

So Ruggedo the Nome sprang upon the flat rock beside Gugu the King, and another roar, gentle this time, showed how astonished the beasts were at the sight of his curious form. His lion's face was surrounded by a mane of pure white hair; his eagle's wings were attached to the shoulders of his monkey body and were so long that they nearly touched the ground; he had powerful arms and legs in addition to the wings, and at the end of his long, strong tail was a golden ball. Never had any beast beheld such a curious creature before, and so the very sight of the stranger, who was said to be a great magician, filled all present with awe and wonder.

Kiki stayed down below and, half hidden by the shelf of rock, was scarcely noticed. The boy realized that the old Nome was helpless without his magic power, but he also realized that Ruggedo was the best talker. So he was willing the Nome should take the lead.

"Beasts of the Forest of Gugu," began Ruggedo the Nome, "my comrade and I are your friends. We are magicians, and from our home in the sky we can look down into the Land of Oz and see everything that is going on. Also we can hear what the people below us are saying. That is how we heard Ozma, who rules the Land of Oz, say to her people: 'The beasts in the Forest of Gugu are lazy and are of no use to us. Let us go to their forest and make them all our prisoners. Let us tie them with ropes, and beat them with sticks, until they work for us and become our willing slaves.' And when the people heard Ozma of Oz say this, they were glad and raised a great shout and said: 'We will do it! We will make the beasts of the Forest of Gugu our slaves!'"

The wicked old Nome could say no more, just then, for such a fierce roar of anger rose from the multitude of beasts that his voice was drowned by the clamor. Finally the roar died away, like distant thunder, and Ruggedo the Nome went on with his speech.

"Having heard the Oz people plot against your liberty, we watched to see what they would do, and saw them all begin making ropes—ropes long and short—with which to snare our friends the beasts. You are angry, but we also were angry, for when the Oz people became the enemies of the beasts they also became our enemies; for we, too, are beasts, although we live in the sky. And my comrade and I said: 'We will save our friends and have revenge on the Oz people,' and so we came here to tell you of your danger and of our plan to save you."

"We can save ourselves," cried an old elephant. "We can fight."

"The Oz people are fairies, and you can't fight against magic unless you also have magic," answered the Nome.

"Tell us your plan!" shouted the huge Tiger, and the other beasts echoed his words, crying: "Tell us your plan."

"My plan is simple," replied Ruggedo. "By our magic we will transform all you animals into men and women—like the Oz people—and we will transform all the Oz people into beasts. You can then live in the fine houses of the Land of Oz, and eat the fine food of the Oz people, and wear their fine clothes, and sing and dance and be happy. And the Oz people, having become beasts, will have to live here in the forest and hunt and fight for food, and often go hungry, as you now do, and have no place to sleep but a bed of leaves or a hole in the ground. Having become men and women, you beasts will have all the comforts you desire, and having become beasts, the Oz people will be very miserable. That is our plan, and if you agree to it, we will all march at once into the Land of Oz and quickly conquer our enemies."

When the stranger ceased speaking, a great silence fell on the assemblage, for the beasts were thinking of what he had said. Finally one of the walruses asked:

"Can you really transform beasts into men, and men into beasts?"

"He can—he can!" cried Loo the Unicorn, prancing up and down in an excited manner. "He transformed me, only last evening, and he can transform us all."

Gugu the King now stepped forward.

"You have heard the stranger speak," said he, "and now you must answer him. It is for you to decide. Shall we agree to this plan, or not?"

"Yes!" shouted some of the animals.

"No!" shouted others.

And some were yet silent.

Gugu looked around the great circle.

"Take more time to think," he suggested. "Your answer is very important. Up to this time we have had no trouble with the Oz people, but we are proud and free, and never will become slaves. Think carefully, and when you are ready to answer, I will hear you."

CHAPTER XII

KIKI USES HIS MAGIC

THEN AROSE A GREAT CONFUSION OF SOUNDS AS all the animals began talking to their fellows. The monkeys chattered and the bears growled and the voices of the jaguars and lions rumbled, and the wolves yelped and the elephants had to trumpet loudly to make their voices heard. Such a hubbub had never been known in the forest before, and each beast argued with his neighbor until it seemed the noise would never cease.

Ruggedo the Nome waved his arms and fluttered his wings to try to make them listen to him again, but the beasts paid no attention. Some wanted to fight the Oz people, some wanted to be transformed, and some wanted to do nothing at all.

The growling and confusion had grown greater than ever when in a flash silence fell on all the beasts present, the arguments were hushed, and all gazed in astonishment at a strange sight.

For into the circle strode a great Lion—bigger and more powerful than any other lion there—and on his back rode a little girl who smiled fearlessly at the multitude of beasts. And behind the Lion and the little girl came another beast—a monstrous Tiger, who bore upon his back a funny little man carrying a black bag. Right past the rows of wondering beasts the strange animals walked, advancing until they stood just before the rock throne of Gugu.

Then the little girl and the funny little man dismounted, and the great Lion demanded in a loud voice:

"Who is King in this forest?"

"I am!" answered Gugu, looking steadily at the other. "I am Gugu the Leopard, and I am King of this forest."

"Then I greet Your Majesty with great respect," said the Lion. "Perhaps you have heard of me, Gugu. I am called the 'Cowardly Lion,' and I am King of all Beasts, the world over."

Gugu's eyes flashed angrily.

"Yes," said he, "I have heard of you. You have long claimed to be King of Beasts, but no beast who is a coward can be King over me."

"He isn't a coward, Your Majesty," asserted the little girl, "he's just cowardly, that's all."

Gugu looked at her. All the other beasts were looking at her, too.

"Who are you?" asked the King.

"Me? Oh, I'm just Dorothy," she answered.

"How dare you come here?" demanded the King.

"Why, I'm not afraid to go anywhere, if the Cowardly Lion is with me," she said. "I know him pretty well, and so I can trust him. He's always afraid, when we get into trouble, and that's why he's cowardly; but he's a terrible fighter, and that's why he isn't a coward. He doesn't like to fight, you know, but when he has to, there isn't any beast living that can conquer him."

Gugu the King looked at the big, powerful form of the Cowardly Lion, and knew she spoke the truth. Also the other Lions of the forest now came forward and bowed low before the strange Lion.

"We welcome Your Majesty," said one. "We have known you many years ago, before you went to live at the Emerald City, and we have seen you fight the terrible Kalidahs and conquer them, so we know you are the King of all Beasts."

"It is true," replied the Cowardly Lion; "but I did not come here to rule the beasts of this forest. Gugu is King here, and I believe he is a good King and just and wise. I come, with my friends, to be the guest of Gugu, and I hope we are welcome."

That pleased the great Leopard, who said very quickly:

"Yes; you, at least, are welcome to my forest. But who are these strangers with you?"

"Dorothy has introduced herself," replied the Lion, "and you are sure to like her when you know her better. This man is the Wizard of Oz, a friend of mine who can do wonderful tricks of magic. And here is my true and tried friend, the Hungry Tiger, who lives with me in the Emerald City."

"Is he *always* hungry?" asked Loo the Unicorn.

"I am," replied the Tiger, answering the question himself. "I am always hungry for fat babies."

"Can't you find any fat babies in Oz to eat?" inquired Loo, the Unicorn.

"There are plenty of them, of course," said the Tiger, "but unfortunately I have such a tender conscience that it won't allow me to eat babies. So I'm always hungry for 'em and never can eat 'em, because my conscience won't let me."

Now of all the surprised beasts in that clearing, not one was so much surprised at the sudden appearance of these four strangers as Ruggedo the Nome. He was frightened, too, for he recognized them as his most powerful enemies; but he also realized that they could not know he was the former King of the Nomes, because of the beast's form he wore, which disguised him so effectually. So he took courage and resolved that the Wizard and Dorothy should not defeat his plans.

It was hard to tell, just yet, what the vast assemblage of beasts thought of the new arrivals. Some glared angrily at them, but more of them seemed to be curious and wondering. All were interested, however, and they kept very quiet and listened carefully to all that was said.

Kiki Aru, who had remained unnoticed in the shadow of the rock, was at first more alarmed by the coming of the strangers than even Ruggedo was, and the boy told himself that unless he acted quickly and without waiting to ask the advice of the old Nome, their conspiracy was likely to be discovered and all their plans to conquer and rule Oz be defeated. Kiki didn't like the way Ruggedo acted either, for the former King of the Nomes wanted to do everything his own way, and made the boy, who alone possessed the power of transformations, obey his orders as if he were a slave.

Another thing that disturbed Kiki Aru was the fact that a real Wizard had arrived, who was said to possess many magical powers, and this Wizard carried his tools in a black bag, and was the friend of the Oz people, and so would probably try to prevent war between the beasts of the forest and the people of Oz.

All these things passed through the mind of the Hyup boy while the Cowardly Lion and Gugu the King were talking together, and that was why he now began to do several strange things.

He had found a place, near to the point where he stood, where there was a deep hollow in the rock, so he put his face into this hollow and whispered softly, so he would not be heard:

"I want the Wizard of Oz to become a fox—**Pyrzqxgl!**"

The Wizard, who had stood smilingly beside his friends, suddenly felt his form change to that of a fox, and his black bag fell to the ground. Kiki reached out an arm and seized the bag, and the Fox cried as loud as it could:

"Treason! There's a traitor here with magic powers!"

Everyone was startled at this cry, and Dorothy, seeing her old friend's plight, screamed and exclaimed: "Mercy me!"

But the next instant the little girl's form had changed to that of a lamb with fleecy white wool, and Dorothy was too bewildered to do anything but look around her in wonder.

The Cowardly Lion's eyes now flashed fire; he crouched low and lashed the ground with his tail and gazed around to discover who the treacherous magician might be. But Kiki, who had kept his face in the hollow rock, again whispered the Magic Word, and the great lion disappeared and in his place stood a little boy dressed in Munchkin costume. The little Munchkin boy was as angry as the lion had been, but he was small and helpless.

Ruggedo the Nome saw what was happening and was afraid Kiki would spoil all his plans, so he leaned over the rock and shouted: "Stop, Kiki—stop!"

Kiki would not stop, however. Instead, he transformed the Nome into a goose, to Ruggedo's horror and dismay. But the Hungry Tiger had witnessed all these transformations, and he was watching to see which of those present was to blame for them. When Ruggedo spoke to Kiki, the Hungry Tiger knew that he was the magician, so he made a sudden spring and hurled his great body full upon the form of the Li-Mon-Eag crouching against the rock. Kiki didn't see the Tiger coming because his face was still in the hollow, and the heavy body of the tiger bore him to the earth just as he said "**Pyrzqxgl!**" for the fifth time.

So now the tiger which was crushing him changed to a rabbit, and relieved of its weight, Kiki sprang up and, spreading his eagle's wings, flew into the branches of a tree, where no beast could easily reach him. He was not an instant too quick in

doing this, for Gugu the King had crouched on the rock's edge and was about to spring on the boy.

From his tree Kiki transformed Gugu into a fat Gillikin woman, and laughed aloud to see how the woman pranced with rage, and how astonished all the beasts were at their King's new shape.

The beasts were frightened, too, fearing they would share the fate of Gugu, so a stampede began when Rango the Gray Ape sprang into the forest, and Bru the Bear and Loo the Unicorn followed as quickly as they could. The elephants backed into the forest, and all the other animals, big and little, rushed after them, scattering through the jungles until the clearing was far behind. The monkeys scrambled into the trees and swung themselves from limb to limb, to avoid being trampled upon by the bigger beasts, and they were so quick that they distanced all the rest. A panic of fear seemed to have overtaken the forest people and they got as far away from the terrible Magician as they possibly could.

But the transformed ones stayed in the clearing, being so astonished and bewildered by their new shapes that they could only look at one another in a dazed and helpless fashion, although each one was greatly annoyed at the trick that had been played on him.

"Who are you?" the Munchkin boy asked the Rabbit; and "Who are you?" the Fox asked the Lamb; and "Who are you?" the Rabbit asked the fat Gillikin woman.

"I'm Dorothy," said the woolly Lamb.

"I'm the Wizard," said the Fox.

"I'm the Cowardly Lion," said the Munchkin Boy.

"I'm the Hungry Tiger," said the Rabbit.

"I'm Gugu the King," said the fat Woman.

But when they asked the Goose who he was, Ruggedo the Nome would not tell them.

"I'm just a Goose," he replied, "and what I was before, I cannot remember."

CHAPTER XIII

THE LOSS OF
THE BLACK BAG

KIKI ARU, IN THE FORM OF THE LI-MON-EAG, HAD
scrambled into the high, thick branches of the tree, so
no one could see him, and there he opened the Wizard's
black bag, which he had carried away in his flight.
He was curious to see what the Wizard's magic tools
looked like, and hoped he could use some of them
and so secure more power; but after he had taken the
articles, one by one, from the bag, he had to admit
they were puzzles to him. For, unless he understood
their uses, they were of no value whatever. Kiki Aru,
the Hyup boy, was no wizard or magician at all, and could do nothing
unusual except to use the magic word he had stolen from his father on Mount Munch.
So he hung the Wizard's black bag on a branch of the tree and then climbed down to
the lower limbs that he might see what the victims of his transformations were doing.

They were all on top of the flat rock, talking together in tones so low that Kiki
could not hear what they said.

"This is certainly a misfortune," remarked the Wizard in the Fox's form, "but our transformations are a sort of enchantment which is very easy to break—when you know how and have the tools to do it with. The tools are in my black bag; but where is the bag?"

No one knew that, for none had seen Kiki Aru fly away with it.

"Let's look and see if we can find it," suggested Dorothy the Lamb.

So they left the rock, and all of them searched the clearing high and low without finding the bag of magic tools. The Goose searched as earnestly as the others, for if he could discover it, he meant to hide it where the Wizard could never find it, because if the Wizard changed him back to his proper form, along with the others, he would then be recognized as Ruggedo the Nome, and they would send him out of the Land of Oz and so ruin all his hopes of conquest.

Ruggedo was not really sorry, now that he thought about it, that Kiki had transformed all these Oz folks. The forest beasts, it was true, had been so frightened that they would now never consent to be transformed into men, but Kiki could transform them against their will, and once they were all in human forms, it would not be impossible to induce them to conquer the Oz people.

So all was not lost, thought the old Nome, and the best thing for him to do was to rejoin the Hyup boy who had the secret of the transformations. So, having made sure the Wizard's black bag was not in the clearing, the Goose wandered away through the trees when the others were not looking, and when out of their hearing, he began calling, "Kiki Aru! Kiki Aru! Quack—quack! Kiki Aru!"

The Boy and the Woman, the Fox, the Lamb and the Rabbit, not being able to find the bag, went back to the rock, all feeling exceedingly strange.

"Where's the Goose?" asked the Wizard.

"He must have run away," replied Dorothy. "I wonder who he was?"

"I think," said Gugu the King, who was the fat Woman, "that the Goose was the stranger who proposed that we make war upon the Oz people. If so, his transformation was merely a trick to deceive us, and he has now gone to join his comrade, that wicked Li-Mon-Eag who obeyed all his commands."

"What shall we do now?" asked Dorothy. "Shall we go back to the Emerald City, as we are, and then visit Glinda the Good and ask her to break the enchantments?"

"I think so," replied the Wizard Fox. "And we can take Gugu the King with us, and have Glinda restore him to his natural shape. But I hate to leave my bag of magic tools behind me, for without it I shall lose much of my power as a Wizard. Also, if I go back to the Emerald City in the shape of a Fox, the Oz people will think I'm a poor Wizard and will lose their respect for me."

"Let us make still another search for your tools," suggested the Cowardly Lion, "and then, if we fail to find the black bag anywhere in this forest, we must go back home as we are."

"Why did you come here, anyway?" inquired Gugu.

"We wanted to borrow a dozen monkeys, to use on Ozma's birthday," explained the Wizard. "We were going to make them small, and train them to do tricks, and put them inside Ozma's birthday cake."

"Well," said the Forest King, "you would have to get the consent of Rango the Gray Ape, to do that. He commands all the tribes of monkeys."

"I'm afraid it's too late, now," said Dorothy, regretfully. "It was a splendid plan, but we've got troubles of our own, and I don't like being a lamb at all."

"You're nice and fuzzy," said the Cowardly Lion.

"That's nothing," declared Dorothy. "I've never been 'specially proud of myself, but I'd rather be the way I was born than anything else in the whole world."

THE GLASS CAT, ALTHOUGH IT HAD SOME DISAGREEABLE WAYS AND MAN-ners, nevertheless realized that Trot and Cap'n Bill were its friends and so was quite disturbed at the fix it had gotten them into by leading them to the Isle of the Magic Flower. The ruby heart of the Glass Cat was cold and hard, but still it was a heart, and to have a heart of any sort is to have some consideration for others. But the queer transparent creature didn't want Trot and Cap'n Bill to know it was sorry for them, and therefore it moved very slowly until it had crossed the river and was out of sight among the trees of the forest. Then it headed straight toward the Emerald City, and trotted so fast that it was like a crystal streak crossing the valleys and plains. Being glass, the cat was tireless, and with no reason to delay its journey, it reached Ozma's palace in wonderfully quick time.

"Where's the Wizard?" it asked the Pink Kitten, which was curled up in the sunshine on the lowest step of the palace entrance.

"Don't bother me," lazily answered the Pink Kitten, whose name was Eureka.

"I must find the Wizard at once!" said the Glass Cat.

"Then find him," advised Eureka, and went to sleep again.

The Glass Cat darted up the stairway and came upon Toto, Dorothy's little black dog.

"Where's the Wizard?" asked the Cat.

"Gone on a journey with Dorothy," replied Toto.

"When did they go, and where have they gone?" demanded the Cat.

"They went yesterday, and I heard them say they would go to the Great Forest in the Munchkin Country."

"Dear me," said the Glass Cat; "that is a long journey."

"But they rode on the Hungry Tiger and the Cowardly Lion," explained Toto, "and the Wizard carried his black bag of magic tools."

The Glass Cat knew the Great Forest of Gugu well, for it had traveled through this forest many times in its journeys through the Land of Oz. And it reflected that the Forest of Gugu was nearer to the Isle of the Magic Flower than the Emerald City was, and so, if it could manage to find the Wizard, it could lead him across the Gillikin Country to where Trot and Cap'n Bill were prisoned. It was a wild country and little traveled, but the Glass Cat knew every path. So very little time need be lost, after all.

Without stopping to ask any more questions the Cat darted out of the palace and away from the Emerald City, taking the most direct route to the Forest of Gugu. Again the creature flashed through the country like a streak of light, and it would surprise you to know how quickly it reached the edge of the Great Forest.

There were no monkey guards among the trees to cry out a warning, and this was so unusual that it astonished the Glass Cat. Going farther into the forest it presently came upon a wolf, which at first bounded away in terror. But then, seeing it was only a Glass Cat, the Wolf stopped, and the Cat could see it was trembling, as if from a terrible fright.

"What's the matter?" asked the Cat.

"A dreadful Magician has come among us!" exclaimed the Wolf, "and he's changing the forms of all the beasts—quick as a wink—and making them all his slaves."

The Glass Cat smiled and said:

"Why, that's only the Wizard of Oz. He may be having some fun with you forest people, but the Wizard wouldn't hurt a beast for anything."

"I don't mean the Wizard," explained the Wolf. "And if the Wizard of Oz is that funny little man who rode a great Tiger into the clearing, he's been transformed himself by the terrible Magician."

"The Wizard transformed? Why, that's impossible," declared the Glass Cat.

"No; it isn't. I saw him with my own eyes, changed into the form of a Fox, and the girl who was with him was changed to a woolly Lamb."

The Glass Cat was indeed surprised.

"When did that happen?" it asked.

"Just a little while ago in the clearing. All the animals had met there, but they ran away when the Magician began his transformations, and I'm thankful I escaped with my natural shape. But I'm still afraid, and I'm going somewhere to hide."

With this the Wolf ran on, and the Glass Cat, which knew where the big clearing was, went toward it. But now it walked more slowly, and its pink brains rolled and tumbled around at a great rate because it was thinking over the amazing news the Wolf had told it.

When the Glass Cat reached the clearing, it saw a Fox, a Lamb, a Rabbit, a Munchkin boy and a fat Gillikin woman, all wandering around in an aimless sort of way, for they were again searching for the black bag of magic tools.

The Cat watched them a moment and then it walked slowly into the open space. At once the Lamb ran toward it, crying:

"Oh, Wizard, here's the Glass Cat!"

"Where, Dorothy?" asked the Fox.

"Here!"

The Boy and the Woman and the Rabbit now joined the Fox and the Lamb, and they all stood before the Glass Cat and speaking together, almost like a chorus, asked: "Have you seen the black bag?"

"Often," replied the Glass Cat, "but not lately."

"It's lost," said the Fox, "and we must find it."

"Are you the Wizard?" asked the Cat.

"Yes."

"And who are these others?"

"I'm Dorothy," said the Lamb.

"I'm the Cowardly Lion," said the Munchkin boy.

"I'm the Hungry Tiger," said the Rabbit.

"I'm Gugu, King of the Forest," said the fat Woman.

The Glass Cat sat on its hind legs and began to laugh. "My, what a funny lot!" exclaimed the Creature. "Who played this joke on you?"

"It's no joke at all," declared the Wizard. "It was a cruel, wicked transformation, and the Magician that did it has the head of a lion, the body of a monkey, the wings of an eagle and a round ball on the end of his tail."

The Glass Cat laughed again. "That Magician must look funnier than you do," it said. "Where is he now?"

"Somewhere in the forest," said the Cowardly Lion. "He just jumped into that tall maple tree over there, for he can climb like a monkey and fly like an eagle, and then he disappeared in the forest."

"And there was another Magician, just like him, who was his friend," added Dorothy, "but they probably quarreled, for the wickedest one changed his friend into the form of a Goose."

"What became of the Goose?" asked the Cat, looking around.

"He must have gone away to find his friend," answered Gugu the King. "But a Goose can't travel very fast, so we could easily find him if we wanted to."

"The worst thing of all," said the Wizard, "is that my black bag is lost. It disappeared when I was transformed. If I could find it I could easily break these enchantments by means of my magic, and we would resume our own forms again. Will you help us search for the black bag, Friend Cat?"

"Of course," replied the Glass Cat. "But I expect the strange Magician carried it away with him. If he's a magician, he knows you need that bag, and perhaps he's afraid of your magic. So he's probably taken the bag with him, and you won't see it again unless you find the Magician."

"That sounds reasonable," remarked the Lamb, which was Dorothy. "Those pink brains of yours seem to be working pretty well to-day."

"If the Glass Cat is right," said the Wizard in a solemn voice, "there's more trouble ahead of us. That Magician is dangerous, and if we go near him he may transform us into shapes not as nice as these."

"I don't see how we could be any worse off," growled Gugu, who was indignant because he was forced to appear in the form of a fat woman.

"Anyway," said the Cowardly Lion, "our best plan is to find the Magician and try to get the black bag from him. We may manage to steal it, or perhaps we can argue him into giving it to us."

"Why not find the Goose, first?" asked Dorothy. "The Goose will be angry at the Magician, and he may be able to help us."

"That isn't a bad idea," returned the Wizard. "Come on, Friends; let's find that Goose. We will separate and search in different directions, and the first to find the Goose must bring him here, where we will all meet again in an hour."

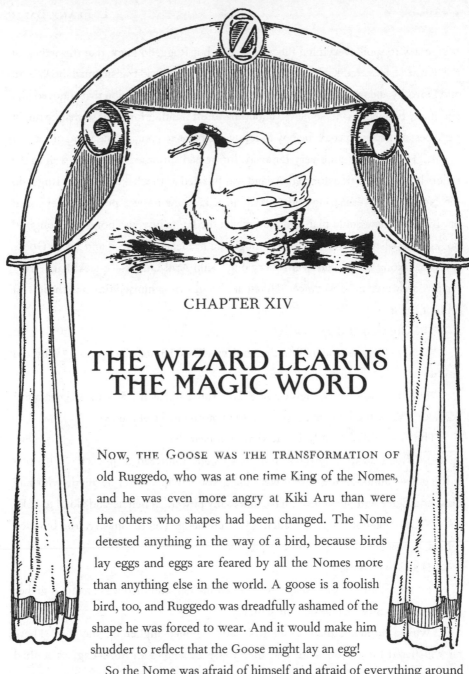

CHAPTER XIV

THE WIZARD LEARNS THE MAGIC WORD

NOW, THE GOOSE WAS THE TRANSFORMATION OF old Ruggedo, who was at one time King of the Nomes, and he was even more angry at Kiki Aru than were the others who shapes had been changed. The Nome detested anything in the way of a bird, because birds lay eggs and eggs are feared by all the Nomes more than anything else in the world. A goose is a foolish bird, too, and Ruggedo was dreadfully ashamed of the shape he was forced to wear. And it would make him shudder to reflect that the Goose might lay an egg!

So the Nome was afraid of himself and afraid of everything around him. If an egg touched him he could then be destroyed, and almost any animal he met in the forest might easily conquer him. And that would be the end of old Ruggedo the Nome.

Aside from these fears, however, he was filled with anger against Kiki, whom he had meant to trap by cleverly stealing from him the magic word. The boy must have been crazy to spoil everything the way he did, but Ruggedo knew that the arrival of the Wizard had scared Kiki, and he was not sorry the boy had transformed the Wizard and Dorothy and made them helpless. It was his own transformation that annoyed him and made him indignant, so he ran about the forest hunting for Kiki, so that he might get a better shape and coax the boy to follow his plans to conquer the Land of Oz.

Kiki Aru hadn't gone very far away, for he had surprised himself as well as the others by the quick transformations and was puzzled as to what to do next. Ruggedo the Nome was overbearing and tricky, and Kiki knew he was not to be depended on; but the Nome could plan and plot, which the Hyup boy was not wise enough to do, and so, when he looked down through the branches of a tree and saw a Goose waddling along below and heard it cry out, "Kiki Aru! Quack—quack! Kiki Aru!" the boy answered in a low voice, "Here I am," and swung himself down to the lowest limb of the tree.

The Goose looked up and saw him.

"You've bungled things in a dreadful way!" exclaimed the Goose. "Why did you do it?"

"Because I wanted to," answered Kiki. "You acted as if I was your slave, and I wanted to show these forest people that I am more powerful than you."

The Goose hissed softly, but Kiki did not hear that.

Old Ruggedo quickly recovered his wits and muttered to himself: "This boy is the goose, although it is I who wear the goose's shape. I will be gentle with him now, and fierce with him when I have him in my power." Then he said aloud to Kiki:

"Well, hereafter I will be content to acknowledge you the master. You bungled things, as I said, but we can still conquer Oz."

"How?" asked the boy.

"First give me back the shape of the Li-Mon-Eag, and then we can talk together more conveniently," suggested the Nome.

"Wait a moment, then," said Kiki, and climbed higher up the tree. There he whispered the magic word and the Goose became a Li-Mon-Eag, as he had been before.

"Good!" said the Nome, well pleased, as Kiki joined him by dropping down from the tree. "Now let us find a quiet place where we can talk without being overheard by the beasts."

So the two started away and crossed the forest until they came to a place where the trees were not so tall nor so close together, and among these scattered trees was another clearing, not so large as the first one, where the meeting of the beasts had been held. Standing on the edge of this clearing and looking across it, they saw the trees on the farther side full of monkeys, who were chattering together at a great rate of the sights they had witnessed at the meeting.

The old Nome whispered to Kiki not to enter the clearing or allow the monkeys to see them.

"Why not?" asked the boy, drawing back.

"Because those monkeys are to be our army—the army which will conquer Oz," said the Nome. "Sit down here with me, Kiki, and keep quiet, and I will explain to you my plan."

Now, neither Kiki Aru nor Ruggedo had noticed that a sly Fox had followed them all the way from the tree where the Goose had been transformed to the Li-Mon-Eag. Indeed, this Fox, who was none other than the Wizard of Oz, had witnessed the transformation of the Goose and now decided he would keep watch of the conspirators and see what they would do next.

A Fox can move through a forest very softly, without making any noise, and so the Wizard's enemies did not suspect his presence. But when they sat down by the edge of the clearing, to talk, with their backs toward him, the Wizard did not know whether to risk being seen, by creeping closer to hear what they said, or whether it would be better for him to hide himself until they moved on again.

While he considered this question he discovered near him a great tree which had a hollow trunk, and there was a round hole in this tree, about three feet above the ground. The Wizard Fox decided it would be safer for him to hide inside the hollow tree, so he sprang into the hole and crouched down in the hollow, so that his eyes just came to the edge of the hole by which he had entered, and from here he watched the forms of the two Li-Mon-Eags.

"This is my plan," said the Nome to Kiki, speaking so low that the Wizard could only hear the rumble of his voice. "Since you can transform anything into any form you wish, we will transform these monkeys into an army, and with that army we will conquer the Oz people."

"The monkeys won't make much of an army," objected Kiki.

"We need a great army, but not a numerous one," responded the Nome. "You will transform each monkey into a giant man, dressed in a fine uniform and armed with a sharp sword. There are fifty monkeys over there and fifty giants would make as big an army as we need."

"What will they do with the swords?" asked Kiki. "Nothing can kill the Oz people."

"True," said Ruggedo. "The Oz people cannot be killed, but they can be cut into small pieces, and while every piece will still be alive, we can scatter the pieces around so that they will be quite helpless. Therefore, the Oz people will be afraid of the swords of our army, and we will conquer them with ease."

"That seems like a good idea," replied the boy, approvingly. "And in such a case, we need not bother with the other beasts of the forest."

"No; you have frightened the beasts, and they would no longer consent to assist us in conquering Oz. But those monkeys are foolish creatures, and once they are transformed to Giants, they will do just as we say and obey our commands. Can you transform them all at once?"

"No, I must take one at a time," said Kiki. "But the fifty transformations can be made in an hour or so. Stay here, Ruggedo, and I will change the first monkey—that one at the left, on the end of the limb—into a Giant with a sword."

"Where are you going?" asked the Nome.

"I must not speak the magic word in the presence of another person," declared Kiki, who was determined not to allow his treacherous companion to learn his secret, "so I will go where you cannot hear me."

Ruggedo the Nome was disappointed, but he hoped still to catch the boy unawares and surprise the magic word. So he merely nodded his lion head, and Kiki got up and went back into the forest a short distance. Here he spied a hollow tree, and by chance it was the same hollow tree in which the Wizard of Oz, now in the form of a Fox, had hidden himself.

As Kiki ran up to the tree the Fox ducked its head, so that it was out of sight in the dark hollow beneath the hole, and then Kiki put his face into the hole and whispered: "I want that monkey on the branch at the left to become a Giant man fifty feet tall, dressed in a uniform and with a sharp sword—**Pyrzqxgl!**"

Then he ran back to Ruggedo, but the Wizard Fox had heard quite plainly every word that he had said.

The monkey was instantly transformed into the Giant, and the Giant was so big that as he stood on the ground his head was higher than the trees of the forest. The monkeys raised a great chatter but did not seem to understand that the Giant was one of themselves.

"Good!" cried the Nome. "Hurry, Kiki, and transform the others."

So Kiki rushed back to the tree and putting his face to the hollow, whispered:

"I want the next monkey to be just like the first **Pyrzqxgl!**"

Again the Wizard Fox heard the magic word, and just how it was pronounced. But he sat still in the hollow and waited to hear it again, so it would be impressed on his mind and he would not forget it.

Kiki kept running to the edge of the forest and back to the hollow tree again until he had whispered the magic word six times and six monkeys had been changed to six great giants. Then the Wizard decided he would make an experiment and use the magic word himself. So, while Kiki was running back to the Nome, the Fox stuck his head out of the hollow and said softly: "I want that creature who is running to become a hickory-nut—**Pyrzqxgl!**"

Instantly the Li-Mon-Eag form of Kiki Aru the Hyup disappeared and a small hickory-nut rolled upon the ground a moment and then lay still.

The Wizard was delighted, and leaped from the hollow just as Ruggedo looked around to see what had become of Kiki. The Nome saw the Fox but no Kiki, so he hastily rose to his feet. The Wizard did not know how powerful the queer beast might be, so he resolved to take no chances.

"I want this creature to become a walnut—**Pyrzqxgl!**" he said aloud. But he did not pronounce the magic word in quite the right way, and Ruggedo's form did not change. But the Nome knew at once that **"Pyrzqxgl!"** was the magic word, so he rushed at the Fox and cried:

"I want you to become a Goose—**Pyrzqxgl!**"

But the Nome did not pronounce the word aright, either, having never heard it spoken but once before, and then with a wrong accent. So the Fox was not transformed, but it had to run away to escape being caught by the angry Nome.

Ruggedo now began pronouncing the magic word in every way he could think of, hoping to hit the right one, and the Fox, hiding in a bush, was somewhat troubled by the fear that he might succeed. However, the Wizard, who was used to magic arts, remained calm and soon remembered exactly how Kiki Aru had pronounced the word. So he repeated the sentence he had before uttered and Ruggedo the Nome became an ordinary walnut.

The Wizard now crept out from the bush and said: "I want my own form again—**Pyrzqxgl!**"

Instantly he was the Wizard of Oz, and after picking up the hickory-nut and the walnut, and carefully placing them in his pocket, he ran back to the big clearing.

Dorothy the Lamb uttered a bleat of delight when she saw her old friend restored to his natural shape. The others were all there, not having found the Goose. The fat Gillikin woman, the Munchkin boy, the Rabbit and the Glass Cat crowded around the Wizard and asked what had happened.

Before he explained anything of his adventure, he transformed them all—except, of course, the Glass Cat—into their natural shapes, and when their joy permitted them to quiet somewhat, he told how he had by chance surprised the Magician's secret and been able to change the two Li-Mon-Eags into shapes that could not speak, and therefore would be unable to help themselves. And the little Wizard showed his astonished friends the hickory-nut and the walnut to prove that he had spoken the truth.

"But—see here!"—exclaimed Dorothy. "What has become of those Giant Soldiers who used to be monkeys?"

"I forgot all about them!" admitted the Wizard; "but I suppose they are still standing there in the forest."

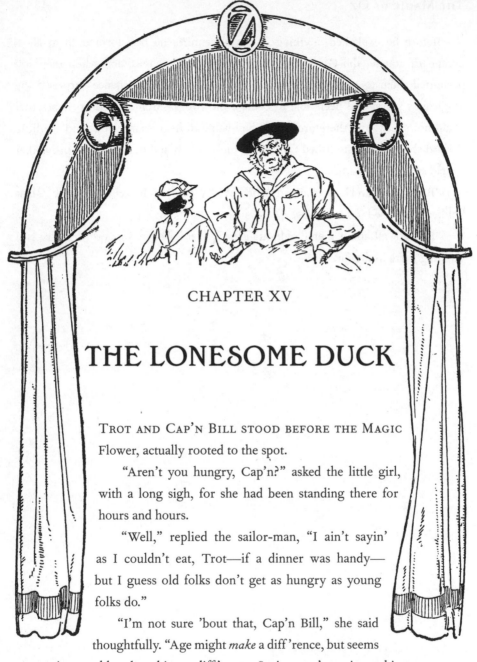

CHAPTER XV

THE LONESOME DUCK

TROT AND CAP'N BILL STOOD BEFORE THE MAGIC
Flower, actually rooted to the spot.

"Aren't you hungry, Cap'n?" asked the little girl,
with a long sigh, for she had been standing there for
hours and hours.

"Well," replied the sailor-man, "I ain't sayin'
as I couldn't eat, Trot—if a dinner was handy—
but I guess old folks don't get as hungry as young
folks do."

"I'm not sure 'bout that, Cap'n Bill," she said
thoughtfully. "Age might *make* a diff'rence, but seems
to me size would make a bigger diff'rence. Seeing you're twice as big as me, you
ought to be twice as hungry."

"I hope I am," he rejoined, "for I can stand it a while longer. I do hope the Glass
Cat will hurry, and I hope the Wizard won't waste time a-comin' to us."

Trot sighed again and watched the wonderful Magic Flower, because there was
nothing else to do. Just now a lovely group of pink peonies budded and bloomed,

but soon they faded away, and a mass of deep blue lilies took their place. Then some yellow chrysanthemums blossomed on the plant, and when they had opened all their petals and reached perfection, they gave way to a lot of white floral balls spotted with crimson—a flower Trot had never seen before.

"But I get awful tired watchin' flowers an' flowers an' flowers," she said impatiently.

"They're mighty pretty," observed Cap'n Bill.

"I know; and if a person could come and look at the Magic Flower just when she felt like it, it would be a fine thing, but to have to stand and watch it, whether you want to or not, isn't so much fun. I wish, Cap'n Bill, the thing would grow fruit for a while instead of flowers."

Scarcely had she spoken when the white balls with crimson spots faded away and a lot of beautiful ripe peaches took their place. With a cry of mingled surprise and delight Trot reached out and plucked a peach from the bush and began to eat it, finding it delicious. Cap'n Bill was somewhat dazed at the girl's wish being granted so quickly, so before he could pick a peach they had faded away and bananas took their place. "Grab one, Cap'n!" exclaimed Trot, and even while eating the peach she seized a banana with her other hand and tore it from the bush.

The old sailor was still bewildered. He put out a hand indeed, but he was too late, for now the bananas disappeared and lemons took their place.

"Pshaw!" cried Trot. "You can't eat those things; but watch out, Cap'n, for something else."

Cocoanuts next appeared, but Cap'n Bill shook his head.

"Ca'n't crack 'em," he remarked, "'cause we haven't anything handy to smash 'em with."

"Well, take one, anyhow," advised Trot; but the cocoanuts were gone now, and a deep, purple, pear-shaped fruit which was unknown to them took their place. Again Cap'n Bill hesitated, and Trot said to him:

"You ought to have captured a peach and a banana, as I did. If you're not careful, Cap'n, you'll miss all your chances. Here, I'll divide my banana with you."

Even as she spoke, the Magic Plant was covered with big red apples, growing on every branch, and Cap'n Bill hesitated no longer. He grabbed with both hands and picked two apples, while Trot had only time to secure one before they were gone.

"It's curious," remarked the sailor, munching his apple, "how these fruits keep good when you've picked 'em, but dis'pear inter thin air if they're left on the bush."

"The whole thing is curious," declared the girl, "and it couldn't exist in any country but this, where magic is so common. Those are limes. Don't pick 'em, for they'd pucker up your mouth and—Ooo! here come plums!" and she tucked her apple in her apron pocket and captured three plums—each one almost as big as an egg—before they disappeared. Cap'n Bill got some too, but both were too hungry to fast any longer, so they began eating their apples and plums and let the magic bush bear all sorts of fruits, one after another. The Cap'n stopped once to pick a fine cantaloupe, which he held under his arm, and Trot, having finished her plums, got a handful of cherries and an orange; but when almost every sort of fruit had appeared on the bush, the crop ceased and only flowers, as before, bloomed upon it.

"I wonder why it changed back," mused Trot, who was not worried because she had enough fruit to satisfy her hunger.

"Well, you only wished it would bear fruit 'for a while,'" said the sailor, "and it did. P'raps if you'd said 'forever,' Trot, it would have always been fruit."

"But why should my wish be obeyed?" asked the girl. "I'm not a fairy or a wizard or any kind of a magic-maker."

"I guess," replied Cap'n Bill, "that this little island is a magic island, and any folks on it can tell the bush what to produce, an' it'll produce it."

"Do you think I could wish for anything else, Cap'n, and get it?" she inquired anxiously.

"What are you thinkin' of, Trot?"

"I'm thinking of wishing that these roots on our feet would disappear, and let us free."

"Try it, Trot."

So she tried it, and the wish had no effect whatever.

"Try it yourself, Cap'n," she suggested.

Then Cap'n Bill made the wish to be free, with no better result.

"No," said he, "it's no use; the wishes only affect the Magic Plant; but I'm glad we can make it bear fruit, 'cause now we know we won't starve before the Wizard gets to us."

"But I'm gett'n' tired standing here so long," complained the girl. "If I could only lift one foot, and rest it, I'd feel better."

"Same with me, Trot. I've noticed that if you've got to do a thing, and can't help yourself, it gets to be a hardship mighty quick."

"Folks that can raise their feet don't appreciate what a blessing it is," said Trot thoughtfully. "I never knew before what fun it is to raise one foot, an' then another, any time you feel like it."

"There's lots o' things folks don't 'preciate," replied the sailor-man. "If somethin' would 'most stop your breath, you'd think breathin' easy was the finest thing in life. When a person's well, he don't realize how jolly it is, but when he gets sick he 'members the time he was well, an' wishes that time would come back. Most folks forget to thank God for givin' 'em two good legs, till they lose one o' 'em, like I did; and then it's too late, 'cept to praise God for leavin' one."

"Your wooden leg ain't so bad, Cap'n," she remarked, looking at it critically. "Anyhow, it don't take root on a Magic Island, like our meat legs do."

"I ain't complainin'," said Cap'n Bill. "What's that swimmin' toward us, Trot?" he added, looking over the Magic Flower and across the water.

The girl looked, too, and then she replied.

"It's a bird of some sort. It's like a duck, only I never saw a duck have so many colors."

The bird swam swiftly and gracefully toward the Magic Isle, and as it drew nearer its gorgeously colored plumage astonished them. The feathers were of many hues of glistening greens and blues and purples, and it had a yellow head with a red plume, and pink, white and violet in its tail. When it reached the Isle, it came ashore and approached them, waddling slowly and turning its head first to one side and then to the other, so as to see the girl and the sailor better.

"You're strangers," said the bird, coming to a halt near them, "and you've been caught by the Magic Isle and made prisoners."

"Yes," returned Trot, with a sigh; "we're rooted. But I hope we won't grow."

"You'll grow small," said the Bird. "You'll keep growing smaller every day, until bye and bye there'll be nothing left of you. That's the usual way, on this Magic Isle."

"How do you know about it, and who are you, anyhow?" asked Cap'n Bill.

"I'm the Lonesome Duck," replied the bird. "I suppose you've heard of me?"

"No," said Trot, "I can't say I have. What makes you lonesome?"

"Why, I haven't any family or any relations," returned the Duck.

"Haven't you any friends?"

"Not a friend. And I've nothing to do. I've lived a long time, and I've got to live forever, because I belong in the Land of Oz, where no living thing dies. Think

of existing year after year, with no friends, no family, and nothing to do! Can you wonder I'm lonesome?"

"Why don't you make a few friends, and find something to do?" inquired Cap'n Bill.

"I can't make friends because everyone I meet— bird, beast or person—is disagreeable to me. In a few minutes I shall be unable to bear your society longer, and then I'll go away and leave you," said the Lonesome Duck. "And, as for doing anything, there's no use in it. All I meet are doing something, so I have decided it's common and uninteresting and I prefer to remain lonesome."

"Don't you have to hunt for your food?" asked Trot.

"No. In my diamond palace, a little way up the river, food is magically supplied me; but I seldom eat, because it is so common."

"You must be a Magician Duck," remarked Cap'n Bill.

"Why so?"

"Well, ordinary ducks don't have diamond palaces an' magic food, like you do."

"True; and that's another reason why I'm lonesome. You must remember I'm the only Duck in the Land of Oz, and I'm not like any other duck in the outside world."

"Seems to me you *like* bein' lonesome," observed Cap'n Bill.

"I can't say I like it, exactly," replied the Duck, "but since it seems to be my fate, I'm rather proud of it."

"How do you s'pose a single, solitary Duck happened to be in the Land of Oz?" asked Trot, wonderingly.

"I used to know the reason, many years ago, but I've quite forgotten it," declared the Duck. "The reason for a thing is never so important as the thing itself, so there's no use remembering anything but the fact that I'm lonesome."

"I guess you'd be happier if you tried to do something," asserted Trot. "If you can't do anything for yourself, you can do things for others, and then you'd get lots of friends and stop being lonesome."

"Now you're getting disagreeable," said the Lonesome Duck, "and I shall have to go and leave you."

"Can't you help us any," pleaded the girl. "If there's anything magic about you, you might get us out of this scrape."

"I haven't any magic strong enough to get you off the Magic Isle," replied the Lonesome Duck. "What magic I possess is very simple, but I find it enough for my own needs."

"If we could only sit down a while, we could stand it better," said Trot, "but we have nothing to sit on."

"Then you will have to stand it," said the Lonesome Duck.

"P'raps you've enough magic to give us a couple of stools," suggested Cap'n Bill.

"A duck isn't supposed to know what stools are," was the reply.

"But you're diff'rent from all other ducks."

"That is true." The strange creature seemed to reflect for a moment, looking at them sharply from its round black eyes. Then it said: "Sometimes, when the sun is hot, I grow a toadstool to shelter me from its rays. Perhaps you could sit on toadstools."

"Well, if they were strong enough, they'd do," answered Cap'n Bill.

"Then, before I go I'll give you a couple," said the Lonesome Duck, and began waddling about in a small circle. It went around the circle to the right three times, and then it went around to the left three times. Then it hopped backward three times and forward three times.

"What are you doing?" asked Trot.

"Don't interrupt. This is an incantation," replied the Lonesome Duck, but now it began making a succession of soft noises that sounded like quacks and seemed to mean nothing at all. And it kept up these sounds so long that Trot finally exclaimed:

"Can't you hurry up and finish that 'cantation? If it takes all summer to make a couple of toadstools, you're not much of a magician."

"I told you not to interrupt," said the Lonesome Duck, sternly. "If you get too disagreeable, you'll drive me away before I finish this incantation."

Trot kept quiet, after the rebuke, and the Duck resumed the quacky muttering. Cap'n Bill chuckled a little to himself and remarked to Trot in a whisper: "For a bird that ain't got anything to do, this Lonesome Duck is makin' consider'ble fuss. An' I ain't sure, after all, as toadstools would be worth sittin' on."

Even as he spoke, the sailor-man felt something touch him from behind and, turning his head, he found a big toadstool in just the right place and of just the right size to sit upon. There was one behind Trot, too, and with a cry of pleasure the little girl sank back upon it and found it a very comfortable seat—solid, yet almost like a cushion. Even Cap'n Bill's weight did not break his toadstool down, and when both were seated, they found that the Lonesome Duck had waddled away and was now at the water's edge.

"Thank you, ever so much!" cried Trot, and the sailor called out: "Much obliged!"

But the Lonesome Duck paid no attention. Without even looking in their direction again, the gaudy fowl entered the water and swam gracefully away.

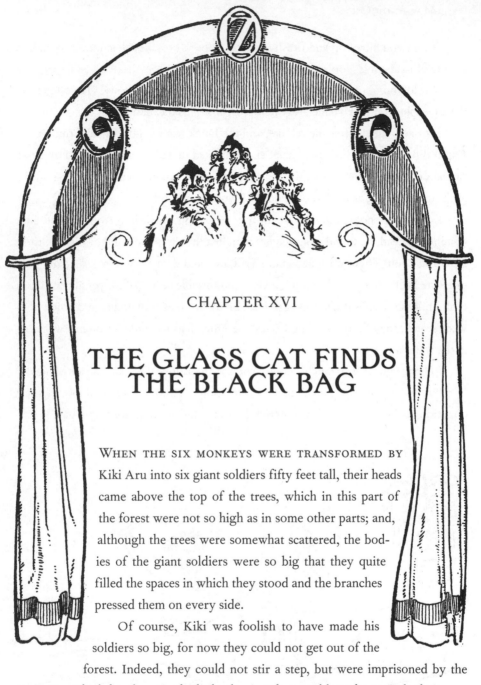

CHAPTER XVI

THE GLASS CAT FINDS THE BLACK BAG

WHEN THE SIX MONKEYS WERE TRANSFORMED BY Kiki Aru into six giant soldiers fifty feet tall, their heads came above the top of the trees, which in this part of the forest were not so high as in some other parts; and, although the trees were somewhat scattered, the bodies of the giant soldiers were so big that they quite filled the spaces in which they stood and the branches pressed them on every side.

Of course, Kiki was foolish to have made his soldiers so big, for now they could not get out of the forest. Indeed, they could not stir a step, but were imprisoned by the trees. Even had they been in the little clearing they could not have made their way out of it, but they were a little beyond the clearing. At first, the other monkeys who had not been enchanted were afraid of the soldiers, and hastily quitted the place; but soon finding that the great men stood stock still, although grunting indignantly at their transformation, the band of monkeys returned to the spot and looked at them curiously, not guessing that they were really monkeys and their own friends.

The soldiers couldn't see them, their heads being above the trees; they could not even raise their arms or draw their sharp swords, so closely were they held by the leafy branches. So the monkeys, finding the giants helpless, began climbing up their bodies, and presently all the band were perched on the shoulders of the giants and peering into their faces.

"I'm Ebu, your father," cried one soldier to a monkey who had perched upon his left ear, "but some cruel person has enchanted me."

"I'm your Uncle Peeker," said another soldier to another monkey.

So, very soon all the monkeys knew the truth and were sorry for their friends and relations and angry at the person—whoever it was—who had transformed them. There was a great chattering among the tree-tops, and the noise attracted other monkeys, so that the clearing and all the trees around were full of them.

Rango the Gray Ape, who was the Chief of all the monkey tribes of the forest, heard the uproar and came to see what was wrong with his people. And Rango, being wiser and more experienced, at once knew that the strange magician who looked like a mixed-up beast was responsible for the transformations. He realized that the six giant soldiers were helpless prisoners, because of their size, and knew he was powerless to release them. So, although he feared to meet the terrible magician, he hurried away to the Great Clearing to tell Gugu the King what had happened and to try to find the Wizard of Oz and get him to save his six enchanted subjects.

Rango darted into the Great Clearing just as the Wizard had restored all the enchanted ones around him to their proper shapes, and the Gray Ape was glad to hear that the wicked magician-beast had been conquered.

"But now, O mighty Wizard, you must come with me to where six of my people are transformed into six great giant men," he said, "for if they are allowed to remain there, their happiness and their future lives will be ruined."

The Wizard did not reply at once, for he was thinking this a good opportunity to win Rango's consent to his taking some monkeys to the Emerald City for Ozma's birthday cake.

"It is a great thing you ask of me, O Rango the Gray Ape," said he, "for the bigger the giants are the more powerful their enchantment, and the more difficult it will be to restore them to their natural forms. However, I will think it over."

Then the Wizard went to another part of the clearing and sat on a log and appeared to be in deep thought.

The Glass Cat had been greatly interested in the Gray Ape's story and was curious to see what the giant soldiers looked like. Hearing that their heads extended above the tree-tops, the Glass Cat decided that if it climbed the tall avocado tree that stood at the side of the clearing, it might be able to see the giants' heads. So, without mentioning her errand, the crystal creature went to the tree and, by sticking her sharp glass claws in the bark, easily climbed the tree to its very top and, looking over the forest, saw the six giant heads, although they were now a long way off. It was, indeed, a remarkable sight, for the huge heads had immense soldier caps on them, with red and yellow plumes and looked very fierce and terrible, although the monkey hearts of the giants were at that moment filled with fear.

Having satisfied her curiosity, the Glass Cat began to climb down from the tree more slowly. Suddenly she discerned the Wizard's black bag hanging to a limb of the tree. She grasped the black bag in her glass teeth, and although it was rather heavy for so small an animal, managed to get it free and to carry it safely down to the ground. Then she looked around for the Wizard and seeing him seated upon the stump she hid the black bag among some leaves and then went over to where the Wizard sat.

"I forgot to tell you," said the Glass Cat, "that Trot and Cap'n Bill are in trouble, and I came here to hunt you up and get you to go and rescue them."

"Good gracious, Cat! Why didn't you tell me before?" exclaimed the Wizard.

"For the reason that I found so much excitement here that I forgot Trot and Cap'n Bill."

"What's wrong with them?" asked the Wizard.

Then the Glass Cat explained how they had gone to get the Magic Flower for Ozma's birthday gift and had been trapped by the magic of the queer island. The Wizard was really alarmed, but he shook his head and said sadly:

"I'm afraid I can't help my dear friends, because I've lost my black bag."

"If I find it, will you go to them?" asked the creature.

"Of course," replied the Wizard. "But I do not think that a Glass Cat with nothing but pink brains can succeed when all the rest of us have failed."

"Don't you admire my pink brains?" demanded the Cat.

"They're pretty," admitted the Wizard, "but they're not regular brains, you know, and so we don't expect them to amount to much."

"But if I find your black bag—and find it inside of five minutes—will you admit my pink brains are better than your common human brains?"

"Well, I'll admit they're better *hunters*," said the Wizard, reluctantly, "but you can't do it. We've searched everywhere, and the black bag isn't to be found."

"That shows how much you know!" retorted the Glass Cat, scornfully. "Watch my brains a minute, and see them whirl around."

The Wizard watched, for he was anxious to regain his black bag, and the pink brains really did whirl around in a remarkable manner.

"Now, come with me," commanded the Glass Cat, and led the Wizard straight to the spot where it had covered the bag with leaves. "According to my brains," said the creature, "your black bag ought to be here."

Then it scratched at the leaves and uncovered the bag, which the Wizard promptly seized with a cry of delight. Now that he had regained his magic tools, he felt confident he could rescue Trot and Cap'n Bill.

Rango the Gray Ape was getting impatient. He now approached the Wizard and said:

"Well, what do you intend to do about those poor enchanted monkeys?"

"I'll make a bargain with you, Rango," replied the little man. "If you will let me take a dozen of your monkeys to the Emerald City, and keep them until after Ozma's

birthday, I'll break the enchantment of the six Giant Soldiers and return them to their natural forms."

But the Gray Ape shook his head.

"I can't do it," he declared. "The monkeys would be very lonesome and unhappy in the Emerald City and your people would tease them and throw stones at them, which would cause them to fight and bite."

"The people won't see them till Ozma's birthday dinner," promised the Wizard. "I'll make them very small—about four inches high, and I'll keep them in a pretty cage in my own room, where they will be safe from harm. I'll feed them the nicest kind of food, train them to do some clever tricks, and on Ozma's birthday I'll hide the twelve little monkeys inside a cake. When Ozma cuts the cake the monkeys will jump out on to the table and do their tricks. The next day I will bring them back to the forest and make them big as ever, and they'll have some exciting stories to tell their friends. What do you say, Rango?"

"I say no!" answered the Gray Ape. "I won't have my monkeys enchanted and made to do tricks for the Oz people."

"Very well," said the Wizard calmly; "then I'll go. Come, Dorothy," he called to the little girl, "let's start on our journey."

"Aren't you going to save those six monkeys who are giant soldiers?" asked Rango, anxiously.

"Why should I?" returned the Wizard. "If you will not do me the favor I ask, you cannot expect me to favor you."

"Wait a minute," said the Gray Ape. "I've changed my mind. If you will treat the twelve monkeys nicely and bring them safely back to the forest, I'll let you take them."

"Thank you," replied the Wizard, cheerfully. "We'll go at once and save those giant soldiers."

So all the party left the clearing and proceeded to the place where the giants still stood among the trees. Hundreds of monkeys, apes, baboons and orangoutangs had gathered round, and their wild chatter could be heard a mile away. But the Gray Ape soon hushed the babel of sounds, and the Wizard lost no time in breaking the enchantments. First one and then another giant soldier disappeared and became an ordinary monkey again, and the six were shortly returned to their friends in their proper forms.

This action made the Wizard very popular with the great army of monkeys, and when the Gray Ape announced that the Wizard wanted to borrow twelve monkeys to take to the Emerald City for a couple of weeks, and asked for volunteers, nearly a hundred offered to go, so great was their confidence in the little man who had saved their comrades.

The Wizard selected a dozen that seemed intelligent and good-tempered, and then he opened his black bag and took out a queerly shaped dish that was silver on the outside and gold on the inside. Into this dish he poured a powder and set fire to it. It made a thick smoke that quite enveloped the twelve monkeys, as well as the form of the Wizard, but when the smoke cleared away the dish had been changed to a golden cage with silver bars, and the twelve monkeys had become about three inches high and were all seated comfortably inside the cage.

The thousands of hairy animals who had witnessed this act of magic were much astonished and applauded the Wizard by barking aloud and shaking the limbs of the trees in which they sat. Dorothy said: "That was a fine trick, Wizard!" and the Gray Ape remarked: "You are certainly the most wonderful magician in all the Land of Oz!"

"Oh, no," modestly replied the little man. "Glinda's magic is better than mine, but mine seems good enough to use on ordinary occasions. And now, Rango, we will say good-bye, and I promise to return your monkeys as happy and safe as they are now."

The Wizard rode on the back of the Hungry Tiger and carried the cage of monkeys very carefully, so as not to joggle them. Dorothy rode on the back of the Cowardly Lion, and the Glass Cat trotted, as before, to show them the way.

Gugu the King crouched upon a log and watched them go, but as he bade them farewell, the enormous Leopard said:

"I know now that you are the friends of beasts and that the forest people may trust you. Whenever the Wizard of Oz and Princess Dorothy enter the Forest of Gugu hereafter, they will be as welcome and as safe with us as ever they are in the Emerald City."

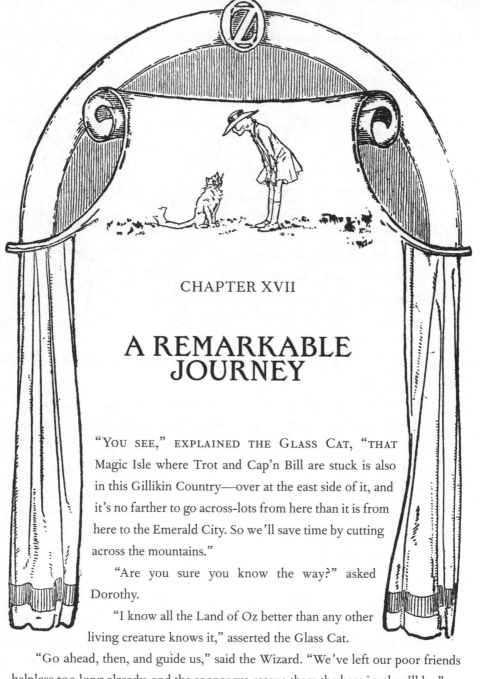

CHAPTER XVII

A REMARKABLE JOURNEY

"You see," explained the Glass Cat, "that Magic Isle where Trot and Cap'n Bill are stuck is also in this Gillikin Country—over at the east side of it, and it's no farther to go across-lots from here than it is from here to the Emerald City. So we'll save time by cutting across the mountains."

"Are you sure you know the way?" asked Dorothy.

"I know all the Land of Oz better than any other living creature knows it," asserted the Glass Cat.

"Go ahead, then, and guide us," said the Wizard. "We've left our poor friends helpless too long already, and the sooner we rescue them the happier they'll be."

"Are you sure you can get 'em out of their fix?" the little girl inquired.

"I've no doubt of it," the Wizard assured her. "But I can't tell what sort of magic I must use until I get to the place and discover just how they are enchanted."

"I've heard of that Magic Isle where the Wonderful Flower grows," remarked the Cowardly Lion. "Long ago, when I used to live in the forests, the beasts told stories about the Isle and how the Magic Flower was placed there to entrap strangers—men or beasts."

"Is the Flower really wonderful?" questioned Dorothy.

"I have heard it is the most beautiful plant in the world," answered the Lion. "I have never seen it myself, but friendly beasts have told me that they have stood on the shore of the river and looked across at the plant in the gold flower-pot and seen hundreds of flowers, of all sorts and sizes, blossom upon it in quick succession. It is said that if one picks the flowers while they are in bloom they will remain perfect for a long time, but if they are not picked they soon disappear and are replaced by other flowers. That, in my opinion, makes the Magic Plant the most wonderful in existence."

"But these are only stories," said the girl. "Has any of your friends ever picked a flower from the wonderful plant?"

"No," admitted the Cowardly Lion, "for if any living thing ventures upon the Magic Isle, where the golden flower-pot stands, that man or beast takes root in the soil and cannot get away again."

"What happens to them, then?" asked Dorothy.

"They grow smaller, hour by hour and day by day, and finally disappear entirely."

"Then," said the girl anxiously, "we must hurry up, or Cap'n Bill an' Trot will get too small to be comf'table."

They were proceeding at a rapid pace during this conversation, for the Hungry Tiger and the Cowardly Lion were obliged to move swiftly in order to keep pace with the Glass Cat. After leaving the Forest of Gugu they crossed a mountain range, and then a broad plain, after which they reached another forest, much smaller than that where Gugu ruled.

"The Magic Isle is in this forest," said the Glass Cat, "but the river is at the other side of the forest. There is no path through the trees, but if we keep going east, we will find the river, and then it will be easy to find the Magic Isle."

"Have you ever traveled this way before?" inquired the Wizard.

"Not exactly," admitted the Cat, "but I know we shall reach the river if we go east through the forest."

"Lead on, then," said the Wizard.

The Glass Cat started away, and at first it was easy to pass between the trees; but before long the underbrush and vines became thick and tangled, and after pushing their way through these obstacles for a time, our travelers came to a place where even the Glass Cat could not push through.

"We'd better go back and find a path," suggested the Hungry Tiger.

"I'm s'prised at you," said Dorothy, eyeing the Glass Cat severely.

"I'm surprised, myself," replied the Cat. "But it's a long way around the forest to where the river enters it, and I thought we could save time by going straight through."

"No one can blame you," said the Wizard, "and I think, instead of turning back, I can make a path that will allow us to proceed."

He opened his black bag and after searching among his magic tools drew out a small axe, made of some metal so highly polished that it glittered brightly even in the dark forest. The Wizard laid the little axe on the ground and said in a commanding voice:

> "Chop, Little Axe, chop clean and true;
> A path for our feet you must quickly hew.
> Chop till this tangle of jungle is passed;
> Chop to the east, Little Axe—chop fast!"

Then the little axe began to move and flashed its bright blade right and left, clearing a way through vine and brush and scattering the tangled barrier so quickly that the Lion and the Tiger, carrying Dorothy and the Wizard and the cage of monkeys on their backs, were able to stride through the forest at a fast walk. The brush seemed to melt away before them and the little axe chopped so fast that their eyes only saw a twinkling of the blade. Then, suddenly, the forest was open again, and the little axe, having obeyed its orders, lay still upon the ground.

The Wizard picked up the magic axe and after carefully wiping it with his silk handkerchief put it away in his black bag. Then they went on and in a short time reached the river.

"Let me see," said the Glass Cat, looking up and down the stream, "I think we are below the Magic Isle; so we must go up the stream until we come to it."

So up the stream they traveled, walking comfortably on the river bank, and after a while the water broadened and a sharp bend appeared in the river, hiding all below from their view. They walked briskly along, however, and had nearly reached the bend when a voice cried warningly: "Look out!"

The travelers halted abruptly and the Wizard said: "Look out for what?"

"You almost stepped on my Diamond Palace," replied the voice, and a duck with gorgeously colored feathers appeared before them. "Beasts and men are terribly clumsy," continued the Duck in an irritated tone, "and you've no business on this side of the river, anyway. What are you doing here?"

"We've come to rescue some friends of ours who are stuck fast on the Magic Isle in this river," explained Dorothy.

"I know 'em," said the Duck. "I've been to see 'em, and they're stuck fast, all right. You may as well go back home, for no power can save them."

"This is the Wonderful Wizard of Oz," said Dorothy, pointing to the little man.

"Well, I'm the Lonesome Duck," was the reply, as the fowl strutted up and down to show its feathers to best advantage. "I'm the great Forest Magician, as any beast can tell you, but even I have no power to destroy the dreadful charm of the Magic Isle."

"Are you lonesome because you're a magician?" inquired Dorothy.

"No; I'm lonesome because I have no family and no friends. But I like to be lonesome, so please don't offer to be friendly with me. Go away, and try not to step on my Diamond Palace."

"Where is it?" asked the girl.

"Behind this bush."

Dorothy hopped off the lion's back and ran around the bush to see the Diamond Palace of the Lonesome Duck, although the gaudy fowl protested in a series of low quacks. The girl found, indeed, a glistening dome formed of clearest diamonds, neatly cemented together, with a doorway at the side just big enough to admit the duck.

"Where did you find so many diamonds?" asked Dorothy, wonderingly.

"I know a place in the mountains where they are thick as pebbles," said the Lonesome Duck, "and I brought them here in my bill, one by one and put them in the river and let the water run over them until they were brightly polished. Then I built this palace, and I'm positive it's the only Diamond Palace in all the world."

"It's the only one I know of," said the little girl; "but if you live in it all alone, I don't see why it's any better than a wooden palace, or one of bricks or cobble-stones."

"You're not supposed to understand that," retorted the Lonesome Duck. "But I might tell you, as a matter of education, that a home of any sort should be beautiful to those who live in it, and should not be intended to please strangers. The Diamond Palace is my home, and I like it. So I don't care a quack whether you like it or not."

"Oh, but I do!" exclaimed Dorothy. "It's lovely on the outside, but—" Then she stopped speaking, for the Lonesome Duck had entered his palace through the little door without even saying good-bye. So Dorothy returned to her friends and they resumed their journey.

"Do you think, Wizard, the Duck was right in saying no magic can rescue Trot and Cap'n Bill?" asked the girl in a worried tone of voice.

"No, I don't think the Lonesome Duck was right in saying that," answered the Wizard, gravely, "but it is possible that their enchantment will be harder to overcome than I expected. I'll do my best, of course, and no one can do more than his best."

That didn't entirely relieve Dorothy's anxiety, but she said nothing more, and soon, on turning the bend in the river, they came in sight of the Magic Isle.

"There they are!" exclaimed Dorothy eagerly.

"Yes, I see them," replied the Wizard, nodding. "They are sitting on two big toadstools."

"That's queer," remarked the Glass Cat. "There were no toadstools there when I left them."

"What a lovely flower!" cried Dorothy in rapture, as her gaze fell on the Magic Plant.

"Never mind the Flower, just now," advised the Wizard. "The most important thing is to rescue our friends."

By this time they had arrived at a place just opposite the Magic Isle, and now both Trot and Cap'n Bill saw the arrival of their friends and called to them for help.

"How are you?" shouted the Wizard, putting his hands to his mouth so they could hear him better across the water.

"We're in hard luck," shouted Cap'n Bill, in reply. "We're anchored here and can't move till you find a way to cut the hawser."

"What does he mean by that?" asked Dorothy.

"We can't move our feet a bit!" called Trot, speaking as loud as she could.

"Why not?" inquired Dorothy.

"They've got roots on 'em," explained Trot.

It was hard to talk from so great a distance, so the Wizard said to the Glass Cat:

"Go to the island and tell our friends to be patient, for we have come to save them. It may take a little time to release them, for the Magic of the Isle is new to me and I shall have to experiment. But tell them I'll hurry as fast as I can."

So the Glass Cat walked across the river under the water to tell Trot and Cap'n Bill not to worry, and the Wizard at once opened his black bag and began to make his preparations.

CHAPTER XVIII

THE MAGIC
OF THE WIZARD

HE FIRST SET UP A SMALL SILVER TRIPOD AND placed a gold basin at the top of it. Into this basin he put two powders—a pink one and a sky-blue one—and poured over them a yellow liquid from a crystal vial. Then he mumbled some magic words, and the powders began to sizzle and burn and send out a cloud of violet smoke that floated across the river and completely enveloped both Trot and Cap'n Bill, as well as the toadstools on which they sat, and even the Magic Plant in the gold flower-pot. Then, after the smoke had disappeared into air, the Wizard called out to the prisoners:

"Are you free?"

Both Trot and Cap'n Bill tried to move their feet and failed.

"No!" they shouted in answer.

The Wizard rubbed his bald head thoughtfully and then took some other magic tools from the bag.

First he placed a little black ball in a silver pistol and shot it toward the Magic Isle. The ball exploded just over the head of Trot and scattered a thousand sparks over the little girl.

"Oh!" said the Wizard, "I guess that will set her free."

But Trot's feet were still rooted in the ground of the Magic Isle, and the disappointed Wizard had to try something else.

For almost an hour he worked hard, using almost every magic tool in his black bag, and still Cap'n Bill and Trot were not rescued.

"Dear me!" exclaimed Dorothy, "I'm 'fraid we'll have to go to Glinda, after all."

That made the little Wizard blush, for it shamed him to think that his magic was not equal to that of the Magic Isle.

"I won't give up yet, Dorothy," he said, "for I know a lot of wizardry that I haven't yet tried. I don't know what magician enchanted this little island, or what his powers were, but I do know that I can break any enchantment known to the ordinary witches and magicians that used to inhabit the Land of Oz. It's like unlocking a door; all you need is to find the right key."

"But s'pose you haven't the right key with you," suggested Dorothy; "what then?"

"Then we'll have to make the key," he answered.

The Glass Cat now came back to their side of the river, walking under the water, and said to the Wizard: "They're getting frightened over there on the island because they're both growing smaller every minute. Just now, when I left them, both Trot and Cap'n Bill were only about half their natural sizes."

"I think," said the Wizard reflectively, "that I'd better go to the shore of the island, where I can talk to them and work to better advantage. How did Trot and Cap'n Bill get to the island?"

"On a raft," answered the Glass Cat. "It's over there now on the beach."

"I suppose you're not strong enough to bring the raft to this side, are you?"

"No; I couldn't move it an inch," said the Cat.

"I'll try to get it for you," volunteered the Cowardly Lion. "I'm dreadfully scared for fear the Magic Isle will capture me, too; but I'll try to get the raft and bring it to this side for you."

"Thank you, my friend," said the Wizard.

So the Lion plunged into the river and swam with powerful strokes across to where the raft was beached upon the island. Placing one paw on the raft, he turned

and struck out with his other three legs and so strong was the great beast that he managed to drag the raft from off the beach and propel it slowly to where the Wizard stood on the river bank.

"Good!" exclaimed the little man, well pleased.

"May I go across with you?" asked Dorothy.

The Wizard hesitated.

"If you'll take care not to leave the raft or step foot on the island, you'll be quite safe," he decided. So the Wizard told the Hungry Tiger and the Cowardly Lion to guard the cage of monkeys until he returned, and then he and Dorothy got upon the raft. The paddle which Cap'n Bill had made was still there, so the little Wizard paddled the clumsy raft across the water and ran it upon the beach of the Magic Isle as close to the place where Cap'n Bill and Trot were rooted as he could.

Dorothy was shocked to see how small the prisoners had become, and Trot said to her friends: "If you can't save us soon, there'll be nothing left of us."

"Be patient, my dear," counselled the Wizard, and took the little axe from his black bag.

"What are you going to do with that?" asked Cap'n Bill.

"It's a magic axe," replied the Wizard, "and when I tell it to chop, it will chop those roots from your feet and you can run to the raft before they grow again."

"Don't!" shouted the sailor in alarm. "Don't do it! Those roots are all flesh roots, and our bodies are feeding 'em while they're growing into the ground."

"To cut off the roots," said Trot, "would be like cutting off our fingers and toes."

The Wizard put the little axe back in the black bag and took out a pair of silver pincers.

"Grow—grow—grow!" he said to the pincers, and at once they grew and extended until they reached from the raft to the prisoners.

"What are you going to do now?" demanded Cap'n Bill, fearfully eyeing the pincers.

"This magic tool will pull you up, roots and all, and land you on this raft," declared the Wizard.

"Don't do it!" pleaded the sailor, with a shudder. "It would hurt us awfully."

"It would be just like pulling teeth to pull us up by the roots," explained Trot.

"Grow small!" said the Wizard to the pincers, and at once they became small and he threw them into the black bag.

"I guess, friends, it's all up with us, this time," remarked Cap'n Bill, with a dismal sigh.

"Please tell Ozma, Dorothy," said Trot, "that we got into trouble trying to get her a nice birthday present. Then she'll forgive us. The Magic Flower is lovely and wonderful, but it's just a lure to catch folks on this dreadful island and then destroy them. You'll have a nice birthday party, without us, I'm sure; and I hope, Dorothy, that none of you in the Emerald City will forget me—or dear ol' Cap'n Bill."

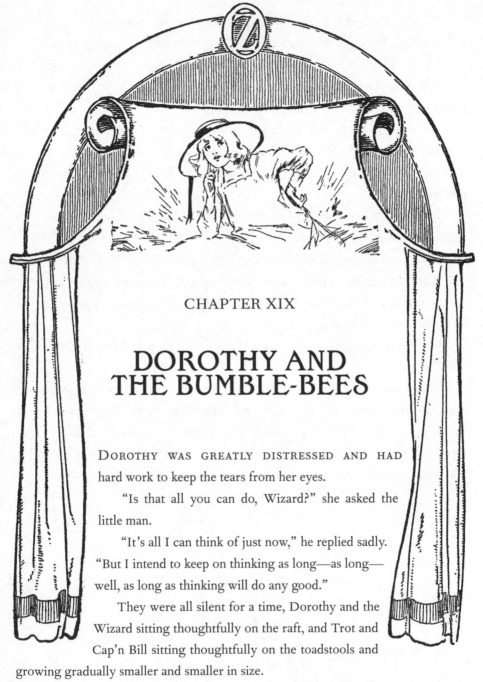

CHAPTER XIX

DOROTHY AND THE BUMBLE-BEES

DOROTHY WAS GREATLY DISTRESSED AND HAD hard work to keep the tears from her eyes.

"Is that all you can do, Wizard?" she asked the little man.

"It's all I can think of just now," he replied sadly. "But I intend to keep on thinking as long—as long—well, as long as thinking will do any good."

They were all silent for a time, Dorothy and the Wizard sitting thoughtfully on the raft, and Trot and Cap'n Bill sitting thoughtfully on the toadstools and growing gradually smaller and smaller in size.

Suddenly Dorothy said: "Wizard, I've thought of something!"

"What have you thought of?" he asked, looking at the little girl with interest.

"Can you remember the magic word that transforms people?" she asked.

"Of course," said he.

"Then you can transform Trot and Cap'n Bill into birds or bumble-bees, and they can fly away to the other shore. When they're there, you can transform 'em into their reg'lar shapes again!"

"Can you do that, Wizard?" asked Cap'n Bill, eagerly.

"I think so."

"Roots an' all?" inquired Trot.

"Why, the roots are now a part of you, and if you were transformed to a bumble-bee the whole of you would be transformed, of course, and you'd be free of this awful island."

"All right; do it!" cried the sailor-man.

So the Wizard said slowly and distinctly:

"I want Trot and Cap'n Bill to become bumble-bees—**Pyrzqxgl!**"

Fortunately, he pronounced the magic word in the right way, and instantly Trot and Cap'n Bill vanished from view, and up from the places where they had been flew two bumble-bees.

"Hooray!" shouted Dorothy in delight; "they're saved!"

"I guess they are," agreed the Wizard, equally delighted.

The bees hovered over the raft an instant and then flew across the river to where the Lion and the Tiger waited. The Wizard picked up the paddle and paddled the raft across as fast as he could. When it reached the river bank, both Dorothy and the Wizard leaped ashore and the little man asked excitedly:

"Where are the bees?"

"The bees?" inquired the Lion, who was half asleep and did not know what had happened on the Magic Isle.

"Yes; there were two of them."

"Two bees?" said the Hungry Tiger, yawning. "Why, I ate one of them and the Cowardly Lion ate the other."

"Goodness gracious!" cried Dorothy horrified.

"It was little enough for our lunch," remarked the Tiger, "but the bees were the only things we could find."

"How dreadful!" wailed Dorothy, wringing her hands in despair. "You've eaten Trot and Cap'n Bill."

But just then she heard a buzzing overhead and two bees alighted on her shoulder.

"Here we are," said a small voice in her ear. "I'm Trot, Dorothy."

"And I'm Cap'n Bill," said the other bee.

Dorothy almost fainted, with relief, and the Wizard, who was close by and had heard the tiny voices, gave a laugh and said:

"You are not the only two bees in the forest, it seems, but I advise you to keep away from the Lion and the Tiger until you regain your proper forms."

"Do it now, Wizard!" advised Dorothy. "They're so small that you never can tell what might happen to 'em."

So the Wizard gave the command and pronounced the Magic Word, and in the instant Trot and Cap'n Bill stood beside them as natural as before they had met their fearful adventure. For they were no longer small in size, because the Wizard had transformed them from bumble-bees into the shapes and sizes that nature had formerly given them. The ugly roots on their feet had disappeared with the transformation.

While Dorothy was hugging Trot, and Trot was softly crying because she was so happy, the Wizard shook hands with Cap'n Bill and congratulated him on his escape. The old sailor-man was so pleased that he also shook the Lion's paw and took off his hat and bowed politely to the cage of monkeys.

Then Cap'n Bill did a curious thing. He went to a big tree and, taking out his knife, cut away a big, broad piece of thick bark. Then he sat down on the ground and after taking a roll of stout cord from his pocket—which seemed to be full of all sorts of things—he proceeded to bind the flat piece of bark to the bottom of his good foot, over the leather sole.

"What's that for?" inquired the Wizard.

"I hate to be stumped," replied the sailor-man; "so I'm goin' back to that island."

"And get enchanted again?" exclaimed Trot, with evident disapproval.

"No; this time I'll dodge the magic of the island. I noticed that my wooden leg didn't get stuck, or take root, an' neither did the glass feet of the Glass Cat. It's only a thing that's made of meat—like man an' beasts—that the magic can hold an' root to the ground. Our shoes are leather, an' leather comes from a beast's hide. Our stockin's are wool, an' wool comes from a sheep's back. So, when we walked on the Magic Isle, our feet took root there an' held us fast. But not my wooden leg. So now I'll put a wooden bottom on my other foot an' the magic can't stop me."

"But why do you wish to go back to the island?" asked Dorothy.

"Didn't you see the Magic Flower in the gold flower-pot?" returned Cap'n Bill.

"Of course I saw it, and it's lovely and wonderful."

"Well, Trot an' I set out to get that magic plant for a present to Ozma on her birthday, and I mean to get it an' take it back with us to the Emerald City."

"That would be fine," cried Trot eagerly, "if you think you can do it, and it would be safe to try!"

"I'm pretty sure it is safe, the way I've fixed my foot," said the sailor, "an' if I should happen to get caught, I s'pose the Wizard could save me again."

"I suppose I could," agreed the Wizard. "Anyhow, if you wish to try it, Cap'n Bill, go ahead and we'll stand by and watch what happens."

So the sailor-man got upon the raft again and paddled over to the Magic Isle, landing as close to the golden flower-pot as he could. They watched him walk across the land, put both arms around the flower-pot and lift it easily from its place. Then he carried it to the raft and set it down very gently. The removal did not seem to affect the Magic Flower in any way, for it was growing daffodils when Cap'n Bill picked it up and on the way to the raft it grew tulips and gladioli. During the time the sailor was paddling across the river to where his friends awaited him, seven different varieties of flowers bloomed in succession on the plant.

"I guess the Magician who put it on the island never thought that any one would carry it off," said Dorothy.

"He figured that only men would want the plant, and any man who went upon the island to get it would be caught by the enchantment," added the Wizard.

"After this," remarked Trot, "no one will care to go on the island, so it won't be a trap any more."

"There," exclaimed Cap'n Bill, setting down the Magic Plant in triumph upon the river bank, "if Ozma gets a better birthday present than that, I'd like to know what it can be!"

"It'll s'prise her, all right," declared Dorothy, standing in awed wonder before the gorgeous blossoms and watching them change from yellow roses to violets.

"It'll s'prise ev'rybody in the Em'rald City," Trot asserted in glee, "and it'll be Ozma's present from Cap'n Bill and me."

"I think *I* ought to have a little credit," objected the Glass Cat. "I discovered the thing, and led you to it, and brought the Wizard here to save you when you got caught."

"That's true," admitted Trot, "and I'll tell Ozma the whole story, so she'll know how good you've been."

CHAPTER XX

THE MONKEYS
HAVE TROUBLE

"Now," said the Wizard, "we must start for home. But how are we going to carry that big gold flower-pot? Cap'n Bill can't lug it all the way, that's certain."

"No," acknowledged the sailor-man; "it's pretty heavy. I could carry it for a little while, but I'd have to stop to rest every few minutes."

"Couldn't we put it on your back?" Dorothy asked the Cowardly Lion, with a good-natured yawn.

"I don't object to carrying it, if you can fasten it on," answered the Lion.

"If it falls off," said Trot, "it might get smashed an' be ruined."

"I'll fix it," promised Cap'n Bill. "I'll make a flat board out of one of these tree trunks, an' tie the board on the lion's back, an' set the flower-pot on the board." He set to work at once to do this, but as he only had his big knife for a tool his progress was slow.

So the Wizard took from his black bag a tiny saw that shone like silver and said to it:

"Saw, little Saw, come show your power;
Make us a board for the Magic Flower."

And at once the Little Saw began to move and it sawed the log so fast that those who watched it work were astonished. It seemed to understand, too, just what the board was to be used for, for when it was completed it was flat on top and hollowed beneath in such a manner that it exactly fitted the Lion's back.

"That beats whittlin'!" exclaimed Cap'n Bill, admiringly. "You don't happen to have two o' them saws; do you, Wizard?"

"No," replied the Wizard, wiping the Magic Saw carefully with his silk handkerchief and putting it back in the black bag. "It's the only saw of its kind in the world; and if there were more like it, it wouldn't be so wonderful."

They now tied the board on the Lion's back, flat side up, and Cap'n Bill carefully placed the Magic Flower on the board.

"For fear o' accidents," he said, "I'll walk beside the Lion and hold onto the flower-pot."

Trot and Dorothy could both ride on the back of the Hungry Tiger, and between them they carried the cage of monkeys. But this arrangement left the Wizard, as well as the sailor, to make the journey on foot, and so the procession moved slowly and the Glass Cat grumbled because it would take so long to get to the Emerald City.

The Cat was sour-tempered and grumpy, at first, but before they had journeyed far, the crystal creature had discovered a fine amusement. The long tails of the monkeys were constantly sticking through the bars of their cage, and when they did, the Glass Cat would slyly seize the tails in her paws and pull them. That made the monkeys scream, and their screams pleased the Glass Cat immensely. Trot and Dorothy tried to stop this naughty amusement, but when they were not looking the Cat would pull the tails again, and the creature was so sly and quick that the monkeys could seldom escape. They scolded the Cat angrily and shook the bars of their cage, but they could not get out and the Cat only laughed at them.

After the party had left the forest and were on the plains of the Munchkin Country, it grew dark, and they were obliged to make camp for the night, choosing a pretty place beside a brook. By means of his magic the Wizard created three tents,

pitched in a row on the grass and nicely fitted with all that was needful for the comfort of his comrades. The middle tent was for Dorothy and Trot, and had in it two cosy white beds and two chairs. Another tent, also with beds and chairs, was for the Wizard and Cap'n Bill, while the third tent was for the Hungry Tiger, the Cowardly Lion, the cage of Monkeys and the Glass Cat. Outside the tents the Wizard made a fire and placed over it a magic kettle from which he presently drew all sorts of nice things for their supper, smoking hot.

After they had eaten and talked together for a while under the twinkling stars, they all went to bed and the people were soon asleep. The Lion and the Tiger had almost fallen asleep, too, when they were roused by the screams of the monkeys, for the Glass Cat was pulling their tails again. Annoyed by the uproar, the Hungry Tiger cried: "Stop that racket!" and getting sight of the Glass Cat, he raised his big paw and struck at the creature. The cat was quick enough to dodge the blow, but the claws of the Hungry Tiger scraped the monkey's cage and bent two of the bars.

Then the Tiger lay down again to sleep, but the monkeys soon discovered that the bending of the bars would allow them to squeeze through. They did not leave the cage, however, but after whispering together they let their tails stick out and all remained quiet. Presently the Glass Cat stole near the cage again and gave a yank to one of the tails. Instantly the monkeys leaped through the bars, one after another, and although they were so small the entire dozen of them surrounded the Glass Cat and clung to her claws and tail and ears and made her a prisoner. Then they forced her out of the tent and down to the banks of the stream. The monkeys had noticed that these banks were covered with thick, slimy mud of a dark blue color, and when they had taken the Cat to the stream, they smeared this mud all over the glass body of the cat, filling the creature's ears and eyes with it, so that she could neither see nor hear. She was no longer transparent and so thick was the mud upon her that no one could see her pink brains or her ruby heart.

In this condition they led the pussy back to the tent and then got inside their cage again.

By morning the mud had dried hard on the Glass Cat and it was a dull blue color throughout. Dorothy and Trot were horrified, but the Wizard shook his head and said it served the Glass Cat right for teasing the monkeys.

Cap'n Bill, with his strong hands, soon bent the golden wires of the monkeys' cage into the proper position and then he asked the Wizard if he should wash the Glass Cat in the water of the brook.

"Not just yet," answered the Wizard. "The Cat deserves to be punished, so I think I'll leave that blue mud—which is as bad as paint—upon her body until she gets to the Emerald City. The silly creature is so vain that she will be greatly shamed when the Oz people see her in this condition, and perhaps she'll take the lesson to heart and leave the monkeys alone hereafter."

However, the Glass Cat could not see or hear, and to avoid carrying her on the journey the Wizard picked the mud out of her eyes and ears and Dorothy dampened her handkerchief and washed both the eyes and ears clean.

As soon as she could speak the Glass Cat asked indignantly: "Aren't you going to punish those monkeys for playing such a trick on me?"

"No," answered the Wizard. "You played a trick on them by pulling their tails, so this is only tit-for-tat, and I'm glad the monkeys had their revenge."

He wouldn't allow the Glass Cat to go near the water, to wash herself, but made her follow them when they resumed their journey toward the Emerald City.

"This is only part of your punishment," said the Wizard, severely. "Ozma will laugh at you, when we get to her palace, and so will the Scarecrow, and the Tin Woodman, and Tik-Tok, and the Shaggy Man, and Button-Bright, and the Patchwork Girl, and—"

"And the Pink Kitten," added Dorothy.

That suggestion hurt the Glass Cat more than anything else. The Pink Kitten always quarreled with the Glass Cat and insisted that flesh was superior to glass, while the Glass Cat would jeer at the Pink Kitten, because it had no pink brains. But the pink brains were all daubed with blue mud, just now, and if the Pink Kitten should see the Glass Cat in such a condition, it would be dreadfully humiliating.

For several hours the Glass Cat walked along very meekly, but toward noon it seized an opportunity when no one was looking and darted away through the long grass. It remembered that there was a tiny lake of pure water near by, and to this lake the Cat sped as fast as it could go.

The others never missed her until they stopped for lunch, and then it was too late to hunt for her.

"I s'pect she's gone somewhere to clean herself," said Dorothy.

"Never mind," replied the Wizard. "Perhaps this glass creature has been punished enough, and we must not forget she saved both Trot and Cap'n Bill."

"After first leading 'em onto an enchanted island," added Dorothy. "But I think, as you do, that the Glass Cat is punished enough, and p'raps she won't try to pull the monkeys' tails again."

The Glass Cat did not rejoin the party of travelers. She was still resentful, and they moved too slowly to suit her, besides. When they arrived at the Royal Palace, one of the first things they saw was the Glass Cat curled up on a bench as bright and clean and transparent as ever. But she pretended not to notice them, and they passed her by without remark.

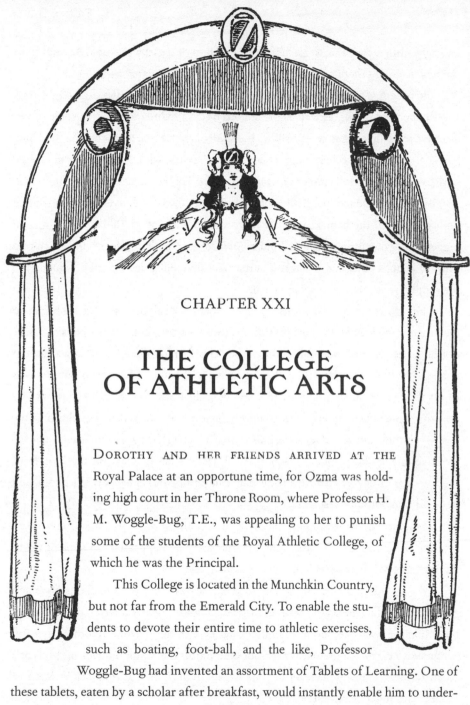

CHAPTER XXI

THE COLLEGE OF ATHLETIC ARTS

DOROTHY AND HER FRIENDS ARRIVED AT THE
Royal Palace at an opportune time, for Ozma was holding high court in her Throne Room, where Professor H.
M. Woggle-Bug, T.E., was appealing to her to punish
some of the students of the Royal Athletic College, of
which he was the Principal.

This College is located in the Munchkin Country,
but not far from the Emerald City. To enable the students to devote their entire time to athletic exercises,
such as boating, foot-ball, and the like, Professor
Woggle-Bug had invented an assortment of Tablets of Learning. One of
these tablets, eaten by a scholar after breakfast, would instantly enable him to understand arithmetic or algebra or any other branch of mathematics. Another tablet eaten
after lunch gave a student a complete knowledge of geography. Another tablet made
it possible for the eater to spell the most difficult words, and still another enabled him
to write a beautiful hand. There were tablets for history, mechanics, home cooking

and agriculture, and it mattered not whether a boy or a girl was stupid or bright, for the tablets taught them everything in the twinkling of an eye.

This method, which is patented in the Land of Oz by Professor Woggle-Bug, saves paper and books, as well as the tedious hours devoted to study in some of our less favored schools, and it also allows the students to devote all their time to racing, base-ball, tennis and other manly and womanly sports, which are greatly interfered with by study in those Temples of Learning where Tablets of Learning are unknown.

But it so happened that Professor Woggle-Bug (who had invented so much that he had acquired the habit) carelessly invented a Square-Meal Tablet, which was no bigger than your little finger-nail but contained, in condensed form, the equal of a bowl of soup, a portion of fried fish, a roast, a salad and a dessert, all of which gave the same nourishment as a square meal.

The Professor was so proud of these Square-Meal Tablets that he began to feed them to the students at his college, instead of other food, but the boys and girls objected because they wanted food that they could enjoy the taste of. It was no fun at all to swallow a tablet, with a glass of water, and call it a dinner; so they refused to eat the Square-Meal Tablets. Professor Woggle-Bug insisted, and the result was that the senior class seized the learned Professor one day and threw him into the river—clothes and all. Everyone knows that a woggle-bug cannot swim, and so the inventor of the wonderful Square-Meal Tablets lay helpless on the bottom of the river for three days before a fisherman caught one of his legs on a fishhook and dragged him out upon the bank.

The learned Professor was naturally indignant at such treatment, and so he brought the entire senior class to the Emerald City and appealed to Ozma of Oz to punish them for their rebellion.

I do not suppose the girl Ruler was very severe with the rebellious boys and girls, because she had herself refused to eat the Square-Meal Tablets in place of food, but while she was listening to the interesting case in her Throne Room, Cap'n Bill managed to carry the golden flower-pot containing the Magic Flower up to Trot's room without it being seen by anyone except Jellia Jamb, Ozma's chief Maid of Honor, and Jellia promised not to tell.

Also the Wizard was able to carry the cage of monkeys up to one of the top towers of the palace, where he had a room of his own, to which no one came unless invited. So Trot and Dorothy and Cap'n Bill and the Wizard were all delighted at the successful end of their adventure. The Cowardly Lion and the Hungry Tiger went to the marble stables behind the Royal Palace, where they lived while at home, and they too kept the secret, even refusing to tell the Wooden Saw-Horse, and Hank the Mule, and the Yellow Hen, and the Pink Kitten where they had been.

Trot watered the Magic Flower every day and allowed no one in her room to see the beautiful blossoms except her friends, Betsy Bobbin and Dorothy. The wonderful plant did not seem to lose any of its magic by being removed from its island, and Trot was sure that Ozma would prize it as one of her most delightful treasures.

Up in his tower the little Wizard of Oz began training his twelve tiny monkeys, and the little creatures were so intelligent that they learned every trick the Wizard tried to teach them. The Wizard treated them with great kindness and gentleness and gave them the food that monkeys love best, so they promised to do their best on the great occasion of Ozma's birthday.

CHAPTER XXII

OZMA'S BIRTHDAY PARTY

IT SEEMS ODD THAT A FAIRY SHOULD HAVE A BIRTH-day, for fairies, they say, were born at the beginning of time and live forever. Yet, on the other hand, it would be a shame to deprive a fairy, who has so many other good things, of the delights of a birthday. So we need not wonder that the fairies keep their birthdays just as other folks do, and consider them occasions for feasting and rejoicing.

Ozma, the beautiful girl Ruler of the Fairyland of Oz, was a real fairy, and so sweet and gentle in caring for her people that she was greatly beloved by them all. She lived in the most magnificent palace in the most magnificent city in the world, but that did not prevent her from being the friend of the most humble person in her dominions. She would mount her Wooden Saw-Horse, and ride out to a farm house and sit in the kitchen to talk with the good wife of the farmer while she did her family baking; or she would play with the children and give them rides on her famous wooden steed;

or she would stop in a forest to speak to a charcoal burner and ask if he was happy or desired anything to make him more content; or she would teach young girls how to sew and plan pretty dresses, or enter the shops where the jewelers and craftsmen were busy and watch them at their work, giving to each and all a cheering word or sunny smile.

And then Ozma would sit in her jeweled throne, with her chosen courtiers all about her, and listen patiently to any complaint brought to her by her subjects, striving to accord equal justice to all. Knowing she was fair in her decisions, the Oz people never murmured at her judgments, but agreed, if Ozma decided against them, she was right and they wrong.

When Dorothy and Trot and Betsy Bobbin and Ozma were together, one would think they were all about of an age, and the fairy Ruler no older and no more "grown up" than the other three. She would laugh and romp with them in regular girlish fashion, yet there was an air of quiet dignity about Ozma, even in her merriest moods, that, in a manner, distinguished her from the others. The three girls loved her devotedly, but they were never able to quite forget that Ozma was the Royal Ruler of the wonderful Fairyland of Oz, and by birth belonged to a powerful race.

Ozma's palace stood in the center of a delightful and extensive garden, where splendid trees and flowering shrubs and statuary and fountains abounded. One could walk for hours in this fascinating park and see something interesting at every step. In one place was an aquarium, where strange and beautiful fish swam; at another spot all the birds of the air gathered daily to a great feast which Ozma's servants provided for them, and were so fearless of harm that they would alight upon one's shoulders and eat from one's hand. There was also the Fountain of the Water of Oblivion, but it was dangerous to drink of this water, because it made one forget everything he had ever before known, even to his own name, and therefore Ozma had placed a sign of warning upon the fountain. But there were also fountains that were delightfully perfumed, and fountains of delicious nectar, cool and richly flavored, where all were welcome to refresh themselves.

Around the palace grounds was a great wall, thickly encrusted with glittering emeralds, but the gates stood open and no one was forbidden entrance. On holidays the people of the Emerald City often took their children to see the wonders of Ozma's gardens, and even entered the Royal Palace, if they felt so inclined, for they knew that they and their Ruler were friends, and that Ozma delighted to give them pleasure.

When all this is considered, you will not be surprised that the people throughout the Land of Oz, as well as Ozma's most intimate friends and her royal courtiers,

were eager to celebrate her birthday, and made preparations for the festival weeks in advance. All the brass bands practiced their nicest tunes, for they were to march in the numerous processions to be made in the Winkie Country, the Gillikin Country, the Munchkin Country and the Quadling Country, as well as in the Emerald City. Not all the people could go to congratulate their Ruler, but all could celebrate her birthday, in one way or another, however far distant from her palace they might be. Every home and building throughout the Land of Oz was to be decorated with banners and bunting, and there were to be games, and plays, and a general good time for every one.

It was Ozma's custom on her birthday to give a grand feast at the palace, to which all her closest friends were invited. It was a queerly assorted company, indeed, for there are more quaint and unusual characters in Oz than in all the rest of the world, and Ozma was more interested in unusual people than in ordinary ones—just as you and I are.

On this especial birthday of the lovely girl Ruler, a long table was set in the royal Banquet Hall of the palace, at which were place-cards for the invited guests, and at one end of the great room was a smaller table, not so high, for Ozma's animal friends, whom she never forgot, and at the other end was a big table where all of the birthday gifts were to be arranged.

When the guests arrived, they placed their gifts on this table and then found their places at the banquet table. And, after the guests were all placed, the animals entered in a solemn procession and were placed at their table by Jellia Jamb. Then, while an orchestra hidden by a bank of roses and ferns played a march composed for the occasion, the Royal Ozma entered the Banquet Hall, attended by her Maids of Honor, and took her seat at the head of the table.

She was greeted by a cheer from all the assembled company, the animals adding their roars and growls and barks and mewing and cackling to swell the glad tumult, and then all seated themselves at their tables.

At Ozma's right sat the famous Scarecrow of Oz, whose straw-stuffed body was not beautiful, but whose happy nature and shrewd wit had made him a general favorite. On the left of the Ruler was placed the Tin Woodman, whose metal body had been brightly polished for this event. The Tin Woodman was the Emperor of the Winkie Country and one of the most important persons in Oz.

Next to the Scarecrow, Dorothy was seated, and next to her was Tik-Tok, the Clockwork Man, who had been wound up as tightly as his clockwork would permit,

so he wouldn't interrupt the festivities by running down. Then came Aunt Em and Uncle Henry, Dorothy's own relations, two kindly old people who had a cozy home in the Emerald City and were very happy and contented there. Then Betsy Bobbin was seated, and next to her the droll and delightful Shaggy Man, who was a favorite wherever he went.

On the other side of the table, opposite the Tin Woodman was placed Trot, and next to her, Cap'n Bill. Then was seated Button-Bright and Ojo the Lucky, and Dr. Pipt and his good wife Margalot, and the astonishing Frogman, who had come from the Yip Country to be present at Ozma's birthday feast.

At the foot of the table, facing Ozma, was seated the queenly Glinda, the good Sorceress of Oz, for this was really the place of honor next to the head of the table where Ozma herself sat. On Glinda's right was the little Wizard of Oz, who owed to Glinda all of the magical arts he knew. Then came Jinjur, a pretty girl farmer of whom Ozma and Dorothy were quite fond. The adjoining seat was occupied by the Tin Soldier, and next to him was Professor H. M. Woggle-Bug, T.E., of the Royal Athletic College.

On Glinda's left was placed the jolly Patchwork Girl, who was a little afraid of the Sorceress and so was likely to behave herself pretty well. The Shaggy Man's brother was beside the Patchwork Girl, and then came that interesting personage, Jack Pumpkinhead, who had grown a splendid big pumpkin for a new head to be worn on Ozma's birthday, and had carved a face on it that was even jollier in expression than the one he had last worn. New heads were not unusual with Jack, for the pumpkins did not keep long, and when the seeds—which served him as brains—began to get soft and mushy, he realized his head would soon spoil, and so he procured a new one from his great field of pumpkins—grown by him so that he need never lack a head.

You will have noticed that the company at Ozma's banquet table was somewhat mixed, but every one invited was a tried and trusted friend of the girl Ruler, and their presence made her quite happy.

No sooner had Ozma seated herself, with her back to the birthday table, than she noticed that all present were eyeing with curiosity and pleasure something behind her, for the gorgeous Magic Flower was blooming gloriously and the mammoth blossoms that quickly succeeded one another on the plant were beautiful to view and filled the entire room with their delicate fragrance. Ozma wanted to look, too, to see what all were staring at, but she controlled her curiosity because it was not proper that she should yet view her birthday gifts.

So the sweet and lovely Ruler devoted herself to her guests, several of whom, such as the Scarecrow, the Tin Woodman, the Patchwork Girl, Tik-Tok, Jack Pumpkinhead and the Tin Soldier, never ate anything but sat very politely in their places and tried to entertain those of the guests who did eat.

And, at the animal table, there was another interesting group, consisting of the Cowardly Lion, the Hungry Tiger, Toto—Dorothy's little shaggy black dog—Hank the Mule, the Pink Kitten, the Wooden Saw-Horse, the Yellow Hen, and the Glass Cat. All of these had good appetites except the Saw-Horse and the Glass Cat, and each was given a plentiful supply of the food it liked best.

Finally, when the banquet was nearly over and the ice-cream was to be served, four servants entered bearing a huge cake, all frosted and decorated with candy flowers. Around the edge of the cake was a row of lighted candles, and in the center were raised candy letters that spelled the words:

OZMA'S

Birthday Cake

from

Dorothy and the Wizard

"Oh, how beautiful!" cried Ozma, greatly delighted, and Dorothy said eagerly: "Now you must cut the cake, Ozma, and each of us will eat a piece with our ice-cream."

Jellia Jamb brought a large golden knife with a jeweled handle, and Ozma stood up in her place and attempted to cut the cake. But as soon as the frosting in the center broke under the pressure of the knife there leaped from the cake a tiny monkey three inches high, and he was followed by another and another, until twelve monkeys stood on the tablecloth and bowed low to Ozma.

"Congratulations to our gracious Ruler!" they exclaimed in a chorus, and then they began a dance, so droll and amusing that all the company roared with laughter and even Ozma joined in the merriment. But after the dance the monkeys performed some wonderful acrobatic feats, and then they ran to the hollow of the cake and took out some band instruments of burnished gold—cornets, horns, drums, and the like—and forming into a procession the monkeys marched up and down the table playing a jolly tune with the ease of skilled musicians.

Dorothy was delighted with the success of her "Surprise Cake," and after the monkeys had finished their performance, the banquet came to an end.

Now was the time for Ozma to see her other presents, so Glinda the Good rose and, taking the girl Ruler by her hand, led her to the table where all her gifts were placed in magnificent array. The Magic Flower of course attracted her attention first, and Trot had to tell her the whole story of their adventures in getting it. The little girl did not forget to give due credit to the Glass Cat and the little Wizard, but it was really Cap'n Bill who had bravely carried the golden flower-pot away from the enchanted Isle.

Ozma thanked them all, and said she would place the Magic Flower in her boudoir where she might enjoy its beauty and fragrance continually. But now she discovered the marvelous gown woven by Glinda and her maidens from strands drawn from pure emeralds, and being a girl who loved pretty clothes, Ozma's ecstasy at being presented with this exquisite gown may well be imagined. She could hardly wait to put it on, but the table was loaded with other pretty gifts and the night was far spent before the happy girl Ruler had examined all her presents and thanked those who had lovingly donated them.

CHAPTER XXIII

THE FOUNTAIN OF OBLIVION

THE MORNING AFTER THE BIRTHDAY FETE, AS THE Wizard and Dorothy were walking in the grounds of the palace, Ozma came out and joined them, saying:

"I want to hear more of your adventures in the Forest of Gugu, and how you were able to get those dear little monkeys to use in Dorothy's Surprise Cake."

So they sat down on a marble bench near to the Fountain of the Water of Oblivion, and between them Dorothy and the Wizard related their adventures.

"I was dreadfully fussy while I was a woolly lamb," said Dorothy, "for it didn't feel good, a bit. And I wasn't quite sure, you know, that I'd ever get to be a girl again."

"You might have been a woolly lamb yet, if I hadn't happened to have discovered that Magic Transformation Word," declared the Wizard.

"But what became of the walnut and the hickory-nut into which you transformed those dreadful beast magicians?" inquired Ozma.

"Why, I'd almost forgotten them," was the reply; "but I believe they are still here in my pocket."

Then he searched in his pockets and brought out the two nuts and showed them to her.

Ozma regarded them thoughtfully.

"It isn't right to leave any living creatures in such helpless forms," said she. "I think, Wizard, you ought to transform them into their natural shapes again."

"But I don't know what their natural shapes are," he objected, "for of course the forms of mixed animals which they had assumed were not natural to them. And you must not forget, Ozma, that their natures were cruel and mischievous, so if I bring them back to life they might cause us a great deal of trouble."

"Nevertheless," said the Ruler of Oz, "we must free them from their present enchantments. When you restore them to their natural forms we will discover who they really are, and surely we need not fear any two people, even though they prove to be magicians and our enemies."

"I am not so sure of that," protested the Wizard, with a shake of his bald head. "The one bit of magic I robbed them of—which was the word of transformation—is so simple, yet so powerful, that neither Glinda nor I can equal it. It isn't all in the word, you know, it's the way the word is pronounced. So if the two strange magicians have other magic of the same sort, they might prove very dangerous to us, if we liberated them."

"I've an idea!" exclaimed Dorothy. "I'm no wizard, and no fairy, but if you do as I say, we needn't fear these people at all."

"What is your thought, my dear?" asked Ozma.

"Well," replied the girl, "here is this Fountain of the Water of Oblivion, and that's what put the notion into my head. When the Wizard speaks that ter'ble word that will change 'em back to their real forms, he can make 'em dreadful thirsty, too, and we'll put a cup right here by the fountain, so it'll be handy. Then they'll drink the water and forget all the magic they ever knew—and everything else, too."

"That's not a bad idea," said the Wizard, looking at Dorothy approvingly.

"It's a very *good* idea," declared Ozma. "Run for a cup, Dorothy."

So Dorothy ran to get a cup, and while she was gone the Wizard said:

"I don't know whether the real forms of these magicians are those of men or beasts. If they're beasts, they would not drink from a cup but might attack us at once and drink afterward. So it might be safer for us to have the Cowardly Lion and the Hungry Tiger here to protect us if necessary."

Ozma drew out a silver whistle which was attached to a slender gold chain and blew upon the whistle two shrill blasts. The sound, though not harsh, was very penetrating, and as soon as it reached the ears of the Cowardly Lion and the Hungry Tiger, the two huge beasts quickly came bounding toward them. Ozma explained to them what the Wizard was about to do, and told them to keep quiet unless danger threatened. So the two powerful guardians of the Ruler of Oz crouched beside the fountain and waited.

Dorothy returned and set the cup on the edge of the fountain. Then the Wizard placed the hickory-nut beside the fountain and said in a solemn voice:

"I want you to resume your natural form, and to be very thirsty—**Pyrzqxgl!**"

In an instant there appeared, in the place of the hickory-nut, the form of Kiki Aru, the Hyup boy. He seemed bewildered, at first, as if trying to remember what had happened to him and why he was in this strange place. But he was facing the fountain, and the bubbling water reminded him that he was thirsty. Without noticing Ozma, the Wizard and Dorothy, who were behind him, he picked up the cup, filled it with the Water of Oblivion, and drank it to the last drop.

He was now no longer thirsty, but he felt more bewildered than ever, for now he could remember nothing at all—not even his name or where he came from.

He looked around the beautiful garden with a pleased expression, and then, turning, he beheld Ozma and the Wizard and Dorothy regarding him curiously and the two great beasts crouching behind them.

Kiki Aru did not know who they were, but he thought Ozma very lovely and Dorothy very pleasant. So he smiled at them—the same innocent, happy smile that a baby might have indulged in, and that pleased Dorothy, who seized his hand and led him to a seat beside her on the bench.

"Why, I thought you were a dreadful magician," she exclaimed, "and you're only a boy!"

"What is a magician?" he asked, "and what is a boy?"

"Don't you know?" inquired the girl.

Kiki shook his head. Then he laughed.

"I do not seem to know anything," he replied.

"It's very curious," remarked the Wizard. "He wears the dress of the Munchkins, so he must have lived at one time in the Munchkin Country. Of course the boy can tell us nothing of his history or his family, for he has forgotten all that he ever knew."

"He seems a nice boy, now that all the wickedness has gone from him," said Ozma. "So we will keep him here with us and teach him our ways—to be true and considerate of others."

"Why, in that case, it's lucky for him he drank the Water of Oblivion," said Dorothy.

"It is indeed," agreed the Wizard. "But the remarkable thing, to me, is how such a young boy ever learned the secret of the Magic Word of Transformation. Perhaps his companion, who is at present this walnut, was the real magician, although I seem to remember that it was this boy in the beast's form who whispered the Magic Word into the hollow tree, where I overheard it."

"Well, we will soon know who the other is," suggested Ozma. "He may prove to be another Munchkin boy."

The Wizard placed the walnut near the fountain and said, as slowly and solemnly as before:

"I want you to resume your natural form, and to be very thirsty—**Pyrzqxgl!**"

Then the walnut disappeared and Ruggedo the Nome stood in its place. He also was facing the fountain, and he reached for the cup, filled it, and was about to drink when Dorothy exclaimed:

"Why, it's the old Nome King!"

Ruggedo swung around and faced them, the cup still in his hand.

"Yes," he said in an angry voice, "it's the old Nome King, and I'm going to conquer all Oz and be revenged on you for kicking me out of my throne." He looked around a moment, and then continued: "There isn't an egg in sight, and I'm stronger than all of you people put together! I don't know how I came here, but I'm going to fight the fight of my life—and I'll win!"

His long white hair and beard waved in the breeze; his eyes flashed hate and vengeance, and so astonished and shocked were they by the sudden appearance of this old enemy of the Oz people that they could only stare at him in silence and shrink away from his wild glare.

Ruggedo laughed. He drank the water, threw the cup on the ground and said fiercely:

"And now—and now—and—"

His voice grew gentle. He rubbed his forehead with a puzzled air and stroked his long beard.

"What was I going to say?" he asked, pleadingly.

"Don't you remember?" said the Wizard.

"No; I've forgotten."

"Who *are* you?" asked Dorothy.

He tried to think. "I—I'm sure I don't know," he stammered.

"Don't you know who we are, either?" questioned the girl.

"I haven't the slightest idea," said the Nome.

"Tell us who this Munchkin boy is," suggested Ozma.

Ruggedo looked at the boy and shook his head.

"He's a stranger to me. You are all strangers. I—I'm a stranger to myself," he said.

Then he patted the Lion's head and murmured, "Good doggie!" and the Lion growled indignantly.

"What shall we do with him?" asked the Wizard, perplexed.

"Once before the wicked old Nome came here to conquer us, and then, as now, he drank of the Water of Oblivion and became harmless. But we sent him back to the Nome Kingdom, where he soon learned the old evil ways again.

"For that reason," said Ozma, "we must find a place for him in the Land of Oz, and keep him here. For here he can learn no evil and will always be as innocent of guile as our own people."

And so the wandering ex-King of the Nomes found a new home, a peaceful and happy home, where he was quite content and passed his days in innocent enjoyment.

GLINDA OF OZ

Glinda
of Oz

CONTENTS

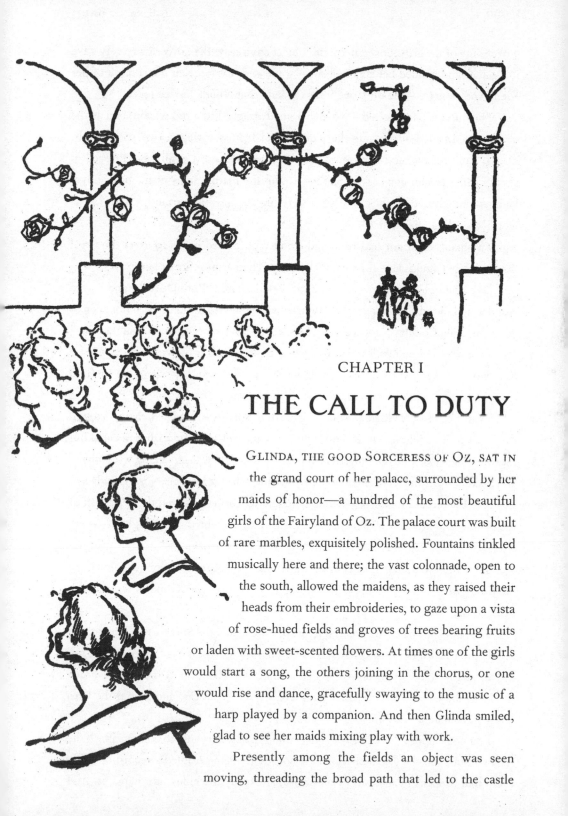

CHAPTER I

THE CALL TO DUTY

GLINDA, THE GOOD SORCERESS OF OZ, SAT IN the grand court of her palace, surrounded by her maids of honor—a hundred of the most beautiful girls of the Fairyland of Oz. The palace court was built of rare marbles, exquisitely polished. Fountains tinkled musically here and there; the vast colonnade, open to the south, allowed the maidens, as they raised their heads from their embroideries, to gaze upon a vista of rose-hued fields and groves of trees bearing fruits or laden with sweet-scented flowers. At times one of the girls would start a song, the others joining in the chorus, or one would rise and dance, gracefully swaying to the music of a harp played by a companion. And then Glinda smiled, glad to see her maids mixing play with work.

Presently among the fields an object was seen moving, threading the broad path that led to the castle

gate. Some of the girls looked upon this object enviously; the Sorceress merely gave
it a glance and nodded her stately head as if pleased, for it meant the coming of her
friend and mistress—the only one in all the land that Glinda bowed to.

Then up the path trotted a wooden animal attached to a red wagon, and as the
quaint steed halted at the gate there descended from the wagon two young girls,
Ozma, Ruler of Oz, and her companion, Princess Dorothy. Both were dressed in
simple white muslin gowns, and as they ran up the marble steps of the palace they
laughed and chatted as gaily as if they were not the most important persons in the
world's loveliest fairyland.

The maids of honor had risen and stood with bowed heads to greet the royal
Ozma, while Glinda came forward with outstretched arms to greet her guests.

"We've just come on a visit, you know," said Ozma. "Both Dorothy and I were
wondering how we should pass the day when we happened to think we'd not been to
your Quadling Country for weeks, so we took the Saw-Horse and rode straight here."

"And we came so fast," added Dorothy, "that our hair is blown all fuzzy, for the
Saw-Horse makes a wind of his own. Usually it's a day's journey from the Em'rald
City, but I don't s'pose we were two hours on the way."

"You are most welcome," said Glinda the Sorceress, and led them through
the court to her magnificent reception hall. Ozma took the arm of her hostess, but
Dorothy lagged behind, kissing some of the maids she knew best, talking with others,
and making them all feel that she was their friend. When at last she joined Glinda and
Ozma in the reception hall, she found them talking earnestly about the condition of
the people, and how to make them more happy and contented—although they were
already the happiest and most contented folks in all the world.

This interested Ozma, of course, but it didn't interest Dorothy very much, so
the little girl ran over to a big table on which was lying open Glinda's Great Book
of Records.

This Book is one of the greatest treasures in Oz, and the Sorceress prizes it more
highly than any of her magical possessions. That is the reason it is firmly attached to
the big marble table by means of golden chains, and whenever Glinda leaves home
she locks the Great Book together with five jeweled padlocks, and carries the keys
safely hidden in her bosom.

I do not suppose there is any magical thing in any fairyland to compare with the
Record Book, on the pages of which are constantly being printed a record of every
event that happens in any part of the world, at exactly the moment it happens. And

the records are always truthful, although sometimes they do not give as many details as one could wish. But then, lots of things happen, and so the records have to be brief or even Glinda's Great Book could not hold them all.

Glinda looked at the records several times each day, and Dorothy, whenever she visited the Sorceress, loved to look in the Book and see what was happening everywhere. Not much was recorded about the Land of Oz, which is usually peaceful and uneventful, but today Dorothy found something which interested her. Indeed, the printed letters were appearing on the page even while she looked.

"This is funny!" she exclaimed. "Did you know, Ozma, that there were people in your Land of Oz called Skeezers?"

"Yes," replied Ozma, coming to her side, "I know that on Professor Woggle-Bug's Map of the Land of Oz there is a place marked 'Skeezer,' but what the Skeezers are like I do not know. No one I know has ever seen them or heard of them. The Skeezer Country is 'way at the upper edge of the Gillikin Country, with the sandy, impassable desert on one side and the mountains of Oogaboo on another side. That is a part of the Land of Oz of which I know very little."

"I guess no one else knows much about it either, unless it's the Skeezers themselves," remarked Dorothy. "But the Book says: 'The Skeezers of Oz have declared war on the Flatheads of Oz, and there is likely to be fighting and much trouble as the result.'"

"Is that all the Book says?" asked Ozma.

"Every word," said Dorothy, and Ozma and Glinda both looked at the Record and seemed surprised and perplexed.

"Tell me, Glinda," said Ozma, "who are the Flatheads?"

"I cannot, Your Majesty," confessed the Sorceress. "Until now I never have heard of them, nor have I ever heard the Skeezers mentioned. In the faraway corners of Oz are hidden many curious tribes of people, and those who never leave their own countries and never are visited by those from our favored part of Oz, naturally are unknown to me. However, if you so desire, I can learn through my arts of sorcery something of the Skeezers and the Flatheads."

"I wish you would," answered Ozma seriously. "You see, Glinda, if these are Oz people they are my subjects and I cannot allow any wars or troubles in the Land I rule, if I can possibly help it."

"Very well, Your Majesty," said the Sorceress, "I will try to get some information to guide you. Please excuse me for a time, while I retire to my Room of Magic and Sorcery."

"May I go with you?" asked Dorothy, eagerly.

"No, Princess," was the reply. "It would spoil the charm to have anyone present."

So Glinda locked herself in her own Room of Magic and Dorothy and Ozma waited patiently for her to come out again.

In about an hour Glinda appeared, looking grave and thoughtful.

"Your Majesty," she said to Ozma, "the Skeezers live on a Magic Isle in a great lake. For that reason—because the Skeezers deal in magic—I can learn little about them."

"Why, I didn't know there was a lake in that part of Oz," exclaimed Ozma. "The map shows a river running through the Skeezer Country, but no lake."

"That is because the person who made the map never had visited that part of the country," explained the Sorceress. "The lake surely is there, and in the lake is an island—a Magic Isle—and on that island live the people called the Skeezers."

"What are they like?" inquired the Ruler of Oz.

"My magic cannot tell me that," confessed Glinda, "for the magic of the Skeezers prevents anyone outside of their domain knowing anything about them."

"The Flatheads must know, if they're going to fight the Skeezers," suggested Dorothy.

"Perhaps so," Glinda replied, "but I can get little information concerning the Flatheads, either. They are people who inhabit a mountain just south of the Lake of the Skeezers. The mountain has steep sides and a broad, hollow top, like a basin, and in this basin the Flatheads have their dwellings. They also are magic-workers and usually keep to themselves and allow no one from outside to visit them. I have learned that the Flatheads number about one hundred people—men, women and children—while the Skeezers number just one hundred and one."

"What did they quarrel about, and why do they wish to fight one another?" was Ozma's next question.

"I cannot tell Your Majesty that," said Glinda.

"But see here!" cried Dorothy, "it's against the law for anyone but Glinda and the Wizard to work magic in the Land of Oz, so if these two strange people are magic-makers they are breaking the law and ought to be punished!"

Ozma smiled upon her little friend.

"Those who do not know me or my laws," she said, "cannot be expected to obey my laws. If we know nothing of the Skeezers or the Flatheads, it is likely that they know nothing of us."

"But they ought to know, Ozma, and we ought to know. Who's going to tell them, and how are we going to make them behave?"

"That," returned Ozma, "is what I am now considering. What would you advise, Glinda?"

The Sorceress took a little time to consider this question, before she made reply. Then she said:

"Had you not learned of the existence of the Flatheads and the Skeezers, through my Book of Records, you would never have worried about them or their quarrels. So, if you pay no attention to these peoples, you may never hear of them again."

"But that wouldn't be right," declared Ozma. "I am Ruler of all the Land of Oz, which includes the Gillikin Country, the Quadling Country, the Winkie Country and the Munchkin Country, as well as the Emerald City, and being the Princess of this fairyland it is my duty to make all my people—wherever they may be—happy and content and to settle their disputes and keep them from quarreling. So, while the Skeezers and Flatheads may not know me or that I am their lawful Ruler, I now know that they inhabit my kingdom and are my subjects, so I would not be doing my duty if I kept away from them and allowed them to fight."

"That's a fact, Ozma," commented Dorothy. "You've got to go up to the Gillikin Country and make these people behave themselves and make up their quarrels. But how are you going to do it?"

"That is what is puzzling me also, Your Majesty," said the Sorceress. "It may be dangerous for you to go into those strange countries, where the people are possibly fierce and warlike."

"I am not afraid," said Ozma, with a smile.

"'Tisn't a question of being 'fraid," argued Dorothy. "Of course we know you're a fairy, and can't be killed or hurt, and we know you've a lot of magic of your own to help you. But, Ozma dear, in spite of all this you've been in trouble before, on account of wicked enemies, and it isn't right for the Ruler of all Oz to put herself in danger."

"Perhaps I shall be in no danger at all," returned Ozma, with a little laugh. "You mustn't imagine danger, Dorothy, for one should only imagine nice things, and we do not know that the Skeezers and Flatheads are wicked people or my enemies. Perhaps they would be good and listen to reason."

"Dorothy is right, Your Majesty," asserted the Sorceress. "It is true we know nothing of these faraway subjects, except that they intend to fight one another, and have a certain amount of magic power at their command. Such folks do not like to submit to interference and they are more likely to resent your coming among them than to receive you kindly and graciously, as is your due."

"If you had an army to take with you," added Dorothy, "it wouldn't be so bad; but there isn't such a thing as an army in all Oz."

"I have one soldier," said Ozma.

"Yes, the soldier with the green whiskers; but he's dreadful 'fraid of his gun and never loads it. I'm sure he'd run rather than fight. And one soldier, even if he were brave, couldn't do much against two hundred and one Flatheads and Skeezers."

"What then, my friends, would you suggest?" inquired Ozma.

"I advise you to send the Wizard of Oz to them, and let him inform them that it is against the laws of Oz to fight, and that you command them to settle their differences and become friends," proposed Glinda. "Let the Wizard tell them they will be punished if they refuse to obey the commands of the Princess of all the Land of Oz."

Ozma shook her head, to indicate that the advice was not to her satisfaction.

"If they refuse, what then?" she asked. "I should be obliged to carry out my threat and punish them, and that would be an unpleasant and difficult thing to do.

I am sure it would be better for me to go peacefully, without an army and armed only with my authority as Ruler, and plead with them to obey me. Then, if they prove obstinate I could resort to other means to win their obedience."

"It's a ticklish thing, anyhow you look at it," sighed Dorothy. "I'm sorry now that I noticed the Record in the Great Book."

"But can't you realize, my dear, that I must do my duty, now that I am aware of this trouble?" asked Ozma. "I am fully determined to go at once to the Magic Isle of the Skeezers and to the enchanted mountain of the Flatheads, and prevent war and strife between their inhabitants. The only question to decide is whether it is better for me to go alone, or to assemble a party of my friends and loyal supporters to accompany me."

"If you go I want to go, too," declared Dorothy. "Whatever happens it's going to be fun—'cause all excitement is fun—and I wouldn't miss it for the world!"

Neither Ozma nor Glinda paid any attention to this statement, for they were gravely considering the serious aspect of this proposed adventure.

"There are plenty of friends who would like to go with you," said the Sorceress, "but none of them would afford Your Majesty any protection in case you were in danger. You are yourself the most powerful fairy in Oz, although both I and the Wizard have more varied arts of magic at our command. However, you have one art that no other in all the world can equal—the art of winning hearts and making people love to bow to your gracious presence. For that reason I believe you can accomplish more good alone than with a large number of subjects in your train."

"I believe that also," agreed the Princess. "I shall be quite able to take care of myself, you know, but might not be able to protect others so well. I do not look for opposition, however. I shall speak to these people in kindly words and settle their dispute—whatever it may be—in a just manner."

"Aren't you going to take *me*?" pleaded Dorothy. "You'll need *some* companion, Ozma."

The Princess smiled upon her little friend.

"I see no reason why you should not accompany me," was her reply. "Two girls are not very warlike and they will not suspect us of being on any errand but a kindly and peaceful one. But, in order to prevent war and strife between these angry peoples, we must go to them at once. Let us return immediately to the Emerald City and prepare to start on our journey early tomorrow morning."

Glinda was not quite satisfied with this plan, but could not think of any better way to meet the problem. She knew that Ozma, with all her gentleness and sweet disposition, was accustomed to abide by any decision she had made and could not easily be turned from her purpose. Moreover she could see no great danger to the

fairy Ruler of Oz in the undertaking, even though the unknown people she was to visit proved obstinate. But Dorothy was not a fairy; she was a little girl who had come from Kansas to live in the Land of Oz. Dorothy might encounter dangers that to Ozma would be as nothing but to an "Earth child" would be very serious.

The very fact that Dorothy lived in Oz, and had been made a Princess by her friend Ozma, prevented her from being killed or suffering any great bodily pain as long as she lived in that fairyland. She could not grow big, either, and would always remain the same little girl who had come to Oz, unless in some way she left that fairyland or was spirited away from it. But Dorothy was a mortal, nevertheless, and might possibly be destroyed, or hidden where none of her friends could ever find her. She could, for instance be cut into pieces, and the pieces, while still alive and free from pain, could be widely scattered; or she might be buried deep underground or "destroyed" in other ways by evil magicians, were she not properly protected. These facts Glinda was considering while she paced with stately tread her marble hall.

Finally the good Sorceress paused and drew a ring from her finger, handing it to Dorothy.

"Wear this ring constantly until your return," she said to the girl. "If serious danger threatens you, turn the ring around on your finger once to the right and another turn to the left. That will ring the alarm bell in my palace and I will at once come to your rescue. But do not use the ring unless you are actually in danger of destruction. While you remain with Princess Ozma I believe she will be able to protect you from all lesser ills."

"Thank you, Glinda," responded Dorothy gratefully, as she placed the ring on her finger. "I'm going to wear my Magic Belt which I took from the Nome King, too, so I guess I'll be safe from anything the Skeezers and Flatheads try to do to me."

Ozma had many arrangements to make before she could leave her throne and her palace in the Emerald City, even for a trip of a few days, so she bade good-bye to Glinda and with Dorothy climbed into the Red Wagon. A word to the wooden Saw-Horse started that astonishing creature on the return journey, and so swiftly did he run that Dorothy was unable to talk or do anything but hold tight to her seat all the way back to the Emerald City.

CHAPTER II

OZMA AND DOROTHY

RESIDING IN OZMA'S PALACE AT THIS TIME WAS A LIVE Scarecrow, a most remarkable and intelligent creature who had once ruled the Land of Oz for a brief period and was much loved and respected by all the people. Once a Munchkin farmer had stuffed an old suit of clothes with straw and put stuffed boots on the feet and used a pair of stuffed cotton gloves for hands. The head of the Scarecrow was a stuffed sack fastened to the body, with eyes, nose, mouth and ears painted on the sack. When a hat had been put on the head, the thing was a good imitation of a man. The farmer placed the Scarecrow on a pole in his cornfield and it came to life in a curious manner. Dorothy, who was passing by the field, was hailed by the live Scarecrow and lifted him off his pole. He then went with her to the Emerald City, where the Wizard of Oz gave him some excellent brains, and the Scarecrow soon became an important personage.

Ozma considered the Scarecrow one of her best friends and most loyal subjects, so the morning after her visit to Glinda she asked him to take her place as Ruler of the Land of Oz while she was absent on a journey, and the Scarecrow at once consented without asking any questions.

Ozma had warned Dorothy to keep their journey a secret and say nothing to anyone about the Skeezers and Flatheads until their return, and Dorothy promised to obey. She longed to tell her girl friends, tiny Trot and Betsy Bobbin, of the adventure they were undertaking, but refrained from saying a word on the subject although both these girls lived with her in Ozma's palace.

Indeed, only Glinda the Sorceress knew they were going, until after they had gone, and even the Sorceress didn't know what their errand might be.

Princess Ozma took the Saw-Horse and the Red Wagon, although she was not sure there was a wagon road all the way to the Lake of the Skeezers. The Land of Oz is a pretty big place, surrounded on all sides by a Deadly Desert which it is impossible to cross, and the Skeezer Country, according to the map, was in the farthest northwestern part of Oz, bordering on the north desert. As the Emerald City was exactly in the center of Oz, it was no small journey from there to the Skeezers.

Around the Emerald City the country is thickly settled in every direction, but the farther away you get from the city the fewer people there are, until those parts that border on the desert have small populations. Also those faraway sections are little known to the Oz people, except in the south, where Glinda lives and where Dorothy has often wandered on trips of exploration.

The least known of all is the Gillikin Country, which harbors many strange bands of people among its mountains and valleys and forests and streams, and Ozma was now bound for the most distant part of the Gillikin Country.

"I am really sorry," said Ozma to Dorothy, as they rode away in the Red Wagon, "not to know more about the wonderful Land I rule. It is my duty to be acquainted with every tribe of people and every strange and hidden country in all Oz, but I am kept so busy at my palace making laws and planning for the comforts of those who live near the Emerald City, that I do not often find time to make long journeys."

"Well," replied Dorothy, "we'll prob'bly find out a lot on this trip, and we'll learn all about the Skeezers and Flatheads, anyhow. Time doesn't make much diff'rence in the Land of Oz, 'cause we don't grow up, or get old, or become sick and die, as they do other places; so, if we explore one place at a time, we'll by-an'-by know all about every nook and corner in Oz."

Dorothy wore around her waist the Nome King's Magic Belt, which protected her from harm, and the Magic Ring which Glinda had given her was on her finger. Ozma had merely slipped a small silver wand into the bosom of her gown, for fairies do not use chemicals and herbs and the tools of wizards and sorcerers to perform their magic. The silver wand was Ozma's one weapon of offense and defense and by its use she could accomplish many things.

They had left the Emerald City just at sunrise and the Saw-Horse traveled very swiftly over the roads toward the north, but in a few hours the wooden animal had to slacken his pace because the farm houses had become few and far between and often there were no paths at all in the direction they wished to follow. At such times they crossed the fields, avoiding groups of trees and fording the streams and rivulets whenever they came to them. But finally they reached a broad hillside closely covered with scrubby brush, through which the wagon could not pass.

"It will be difficult even for you and me to get through without tearing our dresses," said Ozma, "so we must leave the Saw-Horse and the Wagon here until our return."

"That's all right," Dorothy replied, "I'm tired riding, anyhow. Do you s'pose, Ozma, we're anywhere near the Skeezer Country?"

"I cannot tell, Dorothy dear, but I know we've been going in the right direction, so we are sure to find it in time."

The scrubby brush was almost like a grove of small trees, for it reached as high as the heads of the two girls, neither of whom was very tall. They were obliged to thread their way in and out, until Dorothy was afraid they would get lost, and finally they were halted by a curious thing that barred their further progress. It was a huge web—as if woven by gigantic spiders—and the delicate, lacy film was fastened stoutly to the branches of the bushes and continued to the right and left in the form of a half circle. The threads of this web were of a brilliant purple color and woven into numerous artistic patterns, but it reached from the ground to branches above the heads of the girls and formed a sort of fence that hedged them in.

"It doesn't look very strong, though," said Dorothy. "I wonder if we couldn't break through." She tried but found the web stronger than it seemed. All her efforts could not break a single thread.

"We must go back, I think, and try to get around this peculiar web," Ozma decided.

So they turned to the right and, following the web, found that it seemed to spread in a regular circle. On and on they went until finally Ozma said they had returned to the exact spot from which they had started. "Here is a handkerchief you dropped when we were here before," she said to Dorothy.

"In that case, they must have built the web behind us, after we walked into the trap," exclaimed the little girl.

"True," agreed Ozma, "an enemy has tried to imprison us."

"And they did it, too," said Dorothy. "I wonder who it was."

"It's a spider-web, I'm quite sure," returned Ozma, "but it must be the work of enormous spiders."

"Quite right!" cried a voice behind them. Turning quickly around they beheld a huge purple spider sitting not two yards away and regarding them with its small bright eyes.

Then there crawled from the bushes a dozen more great purple spiders, which saluted the first one and said:

"The web is finished, O King, and the strangers are our prisoners."

Dorothy did not like the looks of these spiders at all. They had big heads, sharp claws, small eyes and fuzzy hair all over their purple bodies.

"They look wicked," she whispered to Ozma. "What shall we do?"

Ozma gazed upon the spiders with a serious face.

"What is your object in making us prisoners?" she inquired.

"We need someone to keep house for us," answered the Spider King. "There is sweeping and dusting to be done, and polishing and washing of dishes, and that is work my people dislike to do. So we decided that if any strangers came our way we would capture them and make them our servants."

"I am Princess Ozma, Ruler of all Oz," said the girl with dignity.

"Well, I am King of all Spiders," was the reply, "and that makes me your master. Come with me to my palace and I will instruct you in your work."

"I won't," said Dorothy indignantly. "We won't have anything to do with you."

"We'll see about that," returned the Spider in a severe tone, and the next instant he made a dive straight at Dorothy, opening the claws in his legs as if to grab and

pinch her with the sharp points. But the girl was wearing her Magic Belt and was not harmed. The Spider King could not even touch her.

He turned swiftly and made a dash at Ozma, but she held her Magic Wand over his head and the monster recoiled as if it had been struck.

"You'd better let us go," Dorothy advised him, "for you see you can't hurt us."

"So I see," returned the Spider King angrily. "Your magic is greater than mine. But I'll not help you to escape. If you can break the magic web my people have woven you may go; if not you must stay here and starve." With that the Spider King uttered a peculiar whistle and all the spiders disappeared.

"There is more magic in my fairyland than I dreamed of," remarked the beautiful Ozma, with a sigh of regret. "It seems that my laws have not been obeyed, for even these monstrous spiders defy me by means of magic."

"Never mind that now," said Dorothy; "let's see what we can do to get out of this trap."

They now examined the web with great care and were amazed at its strength. Although finer than the finest silken hairs, it resisted all their efforts to work through, even though both girls threw all their weight against it.

"We must find some instrument which will cut the threads of the web," said Ozma, finally. "Let us look about for such a tool."

So they wandered among the bushes and finally came to a shallow pool of water, formed by a small bubbling spring. Dorothy stooped to get a drink and discovered in the water a green crab, about as big as her hand. The crab had two big, sharp claws, and as soon as Dorothy saw them she had an idea that those claws could save them.

"Come out of the water," she called to the crab; "I want to talk to you."

Rather lazily the crab rose to the surface and caught hold of a bit of rock. With his head above the water he said in a cross voice:

"What do you want?"

"We want you to cut the web of the purple spiders with your claws, so we can get through it," answered Dorothy. "You can do that, can't you?"

"I suppose so," replied the crab. "But if I do what will you give me?"

"What do you wish?" Ozma inquired.

"I wish to be white, instead of green," said the crab. "Green crabs are very common, and white ones are rare; besides the purple spiders, which infest this hill-side, are afraid of white crabs. Could you make me white if I should agree to cut the web for you?"

"Yes," said Ozma, "I can do that easily. And, so you may know I am speaking the truth, I will change your color now."

She waved her silver wand over the pool and the crab instantly became snow-white—all except his eyes, which remained black. The creature saw his reflection in the water and was so delighted that he at once climbed out of the pool and began moving slowly toward the web, by backing away from the pool. He moved so very slowly that Dorothy cried out impatiently: "Dear me, this will never do!" Caching the crab in her hands she ran with him to the web.

She had to hold him up even then, so he could reach with his claws strand after strand of the filmy purple web, which he was able to sever with one nip.

When enough of the web had been cut to allow them to pass, Dorothy ran back to the pool and placed the white crab in the water, after which she rejoined Ozma. They were just in time to escape through the web, for several of the purple spiders now appeared, having discovered that their web had been cut, and had the girls not rushed through the opening the spiders would have quickly repaired the cuts and again imprisoned them.

Ozma and Dorothy ran as fast as they could and although the angry spiders threw a number of strands of web after them, hoping to lasso them or entangle them in the coils, they managed to escape and clamber to the top of the hill.

CHAPTER III

THE MIST MAIDENS

FROM THE TOP OF THE HILL OZMA AND Dorothy looked down into the valley beyond and were surprised to find it filled with a floating mist that was as dense as smoke. Nothing in the valley was visible except these rolling waves of mist, but beyond, on the other side, rose a grassy hill that appeared quite beautiful.

"Well," said Dorothy, "what are we to do, Ozma? Walk down into that thick fog, an' prob'bly get lost in it, or wait till it clears away?"

"I'm not sure it will clear away, however long we wait," replied Ozma, doubtfully. "If we wish to get on, I think we must venture into the mist."

"But we can't see where we're going, or what we're stepping on," protested Dorothy. "There may be dreadful things mixed up in that fog, an' I'm scared just to think of wading into it."

Even Ozma seemed to hesitate. She was silent and thoughtful for a little while, looking at the rolling drifts that were so gray and forbidding. Finally she said:

"I believe this is a Mist Valley, where these moist clouds always remain, for even the sunshine above does not drive them away. Therefore the Mist Maids must live here, and they are fairies and should answer my call."

She placed her two hands before her mouth, forming a hollow with them, and uttered a clear, thrilling, bird-like cry. It floated far out over the mist waves and presently was answered by a similar sound, as of a far-off echo.

Dorothy was much impressed. She had seen many strange things since coming to this fairy country, but here was a new experience. At ordinary times Ozma was just like any little girl one might chance to meet—simple, merry, lovable as could be—yet with a certain reserve that lent her dignity in her most joyous moods. There were times, however, when seated on her throne and commanding her subjects, or when her fairy powers were called into use, when Dorothy and all others about her stood in awe of their lovely girl Ruler and realized her superiority.

Ozma waited. Presently out from the billows rose beautiful forms, clothed in fleecy, trailing garments of gray that could scarcely be distinguished from the mist. Their hair was mist-color, too; only their gleaming arms and sweet, pallid faces proved they were living, intelligent creatures answering the call of a sister fairy.

Like sea nymphs they rested on the bosom of the clouds, their eyes turned questioningly upon the two girls who stood upon the bank. One came quite near and to her Ozma said:

"Will you please take us to the opposite hillside? We are afraid to venture into
the mist. I am Princess Ozma of Oz, and this is my friend Dorothy, a Princess of
Oz."

The Mist Maids came nearer, holding out their arms. Without hesitation Ozma
advanced and allowed them to embrace her and Dorothy plucked up courage to
follow. Very gently the Mist Maids held them. Dorothy thought the arms were cold
and misty—they didn't seem real at all—yet they supported the two girls above the
surface of the billows and floated with them so swiftly to the green hillside opposite
that the girls were astonished to find themselves set upon the grass before they realized they had fairly started.

"Thank you!" said Ozma gratefully, and Dorothy also added her thanks for the
service.

The Mist Maids made no answer, but they smiled and waved their hands in
good-bye as again they floated out into the mist and disappeared from view.

CHAPTER IV

THE MAGIC TENT

"WELL," SAID DOROTHY WITH A LAUGH, "THAT was easier than I expected. It's worth while, sometimes, to be a real fairy. But I wouldn't like to be that kind, and live in a dreadful fog all the time."

They now climbed the bank and found before them a delightful plain that spread for miles in all directions. Fragrant wild-flowers were scattered throughout the grass; there were bushes bearing lovely blossoms and luscious fruits; now and then a group of stately trees added to the beauty of the landscape. But there were no dwellings or signs of life.

The farther side of the plain was bordered by a row of palms, and just in front of the palms rose a queerly shaped hill that towered above the plain like a mountain. The sides of this hill were straight up and down; it was oblong in shape and the top seemed flat and level.

"Oh, ho!" cried Dorothy; "I'll bet that's the mountain Glinda told us of, where the Flatheads live."

"If it is," replied Ozma, "the Lake of the Skeezers must be just beyond the line of palm trees. Can you walk that far, Dorothy?"

"Of course, in time," was the prompt answer. "I'm sorry we had to leave the Saw-Horse and the Red Wagon behind us, for they'd come in handy just now; but with the end of our journey in sight a tramp across these pretty green fields won't tire us a bit."

It was a longer tramp than they suspected, however, and night overtook them before they could reach the flat mountain. So Ozma proposed they camp for the night and Dorothy was quite ready to approve. She didn't like to admit to her friend she was tired, but she told herself that her legs "had prickers in 'em," meaning they had begun to ache.

Usually when Dorothy started on a journey of exploration or adventure, she carried with her a basket of food, and other things that a traveler in a strange country might require, but to go away with Ozma was quite a different thing, as experience had taught her. The fairy Ruler of Oz only needed her silver wand—tipped at one end with a great sparkling emerald—to provide through its magic all that they might need. Therefore Ozma, having halted with her companion and selected a smooth, grassy spot on the plain, waved her wand in graceful curves and chanted some mystic words in her sweet voice, and in an instant a handsome tent appeared before them. The canvas was striped purple and white, and from the center pole fluttered the royal banner of Oz.

"Come, dear," said Ozma, taking Dorothy's hand, "I am hungry and I'm sure you must be also; so let us go in and have our feast."

On entering the tent they found a table set for two, with snowy linen, bright silver and sparkling glassware, a vase of roses in the center and many dishes of delicious food, some smoking hot, waiting to satisfy their hunger. Also, on either side of the tent were beds, with satin sheets, warm blankets and pillows filled with swansdown. There were chairs, too, and tall lamps that lighted the interior of the tent with a soft, rosy glow.

Dorothy, resting herself at her fairy friend's command, and eating her dinner with unusual enjoyment, thought of the wonders of magic. If one were a fairy and knew the secret laws of nature and the mystic words and ceremonies that commanded those laws, then a simple wave of a silver wand would produce instantly all that men work hard and anxiously for through weary years. And Dorothy wished in her kindly, innocent heart, that all men and women could be fairies with silver wands, and satisfy all their needs without so much work and worry, for then, she imagined, they would have all their working hours to be happy in. But Ozma, looking into her friend's face and reading those thoughts, gave a laugh and said:

"No, no, Dorothy, that wouldn't do at all. Instead of happiness your plan would bring weariness to the world. If every one could wave a wand and have his wants fulfilled there would be little to wish for. There would be no eager striving to obtain the difficult, for nothing would then be difficult, and the pleasure of earning something longed for, and only to be secured by hard work and careful thought, would be utterly lost. There would be nothing to do, you see, and no interest in life and in our fellow creatures. That is all that makes life worth our while—to do good deeds and to help those less fortunate than ourselves."

"Well, you're a fairy, Ozma. Aren't you happy?" asked Dorothy.

"Yes, dear, because I can use my fairy powers to make others happy. Had I no kingdom to rule, and no subjects to look after, I would be miserable. Also, you must realize that while I am a more powerful fairy than any other inhabitant of Oz, I am not as powerful as Glinda the Sorceress, who has studied many arts of magic that I know nothing of. Even the little Wizard of Oz can do some things I am unable to accomplish, while I can accomplish things unknown to the Wizard. This is to explain that I am not all-powerful, by any means. My magic is simply fairy magic, and not sorcery or wizardry."

"All the same," said Dorothy, "I'm mighty glad you could make this tent appear, with our dinners and beds all ready for us."

Ozma smiled.

"Yes, it is indeed wonderful," she agreed. "Not all fairies know that sort of magic, but some fairies can do magic that fills me with astonishment. I think that is what makes us modest and unassuming—the fact that our magic arts are divided, some being given each of us. I'm glad I don't know everything, Dorothy, and that there still are things in both nature and in wit for me to marvel at."

Dorothy couldn't quite understand this, so she said nothing more on the subject and presently had a new reason to marvel. For when they had quite finished their meal table and contents disappeared in a flash.

"No dishes to wash, Ozma!" she said with a laugh. "I guess you'd make a lot of folks happy if you could teach 'em just that one trick."

For an hour Ozma told stories, and talked with Dorothy about various people in whom they were interested. And then it was bedtime, and they undressed and crept into their soft beds and fell asleep almost as soon as their heads touched their pillows.

CHAPTER V

THE MAGIC STAIRWAY

THE FLAT MOUNTAIN LOOKED MUCH NEARER IN the clear light of the morning sun, but Dorothy and Ozma knew there was a long tramp before them, even yet. They finished dressing only to find a warm, delicious breakfast awaiting them, and having eaten they left the tent and started toward the mountain which was their first goal. After going a little way Dorothy looked back and found that the fairy tent had entirely disappeared. She was not surprised, for she knew this would happen.

"Can't your magic give us a horse an' wagon, or an automobile?" inquired Dorothy.

"No, dear; I'm sorry that such magic is beyond my power," confessed her fairy friend.

"Perhaps Glinda could," said Dorothy thoughtfully.

"Glinda has a stork chariot that carries her through the air," said Ozma, "but even our great Sorceress cannot conjure up other modes of travel. Don't forget what I told you last night, that no one is powerful enough to do everything."

"Well, I s'pose I ought to know that, having lived so long in the Land of Oz," replied Dorothy; "but I can't do any magic at all, an' so I can't figure out e'zactly how you an' Glinda an' the Wizard do it."

"Don't try," laughed Ozma. "But you have at least one magical art, Dorothy: you know the trick of winning all hearts."

"No, I don't," said Dorothy earnestly. "If I really can do it, Ozma, I am sure I don't know *how* I do it."

It took them a good two hours to reach the foot of the round, flat mountain, and then they found the sides so steep that they were like the wall of a house.

"Even my purple kitten couldn't climb 'em," remarked Dorothy, gazing upward.

"But there is some way for the Flatheads to get down and up again," declared Ozma; "otherwise they couldn't make war with the Skeezers, or even meet them and quarrel with them."

"That's so, Ozma. Let's walk around a ways; perhaps we'll find a ladder or something."

They walked quite a distance, for it was a big mountain, and as they circled around it and came to the side that faced the palm trees, they suddenly discovered an entrance way cut out of the rock wall. This entrance was arched overhead and not very deep because it merely led to a short flight of stone stairs.

"Oh, we've found a way to the top at last," announced Ozma, and the two girls turned and walked straight toward the entrance. Suddenly they bumped against something and stood still, unable to proceed farther.

"Dear me!" exclaimed Dorothy, rubbing her nose, which had struck something hard, although she could not see what it was; "this isn't as easy as it looks. What has stopped us, Ozma? Is it magic of some sort?"

Ozma was feeling around, her hands outstretched before her.

"Yes, dear, it is magic," she replied. "The Flatheads had to have a way from their mountain top from the plain below, but to prevent enemies from rushing up the stairs to conquer them, they have built, at a small distance before the entrance a wall of solid stone, the stones being held in place by cement, and then they made the wall invisible."

"I wonder why they did that?" mused Dorothy. "A wall would keep folks out anyhow, whether it could be seen or not, so there wasn't any use making it invisible. Seems to me it would have been better to have left it solid, for then no one would have seen the entrance behind it. Now anybody can see the entrance, as we did. And prob'bly anybody that tries to go up the stairs gets bumped, as we did."

Ozma made no reply at once. Her face was grave and thoughtful.

"I think I know the reason for making the wall invisible," she said after a while. "The Flatheads use the stairs for coming down and going up. If there was a solid stone wall to keep them from reaching the plain they would themselves be imprisoned by the wall. So they had to leave some place to get around the wall, and, if the wall was visible, all strangers or enemies would find the place to go around it and then the wall would be useless. So the Flatheads cunningly made their wall invisible, believing that everyone who saw the entrance to the mountain would walk straight toward it, as we did, and find it impossible to go any farther. I suppose the wall is really high and thick, and can't be broken through, so those who find it in their way are obliged to go away again."

"Well," said Dorothy, "if there's a way around the wall, where is it?"

"We must find it," returned Ozma, and began feeling her way along the wall. Dorothy followed and began to get discouraged when Ozma had walked nearly a quarter of a mile away from the entrance. But now the invisible wall curved in toward the side of the mountain and suddenly ended, leaving just space enough between the wall and the mountain for an ordinary person to pass through.

The girls went in, single file, and Ozma explained that they were now behind the barrier and could go back to the entrance. They met no further obstructions.

"Most people, Ozma, wouldn't have figured this thing out the way you did," remarked Dorothy. "If I'd been alone the invisible wall surely would have stumped me."

Reaching the entrance they began to mount the stone stairs. They went up ten stairs and then down five stairs, following a passage cut from the rock. The stairs were just wide enough for the two girls to walk abreast, arm in arm. At the bottom of the five stairs the passage turned to the right, and they ascended ten more stairs, only to find at the top of the flight five stairs leading straight down again. Again the passage turned abruptly, this time to the left, and ten more stairs led upward.

The passage was now quite dark, for they were in the heart of the mountain and all daylight had been shut out by the turns of the passage. However, Ozma drew her silver wand from her bosom and the great jewel at its end gave out a lustrous, green-tinted light which lighted the place well enough for them to see their way plainly.

Ten steps up, five steps down, and a turn, this way or that. That was the program, and Dorothy figured that they were only gaining five stairs upward each trip that they made.

"Those Flatheads must be funny people," she said to Ozma. "They don't seem to do anything in a bold, straightforward manner. In making this passage they forced everyone to walk three times as far as is necessary. And of course this trip is just as tiresome to the Flatheads as it is to other folks."

"That is true," answered Ozma; "yet it is a clever arrangement to prevent their being surprised by intruders. Every time we reach the tenth step of a flight, the pressure of our feet on the stone makes a bell ring on top of the mountain, to warn the Flatheads of our coming."

"How do you know that?" demanded Dorothy, astonished.

"I've heard the bell ever since we started," Ozma told her. "You could not hear it, I know, but when I am holding my wand in my hand I can hear sounds a great distance off."

"Do you hear anything on top of the mountain 'cept the bell?" inquired Dorothy.

"Yes. The people are calling to one another in alarm and many footsteps are approaching the place where we will reach the flat top of the mountain."

This made Dorothy feel somewhat anxious.

"I'd thought we were going to visit just common, ordinary people," she remarked, "but they're pretty clever, it seems, and they know some kinds of magic, too. They may be dangerous, Ozma. P'raps we'd better stayed at home."

Finally the upstairs-and-downstairs passage seemed coming to an end, for daylight again appeared ahead of the two girls and Ozma replaced her wand in the bosom of her gown. The last ten steps brought them to the surface, where they found themselves surrounded by such a throng of queer people that for a time they halted, speechless, and stared into the faces that confronted them.

Dorothy knew at once why these mountain people were called Flatheads. Their heads were really flat on top, as if they had been cut off just above the eyes and ears. Also the heads were bald, with no hair on top at all, and the ears were big and stuck straight out, and the noses were small and stubby, while the mouths of the Flatheads were well shaped and not unusual. Their eyes were perhaps their best feature, being large and bright and a deep violet in color.

The costumes of the Flatheads were all made of metals dug from their mountain. Small gold, silver, tin and iron discs, about the size of pennies, and very thin, were cleverly wired together and made to form knee trousers and jackets for the men and skirts and waists for the women. The colored metals were skillfully mixed to form stripes and checks of various sorts, so that the costumes were quite gorgeous and reminded Dorothy of pictures she had seen of Knights of old clothed armor.

Aside from their flat heads, these people were not really bad looking. The men were armed with bows and arrows and had small axes of steel stuck in their metal belts. They wore no hats nor ornaments.

CHAPTER VI

FLATHEAD MOUNTAIN

WHEN THEY SAW THAT THE INTRUDERS ON THEIR mountain were only two little girls, the Flatheads grunted with satisfaction and drew back, permitting them to see what the mountain top looked like. It was shaped like a saucer, so that the houses and other buildings—all made of rocks—could not be seen over the edge by anyone standing in the plain below.

But now a big fat Flathead stood before the girls and in a gruff voice demanded:

"What are you doing here? Have the Skeezers sent you to spy upon us?"

"I am Princess Ozma, Ruler of all the Land of Oz."

"Well, I've never heard of the Land of Oz, so you may be what you claim," returned the Flathead.

"This is the Land of Oz—part of it, anyway," exclaimed Dorothy. "So Princess Ozma rules you Flathead people, as well as all the other people in Oz."

The man laughed, and all the others who stood around laughed, too. Some one in the crowd called:

"She'd better not tell the Supreme Dictator about ruling the Flatheads. Eh, friends?"

"No, indeed!" they all answered in positive tones.

"Who is your Supreme Dictator?" answered Ozma.

"I think I'll let him tell you that himself," answered the man

who had first spoken. "You have broken our laws by coming here; and whoever you are the Supreme Dictator must fix your punishment. Come along with me."

He started down a path and Ozma and Dorothy followed him without protest, as they wanted to see the most important person in this queer country. The houses they passed seemed pleasant enough and each had a little yard in which were flowers and vegetables. Walls of rock separated the dwellings, and all the paths were paved with smooth slabs of rock. This seemed their only building material and they utilized it cleverly for every purpose.

Directly in the center of the great saucer stood a larger building which the Flathead informed the girls was the palace of the Supreme Dictator. He led them through an entrance hall into a big reception room, where they sat upon stone benches and awaited the coming of the Dictator. Pretty soon he entered from another room—a rather lean and rather old Flathead, dressed much like the others of this strange race, and only distinguished from them by the sly and cunning expression of his face. He kept his eyes half closed and looked through the slits of them at Ozma and Dorothy, who rose to receive him.

"Are you the Supreme Dictator of the Flatheads?" inquired Ozma.

"Yes, that's me," he said, rubbing his hands slowly together. "My word is law. I'm the head of the Flatheads on this flat headland."

"I am Princess Ozma of Oz, and I have come from the Emerald City to—"

"Stop a minute," interrupted the Dictator, and turned to the man who had brought the girls there. "Go away, Dictator Felo Flathead!" he commanded. "Return to your duty and guard the Stairway. I will look after these strangers." The man bowed and departed, and Dorothy asked wonderingly:

"Is *he* a Dictator, too?"

"Of course," was the answer. "Everybody here is a dictator of something or other. They're all office holders. That's what keeps them contented. But I'm the Supreme Dictator of all, and I'm elected once a year. This is a democracy, you know, where the people are allowed to vote for their Rulers. A good many others would like to be Supreme Dictator, but as I made a law that I am always to count the votes myself, I am always elected."

"What is your name?" asked Ozma.

"I am called the Su-dic, which is short for Supreme Dictator. I sent that man away because the moment you mentioned Ozma of Oz, and the Emerald City, I knew who you are. I suppose I'm the only Flathead that ever heard of you, but that's because I have more brains than the rest."

Dorothy was staring hard at the Su-dic.

"I don't see how you can have any brains at all," she remarked, "because the part of your head is gone where brains are kept."

"I don't blame you for thinking that," he said. "Once the Flatheads had no brains because, as you say, there is no upper part to their heads, to hold brains. But long, long ago a band of fairies flew over this country and made it all a fairy-land, and when they came to the Flatheads the fairies were sorry to find them all very stupid and quite unable to think. So, as there was no good place in their bodies in which to put brains the Fairy Queen gave each one of us a nice can of brains to carry in his pocket and that made us just as intel-ligent as other people. See," he continued, "here is one of the cans of brains the fairies gave us." He took from a pocket a bright tin can having a pretty red label on it which said: "Concentrated Brains, Extra Quality."

"And does every Flathead have the same kind of brains?" asked Dorothy.

"Yes, they're all alike. Here's another can." From another pocket he produced a second can of brains.

"Did the fairies give you a double supply?" inquired Dorothy.

"No, but one of the Flatheads thought he wanted to be the Su-dic and tried to get my people to rebel against me, so I punished him by taking away his brains. One day my wife scolded me severely, so I took away her can of brains. She didn't like that and went out and robbed several women of their brains. Then I made a law that if anyone stole another's brains, or even tried to borrow them, he would forfeit his own brains to the Su-dic. So each one is content with his own canned brains and my wife and I are the only ones on the mountain with more than one can. I have three cans and that makes me very clever—so clever that I'm a good Sorcerer, if I do say it myself. My poor wife had four cans of brains and became a remarkable witch, but alas! that was before those terrible enemies, the Skeezers, transformed her into a Golden Pig."

"Good gracious!" cried Dorothy; "is your wife really a Golden Pig?"

"She is. The Skeezers did it and so I have declared war on them. In revenge for making my wife a Pig I intend to ruin their Magic Island and make the Skeezers the slaves of the Flatheads!"

The Su-dic was very angry now; his eyes flashed and his face took on a wicked and fierce expression. But Ozma said to him, very sweetly and in a friendly voice:

"I am sorry to hear this. Will you please tell me more about your troubles with the Skeezers? Then perhaps I can help you."

She was only a girl, but there was dignity in her pose and speech which impressed the Su-dic.

"If you are really Princess Ozma of Oz," the Flathead said, "you are one of that band of fairies who, under Queen Lurline, made all Oz a fairyland. I have heard that Lurline left one of her own fairies to rule Oz, and gave the fairy the name of Ozma."

"If you knew this why did you not come to me at the Emerald City and tender me your loyalty and obedience?" asked the Ruler of Oz.

"Well, I only learned the fact lately, and I've been too busy to leave home," he explained, looking at the floor instead of into Ozma's eyes. She knew he had spoken a falsehood, but only said:

"Why did you quarrel with the Skeezers?"

"It was this way," began the Su-dic, glad to change the subject. "We Flatheads love fish, and as we have no fish on this mountain we would sometimes go to the

Lake of the Skeezers to catch fish. This made the Skeezers angry, for they declared the fish in their lake belonged to them and were under their protection and they forbade us to catch them. That was very mean and unfriendly in the Skeezers, you must admit, and when we paid no attention to their orders they set a guard on the shore of the lake to prevent our fishing.

"Now, my wife, Rora Flathead, having four cans of brains, had become a wonderful witch, and fish being brain food, she loved to eat fish better than any one of us. So she vowed she would destroy every fish in the lake, unless the Skeezers let us catch what we wanted. They defied us, so Rora prepared a kettleful of magic poison and went down to the lake one night to dump it all in the water and poison the fish. It was a clever idea, quite worthy of my dear wife, but the Skeezer Queen—a young lady named Coo-ee-oh—hid on the bank of the lake and taking Rora unawares, transformed her into a Golden Pig. The poison was spilled on the ground and wicked Queen Coo-ee-oh, not content with her cruel transformation, even took away my wife's four cans of brains, so she is now a common grunting pig without even brains enough to know her own name."

"Then," said Ozma thoughtfully, "the Queen of the Skeezers must be a Sorceress."

"Yes," said the Su-dic, "but she doesn't know much magic, after all. She is not as powerful as Rora Flathead was, nor half as powerful as I am now, as Queen Coo-ee-oh will discover when we fight our great battle and destroy her."

"The Golden Pig can't be a witch any more, of course," observed Dorothy.

"No; even had Queen Coo-ee-oh left her the four cans of brains, poor Rora, in a pig's shape, couldn't do any witchcraft. A witch has to use her fingers, and a pig has only cloven hoofs."

"It seems a sad story," was Ozma's comment, "and all the trouble arose because the Flatheads wanted fish that did not belong to them."

"As for that," said the Su-dic, again angry, "I made a law that any of my people could catch fish in the Lake of the Skeezers, whenever they wanted to. So the trouble was through the Skeezers defying my law."

"You can only make laws to govern your own people," asserted Ozma sternly. "I, alone, am empowered to make laws that must be obeyed by all the peoples of Oz."

"Pooh!" cried the Su-dic scornfully. "You can't make me obey your laws, I assure you. I know the extent of your powers, Princess Ozma of Oz, and I know that I am more powerful than you are. To prove it I shall keep you and your companion

prisoners in this mountain until after we have fought and conquered the Skeezers. Then, if you promise to be good, I may let you go home again."

Dorothy was amazed by this effrontery and defiance of the beautiful girl Ruler of Oz, whom all until now had obeyed without question. But Ozma, still unruffled and dignified, looked at the Su-dic and said:

"You did not mean that. You are angry and speak unwisely, without reflection. I came here from my palace in the Emerald City to prevent war and to make peace between you and the Skeezers. I do not approve of Queen Coo-ee-oh's action in transforming your wife Rora into a pig, nor do I approve of Rora's cruel attempt to poison the fishes in the lake. No one has the right to work magic in my dominions without my consent, so the Flatheads and the Skeezers have both broken my laws—which must be obeyed."

"If you want to make peace," said the Su-dic, "make the Skeezers restore my wife to her proper form and give back her four cans of brains. Also make them agree to allow us to catch fish in their lake."

"No," returned Ozma, "I will not do that, for it would be unjust. I will have the Golden Pig again transformed into your wife Rora, and give her one can of brains, but the other three cans must be restored to those she robbed. Neither may you catch fish in the Lake of the Skeezers, for it is their lake and the fish belong to them. This arrangement is just and honorable, and you must agree to it."

"Never!" cried the Su-dic. Just then a pig came running into the room, uttering dismal grunts. It was made of solid gold, with joints at the bends of the legs and in the neck and jaws. The Golden Pig's eyes were rubies, and its teeth were polished ivory.

"There!" said the Su-dic, "gaze on the evil work of Queen Coo-ee-oh, and then say if you can prevent my making war on the Skeezers. That grunting beast was once my wife—the most beautiful Flathead on our mountain and a skillful witch. Now look at her!"

"Fight the Skeezers, fight the Skeezers, fight the Skeezers!" grunted the Golden Pig.

"I *will* fight the Skeezers," exclaimed the Flathead chief, "and if a dozen Ozmas of Oz forbade me I would fight just the same."

"Not if I can prevent it!" asserted Ozma.

"You can't prevent it. But since you threaten me, I'll have you confined in the bronze prison until the war is over," said the Su-dic. He whistled and four stout Flatheads, armed with axes and spears, entered the room and saluted him. Turning to the men he said: "Take these two girls, bind them with wire ropes and cast them into the bronze prison."

The four men bowed low and one of them asked:

"Where are the two girls, most noble Su-dic?"

The Su-dic turned to where Ozma and Dorothy had stood but they had vanished!

CHAPTER VII

THE MAGIC ISLE

OZMA, SEEING IT WAS USELESS TO ARGUE
with the Supreme Dictator of the Flatheads,
had been considering how best to escape from
his power. She realized that his sorcery might be
difficult to overcome, and when he threatened to cast
Dorothy and her into a bronze prison she slipped her
hand into her bosom and grasped her silver wand. With
the other hand she grasped the hand of Dorothy, but
these motions were so natural that the Su-dic did not
notice them. Then when he turned to meet his four
soldiers, Ozma instantly rendered both herself and
Dorothy invisible and swiftly led her companion
around the group of Flatheads and out of the
room. As they reached the entry and descended
the stone steps, Ozma whispered:

"Let us run, dear! We are invisible, so no one will see us."

Dorothy understood and she was a good runner. Ozma had marked the place where the grand stairway that led to the plain was located, so they made directly for it. Some people were in the paths but these they dodged around. One or two Flatheads heard the pattering of footsteps of the girls on the stone pavement and stopped with bewildered looks to gaze around them, but no one interfered with the invisible fugitives.

The Su-dic had lost no time in starting the chase. He and his men ran so fast that they might have overtaken the girls before they reached the stairway had not the Golden Pig suddenly run across their path. The Su-dic tripped over the pig and fell flat, and his four men tripped over him and tumbled in a heap. Before they could scramble up and reach the mouth of the passage it was too late to stop the two girls.

There was a guard on each side of the stairway, but of course they did not see Ozma and Dorothy as they sped past and descended the steps. Then they had to go up five steps and down another ten, and so on, in the same manner in which they had climbed to the top of the mountain. Ozma lighted their way with her wand and they kept on without relaxing their speed until they reached the bottom. Then they ran to the right and turned the corner of the invisible wall just as the Su-dic and his followers rushed out of the arched entrance and looked around in an attempt to discover the fugitives.

Ozma now knew they were safe, so she told Dorothy to stop and both of them sat down on the grass until they could breathe freely and become rested from their mad flight.

As for the Su-dic, he realized he was foiled and soon turned and climbed his stairs again. He was very angry—angry with Ozma and angry with himself—because, now that he took time to think, he remembered that he knew very well the art of making people invisible, and visible again, and if he had only thought of it in time he could have used his magic knowledge to make the girls visible and so have captured them easily. However, it was now too late for regrets and he determined to make preparations at once to march all his forces against the Skeezers.

"What shall we do next?" asked Dorothy, when they were rested.

"Let us find the Lake of the Skeezers," replied Ozma. "From what that dreadful Su-dic said I imagine the Skeezers are good people and worthy of our friendship, and if we go to them we may help them to defeat the Flatheads."

"I s'pose we can't stop the war now," remarked Dorothy reflectively, as they walked toward the row of palm trees.

"No; the Su-dic is determined to fight the Skeezers, so all we can do is to warn them of their danger and help them as much as possible."

"Of course you'll punish the Flatheads," said Dorothy.

"Well, I do not think the Flathead people are as much to blame as their Supreme Dictator," was the answer. "If he is removed from power and his unlawful magic taken from him, the people will probably be good and respect the laws of the Land of Oz, and live at peace with all their neighbors in the future."

"I hope so," said Dorothy with a sigh of doubt.

The palms were not far from the mountain and the girls reached them after a brisk walk. The huge trees were set close together, in three rows, and had been planted so as to keep people from passing them, but the Flatheads had cut a passage through this barrier and Ozma found the path and led Dorothy to the other side.

Beyond the palms they discovered a very beautiful scene. Bordered by a green lawn was a great lake fully a mile from shore to shore, the waters of which were exquisitely blue and sparkling, with little wavelets breaking its smooth surface where the breezes touched it. In the center of this lake appeared a lovely island, not of

great extent but almost entirely covered by a huge round building with glass walls and a high glass dome which glittered brilliantly in the sunshine. Between the glass building and the edge of the island was no grass, flowers or shrubbery, but only an expanse of highly polished white marble. There were no boats on either shore and no signs of life could be seen anywhere on the island.

"Well," said Dorothy, gazing wistfully at the island, "we've found the Lake of the Skeezers and their Magic Isle. I guess the Skeezers are in that big glass palace, but we can't get at 'em."

CHAPTER VIII

QUEEN COO-EE-OH

PRINCESS OZMA CONSIDERED THE situation gravely. Then she tied her handkerchief to her wand and, standing at the water's edge, waved the handkerchief like a flag, as a signal. For a time they could observe no response.

"I don't see what good that will do," said Dorothy. "Even if the Skeezers are on that island and see us, and know we're friends, they haven't any boats to come and get us."

But the Skeezers didn't need boats, as the girls soon discovered. For on a sudden an opening appeared at the base of the palace and from the opening came a slender shaft of steel, reaching out slowly but steadily across the water in the direction of the place where they stood. To the girls this steel arrangement looked like a triangle, with the base nearest the water. It came toward them in the form of an arch, stretching out from the palace wall until its end reached the bank and rested there, while the other end still remained on the island.

Then they saw that it was a bridge, consisting of a steel footway just broad enough to walk on, and two slender guide rails, one on either side, which were connected with the footway by steel bars. The bridge looked rather frail and Dorothy feared it would not bear their weight, but Ozma at once called, "Come on!" and started to walk across, holding fast to the rail on either side. So Dorothy summoned her courage and followed after. Before Ozma had taken three steps she halted and so forced Dorothy to halt, for the bridge was again moving and returning to the island.

"We need not walk after all," said Ozma. So they stood still in their places and let the steel bridge draw them onward. Indeed, the bridge drew them well into the glass-domed building which covered the island, and soon they found themselves standing in a marble room where two handsomely dressed young men stood on a platform to receive them.

Ozma at once stepped from the end of the bridge to the marble platform, followed by Dorothy, and then the bridge disappeared with a slight clang of steel and a marble slab covered the opening from which it had emerged.

The two young men bowed profoundly to Ozma, and one of them said:

"Queen Coo-ee-oh bids you welcome, O Strangers. Her Majesty is waiting to receive you in her palace."

"Lead on," replied Ozma with dignity.

But instead of "leading on," the platform of marble began to rise, carrying them upward through a square hole above which just fitted it. A moment later they found themselves within the great glass dome that covered almost all of the island.

Within this dome was a little village, with houses, streets, gardens and parks. The houses were of colored marbles, prettily designed, with many stained-glass windows, and the streets and gardens seemed well cared for. Exactly under the center of the lofty dome was a small park filled with brilliant flowers, with an elaborate fountain, and facing this park stood a building larger and more imposing than the others. Toward this building the young men escorted Ozma and Dorothy.

On the streets and in the doorways or open windows of the houses were men, women and children, all richly dressed. These were much like other people in different parts of the Land of Oz, except that instead of seeming merry and contented they all wore expressions of much solemnity or of nervous irritation. They had beautiful homes, splendid clothes, and ample food, but Dorothy at once decided something was wrong with their lives and that they were not happy. She said nothing, however, but looked curiously at the Skeezers.

At the entrance of the palace Ozma and Dorothy were met by two other young men, in uniform and armed with queer weapons that seemed about halfway between pistols and guns, but were like neither. Their conductors bowed and left them, and the two in uniforms led the girls into the palace.

In a beautiful throne room, surrounded by a dozen or more young men and women, sat the Queen of the Skeezers, Coo-ee-oh. She was a girl who looked older than Ozma or Dorothy—fifteen or sixteen, at least—and although she was elaborately dressed as if she were going to a ball she was too thin and plain of feature to be pretty. But evidently Queen Coo-ee-oh did not realize this fact, for her air and manner betrayed her as proud and haughty and with a high regard for her own importance. Dorothy at once decided she was "snippy" and that she would not like Queen Coo-ee-oh as a companion.

The Queen's hair was as black as her skin was white and her eyes were black, too. The eyes, as she calmly examined Ozma and Dorothy, had a suspicious and unfriendly look in them, but she said quietly:

"I know who you are, for I have consulted my Magic Oracle, which told me that one calls herself Princess Ozma, the Ruler of all the Land of Oz, and the other is Princess Dorothy of Oz, who came from a country called Kansas. I know nothing of the Land of Oz, and I know nothing of Kansas."

"Why, *this* is the Land of Oz!" cried Dorothy. "It's a *part* of the Land of Oz, anyhow, whether you know it or not."

"Oh, in-deed!" answered Queen Coo-ee-oh, scornfully. "I suppose you will claim next that this Princess Ozma, ruling the Land of Oz, rules me!"

"Of course," returned Dorothy. "There's no doubt of it."

The Queen turned to Ozma.

"Do you dare make such a claim?" she asked.

By this time Ozma had made up her mind as to the character of this haughty and disdainful creature, whose self-pride evidently led her to believe herself superior to all others.

"I did not come here to quarrel with Your Majesty," said the girl Ruler of Oz, quietly. "What and who I am is well established, and my authority comes from the Fairy Queen Lurline, of whose band I was a member when Lurline made all Oz a fairyland. There are several countries and several different peoples in this broad land, each of which has its separate Rulers, Kings, Emperors and Queens. But all these render obedience to my laws and acknowledge me as the supreme Ruler."

"If other Kings and Queens are fools that does not interest me in the least," replied Coo-ee-oh, disdainfully. "In the Land of the Skeezers I alone am supreme. You are impudent to think I would defer to you—or to anyone else."

"Let us not speak of this now, please," answered Ozma. "Your island is in danger, for a powerful foe is preparing to destroy it."

"Pah! The Flatheads. I do not fear them."

"Their Supreme Dictator is a Sorcerer."

"My magic is greater than his. Let the Flatheads come! They will never return to their barren mountain-top. I will see to that."

Ozma did not like this attitude, for it meant that the Skeezers were eager to fight the Flatheads, and Ozma's object in coming here was to prevent fighting and induce the two quarrelsome neighbors to make peace. She was also greatly disappointed in Coo-ee-oh, for the reports of Su-dic had led her to imagine the Queen more just and honorable than were the Flatheads. Indeed Ozma reflected that the girl might be better at heart than her self-pride and overbearing manner

indicated, and in any event it would be wise not to antagonize her but to try to win her friendship.

"I do not like wars, Your Majesty," said Ozma. "In the Emerald City, where I rule thousands of people, and in the countries near to the Emerald City, where thousands more acknowledge my rule, there is no army at all, because there is no quarreling and no need to fight. If differences arise between my people, they come to me and I judge the cases and award justice to all. So, when I learned there might be war between two faraway people of Oz, I came here to settle the dispute and adjust the quarrel."

"No one asked you to come," declared Queen Coo-ee-oh. "It is my business to settle this dispute, not yours. You say my island is a part of the Land of Oz, which you rule, but that is all nonsense, for I've never heard of the Land of Oz, nor of you. You say you are a fairy, and that fairies gave you command over me. I don't believe it! What I *do* believe is that you are an impostor and have come here to stir up trouble among my people, who are already becoming difficult to manage. You two girls may even be spies of the vile Flatheads, for all I know, and may be trying to trick me.

But understand this," she added, proudly rising from her jeweled throne to confront them, "I have magic powers greater than any fairy possesses, and greater than any Flathead possesses. I am a Krumbic Witch—the only Krumbic Witch in the world—and I fear the magic of no other creature that exists! You say you rule thousands. I rule one hundred and one Skeezers. But every one of them trembles at my word. Now that Ozma of Oz and Princess Dorothy are here, I shall rule one hundred and three subjects, for you also shall bow before my power. More than that, in ruling you I also rule the thousands you say you rule."

Dorothy was very indignant at this speech.

"I've got a pink kitten that sometimes talks like that," she said, "but after I give her a good whipping she doesn't think she's so high and mighty after all. If you only knew who Ozma is you'd be scared to death to talk to her like that!"

Queen Coo-ee-oh gave the girl a supercilious look. Then she turned again to Ozma.

"I happen to know," said she, "that the Flatheads intend to attack us tomorrow, but we are ready for them. Until the battle is over, I shall keep you two strangers prisoners on my island, from which there is no chance for you to escape."

She turned and looked around the band of courtiers who stood silently around her throne.

"Lady Aurex," she continued, singling out one of the young women, "take these children to your house and care for them, giving them food and lodging. You may allow them to wander anywhere under the Great Dome, for they are harmless. After I have attended to the Flatheads I will consider what next to do with these foolish girls."

She resumed her seat and the Lady Aurex bowed low and said in a humble manner:

"I obey Your Majesty's commands." Then to Ozma and Dorothy she added, "Follow me," and turned to leave the throne room.

Dorothy looked to see what Ozma would do. To her surprise and a little to her disappointment Ozma turned and followed Lady Aurex. So Dorothy trailed after them, but not without giving a parting, haughty look toward Queen Coo-ee-oh, who had her face turned the other way and did not see the disapproving look.

CHAPTER IX

LADY AUREX

LADY AUREX LED OZMA AND DOROTHY ALONG a street to a pretty marble house near to one edge of the great glass dome that covered the village. She did not speak to the girls until she had ushered them into a pleasant room, comfortably furnished, nor did any of the solemn people they met on the street venture to speak.

When they were seated Lady Aurex asked if they were hungry, and finding they were summoned a maid and ordered food to be brought.

This Lady Aurex looked to be about twenty years old, although in the Land of Oz where people have never changed in appearance since the fairies made it a fairyland—where no one grows old or dies—it is always difficult to say how many years anyone has lived. She had a pleasant, attractive face, even though it was solemn and sad as the faces of all Skeezers seemed to be, and her costume was rich and elaborate, as became a lady in waiting upon the Queen.

Ozma had observed Lady Aurex closely and now asked her in a gentle tone:

"Do you, also, believe me to be an impostor?"

"I dare not say," replied Lady Aurex in a low tone.

"Why are you afraid to speak freely?" inquired Ozma.

"The Queen punishes us if we make remarks that she does not like."

"Are we not alone then, in this house?"

"The Queen can hear everything that is spoken on this island—even the slightest whisper," declared Lady Aurex. "She is a wonderful witch, as she has told you, and it is folly to criticise her or disobey her commands."

Ozma looked into her eyes and saw that she would like to say more if she dared. So she drew from her bosom her silver wand, and having muttered a magic phrase in a strange tongue, she left the room and walked slowly around the outside of the house, making a complete circle and waving her wand in mystic curves as she walked. Lady Aurex watched her curiously and, when Ozma had again entered the room and seated herself, she asked:

"What have you done?"

"I've enchanted this house in such a manner that Queen Coo-ee-oh, with all her witchcraft, cannot hear one word we speak within the magic circle I have made," replied Ozma. "We may now speak freely and as loudly as we wish, without fear of the Queen's anger."

Lady Aurex brightened at this.

"Can I trust you?" she asked.

"Ev'rybody trusts Ozma," exclaimed Dorothy. "She is true and honest, and your wicked Queen will be sorry she insulted the powerful Ruler of all the Land of Oz."

"The Queen does not know me yet," said Ozma, "but I want you to know me, Lady Aurex, and I want you to tell me why you, and all the Skeezers, are unhappy. Do not fear Coo-ee-oh's anger, for she cannot hear a word we say, I assure you."

Lady Aurex was thoughtful a moment; then she said: "I shall trust you, Princess Ozma, for I believe you are what you say you are—our supreme Ruler. If you knew the dreadful punishments our Queen inflicts upon us, you would not wonder we are so unhappy. The Skeezers are not bad people; they do not care to quarrel and fight, even with their enemies the Flatheads; but they are so cowed and fearful of Coo-ee-oh that they obey her slightest word, rather than suffer her anger."

"Hasn't she any heart, then?" asked Dorothy.

"She never displays mercy. She loves no one but herself," asserted Lady Aurex, but she trembled as she said it, as if afraid even yet of her terrible Queen.

"That's pretty bad," said Dorothy, shaking her head gravely. "I see you've a lot to do here, Ozma, in this forsaken corner of the Land of Oz. First place, you've got to take the magic away from Queen Coo-ee-oh, and from that awful Su-dic, too. My idea is that neither of them is fit to rule anybody, 'cause they're cruel and hateful. So you'll have to give the Skeezers and Flatheads new Rulers and teach all their people that they're part of the Land of Oz and must obey, above all, the lawful Ruler, Ozma of Oz. Then, when you've done that, we can go back home again."

Ozma smiled at her little friend's earnest counsel, but Lady Aurex said in an anxious tone:

"I am surprised that you suggest these reforms while you are yet prisoners on this island and in Coo-ee-oh's power. That these things should be done, there is no doubt, but just now a dreadful war is likely to break out, and frightful things may happen to us all. Our Queen has such conceit that she thinks she can overcome the Su-dic and his people, but it is said Su-dic's magic is very powerful, although not as great as that possessed by his wife Rora, before Coo-ee-oh transformed her into a Golden Pig."

"I don't blame her very much for doing that," remarked Dorothy, "for the Flatheads were wicked to try to catch your beautiful fish and the Witch Rora wanted to poison all the fishes in the lake."

"Do you know the reason?" asked the Lady Aurex.

"I don't s'pose there was any reason, 'cept just wickedness," replied Dorothy.

"Tell us the reason," said Ozma earnestly.

"Well, Your Majesty, once—a long time ago—the Flatheads and the Skeezers were friendly. They visited our island and we visited their mountain, and everything was pleasant between the two peoples. At that time the Flatheads were ruled by three Adepts in Sorcery, beautiful girls who were not Flatheads, but had wandered to the Flat Mountain and made their home there. These three Adepts used their magic only for good, and the mountain people gladly made them their Rulers. They taught the Flatheads how to use their canned brains and how to work metals into clothing that would never wear out, and many other things that added to their happiness and content.

"Coo-ee-oh was our Queen then, as now, but she knew no magic and so had nothing to be proud of. But the three Adepts were very kind to Coo-ee-oh. They built for us this wonderful dome of glass and our houses of marble and taught us to make beautiful clothing and many other things. Coo-ee-oh pretended to be very grateful for these favors, but it seems that all the time she was jealous of the three Adepts and secretly tried to discover their arts of magic. In this she was more clever than anyone suspected. She invited the three Adepts to a banquet one day, and while they were feasting Coo-ee-oh stole their charms and magical instruments and transformed them into three fishes—a gold fish, a silver fish and a bronze fish. While the poor fishes were gasping and flopping helplessly on the floor of the banquet room one of them said reproachfully: 'You will be punished for this, Coo-ee-oh, for if one of us dies or is destroyed, you will become shrivelled and helpless, and all your stolen magic will depart from you.' Frightened by this threat, Coo-ee-oh at once

caught up the three fish and ran with them to the shore of the lake, where she cast them into the water. This revived the three Adepts and they swam away and disappeared.

"I, myself, witnessed this shocking scene," continued Lady Aurex, "and so did many other Skeezers. The news was carried to the Flatheads, who then turned from friends to enemies. The Su-dic and his wife Rora were the only ones on the mountain who were glad the three Adepts had been lost to them, and they at once became Rulers of the Flatheads and stole their canned brains from others to make themselves the more powerful. Some of the Adepts' magic tools had been left on the mountain, and these Rora seized and by the use of them she became a witch.

"The result of Coo-ee-oh's treachery was to make both the Skeezers and the Flatheads miserable instead of happy. Not only were the Su-dic and his wife cruel to their people, but our Queen at once became proud and arrogant and treated us very unkindly. All the Skeezers knew she had stolen her magic powers and so she hated us and made us humble ourselves before her and obey her slightest word. If we disobeyed, or did not please her, or if we talked about her when we were in our own homes she would have us dragged to the whipping post in her palace and lashed with knotted cords. That is why we fear her so greatly."

This story filled Ozma's heart with sorrow and Dorothy's heart with indignation.

"I now understand," said Ozma, "why the fishes in the lake have brought about war between the Skeezers and the Flatheads."

"Yes," Lady Aurex answered, "now that you know the story it is easy to understand. The Su-dic and his wife came to our lake hoping to catch the silver fish, or gold fish, or bronze fish—any one of them would do—and by destroying it deprive Coo-ee-oh of her magic. Then they could easily conquer her. Also they had another reason for wanting to catch the fish—they feared that in some way the three Adepts might regain their proper forms and then they would be sure to return to the mountain and punish Rora and the Su-dic. That was why Rora finally tried to poison all the fishes in the lake, at the time Coo-ee-oh transformed her into a Golden Pig. Of course this attempt to destroy the fishes frightened the Queen, for her safety lies in keeping the three fishes alive."

"I s'pose Coo-ee-oh will fight the Flatheads with all her might," observed Dorothy.

"And with all her magic," added Ozma, thoughtfully.

"I do not see how the Flatheads can get to this island to hurt us," said Lady Aurex.

"They have bows and arrows, and I guess they mean to shoot the arrows at your big dome, and break all the glass in it," suggested Dorothy.

But Lady Aurex shook her head with a smile.

"They cannot do that," she replied.

"Why not?"

"I dare not tell you why, but if the Flatheads come to-morrow morning you will yourselves see the reason."

"I do not think they will attempt to harm the island," Ozma declared. "I believe they will first attempt to destroy the fishes, by poison or some other means. If they succeed in that, the conquest of the island will not be difficult."

"They have no boats," said Lady Aurex, "and Coo-ee-oh, who has long expected this war, has been preparing for it in many astonishing ways. I almost wish the Flatheads would conquer us, for then we would be free from our dreadful Queen; but I do not wish to see the three transformed fishes destroyed, for in them lies our only hope of future happiness."

"Ozma will take care of you, whatever happens," Dorothy assured her. But the Lady Aurex, not knowing the extent of Ozma's power—which was, in fact, not so great as Dorothy imagined—could not take much comfort in this promise.

It was evident there would be exciting times on the morrow, if the Flatheads really attacked the Skeezers of the Magic Isle.

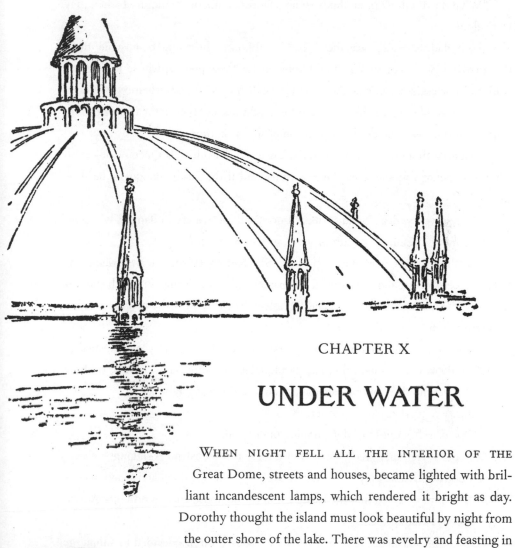

CHAPTER X

UNDER WATER

WHEN NIGHT FELL ALL THE INTERIOR OF THE
Great Dome, streets and houses, became lighted with brilliant incandescent lamps, which rendered it bright as day.
Dorothy thought the island must look beautiful by night from
the outer shore of the lake. There was revelry and feasting in
the Queen's palace, and the music of the royal band
could be plainly heard in Lady Aurex's house,
where Ozma and Dorothy remained with their
hostess and keeper. They were prisoners, but
treated with much consideration.

Lady Aurex gave them a nice supper and
when they wished to retire showed them to a
pretty room with comfortable beds and wished
them a good night and pleasant dreams.

"What do you think of all this, Ozma?" Dorothy anxiously inquired when they were alone.

"I am glad we came," was the reply, "for although there may be mischief done to-morrow, it was necessary I should know about these people, whose leaders are wild and lawless and oppress their subjects with injustice and cruelties. My task, therefore, is to liberate the Skeezers and the Flatheads and secure for them freedom and happiness. I have no doubt I can accomplish this in time."

"Just now, though, we're in a bad fix," asserted Dorothy. "If Queen Coo-ee-oh conquers to-morrow, she won't be nice to us, and if the Su-dic conquers, he'll be worse."

"Do not worry, dear," said Ozma, "I do not think we are in danger, whatever happens, and the result of our adventure is sure to be good."

Dorothy was not worrying, especially. She had confidence in her friend, the fairy Princess of Oz, and she enjoyed the excitement of the events in which she was taking part. So she crept into bed and fell asleep as easily as if she had been in her own cosy room in Ozma's palace.

A sort of grating, grinding sound awakened her. The whole island seemed to tremble and sway, as it might do in an earthquake. Dorothy sat up in bed, rubbing her eyes to get the sleep out of them, and then found it was daybreak.

Ozma was hurriedly dressing herself.

"What is it?" asked Dorothy, jumping out of bed.

"I'm not sure," answered Ozma, "but it feels as if the island is sinking."

As soon as possible they finished dressing, while the creaking and swaying continued. Then they rushed into the living room of the house and found Lady Aurex, fully dressed, awaiting them.

"Do not be alarmed," said their hostess. "Coo-ee-oh has decided to submerge the island, that is all. But it proves the Flatheads are coming to attack us."

"What do you mean by sub-sub-merging the island?" asked Dorothy.

"Come here and see," was the reply.

Lady Aurex led them to a window which faced the side of the Great Dome which covered all the village, and they could see that the island was indeed sinking, for the water of the lake was already half way up the side of the dome. Through the glass could be seen swimming fishes, and tall stalks of swaying seaweeds, for the water was clear as crystal and through it they could distinguish even the farther shore of the lake.

"The Flatheads are not here yet," said Lady Aurex. "They will come soon, but not until all of this dome is under the surface of the water."

"Won't the dome leak?" Dorothy inquired anxiously.

"No, indeed."

"Was the island ever sub-sub-sunk before?"

"Oh, yes; on several occasions. But Coo-ee-oh doesn't care to do that often, for it requires a lot of hard work to operate the machinery. The dome was built so that the island could disappear. I think," she continued, "that our Queen fears the Flatheads will attack the island and try to break the glass of the dome."

"Well, if we're under water, they can't fight us, and we can't fight them," asserted Dorothy.

"They could kill the fishes, however," said Ozma gravely.

"We have ways to fight, also, even though our island is under water," claimed Lady Aurex. "I cannot tell you all our secrets, but this island is full of surprises. Also our Queen's magic is astonishing."

"Did she steal it all from the three Adepts in Sorcery that are now fishes?"

"She stole the knowledge and the magic tools, but she has used them as the three Adepts never would have done."

By this time the top of the dome was quite under water and suddenly the island stopped sinking and became stationary.

"See!" cried Lady Aurex, pointing to the shore. "The Flatheads have come."

On the bank, which was now far above their heads, a crowd of dark figures could be seen.

"Now let us see what Coo-ee-oh will do to oppose them," continued Lady Aurex, in a voice that betrayed her excitement.

The Flatheads, pushing their way through the line of palm trees, had reached the shore of the lake just as the top of the island's dome disappeared beneath the surface. The water now flowed from shore to shore, but through the clear water the dome was still visible and the houses of the Skeezers could be dimly seen through the panes of glass.

"Good!" exclaimed the Su-dic, who had armed all his followers and had brought with him two copper vessels, which he carefully set down upon the ground beside him. "If Coo-ee-oh wants to hide instead of fighting our job will be easy, for in one of these copper vessels I have enough poison to kill every fish in the lake."

"Kill them, then, while we have time, and then we can go home again," advised one of the chief officers.

"Not yet," objected the Su-dic. "The Queen of the Skeezers has defied me, and I want to get her into my power, as well as to destroy her magic. She transformed my poor wife into a Golden Pig, and I must have revenge for that, whatever else we do."

"Look out!" suddenly exclaimed the officers, pointing into the lake; "something's going to happen."

From the submerged dome a door opened and something black shot swiftly out into the water. The door instantly closed behind it and the dark object cleaved its way through the water, without rising to the surface, directly toward the place where the Flatheads were standing.

"What is that?" Dorothy asked the Lady Aurex.

"That is one of the Queen's submarines," was the reply. "It is all enclosed, and can move under water. Coo-ee-oh has several of these boats which are kept in little rooms in the basement under our village. When the island is submerged, the Queen uses these boats to reach the shore, and I believe she now intends to fight the Flatheads with them."

The Su-dic and his people knew nothing of Coo-ee-oh's submarines, so they watched with surprise as the under-water boat approached them. When it was quite

near the shore it rose to the surface and the top parted and fell back, disclosing a boat full of armed Skeezers. At the head was the Queen, standing up in the bow and holding in one hand a coil of magic rope that gleamed like silver.

The boat halted and Coo-ee-oh drew back her arm to throw the silver rope toward the Su-dic, who was now but a few feet from her. But the wily Flathead leader quickly realized his danger and before the Queen could throw the rope he caught up one of the copper vessels and dashed its contents full in her face!

CHAPTER XI

THE CONQUEST OF THE SKEEZERS

QUEEN COO-EE-OH DROPPED THE ROPE, tottered and fell headlong into the water, sinking beneath the surface, while the Skeezers in the submarine were too bewildered to assist her and only stared at the ripples in the water where she had disappeared. A moment later there arose to the surface a beautiful White Swan. This Swan was of large size, very gracefully formed, and scattered all over its white feathers were tiny diamonds, so thickly placed that as the rays of the morning sun fell upon them the entire body of the Swan glistened like one brilliant diamond. The head of the Diamond Swan had a bill of polished gold and its eyes were two sparkling amethysts.

"Hooray!" cried the Su-dic, dancing up and down with wicked glee. "My poor wife, Rora, is avenged at last. You made her a Golden Pig, Coo-ee-oh, and now I have made you a

Diamond Swan. Float on your lake forever, if you like, for your web feet can do no more magic and you are as powerless as the Pig you made of my wife!"

"Villain! Scoundrel!" croaked the Diamond Swan. "You will be punished for this. Oh, what a fool I was to let you enchant me!"

"A fool you were, and a fool you are!" laughed the Su-dic, dancing madly in his delight. And then he carelessly tipped over the other copper vessel with his heel and its contents spilled on the sands and were lost to the last drop.

The Su-dic stopped short and looked at the overturned vessel with a rueful countenance.

"That's too bad—too bad!" he exclaimed sorrowfully. "I've lost all the poison I had to kill the fishes with, and I can't make any more because only my wife knew the secret of it, and she is now a foolish Pig and has forgotten all her magic."

"Very well," said the Diamond Swan scornfully, as she floated upon the water and swam gracefully here and there. "I'm glad to see you are foiled. Your punishment is just beginning, for although you have enchanted me and taken away my powers of sorcery you have still the three magic fishes to deal with, and they'll destroy you in time, mark my words."

The Su-dic stared at the Swan a moment. Then he yelled to his men:

"Shoot her! Shoot the saucy bird!"

They let fly some arrows at the Diamond Swan, but she dove under the water and the missiles fell harmless. When Coo-ee-oh rose to the surface she was far from the shore and she swiftly swam across the lake to where no arrows or spears could reach her.

The Su-dic rubbed his chin and thought what to do next. Near by floated the submarine in which the Queen had come, but the Skeezers who were in it were puzzled what to do with themselves. Perhaps they were not sorry their cruel mistress had been transformed into a Diamond Swan, but the transformation had left them quite helpless. The under-water boat was not operated by machinery, but by certain mystic words uttered by Coo-ee-oh. They didn't know how to submerge it, or how to make the water-tight shield cover them again, or how to make the boat go back to the castle, or make it enter the little basement room where it was usually kept. As a matter of fact, they were now shut out of their village under the Great Dome and could not get back again. So one of the men called to the Supreme Dictator of the Flatheads, saying:

"Please make us prisoners and take us to your mountain, and feed and keep us, for we have nowhere to go."

Then the Su-dic laughed and answered:

"Not so. I can't be bothered by caring for a lot of stupid Skeezers. Stay where you are, or go wherever you please, so long as you keep away from our mountain." He turned to his men and added: "We have conquered Queen Coo-ee-oh and made her a helpless swan. The Skeezers are under water and may stay there. So, having won the war, let us go home again and make merry and feast, having after many years proved the Flatheads to be greater and more powerful than the Skeezers."

So the Flatheads marched away and passed through the row of palms and went back to their mountain, where the Su-dic and a few of his officers feasted and all the others were forced to wait on them.

"I'm sorry we couldn't have roast pig," said the Su-dic, "but as the only pig we have is made of gold, we can't eat her. Also the Golden Pig happens to be my wife, and even were she not gold I am sure she would be too tough to eat."

CHAPTER XII

THE DIAMOND SWAN

WHEN THE FLATHEADS HAD GONE AWAY THE Diamond Swan swam back to the boat and one of the young Skeezers named Ervic said to her eagerly:

"How can we get back to the island, Your Majesty?"

"Am I not beautiful?" asked Coo-ee-oh, arching her neck gracefully and spreading her diamond-sprinkled wings. "I can see my reflection in the water, and I'm sure there is no bird nor beast, nor human as magnificent as I am!"

"How shall we get back to the island, Your Majesty?" pleaded Ervic.

"When my fame spreads throughout the land, people will travel from all parts of this lake to look upon my loveliness," said Coo-ee-oh, shaking her feathers to make the diamonds glitter more brilliantly.

"But, Your Majesty, we must go home and we do not know how to get there," Ervic persisted.

"My eyes," remarked the Diamond Swan, "are wonderfully blue and bright and will charm all beholders."

"Tell us how to make the boat go—how to get back into the island," begged Ervic and the others cried just as earnestly: "Tell us, Coo-ee-oh; tell us!"

"I don't know," replied the Queen in a careless tone.

"You are a magic-worker, a sorceress, a witch!"

"I was, of course, when I was a girl," she said, bending her head over the clear water to catch her reflection in it; "but now I've forgotten all such foolish things as magic. Swans are lovelier than girls, especially when they're sprinkled with diamonds. Don't you think so?" And she gracefully swam away, without seeming to care whether they answered or not.

Ervic and his companions were in despair. They saw plainly that Coo-ee-oh could not or would not help them. The former Queen had no further thought for her island, her people, or her wonderful magic; she was only intent on admiring her own beauty.

"Truly," said Ervic, in a gloomy voice, "the Flatheads have conquered us!"

Some of these events had been witnessed by Ozma and Dorothy and Lady Aurex, who had left the house and gone close to the glass of the dome, in order to see what was going on. Many of the Skeezers had also crowded against the dome, wondering what would happen next. Although their vision was to an extent blurred by the water and the necessity of looking upward at an angle, they had observed the main points of the drama enacted above. They saw Queen Coo-ee-oh's submarine come to the surface and open; they saw the Queen standing erect to throw her magic rope; they saw her sudden transformation into a Diamond Swan, and a cry of amazement went up from the Skeezers inside the dome.

"Good!" exclaimed Dorothy. "I hate that old Su-dic, but I'm glad Coo-ee-oh is punished."

"This is a dreadful misfortune!" cried Lady Aurex, pressing her hands upon her heart.

"Yes," agreed Ozma, nodding her head thoughtfully; "Coo-ee-oh's misfortune will prove a terrible blow to her people."

"What do you mean by that?" asked Dorothy in surprise. "Seems to me the Skeezers are in luck to lose their cruel Queen."

"If that were all you would be right," responded Lady Aurex; "and if the island were above water it would not be so serious. But here we all are, at the bottom of the lake, and fast prisoners in this dome."

"Can't you raise the island?" inquired Dorothy.

"No. Only Coo-ee-oh knew how to do that," was the answer.

"We can try," insisted Dorothy. "If it can be made to go down, it can be made to come up. The machinery is still here, I suppose."

"Yes; but the machinery works by magic, and Coo-ee-oh would never share her secret power with any one of us."

Dorothy's face grew grave; but she was thinking.

"Ozma knows a lot of magic," she said.

"But not that kind of magic," Ozma replied.

"Can't you learn how, by looking at the machinery?"

"I'm afraid not, my dear. It isn't fairy magic at all; it is witchcraft."

"Well," said Dorothy, turning to Lady Aurex, "you say there are other sub-sub-sinking boats. We can get in one of those, and shoot out to the top of the water, like Coo-ee-oh did, and so escape. And then we can help to rescue all the Skeezers down here."

"No one knows how to work the under-water boats but the Queen," declared Lady Aurex.

"Isn't there any door or window in this dome that we could open?"

"No; and, if there were, the water would rush in to flood the dome, and we could not get out."

"The Skeezers," said Ozma, "could not drown; they only get wet and soggy and in that condition they would be very uncomfortable and unhappy. But you are a mortal girl, Dorothy, and if your Magic Belt protected you from death you would have to lie forever at the bottom of the lake."

"No, I'd rather die quickly," asserted the little girl. "But there are doors in the basement that open—to let out the bridges and the boats—and that would not flood the dome, you know."

"Those doors open by a magic word, and only Coo-ee-oh knows the word that must be uttered," said Lady Aurex.

"Dear me!" exclaimed Dorothy, "that dreadful Queen's witchcraft upsets all my plans to escape. I guess I'll give it up, Ozma, and let you save us."

Ozma smiled, but her smile was not so cheerful as usual. The Princess of Oz found herself confronted with a serious problem, and although she had no thought of despairing she realized that the Skeezers and their island, as well as Dorothy and herself, were in grave trouble and that unless she could find a means to save them they would be lost to the Land of Oz for all future time.

"In such a dilemma," said she, musingly, "nothing is gained by haste. Careful thought may aid us, and so may the course of events. The unexpected is always likely to happen, and cheerful patience is better than reckless action."

"All right," returned Dorothy; "take your time, Ozma; there's no hurry. How about some breakfast, Lady Aurex?"

Their hostess led them back to the house, where she ordered her trembling servants to prepare and serve breakfast. All the Skeezers were frightened and anxious over the transformation of their Queen into a swan. Coo-ee-oh was feared and hated, but they had depended on her magic to conquer the Flatheads and she was the only one who could raise their island to the surface of the lake again.

Before breakfast was over several of the leading Skeezers came to Aurex to ask her advice and to question Princess Ozma, of whom they knew nothing except that she claimed to be a fairy and the Ruler of all the land, including the Lake of the Skeezers.

"If what you told Queen Coo-ee-oh was the truth," they said to her, "you are our lawful mistress, and we may depend on you to get us out of our difficulties."

"I will try to do that," Ozma graciously assured them, "but you must remember that the powers of fairies are granted them to bring comfort and happiness to all who appeal to them. On the contrary, such magic as Coo-ee-oh knew and practiced is unlawful witchcraft and her arts are such as no fairy would condescend to use. However, it is sometimes necessary to consider evil in order to accomplish good, and perhaps by studying Coo-ee-oh's tools and charms of witchcraft I may be able to save us. Do you promise to accept me as your Ruler and to obey my commands?"

They promised willingly.

"Then," continued Ozma, "I will go to Coo-ee-oh's palace and take possession of it. Perhaps what I find there will be of use to me. In the meantime tell all the Skeezers to fear nothing, but have patience. Let them return to their homes and

perform their daily tasks as usual. Coo-ee-oh's loss may not prove a misfortune, but rather a blessing."

This speech cheered the Skeezers amazingly. Really, they had no one now to depend upon but Ozma, and in spite of their dangerous position their hearts were lightened by the transformation and absence of their cruel Queen.

They got out their brass band and a grand procession escorted Ozma and Dorothy to the palace, where all of Coo-ee-oh's former servants were eager to wait upon them. Ozma invited Lady Aurex to stay at the palace also, for she knew all about the Skeezers and their island and had also been a favorite of the former Queen, so her advice and information were sure to prove valuable.

Ozma was somewhat disappointed in what she found in the palace. One room of Coo-ee-oh's private suite was entirely devoted to the practice of witchcraft, and here were countless queer instruments and jars of ointments and bottles of potions labeled with queer names, and strange machines that Ozma could not guess the use of, and pickled toads and snails and lizards, and a shelf of books that were written in blood, but in a language which the Ruler of Oz did not know.

"I do not see," said Ozma to Dorothy, who accompanied her in her search, "how Coo-ee-oh knew the use of the magic tools she stole from the three Adept Witches.

Moreover, from all reports these Adepts practiced only good witchcraft, such as would be helpful to their people, while Coo-ee-oh performed only evil."

"Perhaps she turned the good things to evil uses?" suggested Dorothy.

"Yes, and with the knowledge she gained Coo-ee-oh doubtless invented many evil things quite unknown to the good Adepts, who are now fishes," added Ozma. "It is unfortunate for us that the Queen kept her secrets so closely guarded, for no one but herself could use any of these strange things gathered in this room."

"Couldn't we capture the Diamond Swan and make her tell the secrets?" asked Dorothy.

"No; even were we able to capture her, Coo-ee-oh now has forgotten all the magic she ever knew. But until we ourselves escape from this dome we could not capture the Swan, and were we to escape we would have no use for Coo-ee-oh's magic."

"That's a fact," admitted Dorothy. "But—say, Ozma, here's a good idea! Couldn't we capture the three fishes—the gold and silver and bronze ones, and couldn't you transform 'em back to their own shapes, and then couldn't the three Adepts get us out of here?"

"You are not very practical, Dorothy dear. It would be as hard for us to capture the three fishes, from among all the other fishes in the lake, as to capture the Swan."

"But if we could, it would be more help to us," persisted the little girl.

"That is true," answered Ozma, smiling at her friend's eagerness. "You find a way to catch the fish, and I'll promise when they are caught to restore them to their proper forms."

"I know you think I can't do it," replied Dorothy, "but I'm going to try."

She left the palace and went to a place where she could look through a clear pane of the glass dome into the surrounding water. Immediately she became interested in the queer sights that met her view.

The Lake of the Skeezers was inhabited by fishes of many kinds and many sizes. The water was so transparent that the girl could see for a long distance and the fishes came so close to the glass of the dome that sometimes they actually touched it. On the white sands at the bottom of the lake were star-fish, lobsters, crabs and many shell fish of strange shapes and with shells of gorgeous hues. The water foliage was of brilliant colors and to Dorothy it resembled a splendid garden.

But the fishes were the most interesting of all. Some were big and lazy, floating slowly along or lying at rest with just their fins waving. Many with big round eyes looked full at the girl as she watched them and Dorothy wondered if they could hear

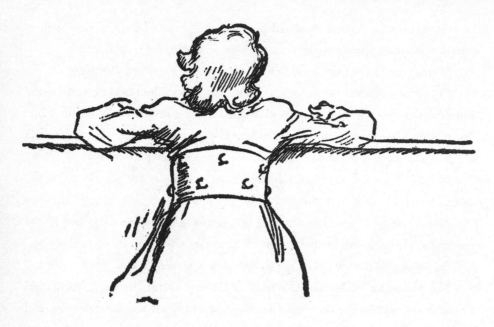

her through the glass if she spoke to them. In Oz, where all the animals and birds can talk, many fishes are able to talk also, but usually they are more stupid than birds and animals because they think slowly and haven't much to talk about.

In the Lake of the Skeezers the fish of smaller size were more active than the big ones and darted quickly in and out among the swaying weeds, as if they had important business and were in a hurry. It was among the smaller varieties that Dorothy hoped to spy the gold and silver and bronze fishes. She had an idea the three would keep together, being companions now as they were in their natural forms, but such a multitude of fishes constantly passed, the scene shifting every moment, that she was not sure she would notice them even if they appeared in view. Her eyes couldn't look in all directions and the fishes she sought might be on the other side of the dome, or far away in the lake.

"P'raps, because they were afraid of Coo-ee-oh, they've hid themselves somewhere, and don't know their enemy has been transformed," she reflected.

She watched the fishes for a long time, until she became hungry and went back to the palace for lunch. But she was not discouraged.

"Anything new, Ozma?" she asked.

"No, dear. Did you discover the three fishes?"

"Not yet. But there isn't anything better for me to do, Ozma, so I guess I'll go back and watch again."

CHAPTER XIII

THE ALARM BELL

GLINDA, THE GOOD, IN HER PALACE IN THE QUADLING Country, had many things to occupy her mind, for not only did she look after the weaving and embroidery of her bevy of maids, and assist all those who came to her to implore her help—beasts and birds as well as people—but she was a close student of the arts of sorcery and spent much time in her Magical Laboratory, where she strove to find a remedy for every evil and to perfect her skill in magic.

Nevertheless, she did not forget to look in the Great Book of Records each day to see if any mention was made of the visit of Ozma and Dorothy to the Enchanted Mountain of the Flatheads and the Magic Isle of the Skeezers. The Records told her that Ozma had arrived at the mountain, that she had escaped, with her companion, and gone to the island of the Skeezers, and that Queen Coo-ee-oh had submerged the island so that it was entirely under water. Then came the statement that the Flatheads had come to the lake to poison the fishes and that their Supreme Dictator had transformed Queen Coo-ee-oh into a swan.

No other details were given in the Great Book and so Glinda did not know that since Coo-ee-oh had forgotten her magic none of the Skeezers knew how to raise the island to the surface again. So Glinda was not worried about Ozma and Dorothy until one morning, while she sat with her maids, there came a sudden clang of the great alarm bell. This was so unusual that every maid gave a start and even the Sorceress for a moment could not think what the alarm meant.

Then she remembered the ring she had given Dorothy when she left the palace to start on her venture. In giving the ring Glinda had warned the little girl not to use its magic powers unless she and Ozma were in real danger, but then she was to turn it on her finger once to the right and once to the left and Glinda's alarm bell would ring.

So the Sorceress now knew that danger threatened her beloved Ruler and Princess Dorothy, and she hurried to her magic room to seek information as to what sort of danger it was. The answer to her question was not very satisfactory, for it was only: "Ozma and Dorothy are prisoners in the Great Dome of the Isle of the Skeezers, and the Dome is under the water of the lake."

"Hasn't Ozma the power to raise the island to the surface?" inquired Glinda.

"No," was the reply, and the Record refused to say more except that Queen Coo-ee-oh, who alone could command the island to rise, had been transformed by the Flathead Su-dic into a Diamond Swan.

Then Glinda consulted the past records of the Skeezers in the Great Book. After diligent search she discovered that Coo-ee-oh was a powerful sorceress, who had gained most of her power by treacherously transforming the Adepts of Magic, who were visiting her, into three fishes—gold, silver and bronze—after which she had them cast into the lake.

Glinda reflected earnestly on this information and decided that someone must go to Ozma's assistance. While there was no great need of haste, because Ozma and Dorothy could live in a submerged dome a long time, it was evident they could not get out until someone was able to raise the island.

The Sorceress looked through all her recipes and books of sorcery, but could find no magic that would raise a sunken island. Such a thing had never before been required in sorcery. Then Glinda made a little island, covered by a glass dome, and sunk it in a pond near her castle, and experimented in magical ways to bring it to the surface. She made several such experiments, but all were failures. It seemed a simple thing to do, yet she could not do it.

Nevertheless, the wise Sorceress did not despair of finding a way to liberate her friends. Finally she concluded that the best thing to do was to go to the Skeezer

Country and examine the lake. While there she was more likely to discover a solution to the problem that bothered her, and to work out a plan for the rescue of Ozma and Dorothy.

So Glinda summoned her storks and her aerial chariot, and telling her maids she was going on a journey and might not soon return, she entered the chariot and was carried swiftly to the Emerald City.

In Princess Ozma's palace the Scarecrow was now acting as Ruler of the Land of Oz. There wasn't much for him to do, because all the affairs of state moved so smoothly, but he was there in case anything unforeseen should happen.

Glinda found the Scarecrow playing croquet with Trot and Betsy Bobbin, two little girls who lived at the palace under Ozma's protection and were great friends of Dorothy and much loved by all the Oz people.

"Something's happened!" cried Trot, as the chariot of the Sorceress descended near them. "Glinda never comes here 'cept something's gone wrong."

"I hope no harm has come to Ozma, or Dorothy," said Betsy anxiously, as the lovely Sorceress stepped down from her chariot.

Glinda approached the Scarecrow and told him of the dilemma of Ozma and Dorothy and she added: "We must save them, somehow, Scarecrow."

"Of course," replied the Scarecrow, stumbling over a wicket and falling flat on his painted face.

The girls picked him up and patted his straw stuffing into shape, and he continued, as if nothing had occurred: "But you'll have to tell me what to do, for I never have raised a sunken island in all my life."

"We must have a Council of State as soon as possible," proposed the Sorceress. "Please send messengers to summon all of Ozma's Counsellors to this palace. Then we can decide what is best to be done."

The Scarecrow lost no time in doing this. Fortunately most of the royal Counsellors were in the Emerald City or near to it, so they all met in the throne room of the palace that same evening.

CHAPTER XIV

OZMA'S COUNSELLORS

NO RULER EVER HAD SUCH A QUEER ASSORTMENT OF advisers as the Princess Ozma had gathered about her throne. Indeed, in no other country could such amazing people exist. But Ozma loved them for their peculiarities and could trust every one of them.

First there was the Tin Woodman. Every bit of him was tin, brightly polished. All his joints were kept well oiled and moved smoothly. He carried a gleaming axe to prove he was a woodman, but seldom had cause to use it because he lived in a magnificent tin castle in the Winkie Country of Oz and was the Emperor of all the Winkies. The Tin Woodman's name was Nick Chopper. He had a very good mind, but his heart was not of much account, so he was very careful to do nothing unkind or to hurt anyone's feelings.

Another Counsellor was Scraps, the Patchwork Girl of Oz, who was made of a gaudy patchwork quilt, cut into shape and stuffed with cotton. This Patchwork Girl was very intelligent, but so full of fun and mad pranks that a lot of more stupid folks thought she must be crazy. Scraps was jolly under all conditions, however grave they might be, but her laughter and good spirits were of value in cheering others and in her seemingly careless remarks much wisdom could often be found.

Then there was the Shaggy Man—shaggy from head to foot, hair and whiskers, clothes and shoes—but very kind and gentle and one of Ozma's most loyal supporters.

Tik-Tok was there, a copper man with machinery inside him, so cleverly constructed that he moved, spoke and thought by three separate clock-works. Tik-Tok was very reliable because he always did exactly what he was wound up to do, but his machinery was liable to run down at times and then he was quite helpless until wound up again.

A different sort of person was Jack Pumpkinhead, one of Ozma's oldest friends and her companion on many adventures. Jack's body was very crude and awkward, being formed of limbs of trees of different sizes, jointed with wooden pegs. But it was a substantial body and not likely to break or wear out, and when it was dressed the clothes covered much of its roughness. The head of Jack Pumpkinhead was, as you have guessed, a ripe pumpkin, with the eyes, nose and mouth carved upon one side. The pumpkin was stuck on Jack's wooden neck and was liable to get turned sidewise or backward and then he would have to straighten it with his wooden hands.

The worst thing about this sort of a head was that it did not keep well and was sure to spoil sooner or later. So Jack's main business was to grow a field of fine pumpkins each year, and always before his old head spoiled he would select a fresh pumpkin from the field and carve the features on it very neatly, and have it ready to replace the old head whenever it became necessary. He didn't always carve it the same way, so his friends never knew exactly what sort of an expression they would find on his face. But there was no mistaking him, because he was the only pumpkin-headed man alive in the Land of Oz.

A one-legged sailor-man was a member of Ozma's council. His name was Cap'n Bill and he had come to the Land of Oz with Trot, and had been made welcome on account of his cleverness, honesty and good nature. He wore a wooden leg to replace the one he had lost and was a great friend of all the children in Oz because he could whittle all sorts of toys out of wood with his big jack-knife.

Professor H. M. Woggle-Bug, T. E., was another member of the council. The "H. M." meant Highly Magnified, for the Professor was once a little bug, who became magnified to the size of a man and always remained so. The "T. E." meant that he was Thoroughly Educated. He was at the head of Princess Ozma's Royal Athletic College, and so that the students would not have to study and so lose much time that could be devoted to athletic sports, such as foot-ball, base-ball and the like, Professor Woggle-Bug had invented the famous Educational Pills. If one of the college students took a Geography Pill after breakfast, he knew his geography lesson in an instant; if he took a Spelling Pill he at once knew his spelling lesson, and an Arithmetic Pill enabled the student to do any kind of sum without having to think about it.

These useful pills made the college very popular and taught the boys and girls of Oz their lessons in the easiest possible way. In spite of this, Professor Woggle-Bug was not a favorite outside his college, for he was very conceited and admired himself so much and displayed his cleverness and learning so constantly, that no one cared to associate with him. Ozma found him of value in her councils, nevertheless.

Perhaps the most splendidly dressed of all those present was a great frog as large as a man, called the Frogman, who was noted for his wise sayings. He had come to the Emerald City from the Yip Country of Oz and was a guest of honor. His long-tailed coat was of velvet, his vest of satin and his trousers of finest silk. There were diamond buckles on his shoes and he carried a gold-headed cane and a high silk hat. All of the bright colors were represented in his rich attire, so it tired one's eyes to look at him for long, until one became used to his splendor.

The best farmer in all Oz was Uncle Henry, who was Dorothy's own uncle, and who now lived near the Emerald City with his wife Aunt Em. Uncle Henry taught the Oz people how to grow the finest vegetables and fruits and grains and was of much use to Ozma in keeping the Royal Storehouses well filled. He, too, was a Counsellor.

The reason I mention the little Wizard of Oz last is because he was the most important man in the Land of Oz. He wasn't a big man in size, but he was a big man in power and intelligence and second only to Glinda the Good in all the mystic arts of magic. Glinda had taught him, and the Wizard and the Sorceress were the only ones in Oz permitted by law to practice wizardry and sorcery, which they applied only to good uses and for the benefit of the people.

The Wizard wasn't exactly handsome but he was pleasant to look at. His bald head was as shiny as if it had been varnished; there was always a merry twinkle in his eyes and he was as spry as a schoolboy. Dorothy says the reason the Wizard is not as powerful as Glinda is because Glinda didn't teach him all she knows, but what the Wizard knows he knows very well and so he performs some very remarkable magic. The ten I have mentioned assembled, with the Scarecrow and Glinda, in Ozma's throne room, right after dinner that evening, and the Sorceress told them all she knew of the plight of Ozma and Dorothy.

"Of course we must rescue them," she continued, "and the sooner they are rescued the better pleased they will be; but what we must now determine is how they can be saved. That is why I have called you together in council."

"The easiest way," remarked the Shaggy Man, "is to raise the sunken island of the Skeezers to the top of the water again."

"Tell me how?" said Glinda.

"I don't know how, your Highness, for I have never raised a sunken island."

"We might all get under it and lift," suggested Professor Woggle-Bug.

"How can we get under it when it rests on the bottom of the lake?" asked the Sorceress.

"Couldn't we throw a rope around it and pull it ashore?" inquired Jack Pumpkinhead.

"Why not pump the water out of the lake?" suggested the Patchwork Girl with a laugh.

"Do be sensible!" pleaded Glinda. "This is a serious matter, and we must give it serious thought."

"How big is the lake and how big is the island?" was the Frogman's question.

"None of us can tell, for we have not been there."

"In that case," said the Scarecrow, "it appears to me we ought to go to the Skeezer Country and examine it carefully."

"Quite right," agreed the Tin Woodman.

"We-will-have-to-go-there-any-how," remarked Tik-Tok in his jerky machine voice.

"The question is which of us shall go, and how many of us?" said the Wizard.

"I shall go of course," declared the Scarecrow.

"And I," said Scraps.

"It is my duty to Ozma to go," asserted the Tin Woodman.

"I could not stay away, knowing our loved Princess is in danger," said the Wizard.

"We all feel like that," Uncle Henry said.

Finally one and all present decided to go to the Skeezer Country, with Glinda and the little Wizard to lead them. Magic must meet magic in order to conquer it, so these two skillful magic-workers were necessary to insure the success of the expedition.

They were all ready to start at a moment's notice, for none had any affairs of importance to attend to. Jack was wearing a newly made Pumpkin-head and the Scarecrow had recently been stuffed with fresh straw. Tik-Tok's machinery was in good running order and the Tin Woodman always was well oiled.

"It is quite a long journey," said Glinda, "and while I might travel quickly to the Skeezer Country by means of my stork chariot the rest of you will be obliged to walk. So, as we must keep together, I will send my chariot back to my castle and we will plan to leave the Emerald City at sunrise to-morrow."

CHAPTER XV

THE GREAT SORCERESS

BETSY AND TROT, WHEN THEY HEARD OF the rescue expedition, begged the Wizard to permit them to join it and he consented. The Glass Cat, overhearing the conversation, wanted to go also and to this the Wizard made no objection.

This Glass Cat was one of the real curiosities of Oz. It had been made and brought to life by a clever magician named Dr. Pipt, who was not now permitted to work magic and was an ordinary citizen of the Emerald City. The cat was of transparent glass, through which one could plainly see its ruby heart beating and its pink brains whirling around in the top of the head.

The Glass Cat's eyes were emeralds; its fluffy tail was of spun glass and very beautiful. The ruby heart, while pretty to look at, was hard and cold and the Glass

Cat's disposition was not pleasant at all times. It scorned to catch mice, did not eat, and was extremely lazy. If you complimented the remarkable cat on her beauty, she would be very friendly, for she loved admiration above everything. The pink brains were always working and their owner was indeed more intelligent than most common cats.

Three other additions to the rescue party were made the next morning, just as they were setting out upon their journey. The first was a little boy called Button-Bright, because he had no other name that anyone could remember. He was a fine, manly little fellow, well mannered and good humored, who had only one bad fault. He was continually getting lost. To be sure, Button-Bright got found as often as he got lost, but when he was missing his friends could not help being anxious about him.

"Some day," predicted the Patchwork Girl, "he won't be found, and that will be the last of him." But that didn't worry Button-Bright, who was so careless that he did not seem to be able to break the habit of getting lost.

The second addition to the party was a Munchkin boy of about Button-Bright's age, named Ojo. He was often called "Ojo the Lucky," because good fortune followed him wherever he went. He and Button-Bright were close friends, although of such different natures, and Trot and Betsy were fond of both.

The third and last to join the expedition was an enormous lion, one of Ozma's regular guardians and the most important and intelligent beast in all Oz. He called himself the Cowardly Lion, saying that every little danger scared him so badly that his heart thumped against his ribs, but all who knew him knew that the Cowardly Lion's fears were coupled with bravery and that however much he might be frightened he summoned courage to meet every danger he encountered. Often he had saved Dorothy and Ozma in times of peril, but afterward he moaned and trembled and wept because he had been so scared.

"If Ozma needs help, I'm going to help her," said the great beast. "Also, I suspect the rest of you may need me on the journey—especially Trot and Betsy—for you may pass through a dangerous part of the country. I know that wild Gillikin Country pretty well. Its forests harbor many ferocious beasts."

They were glad the Cowardly Lion was to join them, and in good spirits the entire party formed a procession and marched out of the Emerald City amid the shouts of the people, who wished them success and a safe return with their beloved Ruler.

They followed a different route from that taken by Ozma and Dorothy, for they went through the Winkie Country and up north toward Oogaboo. But before they got there they swerved to the left and entered the Great Gillikin Forest, the nearest thing to a wilderness in all Oz. Even the Cowardly Lion had to admit that certain parts of this forest were unknown to him, although he had often wandered among

the trees, and the Scarecrow and Tin Woodman, who were great travelers, never had been there at all.

The forest was only reached after a tedious tramp, for some of the Rescue Expedition were quite awkward on their feet. The Patchwork Girl was as light as a feather and very spry; the Tin Woodman covered the ground as easily as Uncle Henry and the Wizard; but Tik-Tok moved slowly and the slightest obstruction in the road would halt him until the others cleared it away. Then, too, Tik-Tok's machinery kept running down, so Betsy and Trot took turns in winding it up.

The Scarecrow was more clumsy but less bother, for although he often stumbled and fell he could scramble up again and a little patting of his straw-stuffed body would put him in good shape again.

Another awkward one was Jack Pumpkinhead, for walking would jar his head around on his neck and then he would be likely to go in the wrong direction. But the Frogman took Jack's arm and then he followed the path more easily.

Cap'n Bill's wooden leg didn't prevent him from keeping up with the others and the old sailor could walk as far as any of them.

When they entered the forest the Cowardly Lion took the lead. There was no path here for men, but many beasts had made paths of their own which only the eyes of the Lion, practiced in woodcraft, could discern. So he stalked ahead and wound his way in and out, the others following in single file, Glinda being next to the Lion.

There are dangers in the forest, of course, but as the huge Lion headed the party he kept the wild denizens of the wilderness from bothering the travelers. Once, to be sure, an enormous leopard sprang upon the Glass Cat and caught her in his powerful jaws, but he broke several of his teeth and with howls of pain and dismay dropped his prey and vanished among the trees.

"Are you hurt?" Trot anxiously inquired of the Glass Cat.

"How silly!" exclaimed the creature in an irritated tone of voice; "nothing can hurt glass, and I'm too solid to break easily. But I'm annoyed at that leopard's impudence. He has no respect for beauty or intelligence. If he had noticed my pink brains work, I'm sure he would have realized I'm too important to be grabbed in a wild beast's jaws."

"Never mind," said Trot consolingly; "I'm sure he won't do it again."

They were almost in the center of the forest when Ojo, the Munchkin boy, suddenly said: "Why, where's Button-Bright?"

They halted and looked around them. Button-Bright was not with the party.

"Dear me," remarked Betsy, "I expect he's lost again!"

"When did you see him last, Ojo?" inquired Glinda.

"It was some time ago," replied Ojo. "He was trailing along at the end and throwing twigs at the squirrels in the trees. Then I went to talk to Betsy and Trot, and just now I noticed he was gone."

"This is too bad," declared the Wizard, "for it is sure to delay our journey. We must find Button-Bright before we go any farther, for this forest is full of ferocious beasts that would not hesitate to tear the boy to pieces."

"But what shall we do?" asked the Scarecrow. "If any of us leaves the party to search for Button-Bright he or she might fall a victim to the beasts, and if the Lion leaves us we will have no protector."

"The Glass Cat could go," suggested the Frogman. "The beasts can do her no harm, as we have discovered."

The Wizard turned to Glinda.

"Cannot your sorcery discover where Button-Bright is?" he asked.

"I think so," replied the Sorceress.

She called to Uncle Henry, who had been carrying her wicker box, to bring it to her, and when he obeyed she opened it and drew out a small round mirror. On the surface of the glass she dusted a white powder and then wiped it away with her handkerchief and looked in the mirror. It reflected a part of the forest, and there, beneath a wide-spreading tree, Button-Bright was lying asleep. On one side of him crouched a tiger, ready to spring; on the other side was a big gray wolf, its bared fangs glistening in a wicked way.

"Goodness me!" cried Trot, looking over Glinda's shoulder. "They'll catch and kill him sure."

Everyone crowded around for a glimpse at the magic mirror.

"Pretty bad—pretty bad!" said the Scarecrow sorrowfully.

"Comes of getting lost!" said Cap'n Bill, sighing.

"Guess he's a goner!" said the Frogman, wiping his eyes on his purple silk handkerchief.

"But where is he? Can't we save him?" asked Ojo the Lucky.

"If we knew where he is we could probably save him," replied the little Wizard, "but that tree looks so much like all the other trees, that we can't tell whether it's far away or near by."

"Look at Glinda!" exclaimed Betsy.

Glinda, having handed the mirror to the Wizard, had stepped aside and was making strange passes with her outstretched arms and reciting in low, sweet tones a

mystical incantation. Most of them watched the Sorceress with anxious eyes, despair giving way to the hope that she might be able to save their friend. The Wizard, however, watched the scene in the mirror, while over his shoulders peered Trot, the Scarecrow and the Shaggy Man.

What they saw was more strange than Glinda's actions. The tiger started to spring on the sleeping boy, but suddenly lost its power to move and lay flat upon the ground. The gray wolf seemed unable to lift its feet from the ground. It pulled first at one leg and then at another, and finding itself strangely confined to the spot began to bark and snarl angrily. They couldn't hear the barkings and snarls, but they could see the creature's mouth open and its thick lips move. Button-Bright, however, being but a few feet away from the wolf, heard its cries of rage, which wakened him from his untroubled sleep.

The boy sat up and looked first at the tiger and then at the wolf. His face showed that for a moment he was quite frightened, but he soon saw that the beasts were unable to approach him and so he got upon his feet and examined them curiously, with a mischievous smile upon his face. Then he deliberately kicked the tiger's head with his foot and catching up a fallen branch of a tree he went to the wolf and gave it a good whacking. Both the beasts were furious at such treatment but could not resent it.

Button-Bright now threw down the stick and with his hands in his pockets wandered carelessly away.

"Now," said Glinda, "let the Glass Cat run and find him. He is in that direction," pointing the way, "but how far off I do not know. Make haste and lead him back to us as quickly as you can."

The Glass Cat did not obey everyone's orders, but she really feared the great Sorceress, so as soon as the words were spoken the crystal animal darted away and was quickly lost to sight.

The Wizard handed the mirror back to Glinda, for the woodland scene had now faded from the glass. Then those who cared to rest sat down to await Button-Bright's coming. It was not long before he appeared through the trees and as he rejoined his friends he said in a peevish tone:

"Don't ever send that Glass Cat to find me again. She was very impolite and, if we didn't all know that she had no manners, I'd say she insulted me."

Glinda turned upon the boy sternly.

"You have caused all of us much anxiety and annoyance," said she. "Only my magic saved you from destruction. I forbid you to get lost again."

"Of course," he answered. "It won't be my fault if I get lost again; but it wasn't my fault this time."

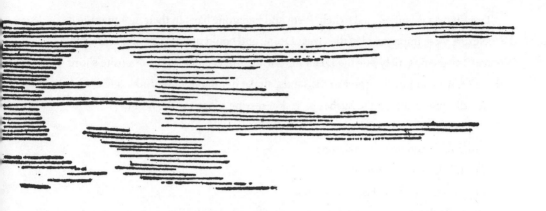

CHAPTER XVI

THE ENCHANTED FISHES

I MUST NOW TELL YOU WHAT HAPPENED TO ERVIC AND THE THREE OTHER Skeezers who were left floating in the iron boat after Queen Coo-ee-oh had been transformed into a Diamond Swan by the magic of the Flathead Su-dic.

The four Skeezers were all young men and their leader was Ervic. Coo-ee-oh had taken them with her in the boat to assist her if she captured the Flathead chief, as she hoped to do by means of her silver rope. They knew nothing about the witchcraft that moved the submarine and so, when left floating upon the lake, were at a loss what to do. The submarine could not be submerged by them or made to return to the sunken island. There were neither oars nor sails in the boat, which was not anchored but drifted quietly upon the surface of the lake.

The Diamond Swan had no further thought or care for her people. She had sailed over to the other side of the lake and all the calls and pleadings of Ervic and his companions were unheeded by the vain bird. As there was nothing else for them to do, they sat quietly in their boat and waited as patiently as they could for someone to come to their aid.

The Flatheads had refused to help them and had gone back to their mountain. All the Skeezers were imprisoned in the Great Dome and could not help even themselves. When evening came, they saw the Diamond Swan, still keeping to the opposite shore of the lake, walk out of the water to the sands, shake her diamond-sprinkled feathers, and then disappear among the bushes to seek a resting place for the night.

"I'm hungry," said Ervic.

"I'm cold," said another Skeezer.

"I'm tired," said a third.

"I'm afraid," said the last one of them.

But it did them no good to complain. Night fell and the moon rose and cast a silvery sheen over the surface of the water.

"Go to sleep," said Ervic to his companions. "I'll stay awake and watch, for we may be rescued in some unexpected way."

So the other three laid themselves down in the bottom of the boat and were soon fast asleep.

Ervic watched. He rested himself by leaning over the bow of the boat, his face near to the moonlit water, and thought dreamily of the day's surprising events and wondered what would happen to the prisoners in the Great Dome.

Suddenly a tiny goldfish popped its head above the surface of the lake, not more than a foot from his eyes. A silverfish then raised its head beside that of the goldfish, and a moment later a bronzefish lifted its head beside the others. The three fish, all in a row, looked earnestly with their round, bright eyes into the astonished eyes of Ervic the Skeezer.

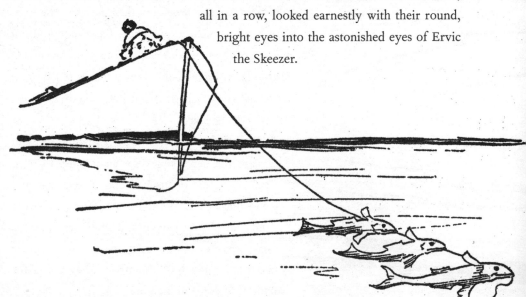

"We are the three Adepts whom Queen Coo-ee-oh betrayed and wickedly transformed," said the goldfish, its voice low and soft but distinctly heard in the stillness of the night.

"I know of our Queen's treacherous deed," replied Ervic, "and I am sorry for your misfortune. Have you been in the lake ever since?"

"Yes," was the reply.

"I—I hope you are well—and comfortable," stammered Ervic, not knowing what else to say.

"We knew that some day Coo-ee-oh would meet with the fate she so richly deserves," declared the bronzefish. "We have waited and watched for this time. Now if you will promise to help us and will be faithful and true, you can aid us in regaining our natural forms, and save yourself and all your people from the dangers that now threaten you."

"Well," said Ervic, "you can depend on my doing the best I can. But I'm no witch, nor magician, you must know."

"All we ask is that you obey our instructions," returned the silverfish. "We know that you are honest and that you served Coo-ee-oh only because you were obliged to in order to escape her anger. Do as we command and all will be well."

"I promise!" exclaimed the young man. "Tell me what I am to do first."

"You will find in the bottom of your boat the silver cord which dropped from Coo-ee-oh's hand when she was transformed," said the goldfish. "Tie one end of that cord to the bow of your boat and drop the other end to us in the water. Together we will pull your boat to the shore."

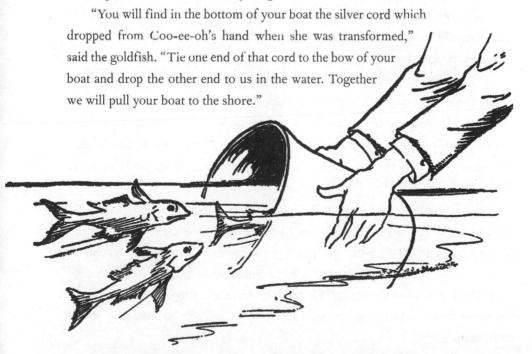

Ervic much doubted that the three small fishes could move so heavy a boat, but he did as he was told and the fishes all seized their end of the silver cord in their mouths and headed toward the nearest shore, which was the very place where the Flatheads had stood when they conquered Queen Coo-ee-oh.

At first the boat did not move at all, although the fishes pulled with all their strength. But presently the strain began to tell. Very slowly the boat crept toward the shore, gaining more speed at every moment. A couple of yards away from the sandy beach the fishes dropped the cord from their mouths and swam to one side, while the iron boat, being now under way, continued to move until its prow grated upon the sands.

Ervic leaned over the side and said to the fishes: "What next?"

"You will find upon the sand," said the silverfish, "a copper kettle, which the Su-dic forgot when he went away. Cleanse it thoroughly in the water of the lake, for it has had poison in it. When it is cleaned, fill it with fresh water and hold it over the side of the boat, so that we three may swim into the kettle. We will then instruct you further."

"Do you wish me to catch you, then?" asked Ervic in surprise.

"Yes," was the reply.

So Ervic jumped out of the boat and found the copper kettle. Carrying it a little way down the beach, he washed it well, scrubbing away every drop of the poison it had contained with sand from the shore.

Then he went back to the boat.

Ervic's comrades were still sound asleep and knew nothing of the three fishes or what strange happenings were taking place about them. Ervic dipped the kettle in the lake, holding fast to the handle until it was under water. The gold and silver and bronze fishes promptly swam into the kettle. The young Skeezer then lifted it, poured out a little of the water so it would not spill over the edge, and said to the fishes: "What next?"

"Carry the kettle to the shore. Take one hundred steps to the east, along the edge of the lake, and then you will see a path leading through the meadows, up hill and down dale. Follow the path until you come to a cottage which is painted a purple color with white trimmings. When you stop at the gate of this cottage we will tell you what to do next. Be careful, above all, not to stumble and spill the water from the kettle, or you would destroy us and all you have done would be in vain."

The goldfish issued these commands and Ervic promised to be careful and started to obey. He left his sleeping comrades in the boat, stepping cautiously over their bodies, and on reaching the shore took exactly one hundred steps to the east. Then he looked for the path and the moonlight was so bright that he easily discovered it, although it was hidden from view by tall weeds until one came full upon it. This path was very narrow and did not seem to be much used, but it was quite distinct and Ervic had no difficulty in following it. He walked through a broad meadow, covered with tall grass and weeds, up a hill and down into a valley and then up another hill and down again.

It seemed to Ervic that he had walked miles and miles. Indeed the moon sank low and day was beginning to dawn when finally he discovered by the roadside a pretty little cottage, painted purple with white trimmings. It was a lonely place—no other buildings were anywhere about and the ground was not tilled at all. No farmer lived here, that was certain. Who would care to dwell in such an isolated place?

But Ervic did not bother his head long with such questions. He went up to the gate that led to the cottage, set the copper kettle carefully down and bending over it asked:

"What next?"

CHAPTER XVII

UNDER THE GREAT DOME

WHEN GLINDA THE GOOD AND HER FOLLOWERS of the Rescue Expedition came in sight of the Enchanted Mountain of the Flatheads, it was away to the left of them, for the route they had taken through the Great Forest was some distance from that followed by Ozma and Dorothy.

They halted awhile to decide whether they should call upon the Supreme Dictator first, or go on to the Lake of the Skeezers.

"If we go to the mountain," said the Wizard, "we may get into trouble with that wicked Su-dic, and then we would be delayed in rescuing Ozma and Dorothy. So I think our best plan will be to go to the Skeezer Country, raise the sunken island and save our friends and the imprisoned Skeezers. Afterward we can visit the mountain and punish the cruel magician of the Flatheads."

"That is sensible," approved the Shaggy Man. "I quite agree with you."

The others, too, seemed to think the Wizard's plan the best, and Glinda herself commended it, so on they marched toward the line of palm trees that hid the Skeezers' lake from view.

Pretty soon they came to the palms. These were set closely together, the branches, which came quite to the ground, being so tightly interlaced that even the Glass Cat could scarcely find a place to squeeze through. The path which the Flatheads used was some distance away.

"Here's a job for the Tin Woodman," said the Scarecrow.

So the Tin Woodman, who was always glad to be of use, set to work with his sharp, gleaming axe, which he always carried, and in a surprisingly short time had chopped away enough branches to permit them all to pass easily through the trees.

Now the clear waters of the beautiful lake were before them and by looking closely they could see the outlines of the Great Dome of the sunken island, far from shore and directly in the center of the lake.

Of course every eye was at first fixed upon this dome, where Ozma and Dorothy and the Skeezers were still fast prisoners. But soon their attention was caught by a more brilliant sight, for here was the Diamond Swan swimming just before them, its long neck arched proudly, the amethyst eyes gleaming and all the diamond-sprinkled feathers glistening splendidly under the rays of the sun.

"That," said Glinda, "is the transformation of Queen Coo-ee-oh, the haughty and wicked witch who betrayed the three Adepts at Magic and treated her people like slaves."

"She's wonderfully beautiful now," remarked the Frogman.

"It doesn't seem like much of a punishment," said Trot. "The Flathead Su-dic ought to have made her a toad."

"I am sure Coo-ee-oh is punished," said Glinda, "for she has lost all her magic power and her grand palace and can no longer misrule the poor Skeezers."

"Let us call to her, and hear what she has to say," proposed the Wizard.

So Glinda beckoned the Diamond Swan, which swam gracefully to a position near them. Before anyone could speak Coo-ee-oh called to them in a rasping voice— for the voice of a swan is always harsh and unpleasant—and said with much pride:

"Admire me, Strangers! Admire the lovely Coo-ee-oh, the handsomest creature in all Oz. Admire me!"

"Handsome is as handsome does," replied the Scarecrow. "Are your deeds lovely, Coo-ee-oh?"

"Deeds? What deeds can a swan do but swim around and give pleasure to all beholders?" said the sparkling bird.

"Have you forgotten your former life? Have you forgotten your magic and witchcraft?" inquired the Wizard.

"Magic witchcraft? Pshaw, who cares for such silly things?" retorted Coo-ee-oh. "As for my past life, it seems like an unpleasant dream. I wouldn't go back to it if I could. Don't you admire my beauty, Strangers?"

"Tell us, Coo-ee-oh," said Glinda earnestly, "if you can recall enough of your witchcraft to enable us to raise the sunken island to the surface of the lake. Tell us that and I'll give you a string of pearls to wear around your neck and add to your beauty."

"Nothing can add to my beauty, for I'm the most beautiful creature anywhere in the whole world."

"But how can we raise the island?"

"I don't know and I don't care. If ever I knew I've forgotten, and I'm glad of it," was the response. "Just watch me circle around and see me glitter!"

"It's no use," said Button-Bright; "the old Swan is too much in love with herself to think of anything else."

"That's a fact," agreed Betsy with a sigh; "but we've got to get Ozma and Dorothy out of that lake, somehow or other."

"And we must do it in our own way," added the Scarecrow.

"But how?" asked Uncle Henry in a grave voice, for he could not bear to think of his dear niece Dorothy being out there under water; "how shall we do it?"

"Leave that to Glinda," advised the Wizard, realizing he was helpless to do it himself.

"If it were just an ordinary sunken island," said the powerful sorceress, "there would be several ways by which I might bring it to the surface again. But this is a Magic Isle, and by some curious art of witchcraft, unknown to any but Queen Coo-ee-oh, it obeys certain commands of magic and will not respond to any other. I do not despair in the least, but it will require some deep study to solve this difficult problem. If the Swan could only remember the witchcraft that she invented and knew as a woman, I could force her to tell me the secret, but all her former knowledge is now forgotten."

"It seems to me," said the Wizard after a brief silence had followed Glinda's speech, "that there are three fishes in this lake that used to be Adepts at Magic and from whom Coo-ee-oh stole much of her knowledge. If we could find those fishes and return them to their former shapes, they could doubtless tell us what to do to bring the sunken island to the surface."

"I have thought of those fishes," replied Glinda, "but among so many fishes as this lake contains how are we to single them out?"

You will understand, of course, that had Glinda been at home in her castle, where the Great Book of Records was, she would have known that Ervic the Skeezer already had taken the gold and silver and bronze fishes from the lake. But that act had been recorded in the Book after Glinda had set out on this journey, so it was all unknown to her.

"I think I see a boat yonder on the shore," said Ojo the Munchkin boy, pointing to a place around the edge of the lake. "If we could get that boat and row all over the lake, calling to the magic fishes, we might be able to find them."

"Let us go to the boat," said the Wizard.

They walked around the lake to where the boat was stranded upon the beach, but found it empty. It was a mere shell of blackened steel, with a collapsible roof that, when in position, made the submarine watertight, but at present the roof rested in slots on either side of the magic craft. There were no oars or sails, no machinery to make the boat go, and although Glinda promptly realized it was meant to be operated by witchcraft, she was not acquainted with that sort of magic.

"However," said she, "the boat is merely a boat, and I believe I can make it obey a command of sorcery, as well as it did the command of witchcraft. After I have given a little thought to the matter, the boat will take us wherever we desire to go."

"Not all of us," returned the Wizard, "for it won't hold so many. But, most noble Sorceress, provided you can make the boat go, of what use will it be to us?"

"Can't we use it to catch the three fishes?" asked Button-Bright.

"It will not be necessary to use the boat for that purpose," replied Glinda. "Wherever in the lake the enchanted fishes may be, they will answer to my call. What I am trying to discover is how the boat came to be on this shore, while the island on which it belongs is under water yonder. Did Coo-ee-oh come here in the boat to meet the Flatheads before the island was sunk, or afterward?"

No one could answer that question, of course; but while they pondered the matter three young men advanced from the line of trees, and rather timidly bowed to the strangers.

"Who are you, and where did you come from?" inquired the Wizard.

"We are Skeezers," answered one of them, "and our home is on the Magic Isle of the Lake. We ran away when we saw you coming, and hid behind the trees, but as you are Strangers and seem to be friendly we decided to meet you, for we are in great trouble and need assistance."

"If you belong on the island, why are you here?" demanded Glinda.

So they told her all the story: How the Queen had defied the Flatheads and submerged the whole island so that her enemies could not get to it or destroy it; how, when the Flatheads came to the shore, Coo-ee-oh had commanded them, together with their friend Ervic, to go with her in the submarine to conquer the Su-dic, and how the boat had shot out from the basement of the sunken isle, obeying a magic word, and risen to the surface, where it opened and floated upon the water.

Then followed the account of how the Su-dic had transformed Coo-ee-oh into a swan, after which she had forgotten all the witchcraft she ever knew. The young men told how, in the night when they were asleep, their comrade Ervic had mysteriously disappeared, while the boat in some strange manner had floated to the shore and stranded upon the beach.

That was all they knew. They had searched in vain for three days for Ervic. As their island was under water and they could not get back to it, the three Skeezers had no place to go, and so had waited patiently beside their boat for something to happen.

Being questioned by Glinda and the Wizard, they told all they knew about Ozma and Dorothy and declared the two girls were still in the village under the Great Dome. They were quite safe and would be well cared for by Lady Aurex, now that the Queen who opposed them was out of the way.

When they had gleaned all the information they could from these Skeezers, the Wizard said to Glinda:

"If you find you can make this boat obey your sorcery, you could have it return to the island, submerge itself, and enter the door in the basement from which it came. But I cannot see that our going to the sunken island would enable our friends to escape. We would only join them as prisoners."

"Not so, friend Wizard," replied Glinda. "If the boat would obey my commands to enter the basement door, it would also obey my commands to come out again, and I could bring Ozma and Dorothy back with me."

"And leave all of our people still imprisoned?" asked one of the Skeezers reproachfully.

"By making several trips in the boat, Glinda could fetch all your people to the shore," replied the Wizard.

"But what could they do then?" inquired another Skeezer. "They would have no homes and no place to go, and would be at the mercy of their enemies, the Flatheads."

"That is true," said Glinda the Good. "And as these people are Ozma's subjects, I think she would refuse to escape with Dorothy and leave the others behind, or to abandon the island which is the lawful home of the Skeezers. I believe the best plan will be to summon the three fishes and learn from them how to raise the island."

The little Wizard seemed to think that this was rather a forlorn hope.

"How will you summon them," he asked the lovely Sorceress, "and how can they hear you?"

"That is something we must consider carefully," responded stately Glinda, with a serene smile. "I think I can find a way."

All of Ozma's Counsellors applauded this sentiment, for they knew well the powers of the Sorceress.

"Very well," agreed the Wizard. "Summon them, most noble Glinda."

CHAPTER XVIII

THE CLEVERNESS OF ERVIC

WE MUST NOW RETURN TO ERVIC THE Skeezer, who, when he had set down the copper kettle containing the three fishes at the gate of the lonely cottage, had asked, "What next?"

The goldfish stuck its head above the water in the kettle and said in its small but distinct voice:

"You are to lift the latch, open the door, and walk boldly into the cottage. Do not be afraid of anything you see, for however you seem to be threatened with dangers, nothing can harm you. The cottage is the home of a powerful Yookoohoo, named Reera the Red, who assumes all sorts of forms, sometimes changing her form several times in a day, according to her fancy. What her real form may be we do not know. This strange creature cannot be bribed with treasure, or coaxed through friendship, or won by pity. She has never assisted anyone, or done wrong to anyone, that we know of. All her wonderful powers are used for her own selfish amusement. She will order you out of the house but you must refuse to go. Remain and watch Reera closely and try to see what she uses to accomplish her transformations. If you can discover the secret whisper it to us and we will then tell you what to do next."

"That sounds easy," returned Ervic, who had listened carefully. "But are you sure she will not hurt me, or try to transform me?"

"She may change your form," replied the goldfish, "but do not worry if that happens, for we can break that enchantment easily. You may be sure that nothing will harm you, so you must not be frightened at anything you see or hear."

Now Ervic was as brave as any ordinary young man, and he knew the fishes who spoke to him were truthful and to be relied upon, nevertheless he experienced a strange sinking of the heart as he picked up the kettle and approached the door of the cottage. His hand trembled as he raised the latch, but he was resolved to obey his instructions. He pushed the door open, took three strides into the middle of the one room the cottage contained, and then stood still and looked around him.

The sights that met his gaze were enough to frighten anyone who had not been properly warned. On the floor just before Ervic lay a great crocodile, its red eyes gleaming wickedly and its wide open mouth displaying rows of sharp teeth. Horned toads hopped about; each of the four upper corners of the room was festooned with a thick cobweb, in the center of which sat a spider as big around as a washbasin, and armed with pincher-like claws; a red-and-green lizard was stretched at full length on the window-sill and black rats darted in and out of the holes they had gnawed in the floor of the cottage.

But the most startling thing was a huge gray ape which sat upon a bench and knitted. It wore a lace cap, such as old ladies wear, and a little apron of lace, but no other clothing. Its eyes were bright and looked as if coals were burning in them. The ape moved as naturally as an ordinary person might, and on Ervic's entrance stopped knitting and raised its head to look at him.

"Get out!" cried a sharp voice, seeming to come from the ape's mouth.

Ervic saw another bench, empty, just beyond him, so he stepped over the crocodile, sat down upon the bench and carefully placed the kettle beside him.

"Get out!" again cried the voice.

Ervic shook his head.

"No," said he, "I'm going to stay."

The spiders left their four corners, dropped to the floor and made a rush toward the young Skeezer, circling around his legs with their pinchers extended. Ervic paid no attention to them. An enormous black rat ran up Ervic's body, passed around his shoulders and uttered piercing squeals in his ears, but he did not wince. The green-and-red lizard, coming from the window-sill, approached Ervic and began spitting a flaming fluid at him, but Ervic merely stared at the creature and its flame did not touch him.

The crocodile raised its tail and, swinging around, swept Ervic off the bench with a powerful blow. But the Skeezer managed to save the kettle from upsetting and he got up, shook off the horned toads that were crawling over him and resumed his seat on the bench.

All the creatures, after this first attack, remained motionless, as if awaiting orders. The old gray ape knitted on, not looking toward Ervic now, and the young Skeezer stolidly kept his seat. He expected something else to happen, but nothing did. A full hour passed and Ervic was growing nervous.

"What do you want?" the ape asked at last.

"Nothing," said Ervic.

"You may have that!" retorted the ape, and at this all the strange creatures in the room broke into a chorus of cackling laughter.

Another long wait.

"Do you know who I am?" questioned the ape.

"You must be Reera the Red—the Yookoohoo," Ervic answered.

"Knowing so much, you must also know that I do not like strangers. Your presence here in my home annoys me. Do you not fear my anger?"

"No," said the young man.

"Do you intend to obey me, and leave this house?"

"No," replied Ervic, just as quietly as the Yookoohoo had spoken.

The ape knitted for a long time before resuming the conversation.

"Curiosity," it said, "has led to many a man's undoing. I suppose in some way you have learned that I do tricks of magic, and so through curiosity you have come here. You may have been told that I do not injure anyone, so you are bold enough to disobey my commands to go away. You imagine that you may witness some of the rites of witchcraft, and that they may amuse you. Have I spoken truly?"

"Well," remarked Ervic, who had been pondering on the strange circumstances of his coming here, "you are right in some ways, but not in others. I am told that you work magic only for your own amusement. That seems to me very selfish. Few people understand magic. I'm told that you are the only real Yookoohoo in all Oz. Why don't you amuse others as well as yourself?"

"What right have you to question my actions?"

"None at all."

"And you say you are not here to demand any favors of me?"

"For myself I want nothing from you."

"You are wise in that. I never grant favors."

"That doesn't worry me," declared Ervic.

"But you are curious? You hope to witness some of my magic transformations?"

"If you wish to perform any magic, go ahead," said Ervic. "It may interest me and it may not. If you'd rather go on with your knitting, it's all the same to me. I am in no hurry at all."

This may have puzzled Red Reera, but the face beneath the lace cap could show no expression, being covered with hair. Perhaps in all her career the Yookoohoo had never been visited by anyone who, like this young man, asked for nothing, expected nothing, and had no reason for coming except curiosity. This attitude practically disarmed the witch and she began to regard the Skeezer in a more friendly way. She knitted for some time, seemingly in deep thought, and then she arose and walked to a big cupboard that stood against the wall of the room. When the cupboard door was opened Ervic could see a lot of drawers inside, and into one of these drawers—the second from the bottom—Reera thrust a hairy hand.

Until now Ervic could see over the bent form of the ape, but suddenly the form, with its back to him, seemed to straighten up and blot out the cupboard of drawers. The ape had changed to the form of a woman, dressed in the pretty Gillikin costume, and when she turned around he saw that it was a young woman, whose face was quite attractive.

"Do you like me better this way?" Reera inquired with a smile.

"You *look* better," he said calmly, "but I'm not sure I *like* you any better."

She laughed, saying: "During the heat of the day I like to be an ape, for an ape doesn't wear any clothes to speak of. But if one has gentlemen callers it is proper to dress up."

Ervic noticed her right hand was closed, as if she held something in it. She shut the cupboard door, bent over the crocodile and in a moment the creature had changed to a red wolf. It was not pretty even now, and the wolf crouched beside its mistress as a dog might have done. Its teeth looked as dangerous as had those of the crocodile.

Next the Yookoohoo went about touching all the lizards and toads, and at her touch they became kittens. The rats she changed into chipmunks. Now the only horrid creatures remaining were the four great spiders, which hid themselves behind their thick webs.

"There!" Reera cried, "now my cottage presents a more comfortable appearance. I love the toads and lizards and rats, because most people hate them, but I would tire of them if they always remained the same. Sometimes I change their forms a dozen times a day."

"You are clever," said Ervic. "I did not hear you utter any incantations or magic words. All you did was to touch the creatures."

"Oh, do you think so?" she replied. "Well, touch them yourself, if you like, and see if you can change their forms."

"No," said the Skeezer, "I don't understand magic and if I did I would not try to imitate your skill. You are a wonderful Yookoohoo, while I am only a common Skeezer."

This confession seemed to please Reera, who liked to have her witchcraft appreciated.

"Will you go away now?" she asked. "I prefer to be alone."

"I prefer to stay here," said Ervic.

"In another person's home, where you are not wanted?"

"Yes."

"Is not your curiosity yet satisfied?" demanded Reera, with a smile.

"I don't know. Is there anything else you can do?"

"Many things. But why should I exhibit my powers to a stranger?"

"I can think of no reason at all," he replied.

She looked at him curiously.

"You want no power for yourself, you say, and you're too stupid to be able to steal my secrets. This isn't a pretty cottage, while outside are sunshine, broad prairies and beautiful wild-flowers. Yet you insist on sitting on that bench and annoying me with your unwelcome presence. What have you in that kettle?"

"Three fishes," he answered readily.

"Where did you get them?"

"I caught them in the Lake of the Skeezers."

"What do you intend to do with the fishes?"

"I shall carry them to the home of a friend of mine who has three children. The children will love to have the fishes for pets."

She came over to the bench and looked into the kettle, where the three fishes were swimming quietly in the water.

"They're pretty," said Reera. "Let me transform them into something else."

"No," objected the Skeezer.

"I love to transform things; it's so interesting. And I've never transformed any fishes in all my life."

"Let them alone," said Ervic.

"What shapes would you prefer them to have? I can make them turtles, or cute little sea-horses; or I could make them piglets, or rabbits, or guinea-pigs; or, if you like I can make chickens of them, or eagles, or bluejays."

"Let them alone!" repeated Ervic.

"You're not a very pleasant visitor," laughed Red Reera. "People accuse me of being cross and crabbed and unsociable, and they are quite right. If you had come here pleading and begging for favors, and half afraid of my Yookoohoo magic, I'd have abused you until you ran away; but you're quite different from that. You're the unsociable and crabbed and disagreeable one, and so I like you, and bear with your grumpiness. It's time for my midday meal; are you hungry?"

"No," said Ervic, although he really desired food.

"Well, I am," Reera declared and clapped her hands together. Instantly a table appeared, spread with linen and bearing dishes of various foods, some smoking hot. There were two plates laid, one at each end of the table, and as soon as Reera seated herself all her creatures gathered around her, as if they were accustomed to be fed when she ate. The wolf squatted at her right hand and the kittens and chipmunks gathered at her left.

"Come, Stranger, sit down and eat," she called cheerfully, "and while we're eating let us decide into what forms we shall change your fishes."

"They're all right as they are," asserted Ervic, drawing up his bench to the table. "The fishes are beauties—one gold, one silver and one bronze. Nothing that has life is more lovely than a beautiful fish."

"What! Am *I* not more lovely?" Reera asked, smiling at his serious face.

"I don't object to you—for a Yookoohoo, you know," he said, helping himself to the food and eating with good appetite.

"And don't you consider a beautiful girl more lovely than a fish, however pretty the fish may be?"

"Well," replied Ervic, after a period of thought, "that might be. If you transformed my three fish into three girls—girls who would be Adepts at Magic, you know they might please me as well as the fish do. You won't do that of course, because you can't, with all your skill. And, should you be able to do so, I fear my troubles would be more than I could bear. They would not consent to be my slaves — especially if they were Adepts at Magic—and so they would command *me* to obey *them*. No, Mistress Reera, let us not transform the fishes at all."

The Skeezer had put his case with remarkable cleverness. He realized that if he appeared anxious for such a transformation the Yookoohoo would not perform it, yet he had skillfully suggested that they be made Adepts at Magic.

CHAPTER XIX

RED REERA,
THE YOOKOOHOO

AFTER THE MEAL WAS OVER AND REERA HAD FED HER pets, including the four monster spiders which had come down from their webs to secure their share, she made the table disappear from the floor of the cottage.

"I wish you'd consent to my transforming your fishes," she said, as she took up her knitting again.

The Skeezer made no reply. He thought it unwise to hurry matters. All during the afternoon they sat silent. Once Reera went to her cupboard and after thrusting her hand into the same drawer as before, touched the wolf and transformed it into a bird with gorgeous colored feathers. This bird was larger than a parrot and of a somewhat different form, but Ervic had never seen one like it before.

"Sing!" said Reera to the bird, which had perched itself on a big wooden peg—as if it had been in the cottage before and knew just what to do.

And the bird sang jolly, rollicking songs with words to them—just as a person who had been carefully trained might do. The songs were entertaining and Ervic enjoyed listening to them. In an hour or so the bird stopped singing, tucked its head under its wing and went to sleep. Reera continued knitting but seemed thoughtful.

Now Ervic had marked this cupboard drawer well and had concluded that Reera took something from it which enabled her to perform her transformations. He thought that if he managed to remain in the cottage, and Reera fell asleep, he could slyly open the cupboard, take a portion of whatever was in the drawer, and by dropping it into the copper kettle transform the three fishes into their natural shapes. Indeed, he had firmly resolved to carry out this plan when the Yookoohoo put down her knitting and walked toward the door.

"I'm going out for a few minutes," said she; "do you wish to go with me, or will you remain here?"

Ervic did not answer but sat quietly on his bench. So Reera went out and closed the cottage door.

As soon as she was gone, Ervic rose and tiptoed to the cupboard.

"Take care! Take care!" cried several voices, coming from the kittens and chipmunks. "If you touch anything we'll tell the Yookoohoo!"

Ervic hesitated a moment but, remembering that he need not consider Reera's anger if he succeeded in transforming the fishes, he was about to open the cupboard when he was arrested by the voices of the fishes, which stuck their heads above the water in the kettle and called out:

"Come here, Ervic!"

So he went back to the kettle and bent over it.

"Let the cupboard alone," said the goldfish to him earnestly. "You could not succeed by getting that magic powder, for only the Yookoohoo knows how to use it. The best way is to allow her to transform us into three girls, for then we will have our natural shapes and be able to perform all the Arts of Magic we have learned and well understand. You are acting wisely and in the most effective manner. We did not know you were so intelligent, or that Reera could be so easily deceived by you. Continue as you have begun and try to persuade her to transform us. But insist that we be given the forms of girls."

The goldfish ducked its head down just as Reera re-entered the cottage. She saw Ervic bent over the kettle, so she came and joined him.

"Can your fishes talk?" she asked.

"Sometimes," he replied, "for all fishes in the Land of Oz know how to speak. Just now they were asking me for some bread. They are hungry."

"Well, they can have some bread," said Reera. "But it is nearly supper-time, and if you would allow me to transform your fishes into girls they could join us at the table and have plenty of food much nicer than crumbs. Why not let me transform them?"

"Well," said Ervic, as if hesitating, "ask the fishes. If they consent, why—why, then, I'll think it over."

Reera bent over the kettle and asked:

"Can you hear me, little fishes?"

All three popped their heads above water.

"We can hear you," said the bronzefish.

"I want to give you other forms, such as rabbits, or turtles or girls, or something; but your master, the surly Skeezer, does not wish me to. However, he has agreed to the plan if you will consent."

"We'd like to be girls," said the silverfish.

"No, no!" exclaimed Ervic.

"If you promise to make us three beautiful girls, we will consent," said the goldfish.

"No, no!" exclaimed Ervic again.

"Also make us Adepts at Magic," added the bronzefish.

"I don't know exactly what that means," replied Reera musingly, "but as no Adept at Magic is as powerful as Yookoohoo, I'll add that to the transformation."

"We won't try to harm you, or to interfere with your magic in any way," promised the goldfish. "On the contrary, we will be your friends."

"Will you agree to go away and leave me alone in my cottage, whenever I command you to do so?" asked Reera.

"We promise that," cried the three fishes.

"Don't do it! Don't consent to the transformation," urged Ervic.

"They have already consented," said the Yookoohoo, laughing in his face, "and you have promised me to abide by their decision. So, friend Skeezer, I shall perform the transformation whether you like it or not."

Ervic seated himself on the bench again, a deep scowl on his face but joy in his heart. Reera moved over to the cupboard, took something from the drawer and returned to the copper kettle. She was clutching something tightly in her right hand, but with her left she reached within the kettle, took out the three fishes and laid them carefully on the floor, where they gasped in distress at being out of water.

Reera did not keep them in misery more than a few seconds, for she touched each one with her right hand and instantly the fishes were transformed into three tall and slender young women, with fine, intelligent faces and clothed in handsome, clinging gowns. The one who had been a goldfish had beautiful golden hair and blue eyes and was exceedingly fair of skin; the one who had been a bronzefish had dark brown hair and clear gray eyes and her complexion matched these lovely features. The one who had been a silverfish had snow-white hair of the finest texture and deep brown eyes. The hair contrasted exquisitely with her pink cheeks and ruby-red lips, nor did it make her look a day older than her two companions.

As soon as they secured these girlish shapes, all three bowed low to the Yookoohoo and said:

"We thank you, Reera."

Then they bowed to the Skeezer and said:

"We thank you, Ervic."

"Very good!" cried the Yookoohoo, examining her work with critical approval. "You are much better and more interesting than fishes, and this ungracious Skeezer would scarcely allow me to do the transformations. You surely have nothing to thank him for. But now let us dine in honor of the occasion."

She clapped her hands together and again a table loaded with food appeared in the cottage. It was a longer table, this time, and places were set for the three Adepts as well as for Reera and Ervic.

"Sit down, friends, and eat your fill," said the Yookoohoo, but instead of seating herself at the head of the table she went to the cupboard, saying to the Adepts: "Your beauty and grace, my fair friends, quite outshine my own. So that I may appear properly at the banquet table I intend, in honor of this occasion, to take upon myself my natural shape."

Scarcely had she finished this speech when Reera transformed herself into a young woman fully as lovely as the three Adepts. She was not quite so tall as they, but her form was more rounded and more handsomely clothed, with a wonderful jeweled girdle and a necklace of shining pearls. Her hair was a bright auburn red, and her eyes large and dark.

"Do you claim this is your natural form?" asked Ervic of the Yookoohoo.

"Yes," she replied. "This is the only form I am really entitled to wear. But I seldom assume it because there is no one here to admire or appreciate it and I get tired admiring it myself."

"I see now why you are named Reera the Red," remarked Ervic.

"It is on account of my red hair," she explained smiling. "I do not care for red hair myself, which is one reason I usually wear other forms."

"It is beautiful," asserted the young man; and then remembering the other women present he added: "But, of course, all women should not have red hair, because that would make it too common. Gold and silver and brown hair are equally handsome."

The smiles that he saw interchanged between the four filled the poor Skeezer with embarrassment, so he fell silent and attended to eating his supper, leaving the others to do the talking. The three Adepts frankly told Reera who they were, how they became fishes and how they had planned secretly to induce the Yookoohoo to transform them. They admitted that they had feared, had they asked her to help, that she would have refused them.

"You were quite right," returned the Yookoohoo. "I make it my rule never to perform magic to assist others, for if I did there would always be crowds at my cottage demanding help and I hate crowds and want to be left alone.

"However, now that you are restored to your proper shapes, I do not regret my action and I hope you will be of use in saving the Skeezer people by raising their island to the surface of the lake, where it really belongs. But you must promise me that after you go away you will never come here again, nor tell anyone what I have done for you."

The three Adepts and Ervic thanked the Yookoohoo warmly. They promised to remember her wish that they should not come to her cottage again and so, with a good-bye, took their departure.

CHAPTER XX

A PUZZLING
PROBLEM

GLINDA THE GOOD, HAVING DECIDED TO
try her sorcery upon the abandoned submarine,
so that it would obey her commands, asked all
of her party, including the Skeezers, to with-
draw from the shore of the lake to the line of
palm trees. She kept with her only the little
Wizard of Oz, who was her pupil and knew
how to assist her in her magic rites. When
they two were alone beside the stranded boat,
Glinda said to the Wizard:

"I shall first try my magic recipe No.
1163, which is intended to make inanimate
objects move at my command. Have you a
skeropythrope with you?"

"Yes, I always carry one in my bag," replied the Wizard. He opened his black bag of magic tools and took out a brightly polished skeropythrope, which he handed to the Sorceress. Glinda had also brought a small wicker bag, containing various requirements of sorcery, and from this she took a parcel of powder and a vial of liquid. She poured the liquid into the skeropythrope and added the powder. At once the skeropythrope began to sputter and emit sparks of a violet color, which spread in all directions. The Sorceress instantly stepped into the middle of the boat and held the instrument so that the sparks fell all around her and covered every bit of the blackened steel boat. At the same time Glinda crooned a weird incantation in the language of sorcery, her voice sounding low and musical.

After a little the violet sparks ceased, and those that had fallen upon the boat had disappeared and left no mark upon its surface. The ceremony was ended and Glinda returned the skeropythrope to the Wizard, who put it away in his black bag.

"That ought to do the business all right," he said confidently.

"Let us make a trial and see," she replied.

So they both entered the boat and seated themselves.

Speaking in a tone of command the Sorceress said to the boat: "Carry us across the lake, to the farther shore."

At once the boat backed off the sandy beach, turned its prow and moved swiftly over the water.

"Very good—very good indeed!" cried the Wizard, when the boat slowed up at the shore opposite from that whence they had departed. "Even Coo-ee-oh, with all her witchcraft, could do no better."

The Sorceress now said to the boat:

"Close up, submerge and carry us to the basement door of the sunken island— the door from which you emerged at the command of Queen Coo-ee-oh."

The boat obeyed. As it sank into the water the top sections rose from the sides and joined together over the heads of Glinda and the Wizard, who were thus enclosed in a water-proof chamber. There were four glass windows in this covering, one on each side and one on either end, so that the passengers could see exactly where they were going. Moving under water more slowly than on the surface, the submarine gradually approached the island and halted with its bow pressed against the huge marble door in the basement under the Dome. This door was tightly closed and it was evident to both Glinda and the Wizard that it would not open to admit the under-water boat unless a magic word was spoken by them or someone from within the basement of the island. But what was this magic word? Neither of them knew.

"I'm afraid," said the Wizard regretfully, "that we can't get in, after all. Unless your sorcery can discover the word to open the marble door."

"That is probably some word only known to Coo-ee-oh," replied the Sorceress. "I may be able to discover what it is, but that will require time. Let us go back again to our companions."

"It seems a shame, after we have made the boat obey us, to be balked by just a marble door," grumbled the Wizard.

At Glinda's command the boat rose until it was on a level with the glass dome that covered the Skeezer village, when the Sorceress made it slowly circle all around the Great Dome.

Many faces were pressed against the glass from the inside, eagerly watching the submarine, and in one place were Dorothy and Ozma, who quickly recognized Glinda and the Wizard through the glass windows of the boat. Glinda saw them, too, and held the boat close to the Dome while the friends exchanged greetings in pantomime. Their voices, unfortunately, could not be heard through the Dome and the water and the side of the boat. The Wizard tried to make the girls understand, through signs, that he and Glinda had come to their rescue, and Ozma and Dorothy understood this from the very fact that the Sorceress and the Wizard had appeared. The two girl prisoners were smiling and in safety, and knowing this Glinda felt she could take all the time necessary in order to effect their final rescue.

As nothing more could be done just then, Glinda ordered the boat to return to shore, and it obeyed readily. First it ascended to the surface of the water, then the roof parted and fell into the slots at the side of the boat, and then the magic craft quickly made the shore and beached itself on the sands at the very spot from which it had departed at Glinda's command.

All the Oz people and the Skeezers at once ran to the boat to ask if they had reached the island, and whether they had seen Ozma and Dorothy. The Wizard told them of the obstacle they had met in the way of a marble door, and how Glinda would now undertake to find a magic way to conquer the door.

Realizing that it would require several days to succeed in reaching the island, raising it and liberating their friends and the Skeezer people, Glinda now prepared a camp half way between the lake shore and the palm trees.

The Wizard's wizardry made a number of tents appear and the sorcery of the Sorceress furnished these tents all complete, with beds, chairs, tables, rugs, lamps and even books with which to pass idle hours. All the tents had the Royal Banner of Oz flying from the centerpoles and one big tent, not now occupied, had Ozma's own banner moving in the breeze.

Betsy and Trot had a tent to themselves, and Button-Bright and Ojo had another. The Scarecrow and the Tin Woodman paired together in one tent and so did Jack Pumpkinhead and the Shaggy Man, Cap'n Bill and Uncle Henry, Tik-Tok and Professor Woggle-Bug. Glinda had the most splendid tent of all, except that reserved for Ozma, while the Wizard had a little one of his own. Whenever it was meal time, tables loaded with food magically appeared in the tents of those who were in the habit of eating, and these complete arrangements made the rescue party just comfortable as they would have been in their own homes.

Far into the night Glinda sat in her tent studying a roll of mystic scrolls in search of a word that would open the basement door of the island and admit her to the Great Dome. She also made many magical experiments, hoping to discover something that would aid her. Yet the morning found the powerful Sorceress still unsuccessful.

Glinda's art could have opened any ordinary door, you may be sure, but you must realize that this marble door of the island had been commanded not to open save in obedience to one magic word, and therefore all other magic words could have no effect upon it. The magic word that guarded the door had probably been invented by Coo-ee-oh, who had now forgotten it. The only way, then, to gain entrance to the sunken island was to break the charm that held the door fast shut. If this could be done no magic would be required to open it.

The next day the Sorceress and the Wizard again entered the boat and made it submerge and go to the marble door, which they tried in various ways to open, but without success.

"We shall have to abandon this attempt, I think," said Glinda. "The easiest way to raise the island would be for us to gain admittance to the Dome and then descend to the basement and see in what manner Coo-ee-oh made the entire island sink or rise at her command. It naturally occurred to me that the easiest way to gain admittance would be by having the boat take us into the basement through the marble door from which Coo-ee-oh launched it. But there must be other ways to get inside the Dome and join Ozma and Dorothy, and such ways we must find by study and the proper use of our powers of magic."

"It won't be easy," declared the Wizard, "for we must not forget that Ozma herself understands considerable magic, and has doubtless tried to raise the island or find other means of escape from it and failed."

"That is true," returned Glinda, "but Ozma's magic is fairy magic, while you are a Wizard and I am a Sorceress. In this way the three of us have a great variety of magic to work with, and if we should all fail it will be because the island is raised and lowered by a magic power none of us is acquainted with. My idea therefore is to seek—by such magic as we possess—to accomplish our object in another way."

They made the circle of the Dome again in their boat, and once more saw Ozma and Dorothy through their windows and exchanged signals with the two imprisoned girls.

Ozma realized that her friends were doing all in their power to rescue her and smiled an encouragement to their efforts. Dorothy seemed a little anxious but was trying to be as brave as her companion.

After the boat had returned to the camp and Glinda was seated in her tent, working out various ways by which Ozma and Dorothy could be rescued, the Wizard stood on the shore dreamily eying the outlines of the Great Dome which showed beneath the clear water, when he raised his eyes and saw a group of strange people approaching from around the lake. Three were young women of stately presence, very beautifully dressed, who moved with remarkable grace. They were followed at a little distance by a good-looking young Skeezer.

The Wizard saw at a glance that these people might be very important, so he advanced to meet them. The three maidens received him graciously and the one with the golden hair said:

"I believe you are the famous Wizard of Oz, of whom I have often heard. We are seeking Glinda, the Sorceress, and perhaps you can lead us to her."

"I can, and will, right gladly," answered the Wizard. "Follow me, please."

The little Wizard was puzzled as to the identity of the three lovely visitors but he gave no sign that might embarrass them.

He understood they did not wish to be questioned, and so he made no remarks as he led the way to Glinda's tent.

With a courtly bow the Wizard ushered the three visitors into the gracious presence of Glinda, the Good.

CHAPTER XXI

THE THREE ADEPTS

THE SORCERESS LOOKED UP FROM HER work as the three maidens entered, and something in their appearance and manner led her to rise and bow to them in her most dignified manner. The three knelt an instant before the great Sorceress and then stood upright and waited for her to speak.

"Whoever you may be," said Glinda, "I bid you welcome."

"My name is Audah," said one.

"My name is Aurah," said another.

"My name is Aujah," said the third.

Glinda had never heard these names before, but looking closely at the three she asked:

"Are you witches or workers in magic?"

"Some of the secret arts we have gleaned from Nature," replied the brown-haired maiden modestly, "but we do not place our skill beside that of the Great Sorceress, Glinda the Good."

"I suppose you are aware it is unlawful to practice magic in the Land of Oz, without the permission of our Ruler, Princess Ozma?"

"No, we were not aware of that," was the reply. "We have heard of Ozma, who is the appointed Ruler of all this great fairyland, but her laws have not reached us, as yet."

Glinda studied the strange maidens thoughtfully; then she said to them:

"Princess Ozma is even now imprisoned in the Skeezer village, for the whole island with its Great Dome, was sunk to the bottom of the lake by the witchcraft of Coo-ee-oh, whom the Flathead Su-dic transformed into a silly swan. I am seeking some way to overcome Coo-ee-oh's magic and raise the isle to the surface again. Can you help me do this?"

The maidens exchanged glances, and the white-haired one replied:

"We do not know; but we will try to assist you."

"It seems," continued Glinda musingly, "that Coo-ee-oh derived most of her witchcraft from three Adepts at Magic, who at one time ruled the Flatheads. While the Adepts were being entertained by Coo-ee-oh at a banquet in her palace, she cruelly betrayed them and after transforming them into fishes cast them into the lake.

"If I could find these three fishes and return them to their natural shapes—they might know what magic Coo-ee-oh used to sink the island. I was about to go to the shore and call these fishes to me when you arrived. So, if you will join me, we will try to find them."

The maidens exchanged smiles now, and the golden-haired one, Audah, said to Glinda:

"It will not be necessary to go to the lake. We are the three fishes."

"Indeed!" cried Glinda. "Then you are the three Adepts at Magic, restored to your proper forms?"

"We are the three Adepts," admitted Aujah.

"Then," said Glinda, "my task is half accomplished. But who destroyed the transformation that made you fishes?"

"We have promised not to tell," answered Aurah; "but this young Skeezer was largely responsible for our release; he is brave and clever, and we owe him our gratitude."

Glinda looked at Ervic, who stood modestly behind the Adepts, hat in hand. "He shall be properly rewarded," she declared, "for in helping you he has helped us all, and perhaps saved his people from being imprisoned forever in the sunken isle."

The Sorceress now asked her guests to seat themselves and a long talk followed, in which the Wizard of Oz shared.

"We are quite certain," said Aurah, "that if we could get inside the Dome we could discover Coo-ee-oh's secrets, for in all her work, after we became fishes, she used the formulas and incantations and arts that she stole from us. She may have added to these things, but they were the foundation of all her work."

"What means do you suggest for our getting into the Dome?" inquired Glinda.

The three Adepts hesitated to reply, for they had not yet considered what could be done to reach the inside of the Great Dome. While they were in deep

thought, and Glinda and the Wizard were quietly awaiting their suggestions, into the tent rushed Trot and Betsy, dragging between them the Patchwork Girl.

"Oh, Glinda," cried Trot, "Scraps has thought of a way to rescue Ozma and Dorothy and all of the Skeezers."

The three Adepts could not avoid laughing merrily, for not only were they amused by the queer form of the Patchwork Girl, but Trot's enthusiastic speech struck them as really funny. If the Great Sorceress and the famous Wizard and the three talented Adepts at Magic were unable as yet to solve the important problem of the sunken isle, there was little chance for a patched girl stuffed with cotton to succeed.

But Glinda, smiling indulgently at the earnest faces turned toward her, patted the children's heads and said:

"Scraps is very clever. Tell us what she has thought of, my dear."

"Well," said Trot, "Scraps says that if you could dry up all the water in the lake the island would be on dry land, an' everyone could come and go whenever they liked."

Glinda smiled again, but the Wizard said to the girls:

"If we should dry up the lake, what would become of all the beautiful fishes that now live in the water?"

"Dear me! That's so," admitted Betsy, crestfallen; "we never thought of that, did we Trot?"

"Couldn't you transform 'em into polliwogs?" asked Scraps, turning a somersault and then standing on one leg. "You could give them a little, teeny pond to swim in, and they'd be just as happy as they are as fishes."

"No indeed!" replied the Wizard, severely. "It is wicked to transform any living creatures without their consent, and the lake is the home of the fishes and belongs to them."

"All right," said Scraps, making a face at him; "I don't care."

"It's too bad," sighed Trot, "for I thought we'd struck a splendid idea."

"So you did," declared Glinda, her face now grave and thoughtful. "There is something in the Patchwork Girl's idea that may be of real value to us."

"I think so, too," agreed the golden-haired Adept. "The top of the Great Dome is only a few feet below the surface of the water. If we could reduce the level of the lake until the Dome sticks a little above the water, we could remove some of the glass and let ourselves down into the village by means of ropes."

"And there would be plenty of water left for the fishes to swim in," added the white-haired maiden.

"If we succeed in raising the island we could fill up the lake again," suggested the brown-haired Adept.

"I believe," said the Wizard, rubbing his hands together in delight, "that the Patchwork Girl has shown us the way to success."

The girls were looking curiously at the three beautiful Adepts, wondering who they were, so Glinda introduced them to Trot and Betsy and Scraps, and then sent the children away while she considered how to carry the new idea into effect.

Not much could be done that night, so the Wizard prepared another tent for the Adepts, and in the evening Glinda held a reception and invited all her followers to meet the new arrivals. The Adepts were greatly astonished at the extraordinary personages presented to them, and marveled that Jack Pumpkinhead and the Scarecrow and the Tin Woodman and Tik-Tok could really live and think and talk just like other people. They were especially pleased with the lively Patchwork Girl and loved to watch her antics.

It was quite a pleasant party, for Glinda served some dainty refreshments to those who could eat, and the Scarecrow recited some poems, and the Cowardly Lion sang a song in his deep bass voice. The only thing that marred their joy was the thought that their beloved Ozma and dear little Dorothy were yet confined in the Great Dome of the Sunken Island.

CHAPTER XXII

THE SUNKEN ISLAND

As soon as they had breakfasted the next morning, Glinda and the Wizard and the three Adepts went down to the shore of the lake and formed a line with their faces toward the submerged island. All the others came to watch them, but stood at a respectful distance in the background.

At the right of the Sorceress stood Audah and Aurah, while at the left stood the Wizard and Aujah. Together they stretched their arms over the water's edge and in unison the five chanted a rhythmic incantation.

This chant they repeated again and again, swaying their arms gently from side to side, and in a few minutes the watchers behind them noticed that the lake had begun to recede from the shore. Before long the highest point of the dome appeared above the water. Gradually the water fell, making the dome appear to rise.

When it was three or four feet above the surface Glinda gave the signal to stop, for their work had been accomplished.

The blackened submarine was now entirely out of water, but Uncle Henry and Cap'n Bill managed to push it into the lake. Glinda, the Wizard, Ervic and the Adepts got into the boat, taking with them a coil of strong rope, and at the command of the Sorceress the craft cleaved its way through the water toward the part of the Dome which was now visible.

"There's still plenty of water for the fish to swim in," observed the Wizard as they rode along. "They might like more but I'm sure they can get along until we have raised the island and can fill up the lake again."

The boat touched gently on the sloping glass of the Dome, and the Wizard took some tools from his black bag and quickly removed one large pane of glass, thus making a hole large enough for their bodies to pass through. Stout frames of steel supported the glass of the Dome, and around one of these frames the Wizard tied the end of a rope.

"I'll go down first," said he, "for while I'm not as spry as Cap'n Bill I'm sure I can manage it easily. Are you sure the rope is long enough to reach the bottom?"

"Quite sure," replied the Sorceress.

So the Wizard let down the rope and climbing through the opening lowered himself down, hand over hand, clinging to the rope with his legs and feet. Below in the streets of the village were gathered all the Skeezers, men, women and children, and you may be sure that Ozma and Dorothy, with Lady Aurex, were filled with joy that their friends were at last coming to their rescue.

The Queen's palace, now occupied by Ozma, was directly in the center of the Dome, so that when the rope was let down the end of it came just in front of the palace entrance. Several Skeezers held fast to the rope's end to steady it and the Wizard reached the ground in safety. He hugged first Ozma and then Dorothy, while all the Skeezers cheered as loud as they could.

The Wizard now discovered that the rope was long enough to reach from the top of the Dome to the ground when doubled, so he tied a chair to one end of the rope and called to Glinda to sit in the chair while he and some of the Skeezers lowered her to the pavement. In this way the Sorceress reached the ground quite comfortably and the three Adepts and Ervic soon followed her.

The Skeezers quickly recognized the three Adepts at Magic, whom they had learned to respect before their wicked Queen betrayed them, and welcomed them as friends. All the inhabitants of the village had been greatly frightened by their imprisonment under water, but now realized that an attempt was to be made to rescue them.

Glinda, the Wizard and the Adepts followed Ozma and Dorothy into the palace, and they asked Lady Aurex and Ervic to join them. After Ozma had told of her adventures in trying to prevent war between the Flatheads and the Skeezers, and Glinda had told all about the Rescue Expedition and the restoration of the three Adepts by the help of Ervic, a serious consultation was held as to how the island could be made to rise.

"I've tried every way in my power," said Ozma, "but Coo-ee-oh used a very unusual sort of magic which I do not understand. She seems to have prepared her witchcraft in such a way that a spoken word is necessary to accomplish her designs, and these spoken words are known only to herself."

"That is a method we taught her," declared Aurah the Adept.

"I can do no more, Glinda," continued Ozma, "so I wish you would try what your sorcery can accomplish."

"First, then," said Glinda, "let us visit the basement of the island, which I am told is underneath the village."

A flight of marble stairs led from one of Coo-ee-oh's private rooms down to the basement, but when the party arrived all were puzzled by what they saw. In the center of a broad, low room, stood a mass of great cog-wheels, chains and pulleys,

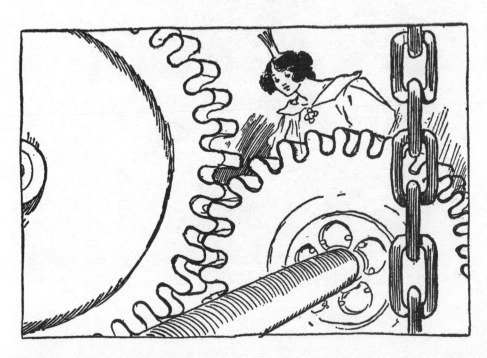

all interlocked and seeming to form a huge machine; but there was no engine or other motive power to make the wheels turn.

"This, I suppose, is the means by which the island is lowered or raised," said Ozma, "but the magic word which is needed to move the machinery is unknown to us."

The three Adepts were carefully examining the mass of wheels, and soon the golden-haired one said:

"These wheels do not control the island at all. On the contrary, one set of them is used to open the doors of the little rooms where the submarines are kept, as may be seen from the chains and pulleys used. Each boat is kept in a little room with two doors, one to the basement room where we are now and the other letting into the lake.

"When Coo-ee-oh used the boat in which she attacked the Flatheads, she first commanded the basement door to open and with her followers she got into the boat and made the top close over them. Then the basement door being closed, the outer door was slowly opened, letting the water fill the room to float the boat, which then left the island, keeping under water."

"But how could she expect to get back again?" asked the Wizard.

"Why the boat would enter the room filled with water and after the outer door was closed a word of command started a pump which pumped all the water from the room. Then the boat would open and Coo-ee-oh could enter the basement."

"I see," said the Wizard. "It is a clever contrivance, but won't work unless one knows the magic words."

"Another part of this machinery," explained the white-haired Adept, "is used to extend the bridge from the island to the mainland. The steel bridge is in a room much like that in which the boats are kept, and at Coo-ee-oh's command it would reach out, joint by joint, until its far end touched the shore of the lake. The same magic command would make the bridge return to its former position. Of course the bridge could not be used unless the island was on the surface of the water."

"But how do you suppose Coo-ee-oh managed to sink the island, and make it rise again?" inquired Glinda.

This the Adepts could not yet explain. As nothing more could be learned from the basement they mounted the steps to the Queen's private suite again, and Ozma showed them to a special room where Coo-ee-oh kept her magical instruments and performed all her arts of witchcraft.

CHAPTER XXIII

THE MAGIC WORDS

MANY INTERESTING THINGS WERE TO BE seen in the Room of Magic, including much that had been stolen from the Adepts when they were transformed to fishes, but they had to admit that Coo-ee-oh had a rare genius for mechanics, and had used her knowledge in inventing a lot of mechanical apparatus that ordinary witches, wizards and sorcerers could not understand.

They all carefully inspected this room, taking care to examine every article they came across.

"The island," said Glinda thoughtfully, "rests on a base of solid marble. When it is submerged, as it is now, the base of the island is upon the bottom of the lake. What puzzles me is how such a great weight can be lifted and suspended in the water, even by magic."

"I now remember," returned Aujah, "that one of the arts we taught Coo-ee-oh was the way to expand steel, and I think that explains how the island is raised and lowered. I noticed in the basement a big steel pillar that passed through the floor and extended upward to this palace. Perhaps the end of it is concealed in this very room. If the lower end of the steel pillar is firmly embedded in the bottom of the lake, Coo-ee-oh could utter a magic word that would make the pillar expand, and so lift the entire island to the level of the water."

"I've found the end of the steel pillar. It's just here," announced the Wizard, pointing to one side of the room where a great basin of polished steel seemed to have been set upon the floor.

They all gathered around, and Ozma said:

"Yes, I am quite sure that is the upper end of the pillar that supports the island. I noticed it when I first came here. It has been hollowed out, you see, and something has been burned in the basin, for the fire has left its marks. I wondered what was under the great basin and got several of the Skeezers to come up here and try to lift it for me. They were strong men, but could not move it at all."

"It seems to me," said Audah the Adept, "that we have discovered the manner in which Coo-ee-oh raised the island. She would burn some sort of magic powder in the basin, utter the magic word, and the pillar would lengthen out and lift the island with it."

"What's this?" asked Dorothy, who had been searching around with the others, and now noticed a slight hollow in the wall, near to where the steel basin stood. As she spoke Dorothy pushed her thumb into the hollow and instantly a small drawer popped out from the wall.

The three Adepts, Glinda and the Wizard sprang forward and peered into the drawer. It was half filled with a grayish powder, the tiny grains of which constantly moved as if impelled by some living force.

"It may be some kind of radium," said the Wizard.

"No," replied Glinda, "it is more wonderful than even radium, for I recognize it as a rare mineral powder called Gaulau by the sorcerers. I wonder how Coo-ee-oh discovered it and where she obtained it."

"There is no doubt," said Aujah the Adept, "that this is the magic powder Coo-ee-oh burned in the basin. If only we knew the magic word, I am quite sure we could raise the island."

"How can we discover the magic word?" asked Ozma, turning to Glinda as she spoke.

"That we must now seriously consider," answered the Sorceress.

So all of them sat down in the Room of Magic and began to think. It was so still that after a while Dorothy grew nervous. The little girl never could keep silent for long, and at the risk of displeasing her magic-working friends she suddenly said:

"Well, Coo-ee-oh used just three magic words, one to make the bridge work, and one to make the submarines go out of their holes, and one to raise and lower the island. Three words. And Coo-ee-oh's name is made up of just three words. One is 'Coo,' and one is 'ee,' and one is 'oh.'"

The Wizard frowned but Glinda looked wonderingly at the young girl and Ozma cried out:

"A good thought, Dorothy dear! You may have solved our problem."

"I believe it is worth a trial," agreed Glinda. "It would be quite natural for Coo-ee-oh to divide her name into three magic syllables, and Dorothy's suggestion seems like an inspiration."

The three Adepts also approved the trial but the brown-haired one said:

"We must be careful not to use the wrong word, and send the bridge out under water. The main thing, if Dorothy's idea is correct, is to hit upon the one word that moves the island."

"Let us experiment," suggested the Wizard.

In the drawer with the moving gray powder was a tiny golden cup, which they thought was used for measuring. Glinda filled this cup with the powder and carefully poured it into the shallow basin, which was the top of the great steel pillar supporting the island. Then Aurah the Adept lighted a taper and touched it to the powder, which instantly glowed fiery red and tumbled about the basin with astonishing energy. While the grains of powder still glowed red the Sorceress bent over it and said in a voice of command: "Coo!"

They waited motionless to see what would happen. There was a grating noise and a whirl of machinery, but the island did not move a particle.

Dorothy rushed to the window, which overlooked the glass side of the dome.

"The boats!" she exclaimed. "The boats are all loose an' sailing under water."

"We've made a mistake," said the Wizard gloomily.

"But it's one which shows we are on the right track," declared Aujah the Adept. "We know now that Coo-ee-oh used the syllables of her name for the magic words."

"If 'Coo' sends out the boats, it is probable that 'ee' works the bridge," suggested Ozma. "So the last part of the name may raise the island."

"Let us try that next then," proposed the Wizard.

He scraped the embers of the burned powder out of the basin and Glinda again filled the golden cup from the drawer and placed it on top the steel pillar. Aurah lighted it with her taper and Ozma bent over the basin and murmured the long drawn syllable: "Oh-h-h!"

Instantly the island trembled and with a weird groaning noise it moved upward— slowly, very slowly, but with a steady motion, while all the company stood by in awed silence. It was a wonderful thing, even to those skilled in the arts of magic, wiz- ardry and sorcery,

to realize that a single word could raise that great, heavy island, with its immense glass Dome.

"Why, we're way *above* the lake now!" exclaimed Dorothy from the window, when at last the island ceased to move.

"That is because we lowered the level of the water," explained Glinda.

They could hear the Skeezers cheering lustily in the streets of the village as they realized that they were saved.

"Come," said Ozma eagerly, "let us go down and join the people."

"Not just yet," returned Glinda, a happy smile upon her lovely face, for she was overjoyed at their success. "First let us extend the bridge to the mainland, where our friends from the Emerald City are waiting."

It didn't take long to put more powder in the basin, light it and utter the syllable "EE!" The result was that a door in the basement opened and the steel bridge moved out, extended itself joint by joint, and finally rested its far end on the shore of the lake just in front of the encampment.

"Now," said Glinda, "we can go up and receive the congratulations of the Skeezers and of our friends of the Rescue Expedition."

Across the water, on the shore of the lake, the Patchwork Girl was waving them a welcome.

CHAPTER XXIV

GLINDA'S TRIUMPH

OF COURSE ALL THOSE WHO HAD JOINED GLINDA'S EXPEDITION AT ONCE crossed the bridge to the island, where they were warmly welcomed by the Skeezers. Before all the concourse of people Princess Ozma made a speech from a porch of the palace and demanded that they recognize her as their lawful Ruler and promise to obey the laws of the Land of Oz. In return she agreed to protect them from all future harm and declared they would no longer be subjected to cruelty and abuse.

This pleased the Skeezers greatly, and when Ozma told them they might elect a Queen to rule over them, who in turn would be subject to Ozma of Oz, they voted for Lady Aurex, and that same day the ceremony of crowning the new Queen was held and Aurex was installed as mistress of the palace.

For her Prime Minister the Queen selected Ervic, for the three Adepts had told of his good judgment, faithfulness and cleverness, and all the Skeezers approved the appointment.

Glinda, the Wizard and the Adepts stood on the bridge and recited an incantation that quite filled the lake with water again, and the Scarecrow and the Patchwork Girl climbed to the top of the Great Dome and replaced the pane of glass that had been removed to allow Glinda and her followers to enter.

When evening came Ozma ordered a great feast prepared, to which every Skeezer was invited. The village was beautifully decorated and brilliantly lighted and there was music and dancing until a late hour to celebrate the liberation of the people. For the Skeezers had been freed, not only from the water of the lake but from the cruelty of their former Queen.

As the people from the Emerald City prepared the next morning to depart Queen Aurex said to Ozma:

"There is only one thing I now fear for my people, and that is the enmity of the terrible Su-dic of the Flatheads. He is liable to come here at any time and try to annoy us, and my Skeezers are peaceful folks and unable to fight the wild and wilful Flatheads."

"Do not worry," returned Ozma, reassuringly. "We intend to stop on our way at the Flatheads' Enchanted Mountain and punish the Su-dic for his misdeeds."

That satisfied Aurex and when Ozma and her followers trooped over the bridge to the shore, having taken leave of their friends, all the Skeezers cheered them and waved their hats and handkerchiefs, and the band played and the departure was indeed a ceremony long to be remembered.

The three Adepts at Magic, who had formerly ruled the Flatheads wisely and considerately, went with Princess Ozma and her people, for they had promised Ozma to stay on the mountain and again see that the laws were enforced.

Glinda had been told all about the curious Flatheads and she had consulted with the Wizard and formed a plan to render them more intelligent and agreeable.

When the party reached the mountain Ozma and Dorothy showed them how to pass around the invisible wall—which had been built by the Flatheads after the Adepts were transformed—and how to gain the up-and-down stairway that led to the mountain top.

The Su-dic had watched the approach of the party from the edge of the mountain and was frightened when he saw that the three Adepts had recovered their natural forms and were coming back to their former home. He realized that his power would soon be gone and yet he determined to fight to the last. He called all the Flatheads together and armed them, and told them to arrest all who came up the stairway and

hurl them over the edge of the mountain to the plain below. But although they feared the Supreme Dictator, who had threatened to punish them if they did not obey his commands, as soon as they saw the three Adepts they threw down their arms and begged their former Rulers to protect them.

The three Adepts assured the excited Flatheads that they had nothing to fear.

Seeing that his people had rebelled the Su-dic ran away and tried to hide, but the Adepts found him and had him cast into a prison, all his cans of brains being taken away from him.

After this easy conquest of the Su-dic, Glinda told the Adepts of her plan, which had already been approved by Ozma of Oz, and they joyfully agreed to it. So, during the next few days, the great Sorceress transformed, in a way, every Flathead on the mountain.

Taking them one at a time, she had the can of brains that belonged to each one opened and the contents spread on the flat head, after which, by means of her arts of sorcery, she caused the head to grow over the brains—in the manner most people wear them—and they were thus rendered as intelligent and good looking as any of the other inhabitants of the Land of Oz.

When all had been treated in this manner there were no more Flatheads at all, and the Adepts decided to name their people Mountaineers. One good result of Glinda's sorcery was that no one could now be deprived of the brains that belonged to him and each person had exactly the share he was entitled to.

Even the Su-dic was given his portion of brains and his flat head made round, like the others, but he was deprived of all power to work further mischief, and with the Adepts constantly watching him he would be forced to become obedient and humble.

The Golden Pig, which ran grunting about the streets, with no brains at all, was disenchanted by Glinda, and in her woman's form was given brains and a round head. This wife of the Su-dic had once been even more wicked than her evil husband, but she had now forgotten all her wickedness and was likely to be a good woman thereafter.

These things being accomplished in a satisfactory manner, Princess Ozma and her people bade farewell to the three Adepts and departed for the Emerald City, well pleased with their interesting adventures.

They returned by the road over which Ozma and Dorothy had come, stopping to get the Saw-Horse and the Red Wagon where they had left them.

"I'm very glad I went to see these peoples," said Princess Ozma, "for I not only prevented any further warfare between them, but they have been freed from the rule of the Su-dic and Coo-ee-oh and are now happy and loyal subjects of the Land of Oz. Which proves that it is always wise to do one's duty, however unpleasant that duty may seem to be."

LITTLE WIZARD STORIES

OF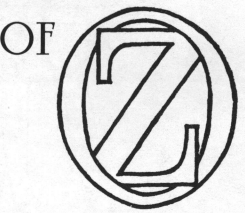

Contents

The Cowardly Lion and the Hungry Tiger

IN THE SPLENDID PALACE OF THE EMERALD CITY, WHICH IS IN THE CENTER of the fairy Land of Oz, is a great Throne Room, where Princess Ozma, the Ruler, for an hour each day sits in a throne of glistening emeralds and listens to all the troubles of her people, which they are sure to tell her about. Around Ozma's throne, on such occasions, are grouped all the important personages of Oz, such as the Scarecrow, Jack Pumpkinhead, Tik-Tok the Clockwork Man, the Tin Woodman, the Wizard of Oz, the Shaggy Man and other famous fairy people. Little Dorothy usually has a seat at Ozma's feet, and crouched on either side the throne are two enormous beasts known as the Hungry Tiger and the Cowardly Lion.

These two beasts are Ozma's chief guardians, but as everyone loves the beautiful girl Princess there has never been any disturbance in the great Throne Room, or anything for the guardians to do but look fierce and solemn and keep quiet until the Royal Audience is over and the people go away to their homes.

Of course no one would dare be naughty while the huge Lion and Tiger crouched beside the throne; but the fact is, the people of Oz are very seldom naughty. So Ozma's big guards are more ornamental than useful, and no one realizes that better than the beasts themselves.

One day, after everybody had left the Throne Room except the Cowardly Lion and the Hungry Tiger, the Lion yawned and said to his friend:

"I'm getting tired of this job. No one is afraid of us and no one pays any attention to us."

"That is true," replied the big Tiger, purring softly. "We might as well be in the thick jungles where we were born, as trying to protect Ozma when she needs no protection. And I'm dreadfully hungry all the time."

"You have enough to eat, I'm sure," said the Lion, swaying his tail slowly back and forth.

"Enough, perhaps; but not the kind of food I long for," answered the Tiger. "What I'm hungry for is fat babies. I have a great desire to eat a few fat babies. Then, perhaps, the people of Oz would fear me and I'd become more important."

"True," agreed the Lion. "It would stir up quite a rumpus if you ate but one fat baby. As for myself, my claws are sharp as needles and strong as crowbars, while my teeth are powerful enough to tear a person to pieces in a few seconds. If I should spring upon a man and make chop suey of him, there would be wild excitement in the Emerald City and the people would fall upon their knees and beg me for mercy. That, in my opinion, would render me of considerable importance."

"After you had torn the person to pieces, what would you do next?" asked the Tiger sleepily.

"Then I would roar so loudly it would shake the earth and stalk away to the jungle to hide myself, before anyone could attack me or kill me for what I had done."

"I see," nodded the Tiger. "You are really cowardly."

"To be sure. That is why I am named the Cowardly Lion. That is why I have always been so tame and peaceable. But I'm awfully tired of being tame," added the Lion, with a sigh, "and it would be fun to raise a row and show people what a terrible beast I really am."

The Tiger remained silent for several minutes, thinking deeply as he slowly washed his face with his left paw. Then he said:

"I'm getting old, and it would please me to eat at least one fat baby before I die. Suppose we surprise these people of Oz and prove our power. What do you say? We will walk out of here just as usual and the first baby we meet I'll eat in a jiffy, and the first man or woman you meet you will tear to pieces. Then we will both run out of the city gates and gallop across the country and hide in the jungle before anyone can stop us."

"All right; I'm game," said the Lion, yawning again so that he showed two rows of dreadfully sharp teeth.

The Tiger got up and stretched his great, sleek body.

"Come on," he said. The Lion stood up and proved he was the larger of the two, for he was almost as big as a small horse.

Out of the palace they walked, and met no one. They passed through the beautiful grounds, past fountains and beds of lovely flowers, and met no one. Then they unlatched a gate and entered a street of the city, and met no one.

"I wonder how a fat baby will taste," remarked the Tiger, as they stalked majestically along, side by side.

"I imagine it will taste like nutmegs," said the Lion.

"No," said the Tiger, "I've an idea it will taste like gumdrops."

They turned a corner, but met no one, for the people of the Emerald City were accustomed to take their naps at this hour of the afternoon.

"I wonder how many pieces I ought to tear a person into," said the Lion, in a thoughtful voice.

"Sixty would be about right," suggested the Tiger.

"Would that hurt any more than to tear one into about a dozen pieces?" inquired the Lion, with a little shudder.

"Who cares whether it hurts or not?" growled the Tiger.

The Lion did not reply. They entered a side street, but met no one.

Suddenly they heard a child crying.

"Aha!" exclaimed the Tiger. "There is my meat."

He rushed around a corner, the Lion following, and came upon a nice fat baby sitting in the middle of the street and crying as if in great distress.

"What's the matter?" asked the Tiger, crouching before the baby.

"I—I—I—lost my m-m-mamma!" wailed the baby.

"Why, you poor little thing," said the great beast, softly stroking the child's head with its paw. "Don't cry, my dear, for mamma can't be far away and I'll help you to find her."

"Go on," said the Lion, who stood by.

"Go on where?" asked the Tiger, looking up.

"Go on and eat your fat baby."

"Why, you dreadful creature!" said the Tiger reproachfully; "would you want me to eat a poor little lost baby, that don't know where its mother is?" And the beast gathered the little one into its strong, hairy arms and tried to comfort it by rocking it gently back and forth.

The Lion growled low in his throat and seemed very much disappointed; but at that moment a scream reached their ears and a woman came bounding out of a house and into the street. Seeing her baby in the embrace of the monster Tiger the woman screamed again and rushed forward to rescue it, but in her haste she caught her foot in her skirt and tumbled head over heels and heels over head, stopping with such a bump that she saw many stars in the heavens, although it was broad daylight. And there she lay, in a helpless manner, all tangled up and unable to stir.

With one bound and a roar like thunder the huge Lion was beside her. With his strong jaws he grasped her dress and raised her into an upright position.

"Poor thing! Are you hurt?" he gently asked.

Gasping for breath the woman struggled to free herself and tried to walk, but she limped badly and tumbled down again.

"My baby!" she said pleadingly.

"The baby is all right; don't worry," replied the Lion; and then he added: "Keep quiet, now, and I'll carry you back to your house, and the Hungry Tiger will carry your baby."

The Tiger, who had approached the place with the child in its arms, asked in astonishment:

"Aren't you going to tear her into sixty pieces?"

"No, nor into six pieces," answered the Lion indignantly. "I'm not such a brute as to destroy a poor woman who has hurt herself trying to save her lost baby. If you are so ferocious and cruel and bloodthirsty, you may leave me and go away, for I do not care to associate with you."

"That's all right," answered the Tiger. "I'm not cruel—not in the least—I'm only hungry. But I thought you were cruel."

"Thank heaven I'm respectable," said the Lion, with dignity. He then raised the woman and with much gentleness carried her into her house, where he laid her upon a sofa. The Tiger followed with the baby, which he safely deposited beside its mother. The little one liked the Hungry Tiger and grasping the enormous beast by both ears the baby kissed the beast's nose to show he was grateful and happy.

"Thank you very much," said the woman. "I've often heard what good beasts you are, in spite of your power to do mischief to mankind, and now I know that the stories are true. I do not think either of you have ever had an evil thought."

The Hungry Tiger and the Cowardly Lion hung their heads and did not look into each other's eyes, for both were shamed and humbled. They crept away and stalked back through the streets until they again entered the palace grounds, where they retreated to the pretty, comfortable rooms they occupied at the back of the palace. There they silently crouched in their usual corners to think over their recent adventure.

After a while the Tiger said sleepily:

"I don't believe fat babies taste like gumdrops. I'm quite sure they have the flavor of raspberry tarts. My, how hungry I am for fat babies!"

The Lion grunted disdainfully.

"You're a humbug," said he.

"Am I?" retorted the Tiger, with a sneer. "Tell me, then, into how many pieces you usually tear your victims, my bold Lion?"

The Lion impatiently thumped the floor with his tail.

"To tear anyone into pieces would soil my claws and blunt my teeth," he said. "I'm glad I didn't muss myself up this afternoon by hurting that poor mother."

The Tiger looked at him steadily and then yawned a wide, wide yawn.

"You're a coward," he remarked.

"Well," said the Lion, "it's better to be a coward than to do wrong."

"To be sure," answered the other. "And that reminds me that I nearly lost my own reputation. For, had I eaten that fat baby I would not now be the Hungry Tiger. It's better to go hungry, seems to me, than to be cruel to a little child."

And then they dropped their heads on their paws and went to sleep.

Little Dorothy and Toto

DOROTHY WAS A LITTLE KANSAS GIRL WHO ONCE ACCIDENTALLY FOUND the beautiful Land of Oz and was invited to live there always. Toto was Dorothy's small black dog, with fuzzy, curly hair and bright black eyes. Together, when they tired of the grandeur of the Emerald City of Oz, they would wander out into the country and all through the land, peering into queer nooks and corners and having a good time in their own simple way. There was a little Wizard living in Oz who was a faithful friend of Dorothy and did not approve of her traveling alone in this way, but the girl always laughed at the little man's fears for her and said she was not afraid of anything that might happen.

One day, while on such a journey, Dorothy and Toto found themselves among the wild wooded hills at the southeast of Oz—a place usually avoided by travelers because so many magical things abounded there. And, as they entered a forest path, the little girl noticed a sign tacked to a tree, which said: "Look out for Crinklink."

Toto could not talk, as many of the animals of Oz can, for he was just a common Kansas dog; but he looked at the sign so seriously that Dorothy almost believed he could read it, and she knew quite well that Toto understood every word she said to him.

"Never mind Crinklink," said she. "I don't believe anything in Oz will try to hurt us, Toto, and if I get into trouble you must take care of me."

"Bow-wow!" said Toto, and Dorothy knew that meant a promise.

The path was narrow and wound here and there between the trees, but they could not lose their way, because thick vines and creepers shut them in on both sides. They had walked a long time when, suddenly turning a curve of the pathway, they came upon a lake of black water, so big and so deep that they were forced to stop.

"Well, Toto," said Dorothy, looking at the lake, "we must turn back, I guess, for there is neither a bridge nor a boat to take us across the black water."

"Here's the ferryman, though," cried a tiny voice beside them, and the girl gave a start and looked down at her feet, where a man no taller than three inches sat at the edge of the path with his legs dangling over the lake.

"Oh!" said Dorothy; "I didn't see you before."

Toto growled fiercely and made his ears stand up straight, but the little man did not seem in the least afraid of the dog. He merely repeated: "I'm the ferryman, and it's my business to carry people across the lake."

Dorothy couldn't help feeling surprised, for she could have picked the little man up with one hand, and the lake was big and broad. Looking at the ferryman more closely she saw that he had small eyes, a big nose and a sharp chin. His hair was blue and his clothes scarlet, and Dorothy noticed that every button on his jacket was the head of some animal. The top button was a bear's head and the next button a wolf's head; the next was a cat's head and the next a weasel's head, while the last button of all was the head of a field-mouse. When Dorothy looked into the eyes of these animals' heads, they all nodded and said in a chorus: "Don't believe all you hear, little girl!"

"Silence!" said the small ferryman, slapping each button head in turn, but not hard enough to hurt them. Then he turned to Dorothy and asked: "Do you wish to cross over the lake?"

"Why, I'd like to," she answered, hesitating; "but I can't see how you will manage to carry us, without any boat."

"If you can't see, you mustn't see," he answered with a laugh. "All you need do is shut your eyes, say the word, and—over you go!"

Dorothy wanted to get across, in order that she might continue her journey.

"All right," she said, closing her eyes; "I'm ready."

Instantly she was seized in a pair of strong arms—arms so big and powerful that she was startled and cried out in fear.

"Silence!" roared a great voice, and the girl opened her eyes to find that he tiny man had suddenly grown to a giant and was holding both her and Toto in a tight embrace while in one step he spanned the lake and reached the other shore.

Dorothy became frightened, then, especially as the giant did not stop but continued tramping in great steps over the wooded hills, crushing bushes and trees beneath his broad feet. She struggled in vain to free herself, while Toto whined and trembled beside her, for the little dog was frightened, too.

"Stop!" screamed the girl. "Let me down!" But the giant paid no attention. "Who are you, and where are you taking me?" she continued; but the giant said not a word. Close to Dorothy's ear, however, a voice answered her, saying: "This is the terrible Crinklink, and he has you in his power."

Dorothy managed to twist her head around and found it was the second button on the jacket—the wolf's head—which had spoken to her.

"What will Crinklink do with me?" she asked anxiously.

"No one knows. You must wait and see," replied the wolf.

"Some of his captives he whips," squeaked the weasel's head.

"Some he transforms into bugs, and other things," growled the bear's head.

"Some he enchants, so that they become doorknobs," sighed the cat's head.

"Some he makes his slaves—even as we are—and that is the most dreadful fate of all," added the field-mouse. "As long as Crinklink exists we shall remain buttons, but as there are no more buttonholes on his jacket he will probably make you a slave."

Dorothy began to wish she had not met Crinklink. Meantime, the giant took such big steps that he soon reached the heart of the hills, where, perched upon the highest peak, stood a log castle. Before this castle he paused to set down Dorothy and Toto, for Crinklink was at present far too large to enter his own doorway. So he made himself grow smaller, until he was about the size of an ordinary man. Then he said to Dorothy, in stern, commanding tones:

"Enter, girl!"

Dorothy obeyed and entered the castle, with Toto at her heels. She found the place to be merely one big room. There was a table and chair of ordinary size near the center, and at one side a wee bed that seemed scarcely big enough for a doll. Everywhere else were dishes—dishes—dishes! They were all soiled, and were piled upon the floor, in all the corners and upon every shelf. Evidently Crinklink had not washed a dish for years, but had cast them aside as he used them.

Dorothy's captor sat down in the chair and frowned at her.

"You are young and strong, and will make a good dishwasher," said he.

"Do you mean me to wash all those dishes?" she asked, feeling both indignant and fearful, for such a task would take weeks to accomplish.

"That's just what I mean," he retorted. "I need clean dishes, for all I have are soiled, and you're going to make 'em clean or get trounced. So get to work and be careful not to break anything. If you smash a dish, the penalty is one lash from my dreadful cat-o'-nine-tails for every piece the dish breaks into," and here Crinklink displayed a terrible whip that made the little girl shudder.

Dorothy knew how to wash dishes, but she remembered that often she carelessly broke one. In this case, however, a good deal depended on being careful, so she handled the dishes very cautiously.

While she worked, Toto sat by the hearth and growled low at Crinklink, and Crinklink sat in his chair and growled at Dorothy because she moved so slowly. He expected her to break a dish any minute, but as the hours passed away and this did not happen Crinklink began to grow sleepy. It was tiresome watching the girl wash dishes and often he glanced longingly at the tiny bed. Now he began to yawn, and he yawned and yawned until finally he said:

"I'm going to take a nap. But the buttons on my jacket will be wide awake and whenever you break a dish the crash will waken me. As I'm rather sleepy I hope you won't interrupt my nap by breaking anything for a long time."

Then Crinklink made himself grow smaller and smaller until he was three inches high and of a size to fit the tiny bed. At once he lay down and fell fast asleep.

Dorothy came close to the buttons and whispered: "Would you really warn Crinklink if I tried to escape?"

"You can't escape," growled the bear. "Crinklink would become a giant, and soon overtake you."

"But you might kill him, while he sleeps," suggested the cat, in a soft voice.

"Oh!" cried Dorothy, drawing back; "I couldn't poss'bly *kill* anything—even to save my life."

But Toto had heard this conversation and was not so particular about killing monsters. Also the little dog knew he must try to save his mistress. In an instant he sprang upon the wee bed and was about to seize the sleeping Crinklink in his jaws when Dorothy heard a loud crash and a heap of dishes fell from the table to the floor. Then the girl saw Toto and the little man rolling on the floor together, like a fuzzy ball, and when the ball stopped rolling, behold! there was Toto wagging his tail joyfully and there sat the little Wizard of Oz, laughing merrily at the expression of surprise on Dorothy's face.

"Yes, my dear, it's me," said he, "and I've been playing tricks on you—for your own good. I wanted to prove to you that it is really dangerous for a little girl to wander alone in a fairy country; so I took the form of Crinklink to teach you a lesson. There isn't any Crinklink, to be sure; but if there had been you'd be severely whipped for breaking all those dishes."

The Wizard now rose, took off the coat with the button heads, and spread it on the floor, wrong side up. At once there crept from beneath it a bear, a wolf, a cat, a weasel and a field-mouse, who all rushed from the room and escaped into the mountains.

"Come on, Toto," said Dorothy; "let's go back to the Emerald City. You've given me a good scare, Wizard," she added, with dignity, "and p'raps I'll forgive you, by'n'by; but just now I'm mad to think how easily you fooled me."

Tik-Tok and the Nome King

THE NOME KING WAS UNPLEASANTLY ANGRY. HE HAD CARELESSLY BITTEN his tongue at breakfast and it still hurt; so he roared and raved and stamped around in his underground palace in a way that rendered him very disagreeable.

It so happened that on this unfortunate day Tik-Tok, the Clockwork Man, visited the Nome King to ask a favor. Tik-Tok lived in the Land of Oz and although he was an active and important person, he was made entirely of metal. Machinery within him, something like the works of a clock, made him move; other machinery made him talk; still other machinery made him think.

Although so cleverly constructed, the Clockwork Man was far from perfect. Three separate keys wound up his motion machinery, his speech works and his thoughts. One or more of these contrivances was likely to run down at a critical moment, leaving poor Tik-Tok helpless. Also some of his parts were wearing out, through much use, and just now his thought machinery needed repair. The skillful little Wizard of Oz had tinkered with Tik-Tok's thoughts without being able to get them properly regulated, so he had advised the Clockwork Man to go to the Nome King and secure a new set of springs, which would render his thoughts more elastic and responsive.

"Be careful what you say to the Nome King," warned the Wizard. "He has a bad temper and the least little thing makes him angry."

Tik-Tok promised, and the Wizard wound his machinery and set him walking in the direction of the Nome King's dominions, just across the desert from the

Land of Oz. He ran down just as he reached the entrance to the underground palace, and there Kaliko, the Nome King's Chief Steward, found him and wound him up again.

"I want to see the King," said Tik-Tok, in his jerky voice.

"Well," remarked Kaliko, "it may be safe for a cast-iron person like you to face His Majesty this morning; but you must announce yourself, for should I show my face inside the jewel-studded cavern where the King is now raving, I'd soon look like a dish of mashed potatoes, and be of no further use to anyone."

"I'm not a-fraid," said Tik-Tok.

"Then walk in and make yourself at home," answered Kaliko, and threw open the door of the King's cavern.

Tik-Tok promptly walked in and faced the astonished Nome King, to whom he said: "Good morn-ing. I want two new steel springs for my thought-works and a new cog-wheel for my speech-pro-du-cer. How a-bout it, your Maj-es-ty?"

The Nome King growled a menacing growl and his eyes were red with rage.

"How dare you enter my presence?" he shouted.

"I dare an-y-thing," said Tik-Tok. "I'm not a-fraid of a fat Nome."

This was true, yet an unwise speech. Had Tik-Tok's thoughts been in good working order he would have said something else. The angry Nome King quickly caught up his heavy mace and hurled it straight at Tik-Tok. When it struck the metal man's breast, the force of the blow burst the bolts which held the plates of his body together and they clattered to the floor in a score of pieces. Hundreds and hundreds of wheels, pins, cogs and springs filled the air like a cloud and then rattled like hail upon the floor.

Where Tik-Tok had stood was now only a scrap-heap and the Nome King was so amazed by the terrible effect of his blow that he stared in wonder.

His Majesty's anger quickly cooled. He remembered that the Clockwork Man was a favorite subject of the powerful Princess, Ozma of Oz, who would be sure to resent Tik-Tok's ruin.

"Too bad! too bad!" he muttered, regretfully. "I'm really sorry I made junk of the fellow. I didn't know he'd break."

"You'd better be," remarked Kaliko, who now ventured to enter the room. "You'll have a war on your hands when Ozma hears of this, and the chances are you will lose your throne and your kingdom."

The Nome King turned pale, for he loved to rule the Nomes and did not know of any other way to earn a living in case Ozma fought and conquered him.

"Do—do you think Ozma will be angry?" he asked anxiously.

"I'm sure of it," said Kaliko. "And she has the right to be. You've made scrap-iron of her favorite."

The King groaned.

"Sweep him up and throw the rubbish into the black pit," he commanded; and then he shut himself up in his private den and for days would see no one, because he was so ashamed of his unreasoning anger and so feared the results of his rash act.

Kaliko swept up the pieces, but he did not throw them into the black pit. Being a clever and skillful mechanic he determined to fit the pieces together again.

No man ever faced a greater puzzle; but it was interesting work and Kaliko suc-ceeded. When he found a spring or wheel worn or imperfect, he made a new one.

Within two weeks, by working steadily night and day, the Chief Steward completed his task and put the three sets of clockworks and the last rivet into Tik-Tok's body. He then wound up the motion machinery and the Clockwork Man walked up and down the room as naturally as ever. Then Kaliko wound up the thought works and the speech regulator and said to Tik-Tok:

"How do you feel now?"

"Fine," said the Clockwork Man. "You have done a ve-ry good job, Kal-i-ko, and saved me from de-struc-tion. Much o-bliged."

"Don't mention it," replied the Chief Steward. "I quite enjoyed the work."

Just then the Nome King's gong sounded, and Kaliko rushed away through the jewel-studded cavern and into the den where the King had hidden, leaving the doors ajar.

"Kaliko," said the King, in a meek voice, "I've been shut up here long enough to repent bitterly the destruction of Tik-Tok. Of course Ozma will have revenge, and send an army to fight us, but we must take our medicine. One thing comforts me; Tik-Tok wasn't really a live person; he was only a machine man, and so it wasn't very wicked to stop his clockworks. I couldn't sleep nights, at first, for worry; but there's no more harm in smashing a machine man than in breaking a wax doll. Don't you think so?"

"I am too humble to think in the presence of Your Majesty," said Kaliko.

"Then get me something to eat," commanded the King, "for I'm nearly starved. Two roasted goats, a barrel of cakes and nine mince pies will do me until dinnertime."

Kaliko bowed and hurried away to the royal kitchen, forgetting Tik-Tok, who was wandering around in the outer cavern. Suddenly the Nome King looked up and saw the Clockwork Man standing before him, and at the sight the monarch's eyes grew big and round and he fell a-trembling in every limb.

"Away, grim Shadow!" he cried. "You're not here, you know; you're only a hash of cogwheels and springs, lying at the bottom of the black pit. Vanish, thou Vision of the demolished Tik-Tok, and leave me in peace—for I have bitterly repented!"

"Then beg my pardon," said Tik-Tok in a gruff voice, for Kaliko had forgotten to oil the speech works.

But the sound of a voice coming from what he thought a mere vision was too much for the Nome King's shaken nerves. He gave a yell of fear and rushed from the room. Tik-Tok followed, so the King bolted through the corridors on a swift run and bumped against Kaliko, who was returning with a tray of things to eat. The sound

of the breaking dishes, as they struck the floor, added to the King's terror and he yelled again and dashed into a great cavern where a thousand Nomes were at work hammering metal.

"Look out! Here comes a phantom clockwork man!" screamed the terrified monarch, and every Nome dropped his tools and made a rush from the cavern, knocking over their King in their mad flight and recklessly trampling upon his prostrate fat body. So, when Tik-Tok came into the cavern, there was only the Nome King left, and he was rolling upon the rocky floor and howling for mercy, with his eyes fast shut so that he could not see what he was sure was a dreadful phantom that was coming straight toward him.

"It oc-curs to me," said Tik-Tok calmly, "that your Maj-es-ty is act-ing like ba-by. I am not a phan-tom. A phan-tom is unreal, while I am the real thing."

The King rolled over, sat up and opened his eyes.

"Didn't I smash you to pieces?" he asked in trembling tones.

"Yes," said Tik-Tok.

"Then you are nothing but a junk-heap, and this form in which you now appear cannot be real."

"It is, though," declared Tik-Tok. "Kal-i-ko picked up my piec es and put me to-geth-er a-gain. I'm as good as new, and perhaps bet-ter."

"That is true, Your Majesty," added Kaliko, who now made his appearance, "and I hope you will forgive me for mending Tik-Tok. He was quite broken up, after you smashed him, and I found it almost as hard a job to match his pieces as to pick turnips from gooseberry bushes. But I did it," he added proudly.

"You are forgiven," announced the Nome King, rising to his feet and drawing a long breath. "I will raise your wages one specto a year, and Tik-Tok shall return to the Land of Oz loaded with jewels for the Princess Ozma."

"That is all right," said Tik-Tok. "But what I want to know is, why did you hit me with your mace?"

"Because I was angry," admitted the King. "When I am angry I always do something that I am sorry for afterward. So I have firmly resolved never to get angry again; unless—unless—"

"Unless what, Your Majesty?" inquired Kaliko.

"Unless something annoys me," said the Nome King. And then he went to his treasure-chamber to get the jewels for Princess Ozma of Oz.

Ozma and the Little Wizard

ONCE UPON A TIME THERE LIVED IN THE BEAUTIFUL EMERALD CITY, WHICH lies in the center of the fairy Land of Oz, a lovely girl called Princess Ozma, who was Ruler of all that country. And among those who served this girlish Ruler and lived in a cosy suite of rooms in her splendid palace, was a little, withered old man known as the Wizard of Oz.

This little Wizard could do a good many queer things in magic; but he was a kind man, with merry, twinkling eyes and a sweet smile; so, instead of fearing him because of his magic, everybody loved him.

Now, Ozma was very anxious that all her people who inhabited the pleasant Land of Oz should be happy and contented, and therefore she decided one morning to make a journey to all parts of the country, that she might discover if anything was amiss, or anyone discontented, or if there was any wrong that ought to be righted. She asked the little Wizard to accompany her and he was glad to go.

"Shall I take my bag of magic tools with me?" he asked.

"Of course," said Ozma. "We may need a lot of magic before we return, for we are going into strange corners of the land, where we may meet with unknown creatures and dangerous adventures."

So the Wizard took his bag of magic tools and the two left the Emerald City and wandered over the country for many days, at last reaching a place far up in the mountains which neither of them had ever visited before. Stopping one morning at a cottage, built beside the rocky path which led into a pretty valley beyond, Ozma asked a man:

"Are you happy? Have you any complaint to make of your lot?"

And the man replied:

"We are happy except for three mischievous Imps that live in yonder valley and often come here to annoy us. If your Highness would only drive away those Imps, I and my family would be very happy and very grateful to you."

"Who are these bad Imps?" inquired the girl Ruler.

"One is named Olite, and one Udent and one Ertinent, and they have no respect for anyone or anything. If strangers pass through the valley the Imps jeer at them and make horrid faces and call names, and often they push travelers out of the path or throw stones at them. Whenever Imp Olite or Imp Udent or Imp Ertinent comes here to bother us, I and my family run into the house and lock all the doors and windows, and we dare not venture out again until the Imps have gone away."

Princess Ozma was grieved to hear this report and the little Wizard shook his head gravely and said the naughty Imps deserved to be punished. They told the good man they would see what could be done to protect him and at once entered the valley to seek the dwelling place of the three mischievous creatures.

Before long they came upon three caves, hollowed from the rocks, and in front of each cave squatted a queer little dwarf. Ozma and the Wizard paused to examine them and found them well-shaped, strong and lively. They had big round ears, flat noses and wide grinning mouths, and their jet-black hair came to points on top of their heads, much resembling horns. Their clothing fitted snugly to their bodies and limbs and the Imps were so small in size that at first Ozma did not consider them at all dangerous. But one of them suddenly reached out a hand and caught the dress of the Princess, jerking it so sharply that she nearly fell down, and a moment later another Imp pushed the little Wizard so hard that he bumped against Ozma and both unexpectedly sat down upon the ground.

At this the Imps laughed boisterously and began running around in a circle and kicking dust upon the Royal Princess, who cried in a sharp voice: "Wizard, do your duty!"

The Wizard promptly obeyed. Without rising from the ground he opened his bag, got the tools he required and muttered a magic spell.

Instantly the three Imps became three bushes—of a thorny, stubby kind—with their roots in the ground. As the bushes were at first motionless, perhaps through

surprise at their sudden transformation, the Wizard and the Princess found time to rise from the ground and brush the dust off their pretty clothes. Then Ozma turned to the bushes and said:

"The unhappy lot you now endure, my poor Imps, is due entirely to your naughty actions. You can no longer annoy harmless travelers and you must remain ugly bushes, covered with sharp thorns, until you repent of your bad ways and promise to be good Imps."

"They can't help being good, now, your Highness," said the Wizard, who was much pleased with his work, "and the safest plan will be to allow them always to remain bushes."

But something must have been wrong with the Wizard's magic, or the creatures had magic of their own, for no sooner were the words spoken than the bushes began to move. At first they only waved their branches at the girl and the little man, but pretty soon they began to slide over the ground, their roots dragging through the earth, and one pushed itself against the Wizard and pricked him so sharply with its thorns that he cried out: "Ouch!" and started to run away.

Ozma followed, for the other bushes were trying to stick their thorns into her legs and one actually got so near her that it tore a great rent in her beautiful dress. The girl Princess could run, however, and she followed the fleeing Wizard until he tumbled head first over a log and rolled upon the ground. Then she sprang behind a tree and shouted: "Quick! Transform them into something else."

The Wizard heard, but he was much confused by his fall. Grabbing from his bag the first magical tool he could find he transformed the bushes into three white pigs. That astonished the Imps. In the shape of pigs—fat, roly-poly and cute—they scampered off a little distance and sat down to think about their new condition.

Ozma drew a long breath and coming from behind the tree she said:

"That is much better, Wiz, for such pigs as these must be quite harmless. No one need now fear the mischievous Imps."

"I intended to transform them into mice," replied the Wizard, "but in my excitement I worked the wrong magic. However, unless the horrid creatures behave themselves hereafter, they are liable to be killed and eaten. They would make good chops, sausages or roasts."

But the Imps were now angry and had no intention of behaving. As Ozma and the little Wizard turned to resume their journey the three pigs rushed forward, dashed between their legs and tripped them up, so that both lost their balance and toppled

over, clinging to one another. As the Wizard tried to get up he was tripped again and fell across the back of the third pig, which carried him on a run far down the valley until it dumped the little man into the river. Ozma had been sprawled upon the ground but found she was not hurt, so she picked herself up and ran to the assistance of the Wizard, reaching him just as he was crawling out of the river, gasping for breath and dripping with water. The girl could not help laughing at his woeful appearance. But he had no sooner wiped the wet from his eyes than one of the impish pigs tripped him again and sent him into the river for a second bath. The pigs tried to trip Ozma, too, but she ran around a stump and so managed to keep out of their way. So the Wizard scrambled out of the water again and picked up a sharp stick to defend himself. Then he mumbled a magic mutter which instantly dried his clothes, after which he hurried to assist Ozma. The pigs were afraid of the sharp stick and kept away from it.

"This won't do," said the Princess. "We have accomplished nothing, for the pig Imps would annoy travelers as much as the real Imps. Transform them into something else, Wiz."

The Wizard took time to think. Then he transformed the white pigs into three blue doves.

"Doves," said he, "are the most harmless things in the world."

But scarcely had he spoken when the doves flew at them and tried to peck out their eyes. When they endeavored to shield their eyes with their hands two of the doves bit the Wizard's fingers and another caught the pretty pink ear of the Princess in its bill and gave it such a cruel tweak that she cried out in pain and threw her skirt over her head.

"These birds are worse than pigs, Wizard," she called to her companion. "Nothing is harmless that is animated by impudent anger or impertinent mischief. You must transform the Imps into something that is not alive."

The Wizard was pretty busy, just then, driving off the birds, but he managed to open his bag of magic and find a charm which instantly transformed the doves into three buttons. As they fell to the ground he picked them up and smiled with satisfaction. The tin button was Imp Olite, the brass button was Imp Udent and the lead button was Imp Ertinent. These buttons the Wizard placed in a little box which he put in his jacket pocket. "Now," said he, "the Imps cannot annoy travelers, for we shall carry them back with us to the Emerald City."

"But we dare not use the buttons," said Ozma, smiling once more now that the danger was over.

"Why not?" asked the Wizard. "I intend to sew them upon my coat and watch them carefully. The spirits of the Imps are still in the buttons, and after a time they will repent and be sorry for their naughtiness. Then they will decide to be very good in the future. When they feel that way, the tin button will turn to silver and the brass to gold, while the lead button will become aluminum. I shall then restore them to their proper forms, changing their names to pretty names instead of the ugly ones they used to bear. Thereafter the three Imps will become good citizens of the Land of Oz and I think you will find they will prove faithful subjects of our beloved Princess Ozma."

"Ah that is magic well worth while," exclaimed Ozma, well pleased. "There is no doubt, my friend, but that you are a very clever Wizard."

Jack Pumpkinhead
and the Saw-Horse

IN A ROOM OF THE ROYAL PALACE OF THE EMERALD CITY OF OZ HANGS A Magic Picture, in which are shown all the important scenes that transpire in those fairy dominions. The scenes shift constantly, and by watching them, Ozma, the girl Ruler, is able to discover events taking place in any part of her kingdom.

One day she saw in her Magic Picture that a little girl and a little boy had wandered together into a great, gloomy forest at the far west of Oz and had become hopelessly lost. Their friends were seeking them in the wrong direction and unless Ozma came to their rescue the little ones would never be found in time to save them from starving.

So the Princess sent a message to Jack Pumpkinhead and asked him to come to the palace. This personage, one of the queerest of the queer inhabitants of Oz, was an old friend and companion of Ozma. His form was made of rough sticks fitted together and dressed in ordinary clothes. His head was a pumpkin with a face carved upon it, and was set on top a sharp stake which formed his neck.

Jack was active, good-natured and a general favorite; but his pumpkin head was likely to spoil with age, so in order to secure a good supply of heads he grew a big field of pumpkins and lived in the middle of it, his house being a huge pumpkin hollowed out. Whenever he needed a new head he picked a pumpkin, carved a face on it and stuck it upon the stake of his neck, throwing away the old head as of no further use.

The day Ozma sent for him Jack was in prime condition and was glad to be of service in rescuing the lost children. Ozma made him a map, showing just where the forest was and how to get to it and the paths he must take to reach the little ones. Then she said:

"You'd better ride the Saw-Horse, for he is swift and intelligent and will help you accomplish your task."

"All right," answered Jack, and went to the royal stable to tell the Saw-Horse to be ready for the trip.

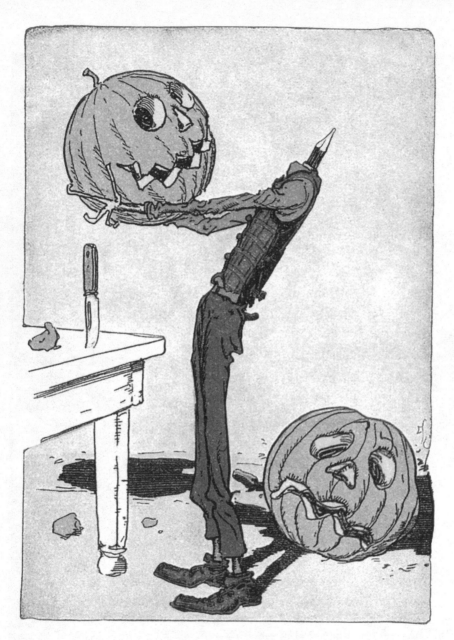

This remarkable animal was not unlike Jack Pumpkinhead in form, although so different in shape. Its body was a log, with four sticks stuck into it for legs. A branch at one end of the log served as a tail, while in the other end was chopped a gash that formed a mouth. Above this were two small knots that did nicely for eyes. The Saw-Horse was the favorite steed of Ozma and to prevent its wooden legs from wearing out she had them shod with plates of gold.

Jack said "Good morning" to the Saw-Horse and placed upon the creature's back a saddle of purple leather, studded with jewels.

"Where now?" asked the horse, blinking its knot eyes at Jack.

"We're going to rescue two babes in the wood," was the reply. Then he climbed into the saddle and the wooden animal pranced out of the stable, through the streets of the Emerald City and out upon the highway leading to the western forest where the children were lost.

Small though he was, the Saw-Horse was swift and untiring. By nightfall they were in the far west and quite close to the forest they sought. They passed the night standing quietly by the roadside. They needed no food, for their wooden bodies never became hungry; nor did they sleep, because they never tired. At daybreak they continued their journey and soon reached the forest.

Jack now examined the map Ozma had given him and found the right path to take, which the Saw-Horse obediently followed. Underneath the trees all was silent and gloomy and Jack beguiled the way by whistling gayly as the Saw-Horse trotted along.

The paths branched so many times and in so many different ways that the Pumpkinhead was often obliged to consult Ozma's map, and finally the Saw-Horse became suspicious.

"Are you sure you are right?" it asked.

"Of course," answered Jack. "Even a Pumpkinhead whose brains are seeds can follow so clear a map as this. Every path is plainly marked, and here is a cross where the children are."

Finally they reached a place, in the very heart of the forest, where they came upon the lost boy and girl. But they found the two children bound fast to the trunk of a big tree, at the foot of which they were sitting.

When the rescuers arrived, the little girl was sobbing bitterly and the boy was trying to comfort her, though he was probably frightened as much as she.

"Cheer up, my dears," said Jack, getting out of the saddle. "I have come to take you back to your parents. But why are you bound to that tree?"

"Because," cried a small, sharp voice, "they are thieves and robbers. That's why!"

"Dear me!" said Jack, looking around to see who had spoken. The voice seemed to come from above.

A big gray squirrel was sitting upon a low branch of the tree. Upon the squirrel's head was a circle of gold, with a diamond set in the center of it. He was running up and down the limbs and chattering excitedly.

"These children," continued the squirrel, angrily, "robbed our storehouse of all the nuts we had saved up for winter. Therefore, being King of all the Squirrels in this forest, I ordered them arrested and put in prison, as you now see them. They had no right to steal our provisions and we are going to punish them."

"We were hungry," said the boy, pleadingly, "and we found a hollow tree full of nuts, and ate them to keep alive. We didn't want to starve when there was food right in front of us."

"Quite right," remarked Jack, nodding his pumpkin head. "I don't blame you one bit, under the circumstances. Not a bit."

Then he began to untie the ropes that bound the children to the tree.

"Stop that!" cried the King Squirrel, chattering and whisking about. "You mustn't release our prisoners. You have no right to."

But Jack paid no attention to the protest. His wooden fingers were awkward and it took him some time to untie the ropes. When at last he succeeded, the tree was full of squirrels, called together by their King, and they were furious at losing their prisoners. From the tree they began to hurl nuts at the Pumpkinhead, who laughed at them as he helped the two children to their feet.

Now, at the top of this tree was a big dead limb, and so many squirrels gathered upon it that suddenly it broke away and fell to the ground. Poor Jack was standing directly under it and when the limb struck him it smashed his pumpkin head into a pulpy mass and sent Jack's wooden form tumbling, to stop with a bump against a tree a dozen feet away.

He sat up, a moment afterward, but when he felt for his head it was gone. He could not see; neither could he speak. It was perhaps the greatest misfortune that could have happened to Jack Pumpkinhead, and the squirrels were delighted. They danced around in the tree in great glee as they saw Jack's plight.

The boy and girl were indeed free, but their protector was ruined. The Saw-Horse was there, however, and in his way he was wise. He had seen the accident and knew that the smashed pumpkin would never again serve Jack as a head. So he said to the children, who were frightened at this accident to their new found friend:

"Pick up the Pumpkinhead's body and set it on my saddle. Then mount behind it and hold it on. We must get out of this forest as soon as we can, or the squirrels may capture you again. I must guess at the right path, for Jack's map is no longer of any use to him since that limb destroyed his head."

The two children lifted Jack's body, which was not at all heavy, and placed it upon the saddle. Then they climbed up behind it and the Saw-Horse immediately turned and trotted back along the path he had come, bearing all three with ease. However, when the path began to branch into many paths, all following different directions, the wooden animal became puzzled and soon was wandering aimlessly about, without any hope of finding the right way. Toward evening they came upon a fine fruit tree, which furnished the children a supper, and at night the little ones lay upon a bed of leaves while the Saw-Horse stood watch, with the limp, headless form of poor Jack Pumpkinhead lying helpless across the saddle.

Now, Ozma had seen in her Magic Picture all that had happened in the forest, so she sent the little Wizard, mounted upon the Cowardly Lion, to save the unfortunates. The Lion knew the forest well and when he reached it he bounded straight through the tangled paths to where the Saw-Horse was wandering, with Jack and the two children on his back.

The Wizard was grieved at the sight of the headless Jack, but believed he could save him. He first led the Saw-Horse out of the forest and restored the boy and girl to the arms of their anxious friends, and then he sent the Lion back to Ozma to tell her what had happened.

The Wizard now mounted the Saw-Horse and supported Jack's form on the long ride to the pumpkin field. When they arrived at Jack's house the Wizard selected a fine pumpkin—not too ripe—and very neatly carved a face on it. Then he stuck the pumpkin solidly on Jack's neck and asked him:

"Well, old friend, how do you feel?"

"Fine!" replied Jack, and shook the hand of the little Wizard gratefully. "You have really saved my life, for without your assistance I could not have found my way home to get a new head. But I'm all right, now, and I shall be very careful not to get this beautiful head smashed." And he shook the Wizard's hand again.

"Are the brains in the new head any better than the old ones?" inquired the Saw-Horse, who had watched Jack's restoration.

"Why, these seeds are quite tender," replied the Wizard, "so they will give our friend tender thoughts. But, to speak truly, my dear Saw-Horse, Jack Pumpkinhead, with all his good qualities, will never be noted for his wisdom."

The Scarecrow
and the Tin Woodman

THERE LIVED IN THE LAND OF OZ TWO QUEERLY MADE MEN WHO WERE THE best of friends. They were so much happier when together that they were seldom apart; yet they liked to separate, once in awhile, that they might enjoy the pleasure of meeting again.

One was a Scarecrow. That means he was a suit of blue Munchkin clothes, stuffed with straw, on top of which was fastened a round cloth head, filled with bran to hold it in shape. On the head were painted two eyes, two ears, a nose and a mouth. The Scarecrow had never been much of a success in scaring crows, but he prided himself on being a superior man, because he could feel no pain, was never tired and did not have to eat or drink. His brains were sharp, for the Wizard of Oz had put pins and needles in the Scarecrow's brains.

The other man was made all of tin, his arms and legs and head being cleverly jointed so that he could move them freely. He was known as the Tin Woodman, having at one time been a woodchopper, and everyone loved him because the Wizard had given him an excellent heart of red plush.

The Tin Woodman lived in a magnificent tin castle, built on his country estate in the Winkie Land, not far from the Emerald City of Oz. It had pretty tin furniture and was surrounded by lovely gardens in which were many tin trees and beds of tin flowers. The palace of the Scarecrow was not far distant, on the banks of a river, and this palace was in the shape of an immense ear of corn.

One morning the Tin Woodman went to visit his friend the Scarecrow, and as they had nothing better to do they decided to take a boat ride on the river. So they got into the Scarecrow's boat, which was formed from a big corncob, hollowed out and pointed at both ends and decorated around the edges with brilliant jewels. The sail was of purple silk and glittered gayly in the sunshine.

There was a good breeze that day, so the boat glided swiftly over the water. By and by they came to a smaller river that flowed from out a deep forest, and the Tin Woodman proposed they sail up this stream, as it would be cool and shady beneath the trees of the forest. So the Scarecrow, who was steering, turned the boat up the stream and the friends continued talking together of old times and the wonderful adventures they had met with while traveling with Dorothy, the little Kansas girl. They became so much interested in this talk that they forgot to notice that the boat was now sailing through the forest, or that the stream was growing more narrow and crooked.

Suddenly the Scarecrow glanced up and saw a big rock just ahead of them.

"Look out!" he cried; but the warning came too late.

The Tin Woodman sprang to his feet just as the boat bumped into the rock, and the jar made him lose his balance. He toppled and fell overboard and being made of tin he sank to the bottom of the water in an instant and lay there at full length, face up.

Immediately the Scarecrow threw out the anchor, so as to hold the boat in that place, and then he leaned over the side and through the clear water looked at his friend sorrowfully.

"Dear me!" he exclaimed; "what a misfortune!"

"It is, indeed," replied the Tin Woodman, speaking in muffled tones because so much water covered him. "I cannot drown, of course, but I must lie here until you find a way to get me out. Meantime, the water is soaking into all my joints and I shall become badly rusted before I am rescued."

"Very true," agreed the Scarecrow; "but be patient, my friend, and I'll dive down and get you. My straw will not rust, and is easily replaced, if damaged, so I'm not afraid of the water."

The Scarecrow now took off his hat and made a dive from the boat into the water; but he was so light in weight that he barely dented the surface of the stream, nor could he reach the Tin Woodman with his outstretched straw arms. So he floated to the boat and climbed into it, saying the while:

"Do not despair, my friend. We have an extra anchor aboard, and I will tie it around my waist, to make me sink, and dive again."

"Don't do that!" called the tin man. "That would anchor you also to the bottom, where I am, and we'd both be helpless."

"True enough," sighed the Scarecrow, wiping his wet face with a handkerchief; and then he gave a cry of astonishment, for he found he had wiped off one painted eye and now had but one eye to see with.

"How dreadful!" said the poor Scarecrow. "That eye must have been painted in water-color, instead of oil. I must be careful not to wipe off the other eye, for then I could not see to help you at all."

A shriek of elfish laughter greeted this speech and looking up the Scarecrow found the trees full of black crows, who seemed much amused by the straw man's one-eyed countenance. He knew the crows well, however, and they had usually been

friendly to him because he had never deceived them into thinking he was a meat man—the sort of man they really feared.

"Don't laugh," said he; "you may lose an eye yourselves, some day."

"We couldn't look as funny as you, if we did," replied one old crow, the king of them. "But what has gone wrong with you?"

"The Tin Woodman, my dear friend and companion, has fallen overboard and is now on the bottom of the river," said the Scarecrow. "I'm trying to get him out again, but I fear I shall not succeed."

"Why, it's easy enough," declared the old crow. "Tie a string to him and all of my crows will fly down, take hold of the string, and pull him up out of the water. There are hundreds of us here, so our united strength could lift much more than that."

"But I can't tie a string to him," replied the Scarecrow. "My straw is so light that I am unable to dive through the water. I've tried it, and knocked one eye out."

"Can't you fish for him?"

"Ah, that is a good idea," said the Scarecrow. "I'll make the attempt."

He found a fishline in the boat, with a stout hook at the end of it. No bait was needed, so the Scarecrow dropped the hook into the water till it touched the Woodman.

"Hook it into a joint," advised the crow, who was now perched upon a branch that stuck far out and bent down over the water.

The Scarecrow tried to do this, but having only one eye he could not see the joints very clearly.

"Hurry up, please," begged the Tin Woodman; "you've no idea how damp it is down here."

"Can't you help?" asked the crow.

"How?" inquired the Tin Man.

"Catch the line and hook it around your neck."

The Tin Woodman made the attempt and after several trials wound the line around his neck and hooked it securely.

"Good!" cried the King Crow, a mischievous old fellow. "Now, then, we'll all grab the line and pull you out."

At once the air was filled with black crows, each of whom seized the cord with beak or talons. The Scarecrow watched them with much interest and forgot that he had tied the other end of the line around his own waist, so he would not lose it while fishing for his friend.

"All together for the good caws!" shrieked the King Crow, and with a great flapping of wings the birds rose into the air.

The Scarecrow clapped his stuffed hands in glee as he saw his friend drawn from the water into the air; but the next moment the straw man was himself in the air, his stuffed legs kicking wildly; for the crows had flown straight up through the trees. On one end of the line dangled the Tin Woodman, hung by the neck, and on the other dangled the Scarecrow, hung by the waist and clinging fast to the spare anchor of the boat, which he had seized hoping to save himself.

"Hi, there—be careful!" shouted the Scarecrow to the crows. "Don't take us so high. Land us on the river bank."

But the crows were bent on mischief. They thought it a good joke to bother the two, now that they held them captive.

"Here's where the crows scare the Scarecrow!" chuckled the naughty King Crow, and at his command the birds flew over the forest to where a tall dead tree stood higher than all the other trees. At the very top was a crotch, formed by two dead limbs, and into the crotch the crows dropped the center of the line. Then, letting go their hold, they flew away, chattering with laughter, and left the two friends suspended high in the air—one on each side of the tree.

Now the Tin Woodman was much heavier than the Scarecrow, but the reason they balanced so nicely was because the straw man still clung fast to the iron anchor. There they hung, not ten feet apart, yet unable to reach the bare tree-trunk.

"For goodness sake don't drop that anchor," said the Tin Woodman anxiously.

"Why not?" inquired the Scarecrow.

"If you did I'd tumble to the ground, where my tin would be badly dented by the fall. Also you would shoot into the air and alight somewhere among the tree-tops."

"Then," said the Scarecrow, earnestly, "I shall hold fast to the anchor."

For a time they both dangled in silence, the breeze swaying them gently to and fro. Finally the tin man said: "Here is an emergency, friend, where only brains can help us. We must think of some way to escape."

"I'll do the thinking," replied the Scarecrow. "My brains are the sharpest."

He thought so long that the tin man grew tired and tried to change his position, but found his joints had already rusted so badly that he could not move them. And his oil-can was back in the boat.

"Do you suppose your brains are rusted, friend Scarecrow?" he asked in a weak voice, for his jaws would scarcely move.

"No, indeed. Ah, here's an idea at last!"

And with this the Scarecrow clapped his hands to his head, forgetting the anchor, which tumbled to the ground. The result was astonishing; for, just as the Tin Man had said, the light Scarecrow flew into the air, sailed over the top of the tree and landed in a bramble-bush, while the tin man fell plump to the ground, and landing on a bed of dry leaves was not dented at all. The Tin Woodman's joints were so rusted, however, that he was unable to move, while the thorns held the Scarecrow a fast prisoner.

While they were in this sad plight the sound of hoofs was heard and along the forest path rode the little Wizard of Oz, seated on a wooden Saw-Horse. He smiled when he saw the one-eyed head of the Scarecrow sticking out of the bramble-bush, but he helped the poor straw man out of his prison.

"Thank you, dear Wiz," said the grateful Scarecrow. "Now we must get the oil-can and rescue the Tin Woodman."

Together they ran to the river bank, but the boat was floating in midstream and the Wizard was obliged to mumble some magic words to draw it to the bank, so the Scarecrow could get the oil-can. Then back they flew to the tin man, and while the Scarecrow carefully oiled each joint the little Wizard moved the joints gently back and forth until they worked freely. After an hour of this labor the Tin Woodman was again on his feet, and although still a little stiff he managed to walk to the boat.

The Wizard and the Saw-Horse also got aboard the corncob craft and together they returned to the Scarecrow's palace. But the Tin Woodman was very careful not to stand up in the boat again.